EDWARD MARSTON was born and brought up in South Wales. A full-time writer for over forty years, he has worked in radio, film, television and the theatre and is a former chairman of the Crime Writers' Association. Prolific and highly successful, he is equally at home writing children's books or literary criticism, plays or biographies.

www.edwardmarston.com

By Edward Marston

THE BRACEWELL MYSTERIES

The Queen's Head • The Merry Devils • The Trip to Jerusalem
The Nine Giants • The Mad Courtesan • The Silent Woman

THE RAILWAY DETECTIVE SERIES

The Railway Detective • The Excursion Train
The Railway Viaduct • The Iron Horse
Murder on the Brighton Express • The Silver Locomotive Mystery
Railway to the Grave • Blood on the Line
The Stationmaster's Farewell • Peril on the Royal Train
The Railway Detective Omnibus:
The Railway Detective, The Excursion Train, The Railway Viaduct

THE CAPTAIN RAWSON SERIES

Soldier of Fortune • Drums of War • Fire and Sword
Under Siege • A Very Murdering Battle

THE RESTORATION SERIES

The King's Evil • The Amorous Nightingale • The Repentant Rake
The Frost Fair • The Parliament House • The Painted Lady

THE HOME FRONT DETECTIVE SERIES

A Bespoke Murder • Instrument of Slaughter

The Nine Giants

An Elizabethan Mystery

EDWARD MARSTON

Allison & Busby Limited
12 Fitzroy Mews
London W1T 6DW
www.allisonandbusby.com

First published in Great Britain in 1991.
This paperback edition published by Allison & Busby in 2013.

A CIP catalogue record for this book is available from
the British Library.

10 9 8 7 6 5 4 3 2

ISBN 978-0-7490-1028-7

Typeset in 10.5/16 pt Sabon
by Allison & Busby Ltd.

The paper used for this Allison & Busby publication
has been produced from trees that have been legally sourced
from well-managed and credibly certified forests.

Printed and bound by
CPI Group (UK) Ltd, Croydon, CR0 4YY

To Lady Diane Pearson

The love I dedicate to your Ladyship is without end: whereof this Book is but a superfluous Moiety. The warrant I have of your Honourable disposition, not the worth of my untutored Lines makes it assured of acceptance. What I have done is yours, what I have to doe is yours, being part in all I have, devoted yours. Were my worth greater, my duety would shew greater, meane time, as it is, it is bound to your Ladyship; to whom I wish long life still lengthned with all happinesse.

The famous Mayor by princely governance
With sword of justice thee ruleth prudently
No lord of Paris, Venice or Florence
In dignity and honour goeth to him nigh.
He is exemplar, lode-star and guy
Principal patron and rose original
Above all mayors as master most worthy
London thou art the flower of cities all.

— WILLIAM DUNBAR

Chapter One

Lawrence Firethorn gazed down in horror at the corpse of his young wife and let out a sigh of utter despair that sent tremors through all who heard it. Swaying over the hapless figure of the child-bride who had been plucked from him on his wedding night, he howled like an animal then held up his hands to heaven in supplication. When no comfort came from above, he was seized with an urge to wreak revenge for the savage murder and he pulled out his dagger to slash wildly at the air. The hopelessness of the gesture made him stand quite still and weep fresh tears of remorse. Then, on impulse, with a suddenness that took everyone by surprise, he turned the point of the dagger on himself and used brute power to plunge it deep into his own breast. Firethorn shuddered and fell to one knee. Though fading with each second, he managed to deliver a speech of sixteen lines with poignant clarity. He was down on both knees when he breathed his last.

Bereft am I of heart and hope, dear bride,
In your foul death, happiness itself has died.
Adieu, cruel world! Farewell, abhorred life!
I quit this void to join my loving wife.

Firethorn hit the ground with a thud that echoed through the taut silence. His outstretched fingertips made a last contact with the pale and forlorn hand of his bride. Anguished servants entered and the two bodies were lifted onto biers with reverential care before being carried out to solemn music. The noble Count Orlando and his adored young Countess would share a marriage bed in the family vault. Harrowed by the tragedy and caught up in its full implications, the onlookers did not dare to move or speak. Mute distress enfolded them.

It was broken in an instant by the reappearance of Lawrence Firethorn, leading out his company to take their bow before the full audience that was packed into the yard at the Queen's Head in Gracechurch Street. He was no stricken aristocrat now, no Italian nobleman who had just committed suicide in a fit of unbearable grief. Firethorn was the finest actor in London, pulsing with vitality and bristling with curiosity, coming out to take his place at the centre of the stage and reap his due reward while at the same time scanning the upper gallery for a particular face. Count Orlando was only one in a long line of tragic heroes played by the acknowledged star of Westfield's Men and it was a role in which he never ceased to work his will upon the raw emotions of the audience. They clapped and cheered and stamped their feet to show their approval of the play. *Death and Darkness* had weaved its magic web once more. Firethorn was being feted.

Applause was the lifeblood of an actor and each member of the cast felt it coursing through his veins. Firethorn might think that all the adulation was being directed solely at him and he was replying with a bow of almost imperious humility but his fellows could dream their dreams as well. The small, squat figure of Barnaby Gill, standing beside him, believed that the ovation was in recognition of his performance as Quaglino, the ancient retainer, the one comic character in a tragic tale, the single filter of light in the prevailing blackness of the play. Edmund Hoode, tall, spare and with a youthful innocence that belied his age, pretended that the applause was in gratitude both for his affecting performance as the doomed lover of the Countess and for his skill as a playwright. *Death and Darkness* was an early piece from his pen but it had stood the test of time and the close scrutiny of many an audience.

And so it was with the rest of the company, right down to its meanest member, George Dart, the tiny assistant stagekeeper, pressed into service as a soldier, proudly wearing the uniform of Count Orlando's guard and quietly congratulating himself on having got his one deathless line – 'My lord, the Duke of Milan waits upon you' – right for the first time in weeks. Though put inconspicuously at the outer limit of the semicircle of actors, he bowed as deep as any of them, feeding hungrily on the sustained clapping while he could, knowing that he would be back to a more meagre diet of chores, complaints, gibes, outright abuse and occasional blows once he left the stage and returned to his accustomed role as the lowliest of the low. Theatre was indeed sweet fancy.

Nicholas Bracewell watched it all from his position behind the curtains. He was a big, well-groomed, handsome man with fair hair and a full beard. As book holder with the company, he stage-managed every performance with an attention to detail that lifted Westfield's Men above so many of their rivals. No matter how generous it might be, applause never penetrated to his domain behind the scenes and this state of affairs suited Nicholas. He had a commanding presence that was offset by a gift for self-effacement and he courted the shadows more than the sun.

While Lawrence Firethorn and the others lapped up the tumultuous admiration, the book holder was still calmly doing his job, noting from his vantage point that Barnaby Gill had torn his hose, that Edmund Hoode had dropped a stitch in the rear of his doublet and that George Dart had somehow lost a buckle off his shoe. Nicholas had also observed in the course of a hectic two hours that entrances had been missed, lines had gone astray and the musicians had not been at their most harmonious. He would have stern words for the offenders afterwards and would even be courageous enough to tell the volatile Firethorn that, during one of his major speeches, the leading man had mistakenly inserted four lines from another play. Nicholas was a relentless perfectionist.

He had also come to know his employer very well.

Even though his view of Firethorn was confined to a bending back and a pair of thrusting buttocks, he could see what was animating Count Orlando. Somewhere in the gallery was a new female face with a roguish charm that had ensnared the actor. Nicholas had spotted the signs earlier when Firethorn was in the tiring-house, working himself up to full pitch, smiling benignly for once on all around him, evincing a confidence that was fringed with nervousness and hogging the mirror even more than usual. The book holder groaned inwardly. It was bad news for the whole company when its actor-manager blundered into yet another romantic entanglement, and it was an extra burden on Nicholas Bracewell because he was invariably used as a reluctant go-between. There was danger in the air.

Lawrence Firethorn confirmed it within a matter of seconds. After taking a last, loving, lingering bow, he blew a kiss to the upper gallery then led his troupe from the stage. As they poured into the tiring-house, they could still hear the tide of approval as it slowly ebbed away. The actors fell into happy chatter and the musicians began to play in their elevated position to cover the noisy departure of their patrons. With his familiar eagerness, Firethorn swooped down on his book holder.

'Nick, dear heart! I have important work for you.'

'There are chores enough to keep me busy, sir.'

'This is a special commission,' said Firethorn. 'It comes direct from Cupid.'

'Can it not wait, master?' said Nicholas, trying to evade

13

a duty that was about to be thrust upon him. 'I am needed here, as you may well judge.'

Firethorn grabbed him by the arm, pushed him towards the curtain then drew it slightly back to give them a view of the yard. His voice was an urgent hiss.

'Find out who she is!'

'Which lady has caught your attention?'

'That creature of pure joy and beauty.'

'There are several to fit that description,' said Nicholas, surveying the crowd as it dispersed. 'How am I to pick her out from such a throng?'

'Are you blind, man!' howled Firethorn, pointing a finger. 'She is there in the upper gallery.'

'Amid three dozen or more fair maids.'

'Outshining them all with her splendour.'

'I fear I cannot pick her out, master.'

'The angel wears blue and pink.'

'As do several others.'

'Enough of this, you wretch!'

Firethorn punched him playfully and Nicholas saw that he could not escape his appointed task by a show of confusion. He had seen the young woman at once and the sight of her had rung a warning bell inside his skull. Even in the blaze of colour provided by the gallants and the ladies all around her, she stood out with ease. Her face was small, oval and exquisitely lovely with none of the cosmetic aids on which others had to rely so heavily. She was quite petite with a delicate vivacity apparent even at a cursory glance. Nicholas put her age at no more than twenty. She wore a dress in the Spanish fashion with a round, stiff-laced collar above a blue bodice that was fitted with sleeves of a darker hue. Pink ribbons flowed down both arms. Her skirt ballooned out with a matching explosion of blue and pink. Jewellery added the final touch to a glittering portrait.

'I think you have marked her now,' said Firethorn with a chuckle. 'Is she not divine?'

'Indeed, yes,' agreed Nicholas. 'But you are not the first to make that observation.'

'How so?'

'She is in the company of two young gentlemen.'

'What should I care?'

'Haply, one of them might be her husband.'

'That will not deter me, Nick. Had she fifty or more husbands, I would still pursue her. It only serves to add spice to the chase. I have something that no other man can offer. True genius upon the stage!'

'The lady has seen you at your peak.'

'Count Orlando has conquered her,' said Firethorn grandly. 'I saw it every time I stepped out upon the boards. I drew tears from those pearls that are her eyes. I made her little heart beat out the tune of love.'

Nicholas Bracewell gave the resigned sigh of someone who had heard it all before. The actor had immense talent but it was matched by immense vanity. Firethorn believed that he simply had to perform one of his major roles in front of a woman and she would fling herself into his bed without reservation or delay. What made his latest target more alarming to Nicholas was the fact that she did not conform to the accepted type. Here was no practised coquette, sending hot glances down to stir Firethorn's ardour. The young woman was self-evidently not the kind of court beauty who enjoyed an occasional dalliance to break up the monotony of an idle and powdered existence. For all her undeniable charms and her gorgeous array, there was a wan simplicity about her, a lack of sophistication, the shy awkwardness of someone who was enthralled by the play without quite knowing how to comport herself at a playhouse.

She was unawakened and Lawrence Firethorn had elected himself as the man to open her eyes.

'Find out who she is, Nick.'

'Leave it with me, sir.'

'About it straight.'

'As you wish.'

A stocky man of medium height, Firethorn filled his lungs to expand his chest and got a last, fleeting glimpse of her before she left the gallery. He had reached an irrevocable decision. Still in the attire of an Italian aristocrat, he stroked his dark, pointed beard and gave a Machiavellian smile.

'I must have her!'

Born and brought up in Richmond with its quiet beauty and its abundant royal associations, Anne Hendrik had never regretted her move to Southwark. It was a dirtier, darker and more populous area with lurking danger in its narrow thoroughfares and the threat of disease in its careless filth. But it was also one of the most colourful and cosmopolitan districts of London, a vibrant place that throbbed with excitement and which had become the home of theatres and bear-baiting arenas and other entertainments which could flourish best outside the city boundaries. Anne had chosen to live there when she married Jacob Hendrik, an immigrant hatmaker, who brought his Dutch skill and conscientiousness to his adopted country. Theirs was a happy marriage that produced no children but which gave birth to a steady flow of fashionable headgear for all classes. The Hendrik name became a seal of quality.

When her husband died, Anne inherited a comfortable house and a thriving business in the adjoining premises. A handsome woman in her thirties, she was expected by almost everyone to mourn for a decent interval before taking another man to the altar and there was no shortage of candidates seeking that honour. Anne Hendrik kept them all at bay with a show of independence that was unlikely in a woman in her position. Instead of taking the softer options posed by remarriage, she picked up the reins of the business and proved that she had more than enough shrewdness and acumen to drive it along. Like her husband before her, she was not afraid to use a judicious crack of the whip over her employees.

'This will not be tolerated much longer,' she said.

'Hans is a good craftsman,' argued her companion.

'Only when he is here.'

'The boy was sent on an errand, mistress.'

'He should have been back this long while.'

'Give him a little more time.'

'I have done that too often, Preben,' she said. 'I will have to speak more harshly to Master Hans Kippel. If he wishes to remain as an apprentice under my roof, then he must mend his ways.'

'Let *me* talk to him in your stead.'

'You are too fond of the boy to scold him.'

Preben van Loew accepted the truth of the charge and nodded sadly. A dour, emaciated man in his fifties, he was the oldest and best of her employees and he had been a close friend of Jacob Hendrik. Though he specialised in making ostentatious hats for the gentry, the Dutchman was soberly dressed himself and wore only a simple cap upon his bulbous head. Hans Kippel was far and away the most able of the apprentices when he put his mind to it but there was a wayward streak in the youth that made for bad timekeeping and lapses of concentration. Entrusted with the task of delivering some hats in the city itself, he should have been back with the money almost an hour ago. Anne liked him enormously but even her affection was not proof against the nudging suspicion that temptation might have been too much for the lad. The money that he was carrying was worth more than three months' wages and he would not have been the first apprentice to abscond.

Preben van Loew read her mind and rushed to the defence of his young colleague.

'Hans is an honest boy,' he said earnestly.

'Let us hope so.'

'I know his family as well as my own. We grew up

18

together in Amsterdam. You can always put your trust in a Kippel. They will never let you down.'

'Then where is he now?'

'On the road back, mistress.'

'By way of Amsterdam?'

She had meant it as a joke but she rued it when his face crumpled. Preben van Loew was the mainstay of the business and she did not want to upset him in any way. At the same time, she could not allow an apprentice too much leeway or he would be bound to take advantage. Anne tried to make amends by praising the handiwork of her senior employee who was about to put the last carefully chosen feather into a tall hat with a curling brim. It was a small masterpiece that would grace the head of a gallant. The Dutchman allowed himself to be mollified then fell into a refrain that she had heard all too often on the lips of her husband.

'They do us wrong to keep us out,' he moaned.

'It is the English way, I fear.'

'Why do they fear the foreigner so?'

'Simply because he is foreign.'

'We make hats as good as theirs but they will not let us join their Guilds. They have the first choice of all the work that is on offer. We have to struggle on down here, outside the city limits, so that we do not offend their noses with our Dutch smell.'

'They are jealous of your skills, Preben.'

'It is unjust, mistress.'

'Jacob said as much every day,' she recalled. 'He went

to them and put his arguments but they were deaf to his entreaties. All they would do was to boast about their history. They told him that the Hatters and the Furriers united with the Haberdashers at the very start of this century. Among those Hatters were the Feltmakers who have been trying to form their own Guild of late.'

'I know, mistress,' he said gloomily. 'But the move has been opposed. What does it matter to us? None of these precious Guilds will appreciate our quality. They just wish to look after themselves and keep us out.'

'It may change in time, Preben.'

'I will not live to see it.'

'Justice will one day be done.'

'It has no place in business.'

Anne Hendrik was unable to reply. Before she could open her mouth, the door flew open and a scrawny youth in buff jerkin and hose came staggering in. Hans Kippel could not have made a more dramatic entrance. Anne moved across to reproach him and Preben van Loew stepped in to protect him then they both took a closer look at the newcomer. He was in great distress. His clothes were torn, his face was bruised and blood was oozing freely from a deep gash in his temple. Hans Kippel could barely stand. They helped him quickly to a seat.

'Rest yourself here,' said Anne.

'What happened?' asked Preben van Loew.

'I will send for a surgeon directly.'

'Tell us what befell you, Hans.'

The boy was trembling with fear. On the verge of

exhaustion, he could barely dredge up strength enough to speak. When the words finally dribbled out, there was a tattered bravery to them.

'I saved . . . it. They . . . did not get . . . the money . . .'

With a ghost of a smile, he pitched forward onto the oak floorboards in a dead faint.

Stanford Place stood in a prime position on the east side of Bishopsgate and dwarfed the neighbouring dwellings. It was built in the reign of Edward IV and had now been arresting eyes and exciting envy for well over a century. With a frontage of almost two hundred feet, it had four storeys, each one jettied out above the floor below. Time had wearied the timber framing somewhat and the beams had settled at a slight angle to give the façade a curiously lopsided look but this only added to the character of the house. It was like a keystone in an arch and the adjacent buildings in Bishopsgate Street leant against it for support with companionable familiarity.

The establishment ran to a dozen bedchambers, a small banqueting hall, a dining parlour, a drawing room, butler's lodging, servants' quarters, kitchens, a bake house, even a tiny chapel. There were also stables, outhouses and an extensive garden. It was around this last impressive feature of the house that its owner was perambulating in the early evening sunlight. Walter Stanford was a big, bluff man with apparel that suggested considerable wealth and a paunch which hinted at too ready an appetite. Yet though his body had succumbed to middle age, his plump face still had a boyish quality to it and the large brown eyes sparkled with childlike glee.

'There is always room for improvement, Simon.'

'Yes, master.'

'No expense must be spared in pursuit of it.'

'That was ever your way, sir.'

'Look to the example of Theobalds,' said Stanford with a lordly wave of his hand. 'When Sir Robert Cecil was gracious enough to invite a party of us there, we were conducted around his garden. Garden, do I say? It was truly a revelation.'

'You have commended it to me before, master.'

'No praise is too high, Simon. Why, man, it beggars all description.' Stanford chortled as he hit his stride. 'The garden at Theobalds is encompassed with a ditch full of water, so broad and inviting that a man could row a boat between the shrubs if he had a mind to. There was a great variety of trees and plants with labyrinths to provide sport and decoration. What pleased me most was the *jet d'eau* with its basin of white marble. I must have such a thing here.'

'Order has already been given for it.'

'Then there were columns and pyramids of wood at every turn. After seeing these, we were taken by the gardener into the summerhouse, in the lower part of which, built, as it were, in a semicircle, are the twelve Roman emperors in white marble, and a table of touchstone. The upper part of it is set round with cisterns of lead into which the water is conveyed through pipes, so that fish may be kept in them, and in summertime they are very convenient for bathing. And so it went on, Simon.'

'Indeed, sir.'

As steward of the household, Simon Pendleton was well acquainted with his master's enthusiasms. Unlike many who make large amounts of money, Walter Stanford was always looking for new ways to spend it and his home provided him with endless opportunities. The steward was a short, slim, unctuous man in his forties with a high forehead and greying beard. Trotting discreetly at the heels of the other, he made a mental note of any new commissions for the garden and there was much to keep him occupied. Every time Stanford paused, he ordered some new trees, shrubs, flowers, or herbs. Whenever a gap presented itself in some quiet corner, he decided to fill it with some statuary or with a pool. Parsimony was unknown to the master of Stanford Place. He was generosity itself when his interest was aroused.

'It must all be ready in time,' he warned.

'I will speak to the gardeners, sir.'

'My hour of triumph comes ever closer, Simon.'

'And much deserved it is,' said the steward with an obsequious bow. 'Your whole establishment is conscious of the honour that you bestow upon them. It will indeed be a privilege to serve the next Lord Mayor of London.'

'It will be the summit of my achievement.'

Stanford was lost for a moment in contemplation of the joys that lay ahead. Like his father before him, he was a Master of the Mercers' Company, the most prestigious Guild in the city, first in order of precedence on all ceremonial occasions, and immortalised by the name of London's revered mayor, Dick Whittington, who had slipped immoveably into the folk-memory of the capital. The great man had also been Master of the Company and it was Stanford's ambition to emulate some of his achievements. He wanted to leave his mark indelibly upon the city.

'He built the largest privy in London,' he mused fondly. 'In the year of our Lord, 1419, Richard Whittington erected a convenience in Vintry Ward with sixty seats for Ladies and for Gentlemen, flushed with piped water. What a legacy to bequeath to old London town!'

Pendleton coughed discreetly and Stanford came out of his reverie. He was about to continue his walk when he saw someone flitting through the apple trees towards him on the tips of her toes. She wore a dress of blue and pink that set off the colour of her eyes and the rosiness of her cheeks. Stanford held his arms wide to welcome her and his steward melted quickly into the undergrowth. The young woman came gambolling excitedly up.

'Matilda!' said Stanford. 'What means this haste?'

'Oh, sir, I have so much to tell you!' she gasped.

'Catch your breath first while I steal a kiss.' He bent over to peck her on the cheek then stood back to admire her. 'You are truly the delight of my life!'

'I have found delights of my own, sir.'

'Where might they be?'

'At the playhouse,' she said. 'We saw Westfield's Men perform this dolorous tragedy at the Queen's Head. It made

24

me weep piteously but it also filled me with such wonder. I beg of you to indulge me. When you are made Lord Mayor of London, let us have a play to mark the occasion.'

'There will be a huge procession, child, a ceremonial parade through the streets of the city. It will lack nothing in pomp and pageant, that I can vouch.'

'But I want a play,' she urged. 'To please me, say that I may have my way in this matter. It was a transport of delight from start to finish. Master Firethorn is the best actor in the whole world and I worship at his feet.' She threw her arms around his neck. 'Do not deny me, sir. I know it is *your* day but I would round it off with a performance of some lively play.'

Walter Stanford gave an indulgent chuckle.

'You shall have your wish, Matilda,' he said.

'Oh, sir! You are a worthy husband!'

'And you, a wife among thousands. I strive to satisfy every whim of my gorgeous young bride.'

Nicholas Bracewell paid the penalty for being so reliable and resourceful. The more competent he proved himself in every sphere, the more onerous became his duties. While he made himself indispensable to the company and thereby attained a degree of security that none of the other hired men could aspire to, he found himself coping with additional responsibilities all the time. Nicholas made light of them. Having run his errand for Lawrence Firethorn, he went straight back to his post to supervise the dismantling of the stage and the storing of the costumes and properties.

Westfield's Men were not due to perform at the Queen's Head until the following week and so their makeshift theatre had to be taken down so that the yard could be returned to its more workaday function as a stabling area for visitors to the inn. The valuable accoutrements of the actor's art had to be carefully gathered up and locked away in a private room that was rented from the landlord.

While marshalling the stagekeepers, Nicholas also had to deal with countless enquiries from members of the company who wanted details of future engagements, repairs made to some hand prop or other, simple praise for their afternoon's work and, most of all, confirmation of when and where they would get their wages. The book holder was also the central repository of complaints and there was never a shortage of these as peevish actors pursued their vendettas or argued their case for a larger role. It was tiring work but Nicholas sailed through it with the quiet smile of a man who revels in his occupation.

When the last complaint had been fielded – George Dart wondering why Count Orlando had boxed him on the ear in the middle of Act Two – Nicholas went on to tackle one of his most daunting tasks. This was his all too regular encounter with Alexander Marwood, the gloomy landlord of the Queen's Head, a man temperamentally unsuited to the presence of actors because he believed, in that joyless wasteland known as his heart, that their avowed purpose in life was to destroy the fabric of his inn, scandalise his patrons and debauch his nubile daughter. That none of these things had so far actually happened did nothing to subdue his restless pessimism or to still his nervous twitch.

Nicholas met this merchant of doom in the taproom and smiled into the cadaverous, ever-mobile face.

'How now, Master Marwood!'

'You do me wrong to vex me so,' said the landlord.

'In what way, sir?'

'Fire, Master Bracewell. Yellow flames of fire. It is not enough that my thatch is at risk from those pipe-smokers who crowd my galleries. Westfield's Men have to bring it onto the stage as well. It was almost *Death and Darkness* indeed for me. Those torches could have set my whole establishment ablaze. Do but consider, I might have lost my inn, my home, my livelihood and my hopes of future happiness.'

'Water was at hand in case of any mishap.'

'Would you burn me to the ground, sir?'

'Indeed not, Master Marwood,' soothed Nicholas. 'We would never destroy that which we hold most dear. Namely, your good opinion which is attested by your contractual dealings with us. In token of which, allow me to pay the rent that is now due. In full, sir.'

He handed over a bag of coins and sought to steal away but the landlord's skeletal fingers clutched at his sleeve to detain him.

'I crave a word with you, Master Bracewell.'

'As many as you wish.'

'It concerns your contract with the Queen's Head.'

'We are anxious to renew it.'

'On what terms, though?'

'On those satisfactory to both parties.'

'Aye, there's the rub,' said Marwood, using a hand to push back a strand of greasy hair from his furrowed brow. 'The case is altered, sir.'

'I am sure that we can come to composition.'

'Westfield's Men bring me many woes.'

Alexander Marwood recited them with morbid glee. It was a litany that Nicholas had heard many times and always with the same wringing of hands, the same sighing of sighs and the same uncontrollable facial contortions. Use of the Queen's Head came at a high price. Westfield's Men had to put up with the sustained hysteria of a landlord who was whipped into action by a nagging wife. Ready to reap the financial advantages of having a theatre company in his yard, Marwood also harvested a bumper crop of outrage and apprehension. He was at his most febrile when the contract was due for renewing, hoping to exact more money and greater assurances of good conduct from the acting fraternity. What disturbed Nicholas was that a new note was being sounded.

'We may have to part company, Master Bracewell.'

'You would drive us away to another inn?'

'No other landlord would be foolish enough to have you,' said Marwood fretfully. 'They lack my patience and forbearance. You'll not easily find another home.'

It was a painful truth. Public performance of plays was forbidden within the city boundaries and it was only municipal weakness in enforcing this decree that allowed companies such as Westfield's Men to flourish unscathed.

More than once, they aroused aldermanic ire by their choice of repertoire or by the bad influence they were alleged to have on their audiences but they had never actually faced prosecution. Though fearing that every day the hand of authority would descend on his bony shoulder, Alexander Marwood, out of naked self-interest, yet ran the risk of contravening regulations. Other publicans would not be so adventurous, quite apart from the fact that their premises, in most cases, were not at all suitable for the presentation of drama. For some years now, the Queen's Head had furnished Westfield's Men with the illusion of having a permanent base. That illusion could be completely shattered.

'Do not make any hasty decision,' said Nicholas.

'It is one that may be forced upon me, sir.'

'For what reason?'

'The Queen's Head may change hands.'

Nicholas was jolted. 'You are leaving?'

'No, sir, but we may yield up ownership. We have received an offer too generous to ignore. It would give us security in our old age and provide a fit dowry for our daughter, Rose.' He attempted a smile but it came out as a hideous leer. 'There is but one main condition.'

'What might that be?'

'If we sell the inn, the new owner insists that Westfield's Men must go.'

'And who is this stern fellow?'

'Alderman Rowland Ashway.'

Nicholas winced. He knew the man by reputation and

liked nothing of what he had heard. Rowland Ashway was not merely one of the most prosperous brewers in London, he was also alderman for the very ward in which the Queen's Head was located. His disapproval of inn-yard theatre did not spring from any puritanical zeal. It arose from notions of prejudice and profit. Like others who felt they created the wealth of the capital city, Ashway had a deep suspicion of an idle aristocracy that fawned away its time at court and held the whiphand over the growing middle class of which he was a prominent member. To his way of thinking, a theatrical company was an indulgence on the part of a highly privileged minority. In ousting Westfield's Men, he could strike a blow at the epicurean Lord Westfield himself.

It was not only social revenge that activated the brewer. In the final analysis, his account book dictated all his business decisions. If he was buying the Queen's Head, he obviously felt that he could more than compensate in other ways for the revenue he would forgo if he expelled the company. Nicholas was seriously alarmed. The resourceful book holder might be thrown out of work by a ruthless book keeper.

'This matter must be discussed in full,' he said.

'I give you but advance warning.'

'Speak with Master Firethorn about it.'

'That I will not,' said Marwood. 'I like not his ranting and raving. My ears buzz for a week after I have talked with him. I would rather treat with you, sir. We have always been congenial to each other.'

Nicholas Bracewell had never met a human being less

congenial than the twitching publican but he did not want to upset the tricky negotiations that lay ahead by saying so. He thanked Marwood for alerting him to the potential danger. In the circumstances, he did not feel like putting more money into Rowland Ashway's pocket by buying a pint of his celebrated ale. Instead, he nodded his farewell and sauntered across to Edmund Hoode who was hunched over a cup of sack in the corner of the taproom.

The two men were good friends and the playwright always consulted the other during the writing of a new work if any special dramatic effects were required. Nicholas had an instinctive feel for the practicalities of theatre and a way of making even the most difficult effects work. The book holder's willingness to confront any technical problems made Hoode's job as resident poet much easier.

Nicholas had intended to pass on the grim tidings he had just gleaned from the landlord but he saw that his friend already had anxieties enough.

'What, Edmund? All amort?'

'In sooth, I am in the pit of misery, Nick.'

'Why so? Your play was as ever a shining success.'

'Actors must quit the stage when they are done.'

'Your meaning?'

'I detest the role I must play now.'

Nicholas understood at once. Edmund Hoode was going through a fallow period in his personal life. A hopeless romantic, he was always losing his heart and dedicating his verses to some new fancy and, although his love was usually unrequited, the blissful agony of infatuation was reward enough in itself. Without a fresh mistress to make him truly unhappy, he was plunged into despair. It took Nicholas well over an hour to instil some hope into his friend. The questing love of Edmund Hoode and the roving lust of Lawrence Firethorn could be equal tyrannies to him.

It was late evening by the time Nicholas finally left the inn and darkness was pulling its malodorous shroud over the city. Instead of walking back home to Southwark by way of London Bridge, he elected to be rowed across by one of the army of watermen who populated the river. As he headed for the wharf, he had time properly to reflect on what Alexander Marwood had told him. Ejection from the Queen's Head would be a disaster for the company and might even lead to its extinction. How serious the threat really was he had no means of knowing but one thing he did resolve upon. He would not spread panic unnecessarily. Insecurity was rife enough in their blighted profession and he did not wish to add to it in any way. The imminent peril should be concealed for the time being until more details emerged because he did not rule out the possibility of finding a way to solve this horrendous problem. He could best do that by working quietly behind the scenes rather than in an atmosphere of communal frenzy. Meanwhile, therefore, Nicholas would have to keep a very dark and very heavy secret to himself.

The Thames was lapping noisily at the timbers of the wharf when he arrived and the moored craft were thudding rhythmically against each other. Daylight turned the river into a floating village and even at this late hour many of the inhabitants were still promenading over the water. Barges, wherries, hoys, fishing smacks and an occasional tilt-boat could be seen and there was a lone coracle wending its way along. Nicholas did not have to choose his means of transport. His pilot came hopping across to him with gruff deference.

'This way, Master Bracewell. Let me serve you, sir.'

'I will do that gladly, Abel.'

'I have missed you for a se'n-night or more.'

'My legs took me home.'

'Sit in my boat and make the journey in style, sir. There is more music to please your ears.'

Abel Strudwick was an unprepossessing individual, a heavy, round-shouldered man of middle height with unkempt hair and a hirsute beard doing their best to hide an ugly, pockmarked face. Though roughly the same age as his favourite passenger, he looked a decade older. Strudwick had the vices and virtues of his breed. Like all watermen, he had a stentorian voice to hail his customers and a savage turn of phrase with which to assault them if they failed to tip him handsomely. On the credit side, he was an honest, reliable citizen who put the strength of his arms and the warmth of his company at the disposal of anyone who sat in the boat.

What set Abel Strudwick apart from the rest and gave him a special relationship with Nicholas Bracewell was his addiction to what he called music. When the book holder was offered fresh melodies, he knew that the waterman had been busy with his pen, for Strudwick had poetic ambitions.

His music came in the form of mundane verse that was always at the mercy of its rhyme scheme and which flowed from him as readily and roughly as the Thames itself. Nicholas was his preferred audience because he always listened with genuine interest and because his connections with the theatre were a distant promise of some kind of literary recognition.

As they got into the boat, Nicholas felt a sailor's surge of excitement at being afloat again, albeit in a modest craft. Before he came into the theatre, he had sailed with Drake on the circumnavigation of the world and it had made a deep impression on him. The experience gave him another bond with the waterman. Though Strudwick had never been more than ten miles upstream, he saw himself as a great voyager like his friend and it fed his invention.

He declaimed his latest piece of music.

'Row on, row on, across the waves,
Thou monarch of the sea.
Steer past those rocks, avoid those caves,
Row on to eternity.'

There was much more to come and Nicholas heard it patiently as he sat in the stern of the boat with his hand trailing gently in the water. Strudwick's methodical rowing was matched by the repetitive banality of his latest verses but his passenger would nevertheless pay him with kind words and encouragement. A warbling poet was milder company than a foul-mouthed waterman.

'A turd in your teeth!'

'How so, Abel?'

'A pox upon your pox-ridden pizzle!'

Strudwick had not lapsed back into his normal mode of speech to berate Nicholas. He was cursing the obstacle which the prow of his boat had struck and which had turned his music to discord. Swearing volubly, he manoeuvred his craft round so that he could see what he was abusing. Nicholas felt it first and it made his blood run cold. His trailing hand met another in the water, five pale, thin, lifeless fingers that touched his own in a clammy greeting. He sat up in the boat and peered into the darkness. Even the roaring Strudwick was frightened into silence.

Caught up in a piece of driftwood was the naked body of a man. There was enough moonlight for them to see that the corpse had met a gruesome death. The head had been battered in and one of the legs was twisted out at an unnatural angle. A dagger was lodged in the throat.

Abel Strudwick was still emptying the contents of a full stomach into the river as Nicholas hauled their sorry cargo aboard.

Chapter Two

Anne Hendrik was not normally given to apprehension. She was a strong-minded woman who had survived all the blows that Fate had dealt her and who always met adversity with resolution. Though her marriage had been sound, it had brought pain and grief to her family who disapproved in frank terms of her choice of husband. London had no love of foreigners and those women who had actually rejected decent English stock in order to marry immigrants were looked upon with disdain, if not outright disgust. Having to cope with the sneers and the cold shoulders had helped to harden Anne in many ways but she was still a sensitive person underneath it all and her emotions could be aroused in a crisis.

The present situation was a case in point. She was very distressed by what had happened to Hans Kippel, her young apprentice, all the more so because the boy had been sent expressly at her command to deliver the order. Anne blamed herself for entrusting such an important duty to such an untried youth. In giving Hans Kippel an extra responsibility, she had exposed him unnecessarily to the dangers of city life. The wounds he got in her service were each a separate reproach to her and she could not bear to look on as they were bathed and bandaged. Preben van Loew tried to assure her that it was not her fault but his words fell on deaf ears. What she needed was the more persuasive, objective, down-to-earth comfort of the man who shared her house with her but he was not there.

The longer she waited, the more convinced she became that he, too, had met with violence on his journey home. As evening became night and night slipped soundlessly into the next day, Anne was almost distraught, pacing the floor of her main room with a candle in her hand and racing to peer through the window every time a footstep was heard on the cobbles outside. The house was not large but she had felt the need for male companionship after her husband's demise and she had taken in a lodger so that she might have the sense of a man about the place once more. It had been a rewarding experiment. The guest had turned out to be not only an exemplary lodger and a loyal friend but – at special moments savoured by both – he had been considerably more. To have lost him at a time when she needed him most would indeed be a cruel stroke of fortune. His movements were uncertain and his hours of work irregular but he should have been back long before now. When there was some unexpected delay, he usually sent word to put her mind at rest.

Where could he be at such a late hour? Bankside was littered with hazards enough in broad daylight. With the cover of darkness, those hazards multiplied a hundredfold. Could he have met the same trouble as Hans Kippel and be lying in his own blood in some fetid lane? Her immediate impulse was to take a lantern and go in search of him but the futility of such a gesture was borne in upon her. It was no use subjecting herself to such grave danger. She was virtually trapped in the house and she had to make the most of it. With a great effort of will, she sat down at the table, put the candle aside, took several deep breaths and told herself to remain calm in the emergency. It worked for a matter of minutes. Worries then flooded back and she was up on her feet again to confront each new horrible possibility that her imagination threw up.

Anne Hendrik was so enmeshed in her concern that she did not hear the key being inserted into the front door. The first she knew of her deliverance was when the solid figure stood before her in the gloom.

Tears came as she flung herself into his arms.

'God be praised!'

'What ails you?'

'Hold me tight, sir. Hold me very tight.'

'So I will, my love.'

'I have been in such dread for your safety.'

'Here I am, unharmed, as you see.'

'Thank the Lord!'

Nicholas Bracewell held her close and kissed the top of

her head softly. It was most unlike her to be so on edge and it took him some time to calm her enough to get the full story out of her. Anne sat opposite him at the table and talked of the deep guilt she felt about Hans Kippel. He heard her out before offering his advice.

'You do yourself an injustice, Anne.'

'Do I, sir?'

'The boy is old enough and sensible enough to take on such a duty. It is all part of his apprenticeship. I warrant that he was delighted when you chose him.'

'Indeed, he was. It got him away from here.'

'Out of the dullness of his workplace and into the excitement of the streets,' said Nicholas. 'Hans will have been a little careless, that is all. He will not make the same mistake again.'

'But that is the trouble of it.'

'What is?'

'Hans does not understand the nature of his error.'

'He was off guard for a moment, surely?'

'Maybe, Nick,' she said. 'But he does not remember. Hans took such a blow on the head that it has knocked the memory out of him. All he can recall is that some men attacked him and that he got away. When, where or why are questions that the lad cannot as yet comprehend.'

'His wounds have been tended?'

'Of course, sir. The surgeon said it is not uncommon to find a lapse of memory in such cases. Hans must be given time to recover. As his body mends, haply his mind will be made whole again.' Anne seized his hands to squeeze them.

'Speak to him, Nick. The boy likes you and looks up to you. Help the poor creature for pity's sake.'

'I will do all that is needful. Trust it well.'

'Your words are a balm to me.'

He leant forward to embrace her then turned to his own story. When he explained what had detained him, Anne was thrown into disarray once more. The injuries of a young apprentice paled beside the discovery of a dead body in the River Thames. Nicholas Bracewell and Abel Strudwick had taken the corpse back to the wharf from which they had departed. After rousing the watch, they had been required to give sworn statements to a magistrate before being allowed to go. Strudwick had then rowed his friend to Bankside in a grim silence that no music could break. Tragedy had knocked all poetic skills out of him.

Anne was in a state of total dismay.

'Who was the man?' she said.

'We have no means of knowing as yet.'

'But why was he stripped of his clothing?'

'The murderer may have thought his apparel worth the taking,' he said. 'And that argues rich garments which could be sold for gain. I think, however, that there could be another reason behind it. His clothing could have helped to identify him and much care was taken to render the poor soul anonymous. The way that his face was beaten to a pulp, his own kin would not be able to recognise him. He went out of this world in the most damnable way.'

'Could nothing be learnt from the corpse, Nick?'

'Only some idea of his age, which I would put around thirty summers. And one thing more, Anne.'

'Well, sir?'

'The body had not long been in the water.'

'How can you be sure of that?'

'By bitter experience,' he said. 'I have seen all too many men who have found a watery grave. *Rigor mortis* sets in after a time and the miserable creatures become bloated in a way too hideous to describe. The person we found tonight was dropped into the river only a short time beforehand.'

'Was any other villainy wreaked upon him?'

'He was stabbed through the neck and one of his legs was horribly broken.' He saw her flinch. 'But these are details enough for you. I would not vex you any more.'

'My joy at seeing you again is blackened by this grim intelligence.' Fresh tears threatened. 'The body in the river could so easily have been yours, Nick.'

'With Abel Strudwick to look after me?' he said with a smile. 'I could not ask for a better guard. A whole armada would not dare to take on Abel when he is afloat. He would give them a broadside with his curses then rake their decks with a fusillade of poems.'

She went back into his arms and hugged him close.

'It has been a long and lonely night for me.'

'I did not stay away from you out of choice, Anne.'

'There is almost too much for me to bear.'

'Let us share the load, my love.'

'That was my hope.'

'Consider it fulfilled.'

'Welcome home, Nick,' she whispered.

They went slowly upstairs to her bedchamber. It was something which they both felt they had deserved.

The change of venue was significant. The meeting was scheduled to take place at Lawrence Firethorn's house in Shoreditch, a rather modest but welcoming abode that gave shelter to the actor's own family and their servants as well as hospitality to the company's four apprentices. What made the establishment function with such relative smoothness was the presiding genius of Margery Firethorn, a redoubtable woman who combined the roles of wife, mother, housekeeper and landlady with consummate ease and who still had enough energy left over to pursue other interests, to maintain a high standard of Christian observance and to terrorise anyone foolhardy enough to stand in her way. Even her husband, fearless in any other way, had been known to quail before her. Indirectly, it was she who had dictated the move to another place and Barnaby Gill spotted this at once.

'Lawrence is on heat again!' he moaned.

'Lord save us!' cried Edmund Hoode.

'That is why he dare not have us at his house. In case Margery gets wind of his new *amour*.'

'Who *is* the luckless creature, Barnaby?'

'I know not and care not,' said Gill with studied indifference. 'Women are all one to me and I like not any of the infernal gender. My passions are dedicated to intimacy

43

on a much higher plane.' He puffed at his pipe and blew out rings of smoke. 'What else did our Creator in his munificence make pretty boys for, I ask?'

It was a rhetorical question and Edmund Hoode would in any case not have been drawn into such a discussion. Barnaby Gill's tendencies were well known and generally tolerated by a company that valued his acting skills and his remarkable comic gifts. Hoode had never plumbed the secret of why his companion – such a gushing fountain of pleasure upon the stage – was so morose and petulant when he left it. The playwright preferred the public clown to the private cynic. They were sitting in a room at the Queen's Head as they waited for Firethorn to arrive. The three men were all sharers with Lord Westfield's Men, ranked players who were named in the royal patent for the company and who took the leading roles in any performance. There were four other sharers but it was this triumvirate that effectively dictated policy and controlled the day-to-day running of the company.

Lawrence Firethorn was the undisputed leader. Even when he burst through the door and gave them an elaborate bow, he was simply asserting his superiority.

'Gentlemen, your servant!'

'You are late as usual, sir,' snapped Gill.

'I was detained by family matters.'

'Your drink awaits you, Lawrence,' said Hoode.

'Thank you, Edmund. I am glad that one of my partners in this enterprise has some concern for me.'

'Oh, *I* have concern in good measure,' said Gill. 'I was

44

a model of concern during yesterday's performance when I feared you might not survive to the end of it.'

'Me, sir?' Firethorn bridled. 'You speak of me?'

'Who else, sir? It was Count Orlando who was puffing and panting so in the heat of the day. And it was that same noble Italian who became so flustered that he inserted four lines from *Vincentio's Revenge*.'

'You lie, you dog!' howled Firethorn.

'Indeed, I do. It was six lines.'

'My Count Orlando was simon pure.'

'Give or take an occasional blemish.'

'You dare to scorn my performance!'

'By no means,' said Gill, ready with a final thrust. 'I thought that your Count Orlando was excellent – but not nearly as fine as your Vincentio in the same play!'

'You viper! You maggot! You pipe-smoking pilchard!'

'Gentlemen, gentlemen,' soothed Hoode. 'We have come together to do business and not to trade abuse.'

'The man is a scurvy rogue!' yelled Firethorn.

'At least I remember my lines,' retorted the other.

'None are worth listening to, sir.'

'My admirers will be the judge of that.'

'You have but one and that is Master Barnaby Gill.'

'I will not brook insults!'

'Then do not wear such ridiculous attire, sir.'

Gill flared up immediately. The one certain way to bring out his choleric disposition was to criticise his appearance because he took such infinite pains with it. Dressed in a peach-coloured doublet and scarlet hose, he wore a tall hat that was festooned with feathers. Rings on almost every finger completed a dazzling effect. Roused to a fever pitch, he now strutted up and down the room, pausing from time to time to stamp a foot in exasperation. Having routed his enemy, Firethorn reclined in the high-backed chair and took his first sip of the Canary wine that stood ready for him.

Hoode, meanwhile, devoted his energy to calming down the anguished clown, an almost daily task in view of the professional jealousy between Gill and Firethorn. Verbal clashes between them were the norm but they were quickly forgotten when the two actors were on stage together. Both were supreme in their own ways and it was from the dynamic between them that Westfield's Men drew much of their motive force.

Edmund Hoode eventually imposed enough calm for the meeting to begin. As they sat around the table, he reached gratefully for his pint of ale to wash away the memory of yet another needless row between his colleagues who had left him feeling that he had been ground into dust by two whining millstones. Lawrence Firethorn, poised and peremptory, opened the business of the day.

'We are met to confirm our future engagements,' he said. 'Tomorrow, as you know, we play *Double Deceit* at The Theatre in Shoreditch. It is a well-tried piece but that is no reason for us to be complacent. We will have a testing rehearsal in the morning to add what polish we may. Westfield's Men must be at their best, sirs.'

'I never give less,' said Gill sulkily.

'As to our immediate future . . .'

Firethorn outlined the programme that lay ahead, most of it confined to the Queen's Head which was their home base. One new performing venue did, however, surface.

'We have received an invitation to visit Richmond,' said Firethorn. 'The date lies some weeks hence but it is important to address our minds to it now.'

'Where will we play?' asked Hoode.

'In the yard of an inn.'

'Its name?'

'The Nine Giants.'

'I have never heard of the place,' sneered Gill.

'That is no bar to it,' said Firethorn easily. 'It is a sizeable establishment, by all accounts, and like to give us all that the Queen's Head can offer. The Nine Giants are nine giant oak trees that grace its paddock.'

Gill snorted. 'You ask me to perform amid trees?'

'Yes, Barnaby,' said his tormentor. 'You simply lift your back leg like any common cur and make water. Even *you* may win a laugh by that device.'

'I am against the whole idea,' said the other.

'Your opposition is a waste of bad breath.'

'The Nine Giants does not get my assent.'

'Too late, sir. I have accepted the invitation on behalf of the company.'

'You had no right to do that, Lawrence!'

'Nor any chance to refuse,' said Firethorn, producing the one reason that could silence Gill. 'It was given by Lord Westfield himself. Our noble patron has commanded us to appear in Richmond.'

'To what particular end?' said Hoode.

'As part of the wedding celebrations of a friend.'

'And what will we play?'

'That is what we must decide, Edmund. Lord Westfield has asked for a comedy that touches upon marriage.'

'There is sense in that,' agreed Gill, reviving at once and seeing a chance to steal some glory. 'The ideal choice must be *Cupid's Folly*.'

'The piece grows stale, sir.'

'How can you say that, Lawrence? My performance as Rigormortis is as fresh as a daisy.'

'Daisies are low, dishonest flowers.'

Barnaby Gill banged the table with irritation. His fondness for *Cupid's Folly* was well founded. A rustic comedy with a farcical impetus, it was the one play in the company's repertoire which gave him a central role that allowed him to dominate throughout. As a result, it was staged whenever they needed to mollify the little actor or to dissuade him for implementing his regular threat to walk out on Westfield's Men. No such exigency obtained here.

'I favour *Marriage and Mischief*,' said Hoode.

'Then you should have wed Margery,' added Firethorn. 'It is an interesting suggestion, Edmund, to be sure, but the play begins to show its age.'

'I stand by *Cupid's Folly*,' said Gill.

'And I by *Marriage and Mischief*,' said Hoode.

'That is why we need a happy compromise.' Firethorn gave a ripe chuckle which showed that the decision had already been made. 'We will favour the nuptials with some sage advice. Let us play *The Wise Widow of Dunstable*.'

It was a compromise indeed and his fellow sharers came to see much virtue in it. Edmund Hoode, fearing that he might be commissioned to write a new play for the occasion, was ready to settle for a seasoned comedy by another hand, especially as it offered him a telling cameo as the ghost of the widow's departed husband. Barnaby Gill, robbed of the opportunity to star in his favourite play, warmed quickly to the idea of a piece which gave him a prominent role and allowed him to execute no less than four of his famous comic jigs. Inevitably, it was Lawrence Firethorn who would shine in the leading part of Lord Merrymouth but there was light enough for others. *The Wise Woman of Dunstable* satisfied all needs.

They discussed their plans in more detail then the meeting broke up. Barnaby Gill was first to leave. When Edmund Hoode tried to follow him out, he was detained by the actor-manager. The glowing countenance of Lawrence Firethorn said it all and the other braced himself.

'I may have work for you, Edmund.'

'Spare me, sir, I pray you.'

'But I am in love, man.'

'I have long admired your beautiful wife.'

'It is not Margery I speak of!' hissed Firethorn. 'Another arrow has been fired into my heart.'

'Pluck it out in the name of marital bliss.'

'Come, come, Edmund. We are men of the world, I hope. Our passions are too fiery to be sated by a single woman. Each of us must spread his love joyously among the sex.'

Hoode sighed. 'Could I but find her, *I* would be faithful to one dear mistress.'

'Then help me secure mine by way of rehearsal.'

'I will not write verses for you, Lawrence.'

'They would be for *her*, man. For a divinity.'

'Offer up prayers instead.'

'I come to you in the name of friendship, Edmund. Do not let me down in my hour of need. Stand by to help, that is all I ask. Nothing is required from you now.'

'Why cannot you do your wooing alone?'

'And throw away the best chance that I have? Your poems are love potions in themselves, Edmund. No woman can resist your honeyed phrases and your sweet sadness.'

Hoode gave a hollow laugh. In recent months, several women had been proof against the most affecting verse that his pen could produce. It would be ironic if his poetic talent helped to ensnare a new victim for the capacious bed of Lawrence Firethorn.

'Who *is* the doomed lady?' he asked.

'That is the beauty of it, man. Nick Bracewell found out her name for me and it has increased my raptures.'

'How can this be?'

Firethorn shook his head. 'I may not tell you until after my prize is secured. But this I will say, Edmund. The lady in question is not only the most splendid creature in London. She will present me with the sternest challenge that I have ever faced. Your assistance will be the difference betwixt success and failure.'

'Or betwixt failure and disaster.'

'I like your spirit,' said Firethorn, slapping his mournful companion between the shoulder blades. 'We are yoke-fellows in this business. Mark my words, sir, we will bed this angel between us.'

'Abandon this folly now, Lawrence.'

'It is my mission in life.'

'Draw back while you still have time.'

'Too late, man. Plans have already been set in motion.'

Nicholas Bracewell set out early next morning with his mind still racing. A night in the arms of Anne Hendrik had lifted his spirits but failed to obliterate his abiding anxieties. The first of these concerned the dead body which he had dragged out of the murky waters on the previous night. As he was rowed back across the Thames in the sunlight, he felt once more the touch of the dead man's hand and saw again the mutilated corpse bobbing about before him. The body had been young, firm and well muscled, sent to its grave before its time with the most grotesque injuries. Nicholas was filled with horror and racked by a sense of waste. The life of some nameless man had been viciously cut short by unknown hands that had worked with malign purpose. Evidently, someone had hated the victim – but who had loved him? Who had borne him and cared for him? What family depended on him? What friends would mourn his absence? Why had he been hacked so cruelly out of existence and sent anonymously to meet his Maker? Over and over again, Nicholas asked himself the question that contained all the others – who *was* he?

One mystery led him on to another. What had really happened to Hans Kippel? He had been given a very incomplete account by Anne Hendrik because she herself did not know the full facts. Something very unpleasant had befallen the apprentice and Nicholas resolved to find out what it was as soon as he was able. He had always liked the boy – despite his lapses – and taken an almost fatherly interest in him. Again, he was upset by Anne's patent agitation and wanted to do all he could to help. It was as important to find Hans Kippel's assailant as it was to identify the body from the Thames.

The boat reached the wharf and he paid the waterman before stepping ashore and making his way towards Gracechurch Street. With his feet on dry land again and his place of work in prospect, he turned to another grim subject. A violent death and a hounded youth had occupied his thoughts this far and those same images still lurked as he considered the walking misery that was Alexander Marwood. The threat of expulsion was indeed real. It was the reputation of Westfield's Men which could meet a violent death if the company was deprived of its home. Sharers and hired men alike would become hounded youths who were driven way from the Queen's Head. Nicholas took a realistic view of possible consequences and shuddered.

Without their base, the company would find it very difficult to survive, certainly in its present form. It might limp along in some attenuated shape for a short while by appearing intermittently at a variety of venues but this could only ever be a temporary expedient. Other companies would move in quickly to pick the bones clean. Outstanding talents such as Lawrence Firethorn, Barnaby Gill and Edmund Hoode would soon be employed elsewhere but lesser mortals would stay out in the cold. Nicholas was confident that he himself would find work somewhere in the theatre but his concern was for his fellows, for the hired men who made up the bulk of the company and who clung to it with the desperate loyalty of those who have tasted the bitterness of neglect. To be thrust once more into unemployment would be a fatal blow to some of them and they might never work again.

Nicholas caught sight of the inn sign outside the Queen's Head and he sighed. Elizabeth Tudor looked as regal and defiant as ever but she might harbour tragedy for some of her subjects. Those least able to defend themselves would be cast adrift in a hostile city. The book holder thought of Thomas Skillen, the old stagekeeper, of Hugh Wegges, the tiremen, of Peter Digby and his consort of musicians. He thought of all the other poor souls to whom Westfield's Men gave a shred of dignity and a semblance of security. One in particular haunted Nicholas.

It was George Dart.

Being a member of a celebrated theatre company was not an unqualified honour. George Dart found that he had to earn his keep and suffer for his art. Even on days when there was no performance, the hard work did not cease and his status as the youngest and smallest of the stagekeepers meant that all the most menial and demanding tasks were assigned to him. It was manifestly unjust and, though that injustice was often reduced by the kindly intercession of Nicholas Bracewell, it could still rankle. George Dart was the company workhorse, the shambling beast of burden onto whom anything and everything could be loaded by uncaring colleagues. In rare moments of introspection, when he could pause to review his lot, he generated such a lather of self-pity that he toyed with the idea of leaving the theatre altogether, a bold move that always evaporated before his eyes when he considered how impossible it would be for him to find employment elsewhere. With all its disadvantages and its insecurities, working with Westfield's Men was the only life he had ever known.

Morning found him attending to one of the jobs that he liked least. He had been sent out early to put up the playbills advertising the performance of *Double Deceit* at the Theatre on the morrow. His first problem was to get the playbills from the printer without having the money to pay for them, assuring the man that Firethorn himself would be around to settle the debt that very day, hoping that the trusting soul was not aware of all the other printers still awaiting payment by Westfield's Men. This time he was lucky and got off lightly with a clip across the ear and a few blood-curdling oaths. Dart left the premises in Paternoster Lane with the playbills under his arm and began the familiar round.

The perils that befall the puny awaited him at every turn. He was jostled by elbows, pushed by hands, tripped by feet, abused by tongues and even chased by a gang of urchins but he continued steadfastly on his way and put up the playbills on every post and fence along the route. The reputation of Westfield's Men went before them and they had built up an appreciable following in a city that was clamouring for lively theatre but that same following needed to be informed of dates and times and places. Though he was involved in unrelieved drudgery, George Dart told himself that he was a vital link between the company and its prospective audience and thereby sought to check his rising sensation of worthlessness.

When the dispiriting work was over, there was one last chore for him. At the command of Lawrence Firethorn himself, he was to deliver the remaining playbill at a house in Bishopsgate. Since it was a continuation of Gracechurch Street, he knew it well but the market was its usual seething mass of humanity and he had to struggle with all his depleted might to make headway. Stanford Place eventually came into sight and he was daunted. Its monstrous size was forbidding and he could hear the barking of dogs from within as he hovered at the threshold. He stepped back involuntarily and was about to turn tail when he remembered the order that had been given to him by Firethorn. Facing his master with the news that he had disobeyed would be worse than hurling his frail body into the midst of a pack of ravening mastiffs. He opted for the lesser punishment and reached out to pull the bell at Stanford Place.

Response was immediate. The barking increased in volume and clawed feet could be heard scrabbling at the other side of the door. When it was opened with a dignified sweep, three dogs let him know that they did not welcome his arrival. They were silenced by a curt command from the slim and supercilious man who was now gazing down his nose at the unsolicited caller. Years as the household steward had given Simon Pendleton an ability to sum up stray visitors in an instant. He felt able to use a tone of complete contempt for the crumpled George Dart.

'Depart from this place at once, boy.'

'But I have business here, sir,' pleaded the other.

'None that need be taken seriously.'

'Do but hear me, master.'

'Away with you and your confounded begging bowl!'

'I ask for nothing,' said Dart hurriedly. 'Except that this be delivered to the mistress of the house.'

Pendleton was taken aback as the handbill was passed over to him. Rolled up into a scroll, it was tied with a piece of pink ribbon to give it a hint of importance. Even though it was covered by the sweaty fingerprints of its bearer, it enforced more serious consideration.

'Who are you?' asked Pendleton.

'A mere messenger, sir.'

'From whom, boy?'

'The lady will understand.'

'I desire further information.'

'My duty has been done,' said Dart gratefully.

And before the dogs could even begin to growl, he swung around and scurried off into the crowd with a speed born of desperation. A typical morning had ended.

* * *

Marriage to a much older man was turning out to have many unforeseen advantages and Matilda Stanford enjoyed the process of discovering what they were. When a young woman consents to wed a partner of more mature years, it is usually more of an arranged match than a case of irresistible love and so it was with her. Doting parents had been delighted when so august a figure as the Master of the Mercers' Company took an interest in their daughter and they encouraged that interest as wholeheartedly as they could. While the father worked sedulously on the potential suitor, the mother began to frame the girl's mind to the concept of marriage as social advance and she had slowly broken down all of Matilda's reservations. Now that she had been a wife for five months, the new mistress of Stanford Place was revelling in her good fortune.

Her husband was kind, attentive and ready to please her with touching eagerness. At the same time, Walter Stanford was a wealthy merchant whose continued success depended on the unremitting work he put into his business affairs. His preoccupation with those – and with the many duties of being Lord Mayor Elect – meant that his wife was given ample free time to spread her wings and to learn the power of his purse. Nor was Matilda put under any undue pressure in the marriage bed. He was a patient and considerate man, never enforcing any conjugal rights that she did not willingly concede and treating her with unflagging respect. There was another element in the relationship. Though devoted to his new wife, Walter Stanford was still, to some degree, in mourning for her predecessor, his first wife,

Alice, mother of his two children, a charming woman who had been killed before her time in a tragic accident some eighteen months earlier.

What pleased Matilda was the fact that she was not expected to be a complete replacement for someone who had shared her husband's life and bed for well over twenty years. Alice Stanford lay in the past. Matilda was the present and future, a rich prize owing to a rich man, an envied catch, a superb item to display in a household that prided itself above all else on the quality of its decoration. She had no illusions about it. Walter Stanford had married her to fill a gap in nature. She was there primarily to be *seen* as a wife rather than to satisfy his lust or provide him with heirs. It was a situation she came to appreciate.

Romance was signally lacking but there had been none of that in her parents' marriage and that was the model on which she based her judgements. Walter Stanford might not be able to stir her emotions but he could impress her with his wealth, please her with his gallantry and amuse her with the way that he showered gifts upon her. Matilda was indeed unawakened but only because she slept so soundly in such a comfortable existence.

'Where shall we go next?'

'I have not recovered from yesterday's outing yet.'

'London has much more to offer,' he said. 'It is the most exciting city in Europe.'

'I am learning that to be true.'

'Let us sail up the river to Hampton Court.'

'Hold on, sir. Do not hurry me so.'

'Then let us go riding together instead.'

'You are so good to me, William.'

'It is because *you* are so good for Father.'

William Stanford was a handsome, upright young man of twenty who had inherited all the best features of his parents. He dressed like a gallant and sought out the pleasures of the day but he also had a shrewd business sense and enjoyed working alongside his father. Shaken by his mother's violent death, he had at first been hostile to the idea of his father's remarriage but Matilda had soon won him over with her beauty and sincerity. She had brought much-needed cheer into the gloom of Stanford Place and, now that she was losing her shyness, she was able to show an effervescence that was delightful. It was William who had taken her to the Queen's Head to watch Westfield's Men in action. He was now anxious to provide further diversions for her.

'Do but wait until Michael returns,' he said.

'When is your cousin due back, sir?'

'At any time now. He has been serving as a soldier in the Low Countries out of sheer bravado.' William gave an affectionate smile. 'You will love Michael. He is the merriest fellow alive and will make you laugh until you beg him to stop lest your sides split.'

'I look forward to meeting him.'

'Michael is the very soul of mirth.'

They were interrupted by a tap on the door. Simon Pendleton oozed into the room with the scroll in his hand and inclined his head in the suspicion of a bow.

'A messenger delivered this for you, mistress.'

'Thank you, sir.'

'He was a ragged creature,' said the steward, handing over the scroll. 'I liked not the look of him and hope that his missive will not cause offence.'

'I do adore surprises,' she said with a giggle and began to untie the ribbon. 'What can it be?'

Pendleton lurked. 'Nothing untoward, I trust.'

'That will be all, Simon,' said William dismissively.

The steward hid his annoyance behind a mask of civility and withdrew soundlessly. Matilda unrolled the playbill and stared at it with sudden ecstasy.

'Dear God, this is wonderful!' she cried.

'May I see?'

'Look, sir. Westfield's Men play again tomorrow.'

'*Double Deceit,*' he noted. 'I have seen the piece before. It is an excellent comedy and well acted.'

'Let us go to this playhouse to see it, William.'

'But I already have another treat in store for you tomorrow. I purposed to take you to The Curtain to watch Banbury's Men go through their paces.'

'I would see Master Firethorn again.'

'He is a brilliant actor, I grant you,' said William, 'but some people believe that Giles Randolph is even better. He has led Banbury's Men to the heights and plays the title role in the *Tragical History of King John.* Take my advice and give Master Randolph his chance.'

'That I will do at some future time,' she promised. 'For tomorrow, I pray, conduct me to The Theatre. It is my earnest wish.' She held up the playbill. 'It would be churlish to refuse such an invitation.'

William quickly agreed then began to tell her something of the plot of *Double Deceit* but his stepmother was not listening. Matilda's mind was racing. She was young and inexperienced in such matters but she sensed that the playbill had been sent for a purpose. Someone was anxious for her to attend a playhouse in Shoreditch on the following day and that set up all sorts of intriguing possibilities. Matilda Stanford was firmly married and she would be going in the company of her stepson but that did not stop her feeling a surge of joyful expectation such as she had never known before.

A grubby playbill had touched her heart.

Hans Kippel had been told to stay at his lodgings and rest but the force of habit was too strong for the lad. It got him out of his bed and along to his workplace early in the morning. Surprised to see him, Preben van Loew had shown a fatherly care for the apprentice and given him only the simplest tasks but even these were beyond his competence. The boy was clearly suffering the after-effects of his ordeal and could not focus his mind on anything for more than a few minutes. The Dutchman tried to probe him for more details of what had occurred on the previous day but none were forthcoming. A blow to the head had locked all memory of the incident inside the young skull of Hans Kippel.

It was early afternoon when Nicholas Bracewell came

back to the house in Bankside. He had spent the morning at The Theatre, finalising the arrangements for the performance of *Double Deceit* and supervising the transfer of costumes and properties from the Queen's Head. With a little spare time at his disposal, he had hurried home to see if he could coax any further information out of the wounded apprentice. Hans Kippel was pleased to see him and shook his hand warmly but the boy's face then became vacant again. Nicholas sat beside him and spoke low.

'We are all very proud of you, Hans.'

'Why so, sir?'

'Because you are a very brave young man.'

'I do not feel brave, Master Bracewell.'

'How do you feel?'

'Sore afraid. I am lost and know not where to turn.'

'You are among friends here, Hans. Safe and sound.'

'Will you protect me, sir?'

'From what?'

The blank face clouded. 'I cannot tell. My mind has cut me adrift. But I know I have enemies.'

'What enemies? Who are they?'

But Hans Kippel had yielded up all that he could. Not even the patient questioning of Nicholas Bracewell could draw anything further out of him. The book holder consulted with Preben van Loew who gave it as his opinion that the boy would be far better off in the comfort of his bed. He was patently not fit for work and needed all the rest that he could get. Nicholas agreed only partly with this, arguing that the apprentice would never make a full recovery until his mind had been cleared of the horror that had possessed it. Since that might not happen of its own volition, he suggested an idea that might help. He volunteered to accompany Hans Kippel as they retraced the steps the boy had taken on the previous day, hoping that somewhere along the way his memory would be restored by the sight of something familiar.

Preben van Loew gave his blessing to the enterprise and waved the two of them off at the door. Hans Kippel was a sad figure with his bandaged head and his limp. It had already occurred to Nicholas that it might have been his nationality which told against the youth. His sober attire, open face and general mien marked him out as a Dutch immigrant and thus the natural target for the resentment of many people. In the company of someone as tall and muscular as Nicholas Bracewell, the boy was not likely to be mocked so openly but he might just recognise the point in the journey at which his humiliation took place. They walked slowly on together.

'Look all about you, Hans,' said Nicholas.

'I will do so, sir.'

'Tell me if you see aught that you remember.'

'My mind is still empty.'

'We will try to put something in it.'

The journey came to an abrupt end. One minute, Hans Kippel was dragging himself along in a daze, the next, he was staring ahead in terror and refusing to move another step. They had come out of the Bankside labyrinth by St Saviour's Church and were heading towards the Bridge.

63

It was one of the finest sights in London, a truly imposing structure that spanned the murky Thames with a series of arches and which housed a miniature city on its broad back. Visitors came from all over Europe to marvel at London Bridge but here was one foreigner who had no sense of wonder. Hans Kippel turned white with fear and let out a scream of intense pain. His trembling finger pointed at the Bridge. Before Nicholas could stop him, he turned around and limped away as fast as his injured legs would carry him.

Chapter Three

Abel Strudwick passed a troubled night in restless contemplation of the incident. Not even the sonorous snoring of the wife who lay beside him could lull him into slumber and this was unusual. As a rule, the waterman enjoyed his sleep to the full, wearied by the physical strains of his working day and by the consumption of ample quantities of bottle ale. He would be dead to the world within minutes and spend a restorative night in dreams of being plucked from the toil of his occupation to become a revered poet. A corpse in the Thames had changed all that. Strudwick had hauled bodies out of the water before now but none had been so gruesome as this one and even his strong stomach had rebelled. Memory turned night into one long, lacerating ordeal.

The next day found him tired and fractious, more ready than ever to burn the ears off his customers with a positive inferno of vituperation. Unlike most watermen, Strudwick plied his trade on his own. The bulk of his fellows took their passengers across the river in six- or eight-oared wherries that enabled them to cope with large parties. Strudwick had only a small rowing boat. He and his son had operated very successfully in it until the latter was press-ganged during the panic that preceded the news of the approach of the Spanish Armada. The loss of their apprentices to the navy was a source of great pain in the watermen's community but their protests went unheard and unregarded. It was not surprising that they therefore resorted to all kinds of stratagems to protect their young men from such a dire fate.

Strudwick paid a young lad to help him from time to time and to sleep in the boat at night to prevent it from being stolen, but the aspiring poet mostly worked alone. The others mocked him cruelly for his ambitions but none dared do so to his face. In contests of verbal abuse and in wharfside brawls, he was a fearsome opponent who could see off the best. Abel Strudwick's black tongue and bulging biceps created the space in which his verse could thrive unhampered. Drink lubricated his creative powers and it was in a tavern that most of his inspiration came.

So it was that afternoon as he sat in the corner of the taproom at the Jolly Sailor and gave his fertile mind free rein. The verse came haltingly at first, then more fluently and, finally, in a torrent that had him leaping up from his stool. Keen to oblige a regular customer, the landlord had pen and ink at the ready for the waterman and Strudwick pulled out the scrap of parchment that he always carried with him for such precious moments. He scratched away happily for half an hour before he felt it was time to return to work. The Bankside theatres would be emptying soon and there would be passengers for every boatman who was moored on the Surrey side of the river.

As Abel Strudwick came tumbling out of the inn, it was another playhouse that caught his attention. Stuck to a post nearby was something which he felt had been put there by the hand of God. It was a playbill advertising the performance of *Double Deceit* by Westfield's Men on the following day and it crystallised a plan which had been forming in his mind for several months. His days as a fumbling amateur in the world of words were numbered. He wanted to see and hear how a professional pen could write verse in a dramatic vein and get the encouragement to fulfil his vaulting ambition. Nicholas Bracewell was a good friend who had never let him down in the past.

It was time to put that friendship to the test.

Margery Firethorn was kept as busy as ever. In addition to her normal household complement of souls, she had to cater for the three actors who were staying with them in Shoreditch and whom she had packed into the attic room to keep them out of the way of the other inhabitants. She ran a tight ship and nobody was allowed to flout her captaincy. When one of the actors dared to ogle a servant girl, Margery gave him a fierce sermon on self-restraint and warned him that his voice would rise by two octaves if ever she caught him fraternising again. Since she was carrying the kitchen knife at the time, he understood her meaning all too well and withdrew hastily to the attic to acquaint his fellows with what had passed. All females in the house were treated with excessive respect from that time on and even the she-cats earned more consideration.

Caught up as she was in feeding and caring for her extended family, Margery yet found time to keep an alert eye on her husband. Lawrence Firethorn had swept her off her feet with one of the most sublime performances of his career then borne her off down the aisle before she could even begin to resist. It had been a magical experience that could still flicker in the memory on rare occasions but it was dulled beneath the accumulated debris that a marriage inevitably builds up. One thing she had learnt at an early stage: her husband had the defects of his virtues. His overwhelming talent as an actor had indeed seduced her but she was realistic enough to see that it had a powerful effect on other women as well. Temptation was ever-present and Firethorn was not always able to resist it. Without her vigilance, he would be led astray by every red lip and arched eyebrow. She sensed that he was beginning to look elsewhere and decided to fire a warning shot across his bows.

'Good morning to you, sir!'

'Good morning, my dove,' he said expansively. 'The sun is streaming down from the heavens to gild the marital couch.'

'You may well say that from where you lie,' she observed tartly, 'but I have been up these two hours to make all ready downstairs. Besides,' she added, 'if our marital couch is so special to you, why did you return to it so late last night?'

'Work and worry kept me away.'

'Does she have a name?'

'Margery! How can you even suggest such a thing?'

He sat up in the four-poster with rumpled dignity and scratched at his beard. His wife stood over him with folded arms and snarled her next question.

'Do you love me, sir?'

'I dote on you, my treasure.'

'But do you dote on me *enough*?'

'My devotion is without human limit.'

'That is my complaint, Lawrence,' she said. 'I would that your devotion was limited to *me* but it flies away like a bird on the wing.'

'Only to return with joy. I am your homing pigeon.'

'You are an eagle, sir, who searches out new prey.'

'These suspicions are unfair and unfounded.'

'Prove it!'

He struck a pose. 'My conscience is clear.'

'You do not possess such a thing.'

'Sweetness,' he said. 'What means this discord so early in the day? What crime have I committed?'

'It still lies festering in your brain.'

'That brain is occupied with fond thoughts of you.'

'Only when I stand before you.'

'And lie beneath me, my little pomegranate.'

He spoke with such tender lechery that even her resolve weakened. A big, buxom, bustling woman in a simple working dress, she let herself be flattered by his words and by the admiring glances he now directed at her. With all its faults, the marriage had never lacked excitement or pleasure. Another episode now beckoned.

'You left my side too soon,' he cooed.

'There was much to be done below.'

'Come back to me for a moment of wild madness.'

'It would be madness indeed at this hour.'

'Let me *show* you how much I love you, Margery.'

Her doubts were temporarily wiped away and she moved in close to be gathered into whirling embrace. She was lifted bodily into the bed and let out a girlish laugh as he rolled on top of her but their joy was short-lived. Before he could plant the first whiskery kiss on her eager lips, pandemonium broke out. A pan boiled over in the kitchen and set off an argument between the two servant girls. The children began a noisy fight and the four apprentices went thundering down the stairs for their breakfast. Worst of all, there was a loud knock on the door of the bedchamber and one of the actors put a decisive end to the snatched happiness.

'I must speak with you at once, sir,' he said.

Firethorn's howl of rage deafened all of Shoreditch.

The Theatre was the first purpose-built public playhouse in London. Situated just north of Holywell Lane, at the angle of Curtain Road and New Inn Yard, it was outside the city boundaries and thus free of its niggling regulations yet close enough to attract the large audiences that came streaming out through Bishopsgate to enjoy its facilities and view its productions. It had been constructed in 1576 under the supervision of James Burbage, a determined man who had begun life as a joiner only to renounce his trade in favour of the theatre. Talent and application helped him to become the leading actor with Leicester's Men but he had a fondness for security and a flair for management that led him to erect The Theatre at an estimated cost of some £666. Even though he bickered thereafter with his partner, John Brayne, a litigious grocer who also happened to be his brother-in-law, the importance of his pioneering work could not be denied. The first permanent home for actors gave their art a new lustre and status. They were at last taken seriously.

Animals influenced humans. For it was the bear- and bull-baiting arenas of Bankside which provided the basic principles of construction. The Theatre was a polygonal building made of stout timber and a modicum of ironwork. Where it differed from the animal-baiting houses was in its imaginative detail. The ring itself was covered with brick and stone, thus turning it into a paved yard with efficient drainage. A stage thrust out boldly into the yard, supported by solid posts rather than by the trestles and barrels used at places like the Queen's Head. At the rear of the stage was a tiring-house which gave the company easy access to the playing area. Above the back section of this area was a cover known as the heavens. Held aloft by tall pillars, it was in turn surmounted by a small hut that could be used to house any suspension gear that was needed for a particular play or, indeed, as a tiny acting area in itself.

The last major difference that separated The Theatre from the standard arena was its use of a third gallery. The Bankside baiting houses were all two-storey buildings that were roughly similar in design. James Burbage did not make his playhouse tower above Shoreditch simply in order to attest its presence. An extra gallery meant an increase in the number of patrons and a corresponding rise in the income that any company could expect. And though the place was an outdoor venue, its cylindrical shape was a form of umbrella against inclement weather and the thatched roofs above the galleries added a great measure of comfort and protection. Much care and thought had gone into the whole venture. It was the brainchild of a true man of the theatre.

Nicholas Bracewell was the first to arrive. His visit to the Queen's Head had only served to deepen his fears that their days at the inn were numbered. With all his appalling faults, Alexander Marwood did actually allow the company to flourish on his premises and the makeshift stage had witnessed some of their finest achievements. If Rowland Ashway acquired the property, he would have no qualms in turning Westfield's Men out into the street. Fresh anxieties surfaced about the likely fate of his fellows. A huge black cloud hung over the future of the company and Nicholas was the only person who knew about it. How long he could keep the fact to himself remained to be seen but it was already causing him profound disquiet.

Thomas Skillen was the next to turn up at The Theatre. The venerable stagekeeper had been with Westfield's Men since their formation but his roots in the drama went much deeper than that. For over forty years now, he had survived in a ruinous profession that had hurled so many people into oblivion, and he had done so by virtue of his quick wits and total reliability. What hope would there be for him if he was driven out of his job now? Advancing age and creaking joints had slowed him down but he could still assert his authority. George Dart found this out when he came running out onto the stage to be given a clip across the ear by the senior man.

'You struck me, Thomas!' he said in alarm.

'Aye, sirrah, I did.'

'For what reason?'

'For none at all, George. The blow was on account.'

'But I have done nothing amiss.'

'You will, sirrah. You will.'

Nicholas stepped in to rescue the injured party and to assign jobs to both men. *Double Deceit* was a highly complicated play which made heavy demands on those behind the scenes. It was an amiable comedy about two pairs of identical twins who get caught up in an escalating series of mistakes and misapprehensions. Inspired by one of the plays of Plautus, it was a glorious romp that never failed to delight its audiences but it called for several scene changes and required an interminable list of properties.

By the time that others began to appear, Thomas Skillen and George Dart had set the stage so that the rehearsal could begin and were attending to a myriad other duties.

Lawrence Firethorn waited until the full company was

assembled before he strode out onto the stage with his characteristic swagger. A raised hand compelled silence.

'Gentlemen,' he announced. 'Let me rid your minds of one abiding error. This is not a rehearsal of an old and ailing text whose sparkle has been dimmed by the passage of time. *Double Deceit* is no plodding nag who asks no more of us than to sit back lazily in the saddle and guide her in the right direction. She is a mettlesome filly whom we take out on her first full gallop today. Wear your spurs, my friends, and do not be shy of using them. We must ride hell for leather into glory!'

Younger members of the cast were stirred by his speech but older hands were more cynical. Barnaby Gill leant over to whisper to Edmund Hoode.

'As I foretold, *she* is coming to the performance.'

'Who?'

'The latest sacrificial victim for his bed,' said Gill sardonically. 'That is why we would put some ginger into *Double Deceit*. He wants to warm the lady up so that she is glowing strongly when he boards her. Westfield's Men are being used as his pimps.'

'Lawrence does not always meet with success.'

'Nor shall he this time, Edmund. This ignoble plot shall be nipped in the bud. I'll act him off the stage and end the matter there.'

The boast was stillborn. It was easier to perform triple somersaults through the eye of a needle than to out-act Lawrence Firethorn when he turned on his full power. For that is what he did at the rehearsal. There was no holding back, no harbouring of his resources for the afternoon. In the twin roles of Argos of Rome and Argos of Florence, he was a soaring comet who dazzled all around him. Barnaby Gill doubled manfully in the parallel roles of the comic servants, Silvio of Rome and Silvio of Florence, but it took all his energy to keep pace with his two masters, let alone try to overtake either.

It was a bold decision to tackle two roles each and it necessitated great concentration and perfect timing to maintain the illusion for the audience. Argos of Rome and his much-maligned companion, Silvio, were a jaded pair who dressed in mean apparel. Argos of Florence, however, and his chirpy servant, Silvio, were bubbling extroverts with vivid attire. As one pair left the stage, the other would step out onto it almost immediately. Lightning changes of cloak, hat and manner worked wonders.

Firethorn's urgency dragged the rest of the cast along behind it. The major technical problem came in Act Five when the two pairs of twins, separated since birth and totally unaware of each other's existence, finally learn the truth and unite in love and laughter. To effect this climactic moment when all four meet together, two other actors had to stand in as one of the duos. The fleeting appearance as Argos of Rome was made by Owen Elias, a sturdy Welshman whose height and build matched those of Firethorn himself. Dressed in the costume of Silvio of Rome, padded out to give him more substance, was none other than George Dart. The substitute twins were a complete contrast. While the Welshman took the stage with overweening confidence, the assistant stagekeeper crept onto it with all the enthusiasm of a snail crawling into a fiery furnace. The latter was mortified when he knocked over a chair in his nervousness and then accidentally pulled the cloak off Silvio of Florence during an embrace with his putative twin. As the play came to an end, Dart waited in trepidation for the acid comments of Firethorn.

But none came. Delighted with his own account of the two roles, and certain that his company would rise to the occasion in front of a large audience, the actor-manager dismissed them all with a few kind words then swept off into the tiring-house. Nicholas Bracewell was not so uncritical of what he had seen and he had many notes to give to erring performers before they slipped away. He had just administered a gentle reprimand to George Dart when Edmund Hoode sidled up to him.

'Tell me her name, Nick.'

'Who?'

'This enchantress who has bewitched Lawrence.'

'That is his business alone.'

'It is ours as well if it affects his conduct here among his fellows. Why, man, he was grinning at us like some lovesick youth just now. If this lady's magic is so potent, we must lure her into the company and pay her to keep the old bear sweet. It would be money well spent.'

Nicholas smiled. 'We all would benefit.'

'So who is this paragon?'

'I may not say, Edmund.'

'But it was you who tracked her down.'

'Master Firethorn has sworn me to secrecy.'

'Can you not divulge the name to me?'

'Neither to you nor to any living soul.'

'But I am your friend, Nick.'

'It is my friendship that holds me back,' said the other seriously. 'You would not thank me for breaking my oath. Better it is that you do not know who the lady is.'

Hoode's eyes widened. 'Do I spy danger here?'

'Acute danger.'

'For Lawrence?'

'For all of us.'

Sir Lucas Pugsley, fishmonger, philanthropist and incumbent Lord Mayor of London, finished another gargantuan meal and washed it down with a glass of French brandy. His guest was still guzzling away at his lunch and taking frequent swigs of beer from the two-pint tankard that stood before him. The Mayor was dining in private for once and sharing confidences with an old friend. Pugsley was as thin as a rake and as pale as a spectre. No matter how much food he ate – and his appetite was gross – he never seemed to put on any weight. The narrow face with its tight lips, its high cheekbones and its tiny black eyes resembled nothing so much as the head of a conger eel. Even in his full regalia, he looked as if he were lying on a slab.

Rowland Ashway was a completely different man. His gormandising had left its mark all too flagrantly upon him. The wealthy brewer had been turned into a human barrel to advertise his way of life. Regular consumption of his own best beer had given the puffed cheeks and the blob of nose such a florid hue that he appeared to be cultivating tomatoes. The two men had a political as well as a personal connection. As Alderman for Bridge Ward Within, the wily Ashway had promoted Pugsley's candidacy for the ultimate civic honour. The fishmonger did not forget such loyalty and it had been rewarded by more than the occasional free meal. Ashway pushed the last mouthful down his throat then emptied his tankard after it. He gave a monstrous belch, laughed merrily and broke wind. It was time for them to sit back in their carved chairs and preen themselves at will.

'My mayoralty has been a triumph,' said Pugsley with easy pomposity. 'I have grown into the role.'

'It fits you like a glove.'

'This city has cause to be grateful to me.'

'Your bounty is in evidence on all sides,' noted the other. 'You have founded schools, built almshouses and donated generously to the Church.'

'Nor have I been slack in my love of country,' said the fishmonger piously. 'Queen Elizabeth herself – God bless her – has been ready to borrow Pugsley money for the defence of the realm. English soldiers are the salt of the earth. I feel honoured that I was able to put uniforms onto their backs and weapons into their hands.'

'A knighthood was a fitting reward, Luke.'

'Sir Lucas, if you please.'

'Sir Lucas.' Ashway fawned obligingly. 'The pity of it is that you cannot remain in place as Lord Mayor.'

'Nothing would please me more, Rowland.'

'We have all been beneficiaries of your term of office and are like to remember it well.'

'There is more still to come. I value friendship above all else and set a true value on it. Aubrey and I were discussing the matter only this morning.'

'Aubrey Kenyon is an upright man,' said the brewer. 'His opinions are to be taken seriously.'

'That is why I always seek them out. My Chamberlain is always the first person I consult on any subject. He is a complete master of the intricacies of municipal affairs and I could not survive for a second without him.'

'You are in safe hands, Sir Lucas.'

'None safer than those of Aubrey Kenyon.'

'Indeed not.' Ashway did some fishing of his own. 'And you say there is something in the wind for me?'

'A small reward for your unfailing loyalty.'

'You are too kind.'

'A trifling matter to a man of your wealth but it may bring some pleasure. You will acquire the control and rent of certain properties in your ward. My Chamberlain advised me on the form of it and he is drawing up the necessary documents.'

'I must thank Master Aubrey Kenyon once again.'

'Where I command, he takes action.'

'Your Chamberlain is truly a paragon.'

'I would trust him like my own brother.' Pugsley took another sip of brandy then appraised his companion. 'Does your business still thrive, Rowland?'

'Assuredly. We go from strength to strength.'

'Feeding off the drunkenness of London!'

'Stout men need strong ale. I simply answer their demand.'

They shared a chuckle then Pugsley fingered his chain with offhand affection. 'I have felt happy and fulfilled as never before in this office,' he said. 'Would that I might stay in it for ever!' A wistful sigh. 'Alas, that is not to be. Election has already been made.'

'*I* did not vote for him, that I swear.'

'Others did.' Pugsley's sadness turned into cold fury. 'It is painful enough to have to retire from office but to be forced to hand over to Walter Stanford is truly galling. I detest the man and all that he represents.'

'You are not alone in that, Sir Lucas.'

'He is unworthy to follow in my footsteps.'

'As for that young wife of his . . .'

'It ought not to be allowed,' said the other in a fit of moral indignation. 'A man should pay for his pleasures in private, not flaunt them before the whole city of London!'

'She is a pretty creature, though, I grant him that.'

'Stanford is bestial!'

'He is not Lord Mayor yet.'

'What do you mean?'

'Many a slip 'twixt cup and lip.'

Sir Lucas Pugsley sat upright in his chair and spat out his words like a snake expelling its venom.

'I would do *anything* to stop him!'

* * *

Fine weather and high expectation saw large crowds of playgoers surging north out of the city. Many of them converged on The Curtain, the other public playhouse in Shoreditch, a circular structure that stood on land that had once been part of Holywell Priory. Banbury's Men were in residence there and the audience flocked to see Giles Randolph as the evil King John. His reputation was overshadowed by that of Lawrence Firethorn, who brought even more spectators hurrying through the doors of The Theatre. Once again, Westfield's Men had the critical edge over its hated rivals.

Abel Strudwick had never been to a play before and he was bewildered by the whole experience. Having paid his penny to one of the gatherers, he went through into the yard and stood as close to the stage as he could. He was soon part of a jostling throng with a carnival spirit and he succumbed willingly to the prevailing atmosphere of mirth. His poems were a source of immense pride to him but he had only so far recited them to his wife and to Nicholas Bracewell. The thought of standing up on that scaffold and entertaining a huge crowd with the work of his creative imagination was quite exhilarating. Long before *Double Deceit* began, he had got his penny's worth.

Matilda Stanford was ushered into the second gallery by her stepson. A friend of his had helped to escort her at the Queen's Head but the young man felt able to look after her alone at The Theatre. William Stanford had opted for a black doublet with a wide-shouldered look and for matching hose. Silver flashes relieved the impression of total darkness and silver feathers adorned his hat. His stepmother had chosen a blend of subtle greens in a dress that displayed all her best features to advantage. Her hair and clothing were perfumed and she carried a pomander to ward off any unpleasant smells that might arise in a packed auditorium. The mask which dangled from her other hand could be used to hide the blushes that were already threatening to come as her presence was noted by the gallants who surrounded her. Compliments and comments ambushed her from all sides.

The keenest attention she received, however, was from Argos of Rome. Costumed for his first entrance, Lawrence Firethorn peered through a chink in the curtain at the rear of the stage to pick out his beloved. She looked even more alluring than before, with those blue eyes and red lips lighting up her porcelain skin. Matilda Stanford had true radiance and he prostrated himself before it.

Nicholas Bracewell came quietly up behind him.

'Stand by, sir.'

'She had my invitation, Nick. She is *here*.'

'So is the hour of two.'

'I knew that she would not disappoint me!'

'Stand by, Argos of Rome!'

'This is earthly paradise.'

'We begin!'

The book holder was firmly in control of the whole operation once the performance started and not even the company's star was allowed to forget that. Firethorn moved quickly across to join Barnaby Gill in readiness for their entrance. The signal was given by Nicholas, the trumpet sounded and the Prologue stepped out in a black cloak to receive a virgin ripple of applause and to outline the plot of *Double Deceit* in rhyming couplets. Argos and Silvio then burst onto the stage in a flurry of arms and legs as the master upbraided his servant and beat him black and blue. Firethorn's voice was hoarse with outrage as he listed his complaints and Gill made the audience collapse with laughter at the hilarious way he fell to the ground each time he was struck. The comic timing and the physical dexterity of the two men was breathtaking. They had won everyone over by the time they made their exit then they reappeared instantly in other guises to win the spectators over even more completely.

Double Deceit had never been played with such panache. There was only one dissentient voice.

'I am wasted in this verminous comedy.'

'Your hour will come, Owen.'

'It is a crime to subdue such talent as mine.'

'Do but wait awhile and it will shine forth.'

'I have waited too long already, Nick.'

'So have many others, I fear.'

'Who cares about those wretches? I am *better*.'

Owen Elias was no shrinking violet. While other hired men took what they could get and were profoundly grateful, he was forever trying to plead his cause. He was without question a far more skilful performer than most of his fellows and his lilting voice was a joy to hear when it was given blank verse to declaim. But his talent as an actor was not matched by his tact as a diplomat. In thrusting himself forward so openly, he jeopardised his already slim chances of advancement. Nicholas liked him immensely for his Celtic charm and forthrightness but he recognised the fatal flaw in his friend. The runaway arrogance made Owen Elias into his own worst enemy.

'Do you see what I mean, Nick?'

'Tell me later, sir.'

'I can do all that Master Firethorn can.'

'You distract me, Owen.'

'They loved me.'

'Stand aside, I pray.'

Nicholas was too busy at his post to listen to the actor at that moment but there was a degree of truth in what the Welshman said. In his brief appearance as Argos of Rome, he not only looked and moved remarkably like Lawrence Firethorn, he even sounded like him. Indeed, the audience was so stunned by the similarity between the two men that they really believed they were looking at a pair of identical twins. It was, literally, a double deceit.

Firethorn was left alone to deliver the Epilogue.

Comedy, our sages oft advise us,
May come accoutred in diverse disguises.
True laughter wears such various attire,
Colour, cut, fashion and style conspire
To catch the eye and to create such mirth,
That heavenly happiness dwells on earth.
In dressing up our offering today
We use twice the apparel of another play.

Behind a cloak hid brooding Argos of Rome,
His twin of Florence lurked beneath a dome . . .

He was leaving the audience in no doubt about the fact
that he had played the two parts. He changed cloaks on
the line about the brooding Argos and put on his other hat
when he referred to a dome. Then he went on to repeat
the process throughout the remainder of the Epilogue, thus
confirming his genius as a theatrical chameleon. It was a
play in itself and the spectators were spellbound.

Abel Strudwick had been hypnotised by it all for
two hours and this final piece of bravura left him totally
awestruck. The furious pace and the freewheeling humour
gave him an experience that altered his whole view of
himself. He wanted somehow to be part of it all, to shed
the onerous burdens of being a waterman and join the
marvellous world of theatre. What had aroused most
wonder in him was the quality of the verse. *Double Deceit*
was written largely in prose but it did contain a number
of speeches in rhyming couplets that struck him as superb.
Delivered by the masterful Firethorn, their shortcomings
were cunningly concealed. Strudwick longed to write such
lines for such an actor, even to become a performer himself.
It was a more honourable existence than rowing incessantly
across the River Thames. Receiving the plaudits of such a
delirious auditorium was infinitely better than dragging
dead bodies out of dark water.

Matilda Stanford was also entranced by the whole
experience. Deeply moved at the Queen's Head, she had

been dizzied by the sheer extravagance of today's frolic. A simple playbill had brought her to The Theatre with a curiosity that was soon satisfied. Lawrence Firethorn himself had sent the invitation and he had left her in no doubt of that. Whether he was playing Argos of Rome or Argos of Florence, he found a way to direct certain lines straight at her by way of tribute. Matilda was utterly enraptured. With his scintillating display in the twin roles, the actor-manager had even surpassed his sublime performance as Count Orlando – and *this* was the man who had deigned to notice her. Concluding the Epilogue, he blew her a kiss and bowed in acknowledgement of her smile. Even in the thunder of the curtain call, Firethorn found time to speak to her with his eyes.

A faithful young wife forgot about her husband.

Walter Stanford was indefatigable. He rose early each day and worked late into the night, attending to his business affairs with jovial energy and pushing out the frontiers of his operations all the time. Sunday was his only day of rest and even then stray thoughts of his latest enterprises mingled with his prayers. The Master of the Mercers' Company did not believe in resting on his many laurels. Expansion was his watchword.

Other men would have been daunted by the additional amount of work entailed in being Lord Mayor Elect but Stanford welcomed it. He simply got up even earlier and laboured longer into the darkness. If fatigue ever laid a hand upon him, he never showed it. If obstacles fell across his path, he leapt nimbly over them. If anything even began to depress his spirits, he invoked the memory of his mentor, Dick Whittington, and carried on with restored vigour. It was impossible to compete with Walter Stanford. He was invincible.

That afternoon found him sitting at the table in his study leafing through some contracts pertaining to the coal mines that he owned up in Newcastle. He checked the figures carefully before entering them into a large account book then he turned to consider another part of his burgeoning empire. It did not worry him in the least that his wife was watching a play at The Theatre while he was slaving on at Stanford Place. He worked so that she might enjoy her leisure and he was content with that arrangement. Rocked by the loss of one wife, he could not believe his luck in being given a second chance of happiness and he did not spurn it. His wife and family were all to him and his industry was at their service.

A knock on the door interrupted his concentration. He looked up as Simon Pendleton sidled into the room carrying a long flat box that was tied with string. A faint whiff in the air made Stanford's nose wrinkle.

'I am sorry to intrude, master,' said the steward.

'What have you brought me?'

'This has just been delivered, sir.'

'By whom?'

'He did not stay to declare himself,' said the other with mild disapproval. 'When I opened the front door, I found this box upon the step. It is addressed to you.'

'What is that strange odour?'

'I am not sure, sir, but it made the dogs sniff their fill. That is why I brought the box straight to you. They would have torn it open else.'

'Thank you, Simon. Put it on the table.'

'Yes, sir.'

Pendleton laid the box down as if he was glad to part with it then stood back so that its pungency did not invade his nostrils any more. Stanford used a knife to cut through the string then lifted the lid with interest. His eyebrows shot up in amazement when he saw what lay inside. It was almost two feet long and weighed several pounds. The silver scales glittered in the light. He took the item out and held it on the palms of both hands to feel its substance and wonder at its meaning. Gifts from friends or debtors were quite common but he had never received an anonymous present of this nature before. Master and steward stared in complete bafflement.

They were looking at a dead fish.

Chapter Four

Nicholas Bracewell was still at The Theatre well after the audience and the cast had departed. With the help of Thomas Skillen and his assistant stagekeepers, he gathered up everything belonging to Westfield's Men and loaded it into a cart. When he had paid the manager for the rental of the playhouse and confirmed details of their next visit to the venue, he drove the cart back towards the city and in through Bishopsgate with his motley crew sitting on the vehicle behind him. As the old horse pulled them on a jolting ride over the cobbles, Nicholas looked up with misgiving at Stanford Place. It was an imposing edifice but perils loitered within for the whole company. George Dart felt it as well. Shrinking away from the house as it appeared on his left, he heard the distant bark of dogs and shivered violently.

They were all glad to reach the Queen's Head where

their effects would be stored until required on the following Monday. Willing hands unloaded and locked everything away then extended themselves towards the book holder with open palms. It was the end of the week and their wages were paid. Most of them went straight off to spend some of their money on ale and to toast the end of another long and tiring stint of work. The solitary exception was George Dart who scampered off home to his lodgings in Cheapside to appease his landlady with his rent and to catch up on some of the sleep that he invariably lost in the service of Westfield's Men.

Nicholas went into the taproom to be pounced on by the egregious publican. Alexander Marwood saw the chance to wallow in further misery.

'One of my serving wenches is with child,' he said. 'I blame Westfield's Men.'

'*All* of them?' queried Nicholas.

'Actors are born lechers.'

'Has the lady named the father?'

'She does not need to, Master Bracewell. The finger points at a member of your company.'

'Then the finger is too hasty in its accusation,' said the book holder. 'Lechery is not confined to our profession. Other men are prey to such urges and you have hundreds of red-blooded customers here during any week. Besides, why must you judge the girl so harshly? Perhaps it was love and not lust that was at work here. Haply, she and her swain plan to wed.'

'There is no talk of that,' said Marwood bitterly. '*She* has lost her virtue and *I* have lost a serving wench. Acting and venery go hand in hand. I will not be loath to see Westfield's Men quit my premises.'

'You are unjust, sir. Do not thrust us out before we have been able to argue our case.'

'What case?'

'Consider how well our arrangement has worked in the past. We have all been beneficiaries.'

'I beg leave to doubt that.'

'Come now,' said Nicholas firmly. 'If our contract did not yield advantage, why did you suffer it these three or four years past? When it suited your purpose, you were quick enough to sign the articles of agreement. All that needs to be done now is to make those provisions a little more appealing to you.'

'The offer comes too late, Master Bracewell.'

'What do you mean?'

'I have another suitor at my door.'

Alexander Marwood gave a sickly grin and pointed towards the corpulent figure at the far end of the bar counter. Rowland Ashway was dispensing some flabby charm on Marwood's wife, impressing her with his aldermanic importance and wooing her with smiling promises about the rosy future that lay ahead if she and her husband agreed to let him take over their inn. A stone-faced harridan was being turned into a compliant woman. The landlord marvelled at the transformation, then hurried across in the hopes of gaining some personal advantage from it. Marwood was soon beaming alternately at his wife and at Rowland Ashway, hanging on the words of both with an almost childlike eagerness.

Nicholas Bracewell was shaken by what he saw. There was an easy arrogance about the brewer which showed how confident he was of landing his prize. Evidently, he was offering them blandishments with which Westfield's Men could not hope to compete. It was going to be extremely difficult to fight off the aldermanic challenge but it had to be done somehow. What troubled Nicholas most was that he was likely to be encumbered rather than helped by his fellows. If he broke the news to Lawrence Firethorn and the other sharers, they would react with such violence that any future dealings with Marwood would be greatly imperilled. For the time being, the book holder was on his own. Yet that situation could not last. Sooner or later, he had to take someone into his confidence. It would have to be done in such a way that hysteria did not spread like wildfire through Westfield's Men.

As he glanced around the taproom, Nicholas could see eight or nine members of the company, relaxing after the exigencies of performance and laughing freely, blissfully unaware of the threat that hung over their livelihood. He did not have the heart to smash their fragile dreams with his grim intelligence. Hiding it deep within him, he went across to a table to join two special friends.

Owen Elias was in the middle of a long monologue but his companion was not listening to a word of it. With his round, clean-shaven moon face aglow, Edmund Hoode stared ahead of him at some invisible object of wonder. When the book holder sat opposite them, the fiery Welshman switched his attack to the newcomer.

'I was telling Edmund here even now,' he said with eyes ablaze. 'I would be Ramon to the life.'

'Ramon?'

'Yes, Nick. The Governor of Cyprus.'

'Ah. You talk of *Black Antonio*.'

'We play it on Monday next. I should be Ramon.'

'The part is already cast.'

'I have the better claim to it.'

'That may well be so,' agreed Nicholas reasonably, 'but it is a major role and must of necessity be played by one of the sharers.'

'Even though I have superior talent?'

'Theatre is not always just, Owen.'

'Support me in this. Take up cudgels on my behalf.'

'I have urged your case a dozen times to Master Firethorn. He is a keen judge of acting and recognises your mettle. But there are other needs to satisfy first.'

'His lice-ridden sharers!'

'It will not help if you abuse your fellows.'

'I am sorry, Nick,' said Elias, lapsing into maudlin vein. 'But it makes my blood boil to see the way that I am held back. In temper and skill, I am the equal of any in the company save Lawrence Firethorn himself yet I languish in the shallows. Take but *Double Deceit*, man. I was partnered with that dolt of a stagekeeper.'

'George Dart does not pretend to be an actor.'

'Others do and get away with murder!'

'Some fall short of greatness, I admit.'

'Help me, Nick,' said the other seriously. 'You are my only hope in this company. Find me the chance to show my genius and they will *beg* me to become a sharer.'

Nicholas doubted it. Owen Elias had many sterling qualities but his relentless self-assertion was a severe handicap. He upset many of his colleagues with his grumbling discontent and would never be accepted by the other sharers, especially as he would show some of them up completely if he were given a sizeable role. Unknown to the Welshman, Nicholas had already saved him from summary dismissal on more than one occasion by pleading on his behalf. The book holder had found an unlikely ally. He had been supported by Barnaby Gill who was highly aware of the potential talent of Owen Elias and who relished the fact that it was akin to that of Lawrence Firethorn. The hired man was no threat at all to Gill but he might steal some of the actor-manager's thunder if he were given the opportunity.

'I grow weary of this damnable life!' said Elias.

'Your hour will come, Owen.'

'Too late, too late. I may not be here to enjoy it.'

He emptied his tankard, hauled himself out of his chair and rolled off towards the exit. His story was typical of so many hired men who toiled in the smaller parts while less able actors scooped the cream. It was one of the many bitter facts of life that had to be accepted by those in the lower ranks of the profession.

Nicholas now turned his attention to Edmund Hoode.

'I am pleased to see you in good spirits.'

'What's that?' Hoode came out of his daydream.

'You have shed your melancholy.'

'No, Nick. It was snatched away from me.'

'By whom?'

'The fairest creature that I ever beheld.'

'That phrase has been on your lips before,' teased the book holder gently.

'This time it finds its mark directly. She has no equal of her sex. I have witnessed perfection.'

'Where did this happen, Edmund?'

'Where else but at The Theatre?'

'During the performance?'

'She condescended to smile down on me.'

'As did the whole assembly. You played your part with great verve and humour.'

'It was dedicated to her,' said Hoode impulsively. 'I noticed her when I had my soliloquy in Act Three. She leant forward in the middle gallery to hear it all the better. Oh, Nick, I all but swooned! She is celestial!'

It was another phrase which he had sometimes used before and not always with discrimination. During an earlier period of frustration in his life, his romantic urge had focused itself wildly and inappropriately on Rose Marwood, the landlord's daughter, an attractive wench with the good fortune to resemble neither of her parents. Like so many of Hoode's attachments, it was wholly unwise and brought him only further grief. Deeply fond of his colleague, Nicholas hoped that another disappointment was not in the offing for him.

Edmund Hoode was back in the playhouse again.

'She sat beside an ill-favoured gallant in black and silver,' he recalled. 'Her own apparel was green, so many hues and each so beautifully blended with the others that she drew my eyes to it. As for her face, it makes all others seem foul and ugly. I will not rest until I have wooed her and won her. Nick, sweet friend, I am in love!'

The poet rhapsodised at length and the book holder's discomfort grew steadily. In every detail, the description tallied with the one given to him by another member of the company and that could only set up the possibility of horrendous complications. Edmund Hoode was unquestionably talking about Matilda Stanford. He was intent on pursuing a young woman who had already been targeted by Lawrence Firethorn. The implications were frightening.

'Help me to find out who she is, Nick!'

'How may I do that?'

'Wait until she visits us again.'

'But the lady may never do that.'

'She will,' said Hoode confidently. 'She will.'

The prospect made Nicholas grit his teeth.

The interior of Stanford Place was even more impressive than its façade. Its capacious rooms were elegantly furnished and given over to an ostentatious display of wealth. Large oak cupboards with intricate carvings all over them were loaded to capacity with gold plate that was kept gleaming. Rich tapestries covered walls and hand-worked carpets of exquisite design softened the clatter of the floors. Gilt-framed oil paintings added colour and dignity. Tables, chairs, benches and cushions abounded and there were no less than three backgammon tables. Huge oak chests bore further quantities of gold plate. Four-branched candelabra were everywhere. The sense of prosperity was overwhelming.

Matilda Stanford saw none of it as she ran through the house in her excitement. Her husband was still in his counting-house and she raced to knock on its door but a firm voice stopped her just in time.

'The master would not be disturbed.'

'But I have such news for him,' she said.

'He left precise instructions.'

'Do they apply to his wife?'

'I fear they do,' said Simon Pendleton with smug deference. 'The late Mistress Stanford knew better than to interrupt him during the working day.'

'Am I to be denied access to my own husband?'

'I do but offer advice.'

Matilda was quite abashed. The steward's manner was so full of polite reproach that it smothered all her vivacity beneath it. When she gave a resigned shrug and began to move away, Pendleton felt that he had won a trial of strength and that was important to him. He was about to congratulate himself when the door opened and Walter Stanford came out. His face beamed indulgently.

'Come to me, my darling,' he said expansively.

'I am not being a nuisance, sir?'

'What an absurd thought!' He glanced at the steward. 'You do not have to protect me from my own wife, Simon.'

'I did what I considered right and proper, sir.'

'For once, your judgement was at fault.'

A hurt bow. 'I apologise profusely.'

'Even the best horse stumbles.'

Putting an arm around his wife, Stanford took her into the room and closed the door behind him. Pendleton's minor triumph had been turned into defeat. It did nothing to endear him to a woman whose presence in the house he resented on a number of grounds. He stalked away to tend to his wounded dignity.

Walter Stanford, meanwhile, had conducted his wife to a chair and stood swaying over her with paternal fondness. She started to recover some of her animation.

'Oh, sir, we have had such a merry afternoon.'

'I am delighted to hear it.'

'William took me to another playhouse.'

'I cannot have my son leading you astray,' he said with mock reproof. 'Where will this levity end?'

'It was the most excellent comedy, sir, and we have not stopped laughing since.'

'Tell me about it, Matilda. I could do with some physic to chase away my seriousness. What play was it?'

'*Double Deceit,* performed by Westfield's Men at The Theatre. Such fun, such frolic, such fireworks!'

She tried to outline the plot but got so hopelessly lost that she exploded into giggles. Her husband was a kind listener who was much more amused at her obvious amusement than at anything in the drama itself. When she had finished, she jumped up to seize his hands in hers.

'You have not forgotten your promise, sir?'

'Which one? There have been so many.'

'This comes first. I want a play.'

'You have had two already this week.'

'A play of my own,' she said, dancing on her toes. 'When you become Lord Mayor, we must have a drama written especially for our entertainment. It will set the seal on a truly memorable day. Say you will oblige me, sir.'

'I will honour my promise.'

'And since it is a happy occasion, I would have a sprightly comedy performed. It will crown the whole event for me. I will be in heaven.'

'With me beside you, my love.'

He gave her a fatherly kiss on the forehead and assured her that he had the matter in hand. Her curiosity bubbled but he would say no more on the subject. Walter Stanford wanted to keep an element of mystery about his plans and this threw her into a paroxysm of pleasure. When her second bout of giggles was over, she remembered another person who would enjoy the projected play.

'William has told me all about his cousin.'

'Has he?'

'I like the sound of this Michael.'

'He has his good points, certainly.'

'William says that he is so blithe and sunny.'

'Indeed, he is,' conceded Stanford, 'and they are good

qualities in a man. But only when they are matched by responsibility and conscientiousness.'

'I hear a note of disapproval in your voice.'

'It is not intended. Michael is very dear to me. He is my sister's pride and joy but he has brought much heartache to his mother.'

'In what way?'

'This merriment of his,' said Stanford. 'It has blighted his young life – except that he is not so young any more. Michael put idle pleasures before honest work and has spent the best part of his inheritance already. Were his father alive, it would never have happened but my sister is a soft, forgiving mother who has no power over her wayward son. Things came to such a pass that she asked me to take Michael to task.'

'What did you say to him?'

'All that was necessary – and in round terms, too, I do assure you. He laughed uproariously but I got my way with him in the end.'

'William told me that he joined the army.'

'That was his final fling,' said her husband. 'He felt that service in the Netherlands would satisfy his spirit of adventure and send him back a more sober man. That is why I have made a place for him.'

'Here?'

'He must learn the rudiments of a real profession.'

'There is not much jollity in business affairs.'

'Michael is resigned to that.'

'Oh!' Her enthusiasm was punctured. 'I knew nothing of

this. William spoke so well of his cousin. I was hoping for another cheerful companion to escort me to the playhouse.' She looked up. 'When is he due home?'

'His ship should have docked by now.'

'Has he left the army?'

'So his letters proclaim.'

'Do not take all the merriment out of him, sir.'

Stanford chuckled. 'No man could do that. Michael is a law unto himself. We may check or control him but we can never subdue his spirit entirely. Nor should we wish to do so because it is the essence of the fellow.' He slipped a fond arm around her shoulders. 'Have no fears on his account. Michael will prance gaily through life until the day he dies.'

The corpse lay on its slab beneath a tattered shroud. It kept grisly company. Other naked bodies were stretched out all around it in varying stages of decomposition. The charnel house was a repository of human decay and not even the herbs that were scattered around could sweeten the prevailing stink. A flight of stone steps led down to the vault. As soon as Nicholas Bracewell entered the dank atmosphere, he felt the hand of death brush across his face. It was not a place he would have chosen to visit but he had been drawn there by curiosity. A few coins put into the hands of the keeper gained him entrance.

'Who did you come to see, sir?' asked the man.

'The poor wretch brought in two nights ago.'

'We had four or five delivered to their slabs.'

'This creature was hauled out of the river,' said Nicholas,

coughing as the stench really hit him. 'His face was battered, his leg smashed most cruelly and there was a dagger in his throat.'

'I remember him well. Follow me.'

He was a thin, hollow-eyed wraith of a man whose grim occupation had given him a deathly pallor and an easy indifference to the cadavers with whom he spent his day. Moving between his prostrate charges like the curator of a museum, he led Nicholas to the slab in the corner and held up his torch to shed flickering light. With a deft flick of the wrist, he pulled the shroud off the corpse. The book holder blenched. Though the body had been washed and laid out, he recognised it immediately as the one that he had dragged out of the Thames. The facial injuries had been hidden beneath bandaging and the dagger had been extracted from the throat but the right leg was still a tortured mass of flesh and bone. For the first time, he noticed something else. There was a long, livid scar on the man's chest, a fairly recent wound that was just starting to heal. Nicholas examined the hands.

'What are you doing?' said the keeper suspiciously.

'Looking at his palms, sir. They are quite smooth and the fingernails are well pared. These are the hands of a gentleman.'

'Not any more. Death treats all as one.'

'This body was strong and upright while it lived.'

'The grave is wide enough for anyone.'

'He would have been able to defend himself.'

'Not any more, sir.'

Nicholas took a last, sad look at the corpse then indicated that it should be covered over again in the name of decency. He headed for the exit with the man shuffling along behind him.

'Will you see anyone else?' said the keeper.

'I have gazed my fill.'

'But we have more interesting sights here.' He plucked at his visitor's sleeve to stop him. 'A young woman was brought in but yesternight. Some punk that was strangled in her bed. She is no more than sixteen with a body as soft and lovely as you could wish. One more coin and I would gladly show you.' He nudged the other. 'If you have money enough, I will let you touch her.'

Nicholas turned away in disgust and stormed out before he gave in to the impulse to hit the man. He vowed to report the incident when he appeared at the Coroner's Court on the following Monday. No matter who they were or what they had been, the dead deserved the utmost respect. He came up into the fresh air and inhaled it gratefully. Light was fading and so he hurried in the direction of the river before it went completely. From the wharf where he had been picked up by Abel Strudwick, he looked out across the water and tried to estimate the point at which they had encountered the body. It was somewhere in mid-stream and he wondered how far it had drifted in order to reach them. He decided that the dead man had been put into the Thames under the cover of darkness but the swift current could still have brought him some distance.

The book holder was no stranger to the wharves and

harbours along the Thames. The son of a West Country merchant, he had fallen in love with the sea at an early age and been on numerous voyages with his father. The bold venture of Francis Drake caught his imagination and he sailed around the world with him for three long years. That experience had brought endless disillusion but it had not entirely stilled the call of the sea. When he first came to London, he would often come down to the river to watch the ships putting in and to talk with the sailors about their voyages and their cargoes. This visit was a far less pleasant one.

His eye inevitably fell on the Bridge. It was an extraordinary sight that never palled and Nicholas felt a surge of admiration for those who conceived and built it. Twenty solid piers supported nineteen arches of varying widths. Islands were created around the piers to protect them from the tide race. These starlings, as they were called, were shaped like great flat boats and narrowed the water channels under the arches so much that the tide race was dramatically increased. Nicholas had not been surprised to learn that the Bridge had taken over thirty years to complete and had claimed the lives of some one hundred and fifty workmen. It had stood for some four centuries and more as a tribute to their craftsmanship. Because it was the only structure to span the broad Thames, it became the most important thoroughfare in London and properties along its length were much coveted. The Bridge was also the healthiest part of the city. When the Black Death was decimating the population in every other ward, it could only boast two recorded deaths among those who lived above the swirling waters of the river.

Respect soon changed to foreboding. It was that same Bridge which had put such deep fear into the heart of Hans Kippel that he could not even stand there and behold it. Two of the most appealing parts of London had taken on a different character for Nicholas. The Bridge held the clue to what had happened to a Dutch apprentice and the River Thames knew the secret of the maimed body that it had washed up into the hands of the book holder. He stood there in deep contemplation until evening had washed the last rays of light from the sky.

A boat took him across to Bankside and he walked briskly along the winding lanes on his way home. Another problem now concentrated his mind. Alexander Marwood had lit a raging bonfire of uncertainty. An impending change of ownership at the Queen's Head was a serious threat to the well-being of Westfield's Men. The landlord was a difficult enough man with whom to bargain but Alderman Rowland Ashway would not even talk terms. Nicholas had thought to confide in Edmund Hoode but his friend was too infected with lovesickness to hear any sense. Lawrence Firethorn would need to be told soon and the book holder resolved to call on him the next day. Trying times lay ahead and they could only be made worse by the fact that a fond poet and a lustful actor had chosen as the object of their passion the same unsuspecting young woman. If tragedy was to be averted, Nicholas would have to provide some highly skilful stage-management.

He walked along between rows of tenements then turned into the street where he lived. The house was still some thirty yards away when he sensed danger and it caused him to slow his pace. Someone was lurking beside the front door, seated on the ground and curled up in an attitude of sleep that he did not trust for a second. Those who walked through the darkness of Southwark were used to the skulking presence of thieves and they used all kinds of tricks to lull the unwary off guard. As Nicholas closed in on the house, one hand fondled the dagger at his waist. The figure on the ground was rough and sturdy with a hat pulled down over his face. There was a sense of crude power about him. Ready for any attack, Nicholas extended a foot to push the man over.

'God's blood! I'll cut your rotten liver out!'

A gushing waterfall of vile abuse came from the man's mouth until he recognised who had roused him from his slumbers. He leapt up at once to issue a stream of apologies and to ingratiate himself with bows and shrugs. Abel Strudwick had waited a long time for his hope of a new future. A broad grin split his hideous face in two and gave it an even more alarming quality.

'You may change my whole life, Master Bracewell.'

'May I?'

'Put me upon the stage, sir!'

Sir Lucas Pugsley never tired of admiring himself in his full regalia as Lord Mayor of London. He paraded up and down in front of the long mirror and watched his black and gold gown trail along the floor. Power had turned an ambitious man into a dangerous one who sought means both to retain and enlarge that power. As Alderman Luke Pugsley of the Fishmongers' Company, he was rich, secure and very influential. When he was elevated to the highest civic office, he became like a demi-god and was consumed with his own self-esteem. Over thirty officers belonged to the Lord Mayor's House. They included the Sword-bearer, the Common Crier, the City Marshall and the Coroner for London as well as the Common Hunt, the Water Bailiff and other assorted bailiffs, sergeants and yeomen. There were always three meal-weighers at his beck and call.

The man on whom he relied most was the Chamberlain.

'Will you put on your chain of office, Lord Mayor?'

'Bring it to me, sir.'

'It becomes you so well.'

'I carry it with dignity and good breeding.'

Aubrey Kenyon was tall, well built and quite stately with greying temples lending an air of distinction to the clear, clean shaven face. The Chamberlain was responsible for the financial affairs of the city but Kenyon's role had enlarged well beyond that. Like his predecessors, the present Lord Mayor found him a source of comprehensive information about civic life and duty, and befriended him early on. Aubrey Kenyon had no airs and graces. Despite the importance of his position, he was happy to perform more menial tasks for the man whom he served. He stood back to appraise the chain.

'It looks exceeding fine,' he said.

'Its weight reminds me of my civic burdens.'

'You have borne them with lightness.'

'Thank you, Aubrey.' He stroked the gold collar. 'This chain was bequeathed to the mayoralty in 1545 by John Allen who held the office twice. I venture to suggest that nobody has worn it with such pride and with such distinction. Am I not the most conscientious Lord Mayor you have ever encountered? Be honest with me, Aubrey, for I trust your opinion above all others. Have I not been a credit to my office?'

'Indeed, indeed.'

Kenyon bowed his agreement then adjusted the chain slightly to make it completely straight. It consisted of twenty-six gold knots, interspersed with roses and the Tudor portcullis and it set off the gold thread which weighted the gown of stiff silk. Beneath his gown, Pugsley wore the traditional court dress of knee breeches, silk stockings and buckled shoes. Aubrey Kenyon held out the mayoral hat with its flurry of ostrich feathers. When it was placed carefully in position, the Lord Mayor of London was ready to attend yet another civic banquet.

'Is everything in order, Aubrey?'

'We await but your august self, Lord Mayor.'

'My wife?'

'She has been standing by this half-hour.'

'That is a welcome change,' said Pugsley with a quiet snigger. 'When we live at home together, it is always *I* who am kept waiting if we are dining out. I like this new order of precedence. A Lord Mayor of London can even put a woman in her place.'

'Unless she be the Queen of England.'

'Even then, sir. I have spoken honestly with Her Majesty before now and she has respected me for it. My generosity is also well known to her.'

'As to the whole city.' The Chamberlain pointed towards the door of the apartment. 'Will you descend? The coach has been at the door this long time.'

'There is no hurry,' said Pugsley grandly. 'Though the Guildhall be full, none will dare to start before me. I claim the privilege of my office in arriving late.'

The Chamberlain smiled quietly and crossed to open the door. Two servants bowed low at the approach of the Lord Mayor. Sir Lucas Pugsley sailed past them and went down the wide staircase to be met by a further display of obeisance in the hall. With his wife on his arm, he left the house and was assisted into the ceremonial coach. The journey to the Guildhall was marred by only one thought. His year of triumph would be over all too soon. Power invaded his brain and gave his resolve a manic intensity.

He had to cling on to office somehow.

Aubrey Kenyon, meanwhile, was pulling a cloak around his shoulders before slipping discreetly out of the house. He walked quickly through the dark lanes until he came to an imposing property in Silver Street near Cripplegate. He was no deferential Chamberlain now but a determined man with an air of self-importance about him. When he knocked at a side-door of the house, he was admitted instantly by a servant and conducted to the main room. His host was waiting anxiously.

'You are a welcome sight, Aubrey!'

'Good even, good sir.'

'We have much to discuss.'

'Time is beginning to run out for us.'

Rowland Ashway dismissed his servant then poured two cups of fine wine. Handing one to his guest, he conducted him to a seat at the long oak table. The portly brewer and the poised Chamberlain were an incongruous pair but they had common interests which tied them indissolubly together.

'How is our mutual friend?' said Ashway.

'Sir Lucas is besotted with his authority. He will not easily yield it up.'

'Nor will we, Aubrey. *You* are the real power behind the Lord Mayor of London and the beauty of it is that Luke is far too addle-brained to notice it.'

'The truth will not escape Walter Stanford.'

'That is why he must never take office. Never, sir!'

The Chamberlain calmly pronounced a death sentence.

'They must find that boy.'

The passage of time had not so far improved the sleeping habits of Hans Kippel. His body had profited from rest but his mind remained a prey to phantoms. The young apprentice was at the mercy of an unknown enemy who would not show his face.

'I will be poor company, Master Bracewell.'

'That is for me to decide.'

'I would not keep you awake.'

'Nor shall you,' said Nicholas with a smile. 'After the day I have endured, I will sleep like a baby.'

'Go upstairs, Hans,' advised Anne Hendrik. 'We have put a truckle bed ready for you.'

'Thank you, mistress. Good night.'

They exchanged farewells and he went off upstairs. Disturbed nights were taking such a toll on the boy that Nicholas volunteered to share a room with him, hoping that his presence might bring a degree of reassurance. At the same time, he wanted to be on hand in case there was any trickle of information from the memory that had so far been completely dammed up. Anne Hendrik was immensely grateful to her lodger.

'It is kindness indeed, Nick.'

'I hate to see that look of terror upon him.'

'As do I.'

'Besides,' he added, 'Hans may still get the worst end of it. If he does fall asleep, my snoring might yet pull him out of his slumbers.'

'You do not snore,' she said fondly.

'How do you know?'

They shared a gentle laugh then he reviewed his day for her. She was fascinated by it all but understandably alarmed at the news about the Queen's Head. If the future of Westfield's Men was in jeopardy, then so was her close relationship with her lodger. He read her concern.

'You will not shake me off so easily, Anne.'

'I hope not, sir.'

'Accompany me through these difficulties.'

'I'll pray in church tomorrow.'

'Add something else while down upon your knees.'

'What do you mean?'

'Abel Strudwick runs mad.'

When he told about how he had been waylaid by the stagestruck waterman, she was torn between laughter and sympathy. Nicholas was placed in a difficult position. He had somehow to deflect his poetic friend without hurting the man's feelings. It was an impossible assignment. As the last of the day dwindled, they parted with a kiss and went off to their separate chambers. When he crept quietly into bed, Nicholas was relieved to hear the steady breathing of Hans Kippel beside him in the dark. The boy was asleep at last. It seemed as if the experiment of bringing him there had worked.

The book holder allowed himself to drift and he was soon lost in a world of floating dreams. How long he stayed there he did not know but when he left there, it was with sudden violence.

'Stop it! No, sirs! Stop it! Stop it!'

Hans Kippel was threshing about in his bed. He sat bolt upright and let out a screech that raised the whole house. He held hands up to defend himself against attack.

'Hold off, sirs! Leave me alone!'

'What is the matter?' said Nicholas, rushing across to him. 'What ails you, lad?'

He put a consoling arm around the apprentice but it

provoked the opposite response. Fearing that he was being grabbed by an assailant, Hans Kippel kicked and fought with all his puny might. Anne Hendrik came rushing into the chamber with a candle to hold over the boy. He was neither awake nor asleep but in some kind of trance. His whole body trembled and perspiration came from every pore. His breathing was faster, deeper and much noisier. Demons of the night turned him into a gibbering wreck. It was a disturbing sight and it destroyed all vain hopes that sleep would restore the pitiable creature.

His delirium was worse than ever.

Night was far kinder to Matilda Stanford. She lay beside her husband in the spacious four-poster that graced their bedchamber and watched moonlight throw ghostly patterns onto the low ceiling. Sleep came imperceptibly and she was led into a land that was full of delight. Sweet songs and lovely images came and went with pulsing beauty and Matilda surrendered to the lackadaisical joy of it all. Greater pleasure yet lay in store for her. A splendid new playhouse appeared before her eyes and she was wafted towards it. When she took up her seat in the topmost gallery, she was part of a large and bubbling audience.

But the play was performed solely for her. Other spectators merely watched from afar. She was engaged from the start. Every gesture was aimed at her, every glance directed her way, every speech laid at her feet in simple homage. Characters came and went with bewildering speed. She saw emperors, kings, soldiers, statesmen, brave

113

knights, bold adventurers and many more besides. Each acted out a story that moved her heart or provoked her laughter, that contained a message for her, that drew her ever closer to the magic of the experience.

And all the parts were played by the same man. He was of solid build and medium height with a fine head and a dark pointed beard. Dazzling apparel changed with each minute as the characters flashed by but his essential quality remained intact throughout. He was Count Orlando about to die, he was Argos of Rome in pensive mood, he was Argos of Florence in hilarious vein, he was here and there to please Matilda in a hundred ways.

Lawrence Firethorn was hers to command.

The next moment she was on the stage beside him, a person in the drama, an anguished young lover greeting the return of her hero from the trials he has undergone on her behalf. She flung herself into his strong arms and lost herself in the power of his embrace. Firethorn's lips touched hers in a kiss of passion that was quite unlike anything she had ever conceived.

It brought her awake in an instant. Matilda Stanford sat up and looked around. It was early morning but her husband had already risen to begin some work before paying his first visit of the day to church. Matilda was stranded alone on the huge, empty beach of their bed. This was the story of their young marriage but it had never caused her any regret before. One dream had altered that. There was a life elsewhere that made her own seem dull and futile. In her own bed, in her own marriage, in one of the finest private houses in London, she was overcome with such a feeling of sadness and loneliness that it made her shudder all over.

Matilda Stanford wept tears of disenchantment. Night had tempered its kindness with a subtle cruelty. She had lost her way. For the first time since she had married Walter Stanford, she realised that she was unhappy.

Chapter Five

Margery Firethorn came into her own on a Sunday and ruled the roost with a brisk religiosity. It was not only her husband, children and servants who were shouted out of bed to attend Matins. The apprentices and the three actors staying at the house in Shoreditch were also dragged protesting from their rooms to give thanks to God. Wearing her best dress and a look of prim respectability that she reserved for the Sabbath alone, she lined up the entire party before they left and admonished them with six lines that she had been forced to learn in her youth.

When that thou come to Church, thy prayers for to say,
See thou sleep not, nor yet talk not, devoutly look to pray,
Nor cast thine eyes to and fro, as things thou wouldst still see
So shall wise men judge you a fool, and wanton for to be.

When thou are in the Temple, see thou do thy Churchly works,
Hear thou God's word with diligence, crave pardon for thy faults.

Her instructions met with only moderate obedience when they reached the Parish Church of St Leonard nearby. Prayers were said, attention wandered, tired souls dozed off. During an interminable sermon based on a text from The Acts of the Apostles ('And the disciples were filled with joy, and with the Holy Ghost') Margery was the only occupant of her pew to hear God's word with anything resembling diligence. The actors slept, the apprentices yawned, the servants suffered, the children bickered in silence and Lawrence Firethorn saw only a naked young woman in the pulpit, shorn of her finery and liberated from her escort, beckoning to him to join her atop a Mount Sinai that was set aside for carnal pleasure. That she was also the wife of the Lord Mayor Elect only served to heighten the joyous feeling of sinfulness.

On the journey home, his wife held confession.

'What were you thinking about in church, sir?'

'Sacred matters.'

'I felt that your mind was wandering.'

'It was on higher things, Margery.'

'The Sabbath is a day of rest.'

'Then must you refrain from scolding your husband.'

'Church is an act of faith.'

He sighed. 'How else could we endure that sermon?'

The party brightened as soon as they entered the house. Breakfast was devoured with chomping gratitude and some of them came properly awake for the first time that day. Firethorn adjourned to the small drawing room to receive the visitor that he had invited. Edmund Hoode had put on his best doublet and hose and sported a new hat that cascaded down the side of his head. Amorous thoughts of his lady love painted a beatific smile on his willing features. Firethorn rubbed the smile off at once.

'Stop grinning at me like a raving madman!'

'I am happy, Lawrence.'

'That is what is so unnatural. You were born to be miserable, Edmund. Nature shaped you especially for that purpose. Embrace your destiny and return to the doe-eyed sadness for which your friends adore you.'

'Do not mock me so.'

'Then do not set yourself up for mockery.' He waved his guest to a chair and sat beside him. 'Let us touch on the business of the day.'

Hoode was wounded. 'I thought you brought me here for the pleasure of my company.'

'And so I did, sir. Now that I have had it, we can turn to more important things.' He glanced around to make sure the door was firmly closed. 'Edmund, dear fellow, I have work for your pen.'

'I have already written two new plays this year.'

'Each one a gem of creation,' flattered the other. 'But no new commission threatens. I wish you merely to compose some verse for me.'

'No, Lawrence.'

'Would you refuse, sir?'

'Yes, Lawrence!'

'This is not my Edmund Hoode that speaks.'

'It is, Lawrence.'

'I am asking you for help. Do not deny me or I will never call you friend again. I am in earnest here.'

'So am I.'

'Write me a sonnet to woo my love.'

'Call in Margery instead and sing her a ballad.'

'Are you a lunatic!' hissed Firethorn. 'What has got into you, sir? I ask but a favour you have done on more than one occasion. Why betray me in this way?'

'Because my verse is reserved for another.'

The actor-manager was livid. Rising to his feet, he released a few expletives then let himself get as angry as he dared without arousing the attention of his wife in the adjoining room. Edmund Hoode was unperturbed. A man whom Firethorn could usually manipulate at will was showing iron resolution for once and would not be moved. There was only one way to bring him to heel.

'Legal process is on my side, Edmund.'

'What do you mean?'

'Your contract with the company.'

'There is nothing in that to make me act as your pandar and fetch in your game with pretty rhymes.'

'Will you push me to violence here!'

'Remember the Sabbath and lead a better life.'

Lawrence Firethorn's rage was about to burst into full flame when he controlled it. What came crackling from his mouth instead were the terms of Edmund Hoode's contract with Westfield's Men, exact in every detail.

'One, that you shall write for no other company.'

'Agreed.'

'Two, that you shall provide three plays a year.'

'I have honoured that clause.'

'Three, that you shall receive five pounds for each new drama performed by Westfield's Men. Four, that you shall publish none of the said plays. Five, that you will receive a weekly wage of nine shillings together with a share of any profit made by the company.'

'All this I accept,' said Hoode. 'Where is my obligation to wear the livery of your wandering eye?'

'I am coming to that.' Firethorn turned the screw with a slow smile. 'Six, that you shall write prologues and epilogues as required. Seven, that you shall add new scenes to revived plays. Eight, that you shall add songs as required. Nine, that you shall write inductions to order. *Finis*!' The smile became a smirk. 'This is covenanted and agreed between us. Do you concede that?'

'Of course.'

'Then must you bow to my purpose here.'

'How can it be enforced?'

'By those same terms I listed even now, Edmund.'

'No lawyer would support you.'

'I think he might.' Firethorn swooped. 'I require you to write prologues and epilogues. I instruct you to add new material to a revived text. I desire that songs be inserted. Inductions will I command. Shall you follow my meaning now, sir? What I demand for public plays I can use for my

121

personal advantage – and I have a legal contract to hold you to your duty.'

'This is treachery!' spluttered Hoode.

'I think I will start with a song.'

'Can you descend to such foul devices?'

'Only upon compulsion,' said the genial Firethorn. 'Now, sir, write me a ballad of love to be included in *Cupid's Folly*. I will sing it before my inamorata.'

'My quill would moult in disgust at such a task!'

'Then cut yourself a new one and pen me a prologue to *Love and Fortune*. Let it touch on the themes of the play and speak tenderly to my lady.'

'You will drain my inspiration dry!' wailed Hoode.

'Do your duty with a gladsome mind.'

'I want to woo my *own* beloved.'

'Watch me, Edmund,' advised Firethorn with avuncular condescension. 'And I will show you how it is done.'

Consternation broke out at Stanford Place to ruffle the smooth piety of a Sunday at home. Matilda was listening to her stepson read from the Bible when her husband came striding into the room. Walter Stanford's affability was for once edged with concern. Without even apologising for the interruption, he held up the letter in his hand.

'I have received disquieting news.'

'From whom?' said Matilda.

'My sister in Windsor. She sends word that Michael has still not returned home. Yet his ship docked at the harbour here some three days ago.'

'That is cause for alarm,' she agreed.

'Not if you know Michael,' said her stepson. 'Do not vex yourselves about him too soon. He has been fighting for his country in the Netherlands. After the hardship of a soldier's lot, he will want to celebrate his return by seeking out the pleasure haunts of the city. That is where we will find him, have no fear.'

'I like not that thought,' said Stanford solemnly. 'Michael promised to turn his back on his idle ways.'

'Give him but a few days of licence, Father.'

'When he shows no consideration to his mother?'

'All will be mended very soon.'

'Not until I have said my piece to him!' Stanford moved between anger and apprehension. 'He is so careless and crack-brained, some ill may have befallen him. If he *has* been carousing all this while, I'll fill his ears with the hot pitch of my tongue. Yet what if he has strayed into danger? I scorn him – yet fear for his safety.'

'Can he not be tracked down?' said Matilda.

'I have already set a search in train, my love.'

'Look that they visit the taverns,' added William.

His father bristled. 'It will be the worse for him if they find him in such a place. Michael was due to report first to me before travelling to see his mother in Windsor. I am not just his uncle now. For my sins, I have elected to be his employer.'

'Then there is the explanation,' said his son with a fatuous grin. 'Michael is in hiding from your strict rule.'

'This is not an occasion for levity, sir!'

'Nor yet for wild surmise, Father.'

'My nephew has been missing for three days. Only accident or dissipation can explain his absence and both give grounds for concern.' He waved the letter. 'There is fresh intelligence here. Michael saw action as a soldier and received a wound.'

'Merciful heavens!' said Matilda. 'Of what nature?'

'He did not say but it bought him his discharge.'

'This throws fresh light,' said William anxiously.

'Indeed, it does,' reinforced his father. 'If my nephew carries an injury, why did he not mention it in his letters to me? How serious is it? Will it disable him from working? Then there is the darkest fear of all.'

'What's that, sir?' asked his wife.

'A wounded man may not defend himself so well.'

Walter Stanford said no more but the implication was frightening. A person whose return had been awaited with such pleasure was unaccountably missing. The even tenor of their Sunday morning had been totally disrupted.

A troubled William spoke for all three of them.

'In God's good name, Michael – where *are* you?'

The burly figure crouched over the corpse and studied the great scar that ran the whole width of the pale chest. Having recovered from one dreadful wound, the man had been subjected to far grosser injuries in the course of his murder. Abel Strudwick had paid his money to view the body and he now stood over it with almost ghoulish interest. A low murmuring sound came from his lips and cut through the

cold silence of the charnel house. The keeper inched closer
with his torch and let the flames illumine his visitor's face.

'Did you say something, sir?'

'Only to myself,' grunted Strudwick.

'What are you doing there?'

'Writing a poem.'

Rowland Ashway finished off a plate of eels and a two-pint
tankard of ale by way of an appetiser for the huge meal that
awaited him at home. He was seated in a private room at
the Queen's Head and gazing around its ornate furnishings
with proprietary satisfaction. It was the finest room at the
inn and was always set aside for Lord Westfield and his
cronies whenever they came to see a play performed in the
yard outside. The rotund Alderman smacked his lips with
good humour. To have penetrated to the inner sanctum
of a disdainful aristocrat was in the nature of a victory. It
remained only to expel Lord Westfield completely and the
triumph would be complete.

Alexander Marwood fluttered around the table like a
moth around a flame, anxious to please a potential owner
yet keen to drive as hard a bargain as he dared. His twitch
was at its most ubiquitous as he moved in close.

'I have been having second thoughts, master.'

'About what?' said Ashway.

'The sale of the Queen's Head.'

'But it is all agreed in principle.'

'That was before I listened to my wife.'

'A fatal error, sir. Wives should be spoken at and not

listened to. They will undo the best plans we may make with their womanly grumbles and their squawking reservations. Ignore the good lady.'

'How, sir?' groaned Marwood. 'It is easier to ignore the sun that shines and the rain that falls. She will give me no sleep in bed at nights.'

'There is but one cure for that!' His crude laugh made the landlord recoil slightly. 'Have your pleasure with her until she succumbs from fatigue.'

'Oh, sir,' said the other, sounding a wistful note. 'You touch on sore flesh there.' He became businesslike. 'And besides, her major objection mirrors my own.'

'What might that be?'

'Tradition. My family has owned the Queen's Head for generations now. I am loath to see that end.'

'Nor shall it, Master Marwood. You and your sweet wife will run the establishment as before with full security of tenure. To all outward appearance, the inn will remain yours.'

'But ownership will transfer to you.'

'In return for a handsome price.'

'Yes, yes,' said Marwood quickly. 'That is very much at the forefront of our minds. You have been most kind and generous in that respect.'

'So what detains you? Sentiment?'

'It has its place, surely.'

'What else?'

'Fear of signing away my birthright.'

'The contract keeps you here until you die.' Rowland

126

Ashway used podgy hands to pull himself up from the table to confront the landlord. 'Do not see me as a threat here. We are equal partners in this enterprise and both of us can profit from the venture.'

'My wife might need more persuasion.'

'Do it in the watches of the night.'

'That is when I am least in command.'

'What *will* content the lady, then?'

Marwood shrugged and started to flutter once more. At one stroke, the brewer cut through the threatened delay to their negotiations.

'I increase my bid by two hundred pounds.'

'You overwhelm me, sir!'

'It is my final offer, mark you.'

'I understand that.'

'Will it please Mistress Marwood?'

'It may do more than that,' said the other as a ray of hope found its way into his desperation. 'I'll raise the matter when we retire tonight.'

'It is settled, then.'

Alderman Rowland Ashway sealed the bargain with a flabby handshake then allowed himself to be conducted down to the yard. Even with the additional payment, he would be getting the inn at a very attractive price and he had already made plans for its improvement. Before new features could be added, however, one old one had to be removed without compunction.

'What of Westfield's Men?' said Ashway. 'Have you acquainted them with their fate?'

'I have mentioned it to their book holder.'

'That will rattle their noble patron.'

'It is Master Firethorn who will roar the loudest.'

'Let him. Rowland Ashway is a match for any man.'

'Rowland Ashway! That barrel of rancid lard! Ashway!'

'This is what I have been told.'

'That fat turd of aldermanic pomposity!'

'The same man, sir.'

'That leech, that vile toad, that bloated threat to every chair he sits upon! I could spit at the wretch as soon as look at him. He should be weighted down with blocks of lead then drowned in a tub of his own beer! Rowland Ashway is a monster in half-human form. Does the creature possess a wife?'

'I believe that he does, master.'

'Then must we pray for her soul. How can the woman endure to be mounted by that elephant, to be pounded to a pulp by that bed-breaker, to be flattened into a wafer by that scvurvy, lousy, red-faced bladder of bilge!'

Lawrence Firethorn had not taken the news well. When Nicholas Bracewell called on him that afternoon, the actor had been pleased to see his colleague and took him into the drawing room in the interests of privacy. That privacy had been rescinded now as Firethorn's voice explored octaves of fury that could be heard half a mile away. Nicholas made a vain attempt to pacify him.

'No contract has as yet been signed, sir.'

'Nor shall it be,' vowed the other. 'My God, I'll grab

that walking nightmare of a landlord and hang him up by his undeserving feet. The traitor, the lily-livered hound, the one-eyed, two-faced, three-toed back-stabber!'

'I think it might be better if you steered well clear of Master Marwood,' suggested Nicholas. 'To lay rough hands upon him will not advance our cause.'

'I demand revenge!' howled Firethorn.

'The crime has not yet been committed.'

'But it is planned, is it not?'

'We may yet be able to avert disaster.'

'Only by a show of force, Nick. Let me at him.'

'I counsel the use of diplomacy.'

'Diplomacy! With a twitching publican and a bloated brewer? I'd sooner play the diplomat with a pair of sabre-toothed tigers. Let them hatch their plot and they'll have us turned out of the Queen's Head without a word of thanks. Is it not perfidious?'

'That is why I felt you should be warned.'

'Indeed, indeed.'

'So that we may take the appropriate action.'

'Aye, Nick. Tie those two villains together back to back and drop them in the Thames to curdle the water.' He prowled around the room as he considered more gruesome deaths for the miscreants then he stopped in his tracks. 'We'll attack them from above.'

'How so?'

'Lord Westfield will be told.'

'Only as a last resort,' urged Nicholas. 'It would be wrong to alarm his lordship with a problem that we may be able to solve ourselves. He would not thank us for dragging him into a wrangle of this nature.'

'You may be right,' admitted Firethorn. 'We must keep that last card up our sleeve then. Meanwhile, I will vent my spleen upon that lizard of a landlord.'

'Then might our case be ruined altogether.'

'Heavens, Nick, this is an insult I will not bear! Our plays have helped to fill his coffers generously these last few years. Our art has put his foul establishment on the map of London. We have *made* the Queen's Head. Instead of selling it to Alderman Rowland Ashway, he should be giving it to us in appreciation.'

'Master Marwood is a businessman.'

Firethorn glowered. 'So am I, sir.'

There was a long pause as the actor-manager fought to subdue his temper and take a more objective view of the crisis into which he was now plunged. Behind all the bombast about the primacy of Westfield's Men there lurked a simple truth. The company's survival depended on the income that it could generate and that would shrink alarmingly if they lost their regular home. Lawrence Firethorn stared blankly ahead as cruel practicalities were borne in upon him. His immediate impulse was to launch an attack but it could bring only short-term benefits. In the long run, they relied on one man.

'What must we do, Nick?' he muttered.

'Move with great stealth.'

'Has anyone else been told of this?'

'No, sir,' said Nicholas. 'Nor should they, except for

Edmund and Master Gill. If we spread panic now, it will show in our work and damage our reputation.'

'You give sound advice as usual.'

'Leave me to work on Master Marwood.'

'I'd do so with the sharpest sword in Christendom!'

'Then would we lose all. We must deal softly with the man or he will take fright and run. It is only by talking to him that we can keep abreast of any moves that are made by Alderman Ashway.'

Firethorn snorted. 'The whole city is aware of any moves made by that spherical gentleman. Whenever he stirs abroad, the very earth does shake. If he stood by the river and broke wind, he could launch a whole armada.' He gave a crumpled smile. 'Help us, Nick.'

'I will do everything in my power.'

'That comforts me greatly.' His eyes moistened. 'I would not lose the Queen's Head for a queen's ransom. That stage has seen the full panoply of my genius. Those boards are sacrosanct. Tarquin has walked there. So have Pompey and Black Antonio. King Richard the Lionheart and Justice Wildboare have strutted their hour. A few days past, it was the turn of Count Orlando and I have burnt dozens of other fine parts into the imagination of my audience.' He looked up. 'I would not have it end like this, dear heart.'

'There has to be a means of escape.'

Lawrence Firethorn's voice faded into a whisper.

'Find it, Nick. Save us from extinction . . .'

* * *

Anne Hendrik's anxiety over her apprentice did not ease. The boy was no better on the following day than he had been during a torrid night. Nor could he provide any clue as to what had upset him so dramatically while he slept. Sunday was no day of rest for Hans Kippel. Watched over carefully by Anne and visited by Preben van Loew, he was unable to do more than hold desultory conversation with either. A depression had settled on his young mind. His face was one large puckered frown and his eyes were dull. All the spirit which had made him so boisterous had been knocked out of him by the experience he had undergone. It would clearly take some time yet before the details of that experience began to emerge.

In the hope that prayer might succeed where all else had failed, Anne took him with her to Evensong at the parish church of St Saviour. It was too close to the Bridge for the boy's complete comfort but far enough away for his attention to be diverted from it by his employer. As the Gothic beauty and the sheer bulk of the building rose up before them, she told him an apocryphal story about its past.

'It was once the Priory church of St Mary Overy,' she explained. 'Do you know how it got its name?'

'No, mistress.'

'From the legend of John Overy, who was the ferryman before ever a bridge was built across the river. Because his ferry was rented by the whole city – small as it must have been in those days – he became exceedingly rich. But there was a problem, Hans.'

'What was it?'

'John Overy was a notorious miser. He hoarded his money and looked for new ways to increase his wealth. Shall I tell you how mean this fellow really was?'

'If you please.'

'He believed that if he pretended to die, his family and servants would fast out of respect and thus save him the expense of a whole day's food for the household.'

'That is meanness indeed.'

'Master Overy put his plan into action,' said Anne. 'But his servants were so overjoyed by his death that they began to feast and make merry. He was so furious that he jumped up out of his bed to scold them. One of the servants, thinking he was the Devil, picked up the butt end of an oar and knocked out his brains.'

'It served him right, mistress.'

'Many thought likewise, Hans. But his daughter was grief-stricken. She used her inheritance to found a convent and retreated into it. That convent became, in time, the Priory of St Mary Overy so his name lingers on.'

The apprentice had listened with interest and almost smiled at one point in the story. Anne had a fleeting sensation of making real contact with him at last, of breaking through the mental barrier which surrounded him. They went into the massive church and walked along the shiny-smooth flagstones of the nave beneath the high, vaulted ceiling. Breathtaking architecture and artistry enveloped them and it was impossible not to be touched by the scrupulous magnificence of it all.

They filed into a pew. As Anne knelt in prayer, she felt

Hans Kippel drop down beside her and start to gabble in Dutch. She could hear the note of alarm in his voice and sense his trembling. Words that she could recognise finally slipped out of the boy.

'Please, God . . . do not let them kill *me* . . .'

The Coroner's Court was held early on Monday morning and among those charged to appear were Nicholas Bracewell and Abel Strudwick. The book holder was the first to give his testimony, speaking under oath and explaining exactly how and when he had found the dead body in the Thames. His friend made more of the opportunity that was offered. The waterman was not content with a simple recital of the facts of the case. He had transformed it into a dramatic event. Standing before the Coroner and the whole court, he responded to the presence of an audience with alacrity.

> The night was dark, the water fast and fierce,
> No moonlight could the inky blackness pierce.
> I rowed full hard, I strove against the flood,
> And Master Bracewell helped me all he could.
> But when we reached the middle of the stream,
> I glimpsed a sight that almost made me scream.
> A naked body floated on the tide
> With mangled limbs and injuries beside.
> What did I do, sirs, at this fateful hour?

They never found out. With stern command, the Coroner ordered him to stop and give his evidence in a more seemly manner. Strudwick was truculent and had to be cowed into obedience by the sternest warnings. When he gave a straightforward account of the incident, it tallied in every respect with that of Nicholas Bracewell. Both were dismissed and hurried out.

The waterman was anxious for some praise at least.

'What did you think of my music?'

'Quite unlike anything I have ever heard, Abel.'

'Will you commend me to Master Firethorn?'

'I shall mention your name.'

'Instruct him in my purpose.'

'I must away. Rehearsal soon begins.'

Nicholas was glad of the chance to break away and race off to Gracechurch Street. Abel Strudwick could be entertaining enough as a versifying waterman. As a prospective member of the theatrical profession, he was a menace. The book holder was going to have to row very carefully with him through choppy waters.

He made up for his late arrival at the Queen's Head by hurling himself into his work. The stage was set up on its trestles, the props, furniture and scenic devices made ready, and the costumes were brought into the room that was used as the tiring-house. *Black Antonio* was another tragedy of revenge with some powerful scenes and some unlikely but effective comedy from the Court Fool. It had been part of their repertoire for some time now and posed no serious problems. The rehearsal was rather flat but without any mishap. Lawrence Firethorn gave them only a touch of the whip before dismissing them from the stage.

Nicholas knew the cause of the general lethargy. The company took its cue from its acknowledged stars and both were jaded. Fear of ejection from the Queen's Head had seeped into the performances of Black Antonio himself and of the Court Fool. They were still in costume as they accosted the book holder.

'Keep that ghoul away from me, Nick,' said Firethorn. 'Or I will slit his ungrateful throat and string up his polecat of a body for all to see.'

'Master Marwood keeps his own counsel, sir.'

'I spurn the ruffian!'

He went out with a swirl of his cloak and left the book holder alone with Barnaby Gill. The latter was no friend of Nicholas but adversity had taken the edge off his animosity. Dressed as the Fool, he advised wisdom.

'Reason closely with the man, sir.'

'I will, Master Gill.'

'Do nothing to provoke this starchy landlord.'

'We may win him around yet.'

'Remind him of the magic of my art. I have reached the heights upon this stage to please the vulgar throng. Master Marwood *owes* it to me to let me continue. Let him know the full quality of my work.'

'It speaks for itself,' said Nicholas tactfully.

'We count on you for our salvation.'

Barnaby Gill gave his arm an affectionate squeeze, an uncharacteristic gesture that showed how upset he was by the shadow hanging over them. As Gill sloped off to the tiring-house, another voice sought the book holder's ear.

'We must talk alone, Nick,' said Edmund Hoode.

'When I have finished here. Meet me in the taproom.'

'It is the worst blow I have ever suffered.'

'We are all still reeling from its force.'

'How can I endure it?'

'Try to put it out of your mind.'

'It sits there like an ogre that will not shift.'

'Master Marwood may be converted to common sense.'

'What use is that?' said Hoode peevishly. 'I want Lawrence Firethorn converted to a eunuch. It is the only way to solve my plight. He compels me to write songs of love to his new doxy when I have a mistress of my own to woo. Come to my aid, Nick. I perish.'

It was hectic. In the short time between rehearsal and performance, Nicholas attended to all his duties, ate a meagre lunch, sympathised with Hoode's predicament, fought off another sally from Owen Elias ('Ramon was a disgrace to the theatre this morning. Let me take over'), managed an exchange of pleasantries with Alexander Marwood then went back to his post to watch the stage being swept and strewn with green rushes. When the audience swarmed in to take up their places in the yard or their seats in the galleries, everything was apparently under control.

The sense of order did not last. *Black Antonio* had never been given such a lacklustre performance. Lawrence Firethorn was strangely muted, Barnaby Gill was curiously dull and Edmund Hoode, who usually sparkled in the role of a duplicitous younger brother, was frankly appalling.

The disease was infectious and the whole company was soon in its grip. They played without conviction and the mistakes began to multiply. But for the book holder's consoling authority behind the scenes, *Black Antonio* might have become a fiasco. As it was, the audience felt so cheated by what it saw that it began to hoot and jeer with gathering displeasure. Only a minor recovery in the fifth act saved the actors from being booed ignominiously off the stage. Westfield's Men had never taken their bows with such indifference.

Lawrence Firethorn came hurtling into the tiring-house to berate everyone in sight for their incompetence only to be told by Edmund Hoode that he himself was the chief offender. The row that developed between them was not only due to the insecurity they now felt at the Queen's Head. There was a deeper reason and Nicholas had noted it from the beginning of the performance. Both men had gone out to act to one person in the packed audience.

Matilda Stanford was not there.

Not even the first hints of calamity could keep Walter Stanford away from home. Though he was still deeply concerned about the fate of his nephew, Michael, he did not interrupt his normal schedule to join in the search. That was now being led by his son who had so far come back empty-handed. Lieutenant Michael Delahaye had indeed disembarked on the previous Thursday but he was only one of hundreds of soldiers who had poured off the ship and into the welcoming bosom of London. Nothing further had been gleaned, not even a description of the wound he had collected in the Netherlands. Medical records had not been kept by the army and Michael was, in any case, no longer a member of it. Discharged into civilian life once again, he had contrived to vanish into thin air.

Walter Stanford put it all to the back of his mind as he walked purposefully into the Royal Exchange on Cornhill. Modelled on the Antwerp Bourse, it was the largest building project undertaken in the city during the Tudor dynasty. Eighty houses had been demolished to clear the site. The Exchange was the work of Thomas Gresham, mercer and financial agent to the Crown, who put some of his vast wealth towards the cost. Enmity between England and Spain had led to trading difficulties with Flanders and created a dire need for a bourse in London. Thomas Gresham obliged and it was duly opened in 1570 by Queen Elizabeth. Its value to the merchant community was inestimable and nobody was more aware of this than Walter Stanford. As he looked around, he was struck yet again by the boldness of the concept.

The Exchange was a long, four-storeyed building that was constructed around a huge courtyard. Its belltower was surmounted by a giant grasshopper which was the emblem of the Gresham crest. Covered walks faced out onto the courtyard and statues of English kings stood in the niches above them. It was an inspiring sight at any time but especially so when it was filled with merchants who stood in groups according to their specialised trading interests. Over the years, the Exchange had also become the haunt of idlers who hung about the gates to mock, jostle, beg, sell their wares or offer their bodies but even this did not detract from the bustling dignity that still prevailed.

Walter Stanford mingled happily and struck many deals that Monday morning. Well known and much respected, his position as Lord Mayor Elect made him a popular target and he was courted on every side. Productive hours soon scudded by but it was not only profit that interested him. A gnarled face in the crowd reminded him of a promise to his young wife.

'Good day to you, Gilbert.'

'Well met, sir.'

'Are you not too old for this madhouse?'

'I will come to the Exchange until I drop, Walter.'

Gilbert Pike was by far the most ancient of the wardens of the Mercers' Company. Thin, silver-haired and decrepit, he was bent almost double and hobbled along with the aid of a stick. But his mind was still as razor-sharp as it had always been and he could more than hold his own in any business deal. There was also another facet to the old man's skills and Walter Stanford drew him aside to gain some advantage from it.

'I need your kind help, Gilbert.'

'Speak on and it is yours.'

'My young wife must be pleased.'

Pike cackled merrily. 'Do not call on me for that!'

'Matilda is adamant. When I become Lord Mayor, she would have a play performed in my honour.'

'Then she is a woman after my own heart,' said the other with croaking enthusiasm. 'The Mercers' Company put on many pageants in times past. I wrote many of them myself and took the leading part.'

'That is why I came to you, Gilbert. Nobody is so well versed in the drama. Would it be possible to stage another piece to brighten up my banquet?'

'It would be an honour!' said Pike eagerly. 'What is more, I have the very play to hand. *The Nine Worthies*.'

'Is that not an antiquated piece?'

'Not in my version, sir.'

'Who are these nine worthies?'

'Three Paynims, three Jews and three Christian men.'

'Explain.'

'Hector of Troy, Alexander the Great and Julius Caesar; then come Joshua, David and Judas Maccabeus; last are Arthur, Charlemagne and Godefroi de Bouillon.'

'I see no comedy there,' said Stanford. 'Matilda orders laughter. Have you no more lively piece?'

'*The Nine Worthies* is my finest invention.'

'I'm sure it is, Gilbert, but it does not suit our purpose here. Unless . . .' An idea took root in his mind and blossomed spontaneously. 'Unless we change these nine fellows to fit our purpose and advance our Guild.'

'How say you?'

'Supposing those same gentlemen wore the livery of the

141

Mercers' Company? Do you follow my inspiration here? Instead of Hector and the rest, we choose nine persons who have brought our Guild most honour as Lord Mayors of London. I like it well. Richard Whittington must be our first worthy, of that there is no question.'

Gilbert Pike took a few minutes to understand and adapt to the notion but he welcomed it with a toothless grin and clapped his claw-like hands. Other names sprang from him for consideration.

'Richard Gardener, Lionel Duckett and John Stockton. Ralph Dodmer should be there and even Geoffrey Boleyn that was a hatter first and then a mercer. John Allen must be there, who presented the mayoral collar. Then there is Richard Malorye and many more besides.' The gums came into view again. 'Nor must we forget the worthiest man of our own day.'

'Who is that, Gilbert?'

'Who else but you, sir?' The old man was warming to the idea rapidly. 'Walter Stanford. You shall be the ninth in the line. It will be a fitting climax.'

'And a wonderful surprise for Matilda,' agreed the other. 'But can this play have humour in it, too? May not these nine honourable men make us laugh as well?'

'They will provide drama and mirth, sir.'

'This is truly excellent, Gilbert!'

'And my title remains – *The Nine Worthies*.'

'No,' said Stanford. 'It would serve to confuse. That title is too familiar. We must find a new one.'

'But it describes the play so well,' argued the old man.

'Are these men not worthy? And are there not nine of them in number? Each one a giant of the company? What is the objection to my title?'

'You have just given me a better one.'

'Have I, sir?'

'Yes, Gilbert. *That* is what the play will be called.'

'What?'

'*The Nine Giants*!'

Chapter Six

Even after the best part of a year in office, Sir Lucas Pugsley was still thrilled at the privileges showered upon him as Lord Mayor of London. The city had always jealously guarded its independence even though this often led to friction with the court and the Parliament at Westminster. Within the city walls, the Lord Mayor ranked above everyone except the Sovereign herself, including princes of the Blood Royal. No fishmonger could ask for more than that. Among his many titles, Pugsley was head of the City Corporation, its chief magistrate, and the chairman of its two governing bodies, the Court of Alderman and the Court of Common Council. Perquisites flourished on all sides but there was one that brought him special delight. He was entitled to any sturgeon caught below London Bridge.

Two features of the office conspired to deter many a possible contender. A year as Lord Mayor was extremely costly since it took you away from your business affairs and involved a great deal of incidental expense. To avoid all this, there had been cases in the past of aldermen bribing their way out of election, paying hundreds of pounds to avoid an honour that would take even heavier toll on their purse. Those rich enough to afford the luxury could yet be halted by another drawback. Being a Lord Mayor committed you to an enormous amount of work. Civic duties were endless and banquets were too frequent and too lavish for many stomachs.

Sir Lucas Pugsley made light of both handicaps. He was wealthy enough to take the job and hungry enough to do it without loss of appetite. Though it took him away from his own business, it was a profitable investment since it gave him an insight into every area of activity in the city. He had considerable patronage at his disposal and could bestow lucrative offices on friends and relations. The head of the city also got the profits from the sale of appointments which were his to make, and received income from rent farms and market leases. Pugsley was an archetypal Lord Mayor. What made him able to savour his public role was the immense assistance he got in private.

The Chamberlain was a rock at all times.

'I have brought the judicial accounts, Lord Mayor.'

'Thank you, Aubrey.'

'Here also is some correspondence from Amsterdam.'

'I have been awaiting that.'

'You have to deliver a speech this evening.'

'Lord save us! I had quite forgot.'

'That is why I took the liberty of drafting it out for you, Lord Mayor. Three foreign ambassadors dine at your house this night. A speech of welcome is in order. You are too busy to give much time to it yourself.' He handed the documents over. 'I hope that my humble scribblings find favour.'

'Indeed, they do, man. You are my saviour, Aubrey!'

'I try to be of service.'

As Chamberlain to the city of London, he had wide-ranging duties with regard to finance but his omnicompetence raised him above his calling. Like many before him, Pugsley used the man's advice and expertise at every turn and confided in him things that he kept from almost everyone. That was another reassuring trait of Aubrey Kenyon. He was the very soul of discretion.

They were in the palatial room that Pugsley used as his office. He was seated at the long oak table with documents piled high in front of him. Without the aid of his Chamberlain, he could never hope to find his way through them. Power made him capricious.

'Do I have appointments this afternoon?'

'Five in total, Lord Mayor.'

'I am in no mood to receive anyone. Cancel them.'

Kenyon bowed. 'I have already done so.'

'You know my mind better than I,' said Pugsley with a chuckle. 'You have learnt to read me like a book, sir.'

'Then I hope I have read aright.'

'What do you mean?'

'I dismissed only four of your five visitors.'

'And the fifth?'

'He waits outside. I did not think you would wish him to be turned away like the others.'

'Who is the fellow?'

'Alderman Rowland Ashway.'

'Once more, you share my thinking, sir. Rowland Ashway must never be sent away from this door. It is largely because of him that I sit this side of it.' He got up from his chair. 'Admit him at once.'

'I will, Lord Mayor.'

Kenyon bowed, left the room quietly then returned almost at once with the waddling Ashway. With another formal bow, the Chamberlain left them alone to trade warm greetings and even warmer gossip. The old friends were soon chatting away happily about the pleasures of high office. Sir Lucas Pugsley let self-importance get the better of him.

'Nothing can compare with this feeling, Rowland.'

'I trust it well.'

'It is a gift from the gods.'

'And from your admirers on the aldermanic roll.'

'Think, man! A fishmonger who has the Queen's ear.'

'We are two of a kind,' said Ashway complacently.

'In what regard?'

'You have the Queen's ear. *I* have the Queen's Head.'

Nicholas Bracewell bided his time until the landlord came out into the courtyard to speak to one of his ostlers. As Alexander Marwood broke away, the book holder intercepted him. It was early evening at the Queen's Head and the disgruntled audience had long since departed.

Westfield's Men had sullied their glowing reputation.

'Good even, good sir,' said Marwood. 'You gave a paltry account of yourselves here today.'

'Some blame must fall on you, I fear.'

'I am no actor, Master Bracewell.'

'Indeed you are not,' said Nicholas. 'Had you been so, you would know the lurching misery of those without a regular wage or a regular home. The Queen's Head has been a beacon in our darkness, sir. Take but that away and you plunge us into blackest night.'

'I must do the best for myself and my family.'

'Granted, sir. But we are part of that family now and feel cut off. When you threaten to exile us, you lower our spirits and our performance. The result was plain for all to see this afternoon.'

'Do not put this guilt upon me.'

'I appeal only to your finer feelings.'

Marwood's twitch had been quiescent until now, lying dormant while it considered which part of his grotesque face to visit next. It reappeared below his left eye and made him wink with alarming rapidity. Nicholas pursued him for more information.

'Has anything been settled with Alderman Ashway?'

'In broad outline.'

'Our contract still has some weeks to run.'

'It will not be renewed, Master Bracewell.'

'Despite the mutual advantage it has brought?'

'All things must come to an end, sir.'

'Would you surrender ownership so easily?'

His question made the landlord smart and shifted the nervous twitch to his pursed lips which now opened and shut with fish-like regularity. Evidently, he had some misgivings about the new dispensation. Nicholas tried to apply some gentle pressure.

'The proud name of Marwood has favoured this inn for over a century. That is a fine achievement.'

'I know my family history, Master Bracewell.'

'Then have some thought for your forbears. Would any of them have yielded up their inheritance like this?'

'No, sir,' agreed Marwood. 'Nor would they have given shelter to a troupe of bothersome actors. My father would not have let Westfield's Men across the threshold.'

'Would he turn away the custom of our noble patron?'

'He liked not plays and players.'

'You have been a kinder host.'

'It is time to show kindness to myself.'

'By giving away all that you hold most dear?'

'Only at a price.'

Nicholas shrugged. 'That is your privilege, sir. But I wonder that you have not looked more fully into this.'

'More fully?'

'Alderman Ashway is an ambitious man. The Queen's Head will not be the only inn he has gobbled up. Look to the Antelope and to the White Hart in Cheapside.'

'What of them?'

'Talk to the landlords,' said the other. 'See if they are happy that they sold out to the good brewer. You will find them weighed down with regret, I think.'

'That is their fault,' insisted Marwood. 'I have wrested better terms for myself. You cannot frighten me in that way, Master Bracewell. The Antelope is a scurvy hostelry and the White Hart draws in low company. I'll not compare the Queen's Head with them.'

'They all serve Ashway's Beer.'

'You have drunk your share without complaint.'

Nicholas was making no headway. Foreseeing the attack, Marwood had shored up his defences with care. The twitch might travel to and fro across his battlements but his wall would not be breached. Another form of entry had to be found. The book holder searched with care.

'How does your wife face the impending loss?'

'That is a private matter, sir.'

'Mistress Marwood has her doubts, then?'

'She will see sense in time.'

'Would you sign a contract without her approval?'

The landlord fell into a stony silence but his twitch betrayed him completely. It broke out in four different areas simultaneously so that a swarm of butterflies seemed to have settled on his face. As he watched the fibrillating flesh, Nicholas Bracewell saw that there might be a shaft of hope for them after all. The future of Westfield's Men rested on a woman.

Matilda Stanford was in reflective mood as she strolled along the winding paths in the garden. Early autumn was offering floral abundance and bending fruit trees, all wrapped in a heady mixture of sweet fragrances and brought alive by

151

bright sunshine and birdsong. Stanford Place was blessed with one of the largest and most luxuriant gardens in the area, and its blend of privacy and tranquillity was exactly what she needed at that moment. The front of the house looked out on the daily turbulence of Bishopsgate Street but its rear gazed down upon an altogether different world. In the heart of the busiest city in Europe was this haven of pure peace. Matilda had loved it from the start but she came to appreciate it far more now. What had once been a pure delight was today a means of escape. In the twisting walks of the garden, she could find true solitude to relieve the sharpness of her melancholy.

Ever since she had realised she was unhappy, it had been more and more of an effort to pretend otherwise and she was almost glad of the crisis about her husband's missing nephew, Michael, because it relieved her of the need to be so wifely and vivacious. In sharing the general concern, she could conceal her own feelings of loss and disappointment. In worrying about Lieutenant Michael Delahaye, she was expressing a deeper anxiety about someone else who had gone astray. Matilda Stanford was also missing and the search for her was fruitless.

There were moments of joy but they lay in the fond contemplation of one who was for ever beyond her reach. Lawrence Firethorn was unattainable. Though he had sent her a playbill and signalled his admiration during the performance of *Double Deceit*, that was as far as the relationship could realistically go. She was a married woman with no freedom of movement and he was a roving actor.

There was no way that she could return the interest he had shown in her even though the desire to do so grew stronger by the hour. Michael's disappearance was a mortal blow to her fleeting hopes. A man who might have accompanied her to the Queen's Head was making sure that she had no means of going there. It was William Stanford who was leading the hunt and thereby depriving his stepmother of her means of attending a play.

As she looked ahead, her spirits sank even more. Her husband was a wonderful man in so many ways but he did not give her anything of the stimulation she received from a ranting actor upon a makeshift stage. When Walter Stanford became Lord Mayor of London, her situation could only get far worse as she was dragged along behind him into an endless round of social events. She would see even less of him and experience more inner torment. A marriage which had brought her such pleasure was now turning into a comfortable ordeal. She was stifled.

The lifeline was brought by Simon Pendleton.

'Hold there, mistress.'

'What's that?'

'Another missive has arrived for you.'

'Who delivered it?'

'That same miserable creature as before,' said the steward, wrinkling his nose with polite contempt. 'I have brought it to your hand.'

'Thank you, Simon.'

'Will there be anything else, mistress?'

'Not at this time.'

He bowed and glided off into the undergrowth with practised ease. Though Matilda could not bring herself to like the man, she was profoundly grateful to him at the moment because he had fetched the thing she most desired. It was a playbill, rolled up as before and tied with a pink ribbon. As her nervous fingers released it, the scroll unwound and a sealed letter dropped to the ground. Matilda snatched it up immediately. A glance at the playbill told her that Westfield's Men were due to stage *Love and Fortune* at the Queen's Head on the following day but it was the letter that produced the real elation.

As she tore it open, she found herself reading a sonnet in praise of her beauty that itemised her charms with such playful delicacy that she almost swooned. It was unsigned but the sender – presumably the poet – was no less a person than Lawrence Firethorn himself. All her doubts were cast aside. Hers was no wild infatuation for a man beyond her grasp. It was a shared passion that drew them ineluctably together. A second message lay in the choice of play. *Love and Fortune* could be no accidental selection. It reinforced the sentiments of the sonnet and was an invitation to romance.

She read the poem again, weighing each word on the scales of her mind to extract maximum pleasure from it. That she could have inspired such a mellifluous flight of language was dizzying enough on its own. For it to have come from the hand of the man on whom she doted made the whole thing quite intoxicating. Walter Stanford could not be faulted as a loyal husband who treated his wife with respect. But he had no pretty rhymes in his soul.

Tears of joy formed. During her dark night of disenchantment, she had come to see that she was not happy in her marriage. During her walk in the afternoon sun, she made a discovery of equal import and adjusted her own view of herself yet again. In a garden in London, standing beneath a juniper tree, seeing the colour clearly, inhaling the sweet odours, hearing the melodious birdsong, Matilda Stanford had another revelation. Her heart was no longer bound by the vows made on her wedding day because it had not truly been engaged in the ceremony. Fourteen lines of poetry and a cheap playbill taught her something that sent a thrill through her entire being.

She was in love for the first time in her life.

The charnel house had a new keeper. Nicholas Bracewell's formal complaint to the Coroner's Court had led to the dismissal of the man who treated the dead bodies in his charge with such grotesque lack of respect. His hollow-cheeked successor was no more companionable but he had a greater sense of decency and decorum. Conducting the small party to the slab in the corner, he took hold of the tattered shroud and looked up for a signal from the watchman. The latter deferred to the two visitors he had brought into the grim vault. Walter Stanford exchanged a glance with his son and both braced themselves. A nod was then given to the keeper who drew back the shroud with clumsy reverence, unveiling only the head and trunk of the corpse so that the repulsive injuries to the leg remained hidden away.

'Lord help us!' exclaimed Stanford.

'God rest his soul!' said his son.

Both were thunderstruck by what they saw and fought to control their stomachs. Neither of them needed to view a crippled leg to confirm the identity of the battered body. Walter Stanford was looking at the nephew who was due to renounce a hedonistic existence and commit himself to a more responsible life. His son was staring at a beloved cousin whose merriment was its own justification. Grief dazed them both completely. The watchman gestured to the keeper and the shroud was pulled back over the corpse to check the hostile smell of death. There was a long, bruised silence as the visitors were given time to compose themselves. The watchman then spoke.

'Well, sirs?' he said.

'That is him,' whispered Stanford.

'You have no doubt?'

'None at all,' added William.

'Would you like to view him again?'

Walter Stanford winced and held up a large palm.

'We have seen enough,' he said. 'My son and I know our own kin. That is Michael Delahaye.'

It was Anne Hendrik's idea. After what she felt was the relative success of taking Hans Kippel to church, she believed he might now be ready for a more important outing, especially if it could be presented to the boy as

156

something else. Nicholas Bracewell agreed to her plan. Since Westfield's Men were not playing that Tuesday, he managed to find an hour in the middle of the afternoon when he could slip back home to Bankside to join in the expedition. The intention was to help the apprentice to confront his fear of the Bridge. This could not be done by simply taking him there and forcing him to cross it. Anne told him that all three of them were going to visit the market in Cheapside. With two adults at his side, he felt as if he were part of a family setting out on a small adventure. Apprehensions did not surface.

After prior discussion, Nicholas and Anne tried to keep his mind engaged by feeding him with snippets of information about some of the buildings and churches that they passed on the way. Their casual tone did not alter when the Bridge came in sight and the gatehouse loomed up ahead of them. Hans Kippel gulped when he saw the heads of executed traitors crudely exhibited on poles but he did not check his stride. The barbarous custom had always upset and fascinated the boy.

'Thirty-two,' he said.

'What's that, Hans?' asked Anne.

'Thirty-two heads today. I have not seen so many.'

'Have pity on their souls,' said Nicholas.

'Who were they, sir?'

'Misguided men.'

'Did they deserve such treatment?'

'No, Hans. They have paid for their crime already.'

'What was it, Master Bracewell?'

By the time that Nicholas had explained, they were passing through the gate and beneath the sightless eyes of the severed heads. Another feature of the Bridge now rose up to dominate and impress.

'That is Nonesuch House,' said Anne.

'I have admired it often, mistress.'

'Did you know that it was Dutch?'

'There is no mistaking it,' he said with a proud smile. 'I have seen other houses like it in Amsterdam.'

Nonesuch House was well named. No other such house or building stood in the whole of London. Built entirely out of wood, it was a huge, rambling structure that was heavily encrusted with ornament and crowned with carved gables and onion-shaped cupolas. The woodwork was painted with such vivid colours that a remarkable house became quite dazzling in every sense. Nonesuch House was one of the wonders of London and it added immeasurably to the awe-inspiring impact of the Bridge.

Nicholas Bracewell supplied more details for him.

'The foundation stone was laid in 1577,' he said. 'The house was built in Holland and shipped over, section by section, to be reassembled here. Just think, Hans. That building made the same journey as you.'

'Will I be reassembled?' he said plaintively.

'We'll put you together again somehow, lad.'

'It has no nails,' continued Anne. 'That is the real miracle of it. The whole house is held together with wooden pegs. What you see there is Dutch perfection.'

'Like the hats of Jacob Hendrik.'

Nicholas coaxed another smile from the boy and a wink of satisfaction from Anne. Their scheme had so far worked. Instead of rebelling at the very sight of the Bridge, the boy was walking steadily across it. Their afternoon stroll was not unimpeded. As ever, the Bridge was liberally overpopulated. Houses and shops stretched every inch of its length and leant over towards each other with such amiable curiosity that they could almost shake hands. The narrow road was made even narrower by the swirling crowds that moved along it in both directions and horse-drawn traffic had to carve its own rough passage through the human wall. Beautiful to behold from a distance, the Bridge was a dangerous place to cross and rolling wheels all too often brought disfigurement and even death.

It was impossible for the three of them to walk abreast. Holding each by the hand, Nicholas led the way and shouldered a path through the press. There were almost forty shops selling their wares. They included a cutler, a glover, a pouch-maker, a goldsmith, a pinner and a painter but many of the tiny establishments sold articles of apparel Lavishly decorated, the shops faced inwards and advertised their presence with swinging signs. The merchandise was invariably made on the premises and sold by apprentices from a wooden board which was hinged to the open-fronted shop to form a counter. Behind the boards, shrill-throated youths called for attention.

Hans Kippel edged through it all with bemused interest. While Nicholas had one eye on him, Anne kept up her commentary to relax the boy.

'Do you know the tale of William Hewet?' she said.

'No, mistress.'

'He was Lord Mayor of London over thirty years ago. A clothworker,' she explained, pointing a finger, 'who owned that house you see up ahead. Note how the windows hang out over the water. William Hewet's daughter fell from one of them straight into the Thames.'

'What happened, mistress?'

'One of the apprentices dived in after her and dragged her to safety. His name was Edward Osborne. The girl grew up to be a beauty who was much courted but the father turned them away. "Osborne saved her, Osborne shall have her," he said. And so it was, Hans. He married her and inherited the business. Edward Osborne then became Lord Mayor of London himself.'

'Apprentices may yet thrive, then?' said the boy.

'Indeed,' said Nicholas. 'But one detail of the story was missing. The lovely daughter was named Anne.'

He smiled at her by way of compliment and she gave a gracious nod of acknowledgement. In that instant when their attention wandered from the boy, he lost all curiosity in the history of the Bridge. Hans Kippel came to a halt and stared at a house that was boxed in between two shops. Memories came back to test him and to make him gibber soundlessly. He took a few steps towards the house and touched it with his hand as if to make sure that it was the right place. The identification was complete. Mad panic gripped him once again and he turned to race back in the direction of Southwark.

But his way was blocked. A large cart was trundling towards him and it took no account of his youth or his urgency. Before he could get out of the way, the boy was knocked flying by the careless brutality of the vehicle. Nicholas rushed to pick him up in his arms and to search for injury while Anne upbraided the carter roundly. She then joined the little crowd who had gathered around the semi-conscious apprentice. No bones seemed to have been broken and no blood showed but he was severely winded. Nicholas and Anne tended him with concern.

But the keenest interest was shown by someone else. As the sagging body of Hans Kippel was borne away, a pair of dark, malignant eyes stared out from the upstairs window of the house which had alarmed the apprentice so much.

The boy had been found.

Edmund Hoode suffered the pangs of rank injustice. As he toyed with his pint of sack at the Queen's Head, he came to appreciate just how selfish and sadistic Lawrence Firethorn could be. It was unforgivable. After months of emotional stagnation, the poet had finally found someone to rescue him from his plight and supply a focus for the creative energy of his romantic inclinations. His new love had been blighted before it could blossom. Firethorn was exploiting a cruel contractual advantage over him. Instead of releasing his passion in verses dedicated to his own love, Hoode was simply helping to satisfy the actor-manager's libidinous desires. Despair made him groan aloud and turn to Barnaby Gill who was seated beside him on the oak settle.

'Truly, I am out of love with this life.'

'That was ever your theme,' said Gill cynically.

'This time I am in earnest, Barnaby. I would sue to be rid of this wretched existence.'

'Chance may contrive that for you.'

'How say you?'

'Westfield's Men are threatened with execution, sir. If Alderman Rowland Ashway takes possession here, ours will be the first heads on the block.'

'I would welcome the axe.'

'Well, I would not, Edmund,' said the other peevishly. 'Blood would ruin my new doublet and ruff. And I would not have my career cut off by the whim of a brewer. If Marwood sells the inn, I must think the unthinkable.'

'Retire from the stage?'

'My admirers would never countenance that. No, sir, I would need to put survival first and join Banbury's Men.' He saw Hoode's shock and sailed over it. 'Yes, it might be an act of betrayal but my art must take precedence. If Westfield's Men cannot sustain me, I must look to the highest bidder and that must be Giles Randolph. He has coveted my services this long time.'

'What about Lawrence?'

'What about him?' challenged Gill.

Hoode pondered. 'You are right, sir. We owe him no loyalty after the way he has treated us. I'll not let him stroke the bodies of his mistresses with my conceits. Do you know his latest demand?'

'A new prologue for *Love and Fortune*?'

'Even so. It is to contain an intimate message.'

'His intimate messages are all contained in his codpiece,' sneered Gill. 'I wonder that he does not teach it to speak for itself. It cannot declaim lines any worse than he and it holds the major organ of his ambition.'

'I'll not endure it longer, Barnaby!'

'Write sixteen lines for Master Codpiece.'

'Lawrence must relent.'

'Not until Margery bites off his pizzle.'

'He'll use me this way no longer.'

'Free yourself from womankind and learn true love.'

'I'll tell him straight.'

Fortified by the sack and by the conversation, Edmund Hoode leapt up from the table and went in search of his colleague. Firethorn had gone to give instructions about some new costumes to Hugh Wegges, their tireman, who worked with needle and thread in the room where the company's equipment was stored. Hoode strode purposefully in that direction but he soon slowed down. A strident voice began to fill the inn yard.

Now here upon this field of Agincourt
Let each man take his oath to fight with me
And give these French a taste of English steel,
With bravest arrows cutting down their knights,
With stoutest hearts o'ercoming any odds
That angry France can muster 'gainst our will.
March onwards, lads, into the ranks of death,
Until we vanquish, no man pause for breath!

The voice of Lawrence Firethorn thrilled the ear as it reverberated around the empty yard to fill the place with sound and frighten the stabled horses. Edmund Hoode knew the lines well because he had written them himself for *King Henry the Fifth*, a stirring saga of military heroism. Firethorn had always been superb in the role but this time he added some Welsh cadences by way of tribute to the king's birthplace of Monmouth. Stoked up with rage to confront the actor-manager, Hoode yet spared a moment to admire his art afresh. No man could equal Firethorn even when he was just showing off his talent as now. That did not excuse his treatment of his resident poet and it was with seething indignation that Hoode swept out into the yard to tackle the barrel-chested figure who stood right in the middle of it.

'Lawrence!' he said. 'I demand to speak to you!'

'Speak to *me* instead, sir.'

The man turned around with an arrogant smile that stunned Hoode completely. It was not Firethorn at all. The extempore performance had been given by Owen Elias.

Walter Stanford and his son were grief-stricken when they returned home. Michael's death was a shattering blow in itself but the nature of his exit made it unbearably worse. Someone so young and full of promise had been cut down savagely in his prime. Stanford resolved that he would not rest until the murderer had been found and made to pay the full penalty of the law. Vengeful as he was, he did not let his feelings warp his behaviour. In an effort to protect his wife from the full horror, he gave her only an attenuated account of what they had seen. Matilda was devastated by the news. Even though she had never met Michael Delahaye, she had heard enough about him to form some very favourable impressions. Sharing the loss with her husband and stepson, she reserved most sympathy for her sister-in-law.

'What of dear Winifred?' she asked.

'She must be told at once,' said Stanford. 'William and I will ride to Windsor today to break the sad tidings to her. It will be the ruination of poor Win.'

'Let me come with you,' she offered. 'I may be of help at this trying time.'

'Your kindness is appreciated, my love, but this is a task for me alone. I need to frame Win's mind to accept what has happened. It will be a long and arduous business and too distressing for you to witness.'

'Have funeral arrangements been made?'

'They are set in motion,' he said. 'When Michael's body is released, it will be brought to Windsor for burial in the family vault. It is then that I will call upon you for your comfort and company.'

'Take both for granted, Walter.'

'You are a solace to me.'

He gave her a perfunctory embrace then held back tears as he thought about the body on the slab. It had been hauled out of the Thames without a shred of clothing to give it decency in its last moments. A thought struck him with sudden force.

'I see the meaning of it now,' he said.

'Of what, sir.'

'That present I received, Matilda.'

'Present?'

'The salmon.'

'What did it signify?'

'That Michael slept with the fishes.'

Sir Lucas Pugsley chewed happily on a crisp mouthful of whitebait. Being the Lord Mayor of London obliged him to entertain on a regular basis but only a small number of guests were dining at his house that evening. One of them was the massive figure of Rowland Ashway who was tucking into his meal with voracious appetite. Placed at the right hand of his friend, he was able to have private conference with a lowered voice.

'Has that contract been allocated, Sir Lucas?'

'What contract?'

'We spoke of it even yesterday.'

'Ah, that,' said the Lord Mayor airily. 'Have no fears on that score, Rowland. You will get your just deserts. I have instructed Aubrey Kenyon to handle the matter.'

'That contents me. Master Kenyon is most reliable.'

'He is the chiefest part of my regalia. I wear him about my neck like the mayoral collar. My year in office would not have been the same without Aubrey.'

'Haply, he will notice the change as well.'

'Change?'

'When you hand over to Walter Stanford.'

'Perish the thought!' snarled Pugsley.

166

'Master Kenyon must feel the same. You and he have worked hand in glove. He will not have the same kind indulgence from that damnable mercer.'

General laughter interrupted their chat and they were forced to join in the hilarity. It was over half an hour before a lull allowed them another murmured debate. Rowland Ashway was remarkably well informed.

'Have you heard of Stanford's latest plot?'

'What idiocy has he invented now?'

'*The Nine Giants.*'

'Nine, sir? We have but two giants in London.'

'That I know. Gogmagog and Corinaeus.'

'From where do the other seven hail?'

'The Mercers' Company,' said Ashway. 'They are to perform a play at the Lord Mayor's banquet to celebrate the triumph of their master. It is called *The Nine Giants* and shows us nine worthies from the ranks of that Guild.'

Pugsley grunted. 'They do not *have* nine worthies.'

'Dick Whittington is first in number.'

'And the last, Rowland. They have none to follow him. If the mercers would stage a play, let them be honest and call it *The Nine Dwarves*. They have plenty of those in their company. Walter Stanford is bold indeed.'

'You have not heard the deepest cut.'

'Tell me, sir.'

'He himself will be the ninth giant.'

Sir Lucas Pugsley choked on his meat and had to swill down the obstruction with some Rhenish wine. All his hatred and jealousy swelled up to enlarge his eyes and turn his face purple.

'*I* should remain as Lord Mayor,' he growled.

'No question but that you should. But the law stands in your way. It is decreed that no retiring mayor can serve another term of office until seven years has passed.'

'That law might yet be revoked.'

'By whom?'

'By force of circumstance.'

'Speak more openly, Sir Lucas.'

'This is not the time or place,' muttered Pugsley. 'All I will tell you is this. If Walter Stanford were to fall at the very last hurdle – if something serious were to disable his mayoralty – might not your fellow aldermen turn to me to help them in their plight?'

Sir Lucas Pugsley began to laugh. Rowland Ashway enlarged the sound with his throaty chuckle. Others found the hilarity infectious and joined in at will. The whole table was soon rocking with mirth even though most of those around it had no idea at what they were laughing. Such was the power of the Lord Mayor of London.

They moved with great stealth through the dark streets of Bankside. One of them was tall, muscular and well groomed with a patch over his right eye. The other was shorter and more thickset, a bull of a man with rough hands and rough ways. They each carried a bundle of rags that had been soaked in oil to advance their purpose. When they came to the house, they checked all the adjoining lanes to make sure that they were not seen. Revellers delayed their work by blundering out of a nearby tavern and rolling past them in full voice. Only when the sound died away did the two men set about their nefarious business.

The rags were stuffed tight up against the front door of the dwelling then set alight. The accomplices waited until the flames began to get a hold on the timber then they took to their heels and fled into the night. Disaster crackled merrily behind them.

Anne Hendrik's house was on fire.

Chapter Seven

Nicholas Bracewell was the first to become aware of the danger. He had developed a sixth sense where fire was concerned because it was such a constant threat to his livelihood. Sparks from careless pipe-smokers had more than once ignited thatch at the Queen's Head and the other venues used by Westfield's Men, and though most of their performances took place in the afternoon, some continued on beyond the fall of darkness and had to be lit by torches or by baskets of burning tarred rope. Extreme care was needed at all times and Nicholas was particularly vigilant. Even in his sleep, his nostrils maintained a watch and so it was that night. As soon as the first whiff of smoke was encountered, he came awake in a flash and leapt up naked.

His bedchamber was at the front of the house and he saw the fierce glow through the window. Instinct took over. After shaking Hans Kippel out of his slumbers, he pulled on his breeches and raised the alarm in the rest of the house. With no means of escape through the front door, he quickly hustled Anne Hendrik, the two servants and the boy into the little garden at the rear then dashed back to tackle the blaze itself. It had now got a firm hold and long tongues of flame were licking their way into the room. Acrid smoke was starting to billow. The triumphant crackle grew louder.

Nicholas moved with great speed. Having once been caught in a blaze in the hold of a ship, he knew that fumes could be as deadly as fire itself. He therefore dipped a shirt in one of the leather buckets of water that stood in the kitchen, then wound it around his neck and mouth. With a bucket in each hand, he hurried back into the drawing room and looked anxiously around. On the wall was one of Anne's most cherished possessions. It was a beautiful tapestry, depicting the town of Ghent, and given to her as a wedding present by Jacob Hendrik who had commissioned it especially for her in Flanders. She would not willingly have parted with it for anything but sentiment had to give way to survival. Nicholas hurled the water over the tapestry then hastily brought two more buckets from the kitchen to repeat the drenching process.

Tearing down the tapestry, he threw it over the floor to douse the smouldering boards then used it to beat out the flames that were coming in through the door. He was soon given support. Anne Hendrik left her servants to look after the quaking apprentice and came back in to help to save her house. She dipped a broom in the last bucket of water then used it to attack the flames as strenuously as she could manage. Smoke invaded her throat and made her cough. Nicholas rent his sodden shirt in two and gave her a piece to cover her mouth and nostrils. The two of them continued the struggle to save the property.

Noise had now reached deafening proportions. The whole street, then the whole neighbourhood, was roused. Panic was readily abroad. Fire was feared almost as much as the plague and its effects were just as devastating. Like the rest of the city, Bankside was predominantly an area of thatched, timber-built dwellings held together with flimsy lath and plaster. Efforts had been made for well over a century to force people to tile their roofs instead of using reed or straw but the ordinances had scant effect. The only precautions that most householders took were to keep buckets of water on hand or, in far fewer cases, to have firehooks hanging at the ready so that they could be used in an emergency to pull down burning wood or thatch. Organised fire-fighting was virtually unknown and pumps were very rudimentary. In any conflagration, people reacted with unashamed self-interest and looked to their own premises. So it was here.

Nicholas and Anne fought the fire from within while their yelling neighbours did their best to stop it from spreading to their tenements. Because the street was so narrow, the houses opposite were as much at risk as those adjoining and their occupants, too, were contributing freely to the communal hysteria. Water was thrown over thatch and timber to keep the fire at bay. Implements of all kinds were used to beat at the flames. As a ferocious glare lit up the night sky,

173

pandemonium ruled. Children screamed, women howled in fear, men bawled unheard orders at each other. Dogs barked, cats shrieked and wild-eyed horses were led neighing from their stables to clatter on the cobbles and add to the gathering confusion. Everyone was soon involved. One old lady in a house directly opposite even opened the upstairs window to hurl the contents of her chamberpot over the small inferno.

Prompt action slowly won the battle. Having subdued the worst of the flames inside the house, Nicholas was able to kick down the charred remains of the door and get into the street. With a clearer view of the danger, he was able to swish the now steaming tapestry against the front of the building. When a few altruists threw buckets and barrels of water at the house, he was grateful for the soaking that he himself got. It enabled him to withstand the fierce heat and get ever closer to its centre. The tapestry eventually secured victory. Torn beyond belief and blackened beyond recognition, it put out the seat of the fire. Nicholas dropped it wearily to the ground and stamped on it with bare feet to stop it smouldering.

Relief spread as rapidly as the fire itself and a ragged cheer went up. People who had been plucked from their beds by the threat of death now saw some cause for celebration. Those terrified neighbours further along the street who had evacuated their homes completely now began to take their furniture and belongings back inside. New friendships grew out of common adversity. Ear-splitting fear was now replaced by gregarious murmur. The crowd began to disperse until the next emergency.

Anne Hendrik stood panting beside her lodger and tried to regain her breath. She was suffering from the effects of inhaling the smoke, but Nicholas Bracewell was in a far worse state. His breeches were scorched, his feet burnt and his chest a mass of black streaks. Sparks had even had the temerity to singe his beard. His umbered face was running with sweat and crumpled by fatigue but he found the strength to slip an arm around her waist. She leant against him for support and looked up at the ravaged frontage of her house.

'Thank you!' she gasped.

'I could not let my lodging go up in smoke.'

'You saved our lives, Nick.'

'God was at our side.'

'How could the fire have started?' she said between bouts of coughing. 'Some careless passer by?'

'This was no accident, Anne. I see design at work.'

'To what end?'

'Someone here was meant to sleep for ever.'

Anne blanched. 'An attempt on our lives? Why, sir? Who would want to kill us?'

'We may not have been the targets,' said Nicholas as he thought it through. 'It is possible that the fire was lit for someone else – Hans Kippel.'

It was the first night since her marriage that Matilda Stanford had spent entirely alone. With her husband away in Windsor, she had the bed and bedchamber exclusively to herself and she revelled in the new freedom. At the same time, however, she felt even more isolated. The news about Michael Delahaye had been horrific and she was genuinely distressed but it did not touch her heart directly. She had never known the dashing soldier and could not share the desperate loss felt by others. Suffused with real sympathy, she was also distanced from her husband and her stepson as they mourned the death of a loved one and became embroiled in sorrowful duties. Michael had been very much inside the charmed circle of the family. For all her readiness to join in, Matilda remained firmly on the outside.

What kept her awake was not the thought of a dead body pulled from the clutches of the Thames. It was something quite remote from that and it brought its due measure of guilt and recrimination. Indeed, so troubled did she feel that she got up in the middle of the night and went down to the little chapel to pray for guidance and to see if divine intercession could direct her mind to more seemly matters. Even on her knees, she remained unable to sustain more than a passing sigh for the fate of Michael Delahaye. It was another man who occupied her thoughts, not a rotting corpse in a charnel house but a person of almost superhuman vitality, a master of his art, a romantic figure, an imp of magic, a symbol of hope.

Lawrence Firethorn even infiltrated her prayers. Instead of asking for a blessing on a departed soul, she begged for the opportunity to meet her self-appointed lover. Happiness no longer lay beside a wheezing mercer in a four-poster bed. True joy resided at the Queen's Head in the formidable person of an actor-manager. In thinking about him at all, she was repudiating the vows taken during holy matrimony. In speculating about the way that their love might be consummated, she was committing a heinous sin. Doing both of these things while kneeling on a hassock before her Maker was nothing short of vile blasphemy but her Christian conscience did no more than bring a blush of shame to her cheeks. Matilda Stanford made a decision that could have dire consequences for her and for her whole marriage.

She would accept the invitation to the play.

First light found Nicholas Bracewell out in the street to assess the damage to the house and to begin running repairs. Word was sent to Nathan Curtis, master carpenter with Westfield's Men, who lived not far away in St Olave's Street, and he hastened across with tools and materials. The front of the house would need to be partially rebuilt and completely replastered but the two men patched it up between them and gave its occupants a much-needed feeling of security and reassurance. Curtis was rewarded with a hearty breakfast and a surge of gratitude but he would accept none of the money that Anne Hendrik offered. As a friend and colleague of the book holder, he was only too glad to be able to repay some of the kindness and consideration that Nicholas Bracewell had always shown him. He shambled off home with the warm feeling that he had done his good deed for the day.

Hans Kippel had been kept ignorant of his role as the intended victim of the arson. Shocked by the grisly experience on the Bridge, he had withdrawn into himself again and could not explain the rashness of his conduct. In the wake of the fire, he was even more alarmed and they did not add to his afflictions by subjecting him to any interrogation. Instead, Nicholas Bracewell set out for the Bridge and walked to the little house which had provoked such an intense reaction from the boy.

There was no answer when he knocked on the door but he felt that someone was at home and he persisted with his banging. In the shop next door, an apprentice was letting down the board as a counter and laying out a display of haberdashery for the early customers. Nicholas turned to the lad for information.

'Who lives in this house?'

'I do not know, sir.'

'But they are near neighbours of yours.'

'They moved in but recently.'

'Tenants, then? A family?'

'Two men are all that I have seen.'

'Can you describe them, lad?'

'Oh, sir,' said the boy. 'I have no time for idle wonder. My master would beat me if I did not attend to the shop out here. It is so busy on the Bridge that I see hundreds of faces by the hour. I cannot pick out two of them just to please a stranger.'

'Is there nothing you can tell me?' said Nicholas.

The boy broke off to serve his first customer of the day, explaining that a much greater range of wares lay inside the shop. When the woman had made her purchase and

178

moved on with her husband, the apprentice turned back to Nicholas and gave a gesture of helplessness.

'I can offer nought but this, sir.'

'Well?'

'One of them wears a patch over his eye.'

'That is small but useful intelligence.'

'And all that I can furnish.'

'Save this,' said Nicholas. 'Who *owns* the house?'

'That I do know, sir.'

'His name?'

'Sir Lucas Pugsley.'

The Lord Mayor of London awoke to another day of self-congratulation. After breakfast with his family, he spent time with the Common Clerk who handled all secretarial matters for him, then he devoted an hour to the Recorder. The City Marshal was next, a dignified man of military bearing, whose skill as a horseman – so vital to someone whose job was to ride ahead of the Lord Mayor during all processions to clear the way – had been learnt in a dozen foreign campaigns. Among other things, the Marshal headed the Watch and Ward of the city, rounding up rogues and vagabonds as well as making sure that lepers were ejected outside the walls. Sir Lucas Pugsley loved to feed off the respect and homage of a man who wore such a resplendent uniform and plumed helmet. It increased the fishmonger's feeling of real power.

Aubrey Kenyon was the next visitor, cutting a swathe through the dense thickets of the working day with his usual calm efficiency. When they had discussed financial affairs at length, the Chamberlain turned to an area that would normally have been outside his remit had not the Lord Mayor encouraged him to offer opinions on almost every subject of discussion that arose. Kenyon's sage counsel was its own best advertisement.

'Have you taken note of next week, Lord Mayor?'

'Indeed, sir,' said the other pompously. 'I am to have another audience with Her Majesty at the Royal Palace. The Queen seeks my advice once more.'

'I was referring to another event.'

'Next week?'

'On Thursday. It is a public holiday.'

'Ah.'

'You should be forewarned, Lord Mayor.'

Pugsley nodded importantly. The preservation of peace and the maintenance of law and order were his responsibility and they were arduous duties in a city that was notorious for its unruly behaviour. Crimes and misdeameanors flourished on a daily basis and there were parts of London, feared by the authorities, that hid whole fraternities of thieves, whores, tricksters, beggars and masterless men. Cripples, vagrants and discharged soldiers swelled the ranks of those who lived by criminal means. These denizens of the seedy underworld were a perpetual nuisance but the law-abiding could also present serious problems. Public holidays were seized on by many as occasions for riot and excess when the anonymity of the crowd shielded miscreants from punishment at the same time as it fired them on to grosser breaches of the peace. For hundreds of years, the mayoralty had learnt to rue the days when the city was at play.

Aubrey Kenyon had strong views on the matter.

'Wild and licentious behaviour must be quashed.'

'So it shall be, sir.'

'Apprentices so soon get out of hand.'

'I know it well,' said Pugsley with a nostalgic smirk. 'I was one myself, Aubrey, and felt that stirring of the blood on every high day and holiday. The pranks that we lads got up to!' He corrected himself at once. 'But it is a tradition much mocked and abused of late. Harmless pleasure can so easily turn to an affray – and I will not permit that in *my* city.'

'Take steps to ward it off then.'

'You have my word that it shall be done.' His beady eyes lit up. 'I take my cue from Geoffrey Boleyn.'

'He was a brave Mayor indeed, sir.'

'In 1458, the King in his wisdom ordered a council of reconciliation in St Paul's between the rival nobility. During the month it took them to arrive, Mayor Boleyn patrolled the streets by day in full armour and he kept three thousand armed men ready by night.' Pugsley's chest expanded. '*I* would ride out at the head of my constables if you think that it is needful.'

'There are other precautions we may take,' said Kenyon tactfully. 'Your bravery does you credit but you do not have to expose yourself to danger.'

'What are these precautions, Aubrey?'

'Appoint sufficient men to keep watch on the city.'

'It shall be done.'

'Look to the selling of ale that it should not be given to those too young to hold it like a gentleman. Discourage large crowds from gathering. Arrest known troublemakers early in the day before they can work up the apprentices.' Aubrey Kenyon reserved his deepest contempt for another area of social life. 'Subdue what entertainment we can, especially the theatres.'

'Theatres?'

'That is where corruption breeds,' said the Chamberlain. 'If it were left to me, I would close down every playhouse in London.'

Abel Strudwick was ruthless in pursuit of the new career that he now felt awaited him. He was rowing away from a Bankside wharf with two passengers in the stern of his boat when he saw Nicholas Bracewell and Hans Kippel in search of transport. The waterman lost all interest in his current fare and swung the prow of the boat around to head back towards the wharf. His passengers complained bitterly but they were no match for Strudwick. His combination of brawn and bellicosity had them scampering out of the boat and he welcomed Nicholas and the boy instead. All three were soon threading their way through the flotilla of craft that was afloat that day. The waterman was impatient.

'Have you acquainted Master Firethorn with my ambitions?' he asked with hirsute eagerness.

'I mean to speak to him today,' said Nicholas.

'Tell him of my quality.'

'It will not go unremarked, Abel.'

'I would strut upon the scaffold with him.'

'That may not be so easy a wish to fulfil.'

'But I have the trick of it,' said the other. 'Let me come out onto the stage before the play begins to woo the audience with my sweet music.'

Nicholas gave a non-committal nod. Hans Kippel, at first alarmed by Strudwick's grinning ugliness, now took an interest in him.

'Are you a musician, sir?' he said.

'Yes, lad. Would you hear me play?'

'What is your instrument?'

'Lie back in the boat and you shall hear it.'

Before Nicholas could stop him, the poet recited a long narrative about his visit to the Queen's Head and its extraordinary effect on his life. The verse had the same rocking-horse rhythm as usual and it was imprisoned hopelessly in its rhyme scheme. A pun of resounding awfulness brought the saga to a grinding conclusion.

Upon a road did Saul see his new light.
My Damascus was a theatre bright.
A water poet, I am the stuff of fable,
Let Strudwick do all that he is able.

Nicholas manufactured a smile of approval but Hans Kippel was truly impressed. The boy was amazed to hear such fine words coming from such a foul source and he clapped his hands. Abel Strudwick beamed as if he had been given an ovation by a huge audience and he sealed an instant friendship with the Dutch apprentice. The fact was not lost on Nicholas who saw its value at once. He had only brought the boy with him in order to ensure his safety. If Hans Kippel was in danger of attack, he had to be watched over carefully at all times. Taking him away from Southwark had the extra advantage of shifting any threat away from Anne Hendrik. As it was, Nicholas had given Preben van Loew and the other workmen stern orders to be vigilant on her behalf but he did not feel she was now at risk. Unknown to himself, the boy was the target. Friendship with Abel Strudwick meant that there was another safe refuge in the event of an emergency.

They landed, paid their fare and took their leave. The boatman's tuneless music had served another turn. So mesmerised was Hans Kippel that he did not look once towards the Bridge which held such terrors for him. He was in an inquisitive mood and they picked their way through the busy market in Gracechurch Street.

'What is the name of the play, Master Bracewell?'

'*Love and Fortune*.'

'And shall I be able to watch it?'

'Only during the rehearsal, Hans.'

'I have never been to a theatre before,' said the boy. 'Preben van Loew was not happy that I should come to this one today. I was brought up strictly in Amsterdam and such things are frowned upon. Will it cause me harm?'

'I do not think so.'

'Old Preben believes that it will.'

'Do not pay too much heed to him.'

Nicholas smiled fondly as he remembered an occasion when the Protestant rectitude of the Dutch hatmaker was put to the test by Westfield's Men. Preben van Loew had been asked to escort Anne Hendrik to a performance of the controversial piece, *The Merry Devils,* and he had been embarrassed to find just how much he enjoyed it. The book holder was confident that Hans Kippel would get equal pleasure out of the present offering. With a paternal arm around the boy's shoulders, he guided him in through the main entrance of the Queen's Head.

The apprentice was an incongruous figure amid the flamboyance of the actors and he came in for some good-natured ribbing. George Dart warmed to him at once because he recognised a kindred spirit in the waiflike youth with his pale face and his wide-eyed wonder. Nicholas introduced his companion to everyone then left him with Richard Honeydew, the youngest and most talented of the four apprentices, a bright, alert, soft-skinned boy with a mop of fair hair and a friendly grin. While the book holder was busy setting the rehearsal up, the little actor took the visitor under his wing. Inevitably, there was especial interest shown from one quarter.

'Welcome to our humble show, Master Kippel.'

'Thank you, sir.'

'Barnaby Gill, at your service.' He gave a mock bow and appraised the newcomer. 'Is not that jerkin a trifle warm for you in this weather?'

'There is a cold breeze blowing, sir.'

185

'That will not hurt you. Come, let me help you off with it. I promise you will feel more comfortable.'

Hans Kippel did not get the chance to find out. Before the actor could even touch the boy, Nicholas came over to interpose himself between them. Having rescued the lad from an attempt on his young life, he was not going to let him fall into the dubious clutches of Barnaby Gill. One glance from the book holder made the actor back off at once. Neither Hans Kippel nor Richard Honeydew fully understood what had happened in that moment. Their innocence remained intact.

The voice of authority boomed out across the yard.

'Gentlemen, we tarry!' yelled Firethorn.

'All is ready, sir,' said Nicholas.

'Then let us show our mettle.'

With no more ado, the rehearsal began. *Love and Fortune* was a romantic comedy about the dangers of committing the heart too soon and too completely. It featured three sets of lovers and its use of mistaken identity was both deft and effective. Westfield's Men put real spirit into it and the play romped along at speed. Lawrence Firethorn crackled hilariously in the leading role, ably supported by Edmund Hoode as a lovelorn gallant and by Barnaby Gill as an ageing cuckold. The small but demanding part of Lorenzo was played with Celtic ebullience by Owen Elias who tackled the speeches as if he were auditioning for much greater theatrical honours. After their patent failure with *Black Antonio*, the company was determined to vindicate its reputation in the most positive manner. The rehearsal had edge.

Hans Kippel loved every moment of it. Seated on an empty firkin in the middle of the yard, he was the lone spectator of a comedy that made him laugh so loud and so much for two whole hours that he kept falling off his perch. The pace of the action bewildered him but that did not dull his appreciation of the play itself or of the many splendid performances. Without quite knowing why, he was happy for the first time in a week. The only things that puzzled him were the absence of Richard Honeydew and the other boy apprentices, and the sudden appearance of four beautiful young women on the stage. When the most affecting of these creatures – a demure maid in a high-waisted dress of pink taffeta – spoke to him, Hans Kippel felt his cheeks burn with modesty.

'Did you like the entertainment?' she said.

'Yes, yes.'

'Be honest with me, Hans.'

'I liked it exceedingly, good mistress.'

'And did you recognise us all?'

'Well . . .'

The visitor's confusion was total. Richard Honeydew cut through it by taking off his auburn wig to reveal the telltale mop of fair hair. Hans Kippel jumped up with a shock that quickly turned to amusement as he realised how completely he had been fooled by the excellence of the playing. The four apprentices had been so convincing in their female roles that he had never suspected for a moment that they might be anything but young ladies themselves. As he looked at his new friend now, then saw the lantern-jawed

John Tallis ease off the shoulders of his dress to expose a padded bust, he beat out a tattoo of joy on the firkin. This was the funniest thing of all and it put some of the old zest back into the Dutch boy.

Nicholas Bracewell watched with approval from the back of the stage. The decision to bring Hans Kippel to the Queen's Head had been a sound one. It had not only guaranteed his safety, it gave a lift to his spirits that nothing else had been able to do. The antics of *Love and Fortune* might be able to unlock the demons that were chained up in his mind.

Demons of another kind prompted Lawrence Firethorn.

'Nick, dear heart!' he sighed.

'I am here, sir.'

'Have you spoken with that creeping insect yet?'

'Master Marwood will not be moved.'

'Then shall he feel the end of my sword up his mean-spirited arse. That will move him, I vow!'

'We must do nothing rash,' said Nicholas.

'He'll not disown us without a fight.'

'Let me use subtler weapons.'

'They have no power to kill.'

'Yet might they preserve our place here, master.'

'Can you be certain of that, Nick?'

The book holder shook his head and replied honestly.

'No, sir. The portents are bad.'

Alderman Rowland Ashway surveyed the inn yard through the window of an upstairs room. With the fidgeting landlord at his shoulder, he pronounced the death sentence.

'I want them out of here at once,' he said.

'Their contract still has weeks to run, sir.'

The alderman was peremptory. 'My attorneys will find a way out of that. Good lawyers will sniff out a loophole in any document. When you have signed the Queen's Head over to me, we'll have Westfield's Men out on the street before they draw breath to protest.'

'Hold fast,' said Alexander Marwood. 'Do they not deserve a fair warning?'

'Notice of eviction is all that they will get.'

'I have scruples.'

'There is no such thing in business affairs.'

Ashway's easy brutality made the landlord pause to consider his own position. If the alderman dealt with his enemies so callously, how would he handle Marwood himself if the two of them ever fell out? Cunning lawyers who could revoke a legal contract with Westfield's Men could do as much with any document of sale. Security of tenure might turn out to rest on the whim of Rowland Ashway.

'I need more time to think this over,' said Marwood.

'You have had weeks already, sir.'

'Fresh doubts arise.'

'Smother them at birth.'

'I must make safe our future.'

'That is my major concern here,' said the other with adipose affability. 'The Queen's Head is nothing without the name of Marwood and I would not dream of buying one without the other. Your family have a proud heritage, sir. It is my sincerest wish to preserve and honour that.'

'I must peruse the contract with my own attorney.'

'So shall you, Master Marwood.'

'And my wife still has her quibbles.'

'I thought my two hundred pounds took care of them.'

'It helped,' said the landlord with a laugh like a death rattle. 'It helped to soften her inclinations.'

'Work on her earnestly.'

'It has been my life's endeavour.'

Ashway pulled away from the window and walked back into the room. Watching the end of the rehearsal had only deepened his hatred of Westfield's Men. Their very existence was a reminder of the privilege and title from which he was excluded by birth. To oust them would be to promote worth in place of idleness. Theatre was nothing but a distraction from the working world of the city.

He fixed an eye on the squirming publican.

'You have given me your word, Master Marwood.'

'It is my bond, sir.'

'I expected no less.'

'We have always dealt honestly with each other.'

'And both of us have prospered,' noted Ashway. 'Bear that in mind in case your wife has further doubts. I will have the contract sent to you forthwith.'

'Give me time to study it at my leisure.'

'Keep me waiting and my interest will wane.'

'All will be well, I am sure.'

'Good,' said the alderman going back to the window to gaze down. 'I'll take possession of the Queen's Head and throw Westfield's Men back into the gutter where they belong, vile rabble that they are! Let their illustrious patron give them all begging bowls!' Something aroused his curiosity. 'Come here to me.'

'What is it, sir?'

'That man below there.'

'Which one?'

'The sturdy fellow with the boy.'

'I see him.'

'Who is he?'

Alexander Marwood watched the tall, muscular figure take his scrawny young companion across the yard to the stage and hoist him up with one fluent movement of his strong arms. The landlord knew him as the one member of the company whom he could respect and trust.

'Well, sir,' said Ashway. 'Who is he?'

'The book holder.'

'What is his name?'

'Nicholas Bracewell.'

Expectation put colour in her cheeks and rekindled the spark in her eyes. The day was rich with promise and she let it show in her face, her voice and her movements even though she collected some glances of disapproval from the household steward. Matilda Stanford had been stirred by the touch of true love and nothing could subdue her. The staid Simon Pendleton might expect her to share in the family sorrow over the murder of Michael Delahaye but she did not put on a false show of mourning for his benefit. All her thoughts were fixed on the afternoon ahead. *Love and Fortune* was more than just another performance by Westfield's Men. If she had the courage to respond to the message of the sonnet, it was a tryst with her beloved.

'Shall we be safe, mistress?'

'Stay close to me, Prudence.'

'I do not know whether to be excited or afraid.'

'I confess I am a little of each.'

'Would that we had a gentleman to protect us!'

'We shall have. Be patient.'

Prudence Ling was far more than just a maidservant. Small, dark and spry, she was an attractive young woman with lively conversation and plenty of bounce. Most important of all, she was utterly trustworthy. Prudence had been in service with Matilda for some years now and their friendship had reached the point where they could exchange any confidences. The maidservant had no time for moral judgement. If her mistress wished to deceive her husband while he was away, then Prudence was ready to help with all her considerable guile. It was she who had procured the hooded cloaks that the two of them now wore and it was she who had led the way out through the garden gate so that their exit was unobserved by the steward of Stanford Place. Hiding their faces behind masks, they joined the crowd that was converging on the Queen's Head.

'I have but one fear, mistress.'

'Be still, child.'

'What if they mistake us for ladies of pleasure?'

'Think on goodness and ignore them.'

The two women paid their entrance fee and went up to

the middle gallery to claim seats on the front bench. They were wedged in between a couple of leering gallants but their masks gave them concealment and the badinage soon died. Other ladies with more available charms were taking their places nearby to watch the entertainment and to ply their trade at the same time. Prudence sneaked a sideways look at them and giggled her amusement.

The wind had freshened now and the sky was overcast. A full and fractious audience needed a vigorous comedy to warm them up and that is what they were given. Inspired by the speech that Lawrence Firethorn delivered just before they began, Westfield's Men played *Love and Fortune* with a verve and commitment that was lacking from their previous offering. In place of tepid tragedy was a joyous comedy of romantic misunderstanding. Riotous laughter soon filled the makeshift auditorium and hearts were moved by the shifts and sufferings within the drama.

Matilda Stanford was entranced from the moment when Lawrence Firethorn stepped out in a magnificent costume of red and gold velvet to deliver the Prologue in tones of ringing sincerity. Her mask fell from her hand to reveal her in her true beauty and the actor spotted her immediately. Though heard by all, his words were clearly directed at her and she let herself be caressed by the language of pure love. Firethorn continued to woo her throughout in such a way that she was impervious to the presence of other spectators and believed herself to be the sole witness of a command performance. *Love and Fortune* was bursting at the seams with fun and frolic but her attention never wandered from

Lawrence Firethorn. She did not notice the lovelorn swain with his clean-shaven naivety who was also dedicating his performance to her. Nor did she consider for a second that it was he who had written the new Prologue as well as the additional lines which were included for her benefit alone.

Suddenly, it was all over. Matilda was caught up in a torrent of applause that went on for several minutes as Firethorn led his company out onto the stage. His eyes sent further messages of desire to her but she could not fathom their meaning. When the cast vanished behind the curtain and the crowd began to leave, she was plunged into despair. During the play itself, Lawrence Firethorn had been so close to her in spirit that she felt she could reach out to touch him but now he was miles away. Had she taken all those risks to such little purpose? Did her blossoming romance amount simply to this? Was there nothing more?

'A word with you, mistress!'

'Away, sir!' said Matilda.

'But I bring you a letter.'

'Do not trouble me further.'

'It is from Master Firethorn.'

Breathless and battered, George Dart had struggled through the press to get to her with his missive. She snatched it from him and rewarded him with a coin that turned his elfin misery into beaming delight. Matilda opened the letter and read its contents with rising elation. It was an invitation to join Lawrence Firethorn in a private room and share a cup of Canary wine. She accepted on impulse and waved George Dart on so that she and her maidservant might follow. During the journey along the gallery, she showed the letter to Prudence. The maidservant was at once intrigued and concerned.

'Is this wise, mistress?'

'There is only one way to find out, Prudence.'

'What of danger?'

'I embrace it willingly.'

'He is certainly the handsomest of men.'

'Master Firethorn is a god whom I would worship.'

Their guide took them through a maze of corridors until he reached a stout oak door. He paused to knock with timid knuckles. His master's roar came from within. George Dart opened the door for the two ladies to enter then he closed it behind them as Lawrence Firethorn bent low to plant a first delicate kiss on the hand of Matilda Stanford. Having done his office, the stagekeeper was now superfluous and could return to the multifarious tasks that still awaited him below. He made for the stairs but his way was blocked by a looming figure with staring eyes and gaping jaw. Edmund Hoode was aghast.

'Who were those ladies?' he demanded.

'Guests of Master Firethorn, sir.'

'But that was *her*! And she is *mine*!'

'I was sent to bid them here. That is all I know.'

'This is torture indeed!'

'You look ill, sir. Shall I send for help?'

Hoode grabbed him. 'Who *was* she?'

'Which one, master?'

'There *is* only one, George. That beauteous creature

with the luminous skin. That angel from the gallery.' He shook his colleague hard. 'What is her name, man?'

'Matilda Stanford, sir.'

'Matilda, Matilda . . .' Hoode played with the name and smiled fondly. 'Yes, yes, it becomes her. Sweet Matilda. O, Matilda mine. Edmund and Matilda. Matilda and Edmund. How well they flow together!' Titters of amusement came from within the room to darken his face. 'Lawrence and Matilda. There's discord and damnation for you!'

'May I go now, Master Hoode?' whimpered Dart.

'What's that?'

'You are hurting me, sir.'

The poet released his quarry and let him scuttle away down the stairs. His own pain now preoccupied him. The cruel irony of it all lanced his very soul. Hoode's own verses had been used to deliver up his mistress into the steamy embrace of Lawrence Firethorn. Deprived of the chance to write to her himself, he had been doing so unwittingly on another's behalf. It was insupportable and the horror of it made him sway and moan. When he put his ear to the door, he heard flattery and laughter and the betrayal of his greatest hopes. Inside the room, mutual desire was flowering into something more purposive.

Edmund Hoode had murder in his heart.

Chapter Eight

During the performance of *Love and Fortune*, Hans Kippel sat in a corner of the tiring-house and wondered at everything he saw. Actors came and went, changing their costumes, characters and sex with baffling speed. Scenic devices were carried on and off. Stage and hand props were in constant use. Everyone was involved in a hectic event that gained momentum all the time and it was left to the book holder to impose order and sanity on the proceedings. From the stage itself came heightened language and comic songs that were interspersed with waves of laughter and oceans of applause. Swordplay, music and dance added to the magic of it all. In its own way, it was even more thrilling than watching the whole play in rehearsal. Tucked away in the tiring-house, Hans Kippel was part of a strange, new, mad, marvellous world that set fire to his imagination. He believed he was in heaven.

'I am sorry to leave you alone so long, Hans.'

'Do not vex yourself about me, Master Bracewell.'

'There was much for me to do, as you saw.'

'I have never seen anyone work so hard,' said the boy with frank admiration. 'Not even Preben van Loew.'

'Did the others keep an eye on you?'

'Dick Honeydew spoke to me many times though his skirts made him look so like a woman. Master Hoode was very kind and so was Master Gill. I also talked a lot with George Dart and even had a few words with Master Curtis, the carpenter, who helped us at the house this morning.' His face clouded. 'Who started that blaze?'

'I will find out, Hans.'

'But why was it done, sir?'

Nicholas shrugged evasively and brought the boy out into the yard. The experiment of bringing Hans Kippel to the Queen's Head had been an unqualified success but he was now in the way. Having supervised the dismantling of the stage, the book holder now took time off to shepherd the boy back down to the wharf where Abel Strudwick was waiting. Nicholas paid him in advance and charged him with the task of rowing the apprentice back to the Surrey side of the river and of accompanying him safely home. The boatman was delighted with his commission, not least because his passenger was so enthused by the play he had just seen and so willing to listen to more of Strudwick's plangent music. Ambition nudged again.

'What did Master Firethorn say about me?' he asked.

'I go back to raise the matter with him now.'

'Tell him I am at his disposal.'

'He may not have need of you directly, Abel.'

'Shall I bring my verses to him?'

'I will ask.'

Nicholas strode back through the coolness of the early evening to attend to his final duties. He was checking that everything had been securely locked away when a broad palm gave him a hearty slap on the back.

'Nick, my bawcock! A thousand thanks!'

'For what, sir?'

'A thousand acts of goodness,' said Firethorn grandly. 'But none more welcome than the service you performed for me of late.'

'You speak of the lady, I think.'

'And think of her as I speak. Oh, Nick, my friend, she is an empress to my imperial design. I have never met a creature of such flawless perfection and such peerless beauty.' Another slap fell. 'And it was *you* who found out who she was. A thousand thousand thanks!'

Nicholas had grave reservations about his role as go-between and he was uneasy when he heard what had transpired. Matilda Stanford had come to the Queen's Head with no chaperone but a maidservant and the two of them had been greeted by Firethorn in a private room. It boded ill for the young lady herself and for the company.

'Conquest is assured,' said Firethorn dreamily.

'Beware of what might follow, sir.'

'I care nothing for that. The present is all to me.'

'Have concern for the future as well,' warned Nicholas.

'The lady is married and to a man of great wealth and influence. Think what hurt he might inflict if he ever found out about this dalliance.'

'I fear no man alive, sir!'

'It is the company I have in mind. Master Stanford will be Lord Mayor of London before long. He could take his anger out on Westfield's Men and expel us promptly.'

'Only if he is cognisant,' said Firethorn. 'And he will not be. We will pull the wool over his mayoral eyes and make a mockery of him. I am no lusty youth with his codpiece points about to pop. Waiting only enhances the prize and I will bide my time until Richmond.'

'Richmond, sir?'

'The Nine Giants.'

'You have made an assignation?'

'I have but put the sweet thought into her mind.'

'And until then?'

'We simply dote on the ecstasy that lies in store.'

Nicholas was relieved that he was not rushing into his entanglement. Advance notice gave the book holder the opportunity to extricate the young bride. Flushed with excitement, Lawrence Firethorn was in a mood to agree to almost anything and Nicholas plied him with a dozen or more requests concerning company business. When the actor-manager acceded to them all, his employee honoured a promise he had been forced to give.

'I have a friend who writes verses, sir.'

'Let me see them, let me see them.'

'He is but a humble waterman.'

'What of that, Nick?' said the actor proudly. 'I am the son of a common blacksmith yet I have risen to the pinnacle of my profession. Who is this fellow?'

'Abel Strudwick.'

'I will read his work and give my opinion.'

Firethorn waved his farewell and swept off down the corridor. Nicholas was glad that he had mentioned his friend but held out little hope for him. The actor would have forgotten all about the request by the next day. Abel Strudwick would be only one of countless dejected scribes who were spurned by the star of Westfield's Men.

The taproom was the next port of call for the book holder. His intention was to speak to Marwood's wife but someone else claimed his attention first. Edmund Hoode was almost suicidal. Seated alone at a table, he was pouring beer down his throat as if he were emptying a bucket of water into a sink. Nicholas intervened and put the huge tankard aside.

'Give it to me, Nick!' gasped Hoode.

'I think you have drunk enough, sir.'

'Fill it to the brim with poison and make me happy.'

'We love you too well for that, Edmund.'

'You might but *she* does not. I am betrayed.'

'Only by yourself,' said Nicholas gently, sitting beside him. 'You do the lady wrong to expect too much from her. She does not even know of your existence.'

'But she read my sonnet!'

'Sent by another.'

'Yes!' growled Hoode, trying to stand. 'Lawrence has

201

used me cruelly in this matter. On my honour, I will not permit it! I will challenge him to a duel!'

He reached for an invisible sword at his side and fell back ridiculously onto his seat. Nicholas steadied his friend then found himself the object of attack.

'I blame you, sir!' said Hoode.

'For what?'

'Foul deception. Why did you not tell me the truth?'

'I thought to save you from pain.'

'But you have made it all the worse,' howled the poet. 'You *knew* that Lawrence was in pursuit of my fair mistress yet you did not even warn me.'

'I hoped to head him off, Edmund.'

'Head him off, sir? When he is at full gallop? It would be easier to head off a charging bull!'

'Nevertheless, it may still be done.'

Hoode clutched at straws. 'How, Nick? How? How? How?'

'I will bethink me.'

'Matilda Stanford.' Fantasy had returned. 'I could weave such pretty conceits around a name like Matilda. It is a description of a divinity. Matilda the Magnificent. I cannot stop saying it – Matilda, Matilda, Matilda . . .'

'Remember to add her surname,' said the other.

'What?'

'Stanford. Matilda Stanford.'

'She will always be plain Matilda to me.'

'But not to her husband.'

'Husband!' He choked. 'The child is married?'

'To Walter Stanford. Master of the Mercers.'

'I have heard of him.'

'So should you have. He is the Lord Mayor Elect.'

Edmund Hoode stared blankly at the ceiling as he tried to process this new information. It introduced many unforeseen difficulties but romance could overcome them. He fell in love indiscriminately and let nothing stand in the way of his surging passion. The presence of a husband was a problem but it was not insurmountable. Far more serious was the existence of a rival of the calibre of Lawrence Firethorn. He had all the advantages. Hoode shifted his ground dramatically.

'I believe in the sanctity of marriage,' he said.

'So should we all.'

'Matilda must be saved from damnation.'

'That is my wish, too, Edmund.'

'I will protect her from the prickly Firethorn.'

'Do it with cunning.'

'I'll move with stealth,' he said. 'If I cannot have her as mine, she will be returned safe and sound to her lawful husband. Lawrence will fail this time. Should he try to board her, I'll take her by the ankles and pull her out from under him. He will not prevail.'

'We two are agreed on that.'

'Yes, Nick. It will be my mission!'

Abel Strudwick rowed with undiminished gusto across the river and guided his boat around and between the endless bobbing obstacles. Hans Kippel urged him to pull harder and play more music. The waterman was overjoyed. He saw in the Dutch apprentice something of the son who had been snatched from him by the navy and his affection for the boy grew. With a captive audience who appreciated his work so much, he launched into some of his most ambitious poems, long, meandering narratives about life on the Thames and the perils that it presented. His music took them all the way to Bankside then out onto the wharf and up the stone steps. A friendship was being consolidated.

There was one peril that Strudwick did not mention. The man with the patch stood in the open window of a house on the Bridge and applied a telescope to his good eye. He watched the waterman and his young passenger until the two of them had vanished between the tenements then he put the telescope aside and turned to his thickset companion. His voice was slurred but cultured.

'We must make no mistakes next time, sir.'

'I will carve the boy to pieces myself.'

'Look to that friend of his.'

'What was his name again?'

'Bracewell.'

'That's the fellow.'

'Master Nicholas Bracewell.'

Sybil Marwood was proving to be even more unyielding than her husband. She was a stout, sour-faced woman of middle years for whom life was a continuing disappointment. She had little time for Westfield's Men and even less for the arguments that Nicholas Bracewell was now putting on their behalf in the taproom at the Queen's Head. Leaning on the counter with her bulging elbows, she cut him down ruthlessly in mid-sentence.

'Hold your peace, sir.'

'I beg leave to finish, mistress.'

'There is no more to say. We sell the inn.'

'And forfeit your birthright?' he said. 'Once the premises are in the hands of Alderman Ashway, you will be at his mercy.'

'We will have security of tenure.'

'For how long?'

'In perpetuity.'

'Even Master Marwood cannot live for ever,' reasoned Nicholas. 'What will happen to you if he should die?'

'I would remain here in his place.'

'Is that in the terms of the contract?'

'It must be,' she insisted. 'Or Alexander will not be allowed to sign it. I know my rights, sir.'

'Nobody respects them more than us, mistress.'

Nicholas was making no impact on her. Simple greed had mortgaged her finer feelings. Sybil Marwood was so dazzled by the amount of ready capital that she and her husband would receive that she had blocked out all other considerations. The theatre company was a disposable item in her codex. As long as actors were abroad, the virginity of her daughter was under threat. The skulking landlord did at least have some vestigial feelings of loyalty to the troupe that had brought so much custom to the inn over the years but his wife had none. Her cold heart was only warmed by the idea of a healthy profit.

'Can no words prevail with you?' asked Nicholas.

'None that you can utter, sir.'

'What if Alderman Ashway plays the tyrant?'

'Then he will have *me* to face.'

'The deed of sale is drawn up by him.'

'Women have ways to get their desires.'

It was a cynical observation made with the veiled hostility which seemed to encircle her but it also contained some advice on which Nicholas was determined to act. Direct approaches to Marwood and to his wife had borne only diseased fruit. The book holder had to work a different way and he suddenly realised how. There was an element of risk but it had to be discounted. It was the last course of action open to them.

Nicholas took his leave and sauntered across the taproom. Edmund Hoode was still plotting revenge at his table, Owen Elias was regaling colleagues with the story of how he first discovered his vocation as an actor, George Dart was sharing a drink with Thomas Skillen and Nathan Curtis, and the indefatigable Barnaby Gill, dressed in his finery, was half-trying to seduce a young ostler from the stables. All of the company had now learnt of the grim fate that menaced them and an air of despondency filled the room. The book holder was given fresh incentive to put his new plan into action.

He went straight to Shoreditch and swore Margery Firethorn to secrecy. She was thrilled. Fond of Nicholas

Bracewell, she let herself be persuaded by his charm and his reason. It was wonderful to feel that she might be the one person who could turn the tide and she saw at once the personal advantage she would gain at home. The domineering Lawrence Firethorn would no longer be able to crow over a wife if she rescued Westfield's Men by her timely intercession.

'I'll do it, Nicholas!' she said.

'Privily.'

'Lawrence will suspect nothing.'

'He would not understand this manoeuvre.'

'Teach me what I must say.'

'Appeal to Mistress Marwood as a woman.'

'But she is a dragon in skirts, from what I hear.'

'All the more reason to flatter and fondle her.'

Margery chortled. 'You are wicked, sir!'

'I will call you when the time is ripe.'

'You will find me ready.'

She planted a kiss of gratitude on his cheek then sent him on his way. Setting her on Sybil Marwood might just be the solution. They were two of a kind, sisters under the skin, powerful women with red blood in their veins and fire in their bellies. With even moderate luck, Margery might be able to get through to the landlord's wife in a way that no man – not even Marwood himself – could possibly manage. It was all down to the ladies in the case. They spoke the same language.

As Nicholas marched homewards, he reflected on the day and the crisis with which it had begun. Hans Kippel was in grave danger. Enemies who would resort to arson would stop at nothing. Evidently, the boy had witnessed something on the Bridge which he should not have and his life was forfeit as a result. The only way to save him was to unmask his attackers first and bring them to justice. These thoughts took the book holder all the way down Gracechurch Street and back onto the Bridge.

The shops were closed now but there were still plenty of people milling around. Nicholas stood aside as two horses cantered past him. He then walked up to the house which he had visited that morning and appraised it more carefully. It was a small, narrow, two-storey property that consisted of a tiny drawing room, a dining room, two bedchambers, and a kitchen that jutted out over the river so that a supply of water could be hauled up in a bucket tied to the end of a long rope. The dwelling also had its own privy. There was a public convenience on the Bridge itself but most householders took advantage of the site to make their own arrangements. The Thames was its own form of sanitation.

Nicholas saw the light in the downstairs window but he did not immediately knock on the door. Instead, he turned sideways to go down the slender gap between the house and the shop next door so that he could reach the parapet. Directly below was one of the starlings into which the stone pillars which supported the Bridge were set. The swift current foamed the water as it sluiced its way under the arch. Nicholas leant right over to get a better view and discovered that he could see right into the kitchen of the house. Its timber-framing had sagged dramatically and it looked as if it was hanging on to the rest of the building with the tips of its fingers. He bent right over the parapet to peer into the kitchen.

'May I help you, sir?'

The voice was polite but unfriendly. Nicholas swung round to see a short, neat, erect figure blocking the narrow passage. His apparel suggested service in a grand establishment. The man stroked his greying beard.

'You are trespassing here,' he said.

'Do you live in this house, sir?'

'No, I have just been visiting.'

'You know the tenants, then?'

'Why do you ask?' His suspicion was candid. 'Have you any business to be here?'

'I was looking for someone.'

'Indeed, sir?'

'He has a patch over one eye.'

Simon Pendleton stared at him with cool distaste and took some time before he spoke. His tone was offhand.

'That is Master Renfrew,' he said.

'May I speak with him?'

'He is not at home, sir.'

'Will he return soon?' asked Nicholas.

'I fear not,' said the steward dismissively. 'He has gone away for a long time. You will not be able to see Master Renfrew. He is not here in London.'

'Then where is he?'

'Far away, sir. Far, far away.'

* * *

The bed creaked and groaned noisily as they flailed around on top of it at the height of their passion. He was a considerate lover who aroused her patiently by degrees and made her yield herself completely to him. She loved the weight of his body with its firm muscles and its thrusting power. She shared his total lack of fear or inhibition. Here was no ordinary client who tumbled into her arms for five minutes of overeager satisfaction or who rolled off her in a drunken stupor before he could complete the business of the night. Kate had found herself a real lover and she revelled in the discovery.

When it was all over, they lay side by side in a peaceful togetherness. His chest was heaving, her heart was pounding and both of their bodies were lathered with sweat. It was minutes before either could speak. He then propped himself up on his elbow to gaze down at her with his one eye. His smile had a rugged tenderness.

'Thank you, my love,' he said softly.

'Thank *you*, sir.'

'We'll meet again some night.'

'That is my hope.'

'And my intention.'

He leant over to kiss her gently on the lips then he reached across to the chair on which he had tossed his clothes. Fumbling at his purse, he brought back some coins to slip into the palm of her hand. Kate knew their value by touch and was instantly grateful.

'Oh, sir, you are too kind!'

'I repay good service handsomely.'

'Be assured of it here at any time.'

'I will always ask for you in this house.'

Another kiss sealed their friendship. Kate was no common whore from the stews. She was a very beautiful and shapely young woman of seventeen who chose her clients at the Unicorn Tavern with some care. They were always true gentlemen even if they could not always hold their wine or complete their transactions between the sheets. Kate had standards and the latest guest to her perfumed little bedchamber was a prime example of those standards. She even liked the black patch over one eye. It gave him a raffish charm that sorted well with his relaxed manner. This was a man who knew how to please a woman properly.

As he got up from the bed and began to dress, she reached out for the rapier that lay against the chair. It glinted in the light of the candles. Kate pulled it a little way from its scabbard before pushing it slowly back in again. Then she noticed the name that was inscribed in large italics on the handle of the weapon

'James Renfrew,' she read.

'At your service, madam.'

'What do your friends call you, sir?'

'Jamie.'

'Then that shall be my name for you. Jamie.'

'I will come when you call it.'

'Then will you never leave this bed, sir.'

He laughed merrily and pulled her to him in a warm embrace. Kate was the finest company he had found in

Eastcheap and he would not neglect her. Cupping her chin in his hand, he brushed his lips past hers then smiled.

'I will be back soon, Kate.'

'I will be waiting, Jamie.'

Only a small party of foreign visitors was dining at the Lord Mayor's house that evening but they were accorded the lavish hospitality for which Sir Lucas Pugsley was justly famed. He sat beside his wife at the head of the table, fielding compliments and savouring the deference of other nations. Exuding good humour, he made his guests feel thoroughly at home. As soon as they had all left, however, he was able to show his true feelings to Aubrey Kenyon.

'I hate these grinning Italians,' he said.

'You showed them great civility, sir.'

'What else could I do, Aubrey? I am bound by the duties of my office here. But private opinion is another matter and in private, I tell you, these greasy fellows are not to my liking. We have enough aliens of our own.'

'London is a melting-pot of nations.'

'And it does not stop here,' said Pugsley irritably. 'Bristol, Norwich and other towns besides have their own foreign quarters. The rot is slowly spreading.'

'I know it well,' said the Chamberlain. 'There are over five thousand registered aliens here and that does not include the many who conceal the origin and escape the census. We have French, German, Italian, Dutch . . .'

'Dutch! Those are the ones I hate most.'

'An industrious people, sir.'

'Then let them stay in their own country and be industrious, Aubrey. We do not want them here to compete with honest English traders and craftsmen.' He was so animated now that his chain jingled. 'London is fast becoming the sewer of Europe. What other nations spew out, we take in and suffer. It is not good, sir.'

'The city has never welcomed foreigners.'

'Can you blame it?'

Before the Lord Mayor could develop his theme, they were interrupted by the arrival of a friend. Alderman Rowland Ashway was perspiring freely from his exertions. He was conducted into the dining room and rested on the back of a chair while he recovered, letting an expert eye rove around the tempting remains of the banquet. Aubrey Kenyon gave his graceful bow then slid out through the door to leave them alone together.

'What means this haste?' said Pugsley.

'I bring news that may advantage you.'

'Then let me hear it.'

'Walter Stanford is much discomfited.'

'That is sweet music to my ear. How?'

'His nephew has been killed,' said Ashway. 'They pulled the dead body of Lieutenant Michael Delahaye from the Thames. He was cruelly murdered.'

'How has Stanford taken it?'

'Sorely. He had high hopes of the young man and made a place for him in his business. Coming after the death of his first wife, this blow is doubly painful.'

Pugsley smirked. 'This is good news indeed. But will it

make the Master of the Mercers abandon his mayoralty?'

'It will make him think twice.'

'That is some consolation. Thank you, Rowland. You shower many favours on me. I know not how to repay them all. You did well to bring me this intelligence.'

'We must pray that further disasters befall him.'

'If that young wife of his should vanish,' said the Lord Mayor. 'Now that would really cut him to the quick.'

Ashway was thoughtful. 'Most certainly.'

'Lieutenant, you say? The nephew was in the army?'

'Recently discharged.'

'Remind me of his name.'

'Michael Delahaye.'

'Michael Delahaye, sir. A soldier lately returned from the Netherlands.'

'Where is he now?'

'The body was released an hour ago.'

'To whom?'

'His uncle. Alderman Stanford.'

'The Lord Mayor Elect?'

'Even he.'

Nicholas was surprised. Having called at the charnel house to see if the body had yet been identified, he found the old keeper replaced by a more respectful individual and the corpse from the river replaced by one that was hauled out of a ditch. He collected all the details he could then came back up into the living world again. The livid scar on the chest of the dead man could now be explained.

It was patently a wound sustained in battle but its owner had been cut down before it had been allowed to heal. The connection with Walter Stanford intrigued him. It had been a bad week for the mercer. While he was learning of the murder of his nephew, his wife was being courted by Lawrence Firethorn. If the actor were not prevented, Stanford might well find a corpse on the slab of his marriage as well.

Nicholas turned towards Gracechurch Street and strolled on as quickly as he could through the morning crush. No play was being performed that day but he was summoned to a meeting about the planned visit to the Nine Giants in Richmond. Night had been quiet at the house and he had felt it safe to leave Hans Kippel there now. The boy's compatriots took their duties as bodyguards with the utmost seriousness. They had armed themselves with swords or staves in case of attack and Preben van Loew had found an antiquated pike. Under the command of Anne Hendrik, they were a motley but effective crew. Besides, there was no performance at the Queen's Head to amuse the boy this time and he would only be in the way.

The book holder let Abel Strudwick row him across the river from Bankside so that he could thank his friend for taking care of the apprentice on the previous day. The waterman was delighted to have been of help and got what he felt was a rich reward when he was told that his name had indeed been mentioned to Lawrence Firethorn. He could not wait to take his verses to the actor-manager before embracing the stardom that beckoned. Nicholas had tried to dampen his overzealous reaction but to no avail. Strudwick had sensed recognition at last.

As he turned into Gracechurch Street, Nicholas had put all thought of the water poet out of his mind. His preoccupation was with a murdered soldier who had been stripped of his clothes and his dignity then hurled into the Thames without even a face to call his own. Service to his country should have earned Michael Delahaye some kinder treatment than that. Was the soldier killed by his own enemies or did his relationship with the Lord Mayor Elect have any bearing on the case?

So caught up was he in his rumination that he did not observe the thickset man who was trailing him through the crowded market. The first that Nicholas knew of it was when a hand grabbed his arm from behind and the point of a knife pricked his spine.

'Do as I bid,' hissed a voice. 'Or I kill you here.'

'Who are you?'

'One that is sent to bear a message.'

'With a dagger in my back.'

'Walk towards that alley or I finish you here.'

The book holder pretended to agree. In the heaving mass of a market day, he had no choice. His assailant had caught him off guard and was now easing him towards a narrow alley. Once he entered that, Nicholas knew, he would never come out again alive. He tried to distract the man.

'You are Master Renfrew, I think.'

'Then must you think again, sir.'

'There is no patch over your eye?'

'No, sir. I see well enough to stab you in the back.'

'Do you lodge at a house on the Bridge?'

'That is of no concern to you.'

'Did you play with fire the other night?'

'Keep moving,' grunted the man.

As Nicholas was prodded by the dagger again, he reacted with sudden urgency. Hs free arm struck out at the canopy of a market stall while a heel was jabbed hard into the shin of his captor. Wrenching his other arm away at the same time, he lurched forward a few paces then swung around to confront the man who was now hopping on one leg and trying to disentangle himself from the canopy while being abused by the stallholder. Nicholas had only a few seconds to study the swarthy, bearded face before the bull-like frame came hurtling angrily at him. He caught the wrist that held the dagger and grappled with his attacker. Uproar now spread as the two men cannoned off the bodies all around them. The irate stallholder joined in the fight with a broom which he used to belabour both of them.

The assailant was strong but Nicholas was a match for him. Recognising this, the man made a last desperate effort to seize the advantage, angling the dagger towards the other's body and thrusting home with all his might. The book holder took evasive action in the nick of time. He turned the man's wrist sharply and sent the blade towards the latter's stomach. The animal howl of pain was so loud and frightening that it silenced the crowd and even made the stallholder hold off with his broom. With a surge of strength, the man flung off Nicholas and ran off through the crowd with bullocking force. The book holder looked down at the front of his jerkin.

It was spattered with blood that was not his own.

Triumph was followed by setback. After his victory in the field on the previous afternoon, Lawrence Firethorn came off badly in skirmishes the next day. It began at home with a spectacular row over the household accounts. He fought hard but his wife was at her most vehement and sent him off with his ears ringing. No comfort awaited him at the Queen's Head. His first encounter was with Edmund Hoode who refused outright to provide any more verses for the actor-manager's romantic purposes and backed up that refusal with the threat of quitting the company. While Firethorn was still recovering from that shock, Barnaby Gill chose his moment to praise the fine performance given by Owen Elias in *Love and Fortune* and to let his colleague know that he was in danger of being eclipsed by one of the hired men. There was worse to come. Alexander Marwood sidled past with a hideous smile to announce that he had now decided to sign a contract with Rowland Ashway for the sale of the inn.

When he had received Matilda Stanford in a private room, he had felt like a king. That was yesterday. Today his subjects were in armed revolt and he could not put them down. He prowled the yard at the Queen's Head while he tried to compose himself. It was the worst possible time to accost him with a handful of poems.

'Good day, Master Firethorn.'

'Who are you?' snarled the other.

'Abel Strudwick. I believe that you know of me.'

'As much as I care to, sir. Away with you!'

'But Master Bracewell mentioned my name.'

'What care I for that?'

'I am a poet, sir. I would perform on the scaffold.'

'Then get yourself hanged for ugliness,' said the irate Firethorn. 'You may twitch on the gallows and provide good entertainment for the lower sort.'

Strudwick bristled. 'What say you, sir?'

'Avoid my sight, you thing of hair!'

'I am a water poet!'

'Then piss your verses up against a wall, sir.'

'I looked for more civility than this.'

'You have come to the wrong shop.'

'So I see,' said the waterman, casting aside his former reverence for the actor. 'But I'll not be put down by you, sir, you strutting peacock with a face like a dying donkey, you whoreson, glass-gazing, beard trimming cozener!'

'Will you bandy words with me, sir!' roared Firethorn with teeth bared. 'Take that epileptic visage away from here before it frights the souls of honest folk. I'll not talk to you, you knave, you rascal, you rag wearing son of Satan. Stand off, sir, and take that stink with you.'

'I am as wholesome a man as you, Master Firethorn, and will not give way to a brazen-faced lecher who opens his mouth but to fart out villainy.'

'You bawd, you beggar, you slave!'

'Thief, coward, rogue!'

'Dog's-head!'

'Trendle-tail!'

'Hedge-bird!'

'You walking quagmire!'

Abel Strudwick cackled at the insult and circled his man to attack again. Having come to offer poetry, he was instead trading invective. It was exhilarating.

'Your father was a pox-riddled pimp!' he yelled.

'Your mother, Mistress Slither, conceived you in a fathom of foul mud. She was mounted by a rutting boar and dropped you in her next litter, the old sow.'

'Snotty nose!'

'Pig face!'

'Pandar!'

'Mongrel!'

Strudwick grinned. 'Your wife, sir, under pretence of keeping a decent home, cuckolds you with every gamester in the city. Diseased she is, surely, and dragged through the cesspits of whoredom by the hour. Even as we speak, some lusty bachelor is riding her pell mell to damnation!'

Firethorn writhed at the insult and replied in kind. The volume and intensity of the argument had risen so much by now that a small crowd had formed to cheer and jibe and urge the combatants on. It was a fascinating contest with advantage swinging first one way and then the other. Firethorn had clear vocal superiority and used all the tricks of his art to subdue the waterman. Strudwick had greater experience on his side and vituperation gushed out of him in an endless, inventive stream. Actor met streetfighter in a war of words. It was at the point where they were about to exchange blows that Nicholas Bracewell came running across the yard and dived between them to hold them off.

'Peace, sirs!' he exclaimed. 'Stand apart.'

'I'll run this black devil through!' said Firethorn.

'I'll tear his liver out and eat it!' said Strudwick.

'Calm down and talk this over as friends.'

'Friends!' howled the waterman.

'Mortal enemies,' said Firethorn. 'I'd not befriend this whelp if he was the last man alive in creation.'

'Let me be judge of this quarrel,' said Nicholas.

But they were too inflamed for a reasoned discussion of their complaints. They eyed each other aggressively like two dogs bred for fighting. Since the book holder was still keeping them apart, they resolved on another form of attack. Abel Strudwick waved a sheaf of poems in the air and glared at Firethorn.

'I challenge you to a flyting contest, sir!' he said.

'Let it be in public,' retorted the other.

'Upon the stage in this yard.'

'Before a full audience.'

'Name the day and the time.'

'Next Monday,' said Firethorn. 'Be here at one. When the clock strikes the half-hour, we'll begin.'

'My waterman's wit will destroy you utterly.'

'Take care you do not drown yourself in it.'

'I will bring friends to support me.'

'All London knows my reputation.'

'Stop, sirs,' said Nicholas. 'This is madness.'

But his pleas went unheard. Pride dictated terms. Lawrence Firethorn and Abel Strudwick had gone too far to pull back now. They would continue their duel on the following Monday with sharper weapons.

It would be a fight to the death.

Chapter Nine

The sky over Windsor was dark and swollen as the funeral cortège walked solemnly up the path to St John's Church. Only a select gathering of family and friends had been invited to watch Lieutenant Michael Delahaye lowered into his final resting place. The priest led the way in white surplice and black cassock with his prayer book open in his hands. Six bearers carried the elm coffin with its ornate brass handles and its small brass commemorative plate. The widowed mother led the procession, leaning for support on the arm of her brother, Walter Stanford, and weeping copiously. Next came her four daughters, each one stricken by the loss, each one helped along by a husband. Black was the predominant colour and Matilda Stanford, who came next, wore a taffeta dress trimmed with black lace and a matching hat with a black veil. Leaning on the arm of her stepson, she wept genuine tears of sorrow and her sympathy for the bereaved was clear to see. Behind her came more figures in black and more lamentation. Michael Delahaye was going out of the world on a tide of grief.

The service was accompanied throughout by sobs, cries and moans as suffering mourners tried to come to terms both with the death of the dear departed and with the brutal nature of that death. Walter Stanford had deemed it wise to keep back the worst details of the horror. His sister and the rest of the family had enough misery to accommodate as it was. They had all been fearful when Michael had announced his intention of joining the army that set out for the Netherlands. His safe return was a cause for celebration and they had planned a small banquet in his honour. Instead of a long table loaded with rich food and fine wine, they were marking his homecoming with funeral bakemeats.

Matilda Stanford went through it all in a daze. The church was filled with so much high emotion that she was overwhelmed and heard very little of the service that was being intoned by the vicar. Only when the coffin was taken out into the graveyard and interred in the family vault did she come out of her reverie and she felt a stab of shame that gave her a prickly sensation. She was not thinking about Michael Delahaye, nor yet about his poor mother, nor even about her husband's grievous pain. She was not listening to any of the muttered words of comfort that were heard all round her as they began to disperse. She was not succumbing to notions of death itself and how it might visit her when the hour drew near.

At a funeral, in a graveyard, close to her husband and in the midst of a family tragedy, she found herself toying with a vision of Lawrence Firethorn. Guilt made her weep the most bitter tears yet and an arm tightened on hers.

But her mind still belonged to the actor.

After a week of upheavals, it was good to get away from the pressures of the city and out into the freedom of the countryside. A fire at his lodging, an attempt on his life and a puzzling encounter at the house on the Bridge had made Nicholas Bracewell more cautious than ever and he kept glancing over his shoulder to make sure that they were not being followed. It was Sunday morning and he had been instructed by Lawrence Firethorn to ride down to Richmond to take stock of the Nine Giants where the company was due to perform in the near future. Nicholas took Hans Kippel with him so that he could guard the boy and – because she was born there – Anne Hendrik went beside him on the road to Richmond. The book holder was mounted on a chestnut mare with the apprentice clinging on behind him. Anne rode a dapple grey with an easy gait.

It had every appearance of a family outing and this was one of its objects. They had not simply taken on a parental responsibility for Hans Kippel. His damaged mind responded to a sense of familial reassurance and it was only when he was at his most relaxed that his memory began to function properly again. In taking him away from London itself, Nicholas hoped to separate the boy from the well-spring of his malady. The country air of Richmond might do wonders for the lad's power of recall. At all events, they made a happy picture, moving along at a rising trot and urging the horses into a gentle canter when the terrain invited it.

The book holder was relieved to put the week behind him. Quite apart from personal crises, it had been an extremely taxing period. He had stage-managed four very different plays for Westfield's Men as well as coping with sundry other duties. Placating Edmund Hoode had proved to be a time-consuming pastime and the ambitious Owen Elias was another constant drain on his patience. Regular sessions with Alexander Marwood had been another burden and Lawrence Firethorn's demands were endless. Then there was the problem of the versifying waterman.

Hans Kippel raised the problem from the bobbing rump of the horse.

'May I go to the Queen's Head tomorrow?'

'I think not,' said Nicholas.

'But I wish to see Master Strudwick on the stage.'

'It is not for your young eyes,' decided Anne. 'And certainly not for your young ears. London watermen use the vilest language in Christendom.'

'But Master Strudwick makes music.'

Nicholas smiled. 'He has another kind of harmony in mind for tomorrow, Hans. I will report everything back to you, have no fear.'

'Who will win the flyting contest?'

'Neither, if I have my way. It will not take place.'

The boy was disappointed but a half-mile taken at

a canter obliged him to hold on tight and suspend his questioning. It was not long before Richmond Palace came into sight to focus all their attention. Overlooking the Thames with regal condescension, it was a magnificent building in the Gothic style, constructed round a paved court and rising up with turreted splendour. Even on such a dull day, its gilded weathervanes added a romantic sparkle and its superfluity of windows lent it an almost crystalline charm. Hans Kippel was awestruck. Glimpsed over the shoulder of his friend, Richmond Palace had a fairy-tale quality that enchanted him.

The village itself had grown steadily throughout the century as more and more people moved out of the plague-ridden city to its healthier suburbs. Many of the local inhabitants gained their livelihood from the Palace itself and it dominated their existence in every way. Nicholas escorted Anne to a cottage on the far side of the village and stayed long enough to witness the tearful reunion with her parents. Hans Kippel was lifted off the sweating chestnut to share in the hospitality. Nicholas rode back across the wide expanse of village green to get to the inn he had come to visit.

One glance told him that the Nine Giants would be ideal for their purposes. It was larger and altogether more generous in its proportions than the Queen's Head. Erected around a paved courtyard, it had three galleries with thatched roofs. Its timber framing gave it the magpie colouring of most London houses but it was vastly cleaner and more well preserved than its equivalents in the city. Not for the first time, Nicholas reflected on how much filth and pollution a large population could generate. Richmond was truly picturesque. The smile had not been wiped off its face by the crude elbows of the urban multitude. A presenting feature of the inn was the cluster of oak trees which gave it its name. Rising high and wide out of the paddock at the rear, they formed a rough circle of timber that had an almost mystic quality. The nine giants were soon joined by a tenth.

'Good day to you, master.'

'And to you, good sir.'

'Welcome to our hostelry.'

'It is a fine establishment you have here.'

'I'll be with you anon.'

Nicholas had come into the yard to see a huge barrel being carried aloft by a giant of a man in a leather apron. He was loading up a brewer's dray with empty casks from the cellar and the work was making him grunt. The book holder dismounted and tethered his horse to a post. At that moment, the man dropped his barrel onto the dray with a terrifying thud then wiped his hands on his apron. Nicholas saw his face properly for the first time and laughed with sheer astonishment.

'Leonard!'

'Is that you, Master Bracewell?'

'Come here, dear fellow!'

They embraced warmly then stood back to appraise each other. Nicholas could not believe what he saw.

His friend had come back from the grave.

* * *

228

The thickset man lay on the bed with heavy bandaging around his midriff. His self-inflicted wound had been serious but not fatal and he was recovering with the aid of regular flagons of bottle ale. James Renfrew looked down at him with mild disgust.

'Drink wine and cultivate some manners,' he said.

'I'll look to my own pleasures, Jamie.'

'How do you feel today, sir?'

'Better.'

'Can you stand?'

'Stand and walk and carry a weapon.'

'There'll be time enough for that.'

'He is *mine*,' hissed the other.

'Master Bracewell?'

'Look what he did to me. I want him.'

'The boy is our main concern. He is a witness.'

'I'll pluck his Dutch eyes out!' He glanced up at the black patch and blurted out a clumsy apology. 'I am . . . sorry, Jamie. I did . . . not mean to . . .'

'Enough of that!' said Renfrew sharply. 'Hold your peace and get some rest.'

'Has the time been set?'

'It is all in hand.'

'When is it?'

'You will be told, Firk.'

'Give me but a day or two and . . .'

'The plan is conceived, have no fear. We will not move without your help. It will be needed.'

'And Master Bracewell?'

'That will come, too. That will come, too.'

Renfrew crossed to the window of the bedchamber and surveyed the river below. It was a forest of rigging that rose and fell on the undulating surface. He watched a boat being rowed expertly across the Thames and followed it until it vanished from sight behind a larger vessel.

Renfrew threw a nonchalant question over his shoulder. 'Firk . . .'

'What?'

'Have you ever killed a waterman?'

Nicholas Bracewell was delighted to see the mountain of flesh again. Leonard had a natural gentleness to offset his immense bulk and his big, round, freckled face shone with hope. He was still in his twenties with receding hair that exposed a wide forehead and a full beard that was split with a snaggle-toothed grin. They had met in the most trying circumstances. Both had been incarcerated in the Counter in Wood Street, one of the city's worst and most repulsive prisons. Nicholas had been falsely accused of assault by enemies who had wanted him out of the way for a time but his connection with Lord Westfield had soon purchased his release. Even that brief period of custody had been enough to convince him that he must never be locked away in one of the city's hellholes again.

Leonard's case had been far more serious. He faced a murder charge that would lead to certain execution. It was a sad tale of being at the mercy of his own muscles. The genial giant had the most easy temperament and no aggressive instincts. When his workmates took him to Hoxton Fair, however, they decided it was time to goad him into some kind of action. Leonard was cajoled into taking on the invincible wrestler, the Great Mario, a towering Italian with too much guile in combat for any of the challengers who came forward in his booth. Most were dispatched without any difficulty but the newcomer was a tougher proposition.

'I did not think to win the bout,' said Leonard as he recounted the story again. 'I only fought to please my fellows. But the Great Mario did not wrestle fair. He tripped and punched and kicked and bit me. I got angry. Ale had been drunk and the weather was hot. My fellows were shouting me on at the top of their voices.'

'I remember. You grappled with the Great Mario.'

'And broke his neck. It snapped in two.'

'He provoked you to it, Leonard.'

'No matter, sir. They arrested me for murder.'

'How then came you to escape?'

'By the grace of God.'

'Was a general release signed?'

London prisons were notoriously overcrowded and many died inside them from the cramped conditions. Every so often the number of inmates would swell so dramatically that the prisons were bursting at the seams. A general release was sometimes issued to thin out the population in the cells to make room for more malefactors. Leonard would not have been the first alleged murderer to have been granted his freedom in this way but his delivery occurred by a slightly different means.

'The Lord Mayor of London took up my case.'

'In person?'

'Yes, Master Bracewell. I was much honoured.'

'Were you brought to trial?'

'Sir Lucas Pugsley saved me from that.'

'But how, Leonard?'

'I know not but his power is without limit.' He gave a defensive smile. 'One minute, I was lying in the straw at the Counter and saying my prayers. Next minute, the sergeant is taking off my chains and letting me go free. If that is what a Lord Mayor can do, then I bow down to him in all humility.'

'Have you ever met Sir Lucas Pugsley?'

'Indeed, no.'

'Then why did he take an interest in you?'

'Out of the kindness of his heart.'

'There must be more to it than that.'

'My master says it was just good fortune.'

'Your master?'

'He it was who brought the release to the Counter.'

'But how was it obtained?'

'As I told you. From the Lord Mayor's hand.'

Nicholas was puzzled by the intercession from above.

'Who is your master, Leonard?'

'Alderman Ashway. I work for his brewery.'

Rowland Ashway arrived importantly at the Queen's Head early on Monday morning. He brought his lawyer with him who, in turn, brought the contract for the sale of the premises. Alexander Marwood had his own lawyer waiting and the four of them went though the document with painstaking care for a couple of hours. A few doubts were raised, a few objections stated, a few emendations made. When the quibbling was over, both lawyers claimed their fees then withdrew to the other side of the room to leave the others alone. Alderman Ashway loomed over the funereal publican with oily complacence.

'All is therefore settled, Master Marwood.'

'I would like my wife to see the contract.'

'When you have signed it, sir.'

'She may have anxieties.'

'Still them in the marriage bed.'

A retrospective wheeze. 'Times have changed.'

'Nothing now detains us,' said the alderman. 'Our attorneys have pronounced on the document and I have the money waiting for you to collect. Do but scrawl your name and the business is complete.'

'Must it be done today, sir?'

'I grow weary of your prevarication.'

'It shall be signed, it shall be signed,' gabbled the other. 'But I must have a moment to reflect. The Queen's Head was willed to me by my father. I must pray for his guidance and be reconciled with his soul.'

'Will you then reach out for your pen?'

'Most assuredly.'

Marwood bowed obsequiously and rubbed his hands together as if he were grating rotten cheese between them.

He had bought another small delay but Rowland Ashway was determined that it would be the last.

'We will return later,' he announced.

'You are always welcome here.'

'To witness the signature.'

'Well, yes, but . . .'

'This is the day of decision, Master Marwood, and I will brook no more evasion. Append your name and your good will to that same document or I will tear it up and leave you to the mercy of Westfield's Men.'

He sailed out of the room with his lawyer in tow. Alexander Marwood trotted meekly after him and smoothed his acceptance of the ultimatum. When he came out into the yard, however, something stopped the landlord and he became prey to fleeting regret.

The actors were gathering for rehearsal.

Abel Strudwick was a creature of extremes. Once he was committed to a course of action, he went the whole way with no hint of holding back. He had been shocked and wounded by Lawrence Firethorn's cavalier treatment of him at the Queen's Head and felt the pangs of the discarded. As one dream crumbled, however, another came into being. In cutting the actor-manager down in a verbal duel, he would not only be gaining his revenge, he would be showing the world his true merit as a performer. When he had made the final thrust into Firethorn's black heart – he was confident of a swift victory – he intended to bestow the ultimate favour upon the audience by reading some of his poems.

This was no mere flyting contest. It was the harbour from which his new career could be launched.

To this end, the visionary waterman had handbills printed to advertise his feat and distributed them freely to his passengers, around the taverns and among his fellows at the wharfside. Abel Strudwick was pitting his skills against a famous thespian. It was an intriguing prospect and it drew scores of people who would not normally have visited a theatrical event. The large audience which had come to watch *The Queen of Carthage* was thus further enlarged by an influx of rowdy watermen who jockeyed for position near the apron stage. As a prelude to an inspiring tragedy, they were being offered a clash of naked steel.

Somebody was doing his best to spoil their fun.

'It is not too late to change your mind, Abel.'

'That would be cowardly!'

'I talk of a dignified withdrawal.'

'Talk of what you wish, Master Bracewell,' said the angry waterman. 'I have vowed to do battle this day.'

'Both of you will incur severe injury.'

'It matters not, sir.'

'But what if you should lose?' suggested Nicholas. 'This would do harm to your reputation.'

'Defeat is impossible. Rest your tongue.'

They were in the taproom at the Queen's Head not long before the contest was scheduled to take place. The book holder had made several attempts to talk his friend out of the whole thing but the latter was adamant. He had been slighted and sought recompense in the only way that would

235

satisfy him. By way of preparation, he was sinking pints of Ashway's Beer to clear his mind for argument.

Nicholas left him alone and slipped off to the tiring-house to make a last appeal to the other half of the dispute. Like the waterman, Lawrence Firethorn had steadfastly refused to listen to reason so far and he could not be diverted from his purpose now. Before he gave his acclaimed performance as Aeneas in the play, he meant to visit destruction upon the hirsute head of Abel Strudwick. The book holder got short shrift.

'Speak not to me of retreat, Nick.'

'Think of the good name of the company, sir.'

'It is to defend that name that I measure swords with this unbarbered ruffian.'

'You should not descend to a vulgar brawl with him.'

'There will be no brawl,' said Firethorn grandly. 'I will disarm the rogue with my first speech and he will stand there helpless while I cut him to shreds.'

'A little diplomacy might save a lot of pain.'

'Begone, sir! I'll not be flouted out of my purpose.'

Nicholas Bracewell had foreseen the impasse and had evolved a contingency plan. It was time to activate it.

Meanwhile, in another part of the inn, another plan of his was being implemented. Margery Firethorn was paying a call on Sybil Marwood. They were in a private room that overlooked the courtyard and their interview was thus punctuated by the throbbing murmur of the crowd. Margery eschewed her usual over-assertive conversational style and opted for a softer and more confiding approach. She had been well primed by the book holder with information that he had gleaned from his chat at the Nine Giants with his old friend from the Counter. The mighty Leonard had unwittingly provided valuable insights into the working methods of Rowland Ashway.

'I came to express my sympathy, Mistress Marwood.'

'On what account, pray?'

'Why, this betrayal that your husband is about.'

'Betrayal?'

'He intends to sell the inn to Alderman Ashway.'

'For a good price, Mistress Firethorn.'

'What do men know of price?' said Margery with cold scorn. 'When they have money in their hand, they cannot conceive its value. Only a woman can set a true price.'

'That is so,' conceded the other.

'Your husband sells the Queen's Head and gets a fair return for the inn, that is agreed. But, mistress, how much does he get for the home he is also losing? For the good will he has built up here? For the years of sweat and toil that both of you have put into the establishment?' Margery heaved a sympathetic sigh. 'This is a place with historic value. It breathes tradition. Did your spouse exact payment for that?'

'I have not seen the terms of the contract.'

'No?' said the other, driving a wedge between husband and wife. 'That is not considerate. My own dear husband would never dare to sign away our property without my amen to the notion. Master Marwood abuses you. He writes his name on a document and your whole lives are at risk.'

'Risk?' The alarm bell was ringing.

'Surely, your husband has informed you.'

'*What* risk, madam? Speak it plain.'

'Eviction.'

'From our own home!'

'It will belong to Alderman Ashway.'

'The contract will protect us.'

'How do you know when you have not seen it?' Margery got up and headed for the door. 'Thank you for listening to me. I will not take up any more of your time.'

'Wait!' said Sybil Marwood. 'I desire more clarity.'

'It would only distress you further.'

'I wish to know, madam. Advise me in this matter and I will be deeply in your debt.'

Margery turned with queenly charm and smiled at her.

'I talk to you but as a woman.'

'Let me hear you.'

'And I do not take sides in this quarrel. But . . .'

'Well?' said the other impatiently. 'But, but, *but* . . .'

'The Queen's Head is not the only inn that the gluttonous alderman has gobbled up. The Antelope and the White Hart in Cheapside have both been swallowed and the Brazen Serpent is to be his next meal.'

'That is his pleasure. He is a wealthy man.'

'Whence comes this wealth, Mistress Marwood?'

'How do you mean?'

'Alderman Ashway seeks a good profit,' said Margery sweetly, 'but that cannot be obtained if he gives too good a price for the property. Or if he pays too good a wage to his tenant publican. Do you follow me here?'

'I begin to, madam.'

'The landlord of the Antelope was driven out within six months of yielding up ownership. His successor works for longer hours and a lower wage.'

'Can this be so?' gasped the other.

'Look to the suburbs. The alderman bought both the Bull and Butcher in Shoreditch and the Carpenters Arms in Islington. Speak to the unhappy landlords. They are now mere slaves where before they were masters. Would you and your husband wear this humiliation?'

A rousing cheer from the yard below took Margery over to the window but she had done her work. Stung with rage and flustered with fear, Sybil Marwood raced out of the room in search of her husband. She felt that she had been kept wilfully in the dark by the menfolk and it was time to voice her complaint. As she stormed into the taproom, her husband greeted her with open arms.

'Come, Sybil! Our future joy is assured.'

'What say you, sir?'

'I have signed the contract with Alderman Ashway.'

'Tear it up at once!' she yelled.

'Too late, madam.'

'Why?'

'It has been sent back to him by messenger.'

The commotion which drew Margery Firethorn to the window was caused by the appearance onstage of Abel

Strudwick. With the aid of his fellow watermen, he scrambled up onto the scaffold and paraded around like a wrestler showing off his muscles. Good-natured jeers went up and there was a ripple of applause. It was only when Strudwick stopped to acknowledge his reception that he realised how much beer he had consumed. His head was muzzy and he had to splay his legs to prevent himself from swaying. There was another, more immediate problem. Viewed from the yard below, the work of the actors had looked as easy as it was stimulating. Now that he was actually up there himself as the cynosure, he became aware of what a test of nerve it was. A sea of heaving bodies lay below. Galleries of grinning faces stretched above. Shouts and cheers and wild advice came from hundreds of throats. His iron confidence began to melt in the fiery heat of all the attention.

It was not helped by the sonorous bell that chimed the half-hour and made him jump with fright. Before he could recover, there was a fanfare of trumpets and then Lawrence Firethorn made a triumphal entry. Flanked by six resplendent soldiers, he wore golden armour, a golden helmet and golden greaves upon his shins. A glittering sword was held aloft in one hand while the other bore a golden shield. The contrast was startling. On one side of the stage was a dishevelled, bow-legged waterman with a round-shouldered stoop: on the other was a virile warrior who stood straight and proud. As the fanfare ended, the actor delivered his rebuke with imperious force.

Avaunt! Begone, thou ragged pestilence!
'Tis Jupiter, thy god, who spurns thee hence.
Heaven's king am I and lord of all the earth,
I do not deal with curs of lowly birth.
Miscreant wretch, avoid this sacred place,
Do not offend it with thy loathsome face.
I walk on high with pure, ethereal tread,
You row across the stinking Thames instead.
By Saturn's soul and Neptune's majesty,
Base trash art thou. I take my leave of thee.

With the words still echoing around the yard, the
godlike presence turned on his sandalled heel and made his
exit with dignified briskness. Lawrence Firethorn had been
so impressive that he had robbed Strudwick of all power to
reply. It was only when a burst of applause broke out for
Jupiter that the boatman came out of his daze and tried to
strike back. When he lurched after the actor, however, he
found his way barred by the six soldiers in shining armour,
each holding a pike whose blade had been dutifully polished
that morning by George Dart. In the heat of the moment,
Strudwick resorted to intemperate abuse.

'Come back, you hound! You snivelling, sneaking rat!
Come here, you caitiff. Show your monkey's face again and
I will knock off your knavish helmet and put a cuckold's
horns upon your head. 'Twas I that rode your foul fiend of
a wife and had such clamorous sport between her spindly
legs. Thy dame is pizzle-mad, sir, and her oily duckies are
sucked by every gallant in the town!'

241

'WHAT!!!!!'

The scream of fury was so loud and penetrating that it silenced Strudwick and the whole audience at once. Margery Firethorn climbed out through the window like a tiger hurtling out of its lair in search of prey. She pushed her way through the seated spectators in the lower gallery and cocked a leg over the balustrade before jumping down onto the stage itself. Words came hissing out of her like poisonous steam.

'Who are you to speak, you pimp, you goose, you carrion crow! I am that same wife you talk so rudely of and I am as sound a Christian as any woman alive. Fie on your foul tongue, you varlet, on your sewer of a mouth, on that running sore of a mind that you scratch for argument to make it bleed villainy. Out, out, you clod, you tottering wretch, you drunken bawd, you scheming devil, you thrice-ugly beggar, you vile and noisome vapour. Draw off lest you infect us all with this leprous speech of yours!' She stood over him with such fearsome rage that he cowered before her. 'A foul fiend, am I, sir? I will haunt your haunches with my housewife's toe for that. I have spindly legs, you say. They hold me better than those poor, mean sticks of yours that cannot hold up the weight of a beer-filled belly without they bend like longbows at full draw. Pizzle-mad, you claim . . .'

Abel Strudwick's defeat was comprehensive and the audience howled and jeered at his expense. He yet had one card to play. Shrugging off Margery's attack, he ran to the front of the stage and tried to redeem himself by reciting his latest poem about a humble waterman who becomes a famous actor and who plays before the Queen. It was a disastrous remedy. The spectators were provoked to such cruel mirth and ribaldry that missiles soon began to be hurled at the stocky figure. Strudwick kept on, dodging the apple cores and rotten eggs as best he could, caught between death and damnation, between the still-fulminating Margery behind him and the foaming torrent of abuse in front of him. *The Queen of Carthage* rescued him.

Seeing his friend in such a quandary, Nicholas gave the signal to start the play early. The trumpet sounded and the Prologue stepped out in a black cloak. Margery and Strudwick went mute and backed away. When the first scene swirled onto the stage, the two of them nimbly dodged the Carthaginian soldiers to escape. Strudwick dived gratefully forward into the arms of his fellows who felt that he had been somewhat maltreated. Margery beat her retreat through the curtain and hurried into the tiring-house. She made straight for the gold-clad figure of Jupiter and kissed him on the cheek.

'Well spoken, Lawrence! You mammocked him!'

'Thank you, mistress,' said a Welsh voice.

She jumped back. 'You are not my husband!'

'No,' said Owen Elias. 'That honour is denied me.'

'But you were the very image of his Jupiter.'

'That was the intention,' said Nicholas, waving another four soldiers onto the stage. 'I sought to uphold Master Firethorn's reputation while keeping him from any real harm.'

She was bemused. 'He had Lawrence's own voice.'

'But not his luck in love,' said Elias with a touch of gallantry, placing a bearded kiss on her hand. 'Edmund Hoode wrote the words. I but learnt them in the manner of our master.' Celestial music sounded. 'Excuse me, dear lady, Jupiter is needed elsewhere.'

With Ganymede beside him, he made his entry.

Margery began to see how the whole thing had been carefully arranged by the book holder. But for her spirited intervention, the flyting match would never have taken place. As it was, she had conquered a worthy foe in place of her husband. She pulled at Nicholas's sleeve.

'Where is Lawrence?' she whispered.

'He will be here even now.'

'How did you keep him away from that ruffian?'

'See there, mistress.'

Lawrence Firethorn was brought into the tiring-house by four strong men who clung on to him for their lives. Costumed as Aeneas, he was palpitating with anger and spitting out curses. On a nod from Nicholas, the actor was released by his terrified captors.

'Heads will roll for this!' warned Firethorn.

'Stand by, sir,' said Nicholas.

'I'll wreak havoc on the whole lot of you.' He saw his wife. 'Margery! You have no place here, woman.'

'I have acted my scene and bowed out.'

'What do you mean?'

'Your cue, sir,' said the book holder.

'Am I locked in a madhouse?' growled the actor.

'Enter Aeneas.'

Music played and personal suffering was put aside. Lawrence Firethorn went out into the cauldron of the action as the cunning Aeneas and dallied with the affections of Dido, Queen of Carthage, as portrayed with winsome charm by Richard Honeydew. Here was the actor as his admirers really wanted to see him, not trading verbal blows with a contentious waterman, but operating at the very height of his powers and thrilling minds and hearts with uncanny skill. Back in the tiring-house, Margery raised an inquisitive eyebrow. Nicholas smiled.

'All will be explained in time,' he said quietly.

Sir Lucas Pugsley sat before a daunting pile of judicial documents and sifted slowly through them. Aubrey Kenyon was on hand to give any help and advice that was needed. The Lord Mayor had to preside at all meetings of the city's administrative courts. As chief magistrate, he had to act as judge, dealing with an enormous range of cases. Everything from petty law breaking to complex commercial disputes came before him. It was also his avowed task to supervise the conduct of trade in the city and see that it was carried out in accordance with civic regulations. This function of his office often brought him up against the names of his friends.

He studied a new document and gave a wry smirk.

'Rowland Ashway is arraigned again.'

'For what, Lord Mayor?'

'Adulterating his beer. The charge will not stick.'

'His brewery has a good reputation.'

'There will always be those who seek to bring a conscientious man down,' said Pugsley. 'How can one trust the word of a landlord, I ask you? These fellows pour water into their beer then swear it was done at the brewery so that they may claim some recompense. The law here is nothing but a whip with which a guileful publican can beat an honest tradesman.'

'Will the case come to court?'

'Not while I sit in judgement, Aubrey.'

'That is the third time Alderman Ashway is indebted to your wisdom,' said the Chamberlain. 'He has aroused much resentment among jealous landlords.'

'They'll get no help from me.' He put the document aside, picked up another then cast that after the first. 'Enough legality for one day, sir. I sometimes think that London runs on the quibbles of attorneys.' He sat back in his chair. 'We have worked hard, Aubrey. I flatter myself that I do the labour of any three men.'

'At least.'

'Walter Stanford will not be able to keep my pace.'

'He may not wish to try, Lord Mayor.'

'Signs of hesitation?'

'This death in the family has preyed upon his mind. It has slowed down his steps towards the mayoralty.'

'That is the best news yet. What of this play?'

'*The Nine Giants*?'

'Is the monstrous piece still promised?'

'By Gilbert Pike. He has written such plays before.'

'This will tax his imagination most,' said Pugsley sourly. 'Where will they find nine giants among the mercers? Where eight? Five? One?'

'Richard Whittington must be allowed, sir.'

'Even so. But do not mention his name to Rowland.'

'That story still smarts with Alderman Ashway.'

'And so it should,' noted the Lord Mayor. 'When the much-vaunted Whittington sat in my place, he made himself very unpopular with the brewers when he tried to enforce standard sizes for barrels.'

'He also attempted to regulate the price of beer.'

'The brewers got no mercy from a mercer!'

Aubrey Kenyon creased his face at the feeble joke and took the opportunity to work in a reminder of a subject that he took very seriously.

'The noble gentleman did sterling work during his terms of office. He kept the city busy and he kept its citizens well subdued.' He crossed over to Pugsley. 'You have not forgotten the public holiday?'

'This Thursday. Preparations are under way.'

'A strict hand is a sign of a sound mayoralty.'

'Then that is what you will get from me, sir. Let others talk of Dick Whittington. If you want discipline and good government, look no further than Sir Lucas Pugsley. On Thursday I will keep a very careful watch.'

It took an hour to pacify Lawrence Firethorn and only the presence of his wife held him back from reviling his whole company. In his opinion, he was the victim of a dreadful conspiracy that could never be forgotten or forgiven. A stoup of wine, a barrel of flattery and the gentle persuasiveness of Nicholas Bracewell finally made him see the true value of the stratagem. Abel Strudwick had been bested, Firethorn's reputation had been enhanced and the performance of *The Queen of Carthage* scaled peaks it had never before assayed. There could be no better advertisement for the work of Westfield's Men.

Warming to it all, Firethorn summoned George Dart to escort his wife back to Shoreditch then he touched on two important issues with the book holder.

'Has that death's-head of a landlord signed yet?'

'I have not spoken with Master Marwood yet.'

'Give him my compliments and bring him to heel.'

'Alderman Ashway has much influence.'

'See that you counteract it, Nick.' He became secretive. 'First, I have another errand for you. Deliver this letter to Stanford Place.'

'Is this sensible, master?'

'Do as you are bid, sir. The letter is expected and you will present it at the garden gate upon the stroke of five. Someone shall be there to receive it.'

Nicholas was not happy to leave the Queen's Head when such a vital talk with the landlord was imminent but he could not refuse the commission. He hastened out into Gracechurch Street and headed north towards Bishopsgate. Fine drizzle was now falling out of a pockmarked sky. When he reached Stanford Place, he went around to the garden and lurked beside the gate until the chimes of the clock were heard. Prudence Ling was a punctual gatekeeper and snatched the letter from him with a giggle before hiding it under the folds of her cloak. She also gave the visitor an admiring glance. Nicholas did not waste his advantage.

'There is sorrow in the house, we hear.'

'The master's nephew, sir. Most horribly killed.'

'Has the murderer been found?'

'Not yet.'

'Tell me the way of it, mistress.'

Prudence needed no second invitation. She gabbled her way through the details and answered every question that he asked. Ten minutes at a garden gate turned out to be a revelation. Nicholas hated being a party to the projected betrayal of a loyal wife but there had been some consolation. Prudence was a mine of information. There was more value yet in his visit. As he made his way back to the front of the house, a coach was just drawing up and Walter Stanford himself was getting out. He was weighted down with sadness and the spring had gone out of his step but it was not the Lord Mayor Elect who commanded attention. Nicholas was far more interested in the steward who opened the door to welcome his master and who bowed ingratiatingly before him. The book holder felt a thrill of recognition as connections were made.

He had met Simon Pendleton on the Bridge.

Chapter Ten

Domestic tragedy inflicted deep wounds on Walter Stanford and he dragged himself around for days after the funeral. He brought his sister back to Stanford Place so that he could look after her properly and they spent much time together on their knees in the little chapel. His work was not entirely neglected and he burnt large quantities of midnight oil in his counting-house. He also resumed his regular visits to the Royal Exchange. His smiling face hid the pain of an anguished soul, his pleasantries concealed a profound sorrow. Though he had disapproved of much that Michael Delahaye did, he had loved him like a second son and felt that he would at last be able to exert a firm paternal influence on his wayward nephew. That fond hope now lay buried in the family vault at Windsor. *Requiescat in pace.*

The first floor of the Exchange – the pawn, as it was known – had been rented out to shopkeepers whose booths sold such luxury items as horn, porcelain, ivory, silver and watches. It was from one of these shops that Gilbert Pike looked down to espy his friend below and he hurried down to the courtyard as fast as his venerable legs would carry him. He waded out through the waves of bartering humanity until he reached Walter Stanford. Greetings were followed by the old man's condolences but the Lord Mayor Elect did not wish to dwell on sadness. He turned to a more uplifting subject.

'Now, sir, how does my play fare?'

'It is all but finished, Walter,' said the other with enthusiasm. 'I still have the trick of words and I vow that *The Nine Giants* will please you and your good lady mightily.'

'Does it beat the drum for the Mercers' Company?'

'Until every ear be deafened.'

'And humour, Gilbert? I asked for lightness.'

'It will set the table on a roar.'

'That will be welcome at this bleak time,' said the other. 'But tell me now, who are our nine giants?'

'Dick Whittington is first.'

'No man could question that.'

'Then come Geoffrey Boleyn and Hugh Clopton.'

'Both mercers and mayors of high repute.'

'Fine fellows,' agreed Pike. 'Except that Clopton does not lend itself to rhyme. John Allen is the next in line with Ralph Dodmer and Richard Gresham close behind.'

'All six of these are giants indeed.'

'Lionel Duckett, too, and with him Rowland Hill.'

252

'That brings the number up to eight.'

'My ninth giant is Walter Stanford.'

'I pale in such company, Gilbert.'

'You may yet stand taller than all the rest, sir.'

They fell into a discussion of the pageant and its simple structure. The doddering author could not resist quoting from his work. One of the nine giants brought special pleasure to Walter Stanford.

'I like the notion of Ralph Dodmer.'

'Lord Mayor of London in 1529,' said the old man. 'He was a brewer who rebelled against the dominance of the Great Twelve. He refused to translate to one of the dozen leading Guilds even though it was the only way to ensure his mayoralty. No mere brewer could get election.'

'Dodmer suffered for his principles.'

'Indeed, sir. A spell in prison and a heavy fine changed his mind for him. Our brewer saw common sense.'

'And became affiliated to the mercers.'

'Then did he take revenge on all his fellows,' said the chortling Pike. 'He kept the alcconners alert enough. Tavern keepers caught watering the beer or serving short measure were fined and jailed, and had their cheating measures burnt in public. Brewers who tampered with their beer were hauled before the court. An alewife found using pitchers with naughty bottoms was sent to play Bo Peep through a pillory.'

'He swinged the whole profession.'

'*The Nine Giants* will tell it true.'

'Then harp on the brewers, Gilbert,' said his friend.

'That is where we may *score* against a certain alderman. Let Ralph Dodmer scourge his fellows soundly. I would make another brewer squirm in his seat.'

'Rowland Ashway, I think?'

'Turn those red cheeks to a deeper hue.'

'His blushes will light up the Guildhall!'

With his florid cheeks shining almost as brightly as his scarlet nose, Alderman Rowland Ashway stood in the window of a room that overlooked the inn yard. The White Hart in Cheapside had been chosen because of its size and its situation. Preparations were being made against the morrow. Extra benches and trestle tables had been procured. Additional servingmen had been hired. Fresh barrels of Ashway's Best Beer were even now being rolled across the pavestones. The brewer was pleased by what he saw. When there was a knock on the door, he swung round and welcomed the tall figure who entered with a grunt of almost porcine satisfaction.

'Is everything in order, sir?' said the newcomer.

'I have seen to it myself.'

'Then have we no cause for vexation.'

'Unless our plans go awry.'

'They will not,' said the other confidently. 'Errors cannot be tolerated. All will be done as discussed.'

'Good. Here's gold to help your purposes.'

Ashway tossed a bag of coins onto the table and his companion nodded his thanks before picking it up. The man was well favoured and dressed with a lazy elegance that came in sharp contrast to the sartorial pomposity of the brewer. A feathered hat was angled on his head so that its brim came down over one eye that was shielded by a black patch. His chin was clean-shaven. They were not natural friends but mutual advantage had turned them into partners. Rowland Ashway spelt out the terms of that partnership.

'We are in this together, sir, remember that.'

'I do not doubt it.'

'Fail me and you fail yourself even worse.'

'Success attends my mission.'

'And Firk?'

'He is recovered enough to aid me.'

'I hope to hear good news from both of you.'

'And so you shall,' said James Renfrew with a grim smile. 'So you shall, sir.'

Public holidays did not please the city authorities. They were at best occasions for drunken excess and at worst an excuse for violence and destruction of property. Nobody charged with maintaining the peace could rest easy and the more suggestible of their number had nightmares about total loss of control. The main problems came from the apprentices, exuberant young men who chafed under the yoke of their masters and who seized every opportunity to assert their manhoods with unruly behaviour and passages of mob hysteria. Holidays gave law-abiding citizens a chance to rest from their labours and to celebrate a sacred or secular festival. Those same holidays also spilt a deal of blood, clogged up the prisons and led to a rash of unwanted pregnancies.

Shrovetide was carnival time, a final fling before the rigours of Lent. Mothering Sunday came next, a public holiday when those away from home – the rowdy apprentices in the workshops of London – could visit families with gifts and eat the simnel cakes baked for the occasion. Easter solemnity was offset by Hockside fairs and a variety of entertainments. May Day was the major source of concern. This most important spring festival had no Christian foundation at all for the ancient custom of going a-maying was unashamedly pagan. Londoners revelled in its spacious jollity and its sexual freedom. There was often rioting through the bawdy houses or affrays at playhouses or gratuitous attacks on shops and houses. Those who had to enforce order never lost sight of the spectre of Evil May Day in 1517 when a riot saw hundreds of frenzied youths on the rampage, terrorising the city and showing open defiance to authority. Thirteen of the mob were later arrested and hanged in a savage gesture that imprinted the day for ever on the minds of London.

Whitsun and Midsummer Eve produced their potential dangers but none could rival May Day. October was a quieter month but even the occasional saint's day could be fraught with difficulty. Caution was advisable.

'Stay indoors with your mistress, Hans.'

'I would rather visit the play with you, sir.'

'The city is too turbulent a place today.'

'You will keep me safe, Master Bracewell.'

'Remain here at home.'

The apprentice was plainly disappointed. Though he had yet to recover his memory, his youthful instincts had returned intact. He wanted to be off in search of sport with his fellows or, at the very least, to be part of the audience which would come in high humour to the Queen's Head to watch a performance of *The Constant Lover* given by Westfield's Men. Anne Hendrik ruffled the boy's hair affectionately.

'Stay here and keep me company, Hans.'

A resigned nod. 'As you wish, mistress.'

'Preben van Loew and I will dream up games for you.'

'Where is the holiday in that?'

Nicholas Bracewell took his leave of his young friend and was seen off at the front door by Anne. The outside of the house was still bruised and blackened from the fire and the very sight of it was warning enough. He gave her a kiss then set off through the streets. Wanting to visit the house on the Bridge again, he yet felt a strong obligation to cross the river by boat. It had given him no pleasure to see Abel Strudwick so totally outwitted at the flyting contest but he felt that it was a necessary hurt to ward off heavier blows for all of them. When he found the waterman at the wharf, he made an apology that was never completed. Strudwick interrupted with chuckling resilience.

'Nay, sir, do not bother about me. My back is broad though I would rather bend it in the service of these oars than let that harridan beat it with her scoldings. She gave good insults and they were justly deserved.'

'You take your punishment nobly, sir.'

'I spoke out of turn, Master Bracewell,' admitted the other. 'I'll face any man in the kingdom with my curses but I'll not offend a lady if I have choice.'

'Mistress Firethorn is an honest woman.'

'She proved that on my pate.'

Abel Strudwick rowed between two other boats that all but collided with him. Ripe language hit both of them like a tidal wave. Replies were foul and fierce but he got the better of them with the virulence of his tongue. It put him into excellent humour again.

'Have you fresh music?' asked Nicholas.

'My Muse has left me awhile, good sir.'

'She will return again.'

'Then I will keep her here on the water with me,' said the other. 'My verses do not belong on the stage in front of baying clods and sneering gallants.' He looked all around. '*This* is my playhouse, sir. The gulls can hear my music and applaud with their wings. I am author and actor when I am out in midstream. No bawling woman can drag me down in my occupation, however well she swim. I am a true waterman, sir.'

Nicholas was delighted that his friend had bowed so humbly to the reality of the situation and he gave him an extra tip when he disembarked. Other passengers clambered into the boat at once. Holidays turned the Thames into a thousand moving bridges. Abel Strudwick would be kept busy until nightfall. He still found time for a farewell.

'Good fortune attend the play, sir!'

'Thank you, Abel.'

'It is a comedy that you stage, I think.'

'Tragedy is out of place on such a merry day.'

'Pray God some rabble do not spoil your offering.'

'No fear of that, I hope.'

Celebrations began early at the White Hart in Cheapside. Wine, beer and ale were plentiful and there was food enough to satisfy the most gluttonous appetites. As the day wore on, the taproom became so full with boisterous apprentices that they spilt out into the yard and passed the time in japes and jeers and being sick in the privies. Serving wenches were groped, ostlers were mocked and scapegoats had their breeches torn off. Small fights broke out to liven up the occasion and old scores were settled between youths from rival trades. Afternoon found the drunken rowdiness slowly changing into a brawling fever for which the area was famous.

Cheapside was the broadest and straightest of London's streets, a major artery that carried the lifeblood of the city. Along the centre of the street, from St Paul's to the Carfax, was an open market for all manner of goods. Every important public procession passed through Cheapside and shoddily produced goods were traditionally burnt there. It was another kind of procession that now staggered along, a ragged band of apprentices who had been gathered up from other inns and taverns along the street by the industrious Firk who had spread the word that beer was being sold at reduced prices in the White Hart and that a wild time was in store for all who came. As Firk led the way into the yard, the newcomers were given a hostile reception by those already packed in and there was much preliminary pushing and shoving. Abundant supplies of beer and ale were brought out to quench the thirst of all and incite them on to more destructive pleasures. Firk watched until a stew was bubbling furiously and he gave a signal to the man who was watching it all from a room in the upper gallery with his one good eye.

James Renfrew calmly finished his glass of wine and crossed to give the naked woman who lolled on the bed a last kiss. Then he pulled on his doublet and went off downstairs to take charge of the fire that his accomplice was so busily stoking up. With sword in hand, he ran into the yard and jumped up onto a table so that he could stamp on it with his feet to gain attention. Even the swirling revelry was stilled for a second. Renfrew was a striking figure with a voice that knew how to command.

'Friends!' he yelled. 'There's villainy abroad!'

'Where, sir?' shouted Firk on cue.

'Close by this inn. I saw it with my own eyes. Five brawny Dutch apprentices set on one poor English lad and gave him such a drubbing that I fear for his life.'

'Shame!' roared Firk.

'Where are they?' howled a dozen voices.

'They are everywhere!' replied Renfrew, pointing his sword in different directions as he spoke. 'Aliens are taking over London. We have Genoese, we have Venetians, we have cheese-eating Swiss. You may find Germans in every street and Frenchmen in every bawdy house. There are Dutchmen in Billingsgate and Polish in Rotherhithe. We are beset by strangers!'

'Drive the aliens out!' bellowed Firk.

'Vengeance on the strangers!'

'Break their foreign heads!'

'Smash their houses!'

'Kill them! Kill them!'

'London belongs to Londoners!' urged Renfrew.

'Yes! Yes! Yes!'

'We defeated the Spanish Armada,' he said, 'yet those same swarthy gentlemen now swagger through our city and defile our womenfolk! Foreigners out, I say!'

'Foreigners out! Foreigners out!'

Renfrew whipped them up until their bloodlust was so strong it simply wanted direction in order to expend itself. He and Firk led the charge out of the yard. With a hundred or more berserk apprentices at their back, they ran along Eastcheap and into Lombard Street, knocking aside anyone who got in their way, smashing windows out of sheer malice and screaming obscenities. Constables came out to confront them but the ferocity of the mob swept the thin line of authority aside as if it had not been there, surging on into Gracechurch Street then swinging right towards the Bridge with gathering fury. In the space of a few minutes, aimless youths with too much beer in their bellies had been turned into a vicious machine of destruction. It rolled remorselessly on.

* * *

Hans Kippel was close to the wharf when he heard the rising tumult. Frustrated at being kept indoors on a public holiday, he had begged permission to go out into the little garden at the rear of the house and had wandered off down to the river when nobody was looking. The boy hoped to find Abel Strudwick so that he could listen to some more verses but the waterman was nowhere in sight. What he saw instead was a torrent of baying apprentices, leaving a trail of debris on the Bridge as they poured into the object of their hate. Southwark was a haven for immigrants from many lands. Swinging boards from shops advertised craftsmen from all over Europe.

Enraged beyond all control, the mob tore down the boards and kicked in doors and shattered windows. Any opposition was ruthlessly stamped on and innocent bystanders were knocked flying on every side. Hans Kippel was hypnotised by the horror of it all. As the angry crowd ran towards him, he stood there trembling for his young life. Out of the mass of faces that bore down on him, he picked out two that he had seen before and quailed even more. One of the men wore a patch over the eye and the other a stubby beard. A memory which had been trapped inside his brain for a long time was suddenly released and it made him cry out in agony.

He found the strength to run but his flight was in vain. They were too fast and too crazed and too numerous. Before he had gone twenty yards, he was knocked over in the stampede and trampled by a score of feet. Using the cover of the mob, Firk slipped a knife into the boy's back then staggered on after James Renfrew. They had done what they had planned without even having to storm Anne Hendrik's house to get at their prey. The apprentices were still carried along by their own senselessness as the two agitators who had started the riot now vanished quietly around a corner.

Hans Kippel lay motionless. His holiday was over.

In a house of sorrow there was still an avenue of escape. All that Matilda Stanford had to do was to read again the letter which Lawrence Firethorn had sent her. In flowery language and a beautiful hand, he had written to give her details of the performance at the Nine Giants in Richmond the following week. It never occurred to her that he had not actually penned the missive himself but had instead dictated it to Matthew Lipton, the scrivener who was used by Westfield's Men to copy out the sides from the one complete version of any play they staged. Lipton's fine calligraphy was also in evidence in the poem that accompanied the letter. Here again, Firethorn had relied on another to supply his inspiration. Unable to coax any new verses out of Edmund Hoode, the actor-manager had used a poem he had once commissioned from the resident poet while in pursuit of Lady Rosamund Varley at an earlier phase of his lustfulness.

Matilda Stanford knew nothing of this and swooned at his ardour as if it had been new-minted that second. As she sat in her bedchamber with the letter and poem on her knees, she thought only of her lover's irresistible charm and felt the touch of his lips on her hand. Married to a mature and preoccupied husband, she had never known true passion before and could only guess at its implications. Innocence protected her from understanding Firethorn's true intent. All that she knew was that she had been offered an assignation by a prince among men. Though it would be immensely difficult to contrive, she had to find a way to get to Richmond.

Prudence Ling knocked on the door and came tripping in on her toes. Obliged to be sombre elsewhere in the house, she could show her girlish spirits when alone with her mistress. She saw what Matilda was reading and gave a conspiratorial giggle.

'I think I know the way of it,' she said.

'Of what, Prudence?'

'Bringing you to your lover.'

'In Richmond?'

'Even there.'

'Teach me how and I'll adore thee for ever.'

'Then here is the manner of it . . .'

The Constant Lover had displayed the constancy of his love, a volatile audience had been held throughout and the stage was now being dismantled. Nicholas Bracewell was in the thick of the action when Preben van Loew arrived panting in the yard of the Queen's Head. With tears streaming, the Dutchman told his story and begged his friend to come at once. Hans Kippel was close to death and calling for Nicholas. The book holder did not pause for a second.

Leaving Thomas Skillen in charge, he borrowed a horse from the stables and rode home as fast as the thick crowds would allow. All the way across the Bridge, he saw evidence of the furious passage of the apprentices. The noise up ahead was muted now as the riot spent its energy in a raid on some of the Bankside stews. Soldiers had been called out to back up the constables and the sight of organised authority was enough to disperse the remnants of the mob.

Nicholas reined in his horse outside the house and dismounted to race upstairs to the bedchamber. Hans Kippel was lying on the truckle bed with his head cradled lovingly by a distraught Anne Hendrik. The doctor in the background shook his head sadly. He had done what he could but the boy was beyond medical help. Nicholas came to kneel beside the bed and took the hand of his young friend. Weak and fading, Hans Kippel rallied briefly at the sight of the book holder and there was a brave flicker of a smile. Words dribbled out of his mouth with painful slowness

'I . . . saw them . . . again.'

'Who?' whispered Nicholas.

'The . . . two . . . men.'

'From that house on the Bridge?'

'Yes . . .'

'Did one have an eyepatch?'

A faint nod. 'My . . . cap . . .'

'What about your cap, Hans?'

'They . . . took . . . it.'

'The two men?'

'No . . . some . . . boys . . .'

'And what did they do with it?'

'Threw . . . river . . .'

The apprentice was near to expiry. Nicholas tried to fill in some of the gaps to squeeze the last precious bits of information out of him.

'Some boys took your cap. They ran off. You chased them. They threw your cap over the Bridge. Was it by that house? In that narrow passage?' Flickering eyelids confirmed his guess. 'Did your cap land on the starling below?'

'I . . . climbed . . .'

'You climbed down to retrieve it. Then you came up again past the window at the rear of the house. You saw something, Hans. What was it?' Nicholas squeezed his hand to encourage him. 'Try to tell us. Try.'

'They . . . killed . . .'

'The two men murdered someone? With a dagger?'

'Throat . . .'

Hans Kippel let out a deep sigh. The effort of dragging the words out of himself and of confronting the memory that lay behind them had drained the last of his resistance. He slipped gently away and his head flopped to one side. Anne Hendrik sobbed and Nicholas comforted her with his own eyes moist. Then he laid the boy's head gently on the pillow and covered it with a sheet. The doctor stole quietly away to let them share their grief. Racked with remorse, they looked down at the prone figure in the little bed and hugged each other tight. The loss of a child of their own could not have been more painful or poignant because that was what Hans Kippel had become in the last sad days of his doomed life. He had turned lovers into a family and taught them a new kind of love.

The Dutch boy had witnessed a horrific murder and been chased by the killers. He had scrambled to safety for a while but had taken refuge in the dark recesses of his young and impressionable mind. They had caught up with him eventually and the nightmare was relived. The irony of it all was not lost on Nicholas. Mocking youths had snatched off the apprentice's cap and hurled it over the edge of the Bridge. In retrieving it, he had seen something which was to have fatal consequences. If Hans Kippel had not bothered about his cap, he would still be alive and happy. But the pride of a craftsman worked against him. The fledgling hatmaker could not leave his cap to the rising waters of the Thames. It simply had to be rescued somehow.

He had made it himself.

Threat of ejection from the Queen's Head had bonded the company together and lent their performance that holiday afternoon a freshness and defiance that transformed a good play into an enthralling experience. *The Constant Lover* was a form of a reply to a landlord who was neither constant nor loving and who had now sold the home of Westfield's Men from under them. Word had leaked out that the contract with Rowland Ashway had actually been signed and it was only a question of time before the alderman expelled them from his premises. Adversity may have drawn them together onstage. When they came off, it only served to heighten their differences. Edmund Hoode and Lawrence Firethorn chose the empty tiring-house as the venue for their argument. Deep insecurity gave them both an edge of wildness.

'I oppose it with every bone in my body, sir!'

'Take your skeleton away from me.'

'Have you no scruples at all?'

'Come, sir. None of that. You lusted after the lady yourself. You longed to lie in her enchanted garden.'

'I am not married,' said Hoode. 'You are.'

'So is Mistress Stanford. Where are *your* scruples?'

'I intend the lady no harm.'

'It matters not,' said Firethorn airily. 'I am the fitter man for her in every way. Both of us are wed and that gives our love some balance. We take equal risks in this business. One fire consumes us both.'

'It will burn up the whole company!'

'Conquer your jealousy, Edmund, and take your defeat like a man. Think not of yourself in this.'

'Nor do I,' said Hoode forcefully. 'It is the sweet lady herself who occupies my mind. I would save her from the disgrace that beckons.'

'Disgrace!' bawled the other.

'She must only suffer in this enterprise.'

'I offer her my true love.'

'Give her your breeches instead, sir, for that is where it is lodged.'

'Take care, Edmund. I have a temper.'

'Save it for the stage, sir.'

'My devotion to Mistress Stanford comes from a pure heart. I have sent her poems of love.'

'Written by *me*!'

'I have kissed her fair hand.'

'Rape upon rape!'

'She has been shown the utmost respect, sir.'

'Then prove it now by releasing her entirely,' said Hoode with vehemence. 'You have a loyal wife to warm your bed and if her loyalty will not suffice, there are others who clamour for your favours. Take one of them, sir, take two or take them all. But spare this gentle creature.'

'So that *you* may take my place?'

'No! I renounce her here and now.'

'Then stand aside for I do not.'

'Lawrence, this is plain idiocy!'

'Love makes a fool of all of us.'

'She is married to the Lord Mayor Elect,' said the other. 'Nick counselled well. Too much peril follows. The beery alderman may only put us out of the Queen's Head. Walter Stanford may put us out of our profession.'

'*He* is the cause I cannot now pull back.'

'Our new Lord Mayor?'

'Do you know how he intends to enter his mayoralty?' said Firethorn with rolling contempt. 'With a play. His wife requested a drama such as Westfield's Men present and he has replied with some rambling pageant.'

'I do not follow.'

'*We* are the finest company in London. We – and

269

only we – should be summoned to make this occasion memorable. Westfield's Men have performed before the Queen and all her Court. Yet this mercer, this man of no taste, this money-grubbing merchant of a Lord Mayor spurns our talents and turns to amateurs! It is an insult.'

'It is also his prerogative.'

'I do not give a fig for that!' barked Firethorn. 'If he will betray our eminence, then I will gladly betray his. His wife has told me of this pageant that he has arranged. Do you know its subject? Nine worthies of his Guild. What drama lies in that? Was ever such a stale subject foisted upon an audience? And *that* is what has put us in the shade here.'

'You take it as a personal affront.'

'I do, sir. Matilda alone can recompense me.'

'Yet you spoke just now of love.'

'Love of her and love of my profession.'

'You would take revenge on Walter Stanford?'

'Indeed, I will,' said Firethorn heartily. 'Let him have *his* nine giants. In Richmond, I will have *mine*.'

The Bull and Butcher was a small tavern in Shoreditch that offered them an excellent meal in a private room. Rowland Ashway sat on one side of the table and ate with noisy gusto. Seated opposite him, James Renfrew was more interested in the Canary wine than the food. The table was loaded. They started with a dish of boiled carp then had been served with a boiled pudding. Chines of veal and of mutton came next with a calf's-head pie to follow. A leg of beef roasted whole then made its appearance. Capons were then set before them. A dish of tarts helped to sweeten the taste of all the meat and the rich sauces.

Ashway raised a cup to announce a toast.

'To our success, my friend!'

'It is not achieved as yet.'

'We have not far to go,' said the other. 'The boy has been killed and with him goes the fear of discovery. Now we may turn back to the main business of our little partnership. Walter Stanford must be stopped.'

'I thought to have done that already.'

'We have maimed him but not yet cut him down.'

'Do we proceed against him now?'

'With all haste, sir. He cannot and must not be Lord Mayor or all our hopes will founder.' Ashway reached for another tart. 'Luke Pugsley has served my purposes so well that I would keep him there in perpetuity, but the law will not allow it. That is why I chose a successor of like temperament and soft intelligence.'

'Who was that?'

'Henry Drewry, the salter.'

'But you could not secure his election.'

'Stanford won the contest by a single vote. The case was altered cruelly. Instead of a pliant salter, I have to contend with a shrewd mercer and that's not good.'

'What of yourself?' said Renfrew. 'Does your own ambition rise as high as the office?'

Ashway grunted. 'As high and much higher. But the Brewers come fourteenth in the order of precedence. That puts me two places away from the Great Twelve and it is from them that the mayor is chosen.'

'You could translate to another Guild.'

'That is in hand, sir. Why do you think I have been at such pains to woo this fool of a fishmonger? Luke Pugsley has sworn to take me into his Guild and promote me to the mayoralty.' He scowled darkly. 'All that will vanish if this mercer takes the chain.'

'I hate the man,' said Renfrew flatly.

'*Enough*?'

'More than enough.'

The younger man picked up a capon and tore at it with his teeth. There was a violence in him which had not been appeased by the murder of a Dutch apprentice. He was ready to add more deaths to the list in pursuit of his ends. As he emptied another cup of wine, he looked across at the gross figure on whom his future depended.

'What of Master Bracewell?'

'His turn will surely come.'

'Let it be soon. Firk is promised.'

'We may bide our time a little.'

'But this book holder pursues us hotly.'

'He will find nothing,' said Ashway smugly. 'What he may know, he cannot prove. The boy was the witness and his voice has been silenced. Do not concern yourself about this Nicholas Bracewell. He is no threat to us now.'

There was much to do in the aftermath of Hans Kippel's death. The body had to be cleaned and laid out. A report

272

on the circumstances of his death had to be given to the relevant authorities. In the wake of the riot, the city magistrates would be busy the next day but a murder was a more serious matter than assault or damage to property. Nicholas Bracewell was realistic. The chances of the killers being tracked down by official means was very slim indeed since the crime had been committed behind a shield. An outbreak of holiday anarchy had been provoked by guileful men. Nicholas recognised stage-management.

It took him a long time to calm Anne Hendrik down and to convince her that it was not her fault. Even if she had kept the boy locked up at home, he would still have been taken. Men who could set fire to a house could just as easily smash down its front door. He left her with Preben van Loew and set out on what was to be a long journey around the taverns of London. The riot was his starting place and it was not difficult to trace it back to the White Hart. Frightened witnesses from Eastcheap all the way down to Southwark had marked its searing trajectory. The inn was still very busy and the drink was still flowing freely. Nicholas was not surprised to learn how the apprentices were first aroused and he knew at once who had supplied the strong beer.

But he was not in search of unruly youths who had been turned into a marauding pack. His quarry was a man who might be anywhere in the teeming city on that raucous night. With strong legs and a full purse, Nicholas was determined to find him. The first soldiers were in the Antelope, carousing with whores and far too inebriated to give him anything more than the names of other taverns which they frequented. The book holder trailed around them all and bought his information bit by bit with drinks for already drunken men. It was like trying to piece together a jigsaw out of wisps of smoke. Discharged soldiers did not wish to talk about their soldiery. On a public holiday such as this, they simply wanted to submit themselves wholly to the pleasures of the city. Nicholas was therefore sent on what seemed like one long and circuitous tour of every inn, ale-house, stew, ordinary and gambling den within the city walls.

One man half-remembered Michael Delahaye, another had gone whoring with him, a third knew him better but was too sodden to recall any useful details. It was painstaking but each new fact took Nicholas one step closer to the person who could really help him. He got the name at the Royal Oak, the address of his lodgings from the Smithfield Arms then found the man himself after midnight in the taproom of the Falcon Inn. Though he was fatigued by a whole day of celebration, the reveller responded warmly to the offer of a pint of sack and a plate of anchovies and made room for Nicholas on his settle.

Geoffrey Mallard was a small, stooping and rather dishevelled individual with a habit of scratching at his ginger beard. He had been an army surgeon with the English expeditionary force to the Netherlands and his memory was not entirely addled by overindulgence.

'Michael Delahaye? I knew him well.'

'Tell me all you can, sir.'

'Do you ask as a friend?'

'I pulled his dead body from the Thames.'

When Nicholas told his tale, the surgeon was sobered enough by the news to supply all manner of new details. Lieutenant Michael Delahaye had not taken to soldiering at all. The glamour which had attracted him proved to be illusory and the muddy reality of service abroad was a trial to his free spirit. He writhed under the discipline and cursed the privations. There was worse friction.

'He made an enemy of his captain,' said Mallard.

'Why?'

'They loathed each other on sight, sir. Two worthy fellows in their own right who could never lie straight in the same bed together. They were warned and they were threatened but their enmity continued to the point where a gentleman must defend his honour.'

'A duel?'

'A bloody event it was,' said Mallard. 'Had they come to any surgeon but me, they would have been reported and hauled up for court martial. They were there to fight against our foes not against each other.'

'You say it was bloody . . .'

'Both of them were injured.'

'Was there a wound that ran across the chest?' He indicated the direction of the gash. 'Like this, sir?'

'There was indeed. I dressed that wound myself.'

'Then was the body that of Michael Delahaye.'

'How say you?'

'He was dropped into the Thames from the Bridge.'

'It could not have been Michael, sir.'

'No?'

'His wound was on his face,' said Mallard. 'The point of a rapier took the fellow's eye out. He is condemned to wear a patch for the rest of his life.'

'Who, then, was his opponent in the duel?'

'The captain whose chest was sliced open.'

'What was his name?'

'James Renfrew.'

Chapter Eleven

Abel Strudwick sat against a wall in Bishopsgate Street and mused on the vagaries of human existence. When he had tried to be a performer upon the stage, he had been cowed by the haughty Jupiter, flayed by the furious Margery Firethorn and stung by the derision of the audience. It had made him abandon all ambition in that direction. Yet here he was, in the person of a beggar, sitting on the ground at the behest of Nicholas Bracewell and actually getting paid for it. The waterman grinned as he reflected on his promotion. What he was doing was acting of a kind and it was professional in nature. It certainly saved him from spending the day on the river with aching sinews. There were handicaps. He was rained on for an hour, spat upon now and again and – if the dog had not been smacked firmly away – there would have been another soaking for his tattered jerkin. Against all this he could see an unlooked for bonus. Because he sat with one leg tucked under him in a tortured posture, the occasional coin was tossed his way to confirm the success of his portrayal.

His job was to keep on eye on Stanford Place so that he could watch the comings and goings. A few visitors called but all had left by the time that Walter Stanford himself came out to make his way to the Royal Exchange. Strudwick caught a glimpse of Matilda Stanford in an upstairs room but that was all. Various tradesmen called to make deliveries but none stayed more than a few minutes. It was late afternoon before the waterman felt that he was able to earn his money. Out of the house came the man whom Nicholas had described to him so exactly. There was a furtive air about Simon Pendleton and his normal measured gait became an undignified scurry as he weaved his way through the back streets towards the Guildhall.

Strudwick dogged him every inch of the way and hid behind a post when the steward stopped and looked around to make sure that he was not seen. Pendleton then opened a door and stepped smartly into a house. It had nothing like the grandeur of the mansion he had left, but it was a sizeable dwelling that conveyed a degree of prosperity. The waterman made a mental note of the address and then shambled past the front of the house so that he could sneak a glance in through the latticed window. The picture he saw was very expressive.

Simon Pendleton was talking in an agitated manner to a tall, stately individual in dark attire. The steward was pointing back in the direction from which he came as if reporting some disturbing news. His companion reacted with some alarm and reached into a desk to take out a roll of parchment. His quill soon scratched out a letter. Strudwick moved away from the window but remained close to the house. When a man wearing the livery of the Lord Mayor's Household came to the front door, the beggar trotted over to accost him.

'Away, you wretch!' said the man.

'It is not money I want, sir, just a kind word.'

'The kind word will come with a hard blow if you stay. Stand off, sir. Your stink will infect me.'

'I seek but instruction.'

'Then I instruct you to leave.'

'Does Abel Strudwick live in this house?'

'Who?'

'Strudwick, sir. A noble family of some repute.'

'This is the home of the Chamberlain, sir.'

'What name would that be?'

'Master Aubrey Kenyon.'

The man brushed him aside and went into the house. The waterman danced on his toes and clapped his hands together with glee. He was certain that he had just found out a significant piece of information and he had done so by the skill of his performance as an actor. It deserved some recognition. Abel Strudwick turned to an invisible audience and gave a deep bow.

In the busy street, only he could hear the applause.

They met him at the brewhouse and he took them down to the cellar where the barrels of Ashway Beer were kept to await delivery. The familiar aroma made Firk feel very thirsty but James Renfrew had more refined tastes. They found a quiet corner where they could not be overheard. Rowland Ashway had new orders to issue.

'Gentlemen, you travel to Richmond tomorrow.'

'Why there?' said Firk.

'Because I tell you,' said the alderman. 'A play is being staged at an inn called the Nine Giants.'

'By Westfield's Men?' guessed Renfrew.

'The very same.'

Firk was pleased. 'Then I'll go gladly, sir. I have an account to settle with a certain book holder.'

'That is not the main reason I send you, man. Someone else will be in Richmond tomorrow night.'

'Who, sir?'

'Mistress Stanford.'

'The new young bride?' said Renfrew with interest.

'Without her husband.'

'This is good fortune indeed, sir. But what brings the lady to the Nine Giants?'

'My informer does not provide that intelligence. When you listen at doors, you do not hear all, but what he has gleaned is enough in itself.' He chortled aloud. 'I know more about what happens at Stanford Place then Stanford himself. It pays to have friends in the right position.'

'What must we do?' asked Renfrew.

'Seize on this accident that heaven provides.'

'Kill the lady?' said Firk hopefully.

'Kidnap her. That will cause panic enough. With his wife

under lock and key, not even Walter Stanford will have the stomach to become Lord Mayor. We strike a blow where it will damage him the most.'

'Where will she be taken?' said Renfrew.

'That I will decide.'

Firk leered. 'And may she be tampered with?'

'No!' snapped Ashway. 'Mend your manners, sir.' He pulled a letter from his belt. 'And while you are in Richmond, you may do me another favour, sirs. Do you see this letter?' He waved it angrily. 'Shall I tell you who sent it? Shall I tell you who favours me with his royal command? None but Lord Westfield himself.'

'The patron of the players,' said Renfrew.

'He takes up their case as if he is judge and jury. The noble lord has heard of my purchase of the Queen's Head and orders me – orders, mark you, no hint of request here, sirs – he orders me to let Westfield's Men remain. And he does so in such round terms that I am treated less like an owner and more like the meanest lackey.' He tore the letter up and threw the pieces away. 'This is an insult that must be answered forthwith.'

'How?' said Firk.

'I'll put his company out of sorts for good!'

'Chase them out from the Queen's Head?'

'No, sir. Kill their king. Lawrence Firethorn.'

The prospect of an additional murder brought a low cackle from Firk. He had his own grudge against the company and this would help to assuage it. Before they could discuss the matter further, they were interrupted by heavy footsteps as a vast drayman came down the steps to collect a barrel. Ashway glanced across and relaxed.

'Ignore him, sirs. Too stupid to listen and too senseless to remember anything he hears.' He put an arm on each of their shoulders. 'All roads lead to Richmond. In one bold strike, we may finish off Stanford and get revenge on Westfield's Men.'

'Do not forget Master Bracewell,' said Firk.

Ashway smiled. 'Deal with him as you will. Firethorn first then this troublesome book holder.'

'The second will please me most.'

'How will you do it, Firk?'

'Strangling, sir. A very quiet death.'

He gave a macabre laugh and Ashway joined in but their companion remained silent and withdrawn. James Renfrew was staring angrily ahead of him as if viewing an object of extreme hatred with his single eye. His lip curled.

'There is an easier way yet, I think,' he said.

'What is that?' asked the brewer.

'Murder the man himself.'

'Walter Stanford?'

'Cut him down without mercy!'

'No,' said Ashway. 'We can disable his mayoralty by another means. It is far too dangerous to attack him directly. That must only be done as a last resort.'

'By *me*,' insisted Renfrew.

'Why?'

'It is my right and I claim it now. The worthy mercer is

all mine and nobody else must touch him. I have waited a long time to settle my score with him.'

'Do you detest your uncle so much?'

'Beyond all imagining,' said the other. 'He ruined my life. I was young, I was free, I was happy. I spread joy among the ladies of the city and they could not get enough of me. Good Uncle Walter called me to order. He told me that my days in the sun were over. Henceforward, I had to work for him in some dingy room and learn responsibility.'

'Is that why you went in the army?'

Renfrew nodded. 'It was my only escape. My only way of prolonging my freedom – or so I fondly thought. The army was a living hell! Thanks to Walter Stanford, I went through two years of complete misery and ended up looking like this.' He lifted the eye patch to show an ugly, red, raw socket. 'Do you see, sirs? I went into the army as a handsome man with his whole life in front of him. I came out disfigured!' He put the patch back in position. 'My uncle killed the real Michael Delahaye. He deserves to die himself.'

'This wound is deep indeed,' said Ashway.

'He talks of nothing else,' added Firk.

'I share his loathing of Walter Stanford.'

'Nobody could despise him as I do,' said the vengeful nephew. 'I denounce all that he is and all that he stands for and will do anything to maim his chances as Lord Mayor. He has condemned me to a half-life under a stolen name. Two short years ago, ladies flocked to me and showered me with their favours. Now I have to buy their bodies and fornicate in darkness where they cannot see my face. That is what I owe to this monster of goodness, Walter Stanford!'

Rowland Ashway and Firk were mesmerised by the intensity of his anger. None of them saw the drayman lift a barrel onto his shoulder and struggle off upstairs with it. He moved ponderously and took care not to drop his cargo. It was a long and troublesome climb.

Leonard was carrying onerous news.

Walter Stanford made no objection at all when his wife asked permission to visit her cousin near Wimbledon. Acting on her maidservant's advice, Matilda claimed to have been invited to call on her sick relative at the earliest opportunity. Her husband did not even ask the nature of the putative illness because he was too overwhelmed with work and with worry. He simply put his coach at her disposal and told her that he would see her on her return. Grief had aged him visibly and put more distance between him and his wife. Matilda took sad note of it.

'I feel that I no longer know him,' she confided.

'That is often the way in marriage.'

'We seem to be growing apart.'

'Fill your life another way.'

'My husband's work always comes first.'

'That is hardly a compliment to you.'

They were being driven along a bumpy road on a dull afternoon by a coachman who was there only to obey orders. Matilda travelled with Prudence Ling and both were thrilled to get away from the confinements of London life. The verdant acres all around them gave promise of a freedom that neither had enjoyed for some time. On the command of his mistress, the coachman drove on to Richmond and stopped at the Nine Giants. While the ladies went inside to dine, he shared a drink with the ostlers and listened amiably to their country gossip. Matilda and her maidservant, meanwhile, had been shown upstairs to the room that had already been reserved by Lawrence Firethorn. Candles were lit and the table was set but the room was dominated by a large four-poster. Prudence giggled.

'It is big enough for you and him and me besides.'

'For shame, girl!'

'You cannot think this room an accident.'

'Master Firethorn is a gentleman.'

'Then he will say a proper thank you afterwards.'

'Prudence!'

'Why else have we come all this way, mistress?'

'To dine with my love.'

'Meat before supper. You are that supper.'

'I will not hear this vulgarity!'

But Matilda Stanford had heard it in a way that had not impinged upon her consciousness before. Infatuation had made her deceive a kind husband and drive miles to her assignation. What had sustained her all this while was the thought of being alone with the man she loved and admired so that she could feel once again those wonderful sensations that he elicited from her. To dine alone with Lawrence Firethorn was an end in itself to her and she was distressed by the idea that it might only be a means for him. It was a long wait in the upstairs room and the bed seemed to get larger all the time.

Westfield's Men journeyed to Richmond at a slower pace than the coach. Lawrence Firethorn, Barnaby Gill, Edmund Hoode and the other sharers rode their own horses but most of the company travelled on the waggon that was carrying their costumes, properties and scenic devices. George Dart and some of the other menials trotted at the cart's tail and dodged any messages left up ahead by the two carthorses. The imminent departure from the Queen's Head had lowered them all and Nicholas Bracewell tried to lighten the mood of dejection by ordering the musicians to play. Country air and lively ditties soon dispelled the city gloom.

Nicholas drove the cart with Owen Elias beside him.

'You have strange friends, sir,' said the Welshman.

'I would not call you *that* strange, Owen.'

'Not me, man. That mountain who accosted you as we left Gracechurch Street. Diu! I thought that you would harness him and let him pull the waggon alone.'

'And so he might. That was Leonard.'

'What did he want?'

'To show his friendship in the kindest way.'

'One giant sends us off to find the other nine.'

'He did more than that,' said Nicholas, recalling the warning that Leonard had given about the plot against his life. 'We met in peculiar lodgings, he and I. Imprisonment binds two such men together.'

'Do not speak of imprisonment!' moaned Elias. 'I am chained hand and foot in this company.'

'Master Firethorn would release you.'

''Tis he who keeps me in bondage. He takes all the leading roles and I serve my sentence as a galley-slave.'

'*The Wise Woman of Dunstable* offers you a hope.'

'In some small way,' said Elias. 'I have a part in which I may briefly shine but it is not enough, Nick. I would be in the centre of the stage. Look at my Jupiter, sir. I was taken for Master Firethorn himself.'

'No man is great by imitation.'

'I have skills that are all my own but they wither on the vine. Give me the role I covet above all others and I will prove my worth!'

'What role is that, Owen?'

'A Welsh one, sir.'

'Henry the Fifth?'

'Aye, man – Harry of Monmouth!'

Lawrence Firethorn had to mix desire with diplomacy in a way that irked him. The company reached the Nine Giants a mere half an hour after the two ladies and his first impulse was to bound up to his room to claim the favours of his mistress. But Edmund Hoode's sensibilities had to be borne in mind. If he were to learn of Matilda's presence at the inn – let alone of her tryst with Firethorn – he would be uncontrollable. It was important, therefore, to settle him and the rest of the company down before its leading man could slip away to enjoy the spoils of war.

What he did do – while the others were being shown to their accommodation – was to make contact with his beloved to reassure her that all was well.

Matilda Stanford jumped up with a mixture of joy and alarm when he let himself into the room. He showered her hand with kisses and told her that he would return within the hour to dine alone with her, making it very clear that Prudence was expected to withdraw tactfully to the next chamber. He was at once inspiring and frightening, a noble knight with high ideals of chivalry and a lecher in search of a lay. Matilda was thrown into confusion. He swung open the door and paused for effect.

'When I come back, my love,' he said softly, 'I will tap on the door like this.' He knocked three times. 'That is my password to paradise. Do you understand?'

'Yes, sir.'

'How many times?'

'Three.'

'At least!' he said under his breath. 'Admit no other to this chamber until I knock thrice.' He blew her a kiss and withdrew. 'Out, then, into the night.'

The door closed and Matilda clutched at her breast to stop her heart pounding. She wanted him more than ever but not in the way that he had implied. Her plan had been to dine with him alone before being driven on to spend the night near Wimbledon with her cousin, who had been advised by letter in advance of the visit. Firethorn evidently had ideas for her sleeping arrangements and the anxious Matilda did not know how to cope with them. Part of

288

her wanted to flee, another part urged her to stay. A wild suggestion sprang from Prudence.

'To save your honour, I will change places with you.'

'How so?'

'Lend me that dress,' she said, 'and blow out some of the candles. If the room be dark enough, I'll make him think I am you, mistress.' She giggled again. 'And when we lie abed together, he will not know the difference.'

'Prudence!'

'I do it but as an act of sacrifice.'

'Leave off these jests.'

'This way, all three get satisfaction.'

'I will not hear another word,' said Matilda firmly. 'Both of us will stay here. Your presence will shield me from any danger.'

'I beg leave to doubt that.'

Before they could debate it further, they heard footsteps outside the door and craned their necks to listen. There were three loud knocks on the door. They exchanged an astonished look. Firethorn had talked about a delay before his return Obviously, he had dealt with his business much faster than expected. The three knocks were repeated. Matilda gave a signal and Prudence rushed to throw the door wide open.

'Welcome again, good sir!'

The man with the black eyepatch smiled slyly.

'Thank you.'

Westfield's Men were given excellent hospitality by mine host and found another treat in store. Staying at the inn with them were several who were due to be guests at the wedding on the morrow. It was as part of the nuptials that the company were to present their play. Hearing of this, the wedding guests called for some entertainment in advance and were quickly answered. Peter Digby and his musicians played for them, Richard Honeydew sang sweet madrigals, Barnaby Gill made them guffaw with his comic dances and Firethorn obliged with a speech or two off the cuff from his extensive repertoire. Westfield's Men were not only given free cakes and ale. The wedding guests each tossed in a few coins to make their gratitude more substantial. With one exception, the company was thrilled.

That exception was Owen Elias, an eager talent who was proud of abilities that were just never given an opportunity to display themselves. It was others who won the plaudits from the guests. He lurked somnolently on the fringes and drank too much beer. When Gill was asked to perform his jig for a fourth time, Elias could take no more and slunk quietly out into the yard in search of his own audience.

Nicholas was pleased by the turn of events but he had not forgotten Leonard's warning and kept his wits about him. He was much exercised, too, by the information that Abel Strudwick had supplied. If there was a form of conspiracy afoot and the Chamberlain were part of it, then it must reach to the very highest levels of municipal administration. Alderman Rowland Ashway was deeply involved in it and his agents were totally ruthless. If a defenceless young apprentice like Hans Kippel could be murdered, then the killers would stoop to anything – even to an attack on

Lawrence Firethorn. The book holder started as he recalled the warning. Leonard had told him that both he and the actor-manager were marked men. In the middle of a large gathering in the taproom, Nicholas was quite safe but there was no sign of Firethorn. Concern flared up.

A quick search of the ground floor of the premises yielded nothing. Nicholas was about to go upstairs when he heard a distant sound that stilled him somewhat. Out in the darkness was a voice so quintessentially that of Lawrence Firethorn that he relaxed at once. The great man was merely rehearsing under the stars and giving the angels themselves some nocturnal entertainment. Letting himself out in the yard, the book holder realised at once from where the speech was coming. The paddock was a ghostly silhouette in the moonlight. Nine giant oak trees stood in a circle to form a natural amphitheatre. Sublime verse was declaimed with such feeling and ferocity that it sailed upwards into the branches of the trees and came back in weird echoes.

Lawrence Firethorn was truly supreme. Only he could make a speech crackle with such intensity and only he would steal off into the night to rehearse alone and to perfect his art. Nicholas walked towards the paddock so that he might enjoy the treat to the full. It was only when he recognised the play that his panic returned. Henry the Fifth was haranguing his troops before battle in the lilting cadences of a true Celt. Once again, the imitation had been uncanny but this was not the actor-manager in conference with the giant oak trees. It was Owen Elias.

The moment Nicholas realised this, the speech was cut

dead to be replaced by a loud gurgling. He ran towards the paddock as fast as he could but the foliage was so dense and widespread that it shadowed the whole area. Only the terrible noise guided him, the final, fading cries of an actor on the verge of the ultimate exit. Nicholas sprinted all round the circle until he collided with a pair of dangling legs and was knocked to the ground. High above him, swaying to and fro, was the twitching Owen Elias who grasped feverishly at the rope around his neck. For a man whose voice was his own greatest joy, it was a cruel way to die.

The Welshman was an unintended victim. Taken for Lawrence Firethorn, he was at least quitting his life in a leading role. The rope was slung over a branch then secured around the trunk of a tree. Nicholas drew his dagger and hacked through the hemp to bring his friend crashing to the ground.

There was no time to attend to him because Firk leapt out from his hiding place with a sword in his hand. He circled his prey menacingly. Nicholas had only the dagger with which to defend himself. Firk rushed in and slashed the air viciously with his blade, catching the other a glancing blow on the left arm. The stinging pain and the gouting blood made Nicholas change his tactics at once. At their last encounter, his attacker had been stabbed in the stomach and must still be suffering from that injury. The book holder put pressure on the wound. He dodged behind a tree then skipped on to another so that Firk had to waddle after him. Nicholas broke into a run and weaved in and out of the nine giants with the sword whistling at his heels all the way. The further he went, the more he tired his pursuer. Firk was panting violently and threshing the air with increasing fury. Leaves fell at each stroke and whole branches were lopped off. Fatigue eventually slowed him and he leant against a tree to catch his breath, one hand holding the sword while the other grabbed at his wounded stomach.

Nicholas switched from defence to attack, moving in to circle his man with the dagger at the ready. Firk responded with a few murderous swipes but his strength was clearly diminished. He made a sudden lunge at his foe but Nicholas parried the sword with his dagger, stepped back a few yards, flicked the blade into his hand then threw the weapon hard at the advancing Firk. It hit him in the shoulder and spun him round. The rapier dropped to the ground and Firk staggered after it. Nicholas was on to him like a shot, grappling madly and rolling in the grass until both were muddied all over. Even in his weakened state, Firk was still strong but he was up against someone who had more than strength on his side.

New power surged through Nicholas. As well as fighting for his own life, he was avenging the deaths of his friends. He was pitted against the man who had cut down Hans Kippel with callous violence in the street. He was wrestling with the creature who had hanged a poor actor intent on improving his craft. They rolled again and Nicholas finished on top, pinning his opponent to the ground and managing to get both hands to his neck. His first squeeze drew a roar of protest from Firk but that did not halt him. The book holder ignored the punches that rained on his chest and the grasping fingers that tried to pluck out his eyes.

He tightened his grip as hard as he could. The spirit of Hans Kippel lent his puny strength and Owen Elias groaned his encouragement from the ground. Between the three of them, they throttled every semblance of breath out of Firk and left him prone on the ground in an attitude of complete submission. The weary Nicholas hauled himself up and went over to the purple-faced Welshman who was slowly recovering from his brush with death. Loosening the knot around his friend's neck, the book holder pulled the noose off and tossed it over to the corpse.

Owen Elias croaked his gratitude and raised a weak arm in salute. There would be no part for him in the play but at least he would live to act another day.

Lawrence Firethorn, meanwhile, was loping along the passage to the private room where his treasure was stored away. Having spoken to the landlord and ordered that food and wine be sent up, he could now begin the soft preliminaries of love and prepare her for the joyful consummation that was to follow. He paused outside the door to adjust his doublet, smooth his beard and lick his lips then he knocked boldly three times and sailed through the door to claim his prize.

'I have come to you, my love!' he sighed.

But Matilda Stanford was not there to receive him. Most of the candles had been extinguished and the room looked empty in the half-dark. Fierce disappointment then gave way to rekindled lust as her inviting noises came from the four-poster. He crossed to the bed to see her body writhing under the bedclothes to allure and excite. Evidently, she could not wait for the leisurely meal and the long seduction. Her ardour brooked no delay and it produced a like passion in him. Running to the door, he slammed home the bolt so that they would not be disturbed then he began to tear at the hooks on his doublet and pull down his breeches. The sounds from the bed grew more desperate every second and he amplified them with his own grunting and groaning.

Firethorn was half-naked by the time he launched himself onto the four-poster, landing beside his love and pulling back the sheets to behold the beauty of her face. His first kiss was to have ignited her passion to the utmost limit but his lips instead met with cold response. He soon saw why. Instead of holding Matilda Stanford, he had his arms around a squirming maidservant whose mouth was covered with a thick rag.

Prudence Ling had been bound and gagged.

Nicholas Bracewell was hurrying back towards the Nine Giants when the actor-manager came tumbling out in search of him to announce the kidnap. The coachman had now been alerted as well and discovered that his coach had been stolen. Others came pouring out of the inn to see what the commotion was all about. The book holder gave his grisly news then raced off to the stables to find a horse and lead the posse in pursuit of the coach. He had instantly worked out who the driver must be and wanted to take him to task about Hans Kippel as well. A dozen armed men were soon in the saddle. Nicholas split them into two groups so that they could scour the road in both directions. The horses were soon spurred into a mad gallop as the chase began.

It was only twenty minutes before they caught sight of the coach. Nicholas was at the head of the group which rode furiously along the London Road and sent up clods of earth in their wake. When he saw the coach cresting a rise up ahead so that its profile was seen momentarily against the sky, he called for even more speed and commitment from his mount. Though the vehicle was being driven hard, it could never outrun the chasing pack and they closed steadily on it. The driver put his own survival first. Heaving on the reins, he pulled the two horses to a juddering halt then leapt from the box into the saddle of the animal who had been tethered to the coach and pulled along with it. To create a diversion, he yelled at the top of his voice and slapped one of the coach horses on the rump. Both of them bolted at once and the vehicle was taken on a mad, swinging, bumping journey across the grass.

Nicholas's immediate concern was the safety of the passenger inside the coach and he set off after it. With a wave of his hand, he sent his fellows off after the lone rider who was moving at a full gallop towards the shelter of a small wood. The coach was now completely out of control and swayed dangerously from side to side. It lurched high in the air as one of its wheels struck a large stone then it veered over at a crazy angle as it was pulled across a slope. Nicholas knew that it was only a matter of time before the vehicle overturned or smashed into a tree. He used his heels to demand even more from his mount and slowly caught up with the coach, keeping well clear of the whirring wheels as they swung towards him. Above the din, he could hear the screams of the terrified occupant as she was thrown wildly around.

Pulling level with the bolting horses, he timed his moment then dived sideways onto the back of the nearest animal and held on grimly to the harness. When he had hauled himself up and sat astride the horse, he gathered up the reins and applied steady pressure until the headlong flight became a measured canter then eventually diminished to a merciful trot. When he finally pulled them to a stop, he jumped down and ran to open the coach door. Tied hand and foot, Matilda Stanford fell into his arms.

An evening of happiness and light ended in a darker vein. The body of Firk was taken away to the local undertaker and a statement about his death given to the county coroner. Matilda Stanford and Prudence Ling were driven on to Wimbledon by the coachman to pass a restorative night with the cousin. Along with the rest of the company, Lawrence Firethorn was shocked by the attempted hanging of Owen Elias. He took Nicholas Bracewell up to his room so that the full details could emerge in private.

The book holder was explicit and unfolded the tale without any trimmings. Murder, arson, riot, kidnap and municipal corruption were revealed in their true light. Firethorn heard it all with immense interest, feeling for the

297

plight of Owen Elias and coming to see how his own wilful involvement with Matilda Stanford had indirectly led to it. If she had not been enticed to the Nine Giants to satisfy him, then the Welshman would still be able to contribute his skills to the company instead of languishing in bed with a bandaged neck. The actor-manager was ashamed and shaken but his priorities remained unchanged. When Rowland Ashway was named as the architect of all the villainy, Firethorn saw it entirely in personal terms and actually grinned.

'If the alderman be arrested,' he said jauntily, 'then will his contract with Marwood be null and void. Westfield's Men will stay at the Queen's Head. Some good may yet come of all the upset I have borne!'

Nicholas had to exhibit supreme self-control.

Next day found Lawrence Firethorn at his best. He assembled the company early on and delivered a moving speech about the importance of overcoming all the setbacks they had endured. Concern for Owen Elias was understandable but the best way to speed his recovery was to put on the finest performance they could manage. In the space of ten minutes, Firethorn transformed a jaded group of men into an alert and determined theatre company. Nicholas had returned from his earlier visit to the Nine Giants with sketches and measurements of the acting area. It did not take long to erect a stage to begin rehearsal.

They heard the bells from the wedding nearby and gave a rousing welcome to the bride and groom when they arrived at the inn to begin the celebrations. Fine weather enabled the banquet to be served in the yard itself and the whole gathering was in excellent spirits by the time the play was due. Lord Westfield himself was the guest of honour, sitting beside the bride in his flamboyant attire and telling her that he would now give his wedding present. Westfield's Men took over.

The Wise Woman of Dunstable could not have been a more appropriate choice. It was a pastoral comedy about the virtues of true love and fidelity. Three suitors vied for the hand of a rich and beautiful widow who wanted nothing more than to live quietly in happy contemplation of her departed husband. All sorts of stratagems were employed to get her to the altar, the most ludicrous by Lord Merrymouth, an egregious old fop with a game leg. Firethorn showed brilliant comic invention in this role and equipped the posturing peer with all sorts of humorous ailments. The widow herself finally agreed to make a choice and everyone thought it would be between the two young, handsome suitors. But the ghost of her former husband – Edmund Hoode at his best – came back to give her sage advice. She chose Lord Merrymouth.

This not only put the other over-amorous gentlemen to flight, it ensured her widowhood, for the old aristocrat was so overwhelmed with pleasure that he drank himself to a stupor then fell into a pond and drowned. Firethorn even made the death scene unbearably comic. In the title role itself, Richard Honeydew was a wise woman of great charm and lightness of heart. The play ended with a dance then the audience pounded their tables in appreciation.

Westfield's Men bowed in acknowledgement of their rapturous reception then went into their closing dance once more by way of an encore. Led by Firethorn, they directed their final bow at the window through which Owen Elias had watched their performance. Still in pain from his ordeal, he applauded with gusto and the tears ran down his cheeks. Westfield's Men had given him the most exhilarating tonic. He belonged.

Walter Stanford's face was designed for mirth and good humour but it was furrowed by anger and disillusion now. At the suggestion of Nicholas Bracewell, his wife had set up an interview between the two men in a private room at the Royal Exchange so that the household steward at Stanford Place would not be aware of the net that was now closing in on him. The Lord Mayor Elect first thanked the book holder profusely for saving the life of his young bride by stopping the runaway horses, though her reason for being at the Nine Giants in the first place was tactfully concealed from her husband. No intimacy had occurred between her and Firethorn. She would not go astray again.

Nicholas had been right in his instincts. Once the connection between Rowland Ashway and Aubrey Kenyon was made, much was explained. With a sudden increase in wealth, the brewer was able to buy up the inns and taverns to whom he supplied his beer. Stanford suspected a whole network of corruption in the conduct of municipal affairs with the Chamberlain at the centre. Only he would be in a position to mastermind such financial chicanery. With a willing but credulous man like Sir Lucas Pugsley as Lord Mayor, the two men had been able to feather their own nests without the slightest suspicion falling on them. Ashway worked on the fishmonger as a friend while Kenyon used his expertise as an administrator to pull the wool over the latter's eyes. They were a potent combination.

Their reign was threatened by the election of Walter Stanford to office. Whatever his weaknesses, the mercer had tremendous acumen and a nose for any mismanagement. Under his surveillance, the corruption would not only have to cease but its extent during the previous mayoralty would have been uncovered. Ashway and Kenyon were left with only one option. Stanford had to be stopped.

'And so they killed Michael,' he said. 'Because so much of me was invested in my nephew, they hoped that my grief would rob me of the urge to go on.' He looked at Nicholas. 'How was it done, Master Bracewell?'

'The murder was committed in that house on the Bridge,' said the other 'I was deceived for a while when I learnt that it was owned by Sir Lucas Pugsley. It was borrowed from him by Alderman Ashway for the purpose. Though the murder happened by daylight, the body was not disposed of until night. Under the cover of darkness, it was dropped out of the window but it struck the starling on its way to the water.'

'The smashed leg!' said Stanford.

'Yes, sir. It must have been caught in the eddies then buoyed up by a piece of driftwood that carried it downstream. By complete chance, we encountered it.'

'You and your waterman.'

'Abel Strudwick. A sound man with all his faults.'

'One question, sir. Why was my nephew's face so mangled and bloody? We could scarce recognise him.'

'That was the intention.'

'What say you?'

'It was not your nephew, sir.'

'*Not*? But William and I saw him.'

'You saw only what looked like him,' explained the other. 'Michael Delahaye is still alive.'

'But that does not make sense.'

When Nicholas enlarged on his claim, Walter Stanford was forced to accept that it was all too logical. The army surgeon had told the book holder everything. Michael Delahaye was not just another grumbling soldier, he was a complete dissolute who resented his uncle for cutting short his strenuous overindulgence. Joining the army in order to prolong his wasteful ways, the soldier had found it so intolerable and depressing that it had turned a merry gentleman into a malevolent one. Walter Stanford became the target for that malevolence. When Michael Delahaye was offered a chance to strike back at his uncle, he seized it because it gave him the opportunity to escape for ever from the oppression of respectability and start a new life of debauchery under a new name. It also gave him the supreme satisfaction of killing off the mortal enemy he had made in the army.

Cold silence had fallen on Stanford as he listened. To lose a loving nephew was one form of misery. To learn that he was the object of that same person's hate was far worse. The one saving grace was that the whole plot had been exposed by a man of such evident discretion.

'What must I do, Master Bracewell?'

'Nothing, sir.'

'But they will flee the approach of justice.'

'Only if you frighten them away,' said Nicholas. 'We must tempt your nephew out of hiding or this will never be settled. Be ruled by me, sir. Prepare yourself for action but take none yet. Wait but a little while and they will surely strike again. Be patient.'

Stanford thought it over and nodded his agreement. He was deeply disturbed by what he had heard and he needed time to assimilate it all. What really cut him to the quick was the news about Michael Delahaye and he did not try to shuffle off his responsibility in the matter. His intentions had been good but he had applied intense pressure to his nephew to get him to conform and to abandon his wilder ways. He had helped to turn an idle but relatively harmless young man into a monster and it preyed on him. Having been through one grim ordeal, he now faced an even more punitive one.

'What am I to tell my sister?' he asked.

'What she needs to know.'

'She believes her son was hauled out of the river.'

'Then that is what happened, sir,' said Nicholas levelly. 'There is no need for her to learn the full truth. The son whom she loved and knew died in the Netherlands. Do not bring him back to torment her.'

303

Once again, Stanford accepted sage advice and looked across at the other with increased respect. Nicholas clearly had to be given some freedom where the stage-management of everything was concerned. He would know how to flush the villains out of their holes.

'When will they strike?' said Stanford.

'Soon.'

'How soon?'

'At the Lord Mayor's Show.'

Chapter Twelve

Ridings were an integral part of life in the capital. The processions were not merely a source of entertainment and wonder for the commonalty but a means of impressing upon them the dignity and power of their rulers. In medieval times, the most splendid processions were those on royal occasions, especially a coronation or a wedding. By the later years of the reign of Queen Elizabeth, however, the Lord Mayor's Show had come to rival even these, taking the whole city as its stage and encompassing traditions that went back to the very origin of old London town. The Show had now completely taken over from the Midsummer Marching Watch as the main civic annual parade and nobody dared to miss it. Ridings meant public holidays when people could enjoy a dazzling spectacle then go off to celebrate what they had seen in general merry-making.

Extra soldiers and constables were on duty as a result

of the recent riot but nobody expected that there would be any real troubles. A Lord Mayor's Show did not stir up apprentices to attack the immigrant craftsmen of Southwark. It was an attestation of civil power in a city that was nominally ruled by a sovereign, a shared belief that London was the most eminent place in Europe, a time when the whole populace was bathed in feelings of pride and identity and well-being. Walter Stanford was known to be exceptionally keen on civic tradition. The Show which carried him into office promised to be an outstanding one.

Some wanted to make it more memorable still.

'Everything turns on today,' said Rowland Ashway.

Aubrey Kenyon nodded. 'We must not lose our nerves.'

'Indeed, sir, or we are like to lose our heads.'

'Hopefully, that might be Stanford's fate.'

'It *has* to be, Aubrey, or we are undone.'

They were talking in Kenyon's house before going out to take up their places in the procession. The aldermanic robes made Ashway look fatter and more florid than ever whereas the Chamberlain's stateliness was enhanced by his regalia. They looked an ill-matched pair but they were yoked together in crime now and depended critically upon each other. There was someone else upon whom they relied.

'Can he be trusted to do his office?' said Kenyon.

'Nobody is more eager to perform it.'

'He let us down at Richmond.'

'That was the fault of Firk,' sneered Ashway. 'He hanged the wrong man and fell foul of that book holder. Did he but know it, Master Bracewell did us a favour. He killed off Firk and saved us the trouble of doing it ourselves. Delahaye is another kind of man again.'

'Renfrew,' said the other. 'He likes to be called James Renfrew. Lieutenant Delahaye is dead.'

'So will this Captain James Renfrew be in time,' said Ashway quietly. 'When he has done what we have paid him for, we must finish him off as well. He knows too much, Aubrey. It is the only way.'

'And today?'

'We must put our faith in his madness.'

'He hates Stanford even more than we do.'

Ashway smirked. 'I love him for that.'

Since 1453, when Sir John Norman was rowed up the river in a fine barge with silver oars, the Lord Mayor's Show had taken place on both land and water. Both banks of the Thames were thus lined with ranks of spectators who waited expectantly to see a floating marvel. Everyone knew the itinerary. Walter Stanford, Lord Mayor of London, would first tour his ward – that of Cornhill in which the Royal Exchange symbolically stood – then proceed to the nearest stairs where he would embark and be rowed up to Westminster to take his oath in the Exchequer before the judge. After that, he would return by barge to Blackfriars and progress to St Paul's for a service of thanksgiving before going on to the Guildhall for his Banquet. Veteran onlookers knew how to move around the city to get several perspectives on the Show. Newcomers with staring country eyes stayed rooted to the same spot for hours in order to catch a mere glimpse of the pomp and circumstance that marked the occasion.

Walter Stanford himself took it all with the utmost seriousness. Dressed in the traditional robes and wearing the famous mayoral hat, he was for that day alone the father of the whole city but it was his position as an uncle that worried him. Somewhere along the way was a crazed nephew with a grudge against him and a need to nip his mayoralty in the bud. Behind his smiles and his waves and his apparent delight, therefore, was an anxiety that would not leave him. His faith had been placed in a man who was nothing more than a book holder in a theatrical company. Was his trust well founded?

Leaving his ward, he followed the procession along a cheering avenue that led to the river. At the front of the parade were two men who bore the arms of the Mercers' Company. They were followed by a drummer, a flute-player and a man with a fife. Behind them, in blue gowns and caps and hose and blue silk sleeves, were sixteen trumpeters blowing their instruments in strident unison. Horse-drawn floats came next, each one elaborately mounted by an individual Guild and competing with each other in colour and spectacle. The Fishmongers' Ship was among the finest on display, a huge galleon that seemed to sail above the craned heads of the populace as it passed by. Another favoured contender was the Goldsmith's Castle, a quite magnificent structure that was first produced for the coronation of Richard II. And there were many others to keep the fingers pointing and the jaws dropping.

Fittingly, it was the Mercer's Maiden Chariot which outshone them all. This pageant was a Roman chariot, some twenty feet or more high, with sides of embossed silver and surmounted by a golden canopy above which sat Fame blowing her trumpet. In the chariot sat the Mercer's Maiden. This was customarily a young and beautiful gentlewoman with a gold and jewelled coronet on her head. At the Lord Mayor's feast, she dined royally at a separate table. This year, however, there was a significant break with tradition. Instead of choosing some long-haired young lady from one of the mercers' families, Walter Stanford selected his own wife as the Maiden and she was overjoyed. Seated high above the long ribbons of yelling people, Matilda Stanford felt the thrill of being a performer and the extraordinary honour of being wife to the Lord Mayor. The journey in the chariot helped her to forget all about Lawrence Firethorn and find her husband instead.

At the rear of it all came the Lord Mayor himself. He was preceded by the Sword Bearer in his immense fur hat and by the Sergeant-at-Arms who bore the mace. Other ceremonial officers walked close by with the Chamberlain among them but Stanford paid him no attention. It was important not to arouse the suspicions of Aubrey Kenyon or of any of the others until they could all be safely apprehended. When the Lord Mayor was not bestowing a genial wave on the crowd, he was keeping one eye on the soldier who marched just ahead of him. Dressed in an armoured breastplate and wearing a steel helmet, the man trailed his pike in the same manner as his fellows but he was no ordinary member of the guard. Nicholas Bracewell had a duty that went well beyond the ceremonial.

Abel Strudwick had rowed his boat out into the middle of the river to be part of the huge armada that accompanied the procession up to Westminster. All around him were other craft with eager spectators and it gave him a feeling of superiority to think that they had simply come to gawp and goggle. Poetry had put the waterman on the Thames that day. He was there to find inspiration for some new verses, to immortalise a great event with the creative fire of his imagination. From where he sat and bobbed, he had a fine view of the parade as it moved from land to water.

First to set off was the Mercers' Barge with its coat of arms proudly displayed aloft. Behind it came the Bachelors' Barge which was followed in turn by the vessels of the other companies, strictly in order of precedence. Strudwick saw the arms of the Grocers, the Drapers, the Fishmongers – with Sir Lucas Pugsley aboard – the Goldsmiths, the Skinners, the Merchant Taylors, the Haberdashers, the Salters, the Ironmongers, the Vintners and the Clothworkers. No place for Rowland Ashway there. The alderman had to wait upon the Dyers before his Guild could step forward for attention. It was an imposing sight that was made even more vivid by the fact that the companies wore their distinctive liveries.

The waterman felt no verse stirring as yet but he remained confident. What drew his gaze now was a sight that never failed to impress and even frighten a little at a

Lord Mayor's Show. Two huge and grotesque creatures were in the prow of the last barge, pretending to draw a model of Britain's Mount. Strudwick recognised them as Corinaeus and Gogmagog, fabled inhabitants of the city in ancient days.

They were giants.

Walter Stanford was vastly more confident now that he was afloat with his guard all around him. Out in the open street, he felt he was a target for a knife, an arrow, even for a sword if its owner could get close enough. He began to enjoy the procession as it sailed slowly down river between the echoing banks of applause. Nicholas was close enough to him for a brief conversation.

'Your fears were groundless, sir,' said Stanford.

'The day is yet young.'

'What harm could touch us here?'

'None, I hope,' said Nicholas.

But his instincts told him otherwise. The Lord Mayor and his retinue were standing on the upper deck of the barge so that they could be seen more clearly. Corinaeus and Gogmagog were several yards in front of them. The book holder took a professional interest in how the giants had been fashioned. They were about twelve feet high and made out of carved and gilded limewood. Skilful painters had given them hideous leering faces. Corinaeus was dressed like a barbarian warrior and sported a morning star on a chain. Gogmagog wore the costume of a Roman centurion and carried a spear and a shield that was decorated with a symbolic phoenix. Nicholas admired the strength of the men inside each of the models. They were even able to manipulate levers that made their weapons lift and fall in the air.

It was when Walter Stanford stepped forward to take a closer look at the giants that the danger came. Corinaeus made no move but Gogmagog responded at once. Through the slit in the bodywork, the man inside saw his chance and acted. Raising his spear, he tried to jab it hard at Walter Stanford but a soldier was there to parry the blow with his pike. What came next caused even more panic in the barge. Gogmagog rose feet in the air and then hurled himself directly at the Lord Mayor with a force that would have killed him had the giant made contact. But the pike of Nicholas Bracewell again did sterling duty and guided the huge wooden object over the side of the barge and into the water. The splash drenched people for twenty yards around and caused some of the smaller boats nearby to capsize.

Michael Delahaye had failed. He glared at his hated uncle with his one malignant eye then hurled a rope at the advancing guards to beat them back. Before they could get him, he had dived over the side of the barge into the river. It all happened with such speed that everyone was totally confused but Nicholas had his wits about him. Throwing off his helmet and divesting himself of his breastplate, he ran to the side of the barge and flung himself after the would-be assassin. Delahaye was strong and cleaved his way through the water but his pursuer was the better swimmer and clawed back the distance between them. Bewildered spectators on boat and bank watched in silence at the two pinheads that seemed to be floating on the waves. None of them understood the significance of what they were witnessing.

Abel Strudwick was well placed to view the final struggle. When Nicholas caught the kicking legs of his man, the latter turned to fight, pulling a dagger from his belt and hacking madly at his assailant. But the latter got his wrist in a grip of steel that would not slacken. They struggled and splashed with frenetic energy then both disappeared beneath the dark waters. Strudwick rowed in closer and peered down but he could see nothing. Long minutes passed when nothing happened and then blood came up to the surface of the water to brighten its scum. A head soon followed, surging up with desperation so that lungfuls of air could be inhaled. The swimmer then lay on his back to recover from the fatigue of a death-grapple. The waterman rowed in close and helped Nicholas Bracewell into his boat so that he could enjoy some of the cheers of congratulation that were ringing out.

Michael Delahaye did not surface.

The atmosphere at the Queen's Head was vastly lighter now that the threat of eviction had disappeared. With the arrest of Rowland Ashway, the contract to buy the inn was effectively rescinded. The alderman would never be able to take possession of his intended purchase now. Relief was so great and comprehensive that a smile dared to flit across the face of Alexander Marwood. He had not only been reprieved from a deal which turned out to be more disadvantageous than he had thought. The landlord was also reunited with a termagant wife who had badgered him incessantly about the idiocy of his action in signing. Nocturnal reconciliation let Marwood recall happier days.

Edmund Hoode was in a generous mood. He bought pints of sack for himself and his friend then sat at the table opposite him. A week had passed since the Lord Mayor's Show but it still vibrated in the memory.

'You were the hero of the hour, Nick,' said Hoode.

'I thought but of poor Hans Kippel.'

'His death is well revenged now. And all those other villains are locked secure away, including the Chamberlain himself. Who would have thought a man in such a place would have stooped to such crimes?'

'Temptation got the better of him, Edmund.'

'Yes,' said the other harshly. 'The same may be said of Lawrence. But for you again, that dalliance might have led us into further disaster. What an actor, Nick! But what a dreadful lecher, too! Margery has much to endure.'

'She is made of stern stuff.'

They sipped their drinks and enjoyed the comfort of being in their own home again. The Queen's Head might not be as well appointed as some inns but it was their chosen base and its landlord was anxious to renew his dealings with them. Nicholas had negotiated a new contract that favoured the company and he extracted an important concession from Marwood. A job had to be found at the inn for a man who had been an immense help to the book holder and whose occupation was now at risk. Leonard would henceforth be working at the Queen's Head and it would be good to see his friendly face around the establishment.

Nicholas thought of another friend and smiled.

'What do you make of Abel Strudwick?' he said.

'His verse is an abomination,' snapped Hoode.

'Yet he has finally found a market. His ballad on the Lord Mayor's Show is the talk of the town. He describes my fight below the water in more detail than I could myself.'

'The fellow is a bungling wordsmith.'

'Let him have his hour, Edmund.'

'He uses rhyme, like a sword, to hack.'

'There are worse things a man may do.'

Hoode agreed and took a kinder view of the waterman. He felt a vestigial sympathy for him because of the way that he was routed at the flyting contest. It had been a fight between the world of the amateur and that of the professional. Abel Strudwick had no chance. He was entitled to his brief moment of glory as a ballad-maker. Such thoughts led Hoode on to consider the merits of the raw amateur whose passions were not inhibited by too great a knowledge of the technicalities of poetry. He recalled the Lord Mayor's banquet to which Nicholas had been bidden as an honoured guest.

'Tell me, Nick. What was it like?'

'What?'

'This play of theirs – *The Nine Giants*.'

'Do I detect jealousy here?'

'No, no, of course not,' said Hoode quickly. 'I am above

such things, as you well know. My plays have held the stage for years and I fear no rival. I just wish you to tell me what this pageant of the nine worthy mercers was like.' He fished gently. 'Tedious, perhaps? Over-long and underwritten? Basely put together?'

'It was very well received,' said Nicholas.

'By Mistress Stanford?'

'By her especially.'

Hoode drooped. 'Then is my cause truly lost.'

'I liked the piece myself. It had quality.'

'What sort of quality, man?'

'Height and hardness.'

'You lose me here.'

'*The Nine Giants* resembled our own at Richmond.'

'They stood in a circle?'

'They were tall, straight and monstrously wooden.'

Edmund Hoode laughed for an hour.

If you enjoyed *The Nine Giants*, look out for more books
in the Bracewell Mystery series . . .

To discover more historical fiction and to
place an order visit our website at
www.allisonandbusby.com
or call us on
020 7580 1080

The Mad Courtesan

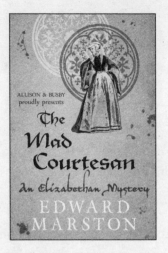

While England is brought low by rumours of Queen Elizabeth's declining health, celebrated theatre company Lord Westfield's Men suffer their own bitter blows. A vicious feud between players causes chaos; a rival company launches a new production; a mysterious beauty reduces their leading actor to a lovelorn wreck; and a brutal murder leaves the group of actors reeling. With matters so fraught, even a performing horse becomes a threat.

Stage manager Nicholas Bracewell, accustomed to damage control, is the only man with the wit to keep the company afloat. As the Queen sinks towards death, Nicholas begins to discern the connections between the company's misfortunes and the larger shadow falling over England . . .

The Silent Woman

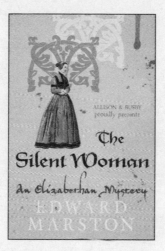

When fire destroys their London theatre, Lord Westfield's players must seek out humbler venues in the countryside. But stage manager Nicholas Bracewell is distracted by a shocking tragedy – a mysterious messenger from his native Devon, murdered by poison. Though the messenger is silenced, Nicholas understands what he must do: return to his birthplace and conclude some unfinished business from his past.

The rest of Westfield's Men, penniless and dejected, ride forth with him on a tour that will perhaps become their valedictory, dogged as they are by plague, poverty, rogues and thieves. And among the sinister shadows that glide silently with them towards Devon is one who means Nicholas never to arrive . . .

STEPHEN J. LEE

ASPECTS OF
EUROPEAN HISTORY
1789–1980

LONDON AND NEW YORK

Again, for Margaret

First published in 1982 by Methuen & Co. Ltd
Reprinted twice
Reprinted 1987

Reprinted 1988, 1990, 1991
by Routledge
11 New Fetter Lane, London EC4P 4EE
29 West 35th Street, New York, NY 10001

© 1982 Stephen J. Lee

Printed in England by
Clays Ltd, St Ives plc

British Library Cataloguing in Publication Data

Lee, Stephen J.
    Aspects of European history 1789–1980.
    1. Europe – History – 1789–1900
    2. Europe – History – 20th century
    I. Title
    940.2'8   D299

    ISBN 0-415-03468-X Pbk (University paperback 764)

Library of Congress Cataloguing in Publication Data

Lee, Stephen J.
    Aspects of European history, 1789–1980.
    Bibliography: p.
    1. Europe – History – 1789–1900.   2. Europe –
    History – 20th century.   I. Title.
    D299.L39   940.2'8   82-6310
    AACR2
    ISBN 0-415-03468-X (Pbk)

Contents

List of illustrations

MAPS

FIGURE

Introduction

This book is a sequel to *Aspects of European History 1494–1789*. It is based on an interpretative approach to some of the topics most commonly encountered in modern European history and is designed to be used in addition to specialist works and standard textbooks. The main intention is to stimulate thought and to assist in the preparation of essays and seminar papers by encouraging the student to develop an angle or an argument, whether in agreement with the chapters or in opposition to them. It is also hoped that the topics and the approach to them will be of interest to the general reader who seeks to understand the background to some of the problems of the modern world.

This volume contains a larger number of contemporary quotations than the first and, in some chapters, more direct reference to recent views of and major controversies among historians.

The chapters suggest a variety of methods by which a theme or argument may be presented.

1 Chapters 6, 9 and 21 stress the ideas, policies and problems of individual statesmen.
2 Chapters 20 and 31 examine an issue from two opposite viewpoints; in Chapter 20 the arguments are separated, in Chapter 31 they are integrated.
3 Chapters 4 and 12 present one viewpoint only and use only carefully selected factual material.
4 Some chapters use the analogy of 'forces' ('internal' and 'external', 'centrifugal' and 'centripetal'); examples are Chapters 1 and 17. Others, like Chapters 4, 18 and 28, emphasize 'contradictions' and 'paradoxes'.
5 Comparisons and contrasts are sometimes drawn; Chapter 9, for example, deals with the ideas and policies of two statesmen.
6 Chapters 33, 34, 35 and 36 provide a survey of four major themes affecting Europe as a whole and other parts of the world.

All the chapters are designed for extensive note-taking. They were built up step by step and the sections and paragraphs of each chapter are each intended to represent a stage in the argument. It should, therefore, be possible to break all the chapters down into their

Aspects of European History 1789–1980

constituent parts. It is hoped that this will ease the task of essay preparation and examination revision.

Because of the problem of compressing such a wide period into a book of this size, the coverage, as in Volume 1, is for the most part political. There is, however, an attempt in many chapters to include economic, social and intellectual trends. Chapters 22, 29 and 32 deal specifically with economic history. Finally, the period since 1945 is dealt with more generally. It is so complex and eventful that detailed analysis would require an entire volume.

1

The Origins of the French Revolution

The purpose of this opening chapter is to provide a synthesis of some of the more important interpretations of the outbreak of the French Revolution.

The 1770s and 1780s brought with them a serious economic depression. This seemed the worse because it followed a long period of mounting prosperity and it caused a sense of resentment and bitterness as all classes faced a decline in their status. The fabric of society was now threatened with rupture by the exertion of two internal forces. These had existed for much of the eighteenth century but were now greatly accentuated by the economic crisis. The first force was the hostility between the Second Estate (aristocracy) and the Third Estate (bourgeoisie, peasantry and urban proletariat) as they pulled further apart from each other. The second force was the simultaneous attempt of both Estates to pull away from the policies of the monarchy and the implications of absolutism. For a while the Estates formed an unnatural alliance against the central power of the monarchy, and so the second force was the stronger. The king, finding himself in serious difficulties, yielded to the combined demands of the different classes, and agreed to summon the Estates General. Now that the central authority seemed to have collapsed, the original antagonism between the Estates reasserted itself so violently that the first force tore through the fabric of the *ancien régime*. The influence of the nobility was now overwhelmed by successive waves of the Third Estate as the bourgeoisie, peasantry

1

and proletariat each pressed for the achievement of their aspirations.

*

It is a common assumption that revolution is caused by misery; Marx certainly believed that worsening conditions create a situation favourable to revolution. In the mid-nineteenth century, however, Alexis de Tocqueville advanced the theory that the French Revolution broke out when conditions were improving. He observed: 'It is not always by going from bad to worse that a country falls into a revolution.' Moreover: 'the state of things destroyed by a revolution is almost always somewhat better than that which immediately precedes it.'[1] In 1962, J. C. Davies used a slightly different approach, but complemented de Tocqueville's view. He suggested that 'revolutions are most likely to occur when a prolonged period of objective economic and social development is followed by a short period of sharp reversal'.[2] This seems to be borne out by the general economic trends of the eighteenth century.

Between 1741 and 1746 France experienced a high overall economic growth rate. Large sections of the bourgeoisie benefited from the threefold increase in trade and the fivefold increase of overseas trade, together with the revived prosperity of ports like Dunkirk, Le Havre, La Rochelle, Bordeaux, Nantes and Marseilles. The increase in prices (estimated at 65 per cent between 1741 and 1765) drove up the value of farm produce and greatly improved the living conditions of the tenant farmers. Although famines did occur, for example in 1725, 1740, 1759 and 1766–8, there was nothing in the 1780s to compare with the catastrophic levels of starvation during the years 1693–4 and 1709–10. In the general upsurge of prosperity, the French bourgeoisie and peasantry seemed distinctly better off than their counterparts in Central and Eastern Europe.

When it came, during the 1770s and 1780s, the slump had a profound effect. France experienced a recession similar to that suffered by other countries; this was probably no more than a temporary dip in a lengthy economic cycle, possibly precipitated by a shortage of bullion from the New World. French industry and commerce were, however, badly affected because of the inadequate nature of French credit facilities. Production therefore declined, unemployment increased and the recession soon spread to agriculture. To make matters worse, there was a severe drought in 1785, and in the following years the peasants were unable to afford the usual quantity of seed, the inevitable result being short yields. The 1788 harvest was ruined by an abnormally wet summer and the position was even worse in 1789. The degree of starvation was lower than it had been at various stages during the reign of Louis XIV, but the suddenness of the decline in the fortunes of each class in the 1770s and 1780s had a far more dangerous psychological impact. The bourgeoisie and the peasantry, in particular, saw the gap between their aspirations and their achievements growing ever wider, while the nobility struggled desperately to hold what they had. The result was deep resentment and growing bitterness, both of them more inflammable revolutionary material than suffering by itself. The social classes looked with increasing suspicion at each other and at the régime itself, trying desperately to recapture their former share of the national wealth and to continue their previous quest for material advancement.

*

The eighteenth century had seen a gradual deterioration in relations between the Second and Third Estates. Each had improved its position economically compared to its own past, but each came to regard the other as a serious threat to its security and well-being. This resentment greatly increased after 1776.

The nobility managed to reassert its influence over the administration and local government by the alliance between the *noblesse d'epée* and the *noblesse de robe*, while positions of authority within the Church had, in the words of Talleyrand, become the preserve *'presque exclusif de la classe noble'.*[3] On the other hand, the nobility feared the ambitions of the wealthy sections of the bourgeoisie and resisted fiercely any attempts by the latter to break the monopoly of the *noblesse de robe* over the administrative offices and the *parlements*. The bourgeoisie regarded their ultimate aim as passage into the Second Estate through the traditional method of ennoblement. Increasingly, however, this form of upward mobility was blocked and with it any chance of gaining political power. Two future leaders of the Revolution showed the effects that disillusionment with this state of affairs could produce. Carnot's radical views followed his unsuccessful attempts to gain ennoblement, while Danton claimed that 'The Old Régime drove us to [revolution] by giving us a good education, without opening any opportunity for our talents'.[4] The peasantry, although lacking the education and economic power of the bourgeoisie, had their own aspirations which were challenged by the rural nobility. Seigneurial rights and dues were extracted to the full, and the peasantry had to suffer the inconveniences and hardships produced by the *banalité du moulin, banalité du four, banalité du pressoir, droit de chasse* and *droit de bauvin*. And, according to one of the *cahiers* of the peasantry in 1789, 'the contempt of the nobility for the commonality is beyond belief'.[5] The nobility therefore came to be regarded as a parasitic element, enjoying seigneurial privileges without carrying out the functions which had once accompanied them.

The rift between the Second and Third Estates widened during the 1770s and 1780s. Under the impact of the recession, the peasantry found the seigneurial dues particularly onerous, while the nobility increasingly tightened up their exactions in order to solve their own difficulties. The burden of the depression was therefore passed downwards to the section of society least able to bear it. The bourgeois complaint about the nobility was more indirect but nevertheless significant for the future. They accused the nobility of resisting any rationalization of the economic and financial structure and of perpetuating anachronistic institutions at a time when reform was most urgently needed.

Yet tensions between the social classes did not result in immediate conflict. For a while they were partially restrained by a temporary and basically artificial coalition against a common target, the absolute power of the monarch.

*

The motives of each class in establishing this common front against the central government differed widely, but each had a fixed idea that the régime in its present form could no longer serve its interests or guarantee it from exploitation. The government had, therefore, to be modified. Precisely how remained a matter of vague speculation until the monarchy actually collapsed under the combined pressure.

The nobility feared absolutism more profoundly in the 1770s and 1780s than ever before. The banning of the *parlements* seemed to be an attack on the most cherished power of the nobility, gained after a long struggle since 1715, namely the questioning of royal legislation. When the *parlements* were restored in 1774 the nobility returned to the offensive, only to be confronted by the appalling

4

The Origins of the French Revolution

spectre of a reforming monarch who, to make matters worse, was served by ministers who openly expressed reservations about the existing fiscal system and the exemptions from taxation. Louis XVI seemed a greater menace than Louis XV because he appeared to be more willing to embark upon an extensive remodelling programme which would reduce the social status of the nobility in a way never even considered before. The nobility therefore used every device available; they fought the reform programme in the *parlements*, in the Court and in the Assembly of Notables. As the financial crisis worsened after 1787, they demanded the convocation of the Estates General. This was merely an appeal to an early precedent, one which the nobility knew the monarch could not ignore. The Estates General would naturally confirm the powers of the nobility, since on the traditional method of voting the First and Second Estates would outnumber the Third.

The bourgeoisie saw matters differently but went along with the tactics of the nobility. To them, the Estates General offered the prospect of fundamental constitutional reform, which would enable the bourgeoisie to exert more control over the political institutions and to redesign the economic structure. After the brief experiments of the Regency with *laissez-faire*, France had seen the return of the mercantilist policies of Colbert from 1726 onwards, and the restoration of the oppressive guild system and internal customs barriers. Then, during the reign of Louis XVI, government policy seemed to lose all sense of overall direction. At the very depth of the economic depression the government seemed prepared to unleash the market forces of Great Britain; by the free trade treaty of 1786 it exposed the struggling French industries to *laissez-faire* at the very time that protection was most needed. If the chaotic economic and fiscal system were to be reorganized, the bourgeoisie would have to play an active role. This could no longer be done by hoping for a special relationship with the monarchy as had existed in the reign of Louis XIV; the nobility had long since blocked the access to political positions. The solution, therefore, had to be found in representative institutions – in a parliamentary monarchy. Much as the bourgeoisie resented the nobility, they therefore resented the latter's demands for the calling of the Estates General.

The peasantry regarded the meeting of the Estates General as a panacea. It would be the means whereby the unequal distribution of taxation would be remedied. The *taille, capitation, vingtième, gabelle* and *aides* would be reassessed or possibly replaced by a graduated land or income tax. The institution of monarchy still commanded respect, but it was felt increasingly that its powers should be limited. The peasantry suspected that the government had been making profits from fluctuations in the price of grain; this and other grievances could now be articulated openly, with greater hope of redress.

In expressing its opposition to the policies of the régime each class made use of the ideas of the leading French *philosophes*. It is often assumed that Montesquieu, Voltaire and Rousseau exerted direct influence on the growth of revolutionary feeling and thereby precipitated the events of 1789. In reality, the growth of dissent was not actually stimulated by the *philosophes*; rather, dissent was expressed with the help of quotations taken liberally from their writings. The Paris *parlement*, for example, used Montesquieu's theories of the balance of power. Sometimes the phrases used closely resembled the American constitution which, in turn, borrowed from the *philosophes*. The *parlement* of Rennes, for example, declared in 1788: 'That man is born free, that originally men are equal, these are truths that have no need of proof',[6] an obvious mixture of Jefferson and Rousseau. The *cahiers* of each social group in 1789 contained examples of an unusually lucid statement of general grievances. It appears, therefore, that Montesquieu and Rousseau had more influence on the expression of opposition than on its actual formation.

*

Such a distinction would have offered little comfort to Louis XVI. During his reign the monarchy not only reached its lowest ebb for two centuries; it eventually proved incapable of presiding over the normal process of government. The main problem was that the monarchy could no longer maintain a careful balance between the divergent social forces for the simple reason that it had no consistent basis of support. Louis XIV had promoted the image of absolutism by elevating the monarchy into a lofty position of isolation. But he had taken care to maintain the support of the bourgeoisie in order to counter the hostility which his policies often invoked from the nobility. After 1851 Napoleon III was to depend on the backing of the peasantry to counterbalance the opposition of the workers. The French monarchy could survive only if it was able to rely upon a

The Origins of the French Revolution

politically significant section of the population, or to pursue the more difficult policy of 'divide and rule'.

The vulnerability of Louis XVI was all the greater because of the financial crisis which lasted throughout his reign, and which proved that he could not maintain his authority without the goodwill, or at least indifference, of his subjects. Intolerable strains had been imposed on the financial structure by the Seven Years' War and the War of American Independence, and he was forced to consider changes in the methods and assessment of taxation. The situation was not without precedent: Louis XIV had had to agree to the introduction of the *dixième* and *capitation* during the War of the League of Augsburg (1688–97) and the War of the Spanish Succession (1701–14). But Louis XVI had to deal only with a relatively docile nobility, and with an impoverished and not yet articulate peasantry. Louis XIV encountered much more wide spread opposition, and in particular a concerted demand, from 1787, for the convocation of the Estates General. In finally giving way in 1788, he acknowledged the collapse of absolutism and the existence of a political vacuum at the centre.

*

Freed from the necessity of having to co-operate against the régime, the Second and Third Estates now expressed their fears of each other more openly, and the crisis became revolution.

The nobility showed their determination to maintain the traditional voting procedures once the Estates General had convened. This brought out into the open their differences with the Third Estate, which proceeded to reconstitute itself as the National Assembly. This was the first sign of institutional revolution, as it was an open defiance of the authority and procedure of a traditional body. From this stage onwards, as G. Lefebvre argues, the momentum was increased by the participation of all the conflicting, rival, disparate elements within the Third Estate. The bourgeoisie appeared to have accepted the new political situation of July 1789 as permanent. The peasantry, however, hastened the destruction of feudal and seigneurial rights in August by a series of riots in the provinces. The artisans and proletariat of Paris pushed the Revolution into the more violent phase of 1791–4, providing solid support for the sweeping changes made by the National Convention.

It is often stated that the Revolution broke out in 1787 as a result of the pressure exerted by the Paris *parlement*. It is possible, however, to put this a different way. For a revolution to begin, a certain momentum is needed. In the nineteenth century, France possessed a large repository of revolutionary experience which exerted the vital push on several occasions (1830, 1848, 1871). During the 1780s there was no such knowledge or leadership; but the nobility, from their position of strength, and as part of their reactionary stance, delivered the first blow. The momentum of this act of political defiance was enough to encourage the different sections of the Third Estate to bring about the destruction of the *ancien régime*, and with it the Second Estate. This seems to confirm the view put forward by Montaigne as far back as 1580 that 'Those who give the first shock to a state are the first overwhelmed in its ruin'.

*

Recent research, particularly by R. R. Palmer and J. Godechot, has placed France in a more general context of revolutionary change which also affected Geneva (1768 and 1792), Ireland (1778 and 1798), the Netherlands (1784–7), Poland (1788–92), the Austrian Netherlands (1787–90) and Hungary (1790), as well as the North American colonies (from 1775). There certainly appear to have been major common problems affecting Europe as a whole. One was a rapid growth of population (100 million to 200 million between 1700 and 1800). Another was a sharp depression in the 1770s and 1780s, following a long period of economic growth. The overall result was increased competition for existing land resources, a huge rise in unemployment, and serious financial problems which confronted virtually every government in Europe and forced a re-examination of the traditional forms of revenue. Given the inability of most governments to deal with a major recession, it is hardly surprising that unrest should have been so widespread.

The majority of the revolutions, however, ended in failure. Palmer emphasizes the importance of a strong bourgeoisie (lacking in Poland and Hungary) and of close co-operation between the different social classes. In Poland and Hungary the huge peasantry remained largely indifferent, while in the Netherlands they backed the forces of counter-revolution. Ultimately, the country which possessed the largest bourgeoisie and the most extensive dissatisfaction within each class was the most likely to experience fundamental change.

The Origins of the French Revolution

That is why, despite the widespread incidence of unrest in the late eighteenth century, it was France which underwent the most violent upheaval and experienced the most advanced political, social and economic reforms.

2

The Course of the French Revolution

The opening years of the French Revolution (1789–92) can be regarded as a period of rapid social and institutional change during which the whole structure of the *ancien régime* was dismantled. This was, however, also the 'moderate' phase, as leaders of the National and Constituent Assemblies endeavoured to control the radicals, and to create a 'balanced' constitution.

The speed with which the changes occurred during the year 1789 was the result of a pendulum reaction between the king's government and the people of Paris. Louis XVI attempted to win back some of the ground he had lost to the recently formed National Assembly by dismissing his most progressive minister, Necker, and reconstituting his government. This provoked demonstrations and riots which culminated, on 14 June, in the fall of the Bastille – an event which symbolized the bankruptcy of royal authority. The king, nevertheless, tried to maintain his powers by rejecting some of the reforming legislation of the National Assembly. The result was the March of the Women (5 October) and the forcible removal of the king from Versailles, the seat of royal power since the 1680s, to Paris. Here the city's populace could exert more continuous and direct pressure on both the king and the National Assembly. Popular participation spread to other areas; as R. R. Palmer states, 'Plain people took part in continuing revolutionary activity at the bottom, while the Constituent Assembly and its successors governed at the top'.[1]

If events in and around Paris resembled the action of a pendulum, the relationship between the capital and the provinces could be

The Course of the French Revolution

described as 'tidal'. Rural unrest and the threat of peasant revolt put considerable pressure on Versailles and Paris to introduce legislation to alter the social structure. Hence the Constituent Assembly abolished feudalism, ended personal obligations and the tithe, formulated the Declaration of the Rights of Man and, in November, put up most of the Church lands for sale. The reverse flow, meanwhile, brought the influence of Paris to the rest of France, resulting in the dismissal of *intendants*, the suspension of *parlements* and the removal of other institutions of the *ancien régime*.

Every effort, however, was made to control the direction of this hectic activity. The 1791 Constitution, for example, reflected the desire for political balance and social harmony. One of its principles was decentralization, which allowed the newly formed *départements* considerable autonomy. Another was the separation, at the centre, of the legislature (in the form of the Constituent Assembly) from the executive (or the king and his ministers). This was in line with the widely accepted theories of Montesquieu and with the proven, if brief, experience of the United States. As a further safeguard against radicalism, the Assembly restricted the franchise to 'active' citizens, who numbered about 4.3 million taxpayers and property owners. The overall intention, therefore, was to reform, but also to hold back; Mirabeau, for example, called himself 'a partisan of order, but not of the old order'.

How long could this harmony and balance be maintained? The 1791 Constitution opened up, in the words of J. Roberts, a 'Pandora's box',[2] from which emerged unforeseen conflicts and complications. Between 1791 and 1792 all prospects of consensus disappeared and France split between Right and Left.

The Right was, of course, based on the king, who had become increasingly disillusioned with the restraints on his authority. He strongly opposed the Assembly's legislation concerning émigrés and non-juring clergy and, in his powerlessness to prevent it, complained: 'What remains to the king other than a vague semblance of royalty?'[3] The Left, meanwhile, had begun to press for a republic, arguing that, as long as France was a monarchy, the legislature and executive would be antagonistic as well as separate. Some deputies were also extremely concerned about the limits placed on reforming legislation; Marat, for example, found his blood 'boiling at the sight of so many decrees . . . which derogate from the Declaration of the Rights of Man and which are mortal to liberty'.[4] Others, like

Robespierre, condemned the limited franchise and 'the monstrous distinction' which makes a citizen 'active or passive'.[5] The conflict between Right and Left was aggravated by the changeover, in 1791, from the Constituent to the Legislative Assembly. A 'self-denying ordinance' ensured that the Legislative Assembly contained none of the deputies of the Constituent, thereby ending the continuity of personnel which had contributed to the political stability of the period 1789–91. Of the new members, 250 were Feuillants, or staunch loyalists, and the rest were radicals, comprising the Girondins and the more extreme Montagnards, of whom the Jacobins were the core. The Feuillants were soon to be pushed aside and the radicals eventually fought among themselves to capture and redirect the Revolution.

*

During its second phase (1792–4) the Revolution became more violent and doctrinaire. The Swiss historian Burckhardt commented that, as the Revolution accelerated, the representatives of the previous stages were cut down as 'moderates'; hence '*La révolution dévore ses enfants*'.

The catalyst for this change was the war. Most sections of the Assembly were enthusiastic about the prospect of taking on France's neighbours; the Feuillants assumed that a national struggle could only strengthen the authority of the king, while the Girondins reasoned that a 'people's war' would destroy the monarchy altogether. Events proved the Girondins correct as, in the words of D. I. Wright, the war 'revolutionized the revolution'.[6] A wave of terror was caused by the impending Prussian invasion, and the search for internal enemies resulted in the notorious massacres of September 1792. In the same month, the right-wing Feuillants were virtually eliminated in the elections for the new National Convention, and power was now shared between 165 Girondins and 145 Montagnards. The Girondins pressed for the indictment of the king, arguing that he was now a rallying point for counter-revolutionaries and that, while he remained on the throne, Austria and Russia would be unlikely to relax their efforts to restore him to his former power. Hence, as a result of the war, a republic was proclaimed on 25 September 1792, and Louis XVI was executed the following January.

By 1793 the Girondins had accomplished their basic aims – a

people's war and a people's republic. It was now time to call a halt and consolidate. After all, asked Brissot, one of the Girondin leaders: 'What more could they [the people] want?'[7] In effect, the Girondins now came to regard themselves as conservatives and they bitterly opposed the attempts of the Left, or Montagnards, to increase the momentum of the Revolution. Brissot and Louvet feared that the Montagnards would open up the National Convention to the influence of the Paris 'mob'; the Girondins would be helpless against this type of popular pressure since their own support came from the *départements* of south-western France. Above all, the Girondins were appalled by the prospects of a Montagnard dictatorship, directed by the tightly-knit Jacobin clubs of Paris. Unfortunately, they lacked the strength to resist the Montagnards or apply a brake to the Revolution. As a party, they were far less cohesive than the Montagnards and they lacked popular support where it really mattered – in the capital. Hence, by June 1793, their position was hopeless. The leading Girondin deputies were dragged from the Convention by a crowd of 20,000 Montagnard supporters and were subsequently tried and executed.

The Montagnards now had the field to themselves, and introduced the phase of the Revolution usually referred to as the 'Terror' (1793–4). This was undoubtedly the most complex period, and it threw up a series of contradictions. For example, the Montagnards made much use of the demonstrations of the *sans-culottes*, particularly the Paris tradesmen, shopkeepers, artisans and wine merchants. And yet they gradually narrowed the actual power-base of their régime by giving all executive powers to a few committees of the Convention. They showed that they were committed to democracy by extending the franchise and removing the distinction between 'active' and 'passive' citizenship. And yet the men who ruled France through the Committees of Public Safety and General Security were less accountable to the electorate than at any other period in the Revolution. There was also an ideological paradox. The Jacobin leaders, especially Marat and Robespierre, explicitly upheld liberty as a key doctrine of the Revolution. But it was the type of liberty which existed only collectively and not in an individual sense. According to Robespierre the will of the people as a whole was 'the natural bulwark of liberty'.[8] Individuals, therefore, could find their freedom only by conforming to the 'general interest'. Robespierre was clearly influenced by the famous argument in Rousseau's *Social Contract* that dissidents, in

13

their very act of disagreeing with the 'general will', were enslaving themselves and that 'it may be necessary to compel a man to be free'.[9]

The principle that freedom could be achieved through compulsion was applied during the course of 1794 by the Committees and the Revolutionary Tribunal. The result was the Terror, a revolutionary device which was justified by the Jacobins provided that the motives were 'pure'. Robespierre, for example, argued that 'virtue' without 'terror' was 'impotent', and Marat urged that 'liberty must be established by violence'.[10] This violence, previously the spontaneous demonstration of mob frustration, was now institutionalized and became the monopoly of the government; hence the guillotine of the Tribunal replaced the butchers' knives of the *sans-culottes*. Terror, however, came to feed upon itself and was used by the Robespierrists to eliminate rival Jacobin factions. The Hébertists, for example, were executed in March 1794, and the Dantonists a month later. Robespierre narrowed the base of power so much that eventually he regarded himself as the personification of the Republic. For this reason, Robespierre has been the subject of greater controversy than any other revolutionary figure.[11] The traditional view is that the Terror perverted the aims of the Revolution and allowed Robespierre to set up a particularly odious dictatorship. To use the analogy of several historians, the French Revolution was a fever, the crisis of which was the Terror; before the patient, or France, could recover, Robespierre had to be cast off. Two French historians have adopted a more positive view of Robespierre: Lefebvre called him 'the resolute and faithful representative of that revolutionary mentality',[12] while Mathiez considered him 'the incarnation of Revolutionary France in its most noble, most generous and most sincere aspects'.[13]

It is also possible to depict the Terror as a period of constructive achievement. The measures taken by the Convention to mobilize the nation and to control the supply of food did more than anything else to turn the tide of the war and therefore to save the Revolution from destruction by foreign armies. Carnot's *levée en masse* created an entirely new approach to warfare and made possible the victories of Bonaparte a few years later. The Montagnards also reinterpreted the objectives of the first phase of the Revolution. Some of the reforms of the Constituent Assembly were reversed; the best example was the end of decentralization, which had brought two years of administrative chaos. Others however were confirmed and

The Course of the French Revolution

years of administrative chaos. Others however were confirmed and extended; these included the Declaration of the Rights of Man, the Civil Constitution of the Clergy and the sale of Church lands. It is often pointed out, however, that the Convention achieved little outside the context of the war or beyond the modification of previous reforms. Of its main innovations, the attempt to introduce the worship of the Supreme Being was a total failure, and the Revolutionary Calendar lasted less than twenty years. The only long lasting non-military reform which originated specifically in the Convention was the metric system of weights and measures.

*

The third period of the Revolution (1794–9) has been extensively reinterpreted. The traditional picture was that the Revolution reached a climax with the overthrow of Robespierre on 9 Thermidor 1794 and that a sharp turn to the right followed, preparing the way for Bonaparte's takeover in 1799. Historians used to dismiss the period 1795–9 as being outside the scope of the Revolution, thus placing it in limbo between two periods which were considered more important and certainly more interesting. Recent works, however, have restored the Thermidorians and the Directory fully to the context of the Revolution. C. Church, for example, called the Directory 'a board of executors for the revolutionary settlement',[14] while 1799, rather than 1794, is now generally taken as the terminal date of the Revolution.

Other assumptions have been challenged as well. There used to be agreement that the *coup d'état* of Thermidor was a right-wing reaction against the radical policies of Robespierre. M. Lyons, however, has argued that some of the plotters, like Tallien, Barras and Fouché, were left-wing Montagnards who considered Robespierre's ideas too moderate. There was also considerable opposition from the atheists within the Committee of General Security to Robespierre's introduction of the Cult of the Supreme Being. For a while, the Thermidorians were even joined by Babeuf and other socialists. 'In a sense, therefore,' says Lyons, 'the *coup* of 9 Thermidor was a revolution of the Left.'[15] There was also a wave of panic among the deputies of the Convention that they would be included in the next batch of Robespierre's victims. The events of 9 Thermidor, therefore, were also a 'revolution in self-defence against impending proscription'.[15] In one respect, Robespierre had only himself to

15

blame; he had narrowed the base of his authority so far that no attempts were made to save him from his fate. It is ironical that the man who claimed to personify the people of Paris was reviled by them on his way to the guillotine.

Thermidor may have been inspired by the Left, but it was the Right which ultimately benefited. Large numbers of moderates resurfaced in the Convention after the overthrow of Robespierre and proceeded to dismantle the institutions of the Terror which had held them, and the Convention itself, in subjection. They also put the Revolution back on the course originally charted between 1789 and 1791 by the Constituent Assembly while, at the same time, retaining Robespierre's policy of central government control over the *départements*. Determined to prevent, in the future, any other Jacobin groups in the Convention from seizing control of the administration, the Jacobins resolved to reintroduce the strict separation of the legislature and executive and also to reduce the influence of the Paris mob by tightening the suffrage. The result was the Constitution of the Year III (1795) which established, as the executive, a Directory of five, and, as the legislature, a bicameral *corps*, comprising the Council of Five Hundred and the Council of Elders. The domestic record of this new régime was not unimpressive. The severely inflated *assignats*, introduced in 1789, were replaced by a new paper currency, the *mandats territoriaux*, and then by the first coin-based currency since the days of the *ancien régime*. From 1797 there were also extensive fiscal reforms, directed by de Nogaret, the minister of finance. Meanwhile, communications were generally improved and attention given at central and local levels to the reorganization of poor relief.

Whatever its achievements, the Directory proved more vulnerable than any of the other revolutionary régimes to military takeover and the emergence of the cult of personality. The success of Bonaparte's *coup d'état* of Brumaire (1799) showed that the Directory had never itself experienced the sort of stability it had brought to the Revolution. For one thing, the separation of the legislature and executive by the 1795 Constitution had ensured that no deputies elected to the Council of Five Hundred would ever serve on the Directory or as a government minister. Since executive posts were not, therefore, allocated on the basis of majorities in the legislature, there was no incentive to organize political parties. This was a serious deficiency in a constitution which otherwise had many of the hallmarks of a liberal democracy. Indeed, the Directors made the mistake of assuming that parties would undermine the régime. La Revellière Lépeaux, for example, argued that it would be preferable 'to die with honour defending the republic and its established government than to . . . live in the muck of parties'.[16] It was because of this obsession with 'faction' that the Directory virtually threw away its authority. By 1799 Siéyès and Ducos had become so alarmed by the prospect of a Jacobin revival that they intrigued with Bonaparte for a revision of the constitution. The result was a further swing to the Right and the beginning of the period known as the Consulate.

3

The Reforms of Napoleon I

Napoleon Bonaparte ruled France as First Consul between 1799 and 1804, and as Emperor between 1804 and 1814–15. He has always been one of the more difficult statesmen to identify with a particular era; indeed, his rule showed aspects of three different phases in European history.

For one thing, he has been called the 'child of the Revolution'. Certainly, he owed his rapid rise from obscurity to political power to the events of the Revolution and to the opportunities which the *ancien régime* could not have provided. His success in the Revolutionary War coincided with the political vulnerability of the Directory, enabling him to seize power by a *coup* which had the tacit support of several ministers. Once installed as First Consul (1799) he proceeded to build on the domestic achievements of the Directory. He stressed that he was the heir to the Revolution, which he had 'stabilized on the principles which began it'.[1]

At the same time, he renounced his own Jacobin connections and cut France off from the doctrinaire period of the Revolution. He rejected the ideology of Rousseau and the attempts made by Robespierre to apply it. In this sense, he considered that his task was 'to close the Romance of the Revolution'.[2] He returned for much of his intellectual inspiration to the earlier philosophers of the Enlightenment – writers like Montesquieu and Voltaire. This gave him much in common with the enlightened despots of Russia, Austria and Prussia; he shared their gloomy view of the 'credulous and criminal' nature of humanity and their belief that the only way to

18

The Reforms of Napoleon I

prevent chaos was the firm and authoritarian enforcement of humane and enlightened policies. Napoleon, therefore, looked back beyond 1779 and some of his measures show the hallmarks of the *ancien régime*. Surveying his career while in exile on St. Helena, he claimed that he had been 'the natural mediator in this struggle of the past against the Revolution'.[3]

He was not, however, merely a revolutionary or merely an enlightened despot; nor was he simply a combination of the two. He fused the Revolution and the *ancien régime* in such a way as to produce an entirely new element. This could be described as 'democratic' or 'plebiscitary' 'dictatorship', achieved by the energies of a self-made man, upheld by a broad base of popular support, sustained by all the trappings of the personality cult, and dedicated to military glory. Bonapartism, therefore, has links with the twentieth century as well as the eighteenth.

The rest of this chapter will elaborate on these three characteristics of Bonapartism in a survey of Napoleon's political, economic and social reforms.

*

The Revolution provided the vital background to Napoleon's political and constitutional changes. It cleared away the obstacles of the *ancien régime*, including the *parlements*, corporations and other vested interests. Napoleon incorporated some of the Revolution's achievements directly into his system. At local government level he kept the *départements* which had been established in 1790 by the Constituent Assembly, and continued the centralizing policies of the National Convention and the Directory. He also built on the Directory's Ministry of the Interior, finding the Ministry's Commissioners particularly useful as government agents in the *départements*. This centralization and uniformity of administration were the basis of Napoleon's authority and, because of the groundwork provided by the Revolution, he possessed more effective powers than had belonged to any of the Bourbon monarchs. The security which his position thus attained enabled him to take liberties with the legislature and executive, although he always claimed that he was, in fact, continuing and rationalizing revolutionary practice. The Constitution of the Year VIII (1799) continued the trend, started by the Constitution of 1795, towards legislatures with more than a single chamber. It should be emphasized, however, that Napoleon went further than the later revolutionaries had ever envisaged; he not only established three chambers instead of two, but also ensured that each had precise and strictly limited powers. The executive, by contrast, was narrowed down, but with the same aim in mind: the quest for personal power. It had originally consisted of the various committees of the National Convention, but had been narrowed down in 1795 to five Directors; Napoleon continued the process by entrusting power to three Consuls. But, even when he made himself First Consul for Life, in 1802, and crowned himself in 1804, he stressed that he was still linked to the Revolution, claiming that 'The government of the Republic is confided to an Emperor'.[4] He was also careful to maintain the appearance of democracy by means of a wide franchise, even if he did elaborate and refine the Directory's formula for making democracy indirect by means of a multiple list system which operated in elections for the legislature.

Napoleon also introduced features which would be more commonly associated with the *ancien régime* and the era of enlightened despotism. He was careful, for example, to avoid any explicit statement of ideology in his constitutions; hence there was no reference to the *liberté, égalité, fraternité* of the Revolution. Like Catherine the Great and Frederick the Great, he considered that a declaration of rights would merely hamstring the authority of the executive. Also, he had a pragmatic approach to constitutional reform which allowed him to use eighteenth-century devices, and hence to blend the Revolution with Bourbon France and Frederician Prussia. Hence he introduced a senate, adapted the old *conseil d'état* and, in local government, resurrected the *intendant* in the form of the prefect and sub-prefect. Above all, he succeeded in combining the power base which he had inherited from the Revolution with the traditional authority of royalty. Like Louis XIV, he was upheld by the concept of Divine Right. An extract from a catechism used by the French Church after 1804 reads: 'God has established him as our sovereign and has made him the minister of His power and His image on earth'.[5] He also adopted, in 1807, the title *le Grand*, thus following the example previously set by eighteenth-century rulers like Peter I, Frederick II and Catherine II.

The title 'Emperor' was not entirely a throwback to the *ancien régime*. It had certain connotations which sound familiar to the twentieth century as well. Napoleon's military success enabled him to maintain a dictatorship based cn massive popular support but

The Reforms of Napoleon I

stripped of the party politics which characterize parliamentary democracies. Refusing to be 'a man of a party', he aimed to depoliticize the régime by destroying 'the spirit of faction' which was 'hurling the nation into an abyss'. Mussolini later developed this approach, claiming that he was cutting the 'Gordian knot' which 'enmeshed' Italian politics, and that he was the focal point for his country's 'most vital forces'. Like Mussolini, Napoleon strengthened his position through the most effective use of the personality cult that Europe had yet seen. He manipulated public opinion by publishing only favourable material and by extensive use of what Hitler later called 'the Big Lie'. Confident in the image created by a carefully controlled press and by the paintings of David and Géricault, Napoleon was able to appeal directly to the people for their support. To do this he used a device which became particularly popular in the Second Empire (1852–70); the plebiscite. This proved a very effective means of seeking popular support for specific issues rather than for a wider range of policies. In 1804, for example, the establishment of the Empire was approved by a vote of 3.57 million to only 2569. As a result, Napoleon made the claim of the type much used by future dictators: 'I did not usurp the crown; I found it in the gutter and the French people put it on my head.'

*

Napoleon openly acknowledged the influence of the Revolution on his economic policies. He intensified the Directory's efforts to bring the *départements* under more effective financial supervision by the central government and maintained the *agence des contributions directes*, set up by the Directory to assess taxes throughout France. He extended this principle of centralization by insisting on the appointment of tax collectors by the Paris administration rather than by the *départements*. To reduce the incidence of tax evasion, he undertook a nationwide survey of capital assets and property, a scheme which had been proposed by the National Convention in 1793 but subsequently shelved. The currency was re-established on a metallic base, along the lines put forward in 1797 by the Directory, and credit was given a more systematic outlet in the Bank of France (1800), again an institution envisaged between 1795 and 1799. The reformed currency was valued in accordance with the decimal system, which had been introduced during the Terror but only sporadically enforced before 1799. Napoleon also promoted and encouraged industry by means of fairs and exhibitions, a practice initiated by the Directory. In general, he made full use of the more constructive policies of the Revolution to ensure that there would be no return to the economic chaos and financial maladministration of the Bourbon era.

In some respects, however, Napoleon's economic thinking was more in tune with eighteenth-century ideas. Although he was popular with the bourgeoisie and relied upon their support, he remained unconverted to the middle-class creed of *laissez-faire* and, like the enlightened despots, preferred the system of mercantilism, with its scope for government intervention. He also retained the eighteenth-century notion that agriculture, rather than industry, was the base of the economy: 'Agriculture is the soul, the foundation of the kingdom; industry ministers to the comfort and happiness of the population. Foreign trade is the superabundance.'[6] Furthermore, the basic principles of his Commercial Code (1808) are reminiscent of the Commercial Ordinance (1673) and the Marine Ordinance (1681) of Colbert. Napoleon also restored some of the financial institutions of the *ancien régime*: the chambers of commerce, suspended in 1791, were reinstated; by 1803 there were twenty-two of these, one allocated to each *département*, to assist in the formulation of policy. Perhaps the most obvious return to the practices of the *ancien régime*, however, was Napoleon's preference for indirect taxation at the expense of direct. He established an Excise Bureau in 1804 and subsequently imposed heavy duties on beer, alcohol, wine and salt. By 1810 he had reversed the Revolution's emphasis on direct taxes and had, apparently, adopted a series of measures similar to those of eighteenth-century Prussia.

Napoleon's dictatorial powers depended, as we have seen, on his military success and personal prestige. This meant that he had to focus his economic policies on providing for a massive war machine which could guarantee his supremacy in Europe. He established several particularly important precedents for the future. The first was the Grand Empire, an economic entity which would feed the French system with tribute and recruits. The second was the Continental System, established by the Berlin and Milan Decrees (1806 and 1807) to seal Europe off from British commerce. These ideas later influenced the ambitious plan, drawn up by Chancellor Bethmann Hollweg during the First World War, for German domination of the whole continent. Hollweg hoped to create a

The Reforms of Napoleon I

Greater Germany through the annexation of neighbouring states, and also an extensive trade area and customs union which would exclude Britain and thereby destroy her commercial base. Thirdly, Napoleon established over industry tighter controls than had ever been achieved before. Mussolini was eventually to take these to their logical conclusion in his 'Corporate State'.

*

The Revolution had made substantial changes to the social structure. These, by and large, Napoleon retained. The power of the bourgeoisie, always latent during the *ancien régime*, was released by a revolution which, according to A. Soboul, established the general principles of bourgeois society and the liberal state.[7] Napoleon continued to elicit the support of the bourgeoisie, who saw in the Consulate an improved and more stable version of the Directory. The peasantry also found Napoleon willing to maintain some of the major achievements of the Revolution like the destruction of feudalism and the sale of Church lands; they were therefore content to support a régime which confirmed their possession of small-holdings. The urban workers were less fortunate; Napoleon expressed little concern about harsh working conditions and frequently legislated in favour of employers. But this was not necessarily out of step with the Revolution; his policy was entirely consistent with, for example, the Chapelier laws of June 1791 which had banned combination and strikes. Besides, the revolutionary leaders had always opposed the more radical elements of the working class, as was shown by the summary treatment of Babeuf and his followers.

The Revolution had also outlined a policy and structure for education and a legal code, but had been too preoccupied with the struggle for survival to carry them through. The National Convention had divided the educational structure into primary, secondary and higher levels. These were confirmed by Napoleon and integrated into the Imperial University after 1808. The Constituent Assembly had, in 1791, resolved to draw up 'A code of civil laws common to the whole kingdom'.[8] The legislation which followed was incomplete, but provided the basic outline for Napoleon's reforms, particularly in the areas of marriage, divorce, property and inheritance. According to J. Godechot, B. Hyslop and D. Dowd,

Aspects of European History 1789–1980

Napoleon's Civil Code 'expressed the great social upheavals of the Revolution and consolidated its great conquests'.[9]

Napoleon was, however, prepared to return to some of the practices of the *ancien régime*, particularly in his re-creation of a French nobility. The *noblesse* had been abolished as a class in June 1790, and even the Directory had introduced laws removing any remaining nobles from administrative posts. From the foundation of the Empire in 1804, Napoleon moved towards the re-establishment of a social élite. He began to confer hereditary fiefs in 1806 and, in 1808, created a new hereditary aristocracy comprising, in descending order, princes, dukes, counts, barons and knights. To some extent, this was a compromise: it retained the career open to talent which had been made possible by the Revolution while, at the same time, reverting to the enlightened despots' emphasis on 'service nobility'. It could also be argued that Napoleon restored the upward mobility between the bourgeoisie and the *noblesse* which had existed during the reign of Louis XIV but ended in the eighteenth century.

There was also compromise over the legal codes and religion. The Civil Code, for example, stressed equality before the law, but also restored, in almost tyrannical form, the authority of the head of the family. There was also a partial return to eighteenth-century property law. The Revolution had banned primogeniture, intending that a will should benefit all children equally. The Civil Code retained this ban but, as a concession, allowed the testator to dispose of 25 per cent of his property as he wished. Napoleon's attitude to women marked a complete departure from the liberalizing tendencies of the Revolution; he insisted on a complete return to Roman Law, and the subjection of wives to their husbands. He also took a backward step with the Code of Criminal Procedure (1808) which virtually revived the notorious *lettres de cachet* of the *ancien régime*, and the Penal Code (1810) which reintroduced branding.

Napoleon's attitude to religion was very similar to that of the enlightened despots. He considered it useful as a social cement, but wished to avoid the dangers of religious controversy. Hence 'I don't see in religion the mystery of the incarnation, but the mystery of the social order'.[5] Concerned with upholding the hierarchy which he had established, Napoleon reasoned: 'Society cannot exist without inequality of fortunes, and inequality of fortunes cannot exist without religion. When a man is dying of hunger alongside another

24

who stuffs himself, it is impossible to make him accede to the difference unless there is an authority which says to him, "God wishes it thus" '.[5] Since religion fulfilled a social function, it had to be carefully directed, which meant that it 'must be in the hands of the government'.[10] The Concordat, formed with the Pope in 1801, ensured government control over the appointment of clergy and minimized papal interference in France. In this respect it also represented the final triumph of Gallicanism in its prolonged conflict, during the seventeenth and eighteenth centuries, with Ultramontanism.

Napoleon's own contribution to the French social structure was a more conscious and deliberate moulding of society than had ever been attempted before. He tried to create a pyramid, a hierarchy of classes, each bound by its own interests to the régime, and each aware of its place. The authority of the emperor would permeate all levels by means of the administrative reorganization and the legal changes, while the people would be committed to the régime emotionally through effective propaganda and military success. The secret police, under the efficient direction of Fouché, could be relied upon to eliminate opposition and discourage dissension. Indeed, this was to be a particularly important precedent. As M. Latey writes, 'the absolute monarchs, who re-established themselves after his fall, learned from Napoleon's techniques and in doing so helped to lay the groundwork of modern totalitarian rule' [11]

*

Napoleon's achievements represent a synthesis of ideas and influences so complex that they are bound to attract an enormous range of historical interpretation. At one extreme, Napoleon appeared as a manifestation of Revolution, especially in those parts of Europe which had not previously been affected by revolutionary upheaval. At the other, the Napoleonic Empire was seen as a perversion of the revolutionary ideal; Trotsky, for example, later used Bonapartism as a term of abuse to describe the capture of a revolution by military reactionaries.

The Napoleonic era was also bound to throw up contradictions. The most important of these was the struggle of the heir to the Revolution, a monarch who had literally made himself, to coexist with rulers whose powers and prerogatives extended far back into the *ancien régime*. This theme will be explored in the next chapter.

4

The Fall of Napoleon I

While in exile on St. Helena, Napoleon composed a memorandum which illuminated his main policies as Emperor between 1804 and 1815. One was 'to reconcile the old France and the new', another 'to reconcile France with Europe'.[1] The implications of the first are dealt with in Chapter 3; this chapter, in examining the reasons for the fall of his régime, explores the meaning of the second.

Throughout his reign Napoleon remained an outcast in Europe. Other rulers declined to accept him as a dynastic equal. The European peoples, whether the middle classes of Italy and Germany, or the peasants of Spain and Russia, came to fear him as a tyrant worse than any lumbering out of the *ancien régime*. Above all, he was despised by Britain and, in his attempts to overcome British opposition, he resorted to devices which eventually unleashed the accumulated resentment of an entire continent.

This resentment was given increasingly effective military expression. Although he possessed clear initial advantages over the rest of Europe, Napoleon gradually lost the initiative as Britain and the powers of the European *anciens régimes* adjusted to the French methods of conscription, learned how to deal with Napoleon's strategy, or took advantage of a series of blunders caused by over-confidence and arrogance.

*

The ruling classes of Europe detested Napoleon because he was a product of the France of the 1790s. Metternich, for example, referred

26

The Fall of Napoleon I

to him as 'the Revolution incarnate'[2] and told Napoleon in 1813 that, between Europe and the latter's aims 'there is an absolute contradiction'.[3] Anna Pavlovna, sister of Tsar Alexander I, spoke of the 'hydra of revolution' and 'this murderer and villain',[4] while Queen Louisa, wife of Frederick William III of Prussia, scorned Napoleon as 'the scum from Hell'.[4]

Napoleon was certainly conscious of his humble origins and the absence of aristocratic pedigree in his genealogy. He was intensely irritated by descriptions like 'the Corsican', 'the usurper' and – the ultimate of insults – the title given to him by the King of Sweden: 'Monsieur Napoleon Bonaparte'. One solution was to establish his own dynasty, and to claim indirect connection with the Bourbons; hence he referred to Louis XIV, curiously, as *mon oncle*, while denying that he was really 'the successor to Robespierre'. Another was to cultivate the Napoleonic Legend, emphasizing the twin virtues of glory and success and disregarding the taunts of the old Europe. In his relations with other states, therefore, he sought to gain permanent acceptance through military victory and a position of diplomatic strength.

There emerged, however, a fundamental contradiction in his attitude to the other European rulers which meant that he and they were ultimately irreconcilable.

On the one hand, it seems that Napoleon did have a genuine desire for acceptance; after meeting the Tsar at Tilsit in 1807 he wrote: 'I like Alexander and he ought to like me'.[5] He also sought permanent links with European royalty to provide a sanction for his power which would transcend mere military conquest. On being refused the Tsar's sister, he married Marie-Louise, daughter of the Emperor Francis of Austria in 1809. The latter regarded this as a 'Sacrifice' necessary to placate Napoleon after the recent French victories in the Austrian War of 1810. Several French marshals, particularly Murat, criticized the marriage on the grounds that Napoleon was betraying the heritage of the Revolution. 'When France raised you to the throne, it believed it had found in you a popular chief, with a title that put you above all the sovereigns of Europe . . . But today you are doing homage to claims of sovereignty which are not yours and which are opposed to your own.' Napoleon remained unmoved. 'You don't like this marriage? I do. I regard it as a great success on a level with the victory of Austerlitz.'[6] He hoped, moreover, that full acceptance by European royalty would follow the birth of his son who was, after all, half Habsburg. He had already taken care to extend the range of his dynasty by installing members of the Bonaparte family on thrones within the Grand Empire; these included Holland, Westphalia, Spain and Naples. 'I am,' he said 'creating a family of kings, or rather of vice-kings.'[7] He also introduced all the outward trappings of kingship, believing that 'sovereigns must always be on show'.[1] Accordingly, on 25 May 1812, he presided over an elaborate ceremony in Dresden in which all his vassal princes, the King of Prussia and the Emperor of Austria, participated. This type of gathering, of which Dresden was the last and the greatest, seemed to imply that Napoleon had gained the recognition which he had sought. Could he keep this permanently?

He never had the opportunity to find out, for another and more destructive element intruded into his diplomacy.

Although he sought acceptance, Napoleon was not prepared to confer partnership. Because he put so much trust in military conquest he never learned how to draw up lasting diplomatic settlements and he frequently had to use further force to overcome resistance to his treaties. He failed to realize that if conquest were to be permanently effective, it must be followed by reconciliation, necessitating concessions by the victor as well as the vanquished. This was later understood by Bismarck and was a course urged upon Napoleon by the astute Talleyrand. In dealing with his three major continental rivals, however, Napoleon drew up a succession of unbalanced settlements which created only resentment, and therefore the incentive for future revolt against him.

He had to subdue Austria five times. The first two wars were a continuation of the struggle between Austria and Revolutionary France, but the other three were the product of insupportable treaties. The Treaty of Lunéville (1801) was forced upon Austria by an extended military campaign to hurry along negotiations. The Emperor Francis' efforts to reverse this in 1805 resulted in military defeat and the still heavier Treaty of Pressburg, by which Austria ceded all her Italian lands to France, and substantial German possessions to Napoleon's satellite states – Bavaria, Baden and Württemberg. Talleyrand urged caution and clemency and his warning was vindicated by another Austrian revolt in 1809. The Treaty of Schonbrünn extracted further territory from Austria, including Illyria and Galicia, and imposed a war indemnity. According to Francis, these terms were 'fatal to the existence of

The Fall of Napoleon I

Austria'.[6] Furthermore, 'From the day when peace is signed we must confine our system to tacking and turning and flattering. Thus alone may we possibly preserve our existence, till the day of general deliverence.'[8] The King of Prussia had even greater grievances Despite his admiration for Frederick the Great (1740–86), Napoleon considered that Prussia was not rightfully one of Europe's major powers, especially since she had grown effete under Frederick William II and Frederick William III. His victory over Prussia in 1806 was followed, in the Treaty of Tilsit (1807), by exceptionally severe terms. Prussia lost half her territory, her western provinces being given to the Kingdom of Westphalia and her Polish lands to the Grand Duchy of Warsaw; her army was limited to an insignificant 42,000 men, and an indemnity was imposed. The King of Prussia played no actual part in the settlement as Napoleon considered that his presence at Tilsit would be superfluous. Even Russia, the power for which Napoleon had most respect, claimed grounds for resentment. The Treaty of Tilsit, negotiated between Alexander I and Napoleon, was intended to divide Europe into two main spheres of influence, confirming French dominance over Western and Central Europe, and give Russian interests an outlet in the East. Between 1807 and 1812, however, Napoleon removed the basis of genuine partnership by refusing to countenance Russian claims to Constantinople. Alexander also reacted with intense hostility to Napoleon's efforts to make Russia adhere to the continental blockade against Britain, and rapidly came to the conclusion that the Tilsit agreement was 'ignominious'.[9]

All this resentment was fully appreciated by Talleyrand, who now began to negotiate secretly with Napoleon's enemies; in 1808, for example, he urged the Tsar to make haste to save Europe from Napoleon. Before 1812, however, Austria and Prussia remained, for the time being, submissive. Then Russian success in the war of 1812 brought about yet another Coalition in 1813, which eventually defeated Napoleon at Leipzig. The powers were, by this time, prepared to overlook the very substantial differences between themselves in their efforts to overthrow the settlements which Napoleon had imposed upon them.

Napoleon's disillusionment became evident in 1814. He had always known that 'between old monarchies and a young republic hostility must always exist'.[10] He had therefore transformed the republic into a monarchy, only to find that this was even more unacceptable. To Napoleon the rulers of Europe had, by 1813, become the revolutionaries. Hence he complained: 'I have behaved to the kings as a sovereign; they have behaved to me like Jacobins'.[3]

Napoleon became no less intensely disliked by the European peoples. He should have possessed some basis of popular appeal as, after all, he claimed that monarchy must be justified by *'l'intérêt des peuples'*.[11] Despite his dynastic interests he did continue the work of the Revolution by reforming institutions throughout the Grand Empire. His positive achievements included the abolition of serfdom where it still existed in Germany and Italy, and the introduction of the Civil Code, which had already been applied in France. At the same time, however, he strongly resisted any move towards 'popular sovereignty',[12] which he associated with the 'principle of rebellion'. He therefore came to be regarded as the heir to enlightened despotism quite as much as the product of the Revolution and, as the war spread after 1808, he came to be seen as a tyrant. Popular movements arose in Spain, where peasants actually co-operated with the nobility against Joseph Bonaparte. The latter said despairingly: 'I haven't a single supporter here.'[13] Napoleon failed to improve the lot of the peasantry in Eastern Europe. Kosciuszko, the leader of the Polish revolt against foreign domination in the early 1790s, complained, 'He thinks of nothing but himself'.[14] Napoleon actually turned his back on the prospect of liberating the Russian serfs, and he condemned 'the brutal nature of this large class of Russian people'.[9] The serfs' opposition to the French was one of the key factors in the failure of Napoleon's 1812 invasion, bringing with it the unexpected and irresistible element of guerrilla warfare. Popular discontent was also widespread in Germany and Italy, where the rigours of the continental blockade alienated the large middle class, and the numerous levies led to growing opposition from men who objected, in the words of an Italian poet, to being 'killed by the enemies of another people'.[15] The sentiment of German and Italian nationalism stirred in opposition to French rule. It is easy to exaggerate the impact of this nationalism, for Napoleon was eventually brought down by kings, not peoples. But the peoples did contribute to the campaigns of 1812 and 1813 and seemed to give some credibility to the kings' claims to be liberating Europe.

The most formidable and consistent of Napoleon's enemies was Britain, the only power to maintain the struggle without compromise between 1803 and 1814. Bonapartism was even more

The Fall of Napoleon I

abhorrent to the English establishment than to the absolute monarchs on the Continent. It seemed to represent the worst threat imaginable to the evolutionary course of British constitutional development so tenaciously upheld in the speeches and writings of Edmund Burke. Few statesmen acknowledged the need for any reform or change in Britain, most agreeing with Lord Braxfield that 'the British constitution is the best that ever was since the beginning of the world, and it is not possible to make it better'.[16] To British leaders like Pitt, Napoleon was the inevitable result of the upheaval of the 1790s, a combination of Terror and Tyranny. Britain could coexist with the absolutism of the *ancien régime*, but not with military absolutism born of revolution.

Napoleon faced enormous difficulties in trying to wear Britain down. He was fully aware of British naval power and relied initially on the invasion scheme of 1803–04. This prospect, however, was destroyed at the Battle of Trafalgar (1805) and the disparity in the naval resources of the two countries grew steadily wider. By 1813, for example, France possessed only seventy-one ships of the line (most of them blockaded in port) to Britain's 235. The implications of this were enormous. Britain maintained and increased her normal commercial links with other continents and was able to land and supply expeditionary forces under Wellington in the Iberian Peninsula.

Eventually, Napoleon had to resort to desperate measures but, in the process, he precipitated more intense opposition from all parts of the Continent. Britain's life-blood was her trade and, in Caulaincourt's words, 'since their trade had ramifications everywhere, he had to pursue them everywhere'.[17] The purpose of the Berlin Decree (1806) and the Milan Decree (1807) was to close the European Continent to British exports; the result would be a crisis of overproduction in Britain, followed by unemployment and rampant inflation. At times the Continental System seemed to come close to success. 1808 and 1811 saw a significant drop in the value of British exports (from £48.8 millions in 1810, to £32.4 millions in 1811). Eventually, however, Napoleon had to admit failure. Two factors were responsible for this: the first was the resilience of British traders, who sought and obtained new outlets in South America and managed, from wartime distribution centres like Heligoland and Malta, to keep illicit commercial contacts with Prussia, Holland, Spain, Naples and other states subject to Napoleon. The second was

31

the inconsistency of Napoleon himself. He seemed to alternate between harsh application of the System, which undoubtedly caused difficulties in Britain, and the granting of special concessions. After 1807, for example, he occupied most of Europe in order to enforce the System. Yet, in 1811, he adopted a more moderate policy. In a year which brought for Britain a chronic shortage of grain and the most unfavourable trade figures of the entire war, he allowed selected imports from Britain on licence, together with the export of grain supplies from France. Napoleon's reasoning was understandable. French commercial interests were also suffering and the selective re-establishment of contacts with Britain would bring relief to French traders and farmers. Hence, 'undoubtedly we must harm our foes, but above all we must live'.[18]

The Continental System had a devastating effect on Napoleon's power and reputation in Europe. In enforcing the blockade, Napoleon over-extended the borders of his influence. The occupation of Spain in 1808 to compel the Iberian Peninsula to close its ports to Britain was a serious mistake: it created, in the Peninsular War, a constant drain on French resources. 'Those devilish Spanish affairs',[19] compounded as they were by guerrilla warfare and the first signs of British military success, kept several hundred thousand troops occupied. These were increasingly needed elsewhere in Europe, for Alexander began to express dissatisfaction with the Tilsit settlement by flouting Napoleon's Continental System. This form of pressure incensed Napoleon to the point of open war with Russia in 1812 – a catastrophic blunder which encouraged other monarchs to rise against him in 1813.

*

Napoleon's military measures against the continental powers at first met with considerable success. The nature of warfare had already been radically altered by the French Revolution, which gave Napoleon an immediate advantage over his rivals. The size of his armies, for example, owed much to Carnot's *levée en masse* (1793), which had produced some 750,000 troops by 1794. This had been modified by Jourdan's Law of 1798 and was finally codified by Napoleon in 1811. Between 1800 and 1812, it has been estimated, 1,100,000 soldiers were mobilized for the Grand Army, or two million between 1800 and 1815. The resulting armies were massive when compared with any raised in the eighteenth century; whereas

The Fall of Napoleon I

Frederick the Great had commanded about 40,000 men at Leuthen (1757) and Kunersdorf (1759), Napoleon led some 190,000 in his Ulm and Jena campaigns. Eventually, however, Napoleon was confronted by two overwhelming problems. One was the growth of mammoth armies in other continental countries, despite the restrictions imposed by the Treaties of Tilsit and Schönbrunn. By 1813, for example, Prussia had introduced conscription for all men between seventeen and forty, mobilizing a total of 300,000 men, while Austria and Russia had the capacity to exceed this figure. The other problem was the resentment caused by Napoleon's conscription of foreigners into the French army, particularly from the vassal states of the Grand Empire. By 1814 only 40 per cent of Napoleon's army consisted of Frenchmen, the rest being drawn from Italy, Germany, Poland and Spain. The result was that the French army became more disunited and less homogeneous at the very time that it was being outnumbered by the forces of the Allies. At the Battle of Leipzig (1813) Russia, Prussia and Austria overwhelmed Napoleon with the colossal figure of 365,000 against 195,000. In 1815, the Allies were able to muster over 600,000 troops for the invasion of France herself. As the Grand Empire contracted, of course, the supply of recruits to the French army dwindled.

Larger armies had originally been introduced in the name of the people. By Carnot's *levée en masse*, for example, 'All Frenchmen are called by their country to defend liberty'.[20] The justification for size was necessarily ideological, and the combination of the two elements revived the practice of destructive warfare after a comparative lull between 1648 and 1792. Again, Napoleon had the early advantage. He took much of Europe by storm and, in his initial success, he came to regard war as a solution for all diplomatic problems, without the impediment of rules. War became virtually self-generating or, in Napoleon's own words, 'war must support war'.[21] France did not, however, retain the monopoly of total war, and there were two notable examples of its use by her enemies. The first was the Russian reaction to the invasion of 1812 – the so-called 'Great Patriotic War' – while the second was the great campaign of 1813. The Battle of Leipzig has been called 'the Battle of Nations'; this aptly describes the extent of European involvement in what was, in terms of numbers, the greatest single pitched battle in the history of mankind.

Napoleon's strategy at first inflicted a series of shocks on the continental powers. He emphasized the importance of forced marches and precisely timed manoeuvres on the battlefield. Everything depended on mobility. As Thiers put it: 'Our Emperor has found out a new way of making war; he no longer makes it with our arms but with our legs.'[22] In many ways he was continuing the policy of the Revolution that armies should be self-sufficient and unimpeded by the type of heavy baggage trains which had accompanied eighteenth-century armies. French troops were expected to supply themselves by foraging in enemy territory. This worked well in the Italian campaigns (1796–7 and 1800), as well as against Austria (1805) and Prussia (1806). The Peninsular War and the Russian Campaign, however, showed the defects of this policy. Despite careful preparations for the 1812 campaign, Napoleon's troops were held up by the dreadful state of Russian roads which slowed down the passage of essential equipment, and by the low standard of Russian agriculture which made foraging much more difficult. Napoleon therefore found himself under severe pressure, and had to seek military confrontation without his usual finesse. The result was the Battle of Borodino, a narrow victory for the French, marred by appalling losses. Worse was to come: the burning of Moscow and the constant harrying of the French army during its retreat. Another paradox emerged. Napoleon, for all his military genius, was entirely unable to comprehend guerrilla warfare, tuned as he was to decisive pitched battles in conditions of his own choosing. He could only, in his own words, 'make war offensively'.[17] What happened in Moscow shocked him profoundly. 'They themselves are setting it afire . . . The barbarians! What a terrible spectacle!'[23] The French performance against guerrillas in Spain was equally ineffectual. Soult and other marshals were also outmanoeuvred by Wellington, who solved the supply problem by using light carts and maintaining continuous contact with the British navy at the mouth of the Tagus. By 1813 the Allies had also learned how to deal with Napoleon's surprise attacks on the battlefield and worked on the principle of evading action until a decisive numerical superiority in the order of two to one could be brought to bear against the French.

Napoleon's battle tactics, in fact, showed the same vulnerability as his campaign strategy. During the late eighteenth century most powers made use of the *ordre mince* (the advance of extended lines), although there was some support for the *ordre profond* (a more

The Fall of Napoleon I

concentrated attack in columns). Napoleon succeeded in confusing the Austrians and Prussians by resorting to a highly effective combination of the two, carried out in such a way as to encourage the enemy to commit itself while, at the same time, concealing his own intentions. The subsequent confusion and the crushing pursuits ensured overwhelming French victories. But Napoleon's mastery of battle formations came to be matched by Wellington, who reintroduced the *ordre mince* in the form of disciplined lines and squares. One British observer, J. W. Croker, had already said of the French strategy, 'I think it is a false one against steady troops'.[24] This assessment was vindicated at the Battles of Vittoria (1813) and Waterloo (1815). Napoleon felt that the Allies had improved their battle tactics, but that he had made no corresponding progress. On St. Helena he remarked, 'I have fought sixty battles and I have learned nothing which I did not know in the beginning'.

Before Tilsit France's greatest military asset was the personal leadership of Napoleon. After Tilsit, however, this became an increasing liability. He succeeded initially because he dared do what others would have feared. He failed eventually because he lost all sense of caution, regarding impossibility as 'a word found only in the dictionary of fools'.[25] After Tilsit he seemed to believe his own officially sponsored legend and told his brother Lucien: 'I can do everything now.'[9] Certainly his ambition increased until, according to Alexander, it knew 'no bounds'. He continued to act on the assumption that military solutions were always attainable. Consequently, as his diplomatic problems increased, his military campaigns became ever more ambitious, stretching French resources to breaking point. His attitude during the Russian campaign is particularly revealing. After the Russian armies had begun to retreat, Napoleon insisted on moving towards Moscow, at whose gates, he was convinced, 'the conclusion of peace awaits me'.[26] His marshals thought otherwise and attempted, unsuccessfully, to dissuade him. Murat warned: 'Moscow will destroy us.' Reminded of the failure of Charles XII and the Swedish army in similar circumstances in 1709, Napoleon revealed an insight into his basic philosophy. 'It is not the rule that creates success, but success that creates the rule, and if I should achieve success by further marches, my new success will create new principles.'[26] Hitler made similar comments in 1941 when reminded of the fate of Napoleon.

Another shortcoming of Napoleon as a leader was his inability to delegate authority effectively. He never seriously considered training a successor and rarely attempted to impart the underlying principles of his military success to his marshals. Thus a huge gap opened between his own strategy and its tactical execution by his subordinates. One result was Ney's failure to turn the advantage created by Napoleon in the Battle of Bautzen into a decisive victory. Another was a series of French disasters in Spain as inexperienced marshals struggled to apply elusive and only partly known Napoleonic rules of warfare. It is ironical that one of the powers which eventually defeated Napoleon had itself been a victim of the same problem. Under Frederick the Great (1740–86) Prussia had been excessively centralized and had become totally dependent on the personality and policies of the king. Frederick's death in 1786 had thrown Prussia into chaos, making possible Napoleon's spectacular victory in 1806. But there then occurred a metamorphosis. Prussian revival was effected by collective leadership and planning, which was followed by deep suspicion for the next fifty years of anything resembling a personality cult. It was France who now became addicted to personal leadership, and even the defeats of 1814 and 1815 were not enough to destroy the Napoleonic Legend. The struggle between Prussia and France was renewed in 1870 and Bonapartism's real Waterloo was the Battle of Sedan.

5

The Concert of Europe 1815–48

The Concert of Europe is the term used to describe various attempts made by the major powers to co-operate, after 1815, in settling possible causes of conflict between themselves in order to prevent the possibility of another large-scale war. At first the European statesmen favoured a conciliar system; according to Article VI of the Quadruple Alliance (1815) 'the High Contracting Powers have agreed to renew at fixed intervals . . . meetings consecrated to great common objects and the examination of such measures as at each one of these epochs shall be judged most salutary for the peace and prosperity of the nations and for the maintenance of the peace of Europe.'[1] This provided the basis for the four further congresses which followed the Congress of Vienna itself, namely Aix-la-Chapelle (1818), Troppau (1820), Laibach (1821) and Verona (1822). By 1823, however, the attempt had broken down, and the idea of relating diplomacy to regular councils had to be abandoned.

A major reason for this was that a gap opened between Britain and the continental autocracies of Austria, Russia and Prussia, caused largely by different policies over the question of intervention against revolutionary movements. Britain's foreign secretaries, Castlereagh and Canning took their stand on a narrow and legalistic interpretation of the Quadruple Alliance, while the absolutist powers held to the Troppau Protocol of 1820 which was, in essence, a reinterpretation of the Holy Alliance of 1815. This conflict ended the possibility of a general conciliar system consisting of both constitutional and autocratic powers. It does not, however, explain why the autocratic powers failed to substitute a regular system of their own, either before or after 1823. The reason for this is twofold. On the one hand, the absolute monarchies had their own rivalries which prevented concerted action at several crucial stages. On the other, there was considerable diplomatic accord between Britain and each of these monarchies at different times and on specific issues. There existed, therefore, no real motive for permanent and concerted opposition to Britain from Russia, Prussia and Austria.

The 1830 revolutions helped inject more unity into the absolutist powers, while there was also some ideological sympathy between Britain and France. But the period between 1830 and 1853 saw much the same general trend as that between 1815 and 1830: ideological formations continued to be undermined by individual interests. After 1830, therefore, no attempt was made to revive conciliarism as a regular device, although concert was still possible over specific issues and at specially convened conferences.

*

The fundamental division in the 'Congress System' had become apparent by 1820; Britain had become increasingly cut off from Russia, Austria and Prussia, while France had contacts with both sides of the divide. The major issue was undoubtedly the use to which the System was to be put in dealing with constitutional movements and revolutions in the various sensitive areas of Europe. This preoccupation was inevitable, partly because all statesmen feared that the French Revolution was still a powerful influence, and partly because the 1815 Vienna Settlement had failed to satisfy widespread aspirations of nationalism and constitutionalism. Metternich, in particular, regarded revolution as a 'terrible social catastrophe' and believed that 'only order produces equilibrium'.[2] Such a balance could be maintained only by the most careful vigilance. Hence, he observed in 1817, 'You see in me the chief Minister of Police in Europe. I keep my eye on everything. My contacts are such that nothing escapes me.'[3] In his *Profession of Political Faith* (1820), Metternich argued that all monarchs should be prepared to take common action. At the Congress of Troppau he was able to make common cause with Alexander I of Russia who, repenting of his earlier liberal views, was now talking of radicalism as 'satanic genius', progressing by 'occult methods' to establish a 'reign of evil'.[4] The Prussian position was less obvious, but Frederick

The Concert of Europe 1815–48

William III had nothing to gain by holding out against the policies of Metternich and Alexander. The overall result, therefore, was the conversion of Alexander's Holy Alliance (1815) with its nebulous and idealistic principles, into the Troppau Protocol of 1820. The latter specifically allowed for the intervention of the major powers in the internal affairs of any state undergoing a constitutional change not sponsored by its ruler.

The British government remained constantly suspicious of this interpretation of the role of the congresses. Castlereagh expressed his contempt for the Tsar's ideal of a mystical union and tried, without success, to get him and his ministers 'to descend from their abstractions'.[5] Profoundly suspicious of the Holy Alliance, Castlereagh took his stand on the Quadruple Alliance (1815), giving it a limited and juridical emphasis by insisting that the only valid purpose of congress diplomacy was to uphold treaty obligations between the powers, and thereby prevent unilateral action by any state to change agreed boundaries. Intervention for any other reason would be a perversion of the Quadruple Alliance. In fact, 'nothing would be more immoral or more prejudicial to the character of government generally than the idea that their force was collectively to be prostituted to the support of established power, without any consideration of the extent to which it was abused'.[6] This argument was used by Lord Stewart, sent to the Congress of Troppau as an observer rather than as a plenipotentiary, to condemn the 1820 Protocol. Stewart added that the policy propounded by the continental powers was 'destructive of all correct notions of internal sovereign authority'.[5] After Castlereagh's death in 1822 and his replacement as Foreign Secretary by Canning, the gap between Britain and the continental autocracies widened. Canning reaffirmed Castlereagh's hostility to collective intervention in equally categorical terms: 'England is under no obligation to interfere, or assist in interfering, in the internal affairs of independent states.' But, whereas Castlereagh had merely distanced Britain from the policies of the continental powers, Canning was entirely happy to break the System altogether by recognizing the new republics in Latin America, and refusing to consider any scheme by which Spanish colonial rule might be restored. He must have had in mind the imminent collapse of congress diplomacy when he justified his American policy with the famous words: 'I called the New World into existence to redress the balance of the Old.'[7]

Aspects of European History 1789–1980

*

The collapse of the Congress System was followed by neither a purely continental conciliar movement, nor by the return to the diplomatic free-for-all of the eighteenth century. The reason was the extraordinary complexity of international diplomacy after 1815, producing unexpected cross currents of rivalry and co-operation. This process can be illustrated by a brief examination of the relations before 1827 between Austria and Russia, Britain and Austria, Britain and Russia, and Britain and France.

For two powers with similar interests in preventing revolution, Austria and Russia had a surprisingly stormy relationship. This was caused, in part, by Metternich's deep suspicion of Alexander's liberal pretensions between 1813 and 1818. Suspicion turned to alarm when Alexander spoke of the 'absurd pretensions of absolute power'.[8] Eventually, Metternich succeeded in restoring Alexander to autocratic principles, aided by the Tsar's revulsion against the assassination of Kotzebue in Germany (1819), the Riego Revolt in Spain (1820), the murder of the duc de Berri in France (1820) and the revolt of the Semyonovski Regiment in St. Petersburg. In October 1820, Alexander renounced his progressive views and confessed to Metternich: 'You have correctly judged the state of affairs. I deplore the waste of time, which we must try to regain.'[8] Metternich said with considerable relief: 'If ever anyone turned from black to white, he has.'[9] Alexander's conversion brought the two countries closer together ideologically at the very time that British policy was at its most obstructive, but it did not eliminate Austro-Russian rivalries altogether. Alexander had always pressed for a more sweeping view than Metternich's of the role of the Congress System and now wanted joint action to suppress the revolutions in Spain and Naples. Metternich, on the other hand, feared the prospect of Europe being inundated with Russian troops and preferred punitive action to be taken unilaterally by the major power most affected. The Greek revolt posed an even more difficult problem, as Alexander had a natural sympathy towards the Balkan Christians which went against Metternich's principle of upholding all authority, including Turkish. Between 1822 and 1825 Metternich succeeded in restraining Russian policy, but the death of Alexander in 1825 meant that this task became more difficult. Nicholas I, anxious to rescue Russia from Austrian tutelage, prepared for measures against

40

Turkey which Metternich considered thoroughly dangerous. The disagreements between the two countries between 1825 and 1830 therefore go a long way towards explaining the absence of any Austro-Russian conciliar system to replace the broader pattern of Congresses.

In theory, it would be difficult to conceive two more contrasting powers than Britain and Austria. Yet several points of limited contact between them did exist. Castlereagh, for example, considered the existence of a strong power in Central Europe essential to restrain France and Russia; in his view the Habsburg Empire was 'the great hinge upon which the fate of Europe must ultimately depend'.[10] Metternich, in turn, greatly respected Castlereagh's emphasis on the 'balance of power' of European states as being the most effective means of preventing the outbreak of future wars. Britain and Austria did, in fact, co operate in 1815 to try to dissuade Russia from annexing Poland and Prussia from claiming Saxony. Furthermore, Castlereagh did not object to all cases of intervention against revolution. He disliked the extent of Metternich's conservatism and opposed the Troppau Protocol, but was also prepared to concede that Austrian intervention in Naples (1821) had a juridical basis, since the Neapolitan revolt destroyed a treaty previously drawn up with the Habsburgs. What really separated Castlereagh from Metternich was the latter's temporary reconciliation with Alexander, and the adoption of a more united ideological stance by the autocratic powers. Even so, there was always the prospect of further contact until Castlereagh's death in 1822. The latter was a disaster for Metternich, since Canning was in no way prepared to compromise with Austria. Metternich's views of the new Foreign Secretary were unequivocal: 'He knocked down and undermined a great deal, but finished nothing.' His views were occasioned partly by Canning's open contempt for the Austrian Chancellor and partly by the more openly opportunist base of British foreign policy which prompted Canning's remark: 'Each country for itself and God for us all.'[4] Yet even Canning did not destroy Britain's links with Austria. Palmerston, although in many aspects of foreign policy a pupil of Canning, was later to revive Castlereagh's concept of the Austrian bulwark against Russia.

The rivalry between Britain and Russia was the deepest and most consistent of all, as might be expected from the world's greatest naval power and the Continent's strongest military state. There was intense mutual mistrust over the operation of the Congress System, and considerable resentment over Castlereagh's contacts with Metternich. Alexander, indeed, tried to create his own balance of power by encouraging the revival of French and Spanish maritime strength to 'group' Britain on the world scene, just as Castlereagh had 'grouped' Russia in Europe. But even Anglo-Russian relations went through more positive periods of co-operation. The accession of Nicholas I in 1825 saw a simultaneous *rapprochement* between Britain and Russia, and alienation between Russia and Austria. In 1826, Canning secured from the Tsar a Protocol which provided the basis of agreed Anglo-Russian action in support of the liberation of Greece from Turkey. The Treaty of London followed in 1827, together with the destruction of the Turkish fleet by Britain, Russia and France at Navarino. The period 1825–7 showed a definite, if temporary, withdrawal from what must have appeared to be entrenched positions on foreign policy. As a result, Russia would have had little motive to construct a rival system of councils with Britain as the target, even assuming that she could have attained the necessary agreement with Austria.

It seemed, in 1820, that Britain and France had much in common. Neither approved of the proposals for intervention and neither sent official representatives to the Congress of Troppau. Could not the two constitutional monarchies of Europe have attempted to establish their own device for regular meetings? Apparently not, for other issues cut across any possibility of close co-operation. France aimed at re-establishing the Bourbon *Pact Famille* with Spain as a prelude to becoming a world power. Naturally, this caused apprehension in the British cabinet, since it might revive the great Anglo-French conflicts of the eighteenth century. Furthermore, Canning was deeply suspicious of French intrigues in the newly independent states of Latin America, one of which was an attempt to instal a Bourbon nominee as King of Buenos Aires in 1820. France, in turn, suspected Britain of trying to monopolize trade with the new republics. French intervention against the Spanish revolutionaries in 1823, despite earlier pronouncements against such a policy, was yet another reason for British reluctance to see in France a permanent ally against Austria, Russia and Prussia.

*

The revolutions which occurred in many parts of Europe in 1830

The Concert of Europe 1815–48

stimulated a brief revival of ideological unity between Austria, Russia and Prussia. Nicholas I's immediate reaction to these was to prepare for an invasion of Central and Western Europe, until his attention was diverted by the Polish Revolt. Metternich considered 1830 a catastrophe, and the three East European monarchs felt impelled through common fears to revive the Holy Alliance and Troppau Protocol by a series of treaties in 1833. At Teplitz, for example, Metternich and Frederick William III agreed to take measures to combat liberalism in the German Confederation. The Münchengrätz Agreement was intended mainly to prevent Austro-Russian misunderstanding over the Eastern Question, but it had an important by-product – the Triple Declaration, which was signed in Berlin in October. This bound Russia, Prussia and Austria to assist any ruler who requested aid in overcoming revolutionary forces. The most successful application of this Treaty was the Russian invasion of Hungary in 1849, following Francis Joseph II's request for help against the Magyar uprising.

Britain, by contrast, sympathized with some of the aspirations of the revolutionaries. Palmerston, in fact, considered 'constitutional states' to be the 'natural allies of this country',[11] and he revived the traditional policy of 'non-interference by force of arms in the affairs of any other country'.[11] The overthrow of the Bourbon monarchy in 1830 gave France a vested interest in liberalism, so that Louis Philippe moved closer to the general principles of Palmerston. Anglo-French co-operation was evident over the Belgian issue (1830) and in the formation of the Quadruple Alliance with Spain and Portugal, in 1834. Metternich and Nicholas regarded these developments with foreboding, emphasizing that the Quadruple Alliance had been set up to counter the Treaties of Münchengrätz.

But once again individual rivalries prevented this ideological gap from becoming permanent. The main irritant during the 1830s was the Eastern Question. Metternich, for example, was always concerned about the prospect of further Russian expansion into Eastern and possibly Central Europe. Relations between Britain and France deteriorated rapidly when Louis Philippe supported the Egyptian Khedive, Mehemet Ali, against the Ottoman Sultan in 1839; this directly challenged British intentions of propping up Turkey as a barrier against Russian expansion into the Eastern Mediterranean. As a result, the Anglo-French understanding, brought about by the Quadruple Alliance, disintegrated into intense mutual suspicion.

Aspects of European History 1789–1980

The 1840s and 1850s saw further disagreements between supposedly friendly powers. Louis Philippe again annoyed Palmerston, this time over the Spanish marriages question (1846), while Austria and Prussia came close to war over Frederick William IV's proposal, in 1850, to establish the Erfurt Union between Prussia and the north German states. Even Russia's assistance to Austria in 1849 brought problems. There were open disagreements between the two armies as they campaigned in Hungary, while the new Austrian Chancellor, Schwarzenberg, was apprehensive about the concessions which he expected Russia to extract in return for her intervention. Indeed, he stated quite openly that 'Austria will surprise the world with her ingratitude'.[12]

Rivalries like these certainly prevented any further experimentation with a regular Congress System. At the same time, however, they gave diplomacy sufficient fluidity to allow for the settlement of the most contentious issues of the day by means of several *ad hoc* conferences in London. In 1830, for example, the three absolutist powers co-operated with Britain and France to secure the separation of Belgium from the Netherlands. Nicholas had little choice because of his preoccupation with the Polish Revolt, while Metternich probably hoped that agreement on Belgium would remove the possibility of Russian troops invading Western Europe. In 1841, Britain, Austria, Russia and Prussia put diplomatic pressure on Louis Philippe to abandon his support for Mehemet Ali, and this co-operation culminated in the Straits Convention, by which all the powers upheld the territorial integrity of the Ottoman Empire, and agreed that the Straits should be closed to warships of all nations. This treaty was among the major diplomatic achievements of the first half of the nineteenth century and gives substance to the view that the Concert of Europe survived long after the collapse of the Congress System.

6

Metternich and the Austrian Empire 1815–48

Clement von Metternich, Minister of Foreign Affairs (1809–48) and Austrian State Chancellor (1821–48), was the most significant conservative statesman in Europe during the period 1815–48. As well as dominating affairs within the Austrian Empire, he often dictated policies within the German Confederation and the Italian peninsula, and directly influenced the pattern of international relations through the medium of the Concert of Europe.

He was regarded, by admirers and opponents alike, as the major spokesman of the first half of the nineteenth century against all forms of revolution. An important theorist of the continental variety of conservatism, Metternich insisted that full monarchical powers should be retained. He returned frequently to his cardinal fear: that the proper restraints imposed on humanity by 'pure and eternal law' were being threatened by the growing presumptions of a dangerous minority who deliberately encouraged violent change rather than a well-ordered evolutionary social and political development. He also seems to have had reservations about man's ability to deal sensibly with technical progress. In his *Political Testament*, written in 1820, he affirmed that the range of human knowledge had widened considerably in recent centuries, but without a corresponding development in human wisdom. Innovations had, therefore, produced unsettling side-effects. Printing, for example, furthered the spread of false and seditious doctrines and ideologies, while the discovery of America had destroyed the traditional notion of landed property as the true source of value, and substituted a more volatile attitude to commercial wealth based on bullion. The ultimate human folly had been the French Revolution, a 'terrible social catastrophe'[1] and an inevitable result of unchecked human presumption.

Although influenced by several theorists of the eighteenth-century Enlightenment, Metternich was in no way an advocate of 'progress'. For him the cosmic principle was equilibrium, whether in politics, society or international relations. He had, after all, lived through an era when equilibrium had been dramatically overturned; he therefore placed particular emphasis after 1815 on order, for 'only order produces equilibrium'.[2] In a time of crisis 'it is above all necessary that something, no matter what, remain steadfast, so that the lost can find a connection and the strayed a refuge'.[3] Despite the restoration settlements of 1815, the danger of revolution in Europe was still considerable. The new menace emanated from liberalism, especially from demands for constitutions and for the recognition of basic rights. He warned of the peril facing any rulers who compromised in any way with such demands by providing written guarantees. *'Parlez d'un contrat social, et la révolution est faite.'*[4] What was most needed was action by monarchs to reimpose equilibrium – internally by responsible policies, and externally by joint action on the basis of treaties like the Troppau Protocol (1820) and the Münchengrätz Agreement (1833).

Metternich's conservatism did not entirely preclude change. After all, 'stability is not immobility'.[5] He did have a positive goal – the gradual and very cautious improvement of the condition of the people, and of the functioning of the administration. Unfortunately, he felt negative measures, like the extension of police powers and the imposition of censorship, had to be used to clear the way. Throughout his period of office, Metternich's negative measures so outweighed any positive achievements that it would be difficult to think of a statesman who had in him less of the reformer.

Two main reasons will be advanced in this chapter for such lack of achievement: the shortcomings of his own analysis on the one hand and, on the other, the serious obstacles impeding those changes which he did propose. He was blind to the former, and vociferously aware of the latter. As the negative policies predominated and the internal problems of the Austrian Empire remained unsolved, Metternich became increasingly disillusioned and full of pessimism about the future.

Metternich and the Austrian Empire 1815–48

*

What measures did Metternich adopt for the administration of the Austrian Empire and its dependent territories? How did these reflect the more negative features of his political philosophy?

The major problem within the Habsburg empire was undoubtedly the existence of a dozen major racial groups within its frontiers; these included Germans, Magyars, Italians, Romanians and Slavs (who were further subdivided into Czechs, Slovaks, Poles, Ruthenes, Serbs, Croats and Slovenes). The main political units of the Empire were the Austrian Hereditary Lands (including Austria, Styria, Carinthia, Carniola and Tyrol), the Bohemian Lands (Bohemia, Moravia and Upper Silesia), Hungary (which also dominated Galicia, Transylvania and Croatia) and the Italian acquisitions of 1815 (Lombardy and Venetia). Metternich was convinced that the variety of aspirations which inevitably result from this diverse make-up presented a constant threat of disruption. He considered that the only means of controlling the centrifugal forces of nationalism was by upholding the one centripetal power, the traditional authority of the Habsburg dynasty. Unfortunately, his measures lacked vision and consistency, while he appeared, at times, profoundly ignorant of the psychological power of national ism in Central Europe.

Metternich had a particular suspicion of the one possible remedy of the internal problem of competing nationalities – federalism. It is true that he had a true conservative's respect for local traditions and that he favoured the full use of existing provincial institutions, but he instinctively opposed anything which suggested liberalism or political and social reform. This meant that there were occasions on which he lost the opportunity to work with moderate reformers like Andrian-Werburg, a widely respected Austrian, and Count Széchenyi. The latter led a large group in the Hungarian Diet which stood between the two extremes of the pro-Austrian conservatives and the radical secessionists. At several stages during the 1820s and 1830s Széchenyi sought Metternich's support for a series of moderate social and political reforms, but received nothing but open discouragement. Indeed, from 1837 Metternich followed a policy which he described as 'salutary terror' designed to 'enlighten' the people of Hungary. Although he decided to abandon this after 1841, enormous damage was done as moderates like Széchenyi lost ground to the extremists. One of the outspoken and anti-Austrian Magyars of the 1840s was Kossuth who described Metternich's influence in vivid and violent terms: 'From the charnel house of the Viennese system a pestilential breath steals over us which paralyzes our nerves and deadens our national spirit.' In 1848 resentment against the unreformed link between Vienna and the provinces erupted openly in Hungary, Bohemia and the Italian states of Lombardy and Venetia. The separatist movement in Hungary was so powerful that Russian troops were needed to restore Habsburg rule. Although Metternich cannot be blamed for not finding an overall solution to the Empire's regional antipathies, he can certainly be accused of shortsightedness in missing opportunities for compromise.

Instead, he followed his own instinctive views on nationalism. Within the Empire he alternated between promoting provincial identities and following a crude version of the principle of 'divide and rule' by encouraging antagonism between the different races. The Emperor Francis gave this policy his full approval, adding: 'From their antipathy will be born order and from their mutual hatred general peace'.[6] Any short-term strategic gains made by such a course were outweighed, in 1848, by the explosion of resentment of Slav against German, Magyar against German, and Slav against Magyar. Outside, and on the periphery of the Empire, Metternich underestimated the capacity of the Germans and Italians to develop closer national links. The Germans, he concluded, were unlikely to develop anything beyond 'provincial patriotism', while the Italians would have to concede that only Austria could maintain public peace and prevent the disintegration of law and order. The inaccuracy and, indeed, complacency of these views was shown by the eventual ejection of Austria from Italy in 1859, and from the German Confederation in 1866.

Metternich opposed federalism largely because he felt that it would have to be accompanied by constitutional concessions in the form of greatly strengthened representative bodies. He never willingly surrendered political powers, believing that the really efficient and successful statesman governs 'so as to avoid a situation in which concessions become necessary'.[3] More fundamentally, he detested the ideological role played by liberalism in sponsoring parliamentarianism; liberalism, in fact, was merely the 'accomplice of demagogy' and invariably prepared the way for popular violence. The section of society most responsible for the spread of 'this moral gangrene' was the middle class, for this promoted political parties which, in turn, prepared demands and applied pressure for constitutional change. The ultimate source of evil was the universities, which taught openly 'the most subversive maxims' and made a virtue of defying authority and undermining tradition. It is hardly surprising, therefore, that Metternich should have been convinced of the necessity for repressive measures. He controlled his own secret police force, which was smaller and more efficient than the official corps of Count Sedlnitzky. He reacted swiftly to internal disturbances within the German Confederation by imposing the Carlsbad Decrees in 1819 and the Six Articles in 1832. Above all, he refused to compromise over censorship. There were, he argued, only two possibilities: either severe censorship or total freedom of the press. Austria would not repeat the mistake made in France of tolerating something between them. After Russia, Austria was the most intransigent autocracy in Europe and seemed unable to follow the periodic examples of Prussia in accommodating to political changes and even experimenting with representative institutions.

Austria lagged behind Prussia also in the treatment of her social problems. Joseph II had been the first of the continental autocrats to abolish serfdom, but his successors in Austria had allowed it to creep back so that, between 1815 and 1848 Austria and Russia were the only major European powers to tolerate feudalism. Metternich refused to follow the example of Stein and Hardenberg, who had ensured its abolition in Prussia after 1807, even though it was becoming increasingly clear that serfdom was counter-productive economically, and unpopular even with some sections of the land-owning nobility. Metternich feared that fundamental social reforms would upset the internal equilibrium of the class structure and prepare the way for destructive revolutionary forces. He did alleviate peasant burdens in Galicia, but this was a tactic designed to alienate them from the Polish nobility who had organized themselves into anti-Austrian nationalist groups in 1846. Elsewhere, peasant grievances mounted; conditions were exacerbated by the depression and the bad harvests of the mid-1840s. It is probable that widespread peasant revolts within the Empire were forestalled only by the outbreak of a wider pattern of revolutions in 1848.

To Metternich, the Austrian Empire was the repository of the only type of conservatism which was likely to succeed in Europe – one which avoided the French pattern of compromise with

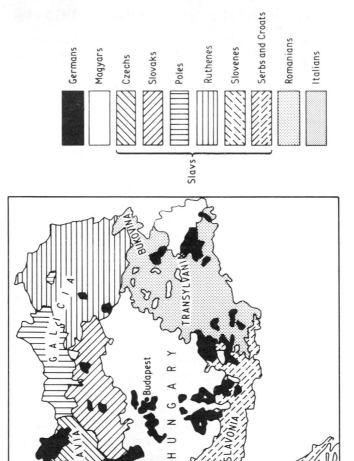

Germans Magyars Czechs Slovaks Poles Ruthenes Slovenes Serbs and Croats Romanians Italians

Slavs

The peoples of the Habsburg Monarchy 1815–1908

constitutionalism and also the more brutal Russian model. Consequently, he projected his ideas and policies beyond a limited domestic scale, hoping to provide a European formula for equilibrium; one of his most celebrated assertions was that Austria was Europe's House of Lords. Even here, however, there were serious defects in his policy; his foreign commitments were not commensurate with Austria's military and economic resources. In part, he adopted this wider scope through desperation, hoping for greater success on the diplomatic level than had proved possible on the domestic. This would explain his confession: 'I have sometimes held Europe in my hands, never Austria.'[1]

*

It could be argued in Metternich's defence that he was confronted with intolerable difficulties which impeded any progressive elements of his political programme. Certainly he was not slow to draw attention to these. Referring to the cumbersome operation of the whole government system, he complained of the obstacles with which he had to contend in the bureaucracy, especially the 'lack of energy'.

He was fortunate in having the support of the Emperor Francis, whose confidence was evident in his Political Will (1835). This urged Ferdinand I to bestow on Metternich the same degree of trust and to take no decision 'on public affairs, or respecting persons, without first hearing him.' Unfortunately, Ferdinand's accession marked the end of any special relationship between Chancellor and Emperor. Ferdinand proved totally incompetent, a mere shell of a ruler. In one minister's words, Austria now had 'an absolute monarchy without a monarch'.[7] The Empire was actually governed by the Conference of State under the chairmanship of the Archduke Ludwig, the rest of the authority being divided between the Archduke Francis Charles, Kolowrat and Metternich. It was a notoriously touchy team, prone to frequent conflict and rarely managing to achieve consensus.

Particularly damaging was the rivalry between Metternich and Kolowrat. The latter had risen to power rapidly during the 1820s and, in the 1830s, headed a series of committees dealing with financial affairs. Metternich complained bitterly that all internal matters were referred to Kolowrat and that his own sphere of responsibility as Chancellor was being steadily reduced. This suspicion was combined with a deep personal animosity and a basic clash of national policies: Kolowrat, a Czech, was strongly inclined to uphold the interests of Bohemia, while Metternich claimed to have a broader and less provincial viewpoint. Metternich found two clashes particularly irksome. The first was Kolowrat's insistence that Austria's military estimates should be reduced; this, of course, would weaken Metternich's position in Europe. The second was provoked by Kolowrat's demands that the Empire's first railway lines should be built within Bohemia; Metternich fought this proposal on the grounds that priority should be given to connecting the Austrian High Command with the vulnerable provinces of Northern Italy. Overall, Metternich accused Kolowrat of being the archetypal bureaucrat, lacking in foresight and imagination and, what was worse, devoting his limited energies to disrupting Metternich's own plans.

These schemes had, in fact, seemed ill-fated throughout his administration. Although he was not renowned as a reformer, Metternich did consider certain constitutional changes necessary to sharpen the Austrian bureaucracy. In 1814, for example, he proposed the replacement of the traditional colleges by modern ministries. The scheme was largely shelved, as Francis had little taste for innovation. In 1816, Metternich set up a *Kommerz-direktorium* to co-ordinate economic planning, but this faded out in 1824. He submitted to Francis several lengthy memoranda on reform concerning the State Council, the State Conference and a series of new regional chancelleries. Francis took no action and, when pressed after 1830, he pointed to the revolutions which had recently affected Western and Central Europe. 'I want no change,' he insisted. 'This is no time for reforms. The people are like men who have been badly wounded. One must not keep touching and irritating their wounds.'[8] This obstruction was maintained by the other members of the State Conference after the death of Francis in 1835, and showed itself increasingly in economic as well as constitutional terms. During the late 1830s Metternich endeavoured to secure Austrian membership of the *Zollverein*, but the necessary step of lowering the Empire's tariff barriers were fiercely resisted by Kolowrat and the archdukes who acted as the Emperor Leopold's spokesmen. Metternich was reminded, somewhat curtly, that economic matters were not within his competence. It is not difficult to see, therefore, why Metternich attached most of the blame for growing political problems and economic stagnation to the rigid and stubborn leadership of an unreformed administration. He might well have agreed with the opinion of a socialist leader, three-quarters of a century later, that the basis of Habsburg authority was 'absolutism tempered by slovenliness'.

*

The collapse of the old order as a result of the French Revolution and the conquests of Napoleon created in Metternich a profound pessimism about human affairs. As his own failures became more apparent and resistance to his policies ever stronger, he became increasingly outspoken. His third wife described him in 1843 as a Jeremiah, but added, 'no one listens to him'.[9] He appeared convinced that 'our society is on the downward slope,' and that he was devoting his energies to 'underpinning buildings which are mouldering into decay'.[4] Most revealing of all, he believed that the world in which he lived was in a terrible hiatus. After the 1830 revolutions he observed: 'Old Europe is at the beginning of the end ... New Europe, however, has not yet even begun its existence, and between the end and the beginning there will be chaos.'[10]

It could be argued that Metternich's failures were due generally to the incompatibility between his variety of conservatism and the changing conditions of Europe. He frequently used the metaphor of a house which was threatening to collapse; in 1825, for example, he denounced Szechenyi's scheme for reforms in Hungary with the warning 'No, no! Take one stone out of the vaulting and the whole thing collapses.' The description is particularly apt. Austrian conservatism had become totally lifeless and had to be propped up against the forces challenging it from without. By contrast, English conservatism was thriving, strengthened by the theoretical base given to it by the ideas of Burke before the turn of the eighteenth century. Burke had preferred to associate the development of a nation, its society and institutions with the metaphor of a living organism. This being could certainly be damaged by a major upheaval like the French Revolution which, 'like a palsy, has attacked the fountain of life itself'.[11] But it was also capable of sustained growth and needed the occasional sharp corrective to the system like, for example, the Revolution of 1689, which had guaranteed the permanent supremacy of Parliament. 'An irregular, convulsive movement may be necessary to throw off an irregular, convulsive disease. But the course of succession is the healthy habit of the

British constitution.' French conservatism, as expressed by Guizot during the reign of Louis Philippe, also possessed vitality, recognizing the social achievements of the French revolution. Both English and French forms managed to adjust to, and secure the support of, the more constructive sections of their societies. Austrian conservatism possessed no such positive spirit.

Metternich's own explanation for his failures was naturally somewhat different. He would never admit to an error of judgement. 'There is a wide sweep about my mind. I am always above and beyond the preoccupations of most public men; I cover a ground much vaster than they can see, or wish to see. I cannot keep myself from saying about twenty times a day, "How right I am and how wrong they are."'[5] The only possible explanation, therefore, was that the rest of the world was wrong or, to put it another way, that he was born into the wrong era. Indeed, he openly wished that he had lived in either the eighteenth century or the twentieth. It is ironical that the man who was most widely regarded as typifying the establishment should have seen himself as an anachronism.

7

The Revolutions of 1848–9

The 1848 revolutions were the most widespread popular disturbances of the nineteenth century; they had a direct impact on France, the German Confederation, Prussia, the Habsburg Empire (especially Austria, Bohemia and Hungary), the Italian states, Wallachia and Moldavia. Other areas were peripherally influenced, including Switzerland, Belgium, Denmark and Spain. Only Russia remained totally unaffected. Yet 1849 was a year of disappointment and anticlimax. The revolutions collapsed in Central Europe, and reactionary régimes recovered their authority and confidence in a way which would have seemed impossible in 1848.

This chapter will deal with two main issues. First, who were the revolutionaries? What drove and inspired them? And why were they at first so successful? Second, why did the Revolutions collapse in 1849? And what enabled the forces of authority to recover so rapidly?

*

The 1848 revolutions were the result of extensive disillusionment within a broad area of society in many continental countries, and of a temporary co-operation between members of different social classes and occupations. Workers, artisans and students provided the activists and the street fighters who manned the barricades in Paris, Berlin and Vienna, and brought fresh intervention when the original impetus began to slow down. The wealthier and more influential elements of society, especially businessmen and lawyers, found themselves in sympathy with the spontaneous rioting of the activists, but soon sought to control what they regarded as dangerously irrational forces and to divert the Revolutions towards achieving more limited and specific objectives. They were ideally placed to do this since they were articulate and influenced the composition of the various provisional governments formed in 1848.

By far the most militant of the revolutionaries of 1848 were the artisans, especially metalworkers in Paris, and weavers in Berlin. They had been a volatile element of the population for several decades because everywhere they were confronted by the problems brought about by economic changes. Increased production in every major European state reduced the emphasis on skilled labour and opened a wide gap between masters and journeymen. A potent revolutionary factor has always been the deterioration of once acceptable conditions and the removal of a long-established means of upward social and economic mobility (see Chapter 1); this was becoming increasingly common by the mid-nineteenth century as industrialization made the progression from journeyman to master more difficult, and threatened to depress the skilled worker to the level of labourer. To make matters worse, the artisans faced increased pressure from below as the population growth in most countries induced migration from the countryside to the towns. Governments were reluctant to consider the interests of the artisans. Indeed, they tried to legislate against them, and the protection provided by the guilds in France, Northern Italy and the western parts of the German Confederation was removed. A rash of artisan disturbances in the 1840s in several German cities, as well as in Paris, Lyons and Marseilles, showed that this section of the population had become sufficiently desperate to resort to direct action. 1848 was a culmination of these activities. The artisans took to the streets of Paris on 22 February, of Vienna and Prague from 11 March, and Berlin from 17 March. They also challenged the policies of the provisional government in Paris, and the recommendations of the Frankfurt Parliament.

Of the rest of the activists, the role of the factoryworker should not be exaggerated. After all, mechanization was still very limited outside the textile industry and affected major cities like Paris, Vienna and Berlin less than the medium-sized towns. It could be said, however, that once the revolutions had broken out, the factory workers provided support for the artisans in the western states of

The Revolutions of 1848–9

Germany. Of greater importance were the very poor and unemployed; although they were too downtrodden and disorganized to take a revolutionary initiative, they had nothing to lose by swelling the numbers behind the barricades at crucial moments in March 1848. More purposeful were the small groups of university students who joined in – and sometimes led – the demonstrations and riots in Vienna, Prague, Munich and the northern Italian cities, articulating the social grievances of the workers and unemployed, and feeding the artisans with radical, sometimes socialist, ideas. The part played in the revolutions by the peasantry provides more contrast and variety. This group certainly had reason to be militant; they were under severe pressure as a result of the population growth and the spread of capital-intensive farming which discriminated against the vast majority of small farmers. In some areas, like southern Italy and Bavaria, the peasantry took direct action, attacking landed proprietors and seizing land. In others, however, they remained passive. In France, for example, they feared the radicalism of the Paris workers more than they resented exploitation by landlords; while in Austria they were bought off by the régime's promise of total emancipation from serfdom.

Meanwhile, the professional and financial sectors of the middle classes had also accumulated their store of resentment against the various governments; it was they who gave the riots a political purpose and who gained most from the embarrassment of the rulers. Their most apparent grievance was political. They were excluded from power in every leading state; even in the France of the so-called 'bourgeois monarchy', high property qualifications restricted the electorate to a mere 240,000. Landed property owners, mostly aristocrats, still dominated the political processes. It is hardly surprising, therefore, that more widely representative institutions should have been the most immediate objective of middle-class leaders in 1848. Behind the political programme, however, lay a series of social and economic grievances. Again, the prospect of upward mobility had been blocked, especially in the bureaucracy. Too few posts were available for the ever-increasing numbers of highly educated lawyers; with luck, constitutional reform would greatly extend the scope of the state apparatus and therefore eliminate this bottleneck. Accompanying legal reforms, including guarantees of *habeas corpus*, would further enhance the role of lawyers by increasing the need for defence attorneys. In Central Europe a change of régime

57

would also help realize some of the economic aspirations of German businessmen. The existing policy of the Prussian government favoured agriculture rather than industry, while even the *Zollverein* proved inadequate commercially. Much more appealing than the existing system would be a constitutional democracy, operating a revised economic policy within the context of a single German state. Writers, professors and teachers formed the final dissident group within the middle class. For some time they had been kicking against the censorship imposed in Austria and in the German Confederation as a result of Metternich's Carlsbad Decrees (1819). All these different groups gradually coalesced, giving a wider purpose to the street fighting by winning constitutions and guarantees of individual rights.

Three powerful forces transformed dissent into revolutionary action. The first was the economic depression of the 1840s. The potato crop of 1845 was ruined, while those between 1846 and 1847 showed little improvement. Similar losses in grain harvests forced prices upwards, creating widespread hardship and misery among the lower classes. The middle classes were affected by a business depression caused by a fall in the population's spending capacity. The different manifestations of the slump provoked revolt or open defiance of authority. The second influence was a widespread feeling of disillusionment following the restored old régime that held sway over much of Europe after 1815. Had the overthrow of Napoleon benefited the majority of Europeans? Byron asked of the Duke of Wellington in *Don Juan*:

> And I shall be delighted to learn who,
> Save you and yours, have gained by Waterloo?

He also maintained that 1815 had served only to 'repair legitimacy's crutch'. The antidote to Metternich and his policies was, of course, the ideals of the French Revolution. Even the mild Lamartine confessed to the power of these: 'France is revolutionary or it is nothing. The Revolution of 1789 is her political religion.'[1] The way in which France could influence the rest of Europe can be seen in the declaration of the people of Wiesbaden in Nassau in March 1848: 'The latest French Revolution . . . has shaken Europe. It is knocking on the doors of Germany.'[2] The third force was confined to Central Europe: the desire for national unification, as in Italy and Germany, or for national self-determination, as in the Habsburg Empire.

The Revolutions of 1848–9

Most of the revolutions of 1848 were disorganized, even haphazard in their immediate origin. The Paris risings, for example, were a spontaneous response to the government's decision to ban the great reform banquet meeting on 22 February. France, in turn, provided the example for movements elsewhere. On 3 March Kossuth demanded in Pressburg constitutions for the whole Habsburg Empire; while, on 12 March, Vienna was the scene of student demonstrations which, in the succeeding weeks, expanded into popular uprisings. By 17 March Berlin was similarly affected and the barricades went up in April. The Italian states had also erupted: Sicily the first area in Europe, in January, and Piedmont, Rome, Venice and Milan in March. Everywhere, authority gave way with remarkably little show of resistance. According to Louis Blanc, Louis Philippe 'let the sceptre slip voluntarily from his hand'.[3] De Tocqueville came to a similar conclusion: 'The government was not overthrown, it was allowed to fall.'[4] Other régimes hastened to make concessions in a manner which would have seemed incredible a year earlier. The Habsburg monarchy promised a constitution for Hungary in March and, in April, for Austria, Bohemia and Moravia. Frederick William IV gave a similar guarantee to Prussia, and an Assembly eventually convened in Berlin in May. Rulers of the smaller German and Italian states also seemed to vie with each other in liberalizing their régimes.

Why did this almost unseemly abdication of authority take place?

The most immediate reason was the element of shock. Metternich, it is true, had warned the monarchs to expect trouble from the bourgeoisie. But, since the latter had been relatively quiet during the 1840s, many rulers assumed that the danger had passed. No one, apparently, saw any immediate danger from the lower orders. Thus complacency affected all the régimes, and this turned to paralysis under the combined and unexpected onslaught of the different social classes in February and March 1848. Metternich observed that the monarchies had 'lost confidence in themselves'. Certainly there were divided counsels in response to street violence. Metternich and Windischgrätz, for example, urged immediate military action, but Emperor Ferdinand I was persuaded, instead, to grant concessions and dismiss Metternich. Frederick William IV of Prussia, on being asked for permission for the army to storm the barricades in Berlin, said: 'Yes, but don't fire!' and followed up with an emotionally worded appeal to 'my dear Berliners'.[5] The immediate result of the absence of clear orders was demoralization, affecting the armies and para-military defence guards in all the major capitals of Western and Central Europe. The Habsburgs had the additional problem of trying to appeal to over a dozen different races, and the initial success of the insurgents owed much to the confusion in Vienna. This was evident in the Proclamation to the Italian people made by the provisional government of Milan after the eviction of the Austrians in March: 'Fellow citizens, we have conquered. We have compelled the enemy to fly, oppressed by his own shame as much as by our valour.'[6] Was there, perhaps, a warning here that the victory was incomplete and that shame can generate revival?

*

By the end of 1848 the revolutions were in disarray and the period 1849–51 brought the hardening of reaction. The Habsburg recovery started with the bombardment by Windischgrätz of Prague in June 1848, and Vienna in October. Franz Joseph, who succeeded Ferdinand as Emperor in December, continued the offensive, closing the Austrian Assembly in March 1849, while General Radetzky subdued the Northern Italian provinces of Lombardy and Venetia between March and August. The final threat, Hungarian separatism, was disposed of with the assistance of Russian troops. Meanwhile, Frederick William IV had recovered his nerve sufficiently to apply the brake to constitutional developments in Prussia, to reject liberal schemes for German unification, and to send Prussian troops against the dissidents in Dresden (May 1849) and Baden (July 1849). France, it is true, did not see the restoration of the previous régime, but she did undergo her own form of reaction. The franchise was restricted in May 1849, and in September censorship was reimposed on the press. There was also a powerful wave against republicanism, beginning with the use of French troops to destroy Garibaldi's Roman Republic in July 1849 and culminating with Louis Napoleon's *coup d'état* of 1851 and the proclamation of the Second Empire in 1852. The dramatic transformation in all these states can be explained by the growing weakness of the revolutionaries and the revival of strong executive powers in the various European capitals.

The initial advantages of the revolutionaries had been the unexpectedness and simultaneity of the uprisings. But these were not accompanied by clarity of purpose and planned action. Mazzini had

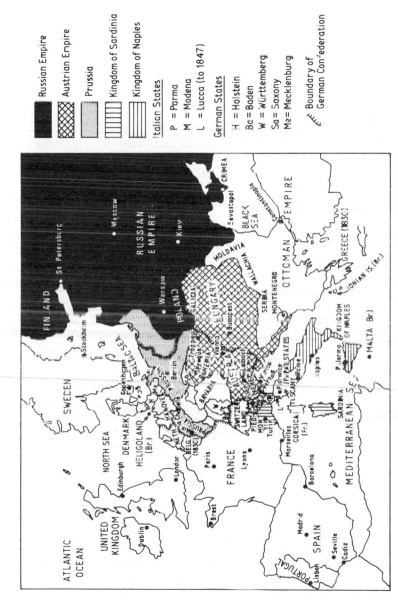

Europe 1815-43

Legend:

Russian Empire

Austrian Empire

Prussia

Kingdom of Sardinia

Kingdom of Naples

Italian States

P = Parma
M = Modena
L = Lucca (to 1847)

German States

H = Holstein
Ba = Baden
W = Württemberg
Sa = Saxony
Me = Mecklenburg

Boundary of German Confederation

laid down in 1831 the basic requirements for a successful conspiracy: 'The security, efficacity and rapid progress of an association, are always in proportion to the determination, clearness and precision of its aims.' Equally important was the 'homogeneity' of the revolutionary elements and the 'perfect concordance . . . as to the path to be followed'.[7] He had also warned that the apparent harmony which existed 'during the work of destruction' might subsequently be undermined by dangerous 'discords'. Mazzini was to have his worst fears confirmed as the revolutionary movements of 1848 split along two lines of cleavage – those of social confrontations and nationalist rivalries.

Referring to the former, E. J. Hobsbawm asserts that 1848 failed because the decisive confrontation was not between the old régime and the united forces of progress, but between order and social revolution.[8] Others have argued that the bourgeoisie aimed at a constitution, with the accompanying liberal requisites of a free press, legal equality and favourable conditions for industrial and commercial progress. The rest of the urban populations, by contrast, wanted more sweeping social changes; on March 26, for example, the workers of Berlin produced demands for universal suffrage, a ministry of labour, a ten-hour working day and a minimum wage. At first the liberal provisional governments deferred to some of the workers' needs. National workshops were set up in Paris, and a road-grading scheme in Vienna guaranteed employment for the destitute. But eventually a conflict developed, revealing two fundamentally different philosophies: *laissez-faire* and state intervention. The former regarded social policies as irreconcilable with economic growth, while the latter argued for certain constraints upon that growth. Everywhere the middle-class liberals gained the greatest representation in the new legislatures. In the French Assembly the April elections returned only eighty-five socialists and radicals (including only thirty workers) out of a total of 876 deputies. The Frankfurt Parliament comprised four journeymen and one peasant, as against thirteen businessmen, ninety-two lawyers, 104 professors and teachers, and one hundred judicial officers.

The previous alliance between the middle and lower classes was now to be torn apart by mutual fear and recrimination. Businessmen and lawyers, who had once welcomed the revolutionary impetus at the barricades, soon came to recognize it as a hostile force. One delegate at the Frankfurt Parliament warned of the consequences of

The Revolutions of 1848–9

radicalism which 'seeks to do away with all natural differences in intellectual and physical endowment and to neutralize their consequences in employment and in the acquisition of wealth'.[9] Dumas, the novelist, used even more emotive words to convey the fears which many members of the French bourgeoisie possessed: 'The terrorists are out to destroy the country, the socialists are out to destroy the family and the communists are out to destroy property.'[10] These words were provoked by the June insurrection in which the workers of Paris defied a government decree closing the National Workshops. Similar fears arose in Vienna in August over protests against the cancellation of the road-grading schemes. In both instances the professional classes welcomed the use of troops against the radicals who, in the meantime, could not even console themselves with the knowledge that the peasantry were behind them. The French peasantry had been largely responsible for the conservative composition of the Assembly, and volunteered in their thousands to join the National Guard to 'put an end to the intolerable dictation of the chronically insurgent Parisian workers'.[11] The key to their behaviour is probably that they were now small landowners and gave priority to defending their property against strange and alarming ideologies. The Austrian peasantry remained totally passive, probably the result of the politic abolition of serfdom by the authorities. Everywhere in Central Europe the tide of opinion ran against radicalism, while, in France, the Second Republic was irreparably damaged; indeed, Lamenais mourned the death of the Republic after the June Days and spoke bitterly of the 'saturnalia of reaction around its bloodstained tomb'.[12]

One reason for the collapse of the revolutions, therefore, was the swift discovery that temporary co-operation between different social groups did not automatically mean a long-term convergence of interest. Another was the confrontation between different nationalities. These can be categorized as external and internal.

External disputes developed between Germans and Slavs (especially Czechs and Poles) and between Magyars and Slavs (especially Serbs and Croats). Among the proposals for a united Germany put forward in the Frankfurt Parliament in 1848 was a scheme whereby the German and Czech areas of Austria would be joined to Prussia and the smaller German states within the German Confederation. This, however, was strongly resisted by the Czechs, and their leader, Palácky, declined an invitation to attend the proceedings. Some Germans preferred a formula which would exclude all Austrian territory, but they came into conflict with another Slav group – the Poles. Delegates at the Frankfurt Parliament justified the inclusion of the Polish-speaking areas in the East by Prussia's 'right of conquest'. The sole Polish member of the parliament, however, warned: 'The Poles have been swallowed up but, by God, it will not be possible to digest them.'[13] Meanwhile, the Magyars, in their attempt to destroy the Habsburg Empire and establish an autonomous Hungary, had fallen foul of the Slavs. Palácky recognized in this Empire a useful means of counter-balancing the pretensions of both the Germans and the Magyars. In a famous defence of the principle of federation he maintained that 'If Austria did not already exist it would be necessary to invent it.'[8] The policy of Austro-Slavism, which saw the future in a reformed and balanced Empire, was also accepted by the Croats, Slovenes and Serbs of the South; they feared and detested the Magyars' contemptuous attitude towards the other races of Hungary. The Magyar reformer, Széchenyi, had warned his compatriots of this as far back as 1847: 'Incite every nationality against the Magyars and you fill to the brim the cup of vengeance with your poison.'[13] Much to the relief of the Emperor, the demands of the Slavs and Magyars were so incompatible that they brought about civil war, in which the Habsburgs were able to enlist the support of one side to defeat the other.

Internal clashes developed among the Germans, Italians and Slavs. The Frankfurt Parliament was divided between pan-Germanism, which aimed at incorporating the whole of German-speaking Europe into the new nation state, and the *Kleindeutsch* movement, which confined itself to the formula of Prussia plus the smaller states of the German Confederation. The Parliament took so long to work out the boundaries of the new state that the revolutionary impetus had dissipated by the time that the leadership was offered to the King of Prussia. The latter killed the whole scheme, in any case. Realizing that his authority would derive from the people rather than from fellow rulers, he bluntly declined to pick the crown of Germany 'from the gutter'. The Italians fared no better in *their* endeavours to create a larger political unit. Charles Albert of Piedmont merely wanted to expand the territories of the House of Savoy, while in the South, Sicily sought separation from mainland Naples; and in the East, the city of Venice remained at odds with mainland Venetia. Even the Slavs, obdurate in their resistance to the claims of the Germans and Magyars, found a common constitutional programme impossible to attain. Slovaks feared the prospect of being overshadowed by Czechs, while Serbs and Croats possessed deep religious and cultural differences.

While these divisions were growing ever wider, the régimes of Central Europe were recovering their confidence, and France was moving towards Bonapartism in a desperate search for order. The Habsburgs and Hohenzollerns owed much to the twin pillars of *vormarz* absolutism, the bureaucracy and the army, neither of which was ever threatened or infiltrated by the revolutionaries. Indeed, the army often took the initiative and, during the course of 1848 and 1849, the Austrian commanders, Jellačić, Windischgrätz and Radetzky were usually a step ahead of the Emperor and his cabinet in their campaigns against the main troublespots. As they recovered their nerve, the governments of Vienna and Berlin followed a more systematic policy, combining well-timed concessions to the middle classes and peasantry with a more determined use of the army against the remaining radicals. Thus, although the initial response of the rulers to the disturbances had been weak and indecisive, their recovery was complete; according to Küdlich, 'Because of a lack of grapeshot they lost their absolute, untouchable position in March, and they won it back in October . . . because of the power of their cannon.'[14]

Since the armies were so much in control in 1848, the revolutionaries, with the possible exception of the Hungarians, never stood much chance of success. The radicals had placed too much confidence in the 'Bastille' tradition and had assumed that a massive turnout in the streets over a short period would be enough to overturn the hated régimes. But the continental powers, although badly shaken, were not sufficiently effete to be toppled by spontaneous demonstrations. It gradually became apparent that a far more effective agency of change was the damage which these powers could inflict on each other; war, rather than revolution, brought some of the desired reforms during the 1860s. Austria, for example, experimented with constitutionalism after her defeat in Italy in 1859, and, by the *Ausgleich*, gave Hungary autonomy as a direct consequence of military defeat by Prussia in 1866. France rejected the Empire in 1870 after the disaster at Sedan. It took the devastation of the First World War to bring down the Habsburgs and Hohenzollerns, while

Russia, also in defeat, eventually succumbed to a revolution which, although it began much as the 1848 revolutions had begun, overthrew an old régime helpless because it had no army left to defend it.

There is one instance of a régime which actually strengthened itself by absorbing some of the influences of 1848 and then using them as antibodies against future revolution. Prussia abandoned the type of reaction which had been upheld by Metternich in favour of a compromise between an authoritarian executive and a broadly based legislature. The shadow of parliamentarianism passed into the 1871 Imperial Constitution while, all the time, Bismarck sought to 'eliminate the liberal and democratic ideas of 1848' (B. E. Schmitt). The Prussian establishment also captured German nationalism, transforming its original association with liberal democracy into a close alliance with conservatism and militarism. In Bismarck's own words, German nationalism was to become 'the moral force with which to expand and buttress the power of the Hohenzollern monarchy'.[15]

8

The Impact of the Crimean War on European Diplomacy

The impact of the Crimean War on Europe was deceptive. At first, it appeared that the Treaty of Paris (1856) might actually revive the prospect of international co-operation, especially since the erring state, Russia, had been brought back into line by Anglo-French policing action, and Turkey was no longer excluded from the diplomatic scene. In addition, the powers seemed to be extending the range of their collective responsibility. Article XV of the Treaty of Paris, for example, provided an international guarantee for freedom of navigation along the Danube; this reaffirmed, in more specific form, the principle laid down in the Treaty of Vienna (1815).

Despite these auspicious signs, it soon became apparent that the Crimean War had brought disruption, not continuity, to nineteenth-century diplomacy wrecking the Concert of Europe, which had existed since 1815, and making possible the extensive territorial changes of the 1860s. The Treaty of Paris did not even solve the problems associated more specifically with the Near East; indeed, for the rest of the century these remained an irritant to diplomacy between the major powers.

*

There is a considerable difference between the periods 1815–54 and 1856–71. The first was the longest period in modern history in which none of the major powers fought a war in Europe. There had, it is true, been numerous rivalries and diplomatic cross-currents which had brought about the collapse of the Congress System. But the common interest which all the powers had in preserving the Vienna Settlement meant that the Congress System was survived by a looser consensus generally known as the Concert of Europe. A delicate diplomatic balance had been maintained, resting on the unstated principle that no one power could be permitted by the others to upset the Settlement. In the general quest for a lasting European peace, all statesmen had seen it in their interest to accept the occasional check and to impose the occasional self-restraint. In complete contrast, the second period saw an explosion of armed conflict as Prussia and Austria each fought three wars and France two.

The reason for this transition was that the Crimean War severely weakened the two traditional guarantors of the *status quo* in Europe, Austria and Russia. The vacuum which resulted gave a unique opportunity to a new generation of statesmen with revisionist aims and a willingness to use force to achieve them: Napoleon III, Cavour and Bismarck.

Despite their many differences and rivalries, Austria and Russia had possessed the same basic interests: the preservation of autocracy, the prevention of territorial change in Central Europe and the suppression of revolution. Metternich had seen Austria as the pivot of European equilibrium, but there were times when Russian diplomatic, even military support had proved essential to enable Austria to fulfil her role as 'Europe's chamber of peers'. Although misunderstandings and diplomatic clashes had prevented a permanent military alliance, there were two particularly important examples of Russian assistance to Austria. The first was Nicholas I's intervention in Hungary in 1849 to put down the Magyar revolt and thereby restore Habsburg authority to Central Europe. The second was Russian diplomatic support for the Austrian Chancellor, Schwarzenberg, against Frederick William IV of Prussia. The latter attempted, by means of the Erfurt Union, to integrate Prussia more closely with some of the smaller German states, but was forced, by the Punctuation of Olmütz (1850) to drop the scheme and agree to the revival of the German Confederation under Austria's presidency. It seemed that as long as Russia was prepared to adhere to the Vienna Settlement and to commit herself ideologically and, if necessary, militarily to its defence, there was little chance of the mould of 1815 being destroyed.

The Crimean War, however, cut the link between Russia and

The Crimean War and European Diplomacy

Austria. Nicholas I had expected Austria to show some gratitude for Russia's military assistance in 1849 by remaining neutral and unresponsive to overtures from Russia's enemies. Instead, Austria proved hostile to Russia throughout the War. In 1854, for example, she joined an alliance with Britain and France (even though this did not actually involve military commitments against Russia), while, in 1855, she demanded the immediate Russian acceptance of the Vienna Four Points. After the War it became clear that the longstanding *entente* between Austria and Russia was over; this was confirmed in Russia by the replacement of an Austrophile foreign minister, Nesselrode, by Gorchakov, an Austrophobe. For the rest of the 1850s and the whole of the 1860s Austria remained in isolation. She now faced the impossible task of preventing political and territorial changes in Central Europe without Russian aid, and with an economic and industrial base which was far smaller than those of Prussia and France.

Austria's difficulties were compounded by another effect of the Crimean War, the destruction of the balance of power which had allowed her ascendancy over Central Europe. This balance had been upheld partly by the peripheral powers of Britain and Russia; indeed, it was the shadow of Russia over Central Europe, just as much as any direct intervention, which had guaranteed the *status quo*. The situation was very different after 1856. Quite apart from her deep alienation from Austria, Russia now had neither the means nor the inclination to revert to her former role. (A. J. P. Taylor argues that the Crimean War destroyed both the myth and the reality of Russian military power, ensuring that Russia would carry less weight in European affairs after 1856 than at any other time since 1721.[1]) Even if she had not been so seriously affected militarily, Russia would no longer have gained anything from upholding the existing system. She could feel no attachment to the Treaty of Paris, the terms of which she found deeply humiliating. From being one of the pillars of the Vienna Settlement, Russia joined the ranks of revisionist powers. She was now prepared to co-operate with any government which appeared willing to lend diplomatic support to her main objective: the repudiation of the Black Sea clauses of the Treaty of Paris.

The contraction of Russia was accompanied by a reduction in the continental role of her great rival, Britain. Although a victor in the Crimean War, Britain drifted through two decades of uncertainty, and her handling of European issues like Italian unification, the Polish uprising (1863) and the Schleswig Holstein dispute (1864) was either indecisive or failed through lack of co-operation from other governments. The more fluid diplomatic conditions which resulted from the weaker roles of the peripheral powers benefited, instead, those states which had not previously been able to dominate the international scene. The way was now open for France, Piedmont and Prussia to attack the one remaining guardian of the 1815 settlement – Austria.

The immediate beneficiary was Napoleon III, who was a revisionist in two ways. First, he aimed at ending the debilitating restraint which the Vienna Settlement imposed on any active French policy. He was even prepared, until the Polish revolt of 1863, to make common cause with Russia, and he observed to Alexander II in 1858: 'You wish to change in part the Treaty of Paris: I would change in part the treaties of 1815'.[2] He hoped that Paris would become the focal point of European diplomacy and that he would be the arbiter of a new network of alignments. Second, he expressed certain sympathies with the nationalist aspirations of the fragmented areas of Central Europe; indeed, he had already published a pamphlet entitled *The New Map of Europe* (1854). The disintegration of the Concert of Europe after the Crimean War gave Napoleon his chance. In 1858, for example, he co-operated with Russia to assist the Romanian independence movement and, in 1859, sent French troops to assist Piedmont to eject the Austrians from Lombardy and, he hoped, set up an independent Northern Italy which would become a French satellite.

Meanwhile, Cavour had also exploited the opportunities offered by both the Crimean War and the Treaty of Paris. It has been argued that he deliberately committed Piedmont to the War as part of a long-term plan to gain international recognition of the Italian cause and to prepare the way for some major power to assist Piedmont. Most historians, however, see Cavour's policy as short-term and opportunist, based on the general hope that an allied victory would bring territorial gain to Piedmont or, at least, a willingness to modify the Vienna Settlement in Italy. To this end he used the forum offered by the Congress of Paris to put Piedmont's case against the Austrian presence in Lombardy. This did not, it is true, produce immediate results; neither the British nor the French governments were prepared to support Piedmont at this stage. But Cavour's

The Crimean War and European Diplomacy

contacts were significant in that they opened up options for the future. By 1858 French and Piedmontese policies had clearly converged, the result partly of Cavour's insistent diplomacy and partly of Napoleon III's growing receptiveness. The latter had by this time come to realize that the Crimean War had effectively isolated Austria and removed the psychological barrier imposed by the Vienna Settlement against territorial revision in Europe. This was the ideal moment for quick and decisive military action, provided, of course, the blame for the outbreak of war could be made to rest with Austria. Hence, by the Pact of Plombières, Napoleon III committed France to the first of the post-Crimea struggles.

By far the most single-minded and effective of the new revisionists, however, was Bismarck, minister president of Prussia from 1862. He rejected the Vienna formula for Germany – a loose confederation under Austria's presidency – and pursued, instead, a policy of Prussian expansion. He made skilful use of the anarchic state of international relations in the 1860s, which proved ideally suited to his pursuit of *Realpolitik* and of the 'strategy of alternatives' (see Chapter 10). Three examples can be given of the way in which he exploited the legacy of the Crimean War. First, he worked on the weakness and isolation of Austria, eventually reversing the Prussian humiliation of Olmütz (1850) by victory at Sadowa (1866). Second, he ensured Russia's neutrality throughout the crucial period of German unification by offering Prussian diplomatic support for the abrogation of the hated Black Sea clauses of the Treaty of Paris. Third, he exploited the diplomatic blunders made by Napoleon III, who had been emboldened by the opportunities offered by the realignment of powers after 1856 but, by the 1860s, had shown that his policies lacked caution and perspective. The Franco–Prussian War (1870–71) destroyed whatever advantages Napoleon had gained in 1856 and showed that Prussia, not France, was the long-term beneficiary of the Crimean War.

This was partly because the international scene after 1856 was uniquely favourable to the short war with specific objectives, a device much more appropriate to Prussia than to France. The Crimean War, for all its blunders and casualties, had been successfully localized and had disproved the fears of those who had drafted the Vienna Settlement that any conflict between major powers must inevitably lead to a general European war. Thus a number of governments came to see warfare not as the penalty for the failure of

71

Aspects of European History 1789–1980

diplomacy but rather as a device to ensure eventual diplomatic success; the famous dictum of Clausewitz that war is the continuation of diplomacy by other means proved to be more applicable to the 1850s and 1860s than to any other period since the middle of the eighteenth century. This approach, however, favoured the state with the greatest potential for military efficiency as well as the strongest industrial base. It was, therefore, fortunate for Bismarck that Prussia's economic growth had been the most rapid in Europe and that her industrial infrastructure was, by the 1860s, second only to that of Britain. Prussia was also armed with justification for aggression. The fulfilment of German unification, one of the motive forces behind the 1848 revolutions, could now be used as a slogan by dynasts on behalf of their subjects, rather than as a means of peoples trying to persuade dynasts. In this sense, the Crimean War made possible the transformation which had eluded the revolutionaries of 1848.

*

In a wider sense the Crimean War marks, in the words of J. A. S. Grenville, a 'point of transition in the history of Europe'.[3] The same cannot, however, be said of its impact on the Balkans and the Near East, the area which had spawned the conflict.

The Treaty of Paris was intended primarily as a solution to the two main problems affecting the Ottoman Empire and its relations with the rest of Europe. The first was the external pressure and the attempts made by Russia to gain control over the Black Sea and uncontested naval access to the Eastern Mediterranean. The Treaty of Paris therefore imposed certain restraints. The Russian land frontier was pulled back in Bessarabia, while Article XI declared: 'The Black Sea is Neutralized'. Consequently, according to Article XIII, 'the maintenance or establishment upon its Coast of Military–Maritime Arsenals becomes alike unnecessary and purposeless'. The second problem was the danger of internal upheaval and the possibility of total disintegration. The British and French delegates assumed that this could be dealt with by extensive internal reforms designed to satisfy the subject peoples of the Balkans. Hence Article IX recorded with approval 'the generous intentions' of His Imperial Majesty the Sultan 'towards the Christian population of his Empire', while Articles XXI, XXII, XXIII, XXVIII and XXIX provided for

The Crimean War and European Diplomacy

greater autonomy within Moldavia, Wallachia and Serbia, although under the sovereignty of the 'Sublime Porte'.

These solutions, however, proved illusory for, in the long term, the Treaty of Paris settled very little. The constraints on Russia could not be enforced; Alexander II succeeded in 1870 in repudiating the Black Sea clauses, while his reconstituted armies were strong enough by 1877 if not perhaps to play a European role then at least to defeat the Turks. Hopes for reform within the Ottoman Empire were also disappointed. Sultan Abdul Aziz (1861–76) assumed that the preservation of his Empire against Russian encroachment would always be a vital strategic consideration for the other powers, and that future assistance would not be made to depend on the degree of progress made towards liberating the subject peoples. He therefore felt that there was a strong case for doing nothing. Moldavia and Wallachia largely escaped Ottoman misrule when, in 1862, they were reconstituted as the autonomous state of Romania. But the other areas of the Empire continued to experience maladministration and neglect. Discontent eventually boiled over, between 1875 and 1876, in a series of revolts in Bosnia, Herzegovina, Bulgaria, Serbia and Montenegro, while the Turkish massacres in Bulgaria demonstrated that the régime was still prepared to resort to brutality. The powers were even hampered by the Treaty of Paris in their attempts to put pressure on Sultan Abdul Hamid II at the 1877 Constantinople Conference. Refusing to accept an international commission to ensure that reforms were implemented, the Sultan took his stand on Article IX, which expressly stated that the powers had no right 'to interfere, either collectively or separately, in the relations of His Majesty the Sultan with his subjects, nor in the Internal Administration of his Empire'. This deadlock precipitated unilateral action by Russia against Turkey and, in 1878, the Congress of Berlin, like the Congress of Paris before it, produced another series of temporary solutions.

During the period 1856–1914 the Eastern Question persistently eluded any lasting settlement. Between 1856 and 1871 it appeared insignificant beside the momentous changes which were taking place in Central Europe. But, by 1871, these changes had worked their way through. Napoleon III had been overthrown in the process, Cavour was dead, and Bismarck was now seeking his objectives by diplomacy rather than by warfare. It was at this stage that the Eastern Question became a constant irritant, inflaming relations between Austria–Hungary and Russia and throwing up major threats to European peace, like the Russo–Turkish War (1877), the Bulgarian Crisis (1885–7), the Bosnian Crisis (1908–9), the Balkan Wars (1912–13) and the Sarajevo assassination (1914).

9

Cavour, Garibaldi and the Unification of Italy

Italy had, for some centuries, been regarded as the part of Europe least likely to be united, and seemed to merit Metternich's observation that it was merely a 'geographical expression'. Yet undercurrents of national sentiment did exist, as did a willingness in all parts to rise against foreign rule or local oppression. There were also theoretical schemes for unification, including the federal scheme of Gioberti and the unitary republicanism of Mazzini. The failure of the 1848 revolutions, however, proved that the expulsion of the foreigner and the reduction of the number of political units required consummate diplomatic and military skills as well.

These were provided by Count Camillo di Cavour (1810–61) and Giuseppe Garibaldi (1807–82) who, between them, succeeded where others had failed. It would be difficult, however, to imagine two more different statesmen. Cavour was an aristocrat, while Garibaldi was the son of a merchant seaman. Cavour's early commitments were to farming and journalism before he became a politician in the 1850s, and he possessed an extensive knowledge of economic and political theory and institutions. Garibaldi spent his early career in the merchant navy. After his hasty withdrawal from Piedmont in 1834, he devoted his attention to guerrilla warfare in South America before returning to Italy in 1848. He was a military leader rather than a politician, with little education and even less pretension to theoretical knowledge.

This chapter will explore three main contrasts in the ideas and activities of Cavour and Garibaldi: their concepts of 'Italy', the base of their power and influence, and their practical contributions to Italian unification.

*

The Kingdom of Italy, which was established in 1860, conformed to the original vision of neither Cavour nor Garibaldi. Indeed, both found it necessary to change their initial conception of 'Italy' and to compromise – Cavour on Italy's geographical extent, and Garibaldi on the type of political structure.

During the 1850s Cavour considered unification of the entire peninsula neither possible nor desirable; he therefore differed fundamentally from Garibaldi, who argued that '*a single Italy* must be our first goal',[1] and who hoped to incorporate the existing states of Piedmont, Sardinia, Lombardy, Venetia, Parma, Modena, Tuscany, the Papal States and Naples. Such was the scope of his vision that Garibaldi was prepared to fight anywhere – in Lombardy against the Austrians in 1848 and 1849, in Rome against the French in 1849, and in Sicily and Naples against Bourbon rule in 1860. Cavour, however, envisaged only an enlarged Piedmont, which would include Lombardy and Venetia. At its most ambitious, his scheme was for an Italian Confederation; this was explicitly stated in a confidential memorandum to Victor Emmanuel explaining the contents of the secret Pact of Plombières with Napoleon III in 1858. Mazzini, fully aware of Cavour's caution, described him as 'the ministerial liberator who taught his master how to prevent the union of Italy'.[2] It does, indeed, appear that Cavour was willing to halt the growth of the Italian nation at a stage already reached by Germany in the loosely structured Confederation.

Between 1859 and 1860, however, Cavour was pushed along irresistibly by the sequence of events and had to adapt his former proposals. His original dislike of total unification had been due largely to his fear of the radical republicans who had made it their ultimate aim. But when Napoleon III withdrew France prematurely from the war with Austria by the Treaty of Villafranca in 1859, Cavour threatened to 'turn revolutionary and conspirator' himself and he resigned his office of prime minister. Until his recall a few months later, Cavour now found himself approving and depending on the activities of Ricasoli, Farini and Azeglio to gain popular acceptance for the incorporation of Tuscany, Modena and Romagna into Piedmont in defiance of the Villafranca settlement. Once

Cavour, Garibaldi and the Unification of Italy

reinstalled as prime minister, this time of a greatly enlarged kingdom in Northern Italy, Cavour was again carried forward by the momentum of change. He was seriously concerned about the activities of Garibaldi and the 'Thousand' in Sicily and Naples (1860) and their threat to the Papal States in Central Italy. He realized that to oppose Garibaldi directly would incur the wrath of Italian patriots everywhere, including Piedmont. To take no action would enable Garibaldi to establish a rival state in the south or, at best, give him the credit for the unification of Italy. Cavour found this prospect abhorrent and was quite adamant that 'The King cannot accept the crown of Italy at the hands of Garibaldi'.[3] The only solution to this dilemma was to take direct military and diplomatic action: to annex the Papal States and to outmanoeuvre Garibaldi into relinquishing his hold on the south. The overall result would have to be a kingdom covering the entire peninsula.

If Cavour's ideas about the extent of Italy underwent a major change, so, too, did Garibaldi's views on the most suitable form of government. Garibaldi had originally agreed with Mazzini's dictum that 'our Italian tradition is essentially republican'.[4] Cavour, on the other hand, opposed republicanism as a dangerous form of radicalism and refused to consider anything but a constitutional monarchy which, in his view, was 'the only type of government which can reconcile liberty with order'.[5] This time the change was made by Garibaldi. As early as 1855 he stated that the main priority must be unification and that all the elements of Italy 'must amalgamate and join whoever is strongest among them'.[1] He applauded the formation of the National Society in 1857, and the decision of many republicans to seek the leadership of the King of Piedmont. His slogan was now: 'Unite yourselves to our programme – *Italy and Victor Emmanuel* – indissolubly.'[6] He also remained on excellent personal terms with the King, affirming in 1860: 'I am truly his friend for life.'[7]

Inevitably both Cavour and Garibaldi had feelings of uneasiness about their changes of plan. Cavour died suddenly and unexpectedly in 1861, before the Kingdom of Italy was more than a few months old; but he had already encountered serious problems over the local administration of the new nation, caused largely by the last-minute inclusion of Naples and the Papal States. He must, therefore, have regretted being pushed by Garibaldi into extending the kingdom in Northern Italy to the Kingdom of Italy. For his part, Garibaldi

77

looked back with some distaste on his surrender of Naples.

> We drove the Bourbon out and took that other,
> Dethroned a corpse, and set up its sick brother.[8]

Indeed, Garibaldi went further, complaining that the Kingdom of Italy was, in the 1870s, corrupt, backward and disunited. Towards the end of his life, therefore, he reaffirmed the ardent republicanism of his youth, and in 1872 declared: 'I am a republican, since I believe this the best kind of government for honest people, the one most generally desired and least dependent on violence or imposture.'[9]

*

Perhaps the greatest contrast between Cavour and Garibaldi lay in the basis of their power and their concept of authority. Cavour was a parliamentarian with an inherent suspicion of mass participation. Garibaldi, on the other hand, was a populist, prepared to appeal directly to the support of the masses. Cavour opposed revolution and radicalism, adopting a stance of conservative liberalism which was similar to the philosophy of Guizot and of the French Orléanist monarchy (1830–48). Garibaldi was one of the great radicals of the nineteenth century, considering himself an ideological descendant of the first French Revolution.

It is hardly surprising that Cavour should have put his faith in parliamentary institutions, since they had shaped his political career. He was elected to the Piedmontese Assembly in 1848, rising in rapid succession to the positions of Minister of Marine and Commerce (1850), and Prime Minister (1852). He owed his power and influence to complex parliamentary manoeuvres. In 1852, for example, he engineered the downfall of Prime Minister Azeglio by building a large centrist *bloc* known as the *connubio* and, for the rest of his life, skilfully maintained a majority for himself. He made full use of his power to take the initiative when dealing with political opponents and this parliamentary *Realpolitik* earned him the grudging acclaim of Gattina (a backbencher): 'Count Cavour is a cross between Sir Robert Peel and Machiavelli.'[10]

Garibaldi, too, had experience of politics in Uruguay before 1847, Rome in 1849, and Turin from 1860. On one famous occasion he clashed with Cavour in the Italian parliament and lost: Cavour was able to drum up a majority against Garibaldi's censure of his

(a) Italy before 1848

	Provinces of the Austrian Empire
	Ruled by members of the Habsburg family
	Kingdom of Piedmont/Sardinia
	Kingdom of the Two Sicilies (Naples)

(Lucca ended 1847)

(b) The stages of unification

	Kingdom of Sardinia in 1858 (plus Savoy and Nice)
	Added to Sardinia after conquest from Austria 1859
	Added to Sardinia after plebiscites 1860
	Conquered by Garibaldi Added to Sardinia 1860
	Garibaldi's route 1860
	Conquered by Sardinia 1860
	Added to Kingdom of Italy 1866
	Added to Kingdom of Italy 1870
	Nice and Savoy (ceded to France 1860)

Kingdom of Italy 1861

The unification of Italy

recent conduct of the war. The two men presented a strange contrast in their powers of oratory. Gattina observed that Cavour was a speaker in the English parliamentary style; his arguments were reasoned but his delivery not particularly impressive. Garibaldi, by contrast, possessed a voice which was renowned throughout Europe and he was at his best when delivering a spontaneous address which appealed to the emotions. For this reason, he found parliamentary debate sterile, and preferred more direct contact with the masses, amongst whom he was known as *il padre dell'Italia*. He had no aspirations to ministerial office and frequently questioned the need for parliamentary sovereignty at all. He went so far as to suggest that dictatorship might be more appropriate to Italy's needs.

This, in fact, was the point of greatest disagreement between Cavour and Garibaldi. Cavour was uncompromising in his hostility to the idea of dictatorship, whether popular or monarchical, revolutionary or reactionary. Besides, Cavour realized, 'parliament enables me to do many things which would be impossible for an absolute ruler'.[11] He found Garibaldi's attachment to dictatorship sinister and alarming; his fear of what Garibaldi might do with this power in Southern Italy induced him, in 1860, to take the extraordinary measures described in the next section. It could be argued, however, that Cavour sometimes misunderstood Garibaldi's motives; the latter was not tempted by power for its own sake, but rather as a means of taking direct action on behalf of the people, thereby reducing the possibility of obstruction and delay which he considered the inherent defects of parliamentarianism. He advocated a return to the constitutional device of Ancient Rome whereby a single leader could assume total authority in times of emergency. He advanced this as a solution to Italy's problems on three occasions. The first was in Rome in 1849, but his path was blocked by the followers of Mazzini. The second was after the conquest of Sicily and Naples in 1860, when Garibaldi ousted the Bourbon administration and ruled by decree, although, according to Crispi, 'by love not by force'.[12] A few months earlier he had urged Victor Emmanuel to take more active measures to complete Italian unification: 'Sire, Italy does not need elections or liberty, but battles; assume the dictatorship!'[13] Victor Emmanuel was not averse to this prospect, but nothing came of it. Cavour had already side-stepped a somewhat clumsy royal attempt to weaken parliament in 1855, and his ministerial position was invulnerable.

Cavour, Garibaldi and the Unification of Italy

Italy's parliamentary institutions were therefore upheld by a conservative, whose contact with the people was indirect and limited, against a radical, whose personal appeal and popularity were unquestioned. Ultimately the traditional concept of legislative checks and balances prevailed over the demand for the personification of the masses by an unfettered executive.

*

What, in practical terms, did Cavour and Garibaldi contribute to the unification of Italy?

The role of Cavour was entirely diplomatic, his fundamental aim being to secure further territory for Piedmont by the expulsion of the Austrians from Northern Italy. Like Bismarck, with whom he is often compared, he showed an uncanny ability to realize his objectives, even if it meant adopting a devious approach and bending to circumstances. Hence his cousin, de la Rive, described him as 'a bar of iron painted like a reed'.[10] Indeed, he was so well versed in the art of diplomacy that Mazzini called him the 'pale ghost of Machiavelli'.[14] Two examples can be used to illustrate this. The first was the provocation of war with Austria in 1859. Cavour was realistic enough to consider French assistance essential if Austria were to be excluded from Northern Italy. Napoleon III, in his own words, was anxious 'to do something for Italy', but, naturally enough, wanted Austria to appear the aggressor. Consequently, the secret Pact of Plombières, drawn up between France and Piedmont in 1858, made French assistance conditional on Austrian aggression. Cavour devoted himself to preparing for war and finding a devious way of stinging Austria into delivering an ultimatum; in his jubilance he said, in a famous mixed metaphor: 'We have Austria in a cleft stick and she cannot get out of it without firing a cannon.' The second example of Cavour's diplomatic art was his invasion of the Papal States in 1860. Although his motive was undoubtedly to prevent Garibaldi from making an attempt on Rome, Cavour manufactured a more appealing excuse. The inhabitants of the Marches were secretly encouraged to rise against the 'brutal oppression' of foreign troops employed by the Pope and to appeal to Piedmont for protection. When the Papacy failed to respond to an ultimatum delivered by Piedmont for the dismissal of foreigners, Cavour sent an army to annex the whole area (with the exception of Rome and the adjacent Patrimony). A frank observation once made by Cavour seems especially appropriate to this sequence of events: 'If we did for ourselves what we do for our country, what rascals we should be!'[2]

Garibaldi, too, had some experience of foreign dealings, his particular ability being to gain the moral backing of other leading statesmen for the cause of Italian unity, but he lacked the unscrupulous element which brought Cavour success. Oliphant called him, in 1860: 'The most amiable, innocent, honest nature possible, and a first rate guerilla chief, but in council a child.'[15] In fact, his real strength was as a soldier. He harassed the Austrians in Northern Lombardy in 1848 and 1859, achieving far greater successes than the regular armies of Piedmont, and bringing to Italy the techniques of guerrilla warfare which he had learned and perfected during his long exile in South America. His campaigns against the Bourbons in Sicily and Naples (1860) were especially important. They enlarged the original plans for unification to embrace the entire peninsula, and also saved Italians from the charge that national unity had been accomplished only by Cavour's manipulation of foreign aid. Garibaldi showed the rest of Europe that Italians could be aroused into sustaining a series of popular campaigns against disciplined armies.

What, in retrospect, appear to be complementary roles, were, at the time, very much in conflict. By 1860 each statesman had developed a profound mistrust of the other. Cavour observed of Garibaldi: 'He is a soldier of fortune, and behind his outward petulance there lies the profound dissimulation of a savage',[16] while Garibaldi described Cavour as 'a low intriguer'. Cavour's attitude to Garibaldi can best be illustrated by his policies towards the Thousand's conquest of Sicily and Naples. He was fundamentally opposed to the expedition because of possible diplomatic complications with France and other powers. But he could not be seen to be too obstructive, as Garibaldi had become enormously popular in Piedmont, as well as in other parts of Italy. Consequently, he allowed the Thousand to sail from Piedmont, but was also determined to keep his options open. 'If the insurrection is put down,' he observed in private, 'we shall say nothing; if it is successful we shall intervene in the name of order and authority.'[3] Garibaldi, however, proved unwilling to hand over Sicily to Piedmont, preferring to proclaim himself temporary dictator and use it as a base from which to conquer mainland Naples. Cavour was now seriously concerned that Garibaldi's conquest of the whole of Southern Italy would threaten 'the national and monarchical character of the Italian movement'.[17] Characteristically, therefore, Cavour now engaged in secret conspiracy to overthrow the Bourbons before Garibaldi's arrival. But the speed of Garibaldi's advance from the Strait of Messina to the city of Naples took Cavour by surprise and negated all his efforts. Fortunately, Garibaldi was prepared, by November, to hand over his conquests to Victor Emmanuel, thus allaying Cavour's fears.

Garibaldi was embittered by the whole episode and subsequently attacked Cavour for his delaying tactics: 'Every possible obstacle was raised in our path between the time we left Genoa and when we arrived at Naples.'[18] Yet he accomplished his victories largely by ignoring Cavour and trusting to the goodwill and support of Victor Emmanuel. Thus, when La Farina was sent by Cavour to Sicily to dissuade the Thousand from crossing to the mainland, Garibaldi ordered his immediate deportation. Throughout his 1860 campaigns, Garibaldi refused to compromise with Cavour, determined that the southern half of the peninsula should be incorporated into a united Italy by his efforts alone. It was an arrogance which Cavour detested but also misunderstood; for Garibaldi was actually working for the extension of Victor Emmanuel's authority and not, as Cavour feared, for the realization of Mazzinian republicanism.

*

Victor Emmanuel's predecessor, Charles Albert, had once maintained *'Italia farà da sè'* ('Italy will do it herself'). Cavour always worked on the assumption that this was totally inappropriate and therefore secured outside help to expel the foreigner. It was Garibaldi, however, who extended the process of unification well beyond the original projections of an enlarged Piedmont. In this sense, it could be argued that Italy *completed* herself.

10

The Unification of Germany

In September 1862 Otto von Bismarck, Prussia's newly appointed Minister President, addressed the Budget Commission of the Prussian *Landtag*. The delegates had recently rejected over-whelmingly an Army Bill, introduced by von Roon, to increase the number of cavalry and infantry regiments. Bismarck now reminded them that if Prussia were to play a dominant role in German affairs, this role must be underpinned by military security. 'Germany', he concluded, 'looks not to Prussia's Liberalism, but to her power . . . The questions of the day will not be decided by speeches and majority decisions . . . but by blood and iron.'[1]

The 'blood and iron' speech passed into mythology as well as history, becoming the phrase most commonly used to describe the method by which a united Germany was eventually created. Until, that is, the British economist John Maynard Keynes challenged the long-held assumption that diplomatic and military factors alone created Germany. Instead, he argued, the long period of economic and industrial preparation must be taken into account, for without this the German nation would have been a mere shell. Hence 'The German Empire was created more by coal and iron than by blood and iron.'[2]

This chapter will weigh up the relative importance in German unification of both influences: diplomatic-military and economic-industrial. It will also look at another controversy. Was the German Empire which emerged in 1871 the model which Bismarck had in

The Unification of Germany

mind from the very start? Or was it the outcome of a series of fortuitous developments?

*

Before unification Germany consisted of a group of smaller states and two major powers, Austria and Prussia.

Until 1806 the smaller states had numbered over 200, but Napoleon I had, in destroying the Holy Roman Empire and substituting his own Confederation of the Rhine, reduced them to sixteen. In 1815, these were incorporated into the German Confederation, which was established by the Congress of Vienna. The opening decades of the nineteenth century were of vital importance for the development of nationalism in these smaller states. In the first place, Napoleon's constitutional consolidation removed the tiny splinter states and free cities which had, for centuries, impeded any form of unity. Secondly, Germans in Hanover, Mecklenburg, Bavaria, Baden, Württemberg, Saxony and other states were conscious of a common role in ejecting French rule. Whether, in fact, Napoleon had been defeated by traditional powers rather than by incipient nationalism, did not really matter. The myth of the patriotic war blended with the common cultural heritage which German Romanticism had given a powerful boost. The result was that 'Germany' exerted, for the first time, a strong emotional and intellectual appeal among liberals, students and a wide cross-section of the middle classes.

The other two components of Germany, Austria and Prussia, each had territory inside and outside the Confederation. Between 1815 and 1848 the two powers remained wary of any manifestations of German nationalism, especially those accompanied by liberal programmes, because these seemed to threaten their more traditional dynastic foundations. There was, therefore, considerable co-operation between the two governments of Berlin and Vienna over policy towards the rest of the Confederation. This period of 'peaceful dualism' was in sharp contrast to the bitter Austro-Prussian rivalries of the eighteenth century. The 1848 revolutions, however, brought dualism to an end and altered the whole nature of the German question.[3] The smaller states had, through their representatives in the Frankfurt parliament, taken the initiative in devising a scheme for a united Germany. Although this was not implemented, it was clear that the clock could not be turned back to 1815 and that extensive revision of the existing German Confederation would be only a matter of time.

The question now arising was: which of the two powers would be able to take charge of and direct this aspiration towards unity? At first sight, Austria might seem the more appropriate. Since she was, herself, a multi-racial and heterogeneous empire, she would be more likely than Prussia to respect the individualism of the smaller German states within a federation. Austrian leadership of Germany would also be in accord with historical evolution. After all, she had dominated the Holy Roman Empire for the second half of its thousand years' existence. Yet it was to Prussia that the majority of German nationalists looked in 1848. Many had deep misgivings about the militarist tradition which Prussia had acquired from Frederick William I (1713–40) and Frederick the Great (1740–86). But the doubters were outnumbered by the *Kleindeutsch* supporters, who saw in Prussia a more cohesive state which was less archaic than Austria in its policies and, above all, more progressive economically. Austrian leadership might be safer, but Prussian leadership would be more in tune with the type of economic progress which the majority of the middle class considered the main priority for the future.

*

Prussia's economy grew steadily between 1815 and 1848 and then, during the 1850s and 1860s, experienced the first industrial revolution on the Continent.

During the earlier period, Prussia had three major advantages. First, she had a tradition of economic reform. Following Prussia's military defeat by Napoleon, ministers like Stein and Hardenberg overhauled the financial system and modified the social structure by abolishing serfdom. What Hardenberg called 'timely reforms from above'[4] gave a vital shove to private enterprise which an unchanged system still held back in Austria. Second, the Congress of Vienna (1815) gave Prussia the coal- and iron-producing areas of the Rhineland in compensation for the Polish provinces annexed by Russia. The Ruhr and Saar regions complemented Silesia in transforming Prussia from a state with relatively few natural resources, to one with the richest mineral deposits in Central and Western Europe. Third, Prussia was able to extend her influence over fellow

The Unification of Germany

German states, from 1834 onwards, by means of the *Zollverein* (customs union), which brought together the Prussian-Hessian, the South German and the Central German Customs Unions. By 1834 many of the smaller German states were linked commercially to Prussia, and were becoming increasingly cut off from Austria (which, of course, was not a member of the *Zollverein*). The middle-class liberals within these states responded enthusiastically to the opportunities offered, and began to think in terms of political unity with Prussia as a means of preserving a larger market and developing Germany as a more powerful economic entity.

During the 1850s the Prussian economy took off, encouraged by the progressive policies of Manteuffel (Minister President), von der Heydt (Minister for Trade) and, above all, Delbrück (an Under-Secretary in the Ministry of Trade). The railway network in Prussia increased from 3869 kilometres in 1850, to 7169 by 1860 and 11,523 by 1870. Coal production in the Saar mines increased from 700,000 tons in 1850 to 2.2 million in 1860 and, in the Ruhr during the same period, from 2 million to 4.3 million. The steel industry, which took full advantage of the Bessemer process (developed in 1856), was further enhanced by the existence of the most highly developed chemical industry in the world. Credit for industrial growth was widely available, whether in the form of investment from abroad or of German joint stock banks like *Disconto-Gesellschaft* (1851), *Darmstadter Bank* (1853) and *Berlin Handelsgesellschaft* (1856). Prussia's economic growth pulled the rest of Germany behind it. The total value of the *Zollverein's* exports, for example, increased between 1853 and 1856 from 356.9 million to 456.1 million thaler, while Germany's combined coal production expanded from 3.2 million tons in 1846 to 12.3 million in 1860.

Meanwhile, Austria had become more and more concerned about the influence being exercised by her rival over the smaller states. To make matters worse, her own economic position was extremely precarious. Between 1853 and 1856, for example, Austrian exports fell from 184.3 million thaler to 150.3 million, while the continental depression which followed the Crimean War had a particularly serious effect on Austria in 1857. The Vienna government awoke, belatedly, to the commercial isolation imposed on Austria by the *Zollverein*. During the 1850s, therefore, Austrian ministers sought to transform the *Zollverein* into a wider customs union covering the whole of Central Europe. Bruck, Minister of Commerce from 1848, hoped eventually to fit Austria into a huge free trade area covering the whole Continent between the Rhine and the Black Sea, with the centre of gravity in Vienna rather than Berlin. Such proposals were, however, doomed to failure. Prussia neatly evaded and side-stepped all proposals to reform the *Zollverein* and, from 1859, Austria became involved in more urgent issues like the Italian War. Austria came out the worse from a further round of negotiations with Prussia in the early 1860s. By 1864 the *Zollverein* was still firmly dominated by Prussia, and Austria had been effectively denied even a treaty of limited accession.

There can be no doubt that Prussia's economic domination of the smaller states was a vital factor in her eventual success in uniting Germany. It was not, however, sufficient. By the early 1860s it had become apparent that the political framework of the German Confederation was acting as an obstacle to any further progress towards unity. By the Olmütz Punctuation (1850) the institutions of the Confederation were restored in full, and Prussia's brief experiment with the Erfurt Union was summarily ended. The Confederation might not be the perfect arrangement for Germany but, to Austria, it was preferable to a closer form of political unity or to allowing the smaller German states to revolve around Prussia. Despite its defects, therefore, the Confederation was the only type of Germany which Austria would tolerate. In the words of Schwarzenberg, Austria's Minister President, 'a threadbare and torn coat is better than no coat at all'.[5] Thus, although Prussia had succeeded by 1860 in preventing Austria from modifying the economic arrangements of the *Zollverein*, Austria had managed, equally effectively, to veto any constitutional change in the Confederation. The progress towards a united Germany had, therefore, reached a political impasse which would have to be resolved by political means.

*

This was to be the achievement of Otto von Bismarck, appointed Minister President by William I in 1862. During the next nine years Prussia found herself at war for the first time since 1815, and against no fewer than three enemies. The first war, against Denmark in 1864, released the Duchies of Schleswig and Holstein for the German Confederation; the second expelled Austria from Germany in 1866, and united the north; while the third resulted, by 1871, in the defeat of France and the incorporation of the south German

The Unification of Germany

states into the new German Empire. By a combination of subtle diplomacy and naked militarism Bismarck appeared to have fulfilled his 1862 prediction that Prussia would unite Germany by 'blood and iron'.

Was this sequence of events carefully engineered by a master strategist of *Realpolitik*? Bismarck himself tried to create the impression that it was. After his retirement in 1890 he stressed the importance of Prussian militarism in German unification and his own role in bringing about the right circumstances. Hence he remarked: 'The Gordian Knot of German circumstances was not to be untied by the gentle methods of dual policy [but] could only be cut by the sword.' Furthermore, 'In order that German patriotism should be active and effective, it needs as a rule to hang on the peg of dependence upon a dynasty.'[6] As for his own role, he provided Disraeli, in 1862, with a much quoted outline of his future intentions. 'When the army has been brought to such a state as to command respect, then I shall take the first opportunity to declare war with Austria, burst asunder the German Confederation, bring the middle and smaller states into subjection, and give Germany a national union under the leadership of Prussia.'[7] Such apparent confidence in his ability to redirect events was clearly intended for the notice of historians and fellow statesmen. Bismarck showed more concern than most about the judgement of posterity and clearly hoped to hang on to his reputation as the most successful, if the most ruthless, diplomat of the entire century.

In fact, most historians present a considerably modified picture of Bismarck's methods. It is important to realize that Bismarck was appointed Minister President in an age of growing uncertainty: the map of Europe could change within the near future in several different ways. No statesman could have complete confidence in dictating the course of this change. On the other hand, there was more scope than usual for a brilliant opportunist who was not afraid of experimentation and, as a last resort, conflict. The key to Bismarck's diplomacy was one of his most moderate assertions that events were part of an irresistible 'time stream' of history. He observed on one occasion: 'One cannot make history.' Nevertheless, it was possible, through an intuitive understanding of the issues involved and decisive action, to achieve certain broad objectives by becoming part of the 'time stream'. In other words, 'Man cannot create the current of events. He can only float with it and steer'.[8] The essential thing,

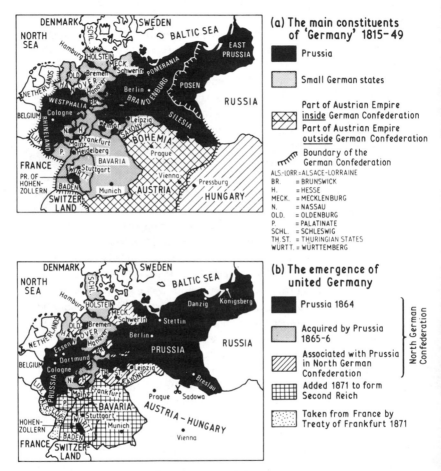

(a) **The main constituents of 'Germany' 1815-49**

■ Prussia

▦ Small German states

▨ Part of Austrian Empire <u>inside</u> German Confederation

▨ Part of Austrian Empire <u>outside</u> German Confederation

ᜤᜤ Boundary of the German Confederation

ALS.-LORR = ALSACE-LORRAINE
BR. = BRUNSWICK
H. = HESSE
MECK. = MECKLENBURG
N. = NASSAU
OLD. = OLDENBURG
P. = PALATINATE
SCHL. = SCHLESWIG
TH. ST. = THURINGIAN STATES
WÜRTT. = WÜRTTEMBERG

(b) **The emergence of united Germany**

■ Prussia 1864

▦ Acquired by Prussia 1865-6

▨ Associated with Prussia in North German Confederation

▦ Added 1871 to form Second Reich

▒ Taken from France by Treaty of Frankfurt 1871

North German Confederation

The unification of Germany

The Unification of Germany

however, was to pursue several alternative policies simultaneously and for as long as possible; 'always have two irons in the fire'.[9] Eventually, one of these would emerge as the only possible course and the others would be eliminated. Where most statesmen erred was in committing themselves too soon to a plan which eventually turned out to be inappropriate. Bismarck's diplomacy, by contrast, was aggressive and devoid of moral restraint but, at the same time, the capacity to defer the vital decision to the last possible moment enabled him to move with history into one of the channels which he had foreseen. In so doing, he gave the impression that he had directed, even divorted, the flow of events. His dealings with Austria and France provide ample evidence of his 'strategy of alternatives'.[9]

Austria had been seen by Bismarck as an obstacle to German unity ever since the Olmütz Punctuation of 1850. There were, however, several methods of dealing with the problem. One was to come to an arrangement between Prussia and Austria, partitioning Germany at the River Main. Another was to aim for Prussian dominance over all the smaller German states, and thereby eject Austria from Germany altogether. Bismarck probably had, in the early 1860s, no clear concept of 'Germany' beyond the enlargement of Prussia at the expense of her immediate neighbours; he therefore followed several policies simultaneously. Between 1864 and 1865, for example, he promoted an alliance with Austria, reasoning that this would allay the fears of the southern German states, who were more naturally inclined towards Vienna than Berlin. This co-operation seemed to reach a climax in 1864 with the joint Austro-Prussian intervention against Denmark and the occupation of Schleswig and Holstein. The 1865 Convention of Gastein between Austria and Prussia was described by Bismarck as 'papering over the cracks' between the two powers. Yet this statement reveals another motive behind Bismarck's diplomacy. He hoped that Austria would concede to Prussia the lion's share of political influence in Northern Germany. If, however, Austria should resist this development, the situation in Schleswig-Holstein could be used to precipitate, at a time of Prussia's own choice, a conflict which would have become inevitable. Meanwhile Bismarck was also hedging his bets in his international diplomacy. His negotiations with France in 1865 and vague hints of territorial gain kept Napoleon III favourably disposed towards Prussia, while Bismarck's moral support for the Russian government over the Polish Revolt won the gratitude of Alexander II. These two powers could, therefore, be relied upon to support Prussia against Austria in any constitutional alterations within the German Confederation. Should Prussia find herself at war with Austria, her two neighbours could be expected to remain neutral. Bismarck's master-stroke was the Italian alliance of 1866. This put Austria under intense diplomatic pressure, outflanked her in the event of war, and gave Bismarck the appearance of taking over from Napoleon III as the benefactor of Italian nationalism. Bismarck's position by 1866 was, therefore, unassailable, for whatever Austria might attempt, he could apply an immediate antidote. As events turned out, he chose to bring on a war from which Prussia forged the North German Confederation.

France is often seen by historians as a target used by Bismarck against which to direct German nationalism as a means of inducing the southern German states to unite with the North. Again, however, Bismarck employed several lines of diplomacy between 1866 and 1870. On the one hand, he hoped that German unification could be completed without force or undue haste. In May 1868, he observed: 'Our whole sympathy belongs to our South German brother to whom we are ready at any time to stretch out a hand, but we neither wish nor ought to force him to grasp it.'[10] Every effort should be made to link the southern states to the North German Confederation by common economic institutions like a Customs Parliament and a Customs Federal Council. On the other hand, Bismarck knew that Bavaria and Württemberg had leanings towards France; consequently, he used several blunders, made by Napoleon III, to alienate the South Germans from their western neighbour. For example, he publicized Napoleon's demands for the Saarland, as well as for Bavarian and Hessian territory in the Rhine area, concessions which Bismarck had once been prepared to consider in exchange for French neutrality in the Austro-Prussian War of 1866. Similarly, he used the Luxemburg crisis of 1867 to discredit France, although not, at this stage, to provoke a war. It seems that, by 1869, Bismarck had come to regard war with France as a distinct possibility, but not one which ought to be forced. Hence he told Werthern: 'I think it probable that German unity will be forwarded through violent events. It is quite another matter, however, to bring about such a violent catastrophe and to bear responsibility for the choice of time for it . . . Such arbitrary interventions in the development of history . . . have always had as

The Unification of Germany

their consequence only the striking down of unripe fruit.'[11] Only a year after this pronouncement, however, Bismarck's deliberate distortion of the message contained in the Ems Telegram goaded Napoleon's government into declaring war on Prussia. It seems that Bismarck had, by this time, come to the conclusion that war was unavoidable. The French government's demand for the withdrawal of Prince Leopold's candidature to the Spanish throne was so aggressively worded that compliance would have brought diplomatic humiliation to the Hohenzollern family as a whole. Besides, Bismarck realized, Prussia had by now outstripped France militarily and the southern German states were ripe for gathering. Bismarck was evidently confident that he could win a 'prize worthy of the sacrifices which every war demands'.[12]

There can be no doubt that Bismarck's success against Austria and France was due partly to the international situation in Europe during the 1860s. None of the powers could seriously consider opposing him or trying to restrain him because they were at loggerheads with each other. Each government had its own problems and priorities; to give one example, Britain was on bad terms with the French and, in any case, possessed during the 1860s a small army and a depleted navy. More than at any other time in the nineteenth century there was a power vacuum in Europe, and Bismarck was able to pursue his own designs unimpeded by the gravitational pull of international diplomacy. There no longer existed even a formal or moral restraint on aggressive statesmanship, as the Concert of Europe, which had maintained a rough balance of power between 1815 and 1854, had ceased to exist, and was not revived until the 1870s.

11

The Reforms of Alexander II

There can be no doubt about the importance of the period 1855–81 in modern Russian history. The 'Tsar Liberator' presided over an 'era of great reforms' which finally dragged Russia into the nineteenth century and provided the background to further changes under Nicholas II (1894–1917). Indeed, the scope of Alexander II's achievement has been compared by some historians with that of Peter the Great or Lenin.

At the same time, his measures were not intended primarily to innovate, but rather to inject new life into a flagging system. Hence there must be at least some reservations about their real effectiveness. This chapter will, on the one hand, point out the extent of change while, on the other, show the continuity between Alexander's ideas and methods and those of his predecessor, Nicholas I. It will also show the limited impact of some of the reforming edicts. The final section will deal with another, but related, duality: is it possible to divide the reign chronologically into two distinct periods, one dominated by reforming zeal, the other stagnating under dreary reaction?

*

Alexander was not by nature, or upbringing, a radical. He had a combination of progressive and traditional views, the result partly of the mixed education which he received from a liberal tutor, Zhukovsky, and a stern father. Although tolerant and always well-intentioned, he imbibed at an early age the autocrat's inherent

The Reforms of Alexander II

pessimism about humanity, once admitting to having 'a very low opinion of the human race in general and in particular'. Inevitably, therefore, he had a limited view of the potential for progressive change. According to D. Field, 'it is hard to find in Alexander the reformer's breadth of vision and harder still to find the strength of will'. Furthermore, 'his autocratic will did not manifest itself in bold strokes, but in passive tenacity'.[1]

When dealing with nineteenth-century Russia, it is worth bearing in mind that the term 'reform' can be given two meanings. First, it can be understood as action against the whole system of autocracy and a modification of the basis of Russia's political institutions; this was certainly the hope of the liberal constitutionalists on the accession of a new and less repressive Tsar in 1855. But clearly Alexander had no intention, at any stage in his reign, of breaking with past political practice. Nicholas I is usually seen as the embodiment of tsarist despotism, yet it was Alexander II who insisted that 'all legislation takes its authority from the unified autocracy'.[2] There was also continuity in their attitudes to parliamentary government and in their desire to uphold the social hierarchy; Nicholas, for example, had affirmed that 'the landowner is the most reliable bulwark of the sovereign',[3] while Alexander similarly regarded the nobility as 'the mainstay of the throne'.[4] The non-Russian fringes of the Empire were also unlikely to experience any radical concessions. To give Poland autonomy and a liberal constitution would only incite demands for similar privileges elsewhere and, in any case, Alexander saw no need to change Nicholas I's policy. When he visited Warsaw in 1856 he told the disappointed Poles: 'I will not change anything; what was done by my father was done well.'[5] He added, in what could be taken as an expression of intent for the whole of Russia: 'My reign will be a continuation of his.'

A second approach to 'reform', however, puts a much more favourable construction on Alexander's achievements. Autocracy would not be undermined, but it would be made to work more efficiently by modernizing and rationalizing the range of social and administrative institutions over which it presided. It was obvious that, by 1855, Russia was in desperate need of overhaul. Alexander had come to the throne at a time when Russia was in grave internal disarray; Nicholas had admitted that 'I am handing you command of the country in a very poor state'.[6] Defeat in the Crimean War showed the structural weakness of the army, the inefficiency of the financial administration and, above all, the dangerously archaic features of serfdom. Alexander was therefore impelled to take action, although what he had in mind was not a break with the past but controlled surgery to save the whole hierarchical body. There is, perhaps, too great a tendency to see Alexander as a tragic, potentially heroic figure struggling to break away from the grip of the tyrannical influence of Nicholas I. Although clearly the more progressive of the two, Alexander had no desire to revolutionize his inheritance. In fact, at times he even made use of the groundwork provided by various projects of reform initiated, but not completed, by Nicholas I.

The first and most important of Alexander's measures, and the one which earned him his unofficial title 'Tsar Liberator', was the emancipation of the serfs, carried against a protesting nobility by the 1861 Edict. From one viewpoint this can be seen as a monumental achievement. (M. S. Anderson states that 'the grant of individual freedom and a minimum of civil rights to twenty million people previously in legal bondage was the greatest single liberating measure in the whole modern history of Europe'.[7]) Peasants could now regulate their own private lives, own property, bring actions through courts and engage in trade. The 1861 Edict accomplished for Russia what had been done in France in 1789, in Prussia in 1807 and in Austria in the 1780s and again in 1849. Its lateral impact was also considerable, for the end of seigneurial jurisdiction necessitated reforms in the entire system of justice, local government and military service. The emancipation of the serfs was therefore the force behind a series of reforms which followed between 1864 and 1881.

From another viewpoint, however, the Edict of Emancipation can be seen as a major reform carried out in a traditional, even cautious, way. Alexander's own intention was to introduce a controlled measure in order to forestall the possibility of more sweeping changes extracted by violence. Hence he told the nobility in 1856: 'It is better to abolish serfdom from above than to wait until the serfs begin to liberate themselves from below'.[8] Moreover, the whole project of emancipation had deep roots within the previous reign. Nicholas I had also disliked serfdom, considering it 'the indubitable evil of Russian life'. He had established a secret committee, consisting of leading reformers like Speransky and Kiselev, to examine the feasibility of gradual liberation. When this committee reported, Nicholas went ahead with the freeing of the state

The Reforms of Alexander II

peasantry (about one half of the total) and, in 1835, added a Fifth Section to the State Chancellery to implement future changes. He placed this under the authority of Kiselev and allocated to it about 1.2 million roubles, the largest sum received by any department except war. From this time onwards, however, obstacles to complete emancipation became increasingly serious so that, in 1843, Nicholas felt obliged to reassure the nobility that no further changes were being contemplated. Alexander derived considerable experience from his service on the committee system and also made extensive use of the surveys which had been carried out on Nicholas's orders. In a sense, therefore, the 1861 Edict was the culmination of a long but intermittent campaign.

The aftermath also illustrates the cautious nature of emancipation. The details of the terms were drafted by the bureaucracy and the main aims were, as always, to uphold the social and economic status of the nobility and to prevent the emergence of a mobile and individualistic peasantry. Hence emancipation was hedged with restrictions and qualifications like redemption payments, which many of the ex-serfs found crippling and far in excess of the value of the small plots which they worked. In addition, the government vested responsibility for peasant affairs in a traditional commune system which, in most areas, organized the payment of taxes and allocated land on the complex principle of repartitional tenure rather than on the more straightforward hereditary basis. The overall result was a peasantry which was still bound, if not by the constraints of serfdom, at least by a system which would not allow the development of simple free enterprise in the rural areas.

What of the changes which followed in the wake of emancipation? The legal system needed a complete overhaul now that the central government could no longer delegate judicial responsibility to the nobility as part of their feudal power. The reforms of 1864 were far-reaching: they introduced key concepts of western jurisprudence like equality before the law, trial by jury and the separation of criminal and civil cases. They also reduced the appalling level of bribery which had affected the courts in the previous reign and did much to modify some of the more savage forms of corporal punishment. Again, however, there were signs of continuity as well as change. Nicholas I, although hardly renowned for his knowledge of judicial procedure, had shown some concern about the extent of corruption and therefore appointed a committee under Bludov, which struggled in vain to reorganize the courts. Alexander's reform may have transcended the narrower vision of earlier administrators and jurists like Bludov and Speransky but it cannot be seen as an entirely new departure. When it came to implementing the change the forces of tradition once again became apparent. The older ecclesiastical and township courts continued to deal with a variety of cases, while the military courts were given considerable powers to deal with cases involving threats to 'public safety'. The 1864 Statute also ensured that the government departments retained the means of initiating proceedings outside the normal court system.

Changes in the structure of local government were also a priority. The emancipation of the serfs broke the hold of the aristocracy on administration and policing and necessitated the emergence of new institutions. The formation of the *zemstvos* in 1864 has been seen as the first step in the evolution of representative institutions in nineteenth-century Russia. This was followed by the Statute of 1870, notable for the establishment of the *dumas*, the urban counterpart of the *zemstvos*. Chapter 18 explains the significance of the latter institution in later constitutional developments, and it is clear that Alexander's reign was an important formative period. Nevertheless, it should also be said that the future uses of the *dumas* and *zemstvos* were not anticipated by Alexander, who tried, as far as possible, to circumscribe their powers and keep them under the supervision of the central government departments. He left them in control of uncontroversial functions, such as the provision of primary education and the improvement of medical facilities, which they discharged with unprecedented zeal and efficiency.

There were two areas in which reforms were less inhibited by tradition, mainly because there was no point at which these reforms could become a threat to autocracy. The first concerned the army. As Minister of War between 1861 and 1881, Milyutin applied the lessons of the Crimean War and also of the Edict of Emancipation; the former showed the need for a chief of general staff and an effective system of regional commands, while the latter forced a complete review of the haphazard and appallingly harsh method of recruitment. Milyutin's reforms paid off more quickly and obviously than any other, with Russia's spectacular victory over the Turks in 1877. Meanwhile, Reutern had come to grips with some of the financial problems which had afflicted Nicholas I and had dragged Russia down during the Crimean War. He ended the wasteful

The Reforms of Alexander II

administration of revenue by separate government departments, introducing, instead, the principle of overall control by the treasury. He also reduced incompetence and corruption by more systematic auditing and a regular budget. The economy as a whole was given a much-needed boost by the import of capital from Western Europe. The main beneficiary was railway construction, and the overall mileage was increased from 660 at the beginning of the reign to 14,000 by the end. But some financial deficiencies, inherited from Nicholas I, were not remedied until much later in the century. Perhaps the most important was the continuing problem of the currency, which had collapsed during the Crimean War and did not recover fully until Witte put Russia on the gold standard in 1896.

*

There has always been a school of thought which has divided the reign of Alexander II into two distinct phases, the first dominated by reform, the second by reaction. The transition from one to the other, it is argued, occurred during the 1860s, with the actual turning point located at 1866, the year in which the ex-student, Karakozov, tried to assassinate the Tsar. It can certainly be shown that attitudes stiffened in response to the Polish Revolt and also to the growing unrest throughout Russia during the early 1860s and the 1870s. Alexander II and his ministers were affected psychologically by the emergence of radicalism, whether in the form of the *raznochintsi*, led by journalists like Chernyshevski, or the violent revolutionary societies of the 1870s, like *Narodnaia Volia* (People's Will). Hence, from the mid-1860s some progressive ministers were being replaced by arch-conservatives. Golovnin, for example, lost the Ministry of Education to Count Dmitri Tolstoy, who cancelled many of the earlier reforms, made sweeping changes in the curriculum of secondary schools, interfered directly with the appointment of university staff, and restored censorship on books, newspapers and pamphlets. Some ministers, who had once been liberal, changed with the times and moved conspicuously to the Right; thus Katkov, who had supported the emancipation of the serfs and the legal and local government reforms, became an important spokesman for reaction. Underpinning the whole edifice was Shuvalov who, from the time he became head of the Imperial Chancellery's notorious Third Section in 1866, did whatever he could to secure the appointment to the bureaucracy of anti-progressives. D. A. Milyutin complained in 1873 that there was a 'devastating and disgusting contrast with the atmosphere in which I entered the government thirteen years ago'.[9]

On the other hand, such changes in attitudes and personnel did not necessarily mean that the whole base of the regime shifted from enlightened reform to unyielding reaction. There are too many threads running through the reign as a whole to allow for such an unqualified break. There is evidence, for example, of the enormous influence of conservative bureaucrats in boiling down the proposals for emancipation before 1861, resulting in widespread discontent with the actual conditions of freedom. There was also a lack of effective co-ordination between the various sections of the unreformed central government, especially between the Departments, Chancellery and Council of State; this tended, from the beginning of the reign, to impede the full implementation of the edicts. The counterpart to reaction in the so-called era of reforms was reform in the phase of reaction. Obvious examples were the Municipal Statute of 1870 and Alexander's decision in 1881 to accept Melikov's plan for a limited consultative assembly of elected representatives of public opinion. The latter, in fact, was cancelled only because of Alexander II's assassination and the imposition of a far more reactionary regime by Alexander III.

A. J. Rieber has emphasized another type of continuity between the beginning and end of the reign. Alexander II's main concerns, the argument runs, were always military and fiscal; these provided the original impetus behind emancipation and continued to dominate all aspects of domestic policy throughout the period. Serfdom, Alexander realized, had 'spawned an outmoded army' and 'crippled the treasury'.[2] Emancipation was therefore a prelude to a more efficient army and a more modern fiscal system, the achievement of which were always given priority throughout the 1860s and 1870s. This argument, while drawing attention away from the value of some of the legal and social changes, does provide the period with a degree of stability and consistency. In any case, like his two immediate predecessors, Alexander II realized that effective autocracy must depend ultimately on sound financial management and military strength. This was a traditional Romanov approach and had as much to do with Alexander's reforms as any enlightened theories.

12

The Collapse of the Second French Empire

On 8 May 1870, the Empereror Napoleon III sought the approval of the French people for recently instituted liberal changes within the Second Empire. The result of the plebiscite was a massive vote of confidence: by 7,358,000 votes to 1,571,000. This was reminiscent of the plebiscite of 1852 which had produced a vote of 7,824,000 to 253,000 in favour of the proclamation of the Empire and the end of the Second Republic.

Only four months later, in one of the most dramatic and unexpected political changes of the entire period, the régime collapsed. France turned away from Bonapartism and drifted into the Third Republic.

The two factors primarily responsible for this reversal were the shock military defeat by Prussia, and the subsequent intervention of the city of Paris to oust a system with which, regardless of the loyalties of the rest of France, it had never really identified. The second development could not have occurred without the first; the first led to the second by exposing weaknesses in the Empire which only its most ardent opponents had previously suspected.

*

French military defeat came in a war which need never have been fought, and which was the climax of a sequence of diplomatic blunders over the issue of the Spanish Candidature.

When Prince Leopold of Hohenzollern Sigmaringen (a distant relative of the King of Prussia) announced his candidature to the

Spanish throne there were misgivings in many European courts. The spectre of a close dynastic connection between Spain and Prussia haunted Britain and Austria-Hungary as well as France. But French diplomacy failed to mobilize this concern and revealed instead the most glaring inconsistency. Indeed, two policies competed for ascendancy in Paris. Gramont and the Empress Eugénie advocated tough measures and immediate pressure, while Ollivier and the Emperor preferred conciliation and caution. What actually happened was a disastrous combination of both courses. The initial application of pressure was followed by conciliation, the benefits of which were destroyed by revived aggression.

This is apparent in the complex sequence of events of July 1870. When the candidature first became public knowledge the French government's immediate reaction was to demand of the King of Prussia an unconditional guarantee of Leopold's total withdrawal. In fact, a more appropriate course would have been to prevail upon the Spanish government to withdraw the offer of the throne, thus omitting Prussia altogether from the negotiations. Only when the King of Prussia had been thoroughly antagonized did Napoleon III force upon his ministers a more moderate approach. In a classic example of the use of roundabout and discreet diplomatic channels, the French Rothschilds were asked to establish secret contacts with Gladstone via the London Rothschilds. The British Prime Minister, in turn, communicated with Leopold II of the Belgians, brother-in-law of Leopold of Hohenzollern Sigmaringen. Meanwhile, Queen Victoria had also been approached to exert some of her influence. The result was highly satisfactory: a quiet withdrawal of Leopold's candidature, with the assent of Prussia. This considerable achievement was, however, destroyed and the crisis was reactivated when Benedetti was instructed to gain from Prussia an assurance that the claim would never be revived. The extent of Napoleon's personal involvement in this has never been precisely established, but it seems that he was pressurized by the French 'hawks'. Certainly the consensus of the *corps legislatif*, the Senate and the government ministers was that Prussia must be seen openly to have capitulated. Prussia's refusal to give this guarantee brought about a state of war-fever in France which was cleverly manipulated by Chancellor Bismarck in the way discussed in Chapter 10.

The advocates of war were noisy and numerous. In the *corps legislatif* Guyot Montpayroux thundered: 'Prussia has forgotten the

The Collapse of the Second French Empire

France of Jena and we must remind her!'[1] For the capitulation of the moderates to this type of reaction two reasons can be given. First, the Emperor was afflicted by a painful bladder condition which sapped his strength and lowered his resistance. Second, both the Emperor and Ollivier claimed to be sensitive to public opinion. Ollivier had stated in 1863 that war was legitimate only 'when it is desired by the whole nation';[2] in July 1870, the nation seemed to be insisting on one. The result was a war without a real cause and at the wrong time. Before the French declaration of war on 19 July, Thiers issued a note of dissent: 'Do you want all Europe to say that although the substance of the quarrel was settled, you have decided to pour out torrents of blood over a mere matter of form?'[1]

Presumably, France was sufficiently prepared to ensure a rapid victory? The majority of the *corps legislatif* seemed to think so, and the Minister of War, Laboouf, promised that the army was at a peak of efficiency. The Emperor, however, was somewhat less confident. Speaking to the Senate, he warned: 'Gentlemen, we are entering upon a long and arduous war.'[3] There were good reasons for his reservations.

It is true that France did not lack experience of warfare during the Second Empire. She had, after all, been involved in the Crimean War (1854–6) and the War for Italian Unification (1859), and had sent overseas expeditions to China, Indochina and Mexico. Indeed, according to Marx, France was guided less by *liberté, égalité, fraternité* than by 'Cavalry, Infantry, Artillery'. In one sense, however, all this experience was inappropriate, since it was based upon far-off ventures rather than on the defence of the homeland. Napoleon I's victories had followed a period of intense national effort during the 1790s, whereas the vulnerability of France in the 1860s to war on her own frontiers was apparent in several ways.

First, there were serious deficiencies in the French system of conscription. The nation which had introduced the *levée en masse* in the 1790s had since lost the initiative to Prussia. Recruitment to the French army was always long-term and based upon a system of ballot. The result was a force devoid of any real contact with the people at large. Indeed, General Trochu openly stated that 'the ideal constitution is that which creates an army whose instincts, beliefs and habits make up a corporation distinct from the rest of the population'.[4] Prussia, by contrast, had long since adopted a system of short-term service and, by applying this universally rather than

Aspects of European History 1789–1980

selectively, had built up a massive reserve power. Napoleon III was certainly aware of the discrepancy in the mobilizing capacity of the two countries and endeavoured, at the Compiegne Conference of November 1866, to gain support for short-term conscription. There was, however, strong resistance in the *corps legislatif*, and it gradually became clear that Napoleon's efforts to liberalize the Empire by strengthening its legislature had only increased the latter's capacity to obstruct military reforms; the middle class, in particular, wanted *La Gloire* but their parliamentary represent-atives would not consider genuine conscription. The eventual com-promise of 1868, and the introduction of the part-time *garde mobile*, could not prevent the French armies from being completely out-numbered in 1870.

Equally serious was the cumbersome method of moving troops to the Front on mobilization. Prussia had adapted her railway network far more effectively to military demands, which meant that the advance of the Prussian armies encountered fewer delays. This was particularly unfortunate as French success would depend on a rapid invasion of the southern German states, to detach them from any alliance with Prussia. During the Franco-Prussian War, von Moltke and Bismarck were astonished at the delay and confusion of the French concentrations (even though French mobilization in 1870 was quicker than it had been in 1854 or 1859). Units from all parts of France reached the Front in disarray, imperfectly merged into their higher formations. The Prussians, who had expected to fight a war of defence, were able to seize the initiative and inflict severe defeats on the French in the Battles of Wissembourg, Fröschwiller and Forbach (August 1870).

The leadership of the French armies was also suspect. There was no shortage of famous names – Bazaine, Canrobert, Macmahon, Trochu. But these commanders formed an élite which resisted change and placed its trust in traditional methods. Napoleon III realized the need for greater co-ordination at the centre but, unlike Wilhelm I, his Prussian counterpart, he failed to form a war cabinet. Matters were made worse by unfortunate policy decisions. On the outbreak of war, for example, the assumption of overall command by Napoleon III destroyed any chance of independent action by the three Rhine armies. Even after the Emperor had been elbowed out of the way by Bazaine, defective decisions were made. The armies were hamstrung by the failure of the Paris government to allow any

The Collapse of the Second French Empire

large-scale adoption of defensive strategy. In August Macmahon's army was prevented from retreating from an insecure position at the Argonne; instead, it was ordered to join Bazaine, with the result that both were defeated at Beaumont. The ultimate catastrophe occurred when Paris urged Napoleon III to remain at the Front and not, as he intended, conduct an orderly withdrawal. Instead of regrouping for the possibility of a defensive victory, the remaining French forces were bottled up and forced to surrender on 2 September. There was to be no Valmy; only Sedan.

The outcome of the war might have been less catastrophic had France been assisted by one or more allies. The complete lack of diplomatic support in 1870 can be attributed to the widespread suspicion aroused by the Emperor's foreign policy. It is ironical that in the opening years of his reign he had been highly successful in gaining the recognition – even support – of other powers. He had always maintained high hopes of serving French territorial interests while, at the same time, harnessing the latent power of nationalism in the belief, expounded by Napoleon I, that: 'The first ruler who appeals to the peoples of Europe will be able to accomplish anything he wishes.'⁵ His ultimate ambition was clearly to reverse the 1815 Vienna Settlement and to re-establish the hegemony of France in Europe.

Unfortunately, the type of revisionism pursued by Napoleon III eventually antagonized every state in Europe, effectively isolating France by 1870. Russia made an agreement with France in 1858, but remained suspicious of Napoleon's support for incipient nationalism. When the Emperor expressed sympathy with the Polish Revolt in 1863, Alexander II broke off diplomatic contacts with France and considered closer co-operation with Prussia instead. A more promising area of permanent friendship was Italy; after all, Napoleon III had committed French troops and resources to the cause of Italian Unification in 1859. The apparent absence of Italian gratitude, one of the great disappointments of Napoleon's reign, was attributable to the suspicion of Cavour and his successors that France had never intended to allow the establishment in the Italian peninsula of anything more than a series of satellite states. Certainly the Italian government never forgot the premature withdrawal of France from the war by the Armistice of Villafranca, while Garibaldi regarded the French garrison supporting Papal power in Rome as a direct betrayal of Italian nationalism, particularly since

Aspects of European History 1789–1980

French troops fired upon two Italian expeditions in the 1860s. Even the moderate Victor Emmanuel turned against France after Napoleon's annexation of Nice and Savoy in 1860 and, like Russia, cultivated closer relations with Prussia. The result was a military alliance between Italy and Prussia, drawn up in 1866.

What of the British attitude to Napoleon III's diplomacy? At first London's reaction was favourable; Palmerston had been so eager to recognize the new régime that he had landed himself in trouble with the Prime Minister and the Queen, although this had been on the question of procedure rather than principle. Within three years, France and Britain were formal allies in the Crimean War and the British government seemed quite content to allow Napoleon III to preside over the Paris Peace Conference of 1856. But five years more brought open British hostility, particularly to Napoleon's scarcely concealed dynastic designs in Italy and hopes of territorial acquisitions in Germany. Palmerston wrote to Russell in 1861: 'The whole drift of our policy is to prevent France from realizing her vast schemes of expansion in a great number of quarters.'[6] The lowest point in Anglo-French relations was reached in 1870. When Bismarck disclosed to the British government French schemes to partition Belgium, Gladstone declared that he was 'shocked and horrified'. British public opinion had been reinfected with its customary francophobia, and even literary circles joined in the castigation of Napoleon. Carlyle, for example, contrasted 'noble, patient, deep, pious and solid Germany' with 'vapouring, vainglorious, gesticulating, quarrelsome, restless and over-sensitive France'.

Of all the European states, Austria had the most cause for resentment against Napoleon III. After all, France had assisted the Italians in ejecting Austrian rule from Lombardy in 1859. Secondly, Napoleon had attempted to negotiate an agreement with Russia in 1858 which would have given autonomy to part of the Austrian Empire. Thirdly, the Austrian royal family had lost one of its members, Maximilian, in Napoleon's catastrophic Mexican venture (1863). Yet Austria also had the best reason for supporting France in 1870. Her own recent defeat by Prussia in the Seven Weeks' War (1866) had resulted in her exclusion from Germany and she would clearly welcome an opportunity to revive her previous connection with the southern German states. French diplomats were therefore active in Vienna in 1870, but they failed to produce any specific

The Collapse of the Second French Empire

commitment. For one thing, Austria was militarily exhausted; for another, she had recently experienced serious constitutional and racial problems which even the 1867 *Ausgleich* had not entirely solved. Napoleon had to be satisfied with a vague undertaking that Austria would make common cause with France once the latter had actually invaded southern Germany. After being acquainted with the French disasters of August 1870, the Emperor Franz Joseph opted for 'friendly neutrality'. He no longer had any choice.

French isolation was symptomatic of the collapse of the basic structure of Napoleon's foreign policy. He had sought and, for a while achieved, dominance by fostering nationalism and reviving the Vienna settlement. But he had assumed that this nationalism would be the product of revolutions against authoritarian régimes and that it would seek ideological inspiration from the French Revolution. In fact, the nationalism which emerged in Germany in the 1860s was carefully pruned by Bismarck of any revolutionary connotations and rendered wholly conservative. France, therefore, was to be the victim of Bismarck's *Realpolitik*, not the benevolent guide and mentor envisaged by Napoleon III. Bismarck systematically exploited Napoleon's rash claims to the left bank of the Rhine, Luxembourg and Belgium, thereby casting France in the role of a predator. This destroyed the self-assurance which Napoleon had once possessed so that, according to von der Goltz, 'the Emperor seemed to have lost his compass'.[7] Thus, to return to the starting point of this section, the outbreak of war in 1870 was, for France, futile and unnecessary. It benefited only Prussia; by using it as a means of uniting Germany Bismarck was applying the dictum of Frederick the Great that 'diplomacy without war is like music without instruments'.

*

Military defeat did not by itself cause the collapse of the Second Empire. When Napoleon III went into captivity after the Battle of Sedan France could have been governed by a temporary regency of the type which had operated during the periods of insanity experienced by George III of England, or Frederick William IV of Prussia. Such an expedient, however, was made impossible by the intervention of Paris in the sequence of events, with the result that a republic was proclaimed on 4 September. It is difficult to over-estimate the hold which Paris had, at certain times, over the rest of the country. Napoleon III believed that for half a century, 'France has gone on only because of the administrative, judicial and financial organization of the Consulate and [First] Empire'.[8] These, of course, had been centred on Paris before 1815, and even the Bourbon and Orléanist monarchies had not reversed the most complete form of centralization existing in any European state. Paris had overthrown Charles X in 1830 and Louis Philippe in 1848. Could Napoleon III escape the same fate?

He had certainly used the confused situation in Paris to climb to power, first as President in 1848, then as President for ten years in 1851, and finally as Emperor in 1852. But, from the start, he had tried to break the influence of Paris on the nation's destiny by projecting himself as a national leader, appealing to all classes and all areas. He hoped to break the vicious circle which Paris seemed to keep in motion: according to Prévost-Paradol: 'France is republican when she is under the Monarchy, and she becomes royalist again when her Constitution is republican.'[7] The extent of his initial support reflected the widespread disillusionment with the failures of the Second Republic. The peasantry were reassured by his guarantee of law and order; the bourgeoisie by his promise of security for the unimpeded operation of market forces; and a large part of the proletariat by his promise of social reform which was motivated by his 'love of the suffering classes'.[9] Napoleon III stressed the importance of balance between all sections of the population. At the basic level France should not be 'incessantly troubled either by demagogic ideas or by monarchist hallucinations'.[10] The underlying ideology was radical but controlled: 'The Napoleonic idea springs from the Revolution . . . it stands for the reconciliation of order, liberty, the rights of the people and the principles of authority, obeying neither the uncertain lead of a party nor the passions of the crowd.'[11] Hence, the 1852 Constitution made the Head of State 'responsible to the nation', but gave him 'free and unfettered authority'. The overwhelming majority of Frenchmen seemed to approve.

But for how long? Election figures for the *corps legislatif* show a significant change in voting habits as the reign progressed. The proportion of the popular vote cast in favour of the government rather than the opposition was as follows:

The Collapse of the Second French Empire

4:1 in the 1852 election
4:1 in the 1857 election
5:2 in the 1863 election
4:3 in the 1869 election

Significantly, the opposition was concentrated in the twenty-two largest towns and cities. Paris elected no Bonapartist deputies after 1857; in fact, the last two elections gave, in Paris, crushing majorities to the republicans, against the national trend. The capital, which was the nerve centre of the imperial administration, therefore contained the most hostile part of the population. This was due partly to the rapid alienation of the urban proletariat by the régime's economic policies, and the deterioration of working conditions and wages in contrast to the growing prosperity of the bourgeoisie. The republicans attacked the Empire for creating a plutocracy; Duchêne, referring to the most powerful 200 families of the banking and merchant classes, complained that 'Antiquity does not contain any examples of an oligarchy so concentrated'.[12] Inflation affected the proletariat more than the middle classes. It has been estimated, for example, that the average wage in Paris rose by 30 per cent during the period of the Empire, while the cost of living increased by 45 per cent and rents by 100 per cent. It is hardly surprising, therefore, that Parisians should return to the anti-monarchist and pro-republican views which they had displayed before the appearance of Napoleon III. The process was accelerated by the propaganda which poured from papers like *La Lanterne* after the relaxation of the press laws in 1868.

Ironically, the opposition intensified as the régime became increasingly moderate. Napoleon III was unique among dictators in liberalizing his institutions and weakening the basis of his own authority. He had probably always intended to implement progressive policies once the opportunity arose; indeed, he considered that the main danger to his position lay in *resisting* change. 'March at the head of the ideas of your century and these ideas will follow and support you. March behind them and they will drag you after them. March against them and they will overthrow you.'[13] This view was also held by Ollivier, who was responsible for implementing the so-called Liberal Empire in 1870. He had argued as far back as 1861 that 'without liberty democracy is but despotism. Without democracy liberty is but privilege'.[14] Yet the concessions, designed to increase the influence of the *corps legislatif* and the Senate, failed to satisfy the republican opposition. In fact, Gambetta regarded the more moderate régime of 1870 merely as 'a bridge between the Republic of 1848 and the Republic of the future'. He added ominously: 'It is a bridge which we intend to cross.'[15]

If anything, Napoleon's reforms actually weakened the Second Empire. The *corps legislatif* and the Senate obstructed much of the Emperor's programme for domestic reform between 1868 and 1870, and resisted his proposals to bring the French army up to full strength. Furthermore, the growth of parliamentarianism undermined the hold of Bonapartism on France. Although Napoleon genuinely believed in democracy, he had always regarded himself as being above and outside the conflicts between the parliamentary groups. He therefore made no attempt to form a cohesive Bonapartist *party* which would pursue a consistent set of policies and become conversant with the intricacies of parliamentary strategy. Hence the Bonapartists were by far the most heterogeneous group within the *corps legislatif*, united only by their loyalty to Napoleon himself. Once the Emperor had been removed, most of them defected to the royalist camp where, at least, monarchist principles managed to survive without being personified.

It is hardly surprising, therefore, that the republicans were able to seize the initiative in 1870. Although they were in a minority in France as a whole, they dominated Paris and could rely upon a tight organization which thrived on opposition. In normal times Napoleon III could fend off attacks on his régime; he could prove that he had the confidence of the population as a whole by means of plebiscites which effectively masked the regional variations of support shown in general election figures. But the Franco-Prussian War brought about the collapse of normal government, and the Bonapartists were insufficiently organized to prevent the republicans from gaining control.

13

Bismarck and the German Political Parties 1871–90

The Constitution of the Second Reich (1871) gave Germany universal suffrage and an elected *Reichstag*, or lower chamber. Since the new state was a conglomeration of several different interests – industrial and agrarian, Protestant and Catholic – it was to be expected that such a major advance would favour the growth of political parties. From the beginning of his Chancellorship, however, Bismarck made every effort to prevent the evolution of parliamentary sovereignty on the British model, with accountability of the executive to the legislature. Above all, he disliked the prospect of party politics, and had no intention of attaching himself permanently to any single faction. On the contrary, he avoided any long term commitments so that he could preserve maximum freedom to manoeuvre between the various party leaders. He once described his objective as 'an understanding with the majority of the deputies that will not at the same time prejudice the future authority and governmental powers of the Crown or endanger the proficiency of the army'.[1]

This chapter will analyse Bismarck's relations with the four major groupings within the *Reichstag*: conservatives, liberals, centrists and socialists. In each case it will summarize the respective attitudes of the party leaders and the Chancellor, and will assess the degree of, and reasons for, the latter's success or failure in achieving his objectives.

*

Being a *Junker* himself, Bismarck had a close attachment to the Prussian Conservatives during the 1860s; with their assistance he purged the Prussian ministry of liberalism and increased the size of the German army in preparation for German unification. There would, therefore, appear to have been a natural basis for close and permanent co-operation.

But the German Chancellor and the Conservatives had, after 1871, what can best be described as a love-hate relationship. Only the Free Conservatives, an offshoot from the main party, guaranteed him permanent support. The Conservatives themselves initially feared for the future of Prussia now that German unification had been achieved. Bismarck had always maintained that unification meant that Germany would be absorbed into Prussia: 'Prussians we are, and Prussians we shall remain.' The Conservatives, on the other hand, considered that Prussia was being poured into Germany, suffering dilution in the process. They were particularly concerned about two of Bismarck's policies in the 1870s. The first was his flirtation with the National Liberals to complete the unification of Germany's legal institutions and currency; this, it was felt, would undermine Prussian predominance by removing the possibility of Prussian separatism. The second was Bismarck's struggle with the Centre Party. The *Kulturkampf* was roundly attacked by the Conservatives, since the state's anti-clerical measures could also recoil on Protestant interests, which conservatives of all types claimed to uphold. Meanwhile, a Conservative publication, *Kreuz-Zeitung*, was criticizing Bismarck as an opportunist upstart, a view held by many right-wing Prussians who felt that Bismarck had abandoned their interests altogether.

By 1878, however, there were signs of reconciliation. Bismarck turned his back on the liberals, agreeing with the Kaiser that 'the time has come to rule on more conservative lines'.[2] He now pursued a combination of economic, social and political objectives which largely succeeded in reassuring the Right. His economic policy was shaped by protective tariffs introduced in 1879. This move was particularly popular with the *Junkers* of East Prussia, who faced heavy competition from large American and Russian grain imports. Indeed, it would be no exaggeration to say that the *Junkers* were saved by protection. The swing away from free trade also benefited the industrialists and hence pleased the Free Conservatives. Aristocrats of both kinds – industrial and agrarian – were confirmed

Bismarck and the German Political Parties

in their control over German society and came together in a formidable alliance between 'steel and rye'. Meanwhile, Bismarck's efforts to eliminate the threat of socialism had earned him much sympathy from the Conservatives and confirmed that he and they still had common ideological objectives. This co-operation was strengthened by political changes made by Bismarck during the 1880s. For example, he recast several government institutions to re-establish the influence of Prussia and, assisted by the Prussian Minister of the Interior, von Puttkamer, he ejected the remaining liberals from the civil service. The vacancies created were naturally filled by right-wingers.

How complete was this reconciliation? The Conservatives and Free Conservatives remained dependable supporters of the Chancellor's policies during the crucial period 1879–89 and, in particular, provided the basis of the electoral alliance known as the *Kartell*. Without them, it is difficult to see how Bismarck could have held his own in the *Reichstag*. On the other hand, the Conservatives never possessed the same degree of influence in the *Reichstag* as in the Prussian Diet; consequently, Bismarck still had to negotiate with parties, like the National Liberals, with which he had less sympathy. Nor were *all* the Conservatives won over. The more traditional elements continued to distrust Bismarck, and they sided with the Kaiser against him in 1890, while Conservatives of all descriptions found it easier to get along with Bismarck's successors.

※

Bismarck used, or abused, the German liberals more completely than any other part of the political spectrum.

He had disliked liberalism ever since his own conversion to conservatism after the failure of the Frankfurt Parliament (1848–9). In 1862 he had clashed with Prussian liberals over military expenditure and had made his position clear in his famous 'blood and iron' speech: 'Germany does not look to Prussia for her liberalism but for her strength.' He had subsequently eradicated the liberals from the state executive, and had conducted a fierce anti-liberal propaganda campaign. Elements of this conflict continued after the creation of the Reich in 1871. Both the National Liberals and the Progressives emphasized the importance of the legislature, and leaders like Bennigsen and Lasker pressed hard to make the

113

Chancellor's cabinet accountable to the *Reichstag*. Another cardinal point in the liberal programme was the control by the legislature of all funds supplied to the executive; this explains the opposition of the majority of the liberal deputies to the Tariff Bill of 1879, which was intended, among other things, to make the government more self-sufficient. The Progressives were also opposed to protection because they upheld *laissez-faire* as another article of faith. Finally, all liberals felt uneasy about Bismarck's heavy-handed measures to deal with the socialist threat. Most National Liberals and all Progressives resisted the first two drafts of the Chancellor's anti-socialist bill (1876 and 1878) on the grounds that they were a crude and discriminatory attack on basic social and constitutional freedoms and rights.

Despite this apparently unbridgeable gap, the period 1871–8 saw a strange co-operation between Bismarck and the larger of the two parties, the National Liberals. The main reason was that the National Liberals' greatest single aim was to complete German unification; since they had already compromised some of their principles by accepting the consequences of a 'blood and iron' policy, they had little to lose by using constitutional means to add the finishing touches to the new *Reich*. Hence they helped the head of the Chancellor's office, von Delbrück, put Germany on the gold standard, introduce a common currency and a code for commerce and industry, and establish the *Reichsbank*. The National Liberals, on their own initiative but with Bismarck's approval, introduced the legislation necessary to give the *Reich* a common civil and criminal law code. They were also prepared to support the central government in any struggle against what appeared to be regional or separatist interests. Hence they co-operated to provide the legislation necessary for the *Kulturkampf* although, it is true, there was a minority of dissident liberals led by Lasker and Bamberger. On the whole, Bismarck gained a great deal from this backing, although it is clear that he never had any intention of becoming permanently committed to liberalism; he valued his freedom of executive action too highly to make himself more accountable to the *Reichstag*.

The liberals, by contrast, suffered severely from their association with Bismarck. 1878 and 1879 proved to be the beginning of a long decline. A large section of the National Liberal Party compromised its belief in constitutional guarantees of individual liberty by supporting Bismarck's third anti-socialist bill in 1878, while 1879

Bismarck and the German Political Parties

saw a deep internal rift over the issue of tariff reform. The Centre Party leader, Windthorst, declared contemptuously that the liberal era had gone bankrupt. This was partly true. The National Liberals had over-zealously supported the establishment, with the result that much of their previous radicalism had disappeared. The 1880s brought further division to the liberal ranks. On the one hand, the National Liberals held on to their upper-middle-class support. Their intellectuals, like Treitschke, transformed the universities into pillars of orthodoxy, while their wealthy voters accepted without demur the closer connections with the Conservatives. The overall result was the growth of a curious and distinctively German phenomenon – right-wing liberalism. On the other hand, the Progressives, and the more radical elements of the National Liberals, reacted sharply against this trend and united, in 1884, to form the *Freisinnige* Party, led efficiently by Richter and dependent for its support on small merchants, minor officials and the more outspoken intellectuals. For a while this put up a better electoral performance than did the National Liberals, winning sixty-seven seats in the 1884 elections to the latter's fifty-one. It also had the patronage of the Crown Prince, the future Frederick III. But its decline from 1887 was rapid, and radicalism took a poor second place to 'conservatized' liberalism.

Bismarck had a great deal to do with this trend. Between 1887 and 1889 he appeared to have an uncanny ability to control the course of events. He had already reduced the National Liberals to manageable numbers and had integrated them electorally with the Conservatives by means of the *Kartell*, which won a large pro-government majority in the 1887 *Reichstag*. He was deeply concerned about the success of the *Freisinnige* Party and feared for his own office once the progressive Crown Prince came to power. His political manoeuvres, however, put paid to both threats. He provoked, in 1887, a conflict with the *Reichstag* over another army bill; this was really an excuse to have the *Reichstag* dissolved and new deputies elected. Because of the complex electoral manipulations of the *Kartell*. the *Freisinnige* lost over half their seats and Bismarck was able to confront the liberal heir to the throne with a predominantly right-wing *Reichstag*. His triumph was completed in 1888 with the death of Frederick III after only four months on the throne. The radical threat had now been eliminated. But Bismarck's success can be seen only in personal terms. The damage inflicted on

115

Germany by the splintering of a large and stable liberal party was incalculable.

*

In his relations with the Catholic Centre Party, Bismarck provoked an unnecessary conflict and eventually had to reverse his policy.

The Centre Party, formed in 1870, was highly critical of the Second Reich and firmly opposed the *Kleindeutsch* (see Chapter 10) pattern of unification because this favoured Protestant Prussia at the expense of the Catholic areas. In the former German Confederation, 52 per cent of the total population had been Catholic, and 48 per cent Protestant. In the Second Reich, as a result of the exclusion of Austria, the corresponding ratio was 37 per cent to 63 per cent. The Centre Party, therefore, found itself simultaneously pan-German, in the sense that it favoured close links with Austria, and particularist, as it defended the rights of individual Catholic states, like Bavaria, against the encroachments of Protestant Prussia. Since it could hardly expect to get Austria included in a new *Grossdeutsch* constitution, it settled for a programme of federalism and decentralization – anything which would dilute Prussian power. The Party also tried to inject a Christian ethic into politics. Its leaders opposed Bismarck's *Realpolitik*, with which the National Liberals had compromised, and also rejected the harsh economic extremes of *laissez-faire*, demanding, instead, protective social and industrial legislation along lines suggested by Father Kolping and Bishop Ketteler. Finally, they were determined to protect the Catholic Church and to act as its political agent.

Bismarck reacted swiftly to what he saw as a Catholic threat. He felt that the Centre Party revived two historic dangers: Ultramontanism and Frondism. The former was the more dangerous since it coincided with the Bull of Papal Infallibility, by which Pius IX hoped to reactivate the spiritual and temporal influence of Rome. This could, Bismarck reasoned, make Catholicism an international power for the first time since the seventeenth century. Needless to say, France and Austria would be involved in this, and this was a potential danger to Germany since the Centre Party could well seek their co-operation in spreading Catholic influence internally. The Frondeur element was also alarming. The Centre Party, Bismarck maintained, would, in resisting the Prussian monarchy, promote disruptive separatism and endeavour to cause the collapse of the

Bismarck and the German Political Parties

Reich. Bismarck's answer was the *Kulturkampf,* intended as a series of surgical measures to weaken the capacity of both the Catholic Church of Germany, and the Centre Party to be receptive to foreign and internal disruptive political influences. Falk's May Laws (1873–4) weakened Church control over education by insisting on government inspection of schools, brought the appointment and training of priests within the competence of the state, and increased the degree of secularization for example, by legalizing civil marriage. Bismarck was careful to emphasize that he was not attacking religion as such. He said in the Upper House of the Prussian Diet, in March 1873: 'The question before us is, in my opinion, distorted, and the light in which we see it is a false one, if we regard it as a religious ecclesiastical question. It is essentially a political question... it is a matter of the conflict which is as old as the human race, between monarchy and priesthood.'³ This line of reasoning was reinforced in 1874 by the historian von Sybel: 'We can see that if ever a state has rebelled against clerical pretensions from sheer necessity, from the duty of self preservation, it is our state.'⁴

The *Kulturkampf* turned into one of the major failures of Bismarck's career. By 1878 he was searching for a way of withdrawing honourably from the conflict and, in 1887, he ended the last vestiges of the struggle. What were the main reasons for this reversal?

The first was the amazing resilience shown by the Centre Party, largely because of the extent and depth of its support. Bismarck fought what he considered to be a national struggle against an enemy which drew its strength from two types of backing. On the one hand, its appeal was supranational; it claimed the allegiance of Catholics everywhere, whether they were nobles, small traders, artisans, peasants or workers. On the other hand, it would also use infranational forces like Polish separatism and the anti-German sentiment of Alsace-Lorraine. The Party was also given an effective strategy by Windthorst, who has been described as the most brilliant parliamentarian in German history. Thus it achieved more consistent results than any other party between 1871 and 1890. In the 1884, 1887 and 1890 elections it won ninety-nine, ninety-eight and 106 seats respectively; this pattern continued beyond Bismarck's resignation, the Centre winning ninety-six, 102, 100 and 105 seats in the elections of 1893, 1898, 1903 and 1907.

The second reason was that Bismarck had planned the

Kulturkampf without his usual thoroughness and attention to detail. He even clashed with Falk over the basic method. The latter preferred to use legislative measures, while Bismarck hoped that the task could be carried out with administrative instruments; this would enable the government to keep to a minimum the contacts with Prussian and German parliaments. But the manoeuvre was badly judged, since it brought much sympathy within the *Reichstag* for a party which appeared to be struggling against heavy-handed and unconstitutional interference from the executive. The scope of the *Kulturkampf* was also inadequately defined. Despite Bismarck's original intentions, the campaign against the Centre did take on the appearance of an attack on the Church, particularly when the May Laws regulated the employment of the clergy and decreed the expulsion of Jesuits. Inevitably, the Catholic Church attracted widespread support, which did much to heal the earlier rifts caused by the controversy over Papal Infallibility. For once, Bismarck had been unable to perpetuate and exploit the divisions within the enemy camp; instead, he had unintentionally effected a reconciliation, as Catholics now hastened to support the Papal encyclical of 1875, which declared the measures of the *Kulturkampf* invalid.

Finally, the Centre Party was fortunate in that Bismarck lost enthusiasm for the struggle. By 1878 he had come to realize that he had overestimated the 'Catholic threat'. The Centre Party, after all, could hardly be called radical, particularly when compared with the SPD. It also seemed much less likely that the Centre would act in association with France which, in any case, was now well on its way to becoming an anti-clerical régime. Furthermore, the Centre Party had two potential assets which could be integrated into Bismarck's policies elsewhere. Its friendship for Austria could be used to good effect in gaining support for Bismarck's proposed rapprochement with the Habsburgs (see Chapter 15). And the support of the Centre Party deputies would, in conjunction with that of the Conservatives, overcome the opposition to protective tariffs from the National Liberals, Progressives and SPD. Hence Bismarck managed to salvage something from the wreck of the *Kulturkampf*. The Centre Party voted for the tariff law, in exchange for government concessions to the Church, and also supported Bismarck's policy of state socialism in the 1880s. Nevertheless, the Centre leaders remained wary of Bismarck's attention, and refused to be drawn into the *Kartell* of 1887. Bismarck, in turn, retained a respect for the Centre which he

Bismarck and the German Political Parties

had never shown the liberals, and his last political act was to attempt in 1890 to persuade Windthorst to form a new pro-government combination in the *Reichstag* which would counter-balance the disillusioned National Liberals and Conservatives. But the Centre wisely refused to convert limited support over specific legislative measures into total subservience to a discredited Chancellor.

*

Bismarck's most consistent opponent throughout his administration was the SPD (*Sozialdemokratische Partei Deutschlands*). This was the only party which he sought to eradicate and with which he never considered the possibility of compromise.

The SPD was an amalgamation between Lassalle's General German Workers' Union and the League of Workers' Clubs led by Liebknecht and Bebel. The Gotha Programme of 1875 showed a combination of Lassallean and Marxist principles, all hostile to the new *Reich*. The existing form of universal suffrage was considered a mere sham, and there was bitter criticism of the aristocratic and bourgeois hold on the economy, since this caused deep social divisions and permanent misery for the proletariat. The solutions proposed by the Gotha Programme were radical, including a 'free state and socialist society', the 'elimination of all social and political inequality', factory restrictions on female and child labour, and 'state supervision of factory, workshop and domestic industry'. The overall strategy of the SPD was, at this stage, twofold: to promote immediate social and political reforms and, in the long term, to bring about a socialist state.

To Bismarck such objectives threatened the entire structure of the new *Reich*. The SPD would subvert the 1871 Constitution, which was based on carefully considered checks and balances, and would also destroy the competitive power of German industry by imposing labour regulations. Above all, it would threaten the national base by fostering an international socialist conspiracy; Bismarck never forgot the moral support given by German socialists to the Paris Commune, nor their opposition to Germany's annexation of Alsace-Lorraine in 1871. Thus the campaign against the Social Democrats assumed the proportions of a crusade. In his determination to crush them Bismarck tried everything, changing his strategy several times in the process. In defence of his domestic *Realpolitik* measures,

119

he once observed: 'In dealing with Social Democracy the state must act in self-defence, and in self-defence one cannot be finicky about the choice of means.'[5] His most consistent policy was repression, embodied in the anti-socialist law of October 1878. This authorized the use of emergency powers for up to a year at a time, prohibited socialist assemblies and fund collections, and censored or banned publications of all kinds. As a result, forty-five out of forty-seven papers were removed from circulation, trade unions were virtually eliminated, and many socialist leaders were arrested. Yet Bismarck also considered it necessary to pursue an additional expedient. He made a bid for the support of the proletariat by a policy of state socialism, in which the government sponsored legislation covering sickness insurance (1883), accident insurance (1884), and old age and disability insurance (1889). Then, in 1889, he returned to the task of repression and sought to renew the anti-socialist law. The result was the crisis of 1890 which forced his resignation.

Bismarck's campaign against the SPD not only failed in its attempt to eliminate socialism but actually contributed to its eventual emergence as the strongest single element in the *Reichstag* by 1913. Bismarck failed to take into consideration the growth of the proletariat, a direct result of Germany's rapid industrialization. Steel production, for example, doubled during the 1880s, a decade which also saw the transformation of the ship building, electrical and chemical industries. Two basic reasons have been given for this industrial take-off: the protection afforded by the 1879 tariff, and the development of new methods of production like the Gilchrist-Thomas method of steel smelting. The effect on the composition of the German population was considerable. In 1830 the ratio of urban to rural inhabitants was about 1:4; this had shifted to 2:3 by 1860, and then accelerated from 3:2 in 1882 to 4:1 by 1895. The change was reflected in the increase in the popular vote for the SPD: 493,000 in 1877, 550,000 in 1884 and 1,427,000 in 1890.

Another factor in the survival of the SPD was the use of evasive tactics to reduce the impact of the anti-socialist law. Secret conferences were held abroad as, for example, in Schoss Wyden in 1880, Copenhagen in 1883 and St. Gall in 1887. Bowling, gymnastic and cycling clubs served as a front for local organizations which maintained close contacts with the party caucus in the *Reichstag*, avoiding government surveillance by elaborate deception. Ideas and propaganda were disseminated through the *Sozialdemokrat*, a newspaper founded in Zurich in 1879, and edited by Vollmar and Bernstein.

Thus, although they frightened some individual socialists, Bismarck's measures evoked a disciplined and purposeful resistance from the Party as a whole. As he came to realize this, he tempered repression with state socialism. Unfortunately for Bismarck, the government received little credit for its initiative and the proletariat refused to be won over. Any advances made were accredited by the workers to the pressures which had been exerted by the SPD and not to any generosity on the Chancellor's part. Besides, Bismarck ignored the real problem of poor working conditions. He was not in favour of restricting the power of the great industrialists by factory legislation, and the workers knew that they could expect no relief from the government in this quarter. It is hardly surprising, there-fore, that state socialism was seen merely as a sop to free enterprise, just as parliamentarism was a 'fig leaf covering the nakedness of absolutism'.[6]

*

The balance sheet by 1889 was in Bismarck's favour. He had the committed support of the Conservatives and Free Conservatives; he had split the liberals and kept the larger section docile; and, although he had not succeeded in undermining the Centre, he encountered little obstruction from this source in the 1880s. Only the SPD remained totally hostile, but the loaded electoral system delayed the socialist take-off until after 1900.

Yet 1890 was the year of Bismark's greatest frustration and eventual failure. The problem was that a new and assertive Kaiser had made inroads into the authority which Bismarck had grown accustomed to wielding. Ironically, the most effective means by which the Chancellor could resist this encroachment was by claiming the support of the *Reichstag*, the very institution which he had for so long tried to weaken. But the crisis over the anti-socialist legislation showed the extent to which Bismarck had lost his political skills. He failed to maintain the *Kartell* which had so convincingly won the 1887 election, and antagonized the National Liberals and Free Conservatives as well as the Kaiser by refusing to compromise on the 'expulsion' clause of the anti-socialist bill. He even considered a *coup* against the *Reichstag*, to be followed by a new constitution which would be based on the consent of the German princes. He then abandoned this scheme in favour of another *Kartell* based on the Centre Party. Such schemes, however, served only to increase his isolation and intensify the demand for his resignation.

In the long term, Bismarck's chancellorship weakened the whole party system. Of all the major parties of the Second Reich, only the Centre and the SPD survived unchanged into the Weimar Republic; the others either disappeared or were re-established as new parties. One of the leaders of the Democratic Party, heir to the *Freisinnige* Party, observed in 1917: 'Bismarck left behind him as his political heritage a nation without any political education, far below the level which, in this respect, it had reached twenty years earlier.'[6]

14
The Survival of the Third French Republic 1870–1914

The Second Empire was replaced by the Third Republic in September 1870. As explained in Chapter 12, this was the achievement of Paris, largely in the face of the pro-imperial loyalties of the rest of France. But the permanence of this victory was by no means guaranteed, and it appeared that the provinces might well swing the pendulum back to authoritarian rule. The National Assembly which convened at Versailles in February 1871 contained an anti-republican majority and, under the temporary leadership of Thiers, took drastic measures to suppress the socialist and radical Commune of Paris. April's notorious 'Bloody Week' saw the massacre of over 20,000 people in the streets of the capital, a virtual re-enactment of the conservative and counter-revolutionary measures of Cavaignac during the 'June Days' of 1849. Cavaignac, in effect, destroyed the Second Republic. It would have come as no surprise had Thiers done the same to the Third.

Yet the Third Republic provided the longest period of continuous constitutional development in modern French history. It survived three periods of danger. The first was the attempt, during the early 1870s, to re-establish a monarchy. The second was the threat, made by Macmahon in the 1870s and Boulanger in the 1880s, to increase the powers of the executive at the expense of those of the legislature. The third was the deep cleavage in French politics and society caused by the Dreyfus Affair, and by the revolutionary dissent of both the extreme Right and the extreme Left at the turn of the century.

Aspects of European History 1789–1980

*

The Republic seemed, before 1875, to stand little chance of survival. Its supporters were compromised by the taint of the Commune and were, in any case, grouped into two antagonistic groups: moderates and radicals. The monarchists had, in 1871, an overall majority in the Assembly, with 400 seats out of 630. Although there were three claimants to the throne, schemes were advanced in 1871 and 1873 whereby the Comte de Chambord would be restored, to be succeeded by the comte de Paris; this formula appeared to reconcile the two main monarchist parties, the Legitimists and Orléanists. Throughout the first part of the 1870s there was no permanent commitment to a republic. The Assembly provided through the septennate of 1873 a temporary solution; it prolonged republican institutions only for a further seven years until a suitable alternative could be hammered out.

What saved the Republic at its inception was a combination of growing contention between the Legitimists, Orléanists and Bonapartists, and the electoral recovery of the anti-monarchists.

The political dispute between the three monarchist wings seemed to encompass many of the issues which had already divided them between 1815 and 1870. At first sight there was no real problem. The Legitimist Manifesto promised universal suffrage and parliamentary monarchy, and seemed content, in Cobban's words, to give up the substance of power in order to retain the shadow. The Orléanists, already committed to constitutional monarchy, found the new attitude of the Legitimists quite acceptable. But the monarchist challenge to the Republic was soon to divide along the seam of the tricoleur controversy (1871–3), despite a desperate mission to attempt to persuade the Legitimist comte de Chambord to give up his demands for the return of the white flag of the Bourbons. The comte, however, was adamant; if he were to be the next king of France he would not 'permit the standard of Henri IV, of Francis I and of Joan of Arc' to be snatched from his hands. The Orléanists were equally staunch in their refusal to abandon the tricoleur, the emblem which France had given herself. Behind this apparently trivial conflict lay deep and divisive constitutional issues, showing that Legitimism, Orléanism and Bonapartism were not easily reconcilable. The Legitimists were clearly resuming the stance of Charles X against the 1789 Revolution, determined to reduce its political and social influence. The Orléanists, by contrast, stood for the fusion of the Revolution with limited monarchy. The Bonapartists intended to restore the imperialist tradition of the Revolution in the form of a plebiscitary dictatorship. Thus, there appeared to be an intractable problem. The Legitimists and Orléanists agreed on the restoration of the kingdom rather than the empire, but the Legitimists held out against the Orléanists and Bonapartists on the issue of the tricolour. Since only a combination of Orléanists and Legitimists could ensure a monarchist restoration, the comte de Chambord, in effect, had the last word. Thiers was to be proved right in his belief that this would 'definitely establish the Republic'.

Religious controversy also played an important role in weakening the monarchist campaign against the Republic. It is true that all three wings supported the Church, and that the *noblesse* and upper bourgeoisie, monarchists to a man, were nearly all devout Catholics. But there were substantial differences of emphasis. The Legitimists wished to revive the temporal authority of the Papacy, even if this meant military intervention against the Italian government. They also laid heavy emphasis on the cult of the *Sacré Coeur*, regarding the construction of the Basilica at Montmartre as an act of national penance for decades of secularism. These attitudes found joint expression in the prayer proposed in 1871 by the French bishops. '*Sauvez Rome et la France au nom du Sacré Coeur.*'[1] The Orléanists and Bonapartists considered this Ultramontanism of the Legitimists entirely unacceptable, but could not find an alternative formula upon which they could agree. Many of the Orléanists were Gallicans, some even Jansenists, while the Bonapartists stood for a powerful Church which would act as a 'social cement' but which would avoid the eighteenth-century conflict between Ultramontane and Gallican interests.

The success of the monarchist offensive depended on speed. The longer the three wings took to agree, the greater the chance of survival they gave to the Republic. Leading members of the Assembly, once monarchists themselves, came to realize that the Republic was a viable alternative to the interminable disputes among the royalist factions. Thiers, who as an Orléanist had served under Louis Philippe and, as a Bonapartist under Napoleon III, now declared himself in favour of the Republic in 1872. His reason represented the feeling of a growing proportion of the Assembly: 'There is only one throne; three men cannot sit on it at the same time.'

Aspects of European History 1789–1980

Meanwhile, the republicans were gradually undermining the monarchist parliamentary majority: through a series of by-election victories between 1871 and 1873, and through the defection of a *bloc* of Orléanists to the republican camp after Chambord's final refusal to accept the tricolour. The Republic also benefited from the slow and cautious changes made by the 1875 Wallon Amendment and the 1875 Constitutional Laws. The institutions established included a seven-year presidency and an Upper Chamber, or Senate, both of which could conceivably be adapted to a monarchy some time in the future. This had a double advantage: on the one hand, it removed the urgency from the monarchist campaign against the Republic; the comte de Paris, for example, said: 'If we cannot make a monarchy we must make something as like to it as possible.' On the other, it gave the Republic a further opportunity for consolidation and retrenchment, even if the semi-monarchical appearance of the Constitution caused one newspaper editor to remark: 'We are entering the Republic backwards.'[2]

*

There is a saying that 'In France nothing lasts as long as what is only temporary'. The Constitutional Laws of 1875 were intended to be a stopgap: in fact, they remained in existence until 1940. Yet the Republic had to continue its struggle for survival for another fifteen years. This time it was confronted by the efforts of two individuals, Macmahon and Boulanger, to weaken the legislature, the main source of republican strength, and create a powerful Executive which would become the preserve of the Right.

President Macmahon's ultimate ambition was to restore the monarchy. In the meantime, he intended to use his own powers to the limits prescribed by the Constitution and to prevent the Republic from becoming more radical. As part of his onslaught against the republicans, he secured the resignation of Simon, the moderate prime minister, and installed the Orléanist duc de Broglie as his successor. When the Chamber of Deputies made it clear that it had no confidence in Broglie, Macmahon resorted to a legal, but typically Bonapartist manoeuvre. In May 1877 he obtained the Senate's assent to the dissolution of the Chamber in the hope that fresh elections would return a more docile majority. In preparation for these, Broglie's government weeded out the non-monarchists in the provincial prefectures and municipal councils. Notwithstanding such precautions, the outcome of the elections was a disaster for Macmahon. His manipulation of the Constitution failed to prevent a substantial victory for the Republicans over the Right by 326 seats to 207. Why?

In the first place, Macmahon was the wrong man for the attempt. Lacking personal charisma, he was unable to project any real appeal or confidence in his measures. His widespread publicity campaign fell flat; the distribution of posters and portraits elicited from the public comments like: 'He has an intelligent eye – the horse I mean.' He was clearly incapable of mounting any direct challenge to the constitution itself and yet, without this, any *coup* could only be, in the words of the Bishop of Poitiers, 'a sword stroke in water'. Indeed, Macmahon and Broglie were actually prisoners of the Constitution. They applied all the sanctions allowed by law against their opponents and used their authority to change the personnel of local government. But such methods served only to provoke more intense republican resistance and to forge unity where little had previously existed.

This reconciliation between the various factions of Republicans proved to be the main reason for the salvation of the Republic. The anti-monarchists adopted the slogan 'No enemies on the Left' to indicate that their factional feuds had ended. Partly responsible for this was the agreement between the different republican leaders. Gambetta, previously a radical, now purged his programme of all revolutionary connotations in an effort to gain the support of the bourgeoisie and the peasantry. His slogan 'We shall be prudent' merged with the promise of the more traditional Grévy that France would be guaranteed a 'safe republic'. Greater unity made possible a more effective attack on the government and its dangerous policies. The Republicans were able to play upon the fear of the growing influence of clericalism, of the possible consequences of any attempt to force the Italian government to restore to the Pope his temporal lands, and the threat posed to the legislature by Macmahon's abuse of the presidential prerogative of dissolution. The attacks were effectively conveyed in newspapers like *La République Française* and in the broadsheets distributed among the peasantry. Above all, Gambetta conducted a masterly campaign of aggressive speeches against the President. Attempts to silence him by prosecution only enhanced his reputation and increased his popularity.

Aspects of European History 1789–1980

Macmahon's failure was significant not only because it provided a further respite for the Republic, but also because it altered the nature of the next threat. Macmahon was replaced by Grévy, who decided to be 'submissive to the great law of parliamentary government'. From 1877 onwards the presidency was too weak to harbour any real opposition to the legislature. Consequently, any anti-republican move would have to come from outside the constitutional framework altogether. This inevitably meant that the next challenge from the Right would be more radical, even revolutionary. General Boulanger came close to destroying the Republic in 1889. After a series of remarkable election victories, he stood poised to seize power in a *coup d'état* which he intended to endorse with a referendum. His programme was anti-parliamentary and aimed at abolishing one of the Chambers, extending presidential powers, and replacing elections by plebiscites. It was the old Bonapartist formula of an authoritarian executive freed from legislative restraints, and deriving its support directly from the masses. Boulanger was a much more dangerous threat than Macmahon because he appealed to the radicals of the Left as well as those of the Right. He was, at first, supported by the Blanquists and Socialists who had become, during the 1880s, disillusioned by the high rate of unemployment and more critical of the parliamentary oligarchy into which they considered the Republic had descended. The Right were attracted by his appeal to national pride. Déroulède's League of Patriots, established in 1884, interpreted Boulangism as a means of achieving *revanche* against Germany for the loss of Alsace-Lorraine in 1871. The Bonapartists found Boulanger readily acceptable, the comte de Paris soon advised the Orléanists to give their support, and the overall campaign was financed by the Legitimist duchesse d'Uzès. The Church, traditionally anti-republican, gave its official sanction to Boulangism and set the seal on the new coalition.

Again, however, the Republic survived. The collapse of the movement was unexpected and dramatic. Boulanger, cowed by a government threat of impeachment, fled France in 1889. The elections of the same year gave the Republicans 366 seats to the Right's 216. In retrospect, the weaknesses of Boulangism are obvious. Its support was so diverse that a specific programme was never really possible. How could the radical Left and the conservative Right ever hope to agree on social and economic policies? How could the different concepts of democracy be reconciled? It seems that Boulanger was a powerful catalyst of discontent rather than the creator of a new ideology; indeed, Meyer called him, in 1889, *un talisman promis à tous les malheureux*'. The movement also had little support beyond Paris and the other major towns. The peasant masses remained indifferent to his appeal, or actively supported the Republic which had guaranteed their property. In this respect, therefore, Boulangism lacked the rural base which had been so vital for Bonapartism. Despite his charisma and electoral appeal, Boulanger lacked the capacity for strong and decisive leadership necessary for the personification of executive authority. Indeed, he was a mass of contradictions. An adventurer and opportunist, he declined three perfect opportunities to seize power. And, although immensely popular in Paris, he remained completely dependent on advisers like Laguerre, Naquet and Thiebaud to create an image for him.

The Republic showed characteristic resilience during the latter phase of the crisis. It mobilized the centre of the political spectrum and eventually managed to regain the support of the radical left. Boulanger's appeal to nationalism and clericalism pushed the Socialists back into the Republican camp and the old slogan 'No enemies on the Left' was revived. The attitude of the Possibilists was typical: 'We workers are ready to forget the sixteen years during which the bourgeoisie has betrayed the hopes of the people, we are ready to defend and conserve by all means the weak germ of our republican institutions against military threats.'[2] The Left also established the *Société des Droits de l'Homme et du Citoyen*, committed to forging an alliance between 'all those who remain faithful to the Republic' and waging a 'merciless struggle against any kind of reaction or dictatorship'.[3] With this range of support, the government was able to take the offensive. In a brilliantly conceived legal campaign it threatened Boulanger with impeachment, exposed his natural timidity, and precipitated his withdrawal. Having eliminated the leadership, it then took proceedings against Déroulède's League of Patriots and other groups which had threatened a *coup d'état*. The Third Republic therefore escaped the eventual fate of the First and Second, largely because Boulanger proved an inadequate successor to the Bonapartes. Never again was it to be severely tested by the cult of personality. By 1890 France seemed to have evolved out of her monarchist and authoritarian phases.

*

Deep divisions, however, remained in the social and political fabric. These were exacerbated between 1890 and 1914 by the Dreyfus Affair and, once this had been resolved, by attacks on the régime from *Action Française* and Syndicalism.

The Affair produced the last major threat to the Republic from the Right before 1914. The army considered that its reputation would be seriously endangered by the rehabilitation of Captain Alfred Dreyfus (who had been wrongly convicted of espionage) and therefore proceeded to cover up the greatest judicial crime of the century. In the process, it expressed quite openly its anti-Republican bias. This, in fact, had become more pronounced than ever before. While the major institutions had gradually been republicanized during the 1880s, the army had remained the preserve of the aristocracy, who now dominated the officer corps and the promotion boards. The army was given extensive support by Church leaders, particularly the Bishop of Toulouse, and by religious orders like the Assumptionists. Many Catholics suspected the Republic of spreading atheism, and Fr Didon saw the army as a possible instrument, 'a holy force whose mission is to make right prevail'. Anti-semitism and nationalism also reappeared, and Déroulède emphasized the link between the treason of Dreyfus the Jew, and the corruption of the Republican government itself. Yet the bitter denunciation of Dreyfus and his supporters was no substitute for a positive and concerted programme on the Right; once again, those who attacked the Republic were unable to offer any real alternative. Once again the Right was brought together by only a negative common denominator – resentment. This time, it even lacked a leader. There was no successor to Macmahon or Boulanger who, despite their shortcomings, had been a focal point for the loyalty of the activists of the different Rightist groups.

If the Dreyfus Affair produced a weaker attack on the Republic from the Right, it promoted a more vigorous response from the Left. This took some time to mobilize because of the initial implication of the Méline and Dupuy ministries (1898–9) in the injustice to Dreyfus, and also because the extreme Left at first regarded the whole Affair as a sordid bourgeois conflict. The turning-point, however, came in 1899, with the appointment of Waldeck-Rousseau as Prime Minister. Rousseau and his successor, Combes (1902–5), took a much tougher line and launched a massive offensive on the army and Church, ensuring, by a series of reforms, that these could never again involve themselves actively in political issues. The ministries were able to deal so confidently with the Right because they had sufficient backing from the different Republican groups to ensure an overall majority in the Chamber of Deputies. The threat from the Right, especially Déroulède's attempts to overthrow the Republic in 1899, had reactivated the old slogan 'No enemies on the Left'. The Radicals co-operated with the Socialists who, under the prompting of Jaurès, halted their campaign against the 'bourgeois Republic'. The Cabinet of Waldeck-Rousseau, in fact, contained the first Socialist to serve in any European government, together with Republicans of all other shades. Combes, in turn, co-operated closely with the *Délégation des Gauches*, a steering committee designed to preserve the unity of the Left. Meanwhile, political activity had been accompanied by extensive anti-Rightist and pro-Dreyfusard propaganda in papers like Clemenceau's *L'Aurore* and Guyot's *Le Siècle*. Organizations like the *Ligue des Droits de l'Homme* were also successful in mobilizing mass support from the lower-middle class and the urban proletariat.

The Republic achieved maturity as a result of the Dreyfus Affair and was evidently accepted by the vast majority of the electorate as the only régime possible for France. Between 1900 and 1914, however, activists continued their harassment of existing institutions. Maurras' newly established pressure group, *Action Française*, combined the most extreme elements of right-wing ideology and launched attacks on democracy, Protestantism, Jews, Freemasons and foreigners. It also pressed for a return to the monarchy and the structured society of the *ancien régime*. Yet Maurras could never expect, at this stage, to issue a major challenge to the Republic. His newspaper never achieved a circulation above 50,000 and the majority of the army and Church leaders considered him too radical. The extreme Left, meanwhile, had withdrawn their support for the Republican government in 1905, voting at the congress of the *Confédération Générale du Travail* to resort to direct action to make the régime more directly socialist. The result was a rash of strikes between 1907 and 1911 and a rapid increase in the influence of Sorel's Syndicalism. These, however, posed less of a threat than has often been maintained. The CGT had less than 400,000 resolute Syndicalists, compared with an estimated 10.6 million workers who were not militant. The government took forceful measures against the strikers. Clemenceau called out the troops in 1909, while Briand pressed railway strikers into the army as reservists in 1910. These measures were popular with the majority of the electorate, who cast a much larger vote for the moderate Republican parties in the 1910 general election.

*

How stable was the Third Republic by 1914? It appears, at first sight, that France had experienced a constant stream of political difficulties. Between 1871 and 1914, for example, there were no fewer than fifty ministries, twenty-six of which served between 1889 and 1914, and eleven between 1909 and 1914. The main factor preventing any real continuity was the absence of specific parties; deputies tended to group themselves more loosely into 'alliances' or 'federations', considering themselves free to move from one to another as circumstances dictated. The concept of party discipline, which divided the legislature between representatives of government and opposition, was alien to France. Consequently, new ministries had to be forged whenever there was a major disagreement on policy.

Three things, however, kept the Republic together throughout its times of crisis. The first was what has been called the stability of ministers rather than ministries.[4] Although governments changed frequently, the personnel who served in them reappeared regularly. Delcassé, for example, was Minister of Foreign Affairs six times between 1898 and 1905. Of the 561 ministers appointed between 1870 and 1940, no fewer than 120 served in five or more governments. Thus France was spared the prospect, which existed in other countries, that a new government might be completely inexperienced, or bring about a major change of course. Second, the French administration remained virtually unchanged throughout the prewar era. The major institutions, including the *conseil d'état* and the Inspectorate of Finance, continued to carry out the normal business of government, no matter what was happening at ministerial level; according to Guérard, 'so long as the bureaucrat is at his desk, France survives!'[4] Third, the majority of the population and, after 1875, over half of the parliamentary deputies, were supporters of the Republic. In quiet times their ideas of what form this Republic should take differed widely, resulting in major rifts between Radicals, Radical-Socialists, Socialists and Syndicalists. But

132

whenever there was a major threat from the Right on the institutions of the Republic, these elements combined temporarily to meet it, apparently confirming the belief of Thiers that 'The Republic is the government which divides us least'.

15

German Foreign Policy
1871–1914

The emergence of Germany as a single state substantially altered the balance of power in Europe. Bismarck's victories had already indicated Germany's military superiority over Austria and France, while the rest of the century saw a rapid acceleration of the German economy, the result of a population explosion and an industrial revolution. It is hardly surprising, therefore, that German statesmen tended, after 1871, to dominate the European scene and that other continental leaders found the threads of their own diplomacy passing through Berlin.

＊

After 1871 Bismarck felt that his task of uniting Germany had been accomplished and that consolidation and retrenchment should now replace conflict and *Realpolitik*. The Second Reich, he insisted, was a sated power; further additions of territory were therefore unnecessary and undesirable. Indeed, what had already been achieved 'could only be jeopardized by pressing for further expansion of German power'.[1] Instead, Germany should be 'appeased and peaceful',[2] for 'when we have arrived in a good harbour, we should be content and cultivate what we have won'.[3] His primary concern now was to anticipate and neutralize any forces which might disrupt the internal harmony of the new state or upset the international balance of power.

He therefore kept a close watch on the situation in both Eastern and Western Europe. He was well aware that his *Realpolitik* and

German Foreign Policy 1871–1914

deliberate aggression, used during the 1860s to unite Germany, had undermined the understanding which had previously existed between Russia, Prussia and Austria. There was now a danger either of Austro-Russian collaboration against Germany, or of an Austro-Russian war some time in the future into which Germany might be dragged. Somehow, therefore, he had to prevent relations between the Austrian and Russian governments from becoming too close or too strained. The situation in Western Europe was more immediately threatening. Throughout the 1870s and 1880s Bismarck was haunted by the prospect of an attempt by France to avenge her defeat of 1871. This had, after all, been a profound psychological shock, given a sharp edge of resentment by the cession, in the Treaty of Frankfurt, of Alsace-Lorraine. By herself, France constituted little military danger to Germany. But what if she could acquire an ally – Russia, perhaps? Bismarck's intention was that all continental disputes should be patched up without recourse to war, for an unsuccessful protagonist might otherwise seek any support available; France's price for *her* support would undoubtedly be an alliance against Germany. To guarantee Germany's security, therefore, France would have to be kept out of the mainstream of European diplomacy. As late as 1887 Bismarck still considered that 'France is the European state most eager for war, and European peace is assured with France's isolation'.[4] At the same time, Germany needed to be integrated into an effective defensive system, so that she was in accord with the majority of the European powers. Hence, he observed, 'when there are five [powers], try to be *à trois*'.[5]

In responding to these challenges, Bismarck tried to keep his options open as long as possible and he reserved the right to change course if necessary. He believed that 'in politics there are no such things as complete certainty and definitive results . . . Everything goes continually uphill, downhill.'[6] The result was a period of great complexity in German diplomacy.

At first Bismarck used ideological factors to restore the *rapprochement* between Germany, Austria and Russia, and to build a solid front against France. One of the agencies of destruction which he feared, and exploited, was revolution. In 1872, therefore, he formed the *Dreikaiserbund*, which committed the three governments to co-operate in their measures against socialism and other radical influences. The *Dreikaiserband* was also a means of fostering monarchical unity against republican France. Bismarck's attitude

135

towards France was typically double-edged. He certainly feared that the republicans would continue to demand revenge against Germany; but, on the other hand, he was reluctant to see France with any other form of government, for this would make her more respectable in the eyes of Austrian and Russian statesmen. In 1873 Bismarck actually reprimanded Arnim, the German ambassador in Paris, for supporting a monarchist bid to gain control in France. Why, he demanded angrily, should Germany seek to undermine a régime whose ideological base had, so far, ensured its own isolation?

Until 1875 Bismarck's measures appeared to be fully vindicated. Austria and Russia remained on good terms with each other, but through the agency of Germany, while no major power showed the least inclination to ally with France. In the second half of the decade, however, a situation developed which tested Bismarck's diplomatic acumen more completely. The Ottoman Empire, in decline for nearly two centuries, underwent a series of internal revolts and a new period of administrative chaos. Bismarck had to contend with two sets of diplomatic ramifications; these concerned Austria and Russia in the Balkans, and France and Italy in the Mediterranean.

Between 1875 and 1877 the Sultan was faced, in the Balkans, with insurrections by Bosnia, Herzegovina, Bulgaria, Serbia and Montenegro. Turkish reprisals reactivated Russia's traditional claim to protect the Balkan Christians which, in turn, aroused Austrian fears of Russian expansion into South-Eastern Europe, an area of special interest to Vienna after the loss of Austria's Italian provinces. Relations between Russia and Austria deteriorated rapidly after Russia declared war on and defeated Turkey. Bismarck now had a problem – and an opportunity. On the one hand, the Balkan imbroglio could easily cause a war between Russia and Austria which would upset the balance of power in Europe and endanger Germany. On the other, the Balkans could be used as an irritant to prevent other powers, including Russia and Austria, from coming together. By working on lesser antagonisms he could, therefore, prevent the build-up of a major confrontation. In an attempt to solve the problem, and seize the opportunity, Bismarck offered his services as an 'honest broker' at the Congress of Berlin (1878), playing a vital role in drawing up the eventual territorial compromise. The outcome, however, was far from satisfactory. The enmity between Austria and Russia was still potentially dangerous, while Alexander II bitterly attacked Bismarck's apparent support

German Foreign Policy 1871–1914

for Austria at the Congress and complained about the parsimonious territorial compensation received by Russia and the trisection of her client state, Bulgaria. Bismarck found that he had to take another initiative – this time the defensive Dual Alliance between Germany and Austria, directed specifically at Russia. There is some evidence that this was a precipitate and short-term measure, designed to break the impending threat of war by offering security to one of the protagonists while, at the same time, actively restraining it from aggression. It is sometimes said that the Dual Alliance represented Bismarck's final choice between Russia and Austria. This is not so. He still intended to keep his options open and hoped to revive the close connection with Russia in order to prevent the growth of a counter-alliance based on France. Bismarck did make a choice in 1879, but it was between Russia and Britain. He turned down the opportunity of a direct agreement with Britain because he knew that this would do more than anything else to alienate Russia permanently.

Meanwhile, the North African territories, over which Turkey had maintained the most tenuous of holds, were now coming under the attentions of the great powers. This time things worked more directly in Bismarck's favour. Britain became heavily involved in Egypt, and France in Tunisia – a situation welcomed by Bismarck because it would distract the Republic's attention from affairs in Europe. In fact, Bismarck used these involvements to promote a series of colonial collisions between France and Britain: he openly admitted to projecting the rivalries between the major powers into a safer continent, while working hard to keep them alive. There was also an immediate return from the Tunisia episode. The Italian government had, for some time, regarded Tunisia as being within its sphere of influence, a fact well known to Bismarck when he had given his blessing to the French annexation. When Italy approached Bismarck for help in 1882, Bismarck was able, by the Triple Alliance, to overcome two of the remaining weaknesses within his system. First, by ending the longstanding enmity between Italy and Austria he removed the threat from the latter's southern flank. Second, although Germany did not gain much from Italy's military support, at least France was deprived of a potential ally who would have given her an immense psychological boost.

During the 1880s Bismarck's policies became more and more tortuous as he had to deal with the complications caused by the Dual

Alliance; he was particularly concerned about the possibility of an alliance between France and Russia and tried everything to prevent it. At first, in 1881, he revived his original expedient of the *Dreikaiserbund*, in the form of the Three Emperors' Alliance. This, however, laid less stress on ideological unity, and more on specific territorial compromise between Austria and Russia in the hope that Russia would not seek accommodation with France through a sense of insecurity and isolation. By the mid-1880s, however, this arrangement (renewed in 1884) was on the verge of collapse because of the revival of the Bulgarian crisis. The threat of war between Austria and Russia was more serious than ever. The Austrian government objected forcefully to Russia's intervention in Bulgaria's internal affairs and her involvement in the abduction of Bulgaria's monarch, Alexander of Battenberg. In 1887 Bismarck resorted to a series of controversial measures designed to neutralize the conflict and to provide Germany with a means of avoiding direct involvement should an Austro-Russian war actually break out. By the Reinsurance Treaty he promised Russia full diplomatic support over Bulgaria. He obtained, in return, a guarantee of Russian neutrality in the event of a French attack on Germany, subject to a similar undertaking by Germany not to assist an Austrian attack on Russia. Bismarck was careful, however, to hedge his bets. His support for Russian claims in Bulgaria would not, he knew, result in a sudden increase in Russian influence in South-Eastern Europe, for Austria, Italy and Britain, who had negotiated the Mediterranean Agreement in the same year, would exert diplomatic pressure to prevent Russia from acquiring the vital Straits area. What he was doing, therefore, was reassuring Russia about Germany's friendship, while relying on others to frustrate Russia's plans in the Balkans. He was also careful to do nothing which would involve the desertion of Austria and the neutrality clause of the Reinsurance Treaty did not, technically, contravene the terms of the Dual Alliance.* He was, however, fully aware that his allies would not appreciate the subtlety of his diplomacy and, in order to avoid their inevitable suspicions about his motives, he kept the Reinsurance Treaty under the wraps of strict secrecy.

How successful was Bismarck's foreign policy? Certain advan-

---

* The Dual Alliance had provided for German support for Austria in the event of an attack on Austria by Russia; the Reinsurance Treaty only guaranteed German neutrality if Russia were attacked by Austria.

tages *could* be claimed for the complex system he developed. France remained completely isolated during the entire period of his chancellorship. He projected himself as the arbiter of Europe and took the credit for drawing the sting from the Balkan crises. He formed, in the Dual and Triple Alliances, a solid *bloc* of German-influenced territory in Central Europe. Yet he managed to prevent the growth of an armed camp based on France by keeping open contacts with Russia; the latter considered the Reinsurance Treaty so useful that she was to request its renewal in 1890.

There must, however, be serious reservations about his diplomacy. Complexity cannot, in itself, be considered a virtue, particularly since Bismarck had taken no measures to train a successor to maintain his system of checks and balances. He had been inflexible and dictatorial to his foreign office and diplomatic staff ('My ambassadors must fall into line like soldiers'[7]) and had systematically uprooted any signs of initiative or independent thought. The strongest personality was Baron von Holstein who, as it happened, strongly opposed Bismarck's Russian policy and, after the old Chancellor's resignation in 1890, instigated a major change of course. Bismarck could only fume at the 'mistakes' of his successors. Overlooking his own part in destroying the continuity of German foreign policy, he spoke of the 'criminal negligence' of Holstein and Caprivi and built up a powerful myth about his own supreme gifts as a statesman. This, in turn, was seized upon, elaborated and perpetuated by contemporary German historians.

It could be argued that the whole system was facing imminent collapse *before* Bismarck's resignation. He spent the last three years of his chancellorship trying desperately to juggle with apparently conflicting policies. His approach to Russia was especially faulty. He certainly exaggerated the importance of the Reinsurance Treaty. Russia was committed to neutrality only if France attacked Germany; she reserved the right, however, to join France if Germany were the aggressor. Hence the Reinsurance Treaty in no way precluded the possibility of a Franco-Russian alliance, a point which Bismarck ignored when he attacked the German cabinet for not renewing the treaty in 1890. Since accommodation between Russia and France was still a technical possibility, Bismarck should have devoted his energies to removing all possible motives. This he signally failed to do. In fact, his refusal to allow German investment in Russian state bonds contributed much to the Tsar's decision to take up French loans at the end of the 1880s. Meanwhile, the fall of Ferry's government in France in 1885 had ended the temporary improvement in Franco-German relations, while the emergence of Boulangism gave a new lease of life to Revanchism. France had, therefore, every reason to look beyond a mere economic agreement with Russia, while the latter had lost, in the welter of investment from Paris, its aversion to the prospect of a republican ally. Bismarck's peripheral arrangements were also looking increasingly unhealthy. Italy was an uncertain ally and, in any case, showed her extreme economic vulnerability during the Franco-Italian tariff war in 1888. The Mediterranean Agreement of 1887 could not be interpreted as a permanent arrangement, and Bismarck's offer in 1889 of a military alliance with Britain met a cold reception from the prime minister, Lord Salisbury. In 1879 Bismarck had foregone an Anglo-German Treaty in order to keep his options open with Russia. Now, in 1889, Russia was moving swiftly towards France, and Britain had long since retracted her offer. At no other time in his chancellorship had Bismarck's policy of being *à trois* appeared so threatened.

Bismarck's 'system' was also seen by a substantial section of the German population as anachronistic. Its dependence on restraint in diplomacy left dissatisfied the ever-increasing number of nationalists, while many of the army leaders had adopted the view that the threat of Germany's encirclement should be countered by military, not diplomatic, action. Above all, powerful economic pressure groups demanded a more active overseas policy to procure outlets for raw materials and markets for manufactured goods. Thus, by 1890, Germany was no longer a sated power. The statesman who had introduced this concept had, unfortunately, neglected to educate the German public into accepting it permanently.

*

The change of course in German foreign policy after Bismarck's resignation should not, therefore, be seen as the cold-blooded abandonment of a thriving system. It was rather a change of tempo, or an acceleration of those forces which made German policy more aggressive and less cautious. With the removal of the master tactician of restraint, three main developments took place. The tenuous connection with Russia was abandoned, resulting in the formation, in 1894, of the Franco-Russian Alliance. Then, from the

German Foreign Policy 1871–1914

mid-1890s, Germany broke the European bounds to which Bismarck had constrained her and became involved in the more ambitious *Weltpolitik*. At the same time, a massive programme of naval construction was started, with the declared intention of challenging Britain's supremacy at sea. Why did these changes occur?

The first reason was that Germany's new leadership had bold designs but lacked the political wisdom to control them. Kaiser William II (1888–1918) was less disciplined and more impetuous than either of his predecessors, William I (1871–88) and Frederick III (1888). Modelling himself on Frederick the Great (1740–86), he showed a definite preference for military matters, giving greater attention to army and navy commanders than to his civilian ministers or to the *Reichstag*. After all, he believed that 'the soldiers and the army, and not the decisions of parliaments, forged the German Reich'.[9] Consequently, the ideas of Tirpitz, Schlieffen and Moltke were accepted without reservation, even though their emphasis on military strategy blunted the weapon upon which Bismarck had relied – diplomacy. The chancellors of the period 1890–1914 could not aspire to Bismarck's influence and were, in any case, a diverse mixture. Caprivi (1890–4) and Chlodwig-Hohenlohe (1894–1900) were inexperienced in foreign affairs, and lost the initiative to advisers like Holstein, as well as to the Kaiser's military circle. Bülow (1900–09) was more forceful but, as a product of the new generation, actively fostered both *Weltpolitik* and the naval programme. The last, Bethmann Hollweg (1909–17) had to struggle, in a period of growing international tension, with his own ignorance, and the pressure of the army commanders to decide Germany's course of action.

Recent historians have emphasized a second reason for the change of policy. They argue that serious internal pressures in German society and politics necessitated some form of distraction if the Second Reich were to survive; in this respect, the dilemmas and solutions of William II were similar to those of Napoleon III and Nicholas II. The inherent contradictions within Bismarck's Germany had become more and more obvious by 1890. The auto-cratic traditions of the Prussian-based monarchy and ruling élite appeared incompatible with the more recent concession of parliamentary democracy. The ruling class lived in fear of revolution from below, or at the least, control by socialists and progressives over the *Reichstag*. The working class, which had been considerably enlarged by Germany's massive industrial growth, resented the almost feudal class structure and suspected that the régime would, given the chance, conduct a *coup* to trim the powers of the legislature and reduce the size of the electorate. In the rest of the political and social spectrum, the middle classes shared the régime's fears of socialism, but were fully committed to upholding parliamentary democracy. The Kaiser and his ministers had become uncomfortably aware of the extent of the political stalemate by 1896. They therefore prepared to release internal pressures and turn them outwards, converting class and party dissension into patriotism and pride in empire. Hence, Foreign Minister Bülow said, in 1897: 'I am putting the main emphasis on foreign policy. Only a successful foreign policy can help to reconcile, pacify, rally, unite.'[9] Government policy was to encourage the aristocracy and the Conservative Party to seek political fulfilment in imperialism and to forget their hopes for an onslaught on the *Reichstag*. The middle classes would, in turn, become less obsessive about parliamentary issues and would respond quickly to the economic advantages offered by imperial expansion. The *Reichstag* could even become the means of disseminating interest in colonial issues and correspondingly fewer debates would be held on domestic problems. Above all, the government hoped to win more widespread popular support for the monarchy and achieve what had previously been considered impossible: the 'mobilization of the masses'. Bülow insisted: 'We must unswervingly wrestle for the souls of our workers.'[10] In this policy 'which mobilizes the best patriotic forces' and 'appeals to the highest national emotions', the government merely had to exploit and encourage the demand for expansion put forward by public pressure groups and by the Colonial, Pan-German and Navy Leagues. Remove Bismarck's constraints, concluded the Kaiser, Tirpitz and Bülow, and Germany could be given a more vigorous role, as a world rather than as a continental power, while domestic harmony could be achieved without repression.

There were, however, to be unforeseen results, for the change of course brought reality to all Bismarck's fears of European anarchy and hostile coalitions.

Throughout the 1890s the main target of Germany's new policy was Britain. Holstein, for example, believed that colonial pressure would force the British government to make concessions and thereby acknowledge the legitimacy of Germany's new world role. A provocative line was therefore pursued; Germany refused to compromise over the Samoan Islands in 1894, challenged Britain's Congolese Treaty in the same year, supported Krüger in the Transvaal crisis of 1896, and seized Kiaochow in 1897. Tirpitz believed that pressure should also be applied to Britain's sea power, for then she would 'concede to Your Majesty such a measure of maritime influence which will make it possible for Your Majesty to conduct a great overseas policy'.[10] A key element of his design was to increase Germany's battleship strength, thereby forcing Britain to protect home waters at the expense of her far-flung imperial commitments. In the process of implementing this 'risk policy', Germany lost an opportunity to come to an agreement with Britain offered, in 1899, by Joseph Chamberlain. Under the influence of Tirpitz, the Kaiser's government was far advanced on a course of direct confrontation and not very well-calculated brinkmanship. In a sense, observes G. A. Craig, Germany's efforts to behave like a world power were clumsy, rude and excessive.[9]

Shortly after the turn of the century this emphasis took its toll. The strategy of forcing British attention back to Europe certainly worked, but in a way which had not been expected by Germany. The British government thought the German threat sufficiently serious to abandon its continental isolation and to form, in 1904, the Entente with France. Further German miscalculation followed. The Kaiser and Bülow tried, by exploiting the Moroccan situation of 1905, to prove that this co-operation was only a temporary phenomenon. Far from splitting the Entente, however, German action at Algeçiras only served to tighten and perpetuate it. There was worse to come. Holstein had shown absolute confidence in the total incompatibility of Britain and Russia: 'Whale and bear could never come together.'[11] Yet, in 1907, the two powers settled their colonial disputes by the Anglo-Russian Convention, while the connection of both countries with France was reaffirmed by the Triple Entente. Even at this stage German diplomacy was basically aggressive. The Agadir Incident and the Second Moroccan Crisis (1911) provoked an official warning to Germany in Lloyd George's Mansion House Speech, and created an atmosphere in which Anglo-French and Anglo-Russian fleet manoeuvres were considered necessary.

Inevitably, this turn of events caused in Germany a fundamental sense of unease and necessitated a re-examination of her overall strategy. Far from improving Germany's position relative to the other powers, the pursuit of *Weltpolitik* and naval expansion had actually provoked Britain's return to continental diplomacy and tightened the alliance between France and Russia. Apprehension about Germany's geographical vulnerability revived, sharpened by the knowledge that *Weltpolitik* had actually drawn resources away from the maintenance of her continental hegemony. Bethmann Hollweg summarized the problem: 'Because of the navy we have neglected the army, and our "naval policy" has created enemies all around us.'[9] The only solution possible was another change of course and the return to a continental strategy which would enable Germany to break out of her encirclement. Unfortunately, this could no longer be achieved by diplomacy, for international relations were far less fluid than they had been in Bismarck's era. This absence of any political solutions enabled the military leadership to exert unprecedented influence on the government in two ways. First, the inflexibility of the Schlieffen Plan (1905), which allowed for a general assault on Russia only after the defeat of France, made it impossible to deal separately with Germany's two hostile neighbours. The sort of situation had arisen which Bismarck had always avoided: diplomatic options were limited by the demands of military schedules. Second, military commanders like Moltke and Ludendorff were, by 1912, putting pressure on the government to use war as a means of breaking out of a stranglehold which the current rearmament of Russia could only intensify in the future. Thus the civilian leadership was caught in a dilemma and resorted to the policies explained in Chapter 16.

16

The Outbreak of the First World War*

The debate on responsibility for the outbreak of the First World War has generated more heated controversy than any other within the survey of this book. The Allied Commission on War Guilt affirmed, in 1919, that 'The War was premeditated by the Central Powers' and that it was 'the result of acts deliberately committed in order to make it unavoidable'.[1] During the 1920s and 1930s the German government promoted a revisionist campaign in an effort to rescind the War Guilt clause of the Treaty of Versailles, by stressing collective responsibility for the outbreak of war in 1914. In this it was assisted by eminent historians like H. Rothfels[2] but, it has been suggested, it allowed only certain documents to be used, concealing any evidence which was likely to impede what had become an active political campaign.[3] Meanwhile, the whole concept of German war guilt had come under scrutiny elsewhere from both politicians and historians. Lloyd George, for example, expressed reservations about the postwar treatment of Germany, while H. E. Barnes,[4] S. B. Fay,[5] and G. P. Gooch[6] all enhanced the academic side of the revisionist case.

---

* The main steps in the outbreak of the First World War were as follows. On 28 June 1914, Franz Ferdinand was assassinated at Sarajevo. The eventual response of Austria-Hungary was an ultimatum to Serbia on 23 July. When Serbia rejected one of the terms of this ultimatum, Austria-Hungary declared war on 28 July. Russia mobilized in support of Serbia on 30 July. Germany declared war on Russia on 1 August and on France on 3 August. As part of her operations against France, Germany's forces entered Belgium; this was followed, on 4 August, by the British declaration of war on Germany. The ring was completed when, on 6 August, Austria-Hungary declared war on Russia. Italy, although allied to Germany and Austria-Hungary, remained neutral in 1914.

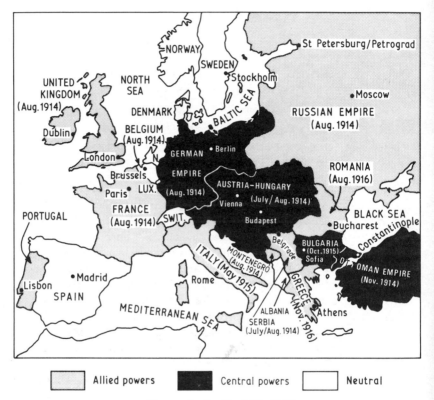

Allied powers   **Central powers**   **Neutral**

Europe in the First World War

The Outbreak of the First World War

During the 1950s the cycle of interpretation moved again towards the position of German responsibility with, for example, the work of A. J. P. Taylor.[7] A further and powerful push in this direction was given by F. Fischer[8] who maintained that Germany deliberately engineered the war in pursuit of expansionist aims which were really a prelude to the designs of Hitler. Fischer's position has, during the late 1960s and the 1970s, been variously challenged and defended. Critics include G. Ritter[9] and, more recently, L. C. F. Turner,[10] while elements of the Fischer thesis have been accepted by I. Geiss,[11] J. Kohl[12] and V. R. Berghahn.[13]

The interpretation presented here has three main ingredients: an assumption of basic German liability, a criticism of the negative policies of the Allies, and a broader survey of the whole system of alliances and war schedules.

*

The most aggressive powers are often the most insecure. Germany was, by 1915, confronted by several dangers. The first, described in Chapter 14, was the threat of containment at best and, at worst, of a war on two Fronts. To make matters worse, the Entente powers, and particularly France and Russia, had been greatly encouraged by the recent diplomatic embarrassment of Germany and Austria-Hungary in the Balkan Wars (1912–13) and were in the process of expanding their military capacity. The French government increased the period of conscription by one year in 1913, while the Russian army was undergoing a major programme of expansion, designed for completion by 1917. The German leadership – civilian and military – felt increasingly trapped between two powers which had considerable military potential and an apparent capacity to recover from internal crises. Russia was particularly worrying. According to Bethmann Hollweg in 1914, 'It grows and grows and hangs over us ever more heavily like a nightmare',[14] a view which was given greater edge by Jagow: 'In a few years, according to expert opinion, Russia will be ready to strike. Then she will crush us with the numbers of her soldiers.'[15] Even the economic front held few bright prospects. Bülow's trade agreement with Russia was about to lapse and, despite her clear industrial lead, Germany had fewer financial resources than France in the struggle to dominate Turkey. In an international situation which had clearly, since 1911, been swinging in favour of the peripheral powers, Germany could not even feel certain of her allies. Italy was unreliable, while Austria was undergoing a serious internal crisis which was exacerbated by the growth of external Slavic pressures and which was rendering her 'weaker and more immobile'.[16] Bismarck's Dual Alliance, so long the lynchpin of German security in Central Europe, was therefore threatened with paralysis. Should the situation in the Balkans deteriorate further Austria might even fall apart, leaving Germany isolated amidst hostile neighbours, the eventuality feared above all others by Bismarck.

Was there a solution? Certainly there was no shortage of pressure groups whose shrill advocacy of forceful action reflected a confidence in the permanence of Germany's European hegemony. But the army clearly thought that such action would have to come sooner than later, for Germany's military advantage would be eliminated during the period 1912–17. On balance, the General Staff favoured a preventive war, although, it must be said, with declining enthusiasm. At a meeting between the Kaiser and his generals, held on 8 December 1912, von Moltke, the Chief of General Staff, said that war was inevitable and, he added, 'the sooner the better'.[17] Some time later, in May 1914, he acknowledged that the French were fast catching up and that 'delay meant a lessening of our chances'.[15] A preventive war could, however, still be won through the implementation of the Schlieffen Plan.

Faced with this unenviable dilemma, Bethmann Hollweg decided on what has been called a 'diagonal' policy; he sought neither to prevent a war by a diplomatic solution, nor to provoke one as openly as the army wished. In encouraging the Austrian government after Sarajevo to take military action against Serbia he was, in effect, taking a calculated risk. If Russia failed to react, Serbia would be destroyed, the Balkan threat would be eliminated, and the Entente would be weakened by a major humiliation. On the other hand, should Austrian action incur Russian retaliation, the war for which the generals were pressing would break out and Germany would smash the Entente by means of the Schlieffen Plan. Bethmann Hollweg, therefore, placed Europe on the brink in the full knowledge of what might happen, fortified by the belief that 'If war must break out, better now than in one or two years' time, when the Entente will be stronger'.[18] His whole attitude was a capitulation to the military leadership, confirming the breakdown of ultimate civilian control.

The Outbreak of the First World War

Indeed, he negated one of Bismarck's most important principles. 'We must both take care', the latter had argued in 1887, 'that the privilege of giving political advice to our monarchs does not in fact slip out of our hands and pass over to the General Staffs.'[19] The collapse of diplomatic options was so complete that Bethmann Hollweg could not pull back from war even though, at the last minute, he had second thoughts about his actions. By the beginning of August, therefore, everything had been subordinated to the most effective means of achieving a military solution. Kurt Breysig later conceded, in March 1919 that, although 'our army was the best in the world [it] perpetrated the world's worst politics'.[20]

What part did Austria-Hungary play in this crisis? The assassination at Sarajevo produced two main reactions. On the one hand, there were those, like the Foreign Minister Berchtold, and the Chief of Staff Conrad, who wanted to settle once and for all the supposed threat from Serbia. They feared that the Balkan Wars of 1912–13 had greatly increased Serbia's power, tempted her into dependence on Russia, and tipped the balance in South-Eastern Europe away from the Central Powers. They also felt that Serbia had the capacity to destabilize Austria-Hungary by inciting rebellion in southern provinces like Bosnia, Herzegovina and Slavonia. The implications of this were enormous: if the Empire's southern Slavs became restless, the northern Slavs, especially the Czechs, Poles, Slovaks and Ruthenes, might also be tempted into rebellion. The Sarajevo incident, therefore, offered an excuse to draw Serbia's sting. On the other hand, the Hungarian Prime Minister, Tisza, was more inclined to caution and negotiation, an attitude shared by some members of the governments in both Vienna and Budapest. For a time, it seemed possible that indecision might allow the assassination to slip into the past without reply. But then the resolve of the 'hawks' was stiffened by Germany's promise of unconditional support. The pendulum swung firmly in favour of those who demanded action, with the result that a harsh ultimatum was despatched to Serbia on 23 July. It is now considered unlikely that Austria-Hungary's leaders hoped that the ultimatum would make Serbia climb down, thereby giving Vienna a major diplomatic victory. Instead, it was intended to provoke Serbia's rejection, and therefore provide a pretext for an Austrian invasion. Berchtold was determined to destroy the Serbian threat not by diplomacy but by direct military action. Whatever the case, the tone of the

149

ultimatum antagonized most of Europe, including Austria's ally, Italy. In fact, the Italian Foreign Minister, San Giuliano, notified Italy's ambassadors in Berlin and Vienna that 'Austria has plainly shown that she means to provoke a war', and that Italy was therefore 'under no obligation to go to the help of Austria' should the latter 'find herself at war with Russia'.[21]

*

Germany may, in collusion with Austria-Hungary, have precipitated the war, but the Allied powers did little to avoid it. Russia and France appeared almost willing to accept the challenge, while British policy, although commendable for its lack of hysteria and pressure, was too equivocal to have any restraining influence.

Nicholas II, in an unusually aggressive mood, once said: 'The Austrians should be forgiven nothing. They must be made to pay for everything.'[22] This typified the intense Austrophobia into which Russia had drifted since the Bosnian Crisis of 1908. This was due partly to increased Russian involvement in the Balkans, itself a reaction to defeat in the Russo-Japanese War of 1905 which had cut off all prospects of further Russian expansion in the Far East. The Tsar now increasingly identified Russian diplomacy with expansionism and with the aspirations of the Balkan peoples in holding their own against the Ottoman and Austro-Hungarian empires. There was also a profound fear that Russia was caught in the grip of, in the words of *Novoe Vremya*, a 'tightening Teutonic ring'. The Tsarist government found this spectre of Austro-German aggression particularly useful as a means of diverting attention from serious internal problems and of creating in the *Duma* a solid *bloc* of government support from the Octobrists and Constitutional Democrats. Little attempt was made, therefore, to moderate the dangerous levels of chauvinism; even Sazonov and Kokovstsev had to abandon, after 1911, Stolypin's pacific diplomacy. By 1914 there was profound pessimism about the prospect of future peace. According to a memorandum by Sazonov, a conference held by the Tsar on 8 (21) February produced a consensus that a general European war was likely, in view of the imminent collapse of Turkey and the impending Austro-Serb conflict. It was in Russia's interest to postpone the collision until 1917 when her rearmament would be

The Outbreak of the First World War

complete, but Serbia should still be supported regardless of the consequences. The public, in the meantime, was assured that 'no clamour will frighten Russia; Russia is prepared for war'.[22] Mobilization plans had also been prepared, giving the same confidence to the Russian General Staff as the Schlieffen Plan gave to the Germans; in January 1914, for example, the Commander-in-Chief, Jhilinski, assured a dubious Kokovstsev that Russia was ready for a 'duel' with her enemies. The constant pressure from the General Staff served, in the long run, to blind the civilian leadership to Russia's military weaknesses. This, in turn, undermined the government's resolve not to react hastily to Austro-German provocation, so that in July 1914, Russia was the first of the major powers to undergo general mobilization.

French policies also had a strong hint of resignation to an impending struggle. Poincaré observed in 1912 that, although 'France does not want war', nevertheless she 'does not fear it'.[23] In a powerful wave of anti-German feeling, the French military leadership under Joffre produced, in 1913, a new offensive plan designed to combat what had been deduced of German intentions. But the French government remained deeply concerned about the prospect of having to bear the brunt of a German attack. Consequently the main purpose of French diplomacy since 1911 had been to commit Russia to invading Germany with all possible speed in the event of war. This explains the virtual 'blank cheque' given to Russia by Paris during the 1912 Balkan Crisis as well as the pressure for Russian mobilization applied, in July 1914, by Laguiche and Paléologue. It would be interesting to speculate on two questions. Would France have been so anxious for Russia to play such an active role in Eastern Europe had she not been so concerned about her own security in the West? And would Russia have committed herself so irrevocably in July 1914, had she not been confident of French support, and comforted by the belief that the destination of most of the German divisions would be Paris?

The role of Britain in the July crisis erred on the side of omission rather than commission. The Foreign Secretary, Sir Edward Grey, is often blamed for not having made clear early enough, and with sufficient force, Britain's readiness to support France in the event of a German attack. There is, however, an alternative viewpoint: that Grey's intention was to defuse the situation by avoiding any aggressive statements of intent. In any case, Germany's course had already

151

been plotted, regardless of whether or not Britain decided to intervene.[24] In a sense, the question of Britain's responsibility for the war is less significant than the change in the character of the struggle caused by her eventual entry. Events up to 1 August culminated in a European war, the result of a rash response from France and Russia to the desperate gamble of Germany and Austria. On 4 August, however, the European war became, with Britain's entry, a world war to be fought at sea and in the colonies as well as in Flanders and Poland. The British government was faced with a major dilemma. As an imperial power, it was not in Britain's interests to become involved in a continental struggle. Yet a German victory over France would destroy the continental balance of power which had enabled Britain to pursue imperial and maritime commitments. By 4 August, the Liberal government made a direct commitment to intervention, although what tipped the scales and prevented the possibility of a cabinet split was the German invasion of Belgium.

*

To move now to more general considerations, the climate in which Europe showed an almost suicidal willingness to rush into war was made up of three constituents. For years the Powers had harboured resentments and grievances, becoming accustomed to pushing claims in order to avoid diplomatic humiliation. This meant that the pursuit of policies of brinkmanship and the growth of a willingness to accept the risk of war. Such policies were carried out within the framework of an alliance system which had a complex pattern of military obligations, but without an international forum for diplomatic pressure. A modern equivalent would be a world in which NATO and the Warsaw Pact existed, but the United Nations Organization did not.

It used to be held that the system of alliances was, in itself, sufficient explanation for the outbreak of war; that the very existence of two armed camps made conflict inevitable sooner or later. But this approach has, for two reasons, an over-simple appreciation of the individual alliances. In the first place, the primary purpose of the alliances was defensive; the 1879 Dual Alliance had committed Germany to supporting Austria only if the latter were attacked by Russia, while the Franco-Russian Alliance

The Outbreak of the First World War

of 1894 also made mutual assistance contingent upon enemy aggression. Such terms could not, in themselves, have led to war; on the contrary, they were more likely to induce one ally to restrain the other from provoking an attack. Second, the way in which war actually broke out bore little relation to treaty obligations. Had the terms of the alliances been carried out to the letter, Germany would not have given Austria a 'blank cheque' after the Sarajevo assassination. Russia had no contractual obligation to assist Serbia and, in any case, her quarrel was with Austria, not Germany. What started as an attempt to mobilize against Austria ended as general mobilization, directed against Germany as well. Had she adhered strictly to the terms of the Alliance of 1894, France would have declared war on Germany as soon as the latter had declared war on Russia. In practice, however, it was Germany who took the initiative against France. Britain had a moral, although not a legal, obligation to assist the Entente powers, but actually entered the struggle after the German invasion of Belgium, a state which was entirely outside the Entente. The alliance system also altered under the impact of the war itself. Italy and Romania pulled away from the Central Powers, later joining the Allies instead, and their place was taken by Turkey, who had had no formal diplomatic ties with Germany before 1914. It seems, therefore, that the alliances were actually less binding than their highly specific terms suggested.

There were, however, two ways in which the alliances *did* affect international relations and contribute to the growth of tension in Europe in the decade before 1914. First, they provided the links across which crises could spread from peripheral areas like North Africa and the Balkans to the major Powers themselves. Normally the dangers were seen and the connections cut; hence the Moroccan crises of 1906 and 1911 were allowed to fizzle out. But, as the sequence of events after Sarajevo showed only too clearly, the means existed whereby a local conflict could be transformed into a continental war. Second, the alliances had a direct bearing on the arms race and the development of military schedules. The Schlieffen Plan, for example, was designed to counter the Franco-Russian offensive which the German High Command assumed to be an integral part of the secret treaty of 1894. Russia would have preferred to concentrate on her major enemy, Austria-Hungary, but the Austro-German Alliance of 1879 forced her to devise a second plan, intended for use against Germany as well. As it happened, these schedules proved so inflexible that general war became inevitable once Russia mobilized on 31 July. The Tsar, faced with the choice of partial mobilization against Austria and total mobilization against Austria and Germany, started with the former but then switched to the latter. The German response was directed by the dead hand of Schlieffen. The military was committed to conquering France before tackling Russia. Thus the Tsar and the Kaiser had found themselves in a terrible dilemma. Russia's quarrel had been with Austria, but partial mobilization would have left Russia exposed to an attack by Germany. Germany's immediate need had been to put pressure on Russia, but this could not be done without first picking a quarrel with France. The military planners had concentrated so carefully on devising a technique to overwhelm the opposing alliance that they had left no room for half-measures. Each camp, obsessed with the fear of containment by the other, had allowed their General Staffs to plan only for total military victory, and not for the application of pressure backed by the threat of limited force. Clausewitz had once argued that military objectives must always be subordinate to diplomacy and that, only as a last resort, should war become 'a continuation of diplomacy by other means'. Unfortunately, the politicians of 1914 lost the initiative to the generals, who were unaccustomed to thinking in diplomatic terms.

There is a school of thought which stresses the parallels with the present nuclear confrontation. Since 1945, armed *blocs* have, as a result of their intense mutual antagonism, developed complex techniques for the deployment of offensive and defensive weapons. Sooner or later, the argument runs, these techniques will break through the political and diplomatic restraints. Political leaders will find themselves entrapped in a situation where the launching of war appears the only way out. Advocates of nuclear weapons, however, put another case. Today the very character of the weapons acts as a deterrent. War would be so fundamentally unacceptable that the balance of terror acts as a powerful restraint. This, it is held, is the basic difference with the situation in 1914. Then, war broke out largely because the prospective struggle was seen in the light of what had gone before – rapid campaigns and limited destruction. There was no new weapon, and the hints as to future developments, provided by the barbed wire in the American Civil War and the trenches in the Russo-Japanese War, had gone unheeded. The concept of the swift, clean kill was still the most powerful of all the

The Outbreak of the First World War

influences on military thinking. Ludendorff, for example, argued in 1910: 'Everything depends on our winning the first battles.'[25] It seems that Europe was looking back to the 1860s and Bismarck's spectacular victories, having, in the meantime, discarded the safeguards which he had attemped to build in the 1870s and 1880s.

17

The Collapse of Austria-Hungary and the Problems of the Successor States

Of the European powers the Ottoman Empire and Austria-Hungary were most directly vulnerable to the threat of internal disintegration. By 1914 the former had been forced to concede independence to its Balkan subjects. Austria-Hungary, however, still held together. More than ever, its existence was imperilled by powerful centrifugal tendencies, but these were, for the time being, restrained by centripetal influences. The future of the Habsburg Empire was literally in the balance.

The most obvious of the centrifugal forces was the Empire's racial tensions. Chapter 6 examined the problem presented to the German Austrians by Hungarian separatism. This had eventually been resolved by the *Ausgleich* (1867), which had granted Hungary autonomy within a federal state which was run by parallel institutions. But, between them, the Germans and the Magyars accounted for only twenty-two million of the Empire's fifty million inhabitants, and a new threat had emerged from the 23.5 million Slavs, who had been excluded from the privileges conferred by the *Ausgleich*. The Austrian half of the Empire, in particular, suffered from the conflict of sectional interests which affected, for example, the dealings between the Bohemian Diets and the Vienna government. Even the grant of universal suffrage in 1907 had not satisfied Slav opinion, for the electoral system was loaded in favour of the German voters. On the other hand, the Germans were still in a minority in the Austrian parliament and any legislative programme could be impeded by determined opposition from the Slavs. The situation was not helped by the Emperor Franz Joseph, who followed the traditional Habsburg dynastic policy of avoiding identification with any individual nationality, and promoting a balance of national antagonisms.

He also reckoned on his dominions being held together by centripetal forces, both internal and external. The strongest internal influence was the accord with Hungary. But there were also many instances of co-operation between the Germans and the Slav aristocracies of Croatia and Polish Galicia who valued their social status more highly than their racial affinities with the Czechs and Serbs. Another bond between the different regions of the Empire was the economic benefit conferred by one of the largest free trade areas in Europe. Hungarian grain, for example, had unrestricted access to Bohemian and Austrian markets, while Bohemian industrial products found outlets in Hungary. The greatest *external* check to disintegration was the existence, on the Empire's eastern frontier, of the Russian autocracy. This had fallen far behind in constitutional development and would, in its expansionist fervour, attempt to dominate any newly emergent state. The peoples of Eastern and Central Europe also feared the prospect of interference by Imperial Germany should Austria-Hungary ever break up. Without exception, therefore, the subject races sought reform within the framework of the existing state. The Nationality Programme, drawn up in Brno in 1899, proposed a new *Ausgleich* which would give the Slavs the same status as that already conceded to the Magyars, while one of the leaders of the Austrian Social Democrats, Bauer, pressed in 1911 for a 'federation of autonomous nations'. When Austria-Hungary went to war in 1914 the main hope of the subject peoples was a rapid victory which would induce a grateful Emperor to preside over the necessary constitutional arrangements. Few people thought in terms of using the war to promote revolution or secession.

By 1918, however, the situation had changed dramatically. Military defeat caused the breakdown of government and consequently destroyed the centripetal influences. This released the centrifugal forces from their restraints and caused the Empire to disintegrate into its national components.

Austria-Hungary experienced a prolonged military crisis from 1915 onwards; the Russians occupied Galicia, and the Italians, who entered the war by the Treaty of London in the same year, threatened the southern frontier. Attempts to negotiate a separate armistice with the Allies failed miserably, and the Empire became totally dependent on Germany for its military survival. Meanwhile, the normal process of government had seized up, with the well-intentioned but inexperienced Emperor Charles being unable to maintain the constitutional ties with Hungary. Within the Austrian half of the monarchy the Slavs were alienated by the introduction of military zones and martial law. Even the economic arguments for imperial unity were fast disappearing. The entire Danubian basin was dislocated as a result of a series of bad harvests and the Allied blockades. Increasingly, therefore, each part of the Empire was forced into self-sufficiency. To make matters worse, the March Revolution of 1917 disposed of the bogy of Tsarist oppression and relieved Austria's Slavs of one of their greatest fears. Russia's new Provisional Government actually gave an incentive to separatism within the Habsburg Empire by openly acknowledging the 'right of the nations to decide their own destinies'. The Bolshevik Revolution (October 1917) seemed to confirm this policy and, in any case, turned Russia in upon herself. The other external restraint on disintegration, Germany, was finally defeated in November 1918. It is no coincidence that the imminence of this defeat accelerated the break-up of Austria-Hungary.

During the course of the war the different nationalities gradually came round to the view that their ends would best be served by complete secession from Habsburg rule. Hence Masaryk and Beneš, Czech leaders in exile, canvassed support in France for the creation of an independent Czechoslovakia, while the Serbs and Croats on the Yugoslav Committee signed the Pact of Corfu with Serbia and made preparations for the establishment of a southern Slav state. International conferences, like the Congress of Oppressed Nationalities held in Rome in April 1918, propagated the arguments for national self-determination and brought Slavs throughout the Empire into contact with their fellows in other countries. These external contacts helped to broaden political perspectives and to undermine any remaining particularist attachments to the Habsburg Empire.

What role did the Western Allies play in all this? The charge was later levelled against them that they deliberately promoted the collapse of Austria-Hungary as a means of guaranteeing victory against Germany in the West. The truth is rather more complex, revealing considerable interplay between the Allies and the nationalities of the Empire. At first the Allied war leaders favoured keeping Austria-Hungary intact as a bulwark against Germany and as a precaution against the 'Balkanization' of Central Europe. But, during the course of 1918, they were gradually convinced by the Slav émigrés and the congresses that the collapse of the Empire was inevitable. A key factor in this change was the failure to negotiate a separate armistice with the Empire; when the Spa Agreement of May 1918 tied the Habsburgs more closely than ever to the Hohenzollerns, the Allied leaders lost patience and became more explicitly in favour of creating separate states in the Danube region. In October 1918, President Wilson refused to accept the Emperor's offer of an armistice on the basis of limited provincial autonomy, insisting, instead, on self-determination, even if new states had to be brought into existence. This policy undoubtedly accelerated the collapse of the Empire as, indeed, it was intended to. By the time of Charles' abdication (11 November), Austria-Hungary no longer existed.

*

The Paris Peace Settlement formally acknowledged the existence of Czechoslovakia as a new state and, by the Treaties of St. Germain and Trianon, confirmed the cession of Galicia to Poland, Transylvania to Romania, Croatia and Bosnia-Herzegovina to Serbia, and the South Tyrol and Trentino to Italy. Austria and Hungary were now merely the German and Magyar rumps of the old Empire. Masaryk, like most of his contemporaries, applauded the new order which had 'shorn nationalism of its negative character by setting oppressed peoples on their feet'.[1] It soon became apparent, however, that the new states were engaged in a desperate struggle for survival, and some observers looked nostalgically back to the days of the multi-national Empire. One of these was the historian E. Eyck, who regarded the 'dismemberment of the Austro-Hungarian state' as a 'basic error'.[2] More recently, A. J. P. Taylor has pointed to the transitory nature of the Empire, but also to the difficulty of managing without it: 'The dynastic Empire sustained central Europe as a plaster cast sustains a broken limb; though it had to be destroyed before movement was possible, its removal did not make movement successful or even easy.'[3]

The Slav peoples of Central Europe were treated generously by the Peace Settlement. The Allies made every effort to implement, in

(a) The structure and composition of Austria–Hungary 1867–1918 (✳=Slavs)

Austria, comprising:
  Germans
  ✳ Czechs
  ✳ Poles
  ✳ Ruthenes
  ✳ Slovenes
  ✳ Serbs and Croats
    Italians
    Romanians
    Magyars

Hungary, comprising:
    Magyars
    Romanians
    Germans
  ✳ Slovaks
  ✳ Croats
  ✳ Serbs
  ✳ Ruthenes
    Others

Bosnia–Herzegovina (annexed by the Empire 1908), comprising:
  ✳ Serbs
  ✳ Croats

(b) The break-up of Austria–Hungary

~ Boundaries shown are those for 1919–38

The extent of Austria–Hungary before break-up

Austria-Hungary and the successor states

their favour, Wilson's principle of national self-determination and, at the same time, to give them frontiers which could be defended and an economic base which had both industrial and agricultural potential. Poland, Czechoslovakia and Yugoslavia all emerged as larger and more populous states than either Austria or Hungary, whose boundaries were pulled back further than even the gloomiest pessimists had feared. Two problems emerged as a result of this disparate treatment. First, the formation of viable states was accomplished only by the inclusion of sizeable minorities. Of the twenty-seven million inhabitants in Poland, only eighteen million were Poles, while Czechoslovakia's 14.5 million people included 3.1 million Sudeten Germans who had been placed under Czech rule because their border area was an integral part of Bohemia's industrial economy. There was, among the advocates of national self-determination, a certain resignation to the inevitability of such anomalies; King Albert of the Belgians, for example, defended the decisions of the statesmen of Paris thus: 'What would you have? They did what they could.'[1] The second problem was the uneasy relationship between the different types of Slavs who had been brought together as co-nationals. Slovaks accused Czechs of monopolizing government positions, a charge which was also levelled in Yugoslavia by the Croats against the Serbs. Some historians consider that the nationalist tensions which existed within the Danube area were worse after the dissolution of the Empire than they had ever been before. And yet the different peoples, with the possible exceptions of the Austrian Germans and the Croatian aristocracy, had no desire to see the restoration of the fallen dynasty.

Inevitably, the new states of Central Europe received dispropor-
tionate amounts of the resources, industries and agricultural land of Austria-Hungary. Czechoslovakia inherited only twenty-seven per cent of the Empire's population but nearly eighty per cent of its heavy industry, sufficient to enable her to compete successfully with many Western industrial states. Hungary was less fortunate; although she received between eighty per cent and ninety per cent of specialized engineering and wood processing plants, these had access to eighty-nine per cent less iron ore and eighty-five per cent less timber. There was also serious disruption in what had, since 1775, been a free trade area of some fifty million inhabitants. The connection between Hungarian agriculture and Austrian and

Bohemian industry has already been noted; the interrelationship could also be more specialized. In the textile industry, for example, most of the spinning was concentrated in Austria, and the weaving in Bohemia. From 1919, however, each of the newly independent nations had to build up those areas of their economies which had not previously been developed in order to create a more balanced agricultural and industrial base. Hence Hungary built up her heavy industry, Austria her weaving and Czechoslovakia her spinning. The result was frantic competition and the emergence of protective tariff barriers. By 1927 Austria's import duties averaged 18.6 per cent, Hungary's 30.7 per cent, Poland's 43.4 per cent and Romania's 99.2 per cent. Attempts *were* made to recreate a Danubian free trade area and to promote co-operation as well as competition, but these invariably foundered. In their struggle for economic survival, the new states of Central and Eastern Europe, with the exception of Czechoslovakia, came to accept the general principles of self-sufficiency and autarky. Whatever success they managed to achieve was, however, wrecked by the Great Depression. The resulting dependence on Germany and its sinister implications are dealt with in Chapter 22.

A great deal of thought had gone into the preparation of the constitutions of the successor states in 1918 and 1919. The view of the Allied leaders, especially President Wilson, was that future peace and stability in Europe would best be preserved by the spread of democracy. Consequently, all the most advanced features of Western democratic thought were enshrined in the new régimes, including universal suffrage, proportional representation, provision for referenda on key issues, and elected presidencies. One of the great disappointments in the inter-war period was that these constitutions failed to work properly in any country in Eastern and Central Europe, with the single exception of Czechoslovakia. Various reasons have been advanced for this. Much of the area had previously experienced only the autocracy of Tsarist Russia or the milder but very limited constitutional monarchy of the Habsburgs. It was, therefore, unduly optimistic to expect that a country like Poland, with no recent experience of self-government, could operate the type of constitution which baffled even the experienced politicians of the Third French Republic. Secondly, the new states, being heterogeneous in their racial composition, were bound to be sectional in their attitude to politics; hence the rivalry between

Austria-Hungary and the Successor States

political parties would often amount to open hatred. And thirdly, the pressure of economic problems, before and after 1929, hastened the emergence of authoritarian régimes. Hungary was the first to swing to the right as the Horthy and Bethlen régimes of the 1920s sought to eliminate the type of radicalism which had, in 1919, been implanted by Bela Kun. Pilsudski virtually scrapped parliamentary democracy in Poland in 1930, while Austria, torn apart by the conflict between Social Democrats and Christian Socialists, eventually succumbed to the corporate policies of Dollfuss and Schuschnigg. The most dramatic trend, however, was the growing reliance of the successor states on the Fascist dictatorships, especially Germany.

This confirmed the worst fears of those Allied leaders who had once argued for the preservation of Austria-Hungary. If, they had insisted, Balkanization occurred, it would be only a matter of time before some expansionist power brought the whole area under its influence. After 1920, two clearly defined *blocs* began to emerge among the successor states. One, which consisted of Austria and Hungary, sought to revise the Versailles Settlement and were the first to gravitate towards Germany during the 1930s, a trend completed by the *Anschluss* and Hungary's membership of Hitler's Anti-Comintern Pact. The second *bloc* comprised Poland, Czechoslovakia, Yugoslavia and Romania. These states formed close diplomatic links with each other and relied upon the guarantee of French protection against any external aggression. During the 1930s, however, French influence in Central and Eastern Europe collapsed dramatically and, as a result, this 'Little Entente' disintegrated. Romania and Poland made their own arrangements with Germany. Only Czechoslovakia held out against German influence, but she was set upon in 1938 by Germany, Hungary and Poland, all intent upon claiming their fellow nationals in the Sudetenland, southern Slovakia and Teschen. Poland, in turn, fell victim to the Nazi war machine in September 1939, and Yugoslavia followed in 1941.

18

The Last Years of Tsarist Russia

This analysis of the final two decades of Imperial Russia will be based on two propositions. The first is that Russia experienced a series of economic and social reforms, which were, particularly between 1905 and 1914, more substantial than is often realized. The second, however, is that the forces of tradition and reaction were a serious impediment to sustained progress. The resulting dichotomy imposed a severe strain on Russian institutions, leaving them exposed to the greatest externally induced crisis in Russian history, the First World War.

*

At first sight, the political and constitutional progress made after 1905 seemed very promising, particularly when contrasted with the negative and inflexible autocracy of Alexander III (1881–94). The October Manifesto (1905) was the first acknowledgement by any Tsar that an elected bicameral legislature had a role to play in Russia's constitutional future. The new state *Duma*, in fact, could be interpreted as a logical, if overdue, development of the concessions made by Alexander II in 1864 and 1870 granting permission for the establishment of provincial *zemstvos* and urban councils. Legislative powers, initially restricted to local government, had now reached the centre. This process did not, however, lead to the decline of local initiative. On the contrary, the early twentieth century saw an increase in reforms carried out by the *zemstvos*, affecting education, health, agriculture and communications, together with

The Last Years of Tsarist Russia

more systematic inter-provincial co-operation in the form of All Russian Congresses. An essential balance, therefore, seemed to have been reached. Local activism, so important in a country the size of Russia, in no way impeded the flow of broader legislative proposals from the *Duma*. Indeed, *Duma* deputies drew from the *zemstvos* experience of constitutional procedure while, at the same time, they broadened and redefined their reforming objectives as national party programmes. The Constitutional Democrats, for example, could be seen as a typical example of Western liberalism, evolving from a series of local interest groups into a cohesive and moderate force for progressive constitutional change. An encouraging sign for Russia's future political stability was that the Constitutional Democrats were usually in broad agreement with the Octobrists, or moderate conservatives. This made possible a broad consensus against attempts to interrupt the evolutionary process made by the extreme Right (especially the Union of Russian People), and by the extreme Left (including the Social Democrats).

Constitutional development was, however, impeded by official conservatism. The latter was given a powerful philosophical base by Pobedonostsev, Procurator-General of the Holy Synod between 1880 and 1905, mentor to Alexander III, and tutor to Nicholas II. His premise that humanity was infinitely corruptible and needed stability in the form of a permanently structured society led him to reject parliamentarism as 'the greatest falsehood of our time',[1] and to stress 'The whole secret of Russian order and prosperity is in the top, in the person of the supreme authority'.[2] His views, like those of Metternich, expressed the established order's growing fear of radical forces, and defined the nature of its response to them. It was unfortunate that the two traditional pillars of Tsarist power, autocracy and bureaucracy, should have been so well equipped with theoretical justification at the very time that the new 'constitutional experiment' was under way.

Nicholas II made it clear that the Constitution which he had been forced to concede as a result of the events of 1905 would not affect his basic powers. In a speech to the *Duma* in 1906 he announced: 'Let it be known to all that I . . . shall maintain the principle of autocracy just as firmly and unflinchingly as did my unforgettable dead father.'[3] This intention was soon embodied in Article 47 of the Fundamental Laws which made 'positive laws, statutes and regulations' directly dependent on 'the Autocratic power'. Everything possible was done to circumscribe the rights of the *Duma*. Although the interpellation of the Tsar's ministers by the *Duma* was a theoretical possibility, their removal was not; this immediately established that the legislature had no real control of the personnel of the executive. Although the budget could be debated, the *Duma* had no means of preventing its enactment, nor even of checking the calculations made by the State Comptroller; this removed the legislature's competence over financial matters. Although the *Duma*, together with the Upper Chamber (the State Council) could pass reforms, the Tsar retained the all-important power of veto; this was extended by Article 87 of the Fundamental Laws into a right to rule by decree when the legislature had been prorogued or dissolved. Thus, concessions granted with one hand had been snatched away by the other, leaving a parliament which was frustrated and embittered by the knowledge that it was a mere shadow of the Western institutions it hoped to emulate. Conflict between the executive and legislature disposed of the First *Duma* in 1906 and the Second in the following year. The alteration of the electoral law in 1907 produced a less belligerent parliament which lasted its full term until 1912, but the Fourth *Duma* (1912–17) revived the claims of the legislature against those of autocracy. One of the tragedies of the whole period was that the liberal intelligentsia were arbitrarily excluded from the reality of power, with the result that it became less and less inclined to co-operate with the Tsar's cabinet and bureaucracy.

The bureaucracy had, after the reforms of Speransky (1809–11), been a progressive force. By the twentieth century, however, many of its features were clearly anachronistic. It failed to co-operate with any representative institutions, and central government officials constantly tried to reduce the authority of the *Duma*, the *zemstvos*, and the numerous voluntary organizations which sprang up after 1900. Hence the volume of reforms produced by the *zemstvos*, although impressive, was far below their real potential. Gradovsky commented: 'In the hands of governmental offices and officials remained power without competence; in the hands of the *zemstvo* institutions was concentrated competence without power'.[4] There was also a serious absence of co-ordination between the various departments of the bureaucracy. The principle of collective ministerial responsibility still did not exist, and the Tsar continued to deal with each department individually. According to Jacob Walkin, the bureaucracy had, by 1914, 'become largely sterile and

The Last Years of Tsarist Russia

obstructive',[5] with urgently needed reforms being delayed or cancelled. The unfortunate complement to a weakened legislature was, therefore, an inefficient executive.

More obvious progress occurred in the Russian economy between 1890 and 1914, the result of a series of ministerial reforms.

Industrial growth is often regarded as the major success of Nicholas II's reign. The initial boost was given by Witte's policies in the 1890s, with their emphasis on government subsidies, derived largely from foreign investment, to heavy industry. The results were spectacular. During the 1890s Russia progressed from fifth to second place among the world powers in terms of railway mileage, while her coal and steel production doubled. By placing Russia on the gold standard in 1896, Witte ensured direct monetary contact with the rest of the world, and took maximum advantage of the prevalent low interest rates. After a depression lasting from 1900 to 1905, Russia experienced, between 1906 and 1913, a second boom, with an annual growth rate of 6 per cent and a corresponding increase in foreign trade. This period saw greater economic flexibility and a lessening of government involvement as conditions for private enterprise became more favourable. These included a greater demand among the peasantry for consumer goods, and a wider availability of domestic capital which reduced the necessity of government action to secure investment from abroad. Many industrialists and economists, inside and outside the country, believed that Russia was well on the way to catching up with the West.

But was she? In many ways, the industrial sector remained sluggish, and it is possible that government involvement, which had given it the initial shove, would eventually have acted as a brake as well. Russian industry found itself in a paradoxical position. On the one hand, there was a smaller entrepreneurial class than elsewhere, which could be supplemented only by government-sponsored activity. On the other hand, this activity was criticized, long before 1914, by the very industrialists it was intended to benefit. There were numerous complaints about inadequate statistical research and unnecessary bureaucratic regulations, while the Congress of the Representatives of Industry and Trade, established in 1906, applied pressure for more direct consultation by the Department of Finance. Above all, there was an underlying suspicion of the motives for industrialization. Nicholas II made no secret of his view that the whole process was intended to renovate and underpin political autocracy. This anti-constitutional motive was separated by a huge gap from the more progressive political ideas which had accompanied industrialization in the West. Conscious of this, many Russian industrialists joined the agitation in the *Duma* for political reform, hoping thereby to exert more direct influence on government policies.

The real test of Russian economic progress was developments in agriculture. Between 1906 and 1910 Stolypin sponsored a series of measures to dispose of the anomalies which remained from Alexander II's emancipation of the serfs. Changes from 1906 enabled peasants to substitute hereditary for repartitional land tenure and to escape the enervating control of the commune. Other laws made available credit throught the Peasant Land Bank, promoted the colonization of Siberia, and abolished redemption payments. By 1913 considerable progress had been made in an economic sector which had induced deep despondency in Witte only fourteen years earlier. Over two million peasants had successfully transferred to hereditary tenure, and there was evidence of more widespread use of new farming implements and fertilizers, the inevitable result being higher yields of crops. At no stage, however, did Russian agriculture even approach the efficiency of that of the West. Moreover, Stolypin's reforms had been highly selective, intended to create a stratum of wealthy peasants which would promote political stability and provide a consumer outlet for industry. Hence, in his own words, his policy was only to 'take account of the sound and the strong'.[5] The poor and the weak, however, still made up the majority of the population, and the totally inadequate distribution of land ensured that the Russian peasantry would never emulate the conservative stability of its French counterpart.

Some historians see in the last years of Tsarist Russia an attempt by the government to spread the social base of its support through a variety of welfare reforms. The 1906 law on associations, for example, conferred basic trade union rights, and a scheme of health insurance was introduced in 1912. Annual expenditure on education quadrupled between 1900 and 1913 and the government showed greater willingness to consider the possibility of factory legislation. When compared with developments in the West, however, these reforms were inadequate and, in any case, hedged with restrictions. There is evidence that the degree of support for autocracy actually

The Last Years of Tsarist Russia

diminished in the first decade of the twentieth century. The proletariat was permanently alienated by the reception given on 22 January 1905 to Gapon's petition, and the inadequacy of government reforms after 1906 made the factory workers an ideal target for Bolshevik propaganda. The professional, commercial and industrial sectors of the middle class all resented the interference of the bureaucracy in the workings of the legislature over political and economic issues, and were made more articulate by the utterings of the intelligentsia. Finally, the nobility, for centuries the pillar of absolutism, was undergoing a crisis of its own. Some members had, out of conviction, joined the more progressive of the *zemstvos* or the liberal parties in the *Duma*, while the reactionary core were exasperated by growing economic problems. Indeed, it would be no exaggeration to say that the aristocracy no longer constituted a homogeneous class, a serious development for a régime which was becoming increasingly isolated from the rest of the people.

*

Judged by its own standards, Imperial Russia had produced some impressive achievements in the twenty years before 1914 and had experienced what was by her standards a rapid rate of evolution. But the obstacles in the way of further progress have led some historians, the 'pessimists', to conclude that revolution was inevitable, with or without the assistance of a catalyst like war. An alternative view, held by the 'optimists', is that Tsarism could have struggled on, at least into the foreseeable future. Even when it lacked the will to transform society and tried to insulate itself from radical pressures by repression, autocracy had considerable resilience and a definite capacity to survive. Revolutionary forces were, by themselves, insufficient to destroy absolutism, as was shown by the triumph of reaction in Central Europe in 1849, and, later, by the triumph of Stalin. An autocracy which was prepared to introduce basic reforms seemed to improve its prospects of overcoming radicalism. Liberals, for example, could be reconciled by the prospect of accelerated evolution; Shidlovsky, a leading representative in the *Duma*, observed before 1914: 'Give us ten more years and we are safe'.[6] To the extreme Left, reforms sponsored by the government were a serious threat. Lenin feared that Stolypin's measures could, if given time to work, insulate most of the peasantry from revolutionary activists. It seems, therefore, that Tsarism did have a chance, provided that it was spared external pressure, and that it could undergo a long period of retrenchment.

The outbreak of the First World War, however, made all the difference. Military collapse had a disastrous effect on the country's political institutions, accentuating the problems already referred to and provoking irreconcilable conflict between the executive and legislature. At the same time, the impact on the economy was so widespread that discontent reached the point of spontaneous eruption. As in Austria-Hungary, therefore, war acted as a catalyst for revolution. It did not actually cause the destruction of the existing régime, but it intensified the internal conflicts to such a degree that the basic capacity for survival was undermined.

*

Russia entered the war unprepared. The army was inadequately supplied, while leaders like the Grand Duke Nicholas, Yanushkevich and Danilov, lacked the experience and expertise of great generals of the past or future, like Kutuzov and Zhukov. The training of the higher officer corps had been seriously defective and there was a grave lack of co-ordination between the Ministry of War and the Front. The inadequacy of the army was fully clear by mid-1915, by which time it had been compounded by a disastrous decision to imitate the scorched earth strategy of withdrawal used against Napoleon in 1812. Since this affected an enormous area, it had a devastating social and economic impact. It was criticized even by the Minister of Agriculture, Krivoshein, who warned: 'Of all the grave consequences of the war this is the most unexpected, the most threatening, the most irreparable.'[7] It also failed to prevent the slow but inexorable disintegration of the Russian army which, after all, was a microcosm of Russian society as a whole.

The collapse of the Russian offensive in 1915 convinced Nicholas II that his greatest duty was to lead the army in person. This had a disastrous impact on the administration, creating a vacuum at the centre which was filled by more irrational and arbitrary manifestations of autocracy in the form of Rasputin and the Empress Alexandra. Although the extent of his influence was exaggerated at the time, Rasputin incurred the bitter opposition of the *Duma*, which formed a Progressive *Bloc* from the Constitutional Democrats and Octobrists to agitate for more direct legislative influence over the process of government. One of the greatest mistakes of the régime, in

The Last Years of Tsarist Russia

fact, was to ignore the efforts of voluntary associations, *Duma* committees and *zemstvo* councils to co-ordinate vital elements of the war effort like fuel, food and transport. Instead, the government assumed openly dictatorial powers, bypassing the *Duma* and issuing nearly 400 special decrees under Article 87 of the Fundamental Laws in two years. When the *Duma* was eventually prorogued until February 1917, its President, Rodzianko, warned that 'only a government that enjoys the confidence of the country could induce it to accept further privations'. Even more important than the conflict with representative institutions, however, was the alienation of the bureaucracy. The virtual abdication of the Tsar by 1915 from administrative responsibilities caused extensive disruption which produced, between 1915 and 1917, no fewer than four premiers: Goremykin, Sturmer, Trepov and Golitsin. This 'ministerial leapfrog' affected the entire bureaucracy causing, by 1917, total paralysis in the face of internal and external threats alike. According to Sazonov, 'the Government was hanging in the air and had no support either from above or below'.

The economic situation also became more and more desperate, rapidly undermining any progress made before 1914. Government policy, never renowned for creating a balance between withdrawal and involvement, now became more inconsistent than ever. At a time when the British and German governments were imposing extensive state control, the Russian administration adopted only half-measures relying, in effect, on a dual system of both state monopolies and private enterprise. These could not coexist, but when the government eventually suppressed the latter, the bureaucracy, depleted by political crisis, failed to adjust to the change. Meanwhile, the lack of systematic planning before the war resulted in serious shortages and contributed to hyper-inflation. Particularly serious was the inadequate supply of raw materials and foodstuffs; this was largely a problem of distribution and reflected badly on the decision, taken before 1914 by the Minister of Transportation, Rukhlov, to slash government expenditure on the railways. These shortages, together with a government decision to print paper money in vast quantities, stimulated price increases without allowing for corresponding adjustments in wages. The deteriorating standard of living inevitably fuelled popular discontent and was the most immediate factor in the February (March) Revolution of 1917.

The events of 23–8 February (8–13 March) were by no means

171

unprecedented in Russian history. The riots, strikes and demonstrations were almost entirely spontaneous and were regarded by the Empress as yet another of the country's 'hooligan movements'. The war, however, made a decisive difference. It swelled the numbers of those who were prepared to take to the streets, thus making impossible the task of enforcing law and order. In 1905 the Tsar had owed the survival of his régime to the backing of the army. By 1917, however, this had been severely weakened; in this respect the impact of the First World War was far greater than that of the Russo-Japanese War, which had left the army intact as an anti-revolutionary force. Finally, the government had become so discredited that the *Duma* was prepared to assume the leadership of the Revolution and put pressure on the Tsar to abdicate. Very little effort was made to resolve the problem of the succession to the throne, an indication that moderate as well as radical opinion now opposed monarchy as well as autocracy.

19

The Bolshevik Seizure and Retention of Power 1917–24

It is often assumed that the Bolshevik Revolution was completed in October 1917. Significant though this date is as one of the great turning points of modern history, the Revolution has to be seen in a broader context.

This chapter will therefore look at the whole period between 1917 and 1924, concentrating on the Bolshevik seizure of power in October 1917, the apparent vulnerability of the new régime in 1918, and its survival between 1918 and 1924.

There is inevitably a profound conflict of opinion over the deeper undercurrent of Russian history in 1917. This is best expressed by two of the leading protagonists in the struggle for power – Trotsky and Kerensky. At one extreme Bolshevik success is seen as part of the dialectical process, and as the completion of a movement towards a higher form of State. Trotsky, for example, argued that it represented 'the transfer of power from one class to another'.[1] The other main view is that the October Revolution was a freak occurrence, a perversion of Russia's historical trends. A well-organized minority group took advantage of administrative and social chaos to force Russian history into one of several alternative channels, and not even the widest one at that. Kerensky believed that the Bolsheviks succeeded 'only by way of conspiracy, only by way of a treacherous and armed struggle'.[2] These two views have since been echoed by

Aspects of European History 1789–1980

Soviet and Western historians who have been separated by the gap between the ideologies which influence their approach.

Despite the controversy about underlying trends, it is possible to find areas of agreement over the objective and immediate reasons for Bolshevik success. The analysis in this chapter will be based on the vulnerability and weaknesses of the Provisional Government, which ruled Russia from March to October, and the efficiency of the Bolsheviks who supplanted it.

The Provisional Government was precipitated into power by the spontaneous revolution in February (March) which, in turn, was the result of Russia's military collapse in the First World War. It had to pick up the pieces and create some sort of order from the chaos which it had inherited and which was not of its own making. A moderate régime, representing the centre and liberal left, it seemed to offer the prospect of reconciliation between Western and Slavic concepts of democracy. But events were against it from the start. As N. Berdyaev maintains, 'moderate people of liberal and humanist principles can never flourish in the elemental sweep of a revolution brought about by war'.[3] The situation in 1917 favoured the group with the firmest resolution, the greatest discipline and the most effective powers of coercion, attributes of the Bolsheviks rather than of liberals and moderate socialists. The collapse of a moderate régime was not, therefore, entirely surprising, especially in view of its extensive flaws.

Its main weakness was its dual base, the result of the emergence of two very different institutions. The Provisional Government itself originated from one of the committees of the *Duma*, and was formally constituted on 1 (14) March. Consisting mainly of liberals, like Lvov, Miliukov and Guchkov, it stood for the development of a Western type of parliamentary democracy. Meanwhile, on 27 February (12 March), the Petrograd Soviet had been set up to represent the working masses. It was dominated by the Left, particularly the Socialist Revolutionaries and Social Democrats who, in turn, had long been divided into Bolsheviks and Mensheviks. It was inevitable that there should be mutual suspicion between the two institutions. The Soviet, it is true, passed an early resolution to co-operate with the Provisional Government's laws 'in so far as they correspond to the interests of the proletariat and the broad democratic masses of the people'. The survival of the régime, however, depended on more than this. What was needed was nothing less than

The Bolshevik Seizure of Power

the gradual convergence of the Provisional Government and Soviet so that any permanent constitution could embody both the parliamentary and mass traditions of Russian democracy.

What in fact happened was more complex. At first co-operation did seem possible as the Provisional Government drew some of its ministers from the Soviet. Kerensky, a Socialist Revolutionary, joined the Provisional Government from the start, while several others were invited into the broad coalition governments of May and July. From July onwards the Provisional Government was dominated by various shades of socialists rather than by its original liberal membership. But this did not guarantee harmony between the Provisional Government and the Soviet. On the contrary, they pulled apart over their conflicting policies on the continuation of the war and the redistribution of land. Kerensky increasingly identified himself with the Provisional Government rather than with the Soviet, which proceeded to move further to the Left. Unfortunately, the Provisional Government appeared less and less homogeneous as Kerensky broke with the liberals as well. The latter actually pulled out of the government in protest against Kerensky's handling of the Kornilov revolt in August. By September, therefore, Kerensky had been left virtually isolated, in charge of a mere rump of a government which was separated by a wide gulf from the Soviet. To make matters worse, Kerensky became more and more aware of the tenuous nature of his claim to power. The Provisional Government was still, in the words of one historian, a 'pre-legitimate régime', as it had not yet been confirmed by parliamentary election. And yet, as Kerensky realized, to call for elections at this stage could only put the Left into power, perhaps irrevocably. He had thus become the guardian of moderation, but without the means of defending it.

Why, it could be asked, did the Socialist Revolutionaries and the Mensheviks in the Soviet not take the initiative and set up, as an alternative to Kerensky's régime, what would after all have been a majority government? The answer is that they stood for different types of socialism which could not readily be reconciled; besides which, neither had the necessary discipline or organization. Hence, the way was open for the Bolsheviks, originally a minority party, to move quickly into action and, by October, to win control of the Soviet. The difference in attitude between the Bolsheviks and the other parties of the Left had been shown in an incident at a meeting of the first All Russian Congress of Soviets in June. One of the Menshevik leaders, Tsereteli, argued that there was no real alternative to the Provisional Government. He concluded: 'At the present moment there is no political party which would say, "Give the power into our hands, go away, we will take your place." There is no such party in Russia.' Lenin was heard to say from his seat, 'There is.'[4]

Indeed, Lenin had for many years prepared for just such a situation and the Bolsheviks were in a unique position to take advantage of the weakness of the régime. Lenin had consistently emphasized the need for a tight party with a core 'of persons engaged in revolution as a profession'.[5] The Bolshevik Party was given a double objective in 1917. The first was to use its organization on behalf of the masses. Trotsky maintained that without this 'the energy of the masses would dissipate like steam not enclosed in a piston box'.[1] The Party would therefore accomplish what the masses by themselves could not: 'Just as a blacksmith cannot seize the red hot iron in his naked hand, so the proletariat cannot directly seize power.'[6] The second role was to take over the Soviet, using it as a front to legitimize the Party's revolutionary activities. From August onwards a process of political osmosis took place; the Provisional Government grew steadily weaker as support drained away from it, while the Soviet came more and more under the control of the Bolsheviks. When the latter actually achieved a numerical majority on 31 August (13 September), Lenin was able to claim that all future Bolshevik actions were to be conducted in the name of the Soviet. He said, for example, on 7 November: 'If we seize power today, we seize it not against the Soviets but for them.'[7]

Effective organization would have been to no avail without a clear overall strategy. The basic principle of the Bolsheviks was to have a fixed long-term objective, but a flexible short-term approach to it. The long-term aim was described in Lenin's *April Theses* as 'the transition from the first stage of the revolution, which gave power to the bourgeoisie ... to the second stage, which should give power into the hands of the proletariat and the poorest strata of the peasantry'.[4] The short-term approach, however, would avoid any rigid or doctrinaire commitments. Three things, in particular, were emphasized. The first was the need for the right degree of force at the right time. Lenin spoke of a judicious alternation between withdrawal and attack, depending on the strengths and weaknesses of the opponent;

The Bolshevik Seizure of Power

the effect, he said later, was 'an overwhelming preponderance of force at the decisive moment in the decisive points'. Secondly, the Bolsheviks should, for the moment, compromise with other parties and, if necessary, adopt elements of their programme. Thus they were prepared to help Kerensky overcome the threat of Kornilov, and they also won substantial support in the Soviet from the Mensheviks and Socialist Revolutionaries. Thirdly, the Bolsheviks made maximum use of any prevailing destructive forces in order to undermine the régime. For example, they promoted or supported regional nationalism in the local Soviets and the army, especially in the Ukraine. They realized that these tactics would break the power of the Provisional Government over all but the core of Russia.

What was the importance of Lenin's personal role in all this? There is general agreement among historians about the vital role played by Lenin during the course of 1917. They all point to his personal charisma and powers of oratory and, even more important, to his influence as the overall leader and strategist. His return from exile in April 1917 ended months of uncertainty and internal divisions within the Party and provided an authoritarian base which promoted a degree of discipline and unity which the other parties lacked. In a sense, Lenin's monolithic power base looked back to the days of the Tsar, providing the only realistic prospect of restoring order after the collapse of Tsarist rule. Above all, Lenin was entirely responsible for the timing of the October Revolution. He had realized that total commitment to the rising in July would have been disastrous, and he therefore urged restraint on that occasion. By October (November), however, he calculated that circumstances had changed sufficiently to warrant immediate action. On 6 November, therefore, he said: 'We must not wait! We may lose everything.'[7] In this respect, Lenin was similar to Napoleon, whose military victories depended on split-second timing. Both leaders illustrate the importance of individuals in promoting or accelerating historical trends.

*

Seizure of power in October (November) 1917 was by no means the end of the matter. The history of revolutions is littered with successful invasions from outside, or with internal Thermidorian reactions. Lenin was fully aware of this. 'It is easy for Russia in the specific, historically very unique situation of 1917 to *start* a Socialist revolution but . . . it will be more difficult for Russia than for the European countries to *continue* and consummate it.'[8] This was said in 1920, after the worst dangers had been overcome. How much bleaker must the situation have seemed in 1918?

There were two particularly serious threats to the new Bolshevik régime. The first was the possible impact of war. The Great War had been the most important catalyst in the destruction of Tsarist rule and also of the Provisional Government. There was now a danger that it would destroy the Bolsheviks as well, especially if, as was likely, it were complemented by civil war and counter-revolution. The second threat was internal. Russia could easily decompose into its national units and a political vacuum would rapidly result. By 1918, in fact, the Bolsheviks controlled an area the size only of fifteenth-century Muscovy, and even here the Socialist Revolutionaries were more popular than the Bolsheviks in electoral terms.

All the ingredients existed for the type of takeover which the Bolsheviks themselves had recently conducted. The Bolsheviks had, therefore, to switch from their previous destructive role to an unfamiliar constructive and defensive strategy. The latter was to prove far more difficult than the former.

*

The most serious danger in 1918 and 1919 was external. Aware of the new régime's vulnerability, Lenin decided to settle one struggle, the Great War, in order to concentrate on the anticipated counter-revolution and civil war. Hence, in the Treaty of Brest Litovsk (1918) he accepted the humiliating terms imposed by the victorious Germans, conceding that 'a disgraceful peace is proper, because it is in the interest of the proletarian revolution and the regeneration of Russia'.[9] The result was that the Bolsheviks were able to concentrate on the offensive launched by the Whites and the Allied powers. After initial difficulties in 1918, the Bolsheviks were, by 1919, close to victory over the White generals; the Allies considered the situation hopeless and therefore withdrew their troops and supplies. Why did this transformation take place?

The first reason was the geographical advantages possessed by the Bolsheviks. At first, they were confined to the rump of European Russia and surrounded on all sides by the enemy. Their location was, however, a source of strength; they were clearly defending the heart of the homeland, while the Whites had to campaign through more

The Bolshevik Seizure of Power

unreliable peripheral areas. The Bolsheviks also controlled the main cities and industries and, above all, Russia's railway network, which radiated outwards from Moscow. The Whites, by contrast, had severe difficulties with transport, especially on the Trans-Siberian railway, which was usually clogged up by complex political and military disputes. The Bolsheviks made full use of their internal lines of communication, switching their defensive units rapidly as one front after another came under attack.

The second factor in the Bolshevik victory was their political homogeneity, a clear contrast to the serious disunity of their opponents. The Bolsheviks had a clear and systematic ideology and used their monopoly over all forms of communication to put across their skilfully prepared propaganda. Their opponents, by contrast, had no overall programme, let alone a single ideology. In fact, they represented the entire range of the political spectrum, ranging from left-wing parties like the Mensheviks and Socialist Revolutionaries, through liberal elements like the Cadets and Octobrists, to right-wing conservatives. Agreement on an alternative régime was out of the question, since the various possibilities were mutually exclusive. How, for example, could the advocates of a socialist republic hope to find common ground with those who wanted the return of Tsarist autocracy? The areas under actual White control were also subject to political problems and divisions – Siberia, for example, had no fewer than nineteen governments early in 1918. Even the Allies, whose interventionist forces were intended to assist the Whites, could not agree on the motives for their involvement, let alone their strategy. Japan and the United States, for instance, found themselves in bitter dispute over economic concessions in Siberia. Eventually the Western powers lost interest in the civil war and those statesmen who, like Churchill and Milner, wanted to continue the anti-Bolshevik crusade, were very much in a minority. By the end of 1920 the British government had heeded the threat of the trade union movement about the possible consequences of further involvement in Russia, while the French government had switched its strategy to containing Communism by preventing its spread to Poland and the rest of Eastern Europe.

Above all, there was an enormous difference between the military efficiency of the Bolsheviks and the shortcomings of the Whites. Trotsky's Red Army, created in 1918, made use of a large number of ex-Tsarist officers, but ensured their permanent loyalty by subordinating them to political commissars who were, in effect, agents of the Party. At the same time, promotion was encouraged from the ranks; this eventually produced top-class generals like Voroshilov, Budyonny, Yakir and Timoshenko. Conscription, introduced in 1918, increased the size of the Red Army from 550,000 in September 1918 to three million in 1919 and 5.5 million in 1920. The Whites, meanwhile, were debilitated by the lack of overall command and of a basic strategy, so that their campaigns invariably fizzled out. Despite the formidable threat implied by Yudenich's advance on Petrograd, Kolchak's move towards the eastern frontier and Deniken's march on Moscow, all the White offences collapsed through poor timing. Even the supporting powers were indecisive; no specific military functions were given to the units landing at Murmansk and Archangel, and the numbers, in any case, were small because of the needs throughout 1918 of the Western Front in France. The Allies also failed to set up an overall War Council to co-ordinate their campaigns. Trotsky pointed out the enormous potential strength of the Allies and stated that when they 'manage to act unanimously and to undertake a campaign against us, we shall be lost'. But, he added, this would 'absolutely not occur'.[10]

In any civil war the attitudes of the civilian population are vitally important. Although they had only minority support in the 1918 elections to the Constituent Assembly, the Bolsheviks came to be seen by the inhabitants in the various war zones as less of a threat than the Whites to their livelihood. The peasantry, for example, feared that the Whites would return the powerful landlords and reimpose the former dues and obligations. Also, the White armies had to live off the land and some of their campaigns produced serious damage through pillage and looting. One of the Whites' major problems was that the peripheral areas under their control were strongly opposed to any programme for reunifying Russia. Self-determination was the key demand of the Ukranians, Poles, Baltic peoples, Caucasians and many others. Thus Deniken and Kolchak, committed to restoring the frontiers of Tsarist Russia, had to deal with highly unstable local politics; indeed Deniken had to divert some of his resources to deal with Ukranian separatists and bands of marauding peasants. Lenin and Trotsky followed a characteristically opportunist policy of supporting this separatism against the Whites and, once the Whites had been cleared out, of crushing it with the Red Army.

The Bolshevik Seizure of Power

Meanwhile, the Bolsheviks had gained firm control over all the institutions of the state. The main development was a move away from a mixed democracy, with different types of representative institutions, towards a more homogeneous base consisting of Soviets and Party. The first casualty of this trend was the Constituent Assembly. At first, the Bolsheviks considered themselves committed to calling this, since Lenin had promised immediate elections. The result, however, was a sweeping majority for the Socialist Revolutionaries, who won 410 seats to the Bolsheviks' 175. Lenin now proceeded to attack the Constituent Assembly as a bourgeois institution, 'an expression of the old relation of political forces which existed when power was held by the compromisers and the Cadets'.[11] He was, therefore, determined to exclude the bourgeoisie from power and to move more directly towards the establishment of a proletarian state. The Constituent Assembly was dissolved and all future legislation was enacted by the Soviets. At the same time, the two new constitutions of 1918 and 1922 subordinated the new hierarchy of Soviets to the corresponding committees of the Party. A new form of democracy had therefore appeared; instead of the Party being forced to work within the constraints of the constitution, the constitution existed to transmit more effectively the policy of the Party. This was the recipe for permanent Bolshevik rule and accorded well with Lenin's concept of the dictatorship of the proletariat.

This process of Bolshevizing Russian democracy was accomplished by two techniques which, although different, were complementary: terror and concessions.

Terror had not originally been an integral part of the Bolshevik programme but, as Lenin was swift to point out, there had been numerous historical precedents, including the famous Jacobin Terror of the French Revolution. The Bolshevik leaders increasingly used violence to destroy all opposition and any remnants of either Western democracy or Tsarism. 'We want', said Lenin, 'to organize violence in the name of the interests of the workers.'[12] The question of the legality of such methods did not arise, for 'Dictatorship is power-based directly upon force, and unrestricted by any laws'.[13] Nor was morality an issue, for 'we say that our morality is wholly subordinated to the interests of the class war waged by the proletariat'.[12] It may well be necessary, Trotsky argued, to use extreme methods to achieve the desired results, for 'we shall not enter into the kingdom of socialism in white gloves on a polished floor'.[14] Hence Bolshevik leaders were convinced of the need for institutions like the *Cheka** and for direct action against the Cadets in 1918 and the Socialist Revolutionaries in 1922. Since they had the complete monopoly of the use of Terror, the Bolsheviks made retaliation impossible; despite the widespread support which they undoubtedly commanded, the Socialist Revolutionaries had no vehicle for transmitting their opposition. The Bolsheviks also managed to avoid turning the Terror inwards. There was no repetition of the internecine conflict which had destroyed Hébert, Danton, Robespierre and other Jacobin leaders between 1793 and 1794.

To ensure that the Bolsheviks did not achieve a reputation for undiluted terror, Lenin also compromised whenever he considered that strategic withdrawal was necessary. Indeed, he seemed to follow the motion of two steps forward, one step backward. The period 1918–24 provides two major examples of this: his attitudes to federalism and the economy. Lenin had originally opposed on principle any form of national self-determination, except as a means of destroying the war effort of the Whites. But in 1918, and again in 1922, he acknowledged that federalism could prevent the threat of future disintegration, and he consented to the formation of the two largest federations in the world, the Russian Socialist Federated Soviet Republic and the Union of Soviet Socialist Republics. At the same time, the price of regional autonomy was close supervision at all levels by the appropriate organs of the Party. Lenin's retreat on economic principles was even more fundamental as in 1921 he transformed war communism into his New Economic Policy. His main reason was that coercion alone could 'ruin the whole course'. There was also an implicit admission that his economic strategy would take longer to achieve than he had originally anticipated because of the inherent conservatism of the peasantry. In the meantime, therefore, tactics should include a form of 'state capitalism', provided, of course, this in no way interfered with Lenin's political changes.

*

The years 1922–4 should have been a highpoint of the Bolshevik régime. The external threat had been overcome and Communism

* Extraordinary Commission for the Suppression of Counter Revolution, Speculation and Sabotage; the forerunner of the NKVD and the KGB.

The Bolshevik Seizure of Power

had been established internally as a permanent and irrevocable system of government. Yet there were already signs of disenchantment. Victor Serge, a French Communist, later complained that 'emergent totalitarianism had already gone half way to crushing us'.[15] Trotsky was by now attacking Stalin for aspiring to personal dictatorship. Lenin, clearly concerned about the possible trend of Bolshevism in the future, tried to demote Stalin and the *Cheka* chief, Dzerzhinsky. One of his main fears in the last year of his life was that the Bolsheviks had revived some of the underlying features of the detested Tsarist régime and had provided 'only a Soviet veneer'.

20
Two Views of the Terms of the Treaty of Versailles

The Treaty of Versailles, which dealt with Germany, was signed on 28 June 1919. In summary, it affirmed, by Article 231, the responsibility of 'Germany and her Allies' for the outbreak of the First World War and, accordingly, made provision for territorial adjustments, demilitarization and economic compensation to the victorious Allies for the losses which they had incurred. Germany was relieved of Alsace-Lorraine, Eupen and Malmedy, Northern Schleswig, Posen, West Prussia, parts of Southern Silesia, and all her overseas colonies. Limits were placed on her naval capacity, her army was restricted to 100,000 volunteers, and the Rhineland was demilitarized. A considerable quantity of rolling stock and merchant shipping was also removed, while France was given exclusive rights to the coal mines of the Saar region. Finally, provision was made for the payment of reparations by the German government, the amount eventually being fixed in 1921 at 136,000 million gold marks. Altogether, it has been estimated, Germany lost 13 per cent of her area, 12 per cent of her population, 16 per cent of her coal, 48 per cent of her iron, 15 per cent of her agricultural land and 10 per cent of her manufactures.

*

Was this a fair settlement? There is a longstanding tradition that it was not. This originated with the forebodings of contemporary diplomats and observers like Harold Nicolson[1] and Norman H. Davies, of the outspoken economist J. M. Keynes,[2] and of the

The Terms of the Treaty of Versailles

historian W. H. Dawson.[3] Although the sympathy for Germany was subsequently diluted by the rise of Hitler, there emerged a feeling that the Versailles Settlement could well have contributed to the destructive phenomenon of Nazism. It then became common to question, in retrospect, the wisdom of visiting the guilt of the Kaiser's Germany upon a moderate republic which had been engaged in a desperate struggle for survival against the forces of the extreme Right. German historiography, meanwhile, had maintained a constant attack on the Versailles *Diktat*, whether from the viewpoint of moderates like Brandenburg and Rothfels, or of the textbook writers for the *Nationalsozialistische Lehrerbund* (Nazi Teachers' Association). Although recent German historians like F. Fischer have, by reviving the whole question of German war guilt (see Chapter 16), brought about a re-examination of the Versailles Settlement, the majority of German writers still favour the traditional view; a typical example of the latter is Hannah Vogt, whose textbook[4] is of the type widely used throughout West Germany, and whose approach to the question is similar to that employed by many teachers in England.

By combining some of these sources it is possible to build up a composite criticism of the Treaty of Versailles. On the question of territorial changes there is some support for the implementation of national self-determination, but considerable criticism of the uneven use of the plebiscite. Why, for example, should this facility have been given to the Danes of Northern Schleswig and the Poles and Czechs of Southern Silesia, but not to the Germans of the Sudetenland or of Austria? Referring to the existence of large and disaffected German minorities in countries like Czechoslovakia and Poland, W. H. Dawson claimed that Germany's frontiers 'are literally bleeding. From them oozes out the life-blood, physical, spiritual and material of large populations'.[5] Poland, in particular, had been treated too generously at Germany's expense, a 'clear perversion' of the thirteenth of President Wilson's Fourteen Points.[5] As for the confiscation of Germany's colonies, many observers pointed to an element of hypocrisy. Wilson's avowed reason for removing regions like South-West Africa and Rwanda-Urundi from German administration was to protect the inhabitants from the proven harshness of German rule. Yet, some of the states which received them as mandates could hardly claim exemplary records: South Africa and Belgium, for example.

Aspects of European History 1789–1980

The most influential critic of the economic provisions of the Treaty was J. M. Keynes. He argued that the Settlement lacked wisdom in its aim to destroy Germany's very means of subsistence. The coal and iron provisions, for example, were 'inexpedient and disastrous'. Germany would be left with a capacity to produce only sixty million tons per annum, whereas in 1913 she had consumed 110 million tons. The situation was aggravated by the damage done to German commerce by the restrictions imposed on ship building and by the new system of protective tariffs against German exports. Above all, the indemnity being considered by the Allies in 1919 was well beyond Germany's means to pay. It was clear to Keynes, who resigned his position in the British delegation in protest, that the real dangers for the future lay not in boundary questions 'but rather in questions of food, coal and commerce'. He remained convinced that 'The Treaty, by overstepping the limits of the possible, has in practice settled nothing'. The subsequent economic crisis suffered by the Weimar Republic, including the collapse of the mark in 1923, seemed to provide immediate evidence to support his prediction.

Why did a treaty of such severity emerge in the first place? The reason most commonly given was that the ideals of President Wilson were heavily diluted by the revanchism of Clemenceau and the pragmatism of Lloyd George. In the words of Harold Nicolson: 'We arrived as fervent apprentices in the school of President Wilson: we left as renegades.'[6] According to H. Vogt, Clemenceau influenced the whole proceedings because 'he knew only one goal: security for France!'[7] The British delegation took a more moderate stance, but Lloyd George was, nevertheless, under heavy pressure from public opinion at home to make Germany pay for all the damage caused during the war. The bargaining position of Wilson was also weakened by disenchantment within the United States with the whole idea of involvement in European affairs. The overall result was inevitably the triumph of expediency over ideals leading, in Nicolson's view, to a 'deterioration of moral awareness'.[6]

There could be only one solution. Contemporary critics of the Settlement were unanimous in their demand for its alteration; according to Keynes, 'the revision of the treaty is the necessary and inevitable first step forward'.[8] There were certainly to be steps in this direction. In 1924, the Dawes Plan modified the method of paying reparations, while the Young Plan of 1930 extended the deadline, and the Lausanne Agreement of 1932 cancelled all out-

The Terms of the Treaty of Versailles

standing reparations. Meanwhile, all occupation forces were withdrawn from the Rhineland by 1930 and provision was made by the League of Nations for the full return of the Saar to Germany by 1935. But critics of the Treaty maintained that these concessions were too late to reconcile German public opinion to a settlement which it bitterly loathed. There was also a strong suspicion that the real beneficiaries of any pangs of conscience aroused in the victorious Allies by Keynes and Nicolson were not so much the statesman of the Weimar Republic as the Nazis who came to power in 1933.

✦

Keynes, Nicolson and Taylor were enormously influential, but it was only to be expected that their views would be contradicted sooner or later. Not surprisingly, the image of a vengeful Clemenceau imposing a 'Carthaginian' settlement was first challenged by the French Prime Minister, Tardieu,[9] some of whose views were later elaborated by E. Mantoux.[10] An American, P. Birdsall[11] also went against the prevailing tendency to attack the Treaty, and they have been followed by many modern historians; examples can be selected from writers on France (like J. Néré[12]), Germany (W. Carr[13] and A. J. Nicholls[14]) and international relations (S. Marks[15] and G. Schulz[16]). The latest wave of interpretation has produced, in the work of M. Trachtenberg[17] and W. A. McDougall,[18] a more or less complete vindication of French policy, together with heavier criticism of Germany and, more controversially, of the United States and Britain.

Another picture of the Treaty of Versailles therefore emerges. By emphasizing three points it is possible to show that the treatment of Germany was not unduly harsh. First, her territorial losses in 1919 were tiny compared with the alterations which a German victory would have brought. According to F. Fischer, Germany's war aims included economic dominance over Belgium, Holland and France; hegemony over Courland, Livonia, Estonia, Lithuania and Poland in Eastern Europe, and over Bulgaria, Romania and Turkey in the Balkans; unification with Austria and the creation of a Greater Germany; and control over the entire Eastern Mediterranean and over a dismantled Russia. In sharp contrast the Allied plenipotentiaries, far from humiliating a defeated country, showed considerable restraint in removing only those ethnic minorities who

187

had clearly suffered from their inclusion in the German Reich. Second, some form of economic compensation was only to be expected, given the appalling scale of French losses; most of the Western Front had been within ten French *départements*, some of which had been totally ravaged by retreating German armies. German industries, by contrast, had largely escaped destruction since the Rhineland and Ruhr never came within the scope of Allied operations. There was, therefore, a straightforward argument for transferring some of the wealth of a complete industrial economy to assist the rebuilding of a shattered one. Third, it has not been proved conclusively that the Treaty of Versailles crippled Germany in the process of compensating France and Belgium. The chronic inflation between 1919 and 1923 was due at least as much to the German government's unrestrained issue of banknotes and to the heavy speculation by the Rhineland industrialists. There remains a strong suspicion that Germany could not meet the reparations bill because she had no intention of doing so. A general increase in taxation could have met all foreign debts and held the mark steady as well. No ministry, however, was prepared to risk the internal opposition which this would have brought; a short-term policy based on the reckless printing of paper money seemed a much easier option.

The role of France and Britain at the Paris Peace Conference has also been extensively re-assessed. (Néré, McDougall and Trachtenberg all refute the charge that France was the intransigent power and a source of constant irritation to the more moderate Britain.) It seems that France had every right to consider herself the aggrieved party between 1918 and 1923. The French originally sought to accomplish two objectives only: economic reconstruction and military security. These could be attained most effectively within the structure of an Atlantic community which would perpetuate the unity of the wartime alliance. Hence the Minister of Commerce, Clémentel, had in 1918 proposed an economic *bloc* which would operate a system of preferential tariffs and come to an agreement on currency matters. As for the future security of France, Tardieu, the French delegate, argued that a neutralized Rhineland would be the best guarantee against future German invasion. This should be related to a permanent pact between the Western powers. Once Western Europe had achieved a new strength and stability as a result of these agreements, Germany could be allowed to regain her economic and industrial status without the

The Terms of the Treaty of Versailles

danger of future aggression and war. Unfortunately, the French scheme collapsed. Clémentel's proposals were rejected by the United States, with the result that France had to depend for her economic recovery entirely on German reparations. Worse followed when, on 19 March 1920, the United States Senate refused to ratify the Treaty of Versailles. This meant that the treaty of mutual guarantee between France, the United States and Britain also crumbled. The United States withdrew from all military commitments in Europe, while Britain, whose membership of the alliance had been tied to American involvement, considered her own obligations to France ended by the Senate's decision. France was now virtually isolated and faced the prospect of containing, by herself, the inevitable revival of Germany. By 1923, moreover, it had become apparent that the German government was doing its utmost to evade fulfilling the terms of the Treaty of Versailles. Was it surprising, therefore, that Poincaré should have tried to restore the French initiative by ordering the occupation of the Ruhr?

Among the main critics of this action was the British government. But, it has been argued, the record of the British delegation at Paris was far from moderate or even consistent. The usual view that Lloyd George was a pragmatist, driven to occasional harshness only by pressure from British public opinion, will not do. If anything, the British position was more extreme than the French. Lloyd George, for example, appeared just as revanchist as Clemenceau; in 1918 he told the Imperial War Cabinet: 'The Terms of Peace must be tantamount to some penalty for the offence.'[17] In one of the sub-commissions, the British representative, Lord Cunliffe, claimed that Germany could afford to pay reparations of 120,000 million dollars, a figure which the French Minister of Industrial Reconstruction, Loucheur, rejected as too high. Although Lloyd George appeared, in his Fontainebleau Memorandum, to have been won over to moderation, the British government still put the reparations figure almost twice as high as did the French, and then complicated the proceedings by demanding the inclusion of war pensions and separations allowances as war damages. Largely because of British intransigence, the reparations figure had to be settled separately and was not announced until 1921. By this time the German government had taken comfort from the evident disintegration of the alliance between the victorious powers and had begun to probe for weaknesses in the Versailles Settlement. The country most seriously affected by this was France, who had taken a consistently reasonable line on the whole reparations issue.

No one could seriously argue that the Treaty of Versailles was a success. But, whereas the Treaty's critics maintained that the major need was fundamental revision, some of its defenders have put the case for more effective enforcement. The Settlement failed not because it was too severe, but because the alliance which formulated it fell apart with the withdrawal of the United States and Britain, and the isolation of France. Although the Treaty was propped up by Collective Security and the Locarno Pact (1925) it remained vulnerable to any German refusal to implement it. The modifications secured by the Dawes Pact (1924) were sufficient to win the temporary co-operation of moderate statesmen like Stresemann. But, in the long term, German public opinion continued to see the whole settlement as a *Diktat* and eventually supported its overthrow by the Nazi régime. Opponents of the Treaty argued that Nazism was one of its legacies; its defenders maintain that Hitler succeeded only because the Treaty was not enforced. Keynes, anticipating future problems, warned of the danger of visiting 'on the children of their enemies the misdoings of parents or of rulers'; Mantoux, looking back on an era of violence, concluded that what in fact happened 'was that the misdoings of a nation were visited on the children of its victims'.[10]

21

Mussolini

A. J. P. Taylor once described Mussolini as 'a vain blundering boaster without either ideas or aims', while the Fascism over which he presided had far less 'drive' than the Nazi movement.[1] This view will provide the basic terms of reference for the examination in this chapter of the career of Italy's dictator between 1922 and 1943. The first section will analyse his rise to power, focusing on his opportunism and the means by which he exploited the weaknesses of the establishment. The second will examine the methods by which he maintained his power, the extent to which he left the previous administrative structure standing, and the aura of the personality cult or 'Mussolinianism'. The third will deal with his decline – the result of personal defects, growing weaknesses within the system, and the damaging effects of the close connection with Nazi Germany.

*

The most striking thing about Mussolini's early years was his commitment to the extreme Left of the Socialist Party. He certainly had orthodox views on class struggle, stating in 1908 that 'the interests of the proletariat are opposed to those of the middle class. No agreement between them is possible. One or the other must disappear.'' He was also uncompromising in his condemnation of nationalism and imperialism, and he said of the Tripolitan venture: 'The national flag is a rag that should be placed in a dunghill'.

By 1922, however, Mussolini's beliefs had been transformed. He abandoned his attachment to the Left and announced in a speech:

191

'We declare war on socialism.'[3] He was also converted to the principles of the free market, claiming that capitalism constituted a
centuries-old and irreplaceable set of values. Imperialism he now
regarded as 'the eternal, immutable law of life',[4] while Catholicism,
which he had once denounced, now became one of the sources of 'the
imperial and Latin tradition of Rome'.[5]

The explanation of this *volte face* is that Mussolini's only really
consistent belief was in the necessity of direct involvement. He
claimed, in 1932, that 'My own doctrine . . . had always been a
doctrine of action'.[2] Explaining his inconsistency over Italy's entry
into the First World War, he argued: 'Only maniacs never change.
New facts call for new positions'.[4] Above all else, therefore, he was an
opportunist, and his real strength lay in his having no overall
system and no ideological straightjacket.

This pragmatism enabled Mussolini to make full use of the chaotic
conditions of post-war Italy. His rise to power was a combination of
parliamentary manoeuvre and extra-parliamentary radical pressure. He played upon the weaknesses and divisions within the
executive and legislature in such a way that the Fascists assumed
far greater importance than the thirty-five seats which they had won
in the 1921 general election would seem to warrant. He also
instructed the local Fascist leaders, like Balbo, to create havoc, and
early results of this activity were the capture of Ferrara by 63,000
Fascists and their successful move against the strike called by the
socialists. The high point of Mussolini's emphasis on 'action',
however, was the so-called 'March on Rome' in 1922, as a result of
which Victor Emmanuel III was pressurized into summoning
Mussolini to form the next government.

During the crucial period between 1919 and 1922 Mussolini had
made the most of a critical economic situation and of the weak
ministries of Orlando, Nitti, Giolitti, Bonomi and Facta. He
launched a blistering attack on all the major parties in the Chamber.
A headline in an issue of his newspaper, *Il Popolo*, warned:
'Gentlemen of the Government, make up your minds to grant the
demands of the working masses.' Socialism he lampooned as 'a new
tyranny that is merciless and also absurd'.[6] As for the liberal parties,
they were basing all their policies on a 'scaffolding', behind which
there was no 'structure'. He offered himself, therefore, as a unifier;
hence 'Fascism draws its sword to cut the many Gordian Knots
which enmesh and strangle Italian life.'[7] The opposition to his

Mussolini

emergence in the Italian parliament was weak and indecisive. Even after Mussolini had been made Prime Minister, Nitti and the moderates were opposed to any form of obstruction: 'The Fascist experiment must be carried out without interference: there must be no opposition from our side'.[8] Even the Left offered little direct opposition, except in the form of individual utterings. Matteotti, who made his own views so clear that he was murdered in 1924, rejected, nevertheless, a proposal from the Communist Party for a united front with the words: 'We are fighting Fascism for freedom: we cannot fight Fascism in the name of another dictatorship.'[8] It is hardly surprising, therefore, that contemporary observers spoke of the 'moral collapse' of parliament. Pietro Neni condemned the whole atmosphere of complacency in the Chamber in which party feuding prevented any form of united action against an organization which threatened the whole basis of the parliamentary system. Indeed, the mistaken impression arose that Mussolini could be used as a pawn in party politics and that he could be restrained from committing any excesses. Hence parliamentarians were 'under the delusion that they were cleverness itself. They fed the flame they should have quenched'.[9]

From which sections of the population did Fascism derive its support? At first it appealed to the displaced or marginal elements; like the Nazis, it was widely accepted among the unemployed. Then it attracted substantial numbers from the lower-middle class, disillusioned by their struggle for survival against the more powerful and better organized élite of the free market system. It also gained support from the demobilized soldiers and officers, students and peasants, who were won over by Fascist promises of grants to individual farmers rather than collectivization on Communist lines. Mussolini made an effort to extend the basis of his support among the urban proletariat by claiming that he agreed with the idea of workers' control of factories. At the same time, his promise to uphold capitalism and his opposition to strikes had the tacit approval of many large business corporations, while his aggressively stated brand of nationalism won favour among conservatives who were antagonized by Italy's parsimonious treatment by the settlement of St. Germain. Mussolini found it possible to appeal to such a wide cross-section of society by avoiding a definite commitment to a fixed ideology. When he finally defined Fascism in 1932, he stated that he had 'no specific doctrinal attitude in mind in these early years'.[10] His success at first was limited; in the 1921 general election, for example, he obtained only 6.5 per cent of the seats in the Chamber. Thereafter, his emphasis on 'action, action, action' paid handsomely, and the appeal of Fascism penetrated more deeply, assisted by a programme of intensive propaganda and the attractions of the cult of *Duce*.

*

How did Mussolini maintain himself in power? On being asked to form a government in 1922, he played the parliamentary game for only a few months before seeking to change the whole façade of the régime. Three constitutional laws ensured that he would not be obstructed by traditional party politics. The 1922 Electoral Law gave an automatic two-thirds majority in the Chamber of Deputies to the governing party, while the Chamber's legislative power was virtually destroyed when, in 1926, Mussolini was enabled to govern by decree. In 1928, a new electoral system was introduced whereby the Fascist Grand Council selected for a *bloc* vote the names of parliamentary candidates from lists drawn up by professional and industrial organizations. Meanwhile, opposition was carefully monitored by the secret police, OVRA. By 1929 Mussolini had shown clearly that 'Fascism is not able, does not know how, and, I add, ought not to become parliamentary'.[11] Furthermore, organized violence was 'more moral than compromise and bargaining'. Similarly, Mussolini implanted his own methods of control over the economy, through a series of 'battles' and public works programmes. Above all, he introduced the 'corporate state' under which syndicates of workers were established and brought within nationwide confederations.

One of the more surprising features of Mussolini's rule, however, is that he left a considerable part of the previous structure intact, especially the system of local prefects. In a circular issued on 5 January 1927, Mussolini ordered that Provincial Prefects must be obeyed completely by all citizens, even by prominent Fascists. The result was that the Prefects exercised far greater control over the Party than the Party possessed over the administration. Indeed, the Fascist Party contributed little to the formulation of policy and Mussolini ensured that it never became as cohesive as the Russian Communist Party or the German Nazi Party by playing off the members of the Grand Council against each other. He also insisted

Mussolini

on widespread membership of the Party, thus deliberately devaluing this privilege. Finally, he made the administrative machine more complex, increased the number of departmental personnel and, in A. Lyttelton's phrase, 'deliberately fostered untidiness and illogicality in the structure of government'.[12] Why?

The main reason was that Mussolini intended to rule by balancing the different elements which made up the state and the Party. His basic fear was that one or more of these elements might eventually challenge his authority, and the greatest immediate threat seemed to come from the Fascist Party itself. Hence he took the drastic but logical step of depoliticizing the régime. The result was a strange paradox: the strength of Fascism depended on the weakness of Fascist organizations or, to put it another way, a movement which was famed for its activism was encouraged by its leader to show inertia. Mussolini was deliberately creating a vacuum in the political and administrative structure where one would normally expect to find a ruling class or élite. The explanation for this was that Mussolini was actually opposed to the emergence of any group which was likely to compete with him for power or public support. The cult of the *Duce*, or Mussolinianism,[14] was not an essential component of the Fascist programme, but rather an elaborate superstructure imposed on top of it. As far as Mussolini was concerned, however, it was the whole point of his rule; indeed, 'if Fascism does not follow me, no one can make me follow Fascism'.[5] Typical of Mussolini's self-projection was his claim to be the 'centre of convergence' for all the major 'forces' of Italy. He emphasized his role in reactivating Italy's glorious past by reintroducing the paraphernalia of ancient Rome, including the *fasces* (the bundle of rods, carried before the high magistrate, as an emblem of authority), the Roman salute, and the devices of the eagle and wolf. At the same time, he constantly emphasized the uniqueness of his personal appeal. He alone had the capacity to appeal directly to the people or to interpret their will. Indeed, he maintained that he possessed an intimate knowledge of crowd psychology, derived partly from the study of Gustav Le Bon's *Psychologie des foules*, and partly from active and extensive experience of mob oratory. Although he did give the impression of being a 'boaster', he was, to some, an impressive figure and the epitome of success. The Archbishop of Canterbury, for example, believed that he was 'the only gigantic figure in Europe'; Churchill called him 'Roman genius in person'. It is not surprising that

Aspects of European History 1789–1980

Emile Henriot should have felt that 'the great man was in the process of becoming God'.[13]

*

This personality cult was also partly responsible for Mussolini's *decline*, for the 'great man' displayed several serious defects of character. He assumed, for example, that he could undertake successfully a vast range of administrative work. In 1929 he was personally responsible for eight key ministries: foreign affairs, the interior, war, navy, aviation, colonies, corporations and public works. By 1943, notwithstanding the pressures of war, he still retained five of these. He showed a lack of detailed administrative knowledge and made what was, for a supposed co-ordinator, an amazing confession: 'I never make a mistake in interpreting the feeling of the masses. I make mistakes in judging men'.[14] His mind was prone to over-simplification and over-confidence, showing little interest in anything which could not be solved by intuitive measures. Eventually, he became caught up in the very success of his own propaganda and convinced himself that he was indeed the focal point of Italy's energies.

Messianic confidence is not, in itself, an inevitable formula for catastrophe. Mussolini might have maintained himself in power indefinitely if no serious pressure had been exerted on his régime. During the 1930s, however, an increasingly active foreign policy put an intolerable strain upon the whole cult of the *Duce*.

During the 1920s Mussolini had seen himself as one of the arbiters of Europe and had played a prominent part in the policy of collective security embodied in the 1925 Locarno Pact. During the 1930s, by contrast, he was seen as one of Europe's aggressors. The root of this transformation was partly economic; the extensive American investments in Italy during the 1920s had restrained Mussolini's hand, but these were withdrawn in 1929 after the Wall Street Crash. During the subsequent depression Mussolini imposed more direct government control over the economy, gearing it for war and expansion. This made his diplomatic movement towards Nazi Germany a logical, if not inevitable, step. In one sense he gave Italy the type of glory which he had always promised: the conquest of Abyssinia and the acquisition of a new African Empire. On the other hand, the Rome–Berlin Axis brought ultimate disaster. Mussolini was hustled prematurely into a world war by his more powerful ally,

Mussolini

and suffered the humiliation of having to be given German support in Greece and North Africa. Military failure had a catastrophic impact on Mussolini's cult of personality; even before the war, the *Duce* had begun to suffer from comparisons made with the *Führer*. The final blow was the reaction of many of the Italian people against the import of Nazi doctrines, especially anti-semitism. By July 1943, Mussolini had been so discredited that he was removed from power by the Fascist Grand Council and the King. At this special session Count Grandi gave Mussolini a curt explanation of what had happened: 'You believe you have the devotion of the people . . . You lost it the day you tied Italy to Germany.'[15]

Why was Mussolini's fall so sudden and dramatic? Did military defeat have to result in so ignominious an end? The answer lies in the delicate balance between the different powers and institutions which Mussolini had been so careful to maintain. Under the strain of war this balance was destroyed, and Mussolini was left without any political protection. During the early 1930s he missed the opportunity of making the Fascist Party more homogeneous and eliminating corruption. He could have delegated this task to the reforming Secretary, Giuriati, but he chose instead to continue his policy of divide and rule. The result was the growth of cliques and factions, which proved to be useful until Mussolini found himself in difficulties in 1943. By this stage he could rely only on a small group led by Farinacci, while the majority of the Fascist Grand Council, under Grandi, turned against him, laying the blame for military defeat on the cult of personality. As Grandi stated in June 1943: 'It is dictatorship, not Fascism, which has lost the War.'[16] Mussolini's vulnerability was in total contrast to the loyalty which Hitler received from most of his subordinates. Hitler had, from the start, an approach which was very different from Mussolini's checks and balances. His aim had been to Nazify the state, not to depoliticize it. Hence all effective internal opposition, real or potential, had been eliminated long before the régime faced military defeat.

Mussolini's vulnerability was intensified by the existence of an alternative leadership in Italy. Unlike Hitler, Mussolini had never assumed the title as well as the effective powers of head of state. The monarchy, which had been left intact, became a rallying point for the Italian army in 1943, while the *coup* against Mussolini was backed and encouraged by Victor Emmanuel himself. It could also be argued that Mussolini had never really made his stamp on the

Italian army; the oath of allegiance, for example, was still to the state and not to the *Duce* in person. Nor had he managed to create an entirely loyal military élite like Hitler's *Waffen* SS. He had also been less careful than Hitler in anticipating trouble from his generals, and had not taken the trouble to shuffle their positions to prevent plotting or the build-up of opposition. Even his intelligence service was defective, for he was taken completely by surprise by the *coup* of July 1943. Despite his known contempt for Mussolini, Hitler was astounded by the *Duce's* fall and asked 'What is this sort of Fascism which melts like snow before the sun?'

22

The Great Depression

J. M. Keynes observed in 1931: 'We are today in the middle of the greatest economic catastrophe – the greatest catastrophe due almost entirely to economic causes – of the modern world.'[1] The Great Depression began in 1929, spreading outwards from the United States until it had affected almost all the countries in the world, whether industrial powers or underdeveloped primary producers. It brought severe dislocation in the form of falling prices, declining production, shrinking trade and rising unemployment. It also had a profound political and psychological impact, inducing in many states a swing away from constitutional democracy towards totalitarianism. The result was a major change in international relations during the 1930s and the envelopment of Europe by a resurgence of the militarism and nationalism which the Frst World War was supposed to have destroyed.

*

How and why did the Depression arise? Any analysis of such a complex phenomenon must be tentative, especially since economic historians still disagree on points of detail. Nevertheless, it is possible to provide a brief synthesis of generally accepted arguments.

The spread of a worldwide crisis presupposes the interdependence of the individual countries and the existence of channels through which influences can operate. Such a connection had developed during the nineteenth century with the spread of international trade and the accompanying search for sources of raw materials, markets for manufactured goods and outlets for investment. This tendency had been interrupted, briefly, by the First World War, but was resumed during the 1920s, providing an ever increasing network across which problems could be transmitted as readily as prosperity. To some extent, these problems were predictable. During the nineteenth century internal (and hence international) economies had experienced cycles in which between seven and ten years of expansion would be followed by a temporary recession. There is some evidence that the major European countries were approaching the peak of a cycle in 1913, but that the war artificially postponed this until 1919–20, a slump following in 1920 and 1921. According to this trend, some sort of recession was likely by the end of the 1920s.

When it eventually came, however, it proved to be no mere 'routine' cyclic Depression. The basic reason was a severe imbalance of world economic development at the time, which meant that behind every appearance of success there lurked a potential crisis. This showed itself in several ways. Industrial production, for example, increased steadily in Europe during the 1920s. There was, however, over-emphasis on the staple industries, particularly coal, ship building and steel; this was largely at the expense of the newer industries which catered more directly for the consumer market. The United States, by contrast, developed the latter, especially the motor vehicle industry, and managed to achieve a growth rate which was considerably larger than Europe's. Hence the industrial progress made by European countries like Britain, France and Germany was actually accompanied by a proportionate decline in their share of the volume of world trade. Agriculture also experienced difficulties: greater efficiency and more widespread mechanization in Europe and North America increased production and lowered prices. This, in turn, had a serious impact on the producers of raw materials, who eventually had to reduce their import of manufactured articles from the industrial countries to compensate for falling revenues. In two sectors of the economy progress in the United States actually impeded the progress of other countries. In the secondary, or industrial sector, it flooded the world markets but remained unwilling to relax its tariff barriers against European goods, while in the primary sector of agriculture and raw materials it remained largely self-sufficient.

The Great Depression

Another contradiction between the capacity for recovery and liability to recession can be seen in the case of foreign investments. On the surface, widespread availability of capital was essential for sustained economic growth, and there was certainly no shortage of funds during the 1920s. American economic supremacy showed itself in the enormous loans to other countries amounting, between 1925 and 1929, to 2900 million dollars to Europe alone. This flow undoubtedly eased the problems of Germany, crippled by the demand for reparations which formed part of the Treaty of Versailles. The German government was able, with the assistance of American investment, to fulfil some of its obligations to Britain and France, and also to increase internal expenditure on industry and public works. In some ways, however, American investment had negative results, establishing what has been called a 'cycle of indebtedness'. There were two examples of this. The first was the pattern whereby American loans were incurred to help Germany pay reparations to Britain and France who, in turn, repaid interest on American wartime investment. The second was the dependence of many of the world's poorer countries on loans from the United States to repay previous loans; the only other form of reimbursement, through a balance of payments surplus, was precluded by American self-sufficiency. The willingness of American investors to export their capital during the second half of the 1920s meant that some countries, industrialized and underdeveloped, were dependent for up to 25 per cent of their assets on external suppliers. Unfortunately, the volume of trade in no way reflected the degree of investment received, which meant that repayment usually had to be in gold reserves. By 1929, the United States had accumulated most of the world's supply of gold and, as a result, distorted the operation of forms of exchange.

This brings us to a third contradiction. Several attempts were made to bring harmony to the international economy, but with little success. Britain, for example, returned sterling to the gold standard in 1925, encouraging other countries to follow her example by 1928. But this process, arguably, increased rather than reduced instability. Governments adjusted their currencies at different levels and at different times, or simply over-valued them and stimulated a further flow of gold to the United States. Long before 1929 there was growing apprehension about monetary, industrial or commercial anarchy. The Geneva Conference, which assembled in 1927 to analyse the problem, found itself unable to suggest any solution, and governments were beginning to find increasingly attractive the prospect of protective legislation, including tariffs and quotas.

During the 1920s two things were, therefore, apparent. One was that the world's economies were closely linked, for good or ill, with that of the United States. The other was that they were all vulnerable. Consequently, an upheaval in the world's wealthiest country would set off a chain reaction. Or, to use a contemporary adaptation of an old metaphor: 'When America sneezes, the rest of the world catches cold.'

This happened in 1929. For a whole decade the rapid growth of American industry had been assisted by the ready availability of money, in part the result of deliberate policy by the Federal Reserve Bank. After 1925 speculation became increasingly common and when, in 1928, the Federal Reserve Bank tried to impose some sort of order by raising the interest rate, large sums invested overseas were immediately repatriated to the American market to swell domestic holdings. As long as the domestic boom continued, this degree of speculation would not actually damage the economy. But the peak of production was reached in July 1929, thus ending hopes that growth could be permanent and uninterrupted. The basic reason was that the supply of goods had finally outstripped consumer demand, necessitating a reduction in output, or an 'inventory recession'. The slump precipitated a crash as the Stock Market reflected a sudden loss of confidence by investors; 40,000 million dollars had been lost by the end of October. The Wall Street Crash, in part a reflection of the slump, also reacted with the slump to bring about 'the slide into depression. Gradually the crisis intensified as banks went under (as many as 1345 in 1930 alone) and the national income fell by 38 per cent between 1929 and 1932.

The impact of these developments on Europe was serious. Some of the industrial economies had already peaked (Germany in April, and Britain in June), while foreign investment was flowing out because of the higher interest rates in the United States from 1928. The Wall Street Crash accelerated this general trend. The sudden crisis of confidence virtually dried up the supply of loans to Europe and resulted in the further recall of investments to America to compensate for home losses. The uncertainty transmitted itself to the world's money markets, making those countries with extensive debts particularly vulnerable to any panic which might occur in the

The Great Depression

future. A major example of this was the 1931 financial crisis, which began with the collapse of the leading Austrian bank, *Credit Anstalt*, spread to the German banking system and then caused a severe strain in London; in the last case, foreign investors withdrew £200 million between July and August. It was obvious that any international monetary system which had ever existed had by now disintegrated. This was confirmed when, in 1931, Britain withdrew from the gold standard, to be followed by many other countries. Financial insecurity brought industrial atrophy which, in turn, led to an upswing in unemployment to 22 per cent of the total workforce in Britain and 44 per cent in Germany. The primary producers of South-Eastern Europe were ruined as the spreading depression eroded the previous price levels by up to 66 per cent and destroyed both external trade and internal consumer markets. Only two countries in Europe seemed, by 1932, to have held out against the depression: one was France, which had the highest level of gold reserves outside the United States, and was therefore able to ride the financial crisis of 1931. By 1934, however, this strength was undermined as France succumbed, belatedly, to the slump. The other exception was the Soviet Union, which was insulated from the international economy by Stalin's isolationist policies.

*

If ever there was a need for a concerted international effort to deal with an economic crisis it was in the early 1930s. It soon became clear, however, that little would be achieved in this direction. The 1932 Lausanne Conference merely confirmed what had for some time been considered inevitable: that payment of German reparations should end. The World Economic Conference, which assembled in London in 1933, achieved nothing at all. Increasingly, therefore, governments resorted to individual rather than collective policies, usually in isolation and often in conflict. Of these the most common was the import tariff, intended to protect domestic industries from foreign competition. Controls were applied vigorously all over Europe and even Britain finally revised eighty-six years of free trade by the Import Duties Act, 1932, and a series of bilateral agreements drawn up with the Dominions as a result of the Ottawa Conference. France adopted a similar, although more tightly organized, preference system with her own colonies. By 1933 the world was divided by a series of tariff walls through which access had to be negotiated by special arrangement.

Apart from the resort to protection, however, European states adopted different techniques, of which three are worth particular mention. The first was the use of deflationary policies. This was confined mainly to Germany until 1932 and France before 1934. In both cases wages were held down or reduced, and public expenditure slashed. In both cases the slump was intensified and prolonged, and the measures eventually had to be reversed. The second method was budgetary control, which applied particularly to Britain. It was less harsh than rigorous deflation, but was probably not all that effective. British economic recovery, which began in 1934, owed something to the availability of cheap money and a favourable atmosphere for private enterprise, in part an achievement of the National Government. But the real factor was the revival of domestic consumer demand which, in turn, promoted those areas of industry which had been relatively neglected during the 1920s. The result was a boom in house building and motor vehicle manufacturing, although this existed side by side with continued depression in the staple industries and the resultant levels of unemployment.

The third approach involved direct government intervention and presupposed the absence of any opposition. The main example was Nazi economic policy, which concentrated on the promotion of heavy industry and public works programmes. The result was the virtual elimination of unemployment as the level dropped from the peak of 44 per cent to 1 per cent in 1938. A new network of markets was established by a series of bilateral trade agreements with the countries of South-Eastern Europe. These guaranteed a flow of essential raw materials to Germany and, in turn, made states like Bulgaria and Romania totally dependent on Hitler. On the whole, German economic growth in the late 1930s was the most rapid in non-communist Europe. Two reservations, however, should be made. The economy was geared to militarism and was built at the cost of the most basic economic freedoms and at the expense of the consumer market; in this respect it moved in the opposite direction of the British economy. Second, the recovery which occurred after 1934 was not the work of the Nazis alone. The hyperinflation which had attacked the Weimar Republic in 1923 had forced many of the weaker industrial firms out of existence, and the remainder used the American investments which became available from 1924 to re-equip and modernize. Hitler therefore inherited an economic base in sound working order and could proceed to add his own super-structure.

*

A broadly accepted historical generalization is that economic crises have political repercussions. The Great Depression had a profound internal and international impact.

Europe consisted, in the 1920s, of a series of parliamentary democracies, many established immediately after the First World War. By the mid-1930s, however, these were confined to Britain, France, the Benelux countries, Scandinavia and Czechoslovakia. Even these countries experienced abnormal political trends; Britain, for example, switched from her normal pattern of single party administrations to a so-called National government, while the ministerial crises in France led, in 1936, to the establishment of Blum's Popular Front government. At the same time, pressure groups built up on the extreme Right to accentuate social insecurity; examples were Mosley's British Fascist Movement, the French Fascist Leagues and the Finnish *Lapua*. More disturbing, however, was the swing of most of Europe to dictatorship. There occurred, on a much wider scale, a repetition of what had brought Mussolini to power in Italy in 1922. Whole classes were destabilized by industrial and agricultural slumps or by financial crises. They gave their support to extremist parties who demonstrated their impatience with the cumbersome operation of parliamentary democracy. Thus the ruined agricultural interests backed right-wing régimes in the Balkans, while the defection of the middle-class voters from the moderate parties brought the Nazis to power in Germany. Italy, Europe's original Fascist régime, experienced what amounted to a second revolution, as Mussolini tightened his grip and imposed the National Council of Corporations. Even the Far East underwent constitutional changes. The initial response of the Japanese govern-ment to the Depression was to attempt a reduction of military estimates. But the Prime Minister, Hamaguchi Yuko, was shot in 1930 and the army became increasingly active in Japanese politics.

The failure to agree on common measures to deal with economic problems contributed, during the 1930s, to the heightening of political tension. Economic anarchy soon led to international anarchy, a process hastened by the three major powers who had emerged from the Great Depression with their economies geared for imperial expansion and war. The Japanese invasion of Manchuria (1931) was the logical outcome of a search for new provinces on the mainland of Asia, but was given extra purpose by the need to control the outlets of the raw materials which were necessary for the new war machine. Italian Fascism, meanwhile, was being converted into an expansionist ideology which underlay the invasions of Abyssinia (1935) and Albania (1939). Partly responsible for this was the withdrawal of American investments after 1929, which had the dual effect of removing all restraints on Italian foreign policy and encouraging Mussolini to reformulate his whole economic strategy. By far the greatest blow to the international system, however, was dealt by Germany. Hitler's Four Year Plan was openly intended to prepare the Reich for war by 1940, and the increase in military expenditure contributed greatly to the growing confidence of Hitler's foreign policy by 1938 and 1939. At the same time, the main barrier to German expansion had been eliminated. The Depression ended French hegemony over Eastern Europe, replacing it with a special relationship between Nazi Germany and the new régimes of Bulgaria, Romania and Hungary. With reliable allies and a ready source of raw materials, Hitler could turn his attention to those states in Central and Eastern Europe which featured in his schemes for a Greater Germany and the achievement of *Lebensraum*. The results were the *Anschluss* (1938), the annexation of Czechoslovakia (1938–9) and the invasion of Poland (1939).

*

The world between the wars was the victim of a basic contradiction: countries were dependent on each other for the fulfilment of their economic needs and yet were not prepared to co-operate with each other, for fear that they might be making major concessions. But without co-operation the fulfilment of needs produced the two extremes of tightly controlled individual economies on the one hand, and a complete absence of international control, either economic or political, on the other. The result was so frightful that extensive efforts have been made, since 1945, to set up more carefully coordinated international institutions and to remove the fears which once led to the building of tariff walls.

23

Hitler's Rise to Power and the Nazi Revolution

Between the two world wars Germany regressed from the constitutional democracy of the Weimar Republic to the ruthless dictatorship of the Third Reich. This change, which occurred with Hitler's rise to power and the implementation of his own ideas, is generally described as 'revolutionary'.

National Socialism brought a profound upheaval to Germany. It directly attacked Western constitutional and libertarian traditions dating back to 1789 and beyond; indeed, Goebbels maintained that the Nazis had 'abolished' the French Revolution. The basic constituents of National Socialism were hardly novel. Pan-Germanism, imperialistic nationalism, the emphasis on race and *Volk* and, above all, anti-semitism, had all existed in the nineteenth century; they had, however, been held under constraint, and their more extreme exposition had been confined to the political fringe. Hitler moulded his own twisted version of these constituents into a cohesive body and, through his demagogic skill, injected it with demonic life.

But how was National Socialism to take control of Germany? Hitler was a resilient opportunist as well as an obsessive fanatic, and fundamentally altered his practical approach to revolution during the course of his career. At first he tried violence and conspiracy: his 1923 Munich *Putsch* was an attempt to overthrow the Weimar Republic as the essential prerequisite for constructing the National Socialist state. Failure at this stage forced him to rethink his method. He aimed, instead, at rising to power by means of the constitution and at introducing revolutionary changes from above once his position was secure. (At the same time, he made no attempt to moderate the frantic tone of his speeches nor the intimidatory power of his mass rallies; his 'pseudo-legal' strategy was in no way intended to weaken what has been called a revolution in the techniques of communication.) His parliamentary success owed much to Germany's internal upheaval, accelerated, from 1929, by the Great Depression. The extension of his power and the systematic destruction of the Weimar Republic were accomplished between 1933 and 1934 by what was officially called the 'National Revolution'.

*

Hitler originally intended that any social and economic changes should be preceded by a military *coup*, the purpose of which was to destroy the existing régime. After all, Mussolini had forced the Italian Government to capitulate by the mere threat of a march on Rome. Hitler felt that he could do the same to the Berlin government. He was determined 'to know neither rest nor peace until the November Criminals had been overthrown'.[1] On 8 November 1923 he issued a communiqué: 'The Government of the November Criminals and the Reich President are declared removed. A new National Government will be nominated this very day here in Munich.'[1] With the revolutionary's concern about the judgement of posterity, he added: 'We can no longer turn back; our action is already inscribed on the pages of world history.'[1]

The whole undertaking was doomed to failure. It was inadequately prepared and confused in its execution. The Bavarian Commissioner-General, Kahr, was not unsympathetic to the Nazi cause, but felt impelled to put down the rising in case his own administration should collapse. Hitler, who had hoped for Kahr's support in acting against the Berlin government, therefore committed a serious error of judgement. He also over-estimated the degree of support for the Nazi Party in the rest of Germany in the early 1920s. In fact, the Nazis had no rating at a national level; they were regarded merely as a paramilitary pressure group, with no seats in the *Reichstag*. They were not even the main party of the Right, a role filled by the National Party. The radical vote was, at this stage, more likely to go to the extreme Left – to the Independent Socialists and the Communists.

Hitler's greatest mistake was to assume that the Republic was in

Hitler's Rise to Power and the Nazi Revolution

danger of collapsing as a direct result of the French occupation of the Ruhr and the inflation of the mark. The problem of 1923 was far more localized and less intense than the Great Depression in 1929 and, once the co-operation of the Allies had been secured, could be dealt with by the issue of the *Rentenmark* in 1923 and by the signing of the Dawes Plan in 1924. Prosperity and moderation were to be the keynote for the next six years, an unhappy time for extremists on both the Right and the Left.

*

The Munich *Putsch* is rightly represented as one of the more ridiculous and ignominious episodes of modern German history, but it was by no means insignificant. Hitler was not prepared to follow the example of another failed revolutionary, Kapp, and fade into obscurity. Ultimately, the *Putsch* was made to serve a triple purpose. First, it established the radical credentials of the Nazi Party, setting it permanently apart from the Establishment. As Hitler later observed: 'Let there be no mistake about it, had we not acted then I would never have been able to found a revolutionary movement. People would have justifiably told me: you talk like all the others and you act as little as they do.'[2] Second, Hitler's trial provided the Nazis with national publicity, enabling Hitler to rail openly against the Republic and to emphasize the constructive nature of his violence: 'If today I stand here as a revolutionary, it is as a revolutionary against the revolution.'[3] Third, the Nazi Party learned during the period of Hitler's imprisonment (1923–5) that it was essentially monolithic and that it would split into several sections unless it were returned to his leadership. On his release Hitler proceeded to eliminate the threat of his main rival, Gregor Strasser, to win over Northerners like Josef Goebbels and to assume complete control over Party strategy. He stated in 1934 that the *Putsch* had enabled him to wage the battle as he wished 'and not otherwise'.[1]

The failure of the *Putsch* also showed the need for a totally different path to power. Even while he was in Landsberg prison, Hitler developed a new strategy. Military revolt would now have to be replaced by participation in regular politics. 'Instead of working to achieve power by an armed *coup*, we shall have to hold our noses and enter the *Reichstag* against Catholic and Marxist deputies.'[4] This did not, however, involve any capitulation to the underlying principles of constitutional democracy. On the contrary, 'for us parliament is not an end in itself, but merely a means to an end.' Hence, 'the consitution prescribes the scene of the battle, but not its aim.' Hitler, in fact, eventually intended to scrap the constitutional process by which he expected to achieve power. As Goebbels put it in 1928: 'We are entering the *Reichstag* in order that we may arm ourselves with the weapons of democracy from its own arsenal. We shall become *Reichstag* deputies in order that the Weimar ideology should itself help us to destroy it . . . We are content to use all legal means to revolutionize the present state of affairs . . . Let no-one think that parliamentarianism is our Damascus. We come as enemies! Like the wolf falling upon a herd of sheep, that's how we come.'[5]

Hitler made no attempt to hide or explain away this double image of Nazism. Instead, he built up what was both a mainstream parliamentary party, with a superficial deference to constitutional principles, and a mass movement, with all the characteristics of a paramilitary pressure group.

On the one hand, Hitler created a more efficient party structure and adopted a more sophisticated attitude towards other parties and interests. Of particular importance was his temporary alliance, from 1928 onwards, with Hugenberg's National Party. Although he had no intention of obliterating the separate identity of the Nazi Party, Hitler was prepared to project a more evolutionary image until he had derived maximum benefit from Hugenberg's considerable resources. The Nazis gained extensive national coverage in Hugenberg's newspaper chain, to say nothing of valuable contacts with Germany's leading industrialists. Ultimately, Hitler's Nazis were to abandon the connection with the National Party, having drained its strength and replaced it as the major party of the Right. The process was accelerated by the injection of funds by major capitalists like the Ruhr coal magnate, Kirdorf, and steel producers Thyssen and Stinnes. They saw the Nazis as the major safeguard against Communism and were encouraged by the new Nazi 'constitutional' image which had already earned Hitler the nickname *Adolphe Légalité*. From 1930 onwards Hitler invested this money in the most extensive electioneering campaigns ever seen in Germany.

On the other hand, Hitler also extended the base of *mass* support for the Nazi movement, by means of a 'revolution in communication'.

Hitler's Rise to Power and the Nazi Revolution

His speeches, for example, reached an enormously wide section of the population; Albert Speer later asserted that 'Hitler was one of the first to be able to avail himself of the means of modern technology'. His speeches identified targets, like 'Jews', 'Bolsheviks' and 'November Criminals', which were oversimplified and caricatured in such a way as to stimulate emotional hatred rather than reasoned opposition. He also projected a sense of collective power, which he contrasted carefully to the insignificance of the individual (and hence of the liberal democratic tradition) and embellished with the imagery of natural forces, especially the survival of the fittest. This power was channelled, through mass meetings and rallies as well as by the violent methods of the S.A., into blind devotion to the leader. Hitler therefore 'personalized' politics and, in the process, appeared as both the prophet of doom and the national saviour.

What were the actual results of Hitler's revised strategy? Success was not instantaneous but, when it did come, it was spectacular. In the *Reichstag* elections of May 1928 the Nazis secured only 2.6 per cent of the popular vote,[6] which the Republic's system of proportional representation translated into twelve seats.[7] Then, from September 1930, the situation changed. The Nazis obtained 18.3 per cent of the vote and 107 seats, finding themselves, after the Social Democrats, the largest party in the *Reichstag*. Encouraged by the apparent success of his tactics, Hitler struck out for the highest office of state, the presidency. In two great election campaigns in 1931 Hitler was defeated by the incumbent, Hindenburg. The Nazis did, however, increase their popular support; in the first presidential election Hitler secured 11.5 million votes to Hindenburg's 18.6 million, while, in the second, Hitler narrowed the gap (13.4 million, to Hindenburg's 19.25 million). After failing to win the presidency, Hitler aimed at the chancellorship. He was assisted by a further boost in the Nazi performance in the *Reichstag* elections of 1932. In July the Nazis became the largest single party with 37.3 per cent of the vote and 230 seats. Goebbels, exasperated that electoral success had not yet produced a Nazi government, complained: 'We'll drop dead from winning elections.'[8] A slight loss of support in November 1932 still left the Nazis, with 33.1 per cent of the vote and 196 seats, easily the major force in the *Reichstag*. Despite his known dislike of the Nazis, President Hindenburg eventually summoned Hitler to the chancellorship in January 1933.

It is, of course, one of the major tragedies of the twentieth century that the Weimar Republic should have handed power to this mass movement posing as a parliamentary party. Two factors were largely responsible for this. The first was an economic catastrophe, the Great Depression, which destroyed the moderate parties and, by 1932, catapulted the Nazis into the position of the largest party in the *Reichstag*. The second was the constant drift of the Republic to the right and the eventual emergence, after 1930, of a series of authoritarian cabinets which had little compunction about doing a political deal with Hitler.

Hitler's tactics had made little headway in the period of comparative economic stability between 1925 and 1928. Something was evidently needed to crack open the whole political and social structure so that Hitler could remould the fragments. German society had, for some time, been vitiated by internal tensions which constantly threatened to break into open conflict; it was, therefore, vulnerable to any major crisis. The Great Depression, which hit Germany from 1929 onwards, released these tensions and cut away much of the previous support for the Weimar Republic. It was the catalyst for a massive change in the voting habits of a large part of the German electorate. The main casualties were the liberal parties – the People's Party (DVP) and the Democratic Party (DDP) – as well as the traditional Nationalists (DNVP). What happened was that the middle classes transferred their support from this area of the political spectrum to the extreme Right, a process caused by demoralization and panic.[9] Farmers, artisans, white-collar workers, shopkeepers and professional men all expressed their disillusionment with the Establishment. Their savings and pensions had been destroyed for the second time within a decade, and the Great Depression was especially hard to bear as it followed a period of economic improvement. They could have transferred their votes to the Social Democrats (SPD), but this would have involved a decline in social status since, at this time, the SPD was primarily a working-class party. Besides, the Nazi Party had concocted an attractive programme which promised much to the different sections of the middle class. In particular, it stressed the importance of the 'small man' as an economic unit, and promised to control some of the more unpredictable forces of capitalism as well as to destroy forever the threat of Communism. Thus the parties which had been involved in most of the Republic's coalition governments were abandoned as a normally stable part of the electorate sought relief in more radical and sweeping programmes, even if their implementation involved the risk of eventual dictatorship.

This contraction of support for the Republic was spectacular but not entirely unprecedented. Ever since its foundation in 1918 the Republic had been opposed by various right-wing interests and political groups. The military, for example, were alienated by the so-called 'stab in the back'. Of the two wartime Commanders-in-Chief, Ludendorff defected to the Nazis, and Hindenburg imposed an authoritarian stamp on the presidency after his election in 1925; other army officers even toyed with the idea of a military *coup*. In some instances whole states rejected the new democratic ethos of the Republic and, like Kahr's Bavaria, remained virtual dictatorships. There were also many right-wing activists and writers: men like Moeller, van den Bruck and Junger, who looked back with nostalgia to the Second Reich and anticipated a Third in the near future. Even the liberals and socialists, who were responsible for drawing up the Republic's constitution, seemed to have reservations about Germany's capacity to sustain democracy indefinitely; they therefore allowed, in Article 48, for the discretionary use of extensive presidential powers in an emergency. According to Theodor Heuss, the first President of the German Federal Republic, 'Germany never conquered democracy for herself',[10] a point which became more and more obvious after 1929. The sudden economic crisis caused by the Great Depression destroyed the previous pattern of coalition cabinets and government by consensus, as the formulation of policy became more and more complicated. Increased reliance was therefore placed on Hindenburg, who was known to favour a paternalist approach to government, and who was impatient of the more complex manoeuvres of party politics. He and Brüning resorted to Article 48 of the Constitution, increasing the number of presidential decrees from five in 1930 to sixty in 1932. During the same period, the sittings of the *Reichstag* decreased from ninety-four to thirteen.[11]

This swing to the Right provided a congenial atmosphere for the suddenly strengthened Nazi Party and made Hitler's emergence as a possible national leader seem less outrageous than it would have been in the 1920s. And yet Hitler actually achieved power in an unexpected manner. He did not acquire it directly, as his attempt to dislodge Hindenburg from the presidency in 1931 had failed. Instead, he became Chancellor after a series of backdoor manoeuvres with and between right-wing Chancellors von Papen and Schleicher, with the connivance of Hindenburg himself. The traditional Right, particularly the Nationalists, tried at first to control the new Right, or Nazis. (Schleicher, for one, hoped to detach leading Nazis, like Gregor Strasser, by offers of posts in his 1932 cabinet.) When it became clear that the Nazi Party could not be divided in this manner, the traditional Right changed its tactics. Schleicher, knowing in January 1933, that his cabinet was about to fall, was in favour of letting Hitler form a government of his own. To try to keep the Nazis out of power much longer might well provoke another *Putsch*. In this event Schleicher, as army commander, would be in the unenviable position of having to put down the revolt in the name of the Republic he hated. Papen had already been prepared to concede Hitler the chancellorship; the Nazis could then be used by the Nationalists to do the dirty work of destroying the fabric of the Republic. Hindenburg was persuaded to appoint Hitler, although he hoped that experience of office would moderate some of Hitler's policies and bring a closer identity between the Nazis and the old Right.

Was there no way of preventing Hitler from being given power in this sordid way? Even allowing for the catastrophic impact of the Great Depression, electoral support for the Nazis could not be guaranteed to remain at 37.3 per cent. Indeed, it showed signs of declining and Hitler reacted with dismay to the 33.1 per cent received by the Nazis in November 1932. A concerted opposition, surely, would have been sufficient to keep Hitler out of power? Could it even have forced Hindenburg to moderate his use of emergency decrees as, according to the last sentence of Article 48, presidential decrees 'may be rescinded on the demand of the *Reichstag*'?[12] After the election of November 1932 the Nazis and National Party had, between them, 247 seats. The moderate parties (People's Party, Centre, Democrats and Social Democrats) controlled 237 seats, while the Communists possessed one hundred. Could a combined front, consisting of the moderates and far Left, therefore, have impeded the progress of the extreme Right? Two main factors prevented this from being a serious possibility. First, the Communists and moderate parties were not prepared to co-operate. The Communists competed directly with the SPD for the vote of the proletariat in the mistaken belief that they could attract the working-class vote in the same way that the Nazis had won the support of the middle class. Second, the use of decree laws *was* attacked by the *Reichstag*. But the chancellors (one of whom, in any case, had been the leader of the Centre Party) could always respond by seeking a dissolution. It does, therefore, seem that any real parliamentary constraints had been severely weakened by the beginning of 1933.

*

Hitler had become Chancellor with a semblance of legality, but had no intention of abiding by the Republic's Constitution. 'We are not', he had always emphasized, 'a parliamentary party.'[13] In fact, 'once we possess the constitutional rights we shall . . . pour the state into the mould which we consider the right one'. The 'National Revolution', therefore, started within weeks of his appointment, gained momentum in 1934 and 1935, and reached its climax after 1941.

Hitler's first priority was to make his authority unassailable by kicking down the ladder by which he had ascended. Ironically, the first stage of Hitler's revolution, the creation of a personal dictatorship, was accomplished by measures which were, technically at least, within the ambit of the Constitution.

The process began on 28 February 1933 with a decree from President Hindenburg which, under Article 48 of the Constitution, suspended normal civil liberties. The pretext was a Communist 'plot', which had included the destruction of the *Reichstag*. Then, in March, Hitler proceeded to shatter the Constitution itself, again by means allowed by the Constitution. The amendment of an entrenched, or constitutional clause, required a two-thirds majority. In the elections of 1933, the Nazis and National Party had won considerably fewer seats than required, although they had a slight overall majority. Hitler solved the problem by using the Decree of 28 February to expel the eighty-three Communist deputies and by negotiating for the support of the Centre Party. The result was a majority, by 441 votes to 94, for the Enabling Law, which empowered the Chancellor to issue legislation for four years without the consent of the *Reichstag*. This eradicated Article 68 of the Weimar Constitution: 'Reich laws shall be enacted by the *Reichstag*.' Other measures followed, including the Law against the New Formation of Parties (July 1933), which wiped out the entire

215

opposition, thus obliterating the principle of legislative restraint on the executive. Although it had not been formally abrogated, the Constitution was now so undermined by the new regulations as to be totally useless. The way was now open for the extension of Nazi control over the whole range of Germany's institutions.

The next stage was hastened by pressure exerted from within the Party by the SA. Röhm and Strasser, in particular, wanted a second revolution in which the SA would take control of the army. Hitler, however, proceeded in his own way. Convinced that a 'brown revolution' would wreck his own position and invite a military counter *coup*, he did a deal with the *Wehrmacht* commanders. In return for weakening the SA in the 'Night of the Long Knives' (30 June 1934) Hitler acquired the direct backing of the *Wehrmacht* for his régime, as well as an oath of loyalty to the person of the *Führer*. The purge of the SA also served to initiate Hitler's own 'second revolution'. It ended the myth of the 'legal changes' and clearly demonstrated that he would depend, in future, on a permanent state of emergency – all designed to uproot the remnants of constitutional democracy. The SS and Gestapo, effectively united in 1934, provided a secure base for the régime, while a new juridical sanction emerged as a result of drastic changes in the concept of justice and the role of the courts. The traditional notion of the law circumscribing the power of the government and the ruling parties was replaced by the principles of 'National Socialist philosophy, especially as expressed by the utterances of our Führer' (Hans Frank).[14] There was now no impediment to the use of coercion and terror and the total destruction of that part of the Weimar Constitution entitled the *Fundamental Rights and Duties of the Germans*. The most extreme departure was the systematic persecution of Jews and other minority groups. Article 109 of the Weimar Constitution had affirmed: 'All Germans are equal before the law.' Article 111 had stated: 'All Germans shall enjoy liberty of travel and residence throughout the Reich.' According to Article 135, 'All inhabitants of the Reich enjoy full religious freedom of conscience.'[12] These safeguards were shredded by the Nuremberg Laws (1935) and by the extensive use of the SS and Gestapo system of concentration camps.

The 'positive' aim of the Nazi system was the creation of a new social order. The emphasis was on expansionist nationalism, which was given extra force by its association with notions of Aryan purity and racial superiority. Attempts were made to subordinate

Hitler's Rise to Power and the Nazi Revolution

every sector of the media and education. Goebbels, who described his aim as 'total propaganda', presided over a new Ministry of Propaganda from March 1933, while draconian measures were taken to ensure ideological conformity by the press. Education was another obvious target; it was through the systematic indoctrination of Germany's youth that the qualities of fanatical loyalty and unquestioning obedience could be implanted into the next generation of citizens. Education was also given a paramilitary emphasis: boys enrolled in the Hitler Youth were rigidly disciplined and, according to the 1936 Law Concerning the Hitler Youth, were to be 'educated physically, mentally and morally in the spirit of National Socialism, to serve the nation and the racial community'.[15] Higher education was also drastically revised. Pure research was replaced by studies intended to uphold Nazi racial concepts – hence the emergence of 'German' or 'Aryan' physics and mathematics. The basic tone was set by the Minister of Culture, who announced to university professors assembled in Munich in 1933: 'From now on it will not be your job to determine whether something is true, but whether it is in the spirit of the National Socialist revolution.' Meanwhile, the Reich Cultural Chamber, created in September 1934, endeavoured to redirect the nation's aesthetic tastes and to eradicate 'degenerate' tendencies in art, literature and music. Underlying the whole process of indoctrination was the moulding of a race which would not question the fact of its superiority. Its aggressiveness and self-confidence were built up by mass rallies and spectacular events like the 1936 Olympics, so that, in the future, war would come to be accepted as a natural means of attaining the extra territory which it would inevitably need. Anticipating future conquest, of course, necessitated an economic policy subordinated to the demands of heavy industry and rearmament, and the Four Year Plan (1936–40) departed from normal practice in western countries by starving the consumer sector.

During the Second World War the Nazi Revolution entered its third and most fanatical phase. Any remaining constraints on expansion and persecution disappeared as Hitler conquered vast areas of *Lebensraum* in Eastern Europe. The annexation of Poland in 1939 and of large parts of European Russia in 1941 brought the Nazis into contact with millions of Jews and tens of millions of 'inferior' Slavs. This intensified the search by Nazi leaders for the ultimate fulfilment of Hitler's ideas, and the views first expressed in

Aspects of European History 1789–1980

Mein Kampf were sublimated in the extermination of much of European Jewry at Auschwitz-Birkenau, Sobibor, Treblinka and other camps. This genocide, organized so methodically by Heydrich, Himmler and Eichmann, went far beyond what is normally understood by the term 'revolution'; it has been seen as nothing less than the overturning of civilization itself. But then, as Hitler once boasted, 'We are ruthless . . . . Yes, we are barbarians! We want to be. That is an honourable epithet. We are the ones who will rejuvenate the world. The old world is done for.'[16]

*

Although Germany experienced, between 1933 and 1945, a profound and even unprecedented upheaval, there is ample evidence of inefficiency and structural weakness in the Nazi Revolution.

One of Hitler's original objectives had been that 'all future institutions of this State must grow out of the [Nazi] movement itself'. This was broadly similar to the Bolshevik aim of replacing state institutions with its own. In practice, however, the Nazis never managed, nor even attempted, such a clean sweep. (K. D. Bracher and others have argued that much within the Third Reich was improvised; 'Almost everywhere the régime operated on two planes simultaneously: penetrating and compromising the old institutions yet at the same time building up new, separate rival machineries above them.'[17]) The traditional civil service, for example, was dominated by, but was still separate from, the new Nazi bureaucracy. As a result, their functions were often duplicated and always complicated. The Nazi political order was inherently untidy and unsystematic, dependent on the *Führer* himself for its continued functioning.

Indeed, the Nazi Revolution as a whole hinged entirely on the personal charisma of one man. This affected the movement in two ways. First, Hitler remained consistently more popular than his Party and there was a serious, if unacknowledged problem concerning the long-term future of the Nazi state. Who else could assume the task of sorting out the 'jurisdictional thicket of party agencies and state machinery'?[17] Second, Nazism was too firmly based on Hitler's personal obsessions to develop into a systematic ideology capable of future growth; in fact, any attempts to make the theory of the Party more scientific incurred Hitler's hostility. During the final phase of the Revolution, Hitler's policies became increas-

218

ingly irrational and, even under the shadow of imminent defeat, one of his main concerns was still the completion of the 'Final Solution'. In April 1945, while Russian artillery pounded Berlin, Hitler urged his successors 'Above all . . . to uphold the racial laws and resist mercilessly the poisoner of all nations, international Jewry'. Deprived of any other rationale and faced with imminent military collapse, the 'Thousand Year Reich' outlived its founder by just one week.

24
German Foreign Policy 1918–39

It is often assumed that 1933, the year in which Hitler came to power, represents a turning point in the development of German foreign policy, and that the objectives of the Third Reich were fundamentally different from those of the Weimar Republic. This chapter will deal with two basic issues arising from this. First, did the Nazis depart completely from the policies of statesmen like Cuno and Stresemann, or is there at least some evidence of continuity? Second, if Hitler's ambitions and projects can be considered essentially new, does it necessarily follow that the Second World War was their inevitable consequence?

*

The Nazi Revolution started, in the domestic sphere, within a year of Hitler's appointment as Chancellor. Changes in foreign policy, however, were at least five years behind, giving politicians in Britain and France cause to hope that National Socialism would eventually apply to Germany's internal problems the moderation apparent in its early diplomacy.

There were two basic reasons for the continuity of Germany's foreign policy during the early and mid-1930s. One was that the governments of the Weimar Republic had been under constant pressure from the more conservative elements of the social spectrum, particularly the National People's Party (DNVP), who had inherited the views and policies of the Conservatives and right-wing National Liberals of the Second Reich. At first, these tradi-

220

tionalists had been kept under control by the coalitions of the 1920s because the Democrats and Social Democrats had considerable electoral support. After 1929, however, the swing to the Right in the *Reichstag* elections put the conservatives into power. While von Schleicher and von Papen were Chancellors, the foreign ministry was filled with men like von Neurath and von Bülow, who constantly looked back to the Wilhelmine era of *Weltpolitik*. The Republic's ambassadors were drawn largely from the former aristocracy and had a similar commitment to seeing Germany re-emerge as a major power. Most of these officials were retained by Hitler during the first four years of the Third Reich, with the result that the continuity of personnel made any sudden and dramatic switch in policy unlikely. Indeed, for a while, Hitler was anxious to establish a reputation as a moderate in diplomacy, and he was actually less outspoken than the National Party leader, Hugenberg. He was also prepared to harmonize his views with those of the conservative leaders of industry, like Thyssen, or of the old-fashioned right-wing economists, like Schacht, even if this meant temporarily ignoring the purists of Nazi theory, like Rosenberg and Strasser. Hitler also found himself in agreement with the decision of the ex-republican leaders of the early 1930s when they accepted limited rearmament as a means of countering the worst effects of the Great Depression; he used this as a stepping stone towards achieving his own more distinctively militarist aims. Given the prevailing right-wing inclination of the Republic's policies and institutions after 1930, it is hardly surprising that Hitler needed to change so little in the early years. He could even keep the existing leaders of the *Reichswehr*, including von Blomberg and Beck, and he went so far as to purge his own radicals, like Röhm, who wanted to Nazify the army immediately.

The second reason for the continuity of German foreign policy during the transition from Republic to Reich was the existence of a common and longstanding programme to revise the Versailles Settlement. The Allies had removed from Germany 12 per cent of her population, 13 per cent of her territory and much of her industrial capacity, as well as imposing on her a total reparations debt of £6600 million. All Germans condemned the Settlement, whether they were moderate supporters of the Republic, traditional conservatives or radical Nazis. Hugo Preuss, a leader of the Democratic Party and architect of the Republic's constitution, referred to the 'criminal madness of the Versailles *Diktat*'.[1] Hence, during the 1920s, Republican statesmen and conservatives alike agreed that a revisionist policy was essential, even though they disagreed bitterly over the measures to be used. The overall aims of the moderate coalitions of the SPD, Centre Party, Democrats and People's Party, were itemized by Stresemann, Foreign Minister between 1923 and 1929. He insisted that the reparations question must be solved in 'a sense tolerable for Germany', that assistance should be given to 'those ten to twelve millions of our kindred who now live under a foreign yoke in foreign lands', and that Germany's eastern frontiers should be liable to 'readjustment'.[2] Von Stülpnagel, head of the *Reichswehr*'s operations section, put a similar case for 'the regaining of full sovereignty over the area retained by Germany' and 'firm acquisition of those areas at present separated from her'.[3] Meanwhile, the High Command was quite happy to evade the ban placed by the Treaty of Versailles on military manoeuvres by arranging for the training of German troops in Russia, a device made possible by the treaties formed with the Soviet Union by Rathenau in 1922, and by Stresemann in 1926.

Thus the elements of revisionism which featured in Hitler's foreign policy were by no means original. Although the moderates had been shocked by his withdrawal from the League of Nations in 1933, they had to admit that his methods did bring spectacular success. The conservative (as distinct from Nazi) Right were more enthusiastic about Hitler's diplomacy than they had ever been about Stresemann's, even though the High Command questioned his lack of military caution over the reoccupation of the Rhineland in 1936. Indeed, a glance at Hitler's diplomatic record before 1939 shows that he had accomplished all the targets of the republican revisionists. Germany had regained full sovereignty over all internal territories, including the Rhineland in 1936; the limitation on armaments had been ignored since 1935; and the Germans of Austria and the Sudetenland had been incorporated into the Reich by the *Anschluss* and the Munich Agreement of 1938. The popularity of his foreign policy was evidenced by the overwhelming majorities which he gained in his plebiscites; 99.08 per cent, for example, voted in favour of the *Anschluss*. Even allowing for a degree of electoral manipulation, it is certain that the German people accepted this early phase of Hitler's diplomacy with greater unanimity than they did his internal measures, perhaps because they were relieved by the

German Foreign Policy 1918–39

apparent harmony of its transition from one régime to another. British and French statesmen, too, regarded the first five years of diplomacy as the moderate face of Nazism and concluded that Hitler, although a radical, had reasonable and fixed objectives.

In retrospect, however, it is obvious that the continuity between the diplomacy of the Weimar Republic and the Third Reich was misleading. The crucial fact, which ultimately showed Nazi foreign policy to be as revolutionary as its domestic counterpart was that Hitler saw revisionism merely as a means of moving towards projects which were well beyond the ambitions of any of the republican statesmen. At the theoretical level, the differences between the aims of the moderates and the conservatives, on the one hand, and the Nazis, on the other, were obvious, although optimism and wishful thinking tended to minimize them. Conservatives, especially in the National Party, looked back to the era of the Second Reich, expecting a revival of *Weltpolitik* with its emphasis on colonies and naval power as well as continental military strength. But the boundaries of Germany herself would be those of 1914; after all, even Bismarck had opposed any drastic territorial changes for fear of weakening the Prussian base of the Reich. The moderates of the Republic faced a dilemma. They did not regret the passing of the Second Reich, and hoped that international co-operation would replace military rivalry. Stresemann, for example, saw Germany as a 'bridge' which would reconcile West and East and bring about the harmonious development of Europe. Consequently, he committed the Republic to a policy of collective security by the formation of the Locarno Pact (1925), and gave Germany a voice in international decisions by securing her membership of the League of Nations (1926). Unfortunately, the conditions of the Treaty of Versailles infused Stresemann's policy with more opportunist and less idealistic tendencies. He felt obliged to resort to covert measures to secure at least the beginning of German rearmament and to open the way for regaining lost territories. At no time, however, did he extend this policy of revisionism into one of expansion for its own sake. His main concern was to 'get the stranglehold off our neck' and not to create an enlarged Reich.

Hitler's aims encompassed nothing less than conquest on a continental scale and the destruction of Germany's neighbours. His views were stated explicitly in *Mein Kampf* and, more lucidly, in his *Secret Book*.[4] The latter contains a number of observations which point to the radicalism of Hitler's basic thought. For example, he claimed that all previous governments had been restricted in their policy by the notion of the 'fixed frontier'. Even the Conservatives and neo-Bismarckians were wrong to hark back to the territorial arrangements of 1914, for 'the German borders of the year 1914 were borders which presented something incomplete'. As an alternative to the 'border policy' of the 'national bourgeois world', the Nazis would follow 'a territorial one', the whole purpose of which would be 'to secure the space necessary to the life of our people'. The limited policies of Bismarck had, perhaps, been necessary to establish and build up the 'power structure' for the future. But Bismarck's successors (the very statesmen who were now being lauded by the Conservatives) had denied Germany her natural process of expansion and had pursued an 'insane' policy of alliance with Austria-Hungary and maritime conflict with Britain. Now the mistakes of history could be rectified, *Lebensraum* could be achieved, and the 'inferior races' could be deprived of the territory to which their low productivity and potential gave them no natural right. Returning to the theme of struggle which had permeated *Mein Kampf*, Hitler affirmed: 'Every healthy, vigorous people sees nothing sinful in territorial acquisition, but something quite in keeping with its nature.' Besides, peace bred submissiveness and there was always the danger that 'whatever will not be a hammer in history, will be an anvil'.

Reduced to more explicit stages, Hitler's objectives were as follows: his first priority was to destroy the Versailles Settlement and revive Germany's military power. With this there was little dissent among his subjects. The next stage was to establish a Greater Reich by dismantling Germany's neighbours. This policy accorded with the views of some of the more extreme members of the National Party, but was generally viewed with reservations when it became apparent. The third step was to take lands in the East, as far as the Urals, for the future settlement of up to 100 million Germans. By this time, Germany's mastery of the Continent would be assured. It has sometimes been suggested that Hitler was considering a fourth aim: world dominance, to be contested, if necessary, against the opposition of Britain and the United States. Clearly, the last two projects would have been discounted by many conservatives as impossible, while Hitler's intentions in relation to the fourth have never been clearly established.

German Foreign Policy 1918–39

How did Hitler progress through these stages? Between 1933 and 1936 he emphasized the importance of firmness in achieving the destruction of the Versailles Settlement, but of moderation in the methods used. It would seem that his main concern was to prevent an Allied attack on Germany, and he warned his generals that 'the most dangerous time is that of the building of the armed forces'.[5] Hence he removed obstacles to German rearmament by withdrawing from the League of Nations Disarmament Commission in 1933, but also affirmed in public speeches that he had no intention of settling disputes with any other country by military means. To back up his self-projection as a man of peace, he formed the Nazi-Polish Non-Aggression Pact in 1934. This was received with undisguised relief by other European powers, but Hitler was merely playing for time and trying to undermine the French security system in Eastern Europe. Indeed, he observed in a moment of frankness, 'All our agreements with Poland have a purely temporary significance. I have no intention of maintaining a serious friendship with Poland.'[6] He showed particular skill in dividing potential opponents and in assessing the likely reaction of other statesmen to a *fait accompli* on his own part. For example, he managed to split the Stresa Front, formed in protest against Germany's announcement of military conscription, by offering a naval agreement which would apparently ensure permanent British superiority. He also affirmed that any departure from the Versailles Settlement should not be construed as a prelude to war, and that he certainly had no intention of annexing Austria. He made similar promises after his reoccupation of the Rhineland in 1936, a *coup* which succeeded because he correctly anticipated that neither the French nor British governments would be prepared to use force to resist.

Greatly encouraged by the success of his diplomacy in these early years, Hitler became increasingly aggressive in his methods and moved into the newer area of territorial expansion. In November 1937, he revealed to the leading personnel of the Foreign Ministry and to military chiefs like Blomberg, Fritsch and Raeder, the basic purpose of his policy, including the schemes for an enlarged Reich and *Lebensraum*. The meeting, recorded as the Hossbach Memorandum, revealed the reservations and even dismay of the non-Nazi elements. Beck, for example, described the programme as 'inconceivable', while Blomberg and Fritsch expressed concern about possible retaliation by Britain and France. Hitler responded by breaking all remaining links with the Weimar Republic. He dismissed those officials who had served it and who were now refusing to see that what had so far been accomplished in foreign policy was only a means to achieving a much greater end. Neurath was replaced as Foreign Minister by von Ribbentrop, while Blomberg and Fritsch were both removed by somewhat devious methods. Altogether, sixteen generals were retired and another fourty-four relocated. In one blow, Hitler had ended the partnership which had previously existed between the Nazis and the *Wehrmacht*; he now transformed the army into yet another institution which he dominated personally. Meanwhile, the economy, too, had been transformed. The pragmatic agreements with the industrialists and with the traditional economists were replaced, from 1936, by the deliberate preparation of a war machine to carry out Hitler's foreign policy. Schacht resigned his post in 1937 and, instead, Goering was given responsibility for the Four Year Plan which was intended to prepare Germany for war by 1940. Hitler's thinking here was revealed in the Hossbach Memorandum. He told his generals that Germany's expansion would have to be accomplished by 1943, or at the latest 1945, for, by this time, Germany's military advantage would have worn off as other countries would have begun to close the gap.

1938 and 1939 saw the completion of Hitler's enlarged Germany and the beginning of the quest for *Lebensraum*. Hitler moved quickly in 1938 because Britain and France hoped that the *Anschluss* and the demand for the Sudetenland were the final stages of a revisionist policy inherited from the Weimar Republic; in fact, they were merely a prelude for the expansion of Germany into Eastern Europe. This was eventually confirmed when, in 1939, Hitler incorporated the whole of Bohemia into the Reich, announced that Slovakia was to be a German protectorate, and launched a full-scale attack on Poland. In November 1939 he finally renounced the use of diplomacy and told his generals: 'All hope for compromise is childish.'[7]

*

The Nuremberg Judgement maintained that the Second World War was the outcome of Nazi policy and of Hitler's resolution 'not to depart from the course he had set for himself'.[8] There are two ways of looking at this whole question of responsibility. The first is that the

German Foreign Policy 1918–39

conflict between 1939 and 1945 was unquestionably 'Hitler's War'. It is true that he had pursued a cautious foreign policy during the first few years after his appointment as Chancellor and that some of his objectives seemed directly in line with the revisionist approach of his predecessors. Yet there is no logical reason why these should not have been short-term measures designed to ease the way for the achievement of a more ambitious scheme – the conquest of Eastern Europe. *Mein Kampf*, the *Secret Book* and the Hossbach Memorandum all point to militarism and virtually unlimited expansion as being the only real objectives of Hitler's policies. Hitler was also obsessed with the notion that struggle and war were fundamental human activities and needs. 'War is the most natural, the most ordinary thing. War is a constant; war is everywhere. There is no beginning, there is no conclusion of peace. War is life. All struggle is war. War is the primal condition.' The logical conclusion, therefore, is that Hitler *wanted* war, partly to achieve his long-term objectives, partly to strengthen the Aryan race. As we have seen, the turn of the decade seemed to offer the best chance of successful aggression, as the rearmament of Germany's main rivals was still at an early stage. The majority of historians have been, and remain, convinced that war was the only possible outcome of Hitler's diplomacy. R. J. Sontag, for example, argued that Hitler's policy in 1939 was, 'like the annexation of Austria and the Sudeten districts of Czechoslovakia, merely preliminary to the task of winning "living space" '.[9] There have been critics of this line of reasoning, the most important being A. J. P. Taylor, who maintained that the war broke out through 'blunder' rather than design. Hitler's projects, as outlined in *Mein Kampf* and the Hossbach Memorandum, were 'in large part day-dreaming, unrelated to what followed in real life'. In his opinion, 'statesmen are too absorbed by events to follow a preconceived plan. They take one step and the next follows from it'.[10] This, however, remained very much a minority viewpoint, and the responsibility of Hitler for the conflict was reaffirmed by H. Trevor Roper, in a critique of Taylor's thesis. He demonstrated Hitler's commitment to long-term aims, all explicitly stated in *Mein Kampf*, and added: 'All the experience of the 1930s showed that Hitler still intended to carry them out.'[11] This line was also followed by a German biographer of Hitler, J. Fest, who reaffirmed the orthodoxy that 'who caused the war is a question that cannot be seriously raised'.[12]

These conclusions do not rule out a degree of responsibility, outside Germany, for the outbreak of war. In this case, however, responsibility is associated less with 'guilt' than with 'misinterpretation', 'inconsistency' and 'default'. It can be argued that Hitler's progress towards war was unintentionally accelerated by Western leaders, paradoxically, because of their very hatred of war. Daladier and Chamberlain, who found war morally repugnant, assumed that the rationale of all diplomacy pointed towards peace. Chamberlain, in particular, made the crucial mistake of assuming that even Hitler had specific objectives, and that if these were conceded to him, the causes of international tension would be removed. Hitler, of course, was greatly encouraged by the pressure exerted on the smaller states by the British and French governments and mistook forbearance in the interests of peace for weakness and diplomatic capitulation. This explains the increasingly aggressive stance which he adopted during the Sudeten crisis of 1938. By 1939 Chamberlain had at last got the true measure of Hitler and decided to extend military guarantees to Poland and Romania. This sudden switch appeared a desperate turn within a bankrupt policy and clearly lacked credibility with the Nazis. Hitler was by no means deterred in his designs against Poland and told his military commanders on 22 August that Britain and France would not, he was certain, react to a full-scale German invasion. B. Liddell Hart drew an analogy with allowing someone to stoke up a boiler until the steam pressure rose to danger point – and then closing the safety-valve; while A. J. P. Taylor considered that British foreign policy fell between two stools: war might possibly have been avoided by 'greater firmness' or 'greater conciliation'.

25

Soviet Foreign Policy 1918–41

This chapter will outline the development of Soviet foreign policy between the wars and provide explanations for the frequent alterations of course made by Lenin and Stalin. At its best, Soviet policy was skilful, confident and effective; at its worst, it was blundering, uncertain and ruinous. Throughout the period there was an internal – it might be said dialectical – conflict between ideological motives on the one hand and, on the other, a pragmatism which bordered on cynicism.

*

The Bolshevik Revolution brought an upheaval in international relations as well as in Russia's domestic situation. There were two reasons for this. The first was that the Bolshevik leaders displayed an intense ideological hostility to the Western powers, believing in the inevitability of their eventual collapse and also in the necessity of this as a precondition for the survival of the new Communist régime. Lenin argued in 1918: 'There can be no doubt that the prospects for final victory of our Revolution would be hopeless if it were to remain alone and if it were not for the revolutionary movement in other countries.'[1] The choice, therefore, was between causing revolution in capitalist states, or sitting back and allowing an eventual capitalist onslaught against Communism. According to Trotsky, 'Either the Russian Revolution will create a revolutionary movement in Europe, or the European powers will destroy the Russian Revolution.'[2]

The second reason was that the Bolshevik Revolution was followed by Russia's withdrawal from the First World War, a development which upset the military strategy of the Western Allies in their struggle against Germany. Lenin had consistently opposed Russia's involvement in what he regarded as a conflict between monopoly capitalists and, on coming to power, he opened the Tsarist archives, published all secret treaties and declared in favour of 'an immediate peace without annexations and without indemnities'.[3] By agreeing to the Treaty of Brest Litovsk with Germany in March 1918, Lenin showed that the Bolsheviks were prepared to suffer a temporary diplomatic humiliation in return for greater freedom to direct the revolutionary forces which would soon render all diplomacy superfluous.

Such calculations soon had to be replaced by a more urgent defensive strategy for survival. For Western reactions to the new Bolshevik régime and to Russia's separate peace with Germany were thoroughly hostile. Russia's capitulation at Brest Litovsk enabled the Germans to launch a new offensive on the Western Front on 21 March 1918, and the Allied Supreme War Council decided at Versailles that Russia should be brought back into the conflict even if this should require military intervention. Hence British expeditionary forces were despatched to Murmansk, Archangel and the Caspian Sea area, the French invaded the Black Sea region, and Eastern Siberia and Vladivostok were occupied by the Japanese and Americans. This intervention rapidly became caught up in support for counter-revolution as aid was given to the White armies of Kolchack, Yudenitch, Deniken and Wrangel. The Bolsheviks, however, managed to contain the threat, combining effective personal leadership with the emergence of the highly effective Red Army from the Revolutionary Military Committee. They had the advantage of complete control over Russia's railway network, which radiated outwards from Moscow, and they succeeded in eliminating most internal opposition to the war effort through the offices of the *Cheka*. But the Soviet régime was less successful in dealing with the Polish threat in 1920; although the Red Army threw back the initial Polish invasion, its own counter-attack was reversed by a second Polish offensive made possible by the reorganization carried out by Marshal Pilsudski and General Weygand. By the Treaty of Riga (1921) Russia suffered a second territorial amputation in three years.

Soviet Foreign Policy 1918–41

These events brought about an important change in Soviet foreign policy. The Bolshevik régime had survived a series of attacks from capitalist and counter-revolutionary forces without collapsing. At the same time, however, the Western powers themselves showed no signs of disintegration under the impact of revolutionary activity. The Spartacist rising in Berlin had been crushed in January 1919 and the Soviet Republic of Bavaria had been destroyed a few months later. Even the Bolshevik-inspired Hungarian revolution had collapsed and there seemed no immediate prospects of workers' risings in any other Eastern or Central European state. It made sense, therefore, to redirect the basic strategy of foreign policy and to think in terms of coexistence. In November 1921, Lenin acknowledged that his predictions of a swift world revolution had not been justified. Hence a period of internal consolidation had now to be the most urgent priority. Furthermore, the civil war had brought home the importance of adequate armaments and a balanced economy. The most direct way of achieving the industrial growth essential for both was through Western investment. According to Kamenev in 1921: 'We can, of course, restore our economy by the heroic effort of the working masses. But we cannot develop it fast enough to prevent the capitalist countries from overtaking us, unless we call in foreign capital.'[4]

Between 1921 and 1924, therefore, Soviet leaders resurrected the art of diplomacy and stunned the West with their mastery of the unexpected *fait accompli*. The target chosen for this activity was Germany, isolated and vulnerable as a result of defeat in the First World War and the harsh terms of the Treaty of Versailles. The Soviet Foreign Minister, Chicherin, conducted secret negotiations with his German counterpart, Rathenau. These reached their climax in Genoa in 1922. Ostensibly, Russia and Germany were themselves the objects of discussion among the other major powers, but the tables were turned when the Russo-German Treaty of Rapallo was announced. Great skill had been shown by the Soviet delegation in using as a lever the German fear that Russia might invoke Article 116 of the Treaty of Versailles unless such an agreement were reached. Although the Rapallo Agreement was not an alliance, it did provide for German investment and valuable military advice.

It should not be assumed, however, that this meant the end of

Aspects of European History 1789–1980

Trotsky's vision of worldwide revolution. On the contrary, the role of *Comintern* was still to foment Communist revolt where possible as, for example, in Germany in 1921 and 1923. Even the use of Western capital could be justified on ideological grounds. According to Kamenev: 'While strengthening Soviet Russia, developing her productive forces, foreign capital will fulfil the role Marx predicted for it when he said that capital was digging its own grave.'[4]

*

When Stalin emerged as Lenin's successor in 1924, Soviet foreign policy became even more complex. Although it is difficult to generalize about the whole spectrum of ideas and methods, certain underlying influences can be detected.

Before 1924 Stalin had had comparatively little contact with diplomacy and had always shown far more concern for the domestic base of socialism than for its external spread. Consequently, he had already come into conflict with Trotsky's belief in 'Worldwide Revolution', maintaining that Russia's only viable course was 'Socialism in One Country'. Stalin was an orthodox Marxist in that he believed in the ultimate, global victory of Communism. He argued, however, that the best way of achieving this was through military methods rather than through external insurrections; war, not revolution, would be the instrument of victory. Russia's role in this ought to be twofold. On the one hand, intensive preparations should be made to develop heavy industry so as to provide a solid military base for victory. On the other, Russia should avoid direct aggression, while being prepared to take advantage of the inevitable conflict between the capitalist powers. He told the Party Central Committee in 1925: 'If war begins . . . we shall have to come out, but we ought to be the last to come out. And we should come out in order to throw the decisive weight on the scales.'[5] How effectively did Stalin carry out these ideas?

*

At first Stalin was content to maintain the policy which had been outlined at Genoa by Chicherin in 1922, 'the parallel existence of the old social order and of the new order now being born'.[6] The Soviet régime obtained, during the course of 1924, recognition from Britain, Italy, France and Japan, and Stalin had high hopes of persuading foreign trade union movements to put pressure on their governments to lessen their ideological animosity towards Russia. He also intended to pursue a moderate course in China. Although Trotsky argued that the Chinese political situation was directly comparable to that in Russia in 1917, Stalin considered that a narrowly-based Communist revolution would be far less likely to succeed than a coalition of different radical forces; hence he urged Mao Tse Tung's Communist Party to join Chiang Kai Shek's organization, the Kuomintang. Before 1927, therefore, Stalin appeared to the capitalist world as a moderating influence and a welcome alternative to the subversive emphasis of Trotsky.

Then came the first of Stalin's changes of strategy. Deutscher maintains that the world had rejected the Bolsheviks as revolutionaries by the end of 1923, and then as conciliators by 1927. Certainly, events had not taken the course Stalin had expected. The major Western governments, with the possible exception of Germany, had grown increasingly hostile; the Soviet embassy in London had been raided and diplomatic relations were severed in 1927. Meanwhile, the Communists in China had broken with the Kuomintang and Stalin's policy of a broad-based coalition had therefore collapsed. There was also a domestic reason for Stalin's change of attitude. By 1927, he had gained complete control over the CPSU and was intent on expelling the rightist element consisting of Bukharin, Kamenev and Zinoviev, as well as the Trotskyists. He intended to abandon Kamenev's attempts to secure loans from the West and to reconstruct the Soviet economy on the radical lines put forward by Preobrazhensky. Agriculture would be collectivized and would subsidize the development of heavy industry in a series of Five Year Plans, the ultimate purpose being to convert the Soviet Union into a major military power. It no longer mattered, therefore, whether foreign powers were unsympathetic, provided that there was no direct military confrontation. In fact, Stalin found it necessary to project the capitalist states in the worst possible light in order to justify his economic upheavals to the Russian people.

How did Stalin explain his new position? In December 1927 he announced that capitalism had entered a phase of instability. This meant that 'the period of peaceful coexistence recedes into the past, giving place to a period of imperialist attacks'.[5] He saw the Great Depression, which struck the capitalist world in 1929, as the fulfilment of his prediction and argued that 'the world economic crisis will turn into a political crisis in a number of countries'.[7] The West, meanwhile, was showing its instability through increased aggression and militarism.

Assuming that his intention was to play a waiting game and, at the same time, to enforce industrialization and rearmament on a backward economy, Stalin's vilification of the West had an unquestionable logic. But he committed a major error in pursuing this logic to its extreme conclusion over Germany. The Great Depression had boosted the electoral performance of the Nazis and, between 1930 and 1933, Hitler made several bids for power, his target being the presidency or, failing that, the chancellorship. Stalin, however, saw little difference between the Nazis and the Social Democrats, the largest obstacle to Hitler and, until 1930, the major party in the *Reichstag*. He regarded them both as fascist; indeed, 'social democracy is objectively the moderate wing of fascism'.[8] He had the word of the German Communist leader, Thälmann, that 'the bourgeoisie would never let Hitler anywhere near power'[8] and, even should this be proved wrong, the real manipulator of the government would be, as always, great industrialists like Thyssen. If Germany moved from the rule of the 'Social fascists' (the SPD) to that of the 'National fascists' (the Nazis), she would be approaching the final internal upheaval which, the dialectic decreed, would destroy capitalism altogether. Consequently, German Communists were instructed not to assist the SPD and other moderate parties in keeping Hitler out of power. From his remote exile, Trotsky issued numerous warnings about the dangers of this policy. He accused the leadership of *Comintern* of 'leading the German proletariat towards an enormous catastrophe' and, in an alternative analysis of fascism, showed that it differed radically from social democracy. Indeed, 'should fascism come to power it will ride over your skulls and spines like a terrific tank . . . only a fighting unity with Social Democratic workers can bring victory. Make haste, you have very little time left!'[5] Trotsky's predictions were entirely accurate. To use another metaphor, Stalin helped create the very monster against which he had been warned.

How did Stalin adapt to the new situation? Although somewhat disconcerted by Hitler's success in 1933, he assumed that coexistence was possible and that Nazi Germany would pursue a Bismarckian policy of restraint towards Russia. After one year, however, Stalin abandoned this view. Hitler's elimination of all internal opposition showed that the Nazi régime was more

Soviet Foreign Policy 1918–41

dangerous than the 'social fascism' of the Weimar Republic. Furthermore, Soviet security seemed imperilled by the 1934 Nazi-Polish Non-Aggression Pact, which provided the basis for a possible anti-Russian alliance. Stalin, therefore, swiftly reverted to diplomacy.

His new policy comprised three elements. The first was a search for collective security in Eastern Europe; this would be made up of interlinked mutual guarantees and would, like the Locarno Pact of 1925, include Germany. When this scheme fell through, Stalin turned to the West for an agreement to outflank Germany. This resulted in the Franco-Soviet Pact and the Soviet-Czechoslovak Pact. These arrangements were accompanied by a third policy, the formation of popular fronts all over Europe to resist the growth of fascism and to prevent any repetition of the internal catastrophe which had befallen Germany. *Comintern* now instructed Communists in Spain, France and elsewhere to sink their differences with social democrats and even liberals. The situation in Spain, however, presented Stalin with a dilemma: the establishment of a Communist régime in order to prevent Franco gaining power would only alienate Western Europe and smash the Soviet Entente with France. He therefore instructed the Spanish Communists to avoid demands for the expropriation of property or state control over industry. He even played along for a while with the principles of the Non-Intervention Committee, until it became obvious that these were being openly flouted by Hitler and Mussolini in their military support to Franco.

By mid-1938, however, Stalin felt that the Western powers were unreliable allies. The Anglo-French response to German territorial expansion was governed by the policy of appeasement, and Stalin was shocked by the ease with which Hitler accomplished the *Anschluss* and absorbed the Sudetenland into the Reich. The Soviet Union alone offered military assistance to Czechoslovakia, but failed to gain French co-operation or permission from Poland or Romania for the transit of Soviet troops. It appeared, therefore, that Germany would be allowed to rearm and expand without hindrance from the Western Allies. To make matters worse, Russian and Japanese troops clashed several times in 1938 and 1939 on the borders of Manchuria and Mongolia. The European problem, therefore, required immediate settlement in case Stalin had to commit divisions to the Far East.

Aspects of European History 1789–1980

What were his options? He could maintain the Soviet relationship with Britain and France, but on revised terms; he could, for example, insist on more definite military commitments. Or he could seek rapprochement with Germany and draw up a territorial settlement which would eliminate any potential causes of conflict with Russia. During the first seven months of 1939 Stalin seemed willing to incline towards either alternative and managed to play off the rival powers with great skill. Foreign Minister Litvinov and General Shaposhnikov offered more clearly defined terms to the Western powers, but their response was too slow. Although Churchill urged the British government to draw up the alliance which Stalin seemed prepared to grant, Chamberlain hesitated, admitting to 'the most profound distrust of Russia'. Meanwhile, Stalin leaked details of these negotiations to Berlin and succeeded in drawing to Moscow a German delegation under von Ribbentrop. The result was the conclusion, on 23 August 1939, of the Nazi-Soviet Non-Aggression Pact, with its secret protocol agreeing to the division of Eastern Europe into Nazi and Soviet spheres of influence. This time Stalin provided no ideological justification; it was obvious to all that this was the most opportunist and pragmatic agreement of the century.

How necessary was the Pact for Russia? Soviet historians today make no mention of Stalin, but argue that 'subsequent events revealed that this step was the only correct one under the circumstances. By taking it, the USSR was able to continue peaceful construction for nearly two years and to strengthen its defences.'[9] There is, however, another view. A modern Western historian[10] maintains that it should not be assumed that, without the Pact, Germany would have attacked Russia in 1939. Hitler was too pre-occupied with Poland, and with the declaration of war by France and Britain, to draw off divisions from the *Wehrmacht* for yet another campaign. More telling is the observation that even if Hitler *had* moved immediately, the Soviet Union would have been better off. By 1941 German military production had grown, proportionately, more rapidly than Russia's, enabling Hitler to launch, in Operation Barbarossa, the sort of offensive which would have been quite impossible in 1939. It would appear that Stalin had simultaneously over-estimated and under-estimated his rival in 1939. He had over-rated German military resources in comparison to Russia's, forgetting that his own Five Year Plans had boosted Soviet heavy industry. But he had underrated the effectiveness of the German

Soviet Foreign Policy 1918–41

Blitzkrieg strategy which shattered Poland and France. Stalin had, in fact, hoped that the final internecine struggle between the capitalist powers had at last arrived. By 1940 he was uncomfortably aware that Hitler had regained the initiative.

Even so, his policy was now to do nothing. For this inactivity during the course of 1940 and 1941 Stalin has been heavily criticized. Khrushchev, for example, said in 1956: 'The threatening danger which hung over our Fatherland in the first period of the war was largely due to the faulty methods of directing the nation and the Party by Stalin himself.'[11] Churchill had earlier described Stalin and his commissars at this stage as 'the most completely outwitted bunglers of the Second World War'.

The indictment rests on Stalin's strange behaviour in the face of the growing threat from Germany. He must have been aware that relations between Russia and Germany were deteriorating rapidly as a result of the Soviet seizure of the Baltic states. Yet he took no action to prepare Russia for the eventuality of war. In April 1941 he received information from Churchill, via British intelligence, that Hitler was moving Panzer divisions to southern Poland, and similar warnings from the United States and his own agents in Berlin. He refused, however, to accept that such manoeuvres were a prelude to a German attack, and he referred in *Tass* to the 'obvious absurdity of these rumours'.[12] He failed to place the Red Army on the alert, concentrating instead on maintaining good relations with Hitler by providing essential supplies of strategic raw materials, even though the Nazis had stopped paying for them. He even issued instructions that the Red Army should not resist any German border incursions in case these provoked a war which he felt that the Germans did not really want. The result of this was that when the *Wehrmacht* did invade, in June 1941, a spectacular Russian collapse occurred, and several million Soviet troops surrendered in the first six months.

This is a summary of the usual interpretation of what happened in 1941. It is, however, possible to adopt a more positive view of Stalin's policies; it could be argued that his appraisal of the situation was wrong not because it was irrational but rather because it was based too heavily on the type of logical reasoning to which he was always accustomed. Stalin doubted whether Hitler had any real motive to attack Russia unless he were actually provoked. It was, therefore, important to keep communications open and to keep stressing that 'The friendship of the peoples of Germany and the Soviet Union, cemented by blood, has every reason to be lasting and firm'.[5] Stalin was convinced that as long as the Soviet Union provided Germany with essential raw materials this coexistence could be maintained indefinitely. At the same time, Soviet policy would be firm and positive in other directions, for Stalin had no intention of adopting the appeasement strategy of Chamberlain. Hence Stalin would remind Hitler of Soviet power by annexing extra territory from Finland, the Baltic states and Romania, thereby strengthening the Russian frontier and cutting off access for a direct German invasion along the coast. Should the two countries appear to be drifting towards war, the symptoms would be recognizable and Stalin could make well-timed concessions to satisfy Hitler. What the Soviet Union had to avoid was alarmism and the possibility of being rushed into war by Churchill, who naturally wanted an ally against Hitler. Stalin did not disbelieve reports about troop movements; but his own interpretation was that they were intended by Hitler as a diplomatic move to put pressure on Russia, possibly as a counter to Russia's territorial annexations. To see in them the beginning of an attack would, in the words of his *Tass* article, be yielding to 'a clumsy propaganda manoeuvre of the forces arrayed against the Soviet Union and Germany'. Up to the very last day, indeed, Stalin was convinced that Hitler could not rationally contemplate widening the scope of the war.

1941, therefore, was dominated by two minds; one tuned to the intricate logic of the dialectic failed entirely to comprehend the other, which was visionary. Then, from the beginning of 1942 onwards, Stalin assumed that the final struggle with capitalism had arrived. It was not in the form which he had intended, but his industrial preparations in the form of the Five Year Plans ensured eventual victory over Nazism.

26

The League of Nations

The League of Nations was established, largely on the initiative of President Wilson, in 1919, the Covenant being drafted at the Paris Peace Conference and subsequently being incorporated into all the treaties which made up the Versailles Settlement. The main institutions were the Council, comprising the major powers and some lesser states elected in rotation; the Assembly, in which all member states were represented; and the Secretariat, which acted as the League's bureaucracy. Associated with the League, but not part of it constitutionally, were the Permanent Court of International Justice, and a series of specialist agencies, like the International Labour Organization. The League's membership totalled forty-one in 1919, rising to fifty by 1924 and sixty by 1934.

This chapter will examine the League of Nations under three main headings: its achievements, the main reasons for its eventual eclipse, and the foundations which it provided for its successor, the United Nations Organization.

*

The League of Nations was not the first attempt to establish institutions for international diplomacy and arbitration; between 1814 and 1914 there had been, under the generic description of 'Concert of Europe', eight Congresses attended by heads of government, and eighteen Conferences of Ambassadors. These had, however, been convened for specific purposes and were intended as an occasion for governments to elaborate their policy rather than as a forum for genuine international debate. They had, moreover, been somewhat exclusive and had represented only the handful of major powers. Other institutions had also been set up during the nineteenth century. These included about 400 non-political organizations and a range of bodies requiring close inter-governmental co-operation, like the International Telegraphic Union (1865) and the Universal Postal Union (1874). Against this background, the League of Nations performed two important functions. It provided a permanent framework for inter-governmental consultation which was more regular and systematic than the *ad hoc* conferences of the nineteenth century. It also extended the range of this framework to incorporate non-political as well as political bodies. The result was greater co-operation, made possible by the unprecedented use of the Secretariat, with all its resources for gathering and collating information and statistics. The system established in 1919 was far from perfect, but it did represent a considerable advance on the scattered institutions of the previous era.

Despite experiencing severe difficulties and eventual collapse, the League achieved several political successes by the mid-1930s. It provided a means whereby a small area could be removed from a defeated power, either temporarily or permanently, without being absorbed by one of the victors as would have been the case before 1914. The Saar, for example, was administered until 1935 by a Governing Commission, and Danzig by a High Commissariat. The League also carried out plebiscites in accordance with the principle of national self-determination embodied in the Treaties of Versailles and St. Germain; three examples were Upper Silesia, Schleswig and East Prussia. In order to give minorities a chance to air any grievances caused by boundary changes, a Minorities Subcommittee of the Council was established, although it possessed no actual jurisdiction within the affected areas. More successful was the action taken by the League, mainly during the 1920s, to settle disputes between some of the lesser states, particularly between Finland and Sweden over the Aaland Islands, Turkey and Iraq over the Mosul, Greece and Bulgaria, and Albania and Yugoslavia. The Commission on Mandates, meanwhile, ensured that those major powers which had received colonies from the defunct German Empire did not cover their administration under a veil of secrecy. Conscious of the League's right to criticize and investigate, if not to interfere directly, the imperial powers refined their colonial governments and took

The League of Nations

care to avoid the type of excesses which had often marred their record before 1914.

The most worthwhile and significant of the League's achievements were undoubtedly in the social field. The Health Organization conducted research into leprosy, gave advice on vaccines and standardized drugs in common use, while the Epidemics Commission dealt with the outbreaks of typhus and cholera which resulted from warfare in Eastern Europe. Refugees, casualties of the same problem, were the subject of the Nansen Report, which tried to ease their absorption into other countries. Various forms of exploitation were also investigated. The League was particularly concerned about the continuing traffic in women and children and the employment of young children in the Persian carpet trade. The International Labour Organization, meanwhile, tried to persuade governments to standardize conditions of labour and to regulate relations between employers and employees; many governments responded by passing the legislation recommended by the Organization's General Conference. Finally, the League sponsored a series of technical organizations which were concerned, above all, with rail transport, inland navigation and electrical power. In general, the League became so heavily committed to non-political activities that the Bruce Report of 1939 recommended extensive institutional changes to cope with the ever increasing volume of work. This came out at a time when the political activities of the League had been all but suspended.

*

In retrospect, it is possible to see the enormous, perhaps unparalleled, difficulties of the inter-war period. Four empires had been destroyed, which had resulted in the most extensive territorial changes for centuries. Powerful ideologies developed on the extreme Left and the extreme Right, the latter assisted by economic catastrophe in the early 1930s. Any international organization was bound to find this environment overwhelmingly hostile, and, if it were to have the remotest chances of success in the political field, it needed the support and goodwill of the majority of the great powers and a structure through which to deal instantly with major disputes, by preventive action where possible, punitive where necessary.

This was not, however, the form taken by the League of Nations. It was not constructed to survive a period of crisis but rather to uphold

241

what was optimistically regarded as an impending period of peace. There was widespread support for the belief of H. G. Wells that the Great War had been the 'war to end wars'; hence Europe had to get away from the traditional view, expressed early in the nineteenth century by Clausewitz, that 'war is the continuation of diplomacy by other means'. War, in fact, was now to be outlawed. By the Kellogg-Briand Pact of 1928, for example, the sixty-five signatories agreed to 'condemn recourse to war for the solution of international controversies and renounce it as an instrument of national policy in their relations with one another'.[1] Britain and the United States, in particular, approached the formation of the League from the assumption that institutions were needed for collective and voluntary agreement rather than for coercion. Hence the League was heavily influenced by Anglo-American notions of liberal democracy, both in the structure of the Council and Assembly and in the responsibilities allocated to them. The French delegates at the session for drafting the Covenant saw matters differently; they pressed for a more tightly knit body, with stronger coercive powers. Eventually, however, the Anglo-American view prevailed. The League would be the medium for peaceful arbitration, with pressure of any kind being used only as a final resort. Since the French amendment to set up a military force was rejected in 1919, the League had no agency with which to enforce its resolutions and therefore relied entirely on the co-operation of the major powers. Hence, in the words of P. Raffo, the League 'depended for its very existence and effectiveness on that unity of purpose and international goodwill which it was itself designed to promote'.[2]

The League Covenant illustrates these deficiencies clearly. Article 10 expressed the basic intention: 'The Members of the League undertake to respect and preserve as against external aggression the territorial integrity and existing political independence of all members of the League.'[3] Article 11 provided that the League should 'take any action that may be deemed wise and effectual to safeguard the peace of nations'. Unfortunately, there was no further ruling on what procedure should be taken in such an emergency. Article 10 stated that the Council should 'advise' on the means whereby members' obligations should be fulfilled, but the effect of this was virtually destroyed by a Canadian resolution in 1923 which gave to each individual government the right to interpret its obligations in its own way. Even more debilitating to

The League of Nations

any form of joint action was Article 5, which stated that 'decisions at any meeting of the Assembly or of the Council shall require the agreement of all the members of the League represented at the meeting'. This 'unanimity clause' severely undermined the League's attempts, under Article 11 to deal with the Japanese invasion of Manchuria (1931) and made it extremely difficult to enforce the sanctions allowed by Article 16. The Covenant assumed throughout that the great powers would always play by the rules even if the process of arbitration should fail; Article 12, for example, provided for a 'cooling off' period of three months before either side in an intractable dispute could resort to war. The events of the 1930s, however, demonstrated that Japan, Italy and Germany acknowledged no rules which could not actually be enforced, and Article 12 made little sense to Fascist régimes which based their foreign policy on surprise and the *fait accompli*.

Two attempts were made, during the 1920s and early 1930s, to make the League more effective as a peacekeeping organization. The first was to reduce the level of international tension through the process of disarmament provided for in Article 8 of the Covenant. The period 1926–34, however, brought total failure. The Commission for the Geneva Disarmament Conference spent five years producing an outline report which contained no details or statistics, while the Conference itself was irreparably damaged by Germany's withdrawal in 1933, and eventually adjourned indefinitely in 1934. The other attempt was more realistic. French pressure from within the League produced proposals for tightening up the procedures for concerted action in a crisis; the most promising were the Draft Treaty of Mutual Assistance and the Geneva Protocol. But these never got off the ground, largely because the British government, supported by the Dominions, attacked them as an unwarranted commitment. Instead, a system of 'collective security' came into existence, based on the 1925 Locarno Pact and guaranteeing the frontiers between France, Belgium and Germany from unilateral revision. The Locarno Pact was not directly connected with the League, although it provided for arbitration by the League in the event of disputes between the three protected states. The device was reasonably effective during the period 1925–9 when German foreign policy was directed by Stresemann, but it was rapidly dismantled by Hitler after 1933. Besides, Collective Security did not cover the more vulnerable and dangerous trouble spots of

Eastern Europe and therefore amounted to no more than a temporary reconciliation between Germany and the countries of Western Europe, giving, in the process, an illusion of safety.

Failure to give the Council any corporate peace-keeping powers confined the League to a role of arbitrating between the lesser states. Acts of aggression by major Powers often invoked a diplomatic response from outside the structure of the League. For example, the 1923 Corfu Crisis, engineered by Mussolini, was eventually resolved by the traditional expedient of a Conference of Ambassadors rather than by the League Council. Attempts by the Council to effect withdrawals from Manchuria by the Japanese, and from Abyssinia by the Italians, failed so dismally that, during the second half of the 1930s, the League was almost always bypassed. Britain and France resorted to a bilateral policy of appeasement towards both Italy and Germany, while the Non-Intervention Committee, set up to prevent the Spanish Civil War from overspilling into the rest of Europe, never came under the League's jurisdiction. (See Chapter 27.) The future of Czechoslovakia was decided, in 1938, by the heads of four governments, and President Beneš did not even bother to appeal to the League against their decision. Of all the states attacked in 1939 only Finland attempted to use the League machinery.

The institutional weaknesses of the League were exacerbated by the policies of the individual powers, to which we now turn. What stands out most clearly is the indecisiveness of the governments who formed and subsequently claimed to uphold the League – the United States, Britain and France – and the mortal wounds inflicted by Japan, Italy and Germany in pursuit of *Lebensraum*.

By far the most ardent advocate of the League of Nations was President Wilson and there can be no doubt of his intention to commit the United States to permanent membership. By 1919, however, the Senate had been captured by the Republicans and, under the forceful leadership of Henry Cabot Lodge, demanded substantial revision of the Covenant which had been submitted to it by the President. The Republicans were particularly concerned about the commitments which the United States would be expected to undertake in terms of Article 10, and stressed that the administration should retain the right to decide for itself in what issues it should become involved. President Wilson, however, rejected this view and undertook an unsuccessful nationwide campaign to seek support for his own interpretation. The outcome was the rejection of

The League of Nations

the Covenant in the Senate and the complete withdrawal of the United States from the League. The impact was enormous; many historians consider the American return to isolation undermined the League from the very beginning. S. Marks, for example, argues that 'In its larger role the League foundered on the twin rocks of the unanimity clause and the absence of America'.[4] Certainly, American isolation made it impossible to consider any specific action over Manchuria in 1931; Austen Chamberlain observed: 'We ought to know by this time that the USA will give us no undertaking to resist by force any action of Japan short of an attack on Hawaii or Honolulu.' Similarly, sanctions against Italy were pointless without American participation, and Roosevelt's refusal to become involved in the European crises of the late 1930s considerably enhanced the cause of fascism.

Britain and France were the only powers to retain their membership of the League throughout its course and, as such, came to be regarded as the organization's main pillars. Unfortunately, serious misunderstandings arose between them, undermining their efforts to keep it going. One of these concerned the very nature of the League. British governments regarded the League as a device for arbitration and as a forum for the expression of different ideas. The French, by contrast, wanted a tight system of security and a means of guaranteeing the 1919 peace settlements; they were therefore bitterly disappointed by Britain's rejection of the Geneva Protocol and refusal to assist the defence of the new frontiers in Eastern Europe. At times, relations between the two states reached rock bottom; Britain was completely out of sympathy with the French search for security in the Ruhr in 1923, while France refused to accept the naval ratio negotiated at the London Conference in 1930. Such disharmony benefited those powers whose main concern was not to place a definitive interpretation on the Covenant but to exploit its loopholes.

The first to do this was Japan. Although she had been one of the original signatories of the League Covenant in 1919, Japan had never been more than a half-hearted member of the League. She resented the heavy-handed refusal by the European members of the League to include within the Covenant an affirmation of racial equality. She was also dissatisfied with the policies of the Western powers, whether inside or outside the League; she was unhappy with the levels of ship building negotiated at the Washington Conference

Aspects of European History 1789–1980

(1921) and the London Conference (1930) and also with the restraints on her commercial expansion into mainland China. The Great Depression acted as a catalyst for change, transforming compliance, but dormant resentment, into defiance, and direct aggression. The economic crisis destroyed the remnants of democratic government and provided opportunities for political intervention by the army. This in turn led to a ruthless and opportunist foreign policy, beginning with military action in Manchuria. The League's reaction was too weak to prevent Japan from establishing the puppet state of Manchukuo, but just strong enough to invoke violent Japanese hostility. The new régime denounced the League as a western clique and ended Japan's membership in March 1933. Thereafter it acknowledged no external restraint on its actions and proceeded in 1937 to attack the rest of China, and in 1941 to dismantle the British, French and Dutch Empires in the Far East.

Italy was another power which had never really been committed to the League. As early as 1923 the British ambassador in Rome had remarked that Italy saw in the League's force antithetical to the vital necessities of her own future expansion'.[5] Mussolini certainly saw in the Covenant an obstacle to his plans for revising the parsimonious treatment of Italy by the Versailles Settlement. Yet, during the 1920s Mussolini followed a cautious policy; he usually projected an image of diplomatic reasonableness, showing an aggressive edge only occasionally, as in the Corfu Incident of 1923. As with Japan, however, the Great Depression brought a transformation. A second 'Fascist Revolution' occurred which, this time, encompassed foreign policy. By 1935 Mussolini was in full pursuit of imperial expansion, helped by the ambivalent attitudes of Britain and France over Abyssinia. On the one hand, he was encouraged by apparent Anglo-French capitulation in the Hoare-Laval Pact; on the other, he was infuriated by the attempt to impose economic sanctions, and withdrew Italy from the League in December 1937. Mussolini has often been seen as the leader who administered the death blow to the League, enabling Hitler to take advantage in the late 1930s of the resulting diplomatic free-for-all.

Germany's attitude to the League underwent a complete change. The statesmen of the parties within the coalition governments of the Weimar Republic favoured and worked for entry, which was eventually accomplished in 1926 by Stresemann. The main intentions were to revise the Treaty of Versailles and gain acceptance for the

The League of Nations

foreign policy objectives described in Chapter 24. By 1929 however, there was widespread dissatisfaction with the League, and growing support for the National Party's charge that the League had never been anything more than a 'syndicate of victors'[6] designed to enforce the Treaty of Versailles to the full. Military leaders like Groener, and diplomats like Bülow, openly stated that the League was irrelevant to Germany's needs; Bülow, for example, argued that if the League's purpose really was the preservation of the *status quo* and the prevention of future wars, then it was 'an objective in which we can have less interest than the other, especially the allied powers'.[7] Hitler, therefore, found a considerable groundswell of opinion against the League, as was demonstrated by the overwhelming majority in the plebiscite approving Germany's withdrawal in October 1933. His subsequent actions revealed open contempt for the League as either the guarantor of the Versailles Settlement or as an arbitrator in disputes. It took time, however, for other governments to realize that the objectives of his foreign policy were incompatible with any form of peaceful diplomacy.

The Soviet Union also underwent a change in its attitude to the League. Lenin had accused the League of upholding the forces of capitalism and colonialism, while Stalin had originally felt that any commitments would place the Soviet Union in an anomalous position: 'We do not want to be either the hammer for the weak nations or the anvil for the mighty ones.'[8] Stalin preferred, during the 1920s, to make his own arrangements, largely with Germany. But the spread of fascism during the 1930s convinced him that he would have to co-operate with the Western democracies. He therefore took the Soviet Union into the League in 1934, hoping that it would provide an alliance with Britain and France. As it turned out, however, the League and Russia gained little from their association with each other. Stalin became disillusioned by the Anglo-French policy of appeasement towards the fascist states, while the British and French governments were disgusted with Stalin's pact with Hitler in August 1939, and his subsequent attacks on Poland and Finland. In December 1939 the League carried out its last decisive act: the termination of Soviet membership.

*

The last session of the League of Nations was held in Geneva on 9 April 1946. One of the speakers, Lord Cecil, concluded with the words: 'The League is dead: long live the United Nations!' This reformulation of the old French salute *Le roi est mort; vive le roi!* was intended to stress the connection between the two organizations; the United Nations had been born in 1945 while the League still existed officially, and the transfer of power was not carried out until August 1946.

Why was it necessary to form a new organization and to go through the rigmarole of transferring power? As we have seen, the League had proved inadequate to deal with the problems which had emerged in the 1930s and the Covenant was regarded as completely outdated. By 1945 the world's leaders were questioning the wisdom of tying an international organization to the specific peace settlement as the statesmen of 1919 had tied the Covenant to the Treaties of Versailles and St. Germain. What was now needed was an institution which would be able to *transcend* a peace settlement and adjust to future problems. At the same time, the great powers wanted to be certain of preserving their own interests without re-enacting the withdrawals of the 1930s. The veto was considered the best safeguard, but this was not provided for within the League Covenant. For this and other reasons, a mere revision of the League would have been inadequate, even if the enormous technical and legal difficulties could have been overcome.

But, although the United Nations would be a new and more complex institution, it would derive much from the League's background. Lord Cecil made this point in his speech of 9 April: 'But for the great experiment of the League, the United Nations could not have come into existence', a view with which a modern historian agrees: 'In most respects, indeed, the United Nations was the recognizable offspring of the League experience.'

This can be illustrated by comparing the institutions of the League and the United Nations. The drafters of the UN Charter kept the basic idea of a Council but decided to allocate its functions more precisely. The League Council was, in effect, replaced by three organs. The first was the Security Council, which was charged specifically with preventing or dealing with disturbances to world peace. The League's emphasis on unanimity was abandoned in favour of majority voting, with each of the five permanent members (the United States, the Soviet Union, Britain, France and China) being given the right of veto. The Security Council was empowered to raise an international peace-keeping force under the command of

The League of Nations

the Military Staff Committee; this remedied one of the greatest deficiencies of the League Covenant. Secondly, the Economic and Social Council was established to assume responsibility for non-political questions. Such an institution had already been recommended by the 1939 Bruce Committee as a means of removing one of the burdens of the League Council. The third new institution, the Trusteeship Council, was also designed to separate a specialized function from the primary task of peace keeping.

Other institutions within the United Nations Organization also had their ancestry within the League. The United Nations General Assembly was clearly the successor to the League Assembly, although experience suggested certain modifications. The General Assembly was given fewer peace-keeping powers but was compensated by a more meaningful role in other areas; it was, for example, given charge of the Trusteeship and Economic and Social Councils. The United Nations maintained with few modifications the League's methods of upholding international law. The League had operated through a Permanent Court of International Justice, although this had been officially outside the League structure. In practice, however, the PCIJ had been fully involved in the life of the League and the fiction of independence was therefore ended by the Charter, which made the new International Court of Justice a primary institution of the United Nations. Direct continuity was also apparent in the case of the Secretariats, although the United Nations version was to become more complex and to have greater responsibility because of the existence of the extra Councils. The UN Secretary General was generally considered more powerful than his League counterpart and, because of deep ideological differences between the major Powers, it became customary to choose candidates from the minor states, a contrast to the League's tendency to select British, French or Russian officials. This, however, can be seen as one of many results of the replacement of a European-based organization by one representing almost every nation on earth.

249

27

The Spanish Civil War

Historians have pointed to two main elements in Spain between 1936 and 1939. The first is a struggle between two broadly-based coalitions, with sharply contrasting ideologies, for the right to shape the country's future social and political institutions. The second is the impact of this struggle on the rest of the Continent. E. H. Carr, in fact, described the Spanish struggle as a 'European Civil War fought on Spanish territory'.[1] This chapter will suggest reasons for the victory of the Right in the domestic conflict and examine the implications for the European powers.

*

Both sides in the Spanish Civil War were heterogeneous and ranged, in each case, from the centre to radical extremes. Since they incorporated such diverse elements, they were described as Fronts. The National Front (or Nationalists) included conservatives, monarchists (especially Carlists), Falangists and other semi-Fascist groups, army commanders, and higher clergy. The Popular Front (or Republicans) comprised liberals, socialists, Communists, and anarchists. Like all broad coalitions, both of these were subject to internal fissures, but the National Front was better able to withstand them and showed the degree of unity necessary to win the war.

In the first place, the Right was susceptible to fewer ideological divisions than the Left. There was, for example, broad agreement between conservatives and Falangists on the necessity for an authoritarian régime. Any disagreements tended to be secondary:

250

The Spanish Civil War

on the precise nature of the authority and on the role of paramilitary organizations. Republican divisions, however, were more fundamental, perhaps because left-wing ideologies are usually more diverse and complex than those of the Right. A three-sided conflict developed between libertarian constitutionalists, authoritarian socialists or Communists, and libertarian anarchists. Any agreement between these was nearly always on a negative basis and was induced by common fear of a Nationalist victory. The National Front possessed greater ideological cohesion, the bond being strengthened by the commitment of the Catholic Church to Franco's victory. Pope Pius XI gave to the Nationalists a crusading zeal, arguing that the enemy had never been so clearly identifiable: 'The first, the greatest and now the general peril, is certainly communism in all its forms and degrees.'[2] The Popular Front, however, was divided between adherents of Marx and Bakunin, or were even, in the case of Azaña and his supporters, admirers of Cromwell. On the whole, the Right were able to implement opportunist policies, and changes of course could be accomplished by its leadership with minimal internal opposition.

The continuity of this leadership was the Right's greatest asset. Franco was not one of the century's great intellects; indeed, Puzzo states that 'His head was a cemetery of dead ideas'.[3] Nevertheless, he was the focal point which the Left lacked. Republican leaders like Azaña, Caballero and Negrin found it impossible to emulate the way in which he held disparate groups together. Franco was expert at rendering disputes superficial and preventing any deeper rift. He gave a meaningful role to all the Nationalist factions, while retaining ultimate power in his own hands. Hence the Carlists were satisfied by the 1938 Clerical Laws and the Falangists by the role assigned to them in propaganda. His first National Council incorporated a complete cross-section of the Right, including twenty Falangists and eight Carlists, and he managed to postpone indefinitely any decision to restore the monarchy, assuming himself Mussolinian powers under the title *Caudillo*. The factions of the Left, by contrast, regarded any attempt to impose a strong leadership as an obstacle to the pursuit of their individual programmes. Hence fighting broke out in Barcelona in 1937 between anarchists, socialists and Communists, while Caballero and Negrin were both ousted from below for attempting to put their own stamp on the Republican war effort.

Aspects of European History 1789–1980

The effectiveness of political organization and the fortunes of war were closely related. The degree of political organization influenced military performance but, equally, military success or failure strengthened or weakened political coalitions. The National Front possessed, in addition to a capacity for greater cohesion, the crucial advantage of extensive assistance from Germany and Italy. German aid was of the highest quality, including 16,000 military advisers, the latest aircraft, and the participation of the Kondor Legion. Italy provided even more assistance: nearly 50,000 troops, 763 aircraft and the use of ninety-one warships. On three occasions all this support was of vital importance to the National Front and held the rebellion together. The first was the transporting of Franco's troops from Morocco to Spain in German and Italian aircraft (1936), an essential preliminary to Franco's conquest of Andalusia. The second was the boost given to Nationalist morale by the sudden inflow of equipment in 1937. The third was the acceleration of Franco's offensive in Catalonia by a final massive consignment of arms and transports in 1939.

The Popular Front, it is true, received much assistance from the Soviet Union and from the thousands of volunteers, from a score of countries, who joined the International Brigades. But it also faced severe disadvantages. Stalin was unwilling to commit Russia too fully; Soviet supply lines were longer and more vulnerable than those of Italy, and Stalin was anxious not to over-commit himself in case he should leave Russia vulnerable to invasion by Germany. It was, however, in its relations with the Western powers that the Republic encountered its greatest obstacles. A series of French governments, headed by Blum and Daladier, carefully avoided involvement in the war for fear that this would destroy the stability achieved by the temporary consensus on the French Left. The British government, meanwhile, established the Non-Intervention Committee in 1936 in an attempt to prevent the provision of either side. Unfortunately, while Britain, the United States and France adhered to the Committee's regulations by not supplying the Republicans, Germany and Italy openly flouted them by assisting Franco. The result was that the transfusions given to the rebel forces were denied to a democratically elected government, a tragic anomaly in international conduct.

*

The Spanish Civil War

The Spanish Civil War reflected the ideological divisions within Europe, and excited intense passions among writers and artists, especially from Malraux, Borkenau, Lorca, Picasso, Cornford, Spender, Auden, Orwell and Hemingway. It also shaped the whole course of international relations between 1936 and 1939 by causing several basic diplomatic trends to converge.

The first of these trends was a growing *rapport* between Europe's two Fascist leaders. Italy had, during the 1920s, been firmly aligned with Britain and France. But a serious rift had opened over the Abyssinian crisis and the application of economic sanctions against Mussolini's régime destroyed the ten-year-old system of collective security. Italian involvement in the Spanish Civil War ensured that this alienation would be permanent and that there would be no reconciliation with the Western democracies. The war, indeed, added a further momentum to this diplomatic change and tipped Italy into the German camp. Hitler skilfully exploited Mussolini's resentment of France and Britain, knowing that the inevitable sense of isolation would result in a major diplomatic realignment. According to Hassell, the German ambassador in Rome: 'The role played by the Spanish conflict as regards Italy's relations with France and England would be similar to that of the Abyssinian conflict, bringing out clearly the actual opposing interests of the Powers. All the more clearly will Italy realize the advisability of confronting the Western Powers shoulder-to-shoulder with Germany.'[4] This expectation was entirely accurate. Ciano, the Italian Foreign Minister, expressed Mussolini's relief at the prospect of a new Italo-German *rapprochement*. 'Italy has broken out of her isolation; she is the centre of the most formidable political and military combination which has ever existed.' This 'combination' included the 'Rome-Berlin Axis', the Anti-Comintern Pact which Italy joined in 1937, and the Pact of Steel, a formal military alliance established in 1939.

Co-operation between Italy and Germany had far-reaching consequences, the most important of which was the removal of Italian constraint on Hitler's policy of expansion in Central Europe. Although he had clearly indicated in *Mein Kampf* that he intended to construct a Greater Germany, Hitler had been impeded by Mussolini's own interest in Austria. Military involvement in Spain, however, absorbed Mussolini's attention, allowing Hitler to carry out, without Italian opposition, the annexation of Austria in 1938.

253

Aspects of European History 1789–1980

Meanwhile, the Spanish Civil War also helped condition the Anglo-French response to Hitler's aggressive diplomacy. Eden, Chamberlain and Daladier all feared that the Spanish Civil War could easily overspill into a European war unless cautious policies were pursued. Eden preferred the principle of containment implicit in the Non-Intervention Committee, while Chamberlain opted for appeasement; both were appalled by the prospect of the damage and loss of life which a mechanized attack would inflict, as had already been demonstrated by the bombing of Guernica and Madrid. These reactions were carefully exploited by Hitler, who had, by the conclusion of the Munich Settlement in 1938, achieved most of his short-term objectives. Anglo-French policies, in turn, provoked a major change in Soviet policy; by 1939 Stalin had decided to abandon the Western powers and seek accommodation with Hitler. (See Chapter 25.) Thus Hitler made enormous gains through the agency of the Spanish Civil War. A new bond existed between Italy and Germany, collective security in the West had been wrecked on the policy of appeasement, and the Franco-Soviet Pact of 1936 was replaced, in August 1939, by the Nazi-Soviet Non-Aggression Pact.

The war also had an important effect on the development of weapons and military strategy. Again, Germany appeared to benefit most directly. Hitler used Spain as a testing ground for the products of his rearmament plan, exploiting especially the opportunity for training German pilots. The German experience derived from the war helped shape the *Blitzkrieg* tactics used against Poland in 1939 and France in 1940, which brought immediate and spectacular success. It is doubtful, however, if Italy received the same benefits. Her commitment was more total than Germany's and the advantages derived from experience were cancelled by the threat of military exhaustion. Mussolini was not unaware that, in 1939, Italy was in no fit state to embark upon another war, and he expressed reservations about Hitler's invasion of Poland. Russia, too, derived no benefit from her involvement in Spain. It could be argued that Russian strategists drew the wrong military conclusions; one of the reasons for the rapidity of the German advance into Russia in 1941 was that Soviet tanks were used, as in Spain, for infantry support, rather than as independent units. If, however, governments erred in their assessment of the war's lessons, many individuals did not. Before 1941 the most active resistance to German occupation came in France and Yugoslavia from partisans, who had served as

The Spanish Civil War

volunteers in the International Brigades.

Finally, the Spanish Civil War further demonstrated the ineffectiveness of the League of Nations as an international organization. The League had already failed to prevent the Japanese occupation of Manchuria, or to secure the withdrawal of Italian troops from Abyssinia. From 1936 onwards, however, the League was even deprived of direct access to major crises. The Non-Intervention Committee, it is true, was inspired by the League Covenant, which insisted that member states should not interfere with each other's internal affairs. But the Committee itself was outside the immediate range of the League's activity. It was a body which reflected the political aims of its founding states and not, as it should have been, an institution with a broader juridical base. Azaña argued, in 1937, that the Committee could in no way substitute for the League, 'for it is not an emanation of that body, it has not the powers of that body, if it is not in conformity . . . with the principles which the Covenant sets forth'.[5] The League was, in effect, cut off from international decision making by *ad hoc* bodies claiming to carry out its principles. The point was later taken by the founders of the United Nations Organization, who took care to ensure that there was a more effective structure of contacts and referral between the different committees and the central institutions.

28

The Contradictions of the Third French Republic 1918–40

This period of French history is often bypassed by the student and general reader, as its fragmented details and enormous complexity make it difficult to generalize about trends and themes. One way out of the problem is to label the period 'France in decline' and then find reasons for French military collapse in 1940. There is much to be said for such an approach but, inevitably, a very one-sided picture will emerge of France between the wars. An alternative method, followed by this chapter, is to highlight the complexities as a series of unresolved contradictions affecting the constitution, the economy, diplomacy and military planning.

*

During the first phase of its existence (1870–1914) the Third Republic had had to struggle to overcome the threats of rightist forces to destroy it. The preoccupation with this had been so intense that the process of contest and reconciliation, essential for the progressive evolution of any political institutions, had been inadequately worked through. The legacy for the second phase (1918–40) was political deadlock. The basic problem, in outline, was a lack of true balance and harmony between the two main components of the Constitution: the legislature and the executive. The 1875 Constitutional Laws had made these of roughly equal status. During the 1870s and 1880s, however, the legislature, or National Assembly, had come into conflict with the executive, or President, and had emerged with greatly enhanced authority. Indeed, the presidency

The Contradictions of the Third French Republic

had been so severely weakened that an alternative form of executive power had to emerge, this time from within the legislature itself. The major executive functions were now assumed by the prime minister and his cabinet colleagues, all of whom were elected members of the National Assembly. At first sight this would seem an ideal compromise, based on the best traditions of parliamentary democracy. But what happened was that the conflict between the Assembly and the President was now replaced by internal strife within the Assembly, between groups which tried to form the country's governments. The result was chronic ministerial instability. Between 1918 and 1939 there were no fewer than thirty-six governments, formed by twenty separate prime ministers; the British record, during the same period, was nine ministries under five prime ministers. Several reasons can be advanced for what amounted to a twenty-two-year crisis.

The first was an example of how the evolution of the French political system had stopped prematurely. Léon Blum, the Socialist leader, pointed to the greatest single deficiency: 'If only there were political parties in France.'[1] To be effective, a legislature must have a well-developed party system, for otherwise, its powers are dissipated in the constant search for a governing majority. In other words, attention comes to be focused on short-term political manoeuvres rather than on long-term legislation.

France did possess the normal range of political ideologies, together with the sort of class divisions which should have promoted party politics. But the major problem was the absence of effective party *organization*. Largely responsible for this was the electoral system, the *scrutin d'arrondissement*, which emphasized the individual candidate rather than any wider loyalties he might have to a party caucus. The result was a somewhat unusual contradiction. France, the most centralized state in Europe, was represented and governed by deputies whose real strength came from narrowly-based provincial support. It is hardly surprising, therefore, that parties were relatively small, and that their leaders found it exceptionally difficult to establish any lasting unity. Blum, for example, had to contend with Pivert and Zyromski, both of whom had strong local support for their virtual secession from the Socialist Party (SFIO) during the late 1930s. The Radical Party, under Herriot and Daladier, was reformed during the 1920s and 1930s in an effort to keep pace with 'changing facts'.[2] Eventually,

257

however, internal divisions reappeared and reforms were pulled apart. The party had too many local interests and conflicting policies; in D. Johnson's phrase, it was 'an amalgam of contradictory ideas'.[3]

Thus the parties were too small and too weak to stand much chance of commanding the sort of parliamentary support that goes with stable government. But was this necessarily a bad thing? Would there not be an inducement to form coalitions and *blocs* which would represent a wider range of views both in the Assembly and among the electorate? Much of the political history of France between the wars concerns the effort to do precisely that. Coalitions of the centrist and right-wing parties included the *Bloc National* formed by Clemenceau in 1919, and the National Union set up by Poincaré in 1926. The Centre and Left combined, under Herriot, in the *Cartel des Gauches* from 1924 and, under Blum, in the Popular Front in 1936. Unfortunately, such attempts to find common ground always failed, for beneath the appearance of co-operation lay another contradiction. On the one hand, the struggle for power continued within the coalitions so that governments rose and fell with undiminished rapidity. On the other hand, this was not, as might be thought, caused by any refusal to compromise on policies, but rather the reverse. All parties had to limit their proposed legislation and abandon any contentious projects of reform. What happened, therefore, was that the parties became less distinctive in their philosophy, but no less competitive in their pursuit of cabinet posts. The paradox applied especially to the Radicals, who supplied ministers for most of the inter-war governments. In the words of a perceptive contemporary, they were reduced to the practice of 'moderation with extreme vehemence'.[1]

The weakness of the party system was made the more serious by the strength of the National Assembly. By the First World War the Assembly had come to dominate the political scene more completely than the 1875 Constitutional Laws had ever envisaged. In the first place, each of its two parts, the Chamber of Deputies and the Senate, had the right to impeach ministers. All governments between the wars faced extensive questioning, and most of them fell as a direct result of the *ordre du jour*, in effect a vote of no confidence. Secondly, the Assembly had developed a series of standing committees which, after the First World War, interfered increasingly in the process of government. The former, says D. Thomson, 'served excellently to sacrifice ministerial stability to parliamentary control over policy'.[4]

The Contradictions of the Third French Republic

Such powers had not, unfortunately, made the Assembly receptive to constitutional reform. The electoral system, for example, was in dire need of change. The introduction of proportional representation might well have tightened the party system by allowing national issues to predominate over local interests. But the Assembly allowed only a limited experiment, and ended even that.

Some constitutions possess a device for emergency government in the event of the normal process seizing up. The French presidency could have fulfilled such a role. Although it had declined dramatically since the days of Macmahon and Grévy, attempts were made by Poincaré from 1913 to give the presidency a meaningful function. The Assembly, however, was anxious to prevent any revival of presidential power, fearing a possible slide into authoritarian government. It therefore voted down all proposals for the election of the president by the public at large, and gave the office to politicians of little standing. Thus, in 1920, the Assembly denied the presidency to Clemenceau, who could have served with distinction as an elder statesman, and gave it to the little known Deschanel, who had to be removed a few months later because of insanity. The presidency had, in effect, become a wasted office and it was unable to take any initiative in reconciling party disputes. This was one more factor which led Reynaud, one-time prime minister, to observe in 1937 that 'the parliamentary régime had failed to function'.[5]

*

Political crises usually coexist with economic problems. In the case of France these were partly brought about by the war, and partly inherited from the period before 1914. The war had affected France more severely than any other Western combatant. She had suffered immense destruction in ten of her north-eastern *départements* and had lost 1.5 million men, including about 30 per cent of her male population between the ages of eighteen and twenty-eight; clearly the latter would have a serious long-term effect by causing a dramatic fall in the future birthrate. Of the inherited problems two were especially serious. France had a much smaller industrial base than her western competitors (in 1913, for example, she was producing only about one-seventh as much coal as Germany). Future expansion would therefore be much more difficult, and would have to be accompanied by extensive modernization. Secondly, the fiscal system was one of the most antiquated in Europe, having changed hardly at all since the days of the Revolution. Many historians have pointed to the selfishness of the wealthy classes and to the ridiculously unfair system of extracting revenue which actually prevented the introduction of income tax until 1920. In 1918, therefore, France faced the double task of reconstruction and renovation. All attention, however, was directed to the former, in the confident expectation that the latter would inevitably follow. Enormous hope was pinned to the reparations which were to be taken from Germany. Not only would these pay for making good the war damage, they would also make possible the modernization of industry, and the adjustment of the whole economy to twentieth-century conditions. France, therefore, suffered a profound psychological shock once it became apparent that these reparations were smaller than had been expected, that they were to spread over a long period, and that they were extremely difficult to enforce.

The first lesson of the early 1920s, therefore, was that there was no straightforward formula for economic recovery or growth. In fact, France faced serious inflation, industrial stagnation and a permanent shortage of revenue which made her social services among the most primitive in Europe. Government attempts to deal with these problems were, for two reasons, cautious and unadventurous. First, no minister could afford to antagonize the bankers or the wealthy sections of the community by proposing extensive fiscal reform, for in the indignant outcry among many deputies and senators, it would undoubtedly be toppled. Second, France was, as yet, completely uninfluenced by recent and progressive economic theory; Keynes, for example, was to make no impact at all. Hence French economists considered it the government's function not to push the economy along, but only to create the environment for natural economic growth. During the late 1920s and early 1930s governments attached overriding importance to a strong currency in the belief that inflation was the worst enemy to economic stability. Thus there was an obsessive determination never to repeat the 1928 devaluation of the franc. By 1931, in fact, industry had picked up, and general economic revival seemed to be indicated by the accumulation of the largest gold reserves anywhere in the world, outside the United States. A strong currency backed by international confidence – this, according to official thought, was a guarantee against future crisis.

Then came a major contradiction. For a while, the strength of the

The Contradictions of the Third French Republic

franc and the huge gold reserves appeared to shield France from the impact of the Great Depression which had hit the rest of the industrialized world by 1931. But, in reality, great damage was to be done by the government's determination to underpin the value of the franc. In the first place, the arrival of the Depression was merely delayed, so that France suffered the worst effects just as other countries were beginning to recover. Secondly, the government made matters far worse by following a policy of savage deflation in order to save the franc from sinking in value, even though governments elsewhere had decided to leave the gold standard and let their national currencies find their own levels. The parties of the French Centre and Right were the victims of defective logic. Deflationary policies, they argued, had protected France for three years against the Depression. Now they must be intensified to push France out of the Depression. What such views failed to realize was that France had been less immediately affected by the Depression not because of the strong franc, but because she had been less heavily industrialized and more self-sufficient than most of the other major economies. Far from being a shield against Depression, deflation exerted a powerful drag against recovery. This was emphasized by the Left, which had the chance to remedy matters when the Popular Front came to power in 1936. Unfortunately, the sudden switch to reflation, government spending and higher wages proved too sudden and only brought further chaos It was not until 1938 that the French economy could really be considered to be on the mend, by which time Britain, the United States and, more ominously, Germany, had widened the gap of industrial production. Compared with these countries, France was now worse off than she had been in 1928.

*

French foreign policy had, since the 1870s and 1880s, been based on avoiding isolation and on forming against Germany alliances with states in Western and Eastern Europe. Unfortunately, such connections proved dangerously unstable between the wars. France's wartime allies in the West both wanted to avoid further European commitments once Germany had been defeated; hence the United States withdrew from the League of Nations into voluntary isolation, while Britain refused to ratify the Geneva Protocol and officially denounced the French invasion of the Ruhr (1923). During the 1930s the British government set the precedent for appeasement, a policy which France had no alternative but to follow. One by one the clauses in the Treaty of Versailles, intended to safeguard France and Belgium, were torn up by Hitler as it became evident that Baldwin and Chamberlain were not prepared to risk war to help France enforce them. Germany proceeded to rearm in 1935, occupied the Rhineland in 1936 and expanded territorially from 1938.

French connections with Eastern Europe proved no more profitable in the long run. The Bolshevik Revolution and Lenin's repudiation of all debts to France caused the French government to abandon the once invaluable Russian alliance. Instead, alliances were built up with the smaller Eastern European states, including Poland (1921 and 1925), Czechoslovakia (1925) and Yugoslavia (1927). But this was a poor substitute for the support of a single major power. Then, during the 1930s, successive French governments found themselves confronted by an impossible dilemma. At the very time that she was being forced on to the defensive by a revived Germany, France was also faced with the appalling prospect of having to contemplate assisting her client states in the East against Hitler. Far from distracting Germany, therefore, the French system looked like draining France. There was one possible solution – reconciliation with Russia. But even the 1935 Franco-Russian Alliance fell apart. Paradoxically, the connection with Russia weakened France still further. Stalin suspected that France expected the Soviet Union to fulfil the role of containing Germany in the East without any corresponding French effort from the West. He watched with alarm as Daladier, conscious of France's vulnerability to German attack, conspired with Chamberlain to abandon Czechoslovakia in 1938. Convinced that the French Alliance offered Russia nothing, he compounded French insecurity by seeking accommodation with Germany instead. By 1939 France had been through the motions of concluding alliances with every state of significance in Eastern Europe and yet had emerged diplomatically enfeebled and dependent once again on the support of Britain, the very power whose lukewarm attitude in the 1920s had pushed France into this hectic activity in the first place.

Then, at the time of greatest French weakness, there occurred a diplomatic revolution. Both Chamberlain and Daladier reversed their appeasement of Nazi Germany and, in 1939, extended a guarantee of protection to Poland. This policy, although honourable, was suicidal, for Germany was growing stronger by the month in the

The Contradictions of the Third French Republic

West and had no longer anything to fear from the French network of alliances in the East, which had long since collapsed. Above all, France was without the lynchpin of her previous war effort against Germany, the support of Russia. But for this backing in the First World War, France could not have won the Battle of the Marne; and the absence of Russian troops to draw off a large part of the German offensive in 1940 must count as the most important single reason for French defeat then.

There is another irony which highlights the muddle of French diplomacy in the 1930s. Although Germany was considered the major enemy and the most serious potential military threat, the French government gave more attention to Italy and the situation in the Mediterranean, for it was generally assumed that the Rhine would be an area of stalemate and defensive strategy. And yet the latter was the only point at which France could exert any pressure in defence of Poland. It seemed, therefore, that France had recovered an active role at the very time that she had lost the means of fulfilling it.

*

How well equipped was France to fight a war in 1939? It used to be thought that the French armies were overwhelmed by superior German forces. More recent estimates, however, have shown that this was not the case at all. Against the 103 German divisions on the Western Front, France mustered ninety-nine which, of course, were supported by British contingents as well. The Allies had a slight superiority in tanks (3000 against 2700) and a massive advantage in large warships (107 against thirteen). The French were able, in addition, to put up 11,200 artillery pieces against the 7710 German guns. The only real deficiency of the Allies was in airpower, where the *Luftwaffe* had a clear advantage.

On paper, therefore, the combatants were evenly matched. Yet France suffered the most rapid and humiliating defeat in her entire history. This was the more shattering because military preparations had been made by strategists who had for years been convinced that war was inevitable. In retrospect, however, we can see the underlying flaws in strategic thought, a sad counterpart to the failure of French foreign policy.

The expectation of a German invasion was entirely in accord with precedent; after all, France had been attacked through Alsace-Lorraine in 1870, and via Belgium in 1914. It also seemed logical that a country with a population of forty million could not reasonably be expected to do more than fend off a power with sixty-five million people and a stronger industrial base. Common sense, therefore, called for effective defences. What emerged, however, was an inflexible system which proved entirely unable to counter Hitler's revolutionary *Blitzkrieg* tactics. The French General Staff put their entire confidence in the Maginot Line, constructed at great expense between the wars. This symbolized France's commitment to fighting a static war across an extended front – a repetition, in other words, of the 1914–18 struggle which had eventually worn down the superior German war machine. But history did not repeat itself. In 1940 the Germans bypassed the Line and punched a hole into the supposedly impenetrable (and therefore lightly defended) Ardennes, before racing to the Channel ports. The French forces were taken by surprise and were unable to manoeuvre with sufficient speed to plug the gaps. By committing themselves so completely to extended linear defences, the French strategists invited a bold and concentrated German blow on a vulnerable section. It is ironical that one of the most expensive and carefully planned defensive walls in history should also have been one of the most useless.

As we have seen, the French army was by no means short of modern equipment. In fact, French tanks were considered superior in armament and firepower to their German rivals, and a concerted effort had been made during the 1930s to keep them rolling off the assembly lines. And yet there was no attempt to integrate the new technology into revised military thinking. A Committee of Generals made the revealing statement in 1936 that 'it does not believe this technical progress sensibly modifies the essential rules hitherto established in the domain of tactics'.[6] Thus, while German commanders like Guderian were establishing independent and highly manoeuvrable tank units, the French view was still, in the words of Major Laporte, that 'the tank must above all be considered as one of the auxiliaries of the foot soldier'.[6] The result was that the heavier and better constructed French machines were, nevertheless, no match for the lighter and more effectively deployed *Panzer* divisions. Similar ignorance was shown over the destructive potential of the aircraft. While the *Luftwaffe* were experimenting, at the expense of Spanish civilians, with *Stuka* dive-bombers, and were devising a strategy to gain control of the air, the French Commander-in-Chief, General Gamelin, believed that 'There is no such thing as an aerial

The Contradictions of the Third French Republic

battle. There is only the battle on the ground'.[6] In view of what happened from 1940 onwards, this must rank as one of modern history's more remarkable statements. If any single factor can be said to have destroyed the morale of the French army in July 1940, it was surely the ease with which the *Luftwaffe* controlled the skies over France.

One of the main defects of the administration was its complexity; much the same can be said of the structure of command within the army. France had her fair share of military statesmen, Weygand and then Gamelin replacing First World War leaders like Joffre, Foch and Pétain. But they were often cut off from their immediate subordinates. Gamelin was desperately anxious to direct personally all aspects of military strategy but, because of his inefficient delegation of duties, ended up controlling very little. This is what de Gaulle had in mind when he referred to Gamelin's headquarters as 'his ivory tower at Vincennes'.

*

Some contemporaries thought that the collapse of France was due to the loss of her previous vitality and the transformation of strength into weakness. Hence Pétain blamed 'our moral laxness', while an English observer considered the Third Republic 'graft-ridden, incompetent, Communistic and corrupt'. The real problem, however, was that France lacked internal harmony because many of its strongest forces were turned inwards. Hence, in the words of Paul Guerin in 1939: 'The régime is paradoxical, conservative in purpose, revolutionary at heart, extremist and idealist in its programmes, opportunist and moderate in its actions.'[7]

29

The Soviet Economy 1917–80

On assuming power in October 1917, the Bolsheviks intended to redirect the Russian economy as quickly as possible according to Marxist principles. The 1918 Constitution of the RSFSR (Russian Socialist Federated Soviet Republic) advanced 'the fundamental aim of abolishing all exploitation of man by man, of eliminating completely the division of society into classes'.[1] Lenin hoped to promote harmony between the industrial and agricultural sectors and exploit all the most modern techniques: 'Communism is the Soviet power plus the electrification of the whole country.' He also intended to promote state ownership through all levels of industry and agriculture, referring, for example, to collectivization as the 'indispensable theoretical truth'.[2]

It soon became obvious, however, that the disturbed time between 1917 and 1929 made impossible any systematic application of Marxist theories. Instead, Lenin's economic policy was based on trial and error, with a changeable mixture of ideology and pragmatism.

At first the emphasis was on caution, as Lenin concentrated on establishing the Bolsheviks politically. Hence the new régime was relatively lenient towards private enterprise in both industry and agriculture. By the middle of 1918 only the banks, foreign trade, and strategic industries like armaments works, had been nationalized. The Decree of November 1917 had even restricted the right of workers on factory committees to representation only, and specifically prevented any contribution to decision making. The peasants

266

The Soviet Economy 1917–80

were allowed considerable concessions. Lenin had allowed them to seize the estates of the nobility in the hope of gaining their political support for the whole Bolshevik programme. Once the estates had changed hands there was no question of the peasantry agreeing to voluntary collectivization. They were fiercely determined to keep possession of their small individual holdings. Lenin realized that he would have to consolidate his own political power before he tried to change their minds.

By the middle of 1918 the Bolsheviks considered that conditions had changed sufficiently to warrant a new approach. Because of the threats of invasion and counter-revolution, Lenin now emphasized the need to tighten up internally. The result, between 1918 and 1921, was the policy of War Communism. This was basically an attempt to replace the free market by state control over all forms of production and distribution. The main measures included the requisitioning of grain to supply the cities, the abolition of banks and credit, the nationalization of all industries, and the allocation of special production targets. This was the first attempt at a state-controlled economy, but it was carried out with inadequate planning and few directives. It resulted in confusion and resistance from the population, especially the peasantry. It also caused a decline in initiative and output; industry, for example, managed in 1921 to reach only 13 per cent of the production level of 1914. Worse still, the Bolsheviks were threatened with widespread disobedience; the 1921 Kronstadt Revolt was based on a demand for 'Soviets without Communists'. Complete failure was imminent. Not only had total state control been ineffectual, it had actually impeded the Bolshevik war effort and clearly had to be reversed. Lenin excused his failure by explaining that the policy had been forced on Russia 'by war and ruin' as 'a temporary measure'.[3]

His strategic withdrawal took the form of the New Economic Policy, announced in 1921. Lenin now emphasized the scale of the problem in moving Russia along the road to socialism, arguing that the time span should be measured not by years but by decades. 'Our poverty and ruin are so great that we cannot *at one stroke* restore full-scale factory, state, socialist production.'[4] To think only in ideological terms was naïve. 'If certain communists were inclined to think it possible in three years to transform the whole economic foundation, to change the very roots of agriculture, they were certainly dreamers.'[5] The basic strategy was now to restore to the economy a degree of capitalism and private enterprise, although no departure was to be allowed from the strict party control over political institutions. About 91 per cent of industrial enterprises were returned to private ownership or trusts, the currency was restored, and requisitioning was replaced by new regulations allowing the peasantry to dispose freely of their surplus produce on payment of a tax. Some concessions were made to socialist principles: every effort was to be made to persuade the peasantry to move away from their obsession with private ownership, and collective farms and co-operatives were to be promoted. The keynote, however, was to be patience.

The early results were disappointing, as the economy experienced further setbacks with a famine in 1921–2 and a financial crisis in 1923. By 1928, however, recovery was substantial. More food was available for the cities, and industrial production had increased steadily: 35.5 million tons of coal were mined in that year, compared with 29.1 million in 1913. But, like all strategic compromises, the New Economic Policy posed the problem of what course was to be followed in the long term.

*

In fact, from the earliest stages of the NEP, the Bolsheviks were divided over the best means of promoting economic growth. During the first half of the 1920s the so-called 'rightists', under Bukharin, argued that the NEP should be maintained for the foreseeable future. The key to future growth was improvements in agriculture; this meant that socialism should be introduced slowly and steadily – 'at the speed of the peasant nag'.[6] The peasantry should be given strong incentives to produce more. 'We have to tell the whole peasantry, and all its strata: "get rich, accumulate, develop your economy".'[7] The 'leftists', who included Trotsky and Preobrazhensky, disagreed with Bukharin's emphasis on agriculture, caution and personal incentives. Preobrazhensky argued that 'We won't be given much time to build',[8] the hostile capitalist states would see to that. To promote private enterprise among the peasantry was asking for trouble because this would inevitably lead to a new bourgeoisie in the form of wealthy peasants, of *kulaks*. These *kulaks* would become hostile to the whole ethos of the Communist régime, and could be expected to identify with 'world

The Soviet Economy 1917–80

capital'. The only strategy to follow, therefore, was to force the pace of industrialization. This would, within a short period, give Russia the means of defending herself against the West and, since all the resources of agriculture could be used by the state to assist the process, the *kulak* class would be eliminated. Far from wishing to prolong the NEP, therefore, the 'leftists' hoped to end it as quickly as possible and return to a more effectively planned form of war Communism.

The man who eventually dictated the course to be followed appeared, during the 1920s, to be inconsistent in his ideas. At first Stalin used Bukharin's ideas to attack the leftists, then, having safely disposed of Trotsky and Preobrazhensky, he turned on Bukharin. It is clear that Stalin's whole approach was based on *political* considerations and that what interested him most was the best means of consolidating his own power. Only gradually did he put together an economic strategy, and even this did not develop any concrete form until after the grain shortage of 1928.[9] From 1929, however, Stalin became more explicit about his economic aims. In the first place, the whole base of the Soviet economy had to be transformed in order to meet the threat of foreign invasion. Only the leadership could design the institutions to achieve this, which fitted in well with Stalin's search for personal power. The whole process would be subsidized by agriculture, which would be reorganized on a collective basis. Although he did not acknowledge it, Stalin had taken over Preobrazhensky's ideas. The main difference was that he intended to go to greater lengths in implementing them.

His instruments were a series of Five Year Plans, the targets for which were devised by Gosplan, with the personal intervention of Stalin himself. The first Five Year Plan (1928–33), which overlapped the collectivization of agriculture, boosted heavy industry. The second (1933–8) extended heavy industry to previously undeveloped areas like the Caucasus and Siberia and also improved major canal and rail networks. The third Plan, launched in 1938, concentrated mainly on the development of strategic industries and armaments. All the Plans were accompanied by state coercion. Stalin revived the *Cheka*, in the form of the OGPU and then the NKVD, dispatched 'dekulakization squads' to overcome peasant resistance to collective farming, reduced trade unions to the status of 'Party transmission belts to the masses', and conducted the most extensive political purges in European history.

269

Aspects of European History 1789–1980

There has been some controversy over the impact of such changes. Stalin's measures were initially praised by Soviet historians and condemned by the West, but recently, as one writer points out, 'the roles are to some extent being reversed'.[10] It is certainly possible to advance both positive and negative arguments.

Stalin's positive achievement was concerned almost entirely with heavy industry. Between 1928 and 1941 steel and coal production increased fourfold and sixfold respectively and, by 1937, the Soviet Union had become the world's second largest manufacturer of heavy vehicles. Even a strong critic of Soviet economic measures, L. Pietromarchi, argues that the credit for setting up the Soviet industrial base must go to Stalin. Indeed, Stalin made three main contributions. First, he accelerated the whole process, breaking away from the much more cautious mentality of Bukharin and perhaps even of Lenin. Second, he extended the range of industrialization by equipping Siberia with plants and factories; these were to be the most important factor in the Russian fight for survival against the Nazis after 1941. Third, he found the resources to transform Russia's economic base without having to seek Western investment. In using agriculture to subsidize industry and squeezing every drop of money out of the ordinary consumer, Stalin devised a ruthless but effective method of accumulating capital.

On the other hand, Stalin's industrial measures are open to extensive criticism. There is evidence that he exaggerated Russia's industrial deficiency in 1929. The Tsars had developed a considerable industrial capacity, based on five main centres: Moscow (textiles), Petrograd (heavy industry), the Donetz region (coalfields), Baku (oil) and the Ukraine (iron and steel).[11] In a sense, the spadework had already been done, so that it is not altogether surprising that Stalin should have achieved such rapid results. He was also reluctant to acknowledge that most of his plans for widespread electrification and the development of Siberia were inherited from Lenin. At times Stalin became so obsessed with the statistics of production that some of the advances were cosmetic. Worst of all was the severe deprivation which accompanied industrial growth. Russia was unique in European economic history in experiencing an industrial revolution without corresponding improvements in the quality of life of the inhabitants. The serious shortage of consumer goods of all types was reflected in a popular riddle of the time: 'Why were Adam and Eve like Soviet citizens? Because they lived in

The Soviet Economy 1917–80

Paradise and had nothing to wear.'

The case against Stalin's agricultural measures is even more substantial. In the first place, he launched collective farming with inadequate information and statistics. He then sought to absolve himself from responsibility for the ensuing chaos by blaming local officials for being over-zealous. Secondly, collectivization policies inflicted appalling suffering on the peasantry, both through the activities of the dekulakization squads and the confiscation of grain supplies by the state. It is hardly surprising that the early 1930s should have seen massive resistance from the peasantry, who destroyed up to 50 per cent of the grain crop, 50 per cent of the total number of horses and 66 per cent of the sheep and goats. There was a greater threat of rebellion during the 1930s than there had ever been in the 1920s. Many peasants were even prepared to welcome the Germans in 1941, until they discovered that Hitler's plans for them were even nastier than Stalin's. Finally, Stalin could be charged with having set back agricultural production by twenty-five years, and with having set a dreadful precedent for the future.

The special problems following the Second World War make it difficult to integrate the last phase of Stalin's rule (1945–53) with the preceding period. Priority had to be given to reconstruction, with the emphasis again being placed on heavy industry. In the fourth and fifth Five Year Plans the consumer continued to suffer, partly because of post-war conditions, and partly because Stalin was determined not to weaken his resolve. Agriculture was reorganized into new collectives, but production remained as low as ever. By 1953 the total agricultural production was only 10 per cent more than it had been in 1914, while the number of livestock was 10 per cent down.

Referring to Russia's historically agricultural base, Stalin had once claimed that the country was 'walking on two unequal legs'.[9] By 1953 he had made the USSR the world's second industrial power, but the strengthening of this leg had been accomplished by crippling the other.

*

Considerable efforts were made after 1953 to redress the balance and to develop both sectors of the economy. At the same time, policies became more pragmatic and varied from one period to another. The main reason for this was the end of the long era of monolithic

271

dictatorship. Stalin's successors (Malenkov until 1955, Khruschev until 1964, and the collective leadership of Brezhnev and Kosygin after 1964) possessed fewer powers and took care to avoid the extremes of Stalinist coercion.

The strongest area of the Soviet economy was still heavy industry. No real alteration of Stalin's emphasis was envisaged except, for a short period, by Malenkov, who hoped to promote the consumer industries. Khruschev, however, pulled the economy back on course after Malenkov had been off-loaded as a 'deviationist'. Production figures were as impressive as ever and, by the 1960s, the Soviet Union led the world in hydro-electric schemes and in heavy engineering, especially in turbines. It also had the capacity to sustain an enormous conventional war machine and to deploy nuclear weapons. By the 1970s it had achieved parity with the United States in the military and heavy industrial spheres.

An examination of the whole range of Soviet industry, however, reveals three problems. The first is the complexity and sometimes the inefficiency of its organization. Soviet leaders were always conscious of this and, from time to time, tried to alter the structure. Khrushchev, for example, scrapped the various ministries in 1957 and substituted 105 regional economic councils. But Brezhnev and Kosygin considered these inadequate and so devised another system. This, too, proved less than fully efficient as a vehicle for state planning. The second problem was that industrial growth still penalized the consumer. Malenkov tried to give a boost to light industry, but Khrushchev postponed any further improvements until the ill-fated Five Year Plan of 1956. Brezhnev and Kosygin did rather more; the Five Year Plan of 1971–5 gave priority to consumer industries. There remained, however, a large gap in consumer goods between the Soviet Union on the one hand and the West, or even the rest of Eastern Europe, on the other. The third snag was that industry generally became, during the 1960s and 1970s more and more dependent on advanced technology. In the 'high priority' areas like weapons and space research, Soviet technology was well-advanced, but during the 1970s the West opened up a lead in electronics and computers,[12] especially where these were related to the consumer market.

Agriculture, since the death of Stalin, experienced a major change of policy. It was no longer considered merely as a means to subsidize industrial growth and was given recognition in its own right.

The Soviet Economy 1917–80

Khrushchev gave it particular attention as, indeed, he had strong personal connections with agriculture. He increased investment and promoted the exploitation of virgin lands and the planting of alternative crops like maize. He also guaranteed higher prices and wages and encouraged a rapid increase in the output of meat and milk. The result, between 1953 and 1958, was a period of unprecedented agricultural growth, which raised hopes of overtaking the West. But this was to prove only a temporary phenomenon and problems re-emerged between 1959 and 1963. The exploitation of the virgin lands had been unbalanced, leading to widespread soil erosion; maize had been imposed, by central decision, on many areas for which it was quite inappropriate; and meat production had outstripped the availability of animal feed, necessitating the slaughter of thirty million out of seventy million pigs. To make matters worse, there was a harvest failure in 1963. Khrushchev's reputation had been so badly damaged by the slide that he was edged out of power in 1964. Brezhnev and Kosygin tried to force recovery by pouring in new investment, estimated as one-quarter of the total capital available in the eighth and ninth Five Year Plans (1966–75). The results were varied, with an apparent alternation between good years (1968, 1970 and 1973) and bad ones (especially 1972).

Western observers agreed that agriculture was consistently the weakest area of the Soviet economy and that comparisons with the United States were distinctly unfavourable. In the 1960s the United States had two-thirds of the Soviet cultivated area and one-fifth of the Soviet labour force, yet produced about three-fifths more.[13] It was also estimated that about five times as much investment had to be put into Soviet agriculture to achieve a return comparable to the United States.[14] The Soviet leadership saw the solution in technical developments and the improvement of collective and state farms. American opinion, however, questioned whether this policy could work satisfactorily. State control had clearly produced results in industry but, it was argued, agriculture is a different matter. There is always a greater need for individual judgement in the field than on the assembly line. It is also more difficult to direct agriculture efficiently from the centre because local peculiarities make it impossible to standardize production on anything like the same scale as in industry. Naturally, such an interpretation was rejected by the Soviet leadership, not least because any extensive decentralization would mean a step backwards towards the NEP.

Solutions, therefore, would have to be sought within the existing ideological framework.

In other ways, the leadership proved more adaptable. One of the major changes after 1963 was in the Soviet attitude towards the West. Stalin had always maintained a policy of strict isolation, whereas Brezhnev and Kosygin specifically sought economic contacts with the West. A change in United States policy made it possible for the West to reciprocate. Originally, American Presidents saw any large-scale commercial contacts with the Eastern *bloc* as a means of helping the Soviet advance towards industrial and military parity with the United States. By the late 1960s, however, it was obvious that this parity would soon be achieved anyway and that economic contacts would make little difference.[15] The commercial agreements which followed Nixon's visit to Moscow in 1972 were of particular importance to two areas. First, the consumer could be protected against the results of bad harvests by huge imports of grain from North America – a sharp contrast with the indifference of Stalin's régime to the suffering caused by shortages. Second, the purchase of computers and electronic technology made up for some of the deficiencies in Soviet industry.[16] Such contacts could not, however, eliminate the under-lying structural weaknesses of the Soviet economy. These were to become so serious during the next decade that Gorbachev, who came to power in 1985, initiated a policy of reforming the whole political and economic system through extensive restructuring, or 'perestroika'. He concentrated especially on addressing the inefficiencies of central planning and injecting some of the principles of the market economy. In the process, he was obliged to abandon some of the policies of Stalin, Khrushchev and Brezhnev and to seek a much closer relationship with the West.

30
The Defeat of Nazi Germany

By June 1940 Hitler had conquered a greater area of Europe than any other leader in history. Under direct Nazi rule lay Poland, Slovakia, Norway, Denmark, the Benelux countries and France. Bohemia and Austria had become provinces of the Reich; while Italy, Hungary and Romania were military allies. Hitler had also demonstrated the effectiveness of the revolutionary *Blitzkrieg* and had modified the old Schlieffen Plan to achieve the stunning victory which had eluded the German High Command in 1914.

Yet, in under five years, the Third Reich lay in ruins and German military paramountcy had been destroyed. The period from 1941 onwards is a classic example of the misuse of a nation's resources in the pursuit of unrealistic and inappropriate policies. This chapter will concentrate particularly on Hitler's strategic and military errors, and upon the huge industrial disparity between Germany on the one hand, and the two major Allied powers on the other.

*

Although his war designs succeeded brilliantly against Poland and France, Hitler badly mismanaged the conflict against Britain, the Soviet Union and the United States.

Britain he had never regarded as a total enemy; indeed, in his *Secret Book*, he had referred to Britain as 'Germany's natural friend'. Consequently, he was always prepared to seek reconciliation, even 'on the basis of partitioning the world'.[1] His early strategy was based on forcing Britain back into neutrality, and he made the grave blunder of not committing Germany's total military capacity in 1940 to the invasion of Britain. Britain's survival was the first step towards the ultimate decline of Hitler's Reich. Alone, she did not possess the military or industrial capacity to defeat Germany. She was the wrong type of power in that her real strength was maritime rather than continental. But, as during the Napoleonic Wars, this gave her the potential for prolonged resistance. Churchill's crucial role was to keep the war going in the West and to extend the conflict to the periphery, especially North Africa and the Atlantic. Hitler made some effort to come to terms with this strategy, including an unsuccessful attempt to engage Franco's Spain in an offensive against Gibraltar. But he reacted with little interest to Admiral Raeder's proposals for breaking British contacts with the Empire and for an all-out campaign against Malta, Suez and North Africa. He also rejected Raeder's advice that further projects in the East should be postponed to ensure the mobilization of all Germany's resources for the struggle in the West. The effect of Britain's role in the war gradually became more serious as German commitments in North Africa and, after 1942, in Italy, weakened the *Wehrmacht's* offensive in Russia. Britain also acted as a stepping-stone for the United States' bombing attacks on Germany as well as a base for the combined Allied invasion of Normandy in 1944.

The invasion of Russia (1941) was undoubtedly the major mistake of Hitler's career, the decision being taken against the advice of the General Staff who stressed that country's hostile geography and climate. It appears, however, that Hitler was immovably committed to his ultimate design which would simultaneously give the Aryan race its promised *Lebensraum* and eradicate the centre of European Jewry and international Bolshevism. His strategic justification was more rational but no less questionable. He argued, for example, that the invasion of Russia would isolate Britain and that 'if Russia is destroyed, Britain's last hope will be shattered'.[2] This, however, directly contravened his opinion of November 1939 that 'We can oppose Russia only when we are free in the West'.[3] His premature invasion undid all the gains of the Nazi-Soviet Non-Aggression Pact, and brought about the very problem which much of his diplomacy in the 1930s had sought to avoid, a war involving Germany against major powers on two fronts. His claim that he had to have direct access to the oil supplies of the Caspian Sea area was also unconvincing, for Stalin had shown no signs of interfering with

The Defeat of Nazi Germany

the flow of fuel and essential minerals. The effect of 'Operation Barbarossa' was to commit Germany to war with a power which was three times her size in population, eighty times as large in area, and of much greater industrial capacity. It is hardly surprising that the major military setbacks experienced by the *Wehrmacht* occurred in Russia. These, in turn, took the pressure off Britain and greatly assisted the latter's peripheral war effort in the Mediterranean and North Africa.

Hitler showed his greatest ignorance over the United States, on which he declared war in 1941. He was convinced that her ethnic and racial mixture made America a degenerate power and that, as a result, she was 'permanently on the brink of revolution'.[4] He also assumed that the US war effort would be confined to the Pacific in a struggle which the Japanese were bound to win. Here Hitler made another great mistake. In January 1942 Roosevelt pledged to Churchill that he would give priority to the defeat of Germany, his reasoning being that American concentration on Japan might result in a Nazi victory over Russia and Britain. The Western Allies also agreed to co-ordinate their strategy and High Commands in the Combined Chiefs-of-Staffs Committee: in effect, they fought the war as one power, and achieved a degree of unity which never existed between Hitler, Mussolini and Tojo. The entry of the United States reactivated the war in the West, and made possible a more direct southern strategy which included the invasion of Italy in 1943. Throughout 1943 and 1944 Germany also suffered numerous bombing raids which demonstrated, in Roosevelt's words, that Hitler's 'fortress Europe' was a fortress 'without a roof'. Meanwhile, Hitler was unable to attack the United States directly, which meant American industrial output was never disrupted by air-raids. The climax of the Anglo-American war effort came with the opening of the Western Front in France in 1944. Instead of remaining an anvil for the Russian hammer, the Western powers had now become a hammer in their own right.

Hitler's mistakes of strategy were monumental. This was characteristic of a mind which encompassed the extremes of bold generalization and obsession with finicky detail, but which was guided by intuition rather than reason. After his initial successes in 1939 and 1940, Hitler became over-confident, developing, in Jödl's words, an 'almost mystical conviction of his own infallibility as leader of the nation and of the war'.[5] Manstein criticized his lack of

277

method in similar terms: 'Ultimately, to the concept of the art of war, he opposed that of crude force, and the full effectiveness of this force was supposed to be guaranteed by the strength of will behind it.'[6] His conduct of military operations showed the same shortcomings. Convinced that 'the fate of the Reich depends only on me',[7] he destroyed any independence left to his commanders by assuming complete control of the *Wehrmacht* in December 1941. Since he had no personal experience of military command, he possessed no real understanding of the problems confronting generals on the front, and only impeded their initiative by refusing to allow them to take emergency measures without his permission.

Several examples can be given of Hitler's weakness as a military leader. The first was his total mismanagement of the campaign against Britain in 1940 and 1941. Goering had promised the destruction of British air defences within four days and conditions which would be ideal for invasion within four weeks. The *Luftwaffe*, however, was diverted from destroying air bases to bombing cities and industrial targets, with the result that the RAF survived what could have been a sudden and crushing blow. Although outnumbered numerically, the RAF gradually gained the ascendancy, largely through the superior training of its pilots, the greater manoeuvrability of British fighters like the *Spitfire* and *Hurricane*, and the early use of radar as a warning system. Hitler was unable to use the *Luftwaffe* to its greatest effect, mainly because it had been designed to back up ground forces in a *Blitzkrieg* operation rather than to fight as an independent unit of command. He also failed to learn from his mistakes and to devote his attention to redesigning the *Luftwaffe* and eliminating the British scientific lead. Instead, he lost interest in the unfamiliar theatre of aerial warfare and returned to his tested ground tactics.

But the Russian campaign also revealed the negative qualities of Hitler's military command. He was utterly convinced that 'Operation Barbarossa' would be concluded before the end of 1941, for 'we have only to kick in the door and the whole rotten structure will come crashing down'.[8] Consequently, German troops were not even equipped with winter uniforms, despite the delay in launching the campaign caused by the necessity of dealing with the trouble in the Balkans in the summer of 1941. Hitler also changed his mind over the most important objectives to be attained. Originally he emphasized the importance of Leningrad, whereas Brauchitsch,

The Defeat of Nazi Germany

Halder, Book, Guderian and Hoth all urged a massive attack on Moscow. He then switched his attention to the Ukraine and, according to Halder, lost the opportunity of knocking Russia out of the war in 1941 by his inconsistency. The Soviet leadership made full use of the breathing space granted by the reprieve of Moscow, to gather strength and launch a counter attack. In the ensuing battle for Stalingrad, Hitler refused to allow von Paulus to conduct an orderly withdrawal, with the result that Zhukov was able to surround the Sixth Army and force it to surrender in January 1943.

Stalingrad was undoubtedly the turning point of the war. From 1943 onwards Hitler was increasingly on the defensive, a role which he found distasteful and difficult. Instead of an orderly contraction of all his front lines, he adopted what Schramm has called the 'wave-break doctrine', whereby positions had to be held even after the enemy had swept past and isolated them. He also placed undue confidence in inadequate defences like the 'Atlantic Wall', despite the misgivings frequently voiced by commanders on the spot, like von Rundstedt. By 1945 German units were spread all over Europe, which meant that the Reich was under-defended against invasion by Soviet, American and British troops. The reason for this strange policy is that Hitler never lost hope of victory, hoping to switch from defence to attack at the first favourable opportunity; thus his advance positions had to be maintained whatever the cost. He likened his situation to that of Frederick the Great in 1761, and awaited the deliverance which, he felt, would follow the inevitable break-up of the Alliance opposing him. He told his generals in 1944: 'All of the coalitions in history have disintegrated sooner or later. The only thing is to wait for the right moment.'[9] In the meantime, he hoped to grind his enemies down by a war of attrition. These, however, were policies born of desperation and delusion. The Soviet Union and the Western Allies did not allow their differences to stand in the way of crushing the Third Reich, whilst attrition proved far more damaging to the defenders than to the invaders.

*

The Second World War was primarily a mechanized war. Although he controlled the finest war machine in Europe in 1939 and 1940, Hitler lost the advantage from 1941 onwards as Germany faced the two greatest industrial powers in history.

The Soviet Union had been caught by surprise by 'Operation

279

Barbarossa' in 1941, but her subsequent recovery owed much to Stalin's economic policies since 1929. The Five Year Plans had transformed Russia's economic base, and had established the plant for sustained industrial production. The transition to a wartime economy was accomplished with remarkable speed. The commissariats of armaments supervised the switch to the mass production of tanks and aircraft in factories which had been removed from European Russia and reassembled, beyond the range of the *Luftwaffe*, in the Urals, Kazakhstan, Western Siberia and Central Asia. The constant supply of war material to the Red Army from 1942 onwards meant that the *Wehrmacht* had to fight against increasing odds. Hence Tippelskirch admitted: 'After 1943 it was no longer possible to upset the enemy's absolute control in the air over the regions of military operations.'[10] The same applied to ground equipment; Soviet tanks had an unassailable numerical advantage at the Battle of Kursk, and Guderian came to the conclusion that the Russian KV and T–34 tanks were superior in performance to the German equivalents. Soviet field artillery was also more advanced, and included the BM–13 rockets (or *Katyusha*) which were employed with devastating results at Stalingrad and later at Berlin. Altogether, the Soviet Union acquired an unassailable lead in the armaments race, as the total production figures for 1942 indicate:

	USSR	Germany
Tanks	24,700	9,300
Aircraft	25,400	14,700
Artillery	127,000	12,000

Of the two totalitarian ideologies, Communism proved more adept than National Socialism at regulating all areas of the economy and subordinating them to the quest for military victory. At no stage did Nazi Germany even approach the level of Soviet military expenditure which amounted to 57 per cent of the 1942 budget.

The transformation of the American economy to wartime production followed an entirely different pattern. Indeed, Goering doubted whether it could be accomplished at all, adding: 'The Americans can't build planes, only ice boxes and razor blades.' By 1941, however, the assembly-line techniques which had produced a constant flow of consumer goods, had been regeared for the manufacture of weapons. This transition was accomplished not by Five

The Defeat of Nazi Germany

Year Plans, but by Roosevelt's Lend-Lease policy. The intention had been to subsidize American armaments industries in order to provide assistance to any country whose integrity was considered vital to that of the United States. Thus, by the time she had entered the war, America had already become the 'arsenal of democracy' and her armaments production soon exceeded that of all the Axis powers together. Between 1940 and 1945 American factories and plans manufactured 300,000 aircraft, 86,000 tanks and 71,000 naval ships. During the course of 1942 German aircraft production was only thirty-one per cent of that of the United States, a factor which gave the Allies air superiority over Germany from 1943 onwards.

The German economy, meanwhile, faced increasing difficulties. Although it had been converted to a war footing by the Four Year Plan of 1936, it relied essentially on plundering other countries rather than on making maximum use of domestic resources. It is true that the German people experienced none of the hardships of the Russians under Stalin's Five Year Plans, but the cost was that the German economy was never intensively exploited until it was too late. Speer, Hitler's Armaments Minister, maintained that the *Wehrmacht* could have been twice as well supplied in 1941, and he constantly criticized the reluctance of Nazi officialdom to employ German women in munitions factories as a means of releasing up to three million men for active service. Germany's dependence on foreign resources and labour was partly responsible for the rapidity of her defeat from 1943 onwards. Deprived by Zhukov's victories of her *Lebensraum* in the East, she could not hope to match the resources and armaments of the two industrial giants who were inexorably rolling back her frontiers.

31

The Cold War to 1980

'Cold War' is a term used to describe the confrontation of the two power *blocs* organized into defensive pacts, armed with nuclear weapons and guarding spheres of influence. This rivalry took shape during the Second World War, or more specifically, with the involvement of the Soviet Union and the United States. At first there was co-operation between Russia and the West against a common enemy. Churchill, for example, said in June 1941: 'The Russian danger is our danger.'[1] There was a possibility of permanent reconciliation and Roosevelt, in particular, favoured institutional experiments and the construction of the United Nations Organizations on the foundations of the wartime Alliance. Gradually, however, a darker side emerged, as Russia and the West attached different interpretations to agreements negotiated at wartime conferences like Yalta and Potsdam, or clashed over the treatment of the defeated powers and liberated states. Attitudes hardened, especially when the self-proclaimed moderate Roosevelt was succeeded by Truman, whose tougher policies resembled more closely those of Churchill.

If the Cold War emerged during the last phase of the struggle against Nazi Germany, it had roots which extended back to the second decade of the century. The confrontation of armed alliances was made more intense by the existence of profound and long-standing ideological differences. Trotsky had once personalized the gulf between Russia and the West by calling Lenin and Wilson 'the apocalyptic antipodes of our time'.[2]

The Cold War to 1980

It is customary to see the Cold War as the response of one side to the aggression of the other. This chapter will retain that approach, examining the attitudes of *both* sides. It will concentrate particularly on the long background of mutual distrust, the concern about strategic security, and the different ideas about freedom and democracy. The final section will consider briefly the main developments between 1962 and 1980.

Notwithstanding their temporary co operation during the Second World War, there was deep mistrust between the two sides, based on historical precedent. The Western suspicion of the Soviet Union derived from two sources. The first was a traditional fear of Russian expansionism which the Bolsheviks were suspected of having inherited from the nineteenth century. Hence the French Minister of the Interior, Sarraut, complained in 1927 that 'the leaders of Muscovite Communism hope to bring forth a new imperialism out of some vast Slavic hegemony'.[3] Secondly, the West was profoundly disturbed by the Trotskyist policy of 'worldwide revolution' and the Leninist maxim that ideological differences made conflict inevitable. Despite the threat of Fascism, therefore, there was a marked reluctance to trust Soviet diplomacy during the 1930s. Besides, the Soviet leadership was notorious for its changes of course in foreign policy and seemed, at times, to be blinded by inflexible dogma. Stalin actually believed in the late 1920s and early 1930s that Germany's Social Democrats were, like the Nazis, a manifestation of Fascism. This was hardly likely to inspire confidence in those democracies which possessed moderate socialist political parties. Chamberlain summed up the prevalent view in 1939 when he confessed to 'the most profound distrust of Russia'.[4]

There was no less suspicion on the Soviet side. Western intervention against the new Bolshevik régime in the civil war had come as a savage blow and did much to shape the subsequent view of the West as aggressive and militarist. Western European states were also seen as unreliable diplomatic partners during the 1930s. Litvinov, the Soviet Foreign Minister, observed in 1938 that Britain and France preferred to coexist with Italian Fascism and German Nazism and to make 'endless concessions to them'.[5] He considered the Munich agreement the ultimate folly of appeasement, leaving Russia with no alternative but to make her own arrangements with

283

Germany. Even when the Soviet Union and Western capitalism sank their differences in 1941, Stalin remained convinced that Churchill and Roosevelt were deliberately using the Russian war effort for their own ends. From 1941 onwards, Stalin consistently urged Britain and the United States to open a second Front against Hitler by invading France. He regarded Churchill's 'soft underbelly' strategy against Italy as an easy option for the West and as a means of using up Russian lives. 'All is clear,' Stalin said in August 1942. 'They want us to bleed white in order to dictate to us their terms later on.'[6] When Roosevelt announced that the invasion of France could not take place until 1944, Stalin bitterly reproached his Allies: 'Your decision . . . leaves the Soviet Army, which is fighting not only for its own country, but also for its Allies, to do the job alone.'

Against this atmosphere of mutual recrimination, the Grand Alliance against Hitler can be seen as an artificial and short-term expedient. There was little possibility of a permanent compromise; even before the ashes of the Third Reich had cooled, the Alliance had disintegrated under the impact of strategic rivalries and ideological differences.

*

The major factor in the development of the Cold War was undoubtedly a preoccupation with military security. As a direct result of the war against Germany, both the United States and the Soviet Union projected themselves more forcefully onto the world political and military scene. The former abandoned the isolationism of the inter-war period, while Stalin revised his previous policy of waiting on the sidelines to pick up whatever was left after the 'death struggle' he anticipated between the capitalist countries. Hitler had unwittingly mobilized the two greatest industrial and military giants in history. It is hardly surprising that these superpowers should have turned on each other with a display of power politics on an unprecedented scale.

The confrontation was intensified by the analysis made by each side of the motives and methods of the other. The United States was influenced by detailed theoretical analysis of Soviet diplomacy by experts like G. F. Kennan. Soviet conduct, it was believed, was based on supreme confidence of ultimate victory. Hence 'the Kremlin is under no ideological compulsion to accomplish its purpose in a hurry';[7] it could apply pressure wherever possible, withdrawing

 Members of the European Community

 Members of the European Free Trade Association
(Norway, Sweden, Switzerland, Austria, Portugal, Iceland, Finland)

 Full members of the North Atlantic Treaty Organization

Members of the Warsaw Pact

 Members of the Council for Mutual Economic Assistance (Comecon)

Military and economic alignments in Europe in 1973

when this became counter-productive. The only way of countering this was by adopting a deliberate policy of containment. This confirmed the views of Truman, although he had argued with much greater force in 1946: 'Unless Russia is faced with an iron fist and strong language, another war is in the making. Only one language do they understand – "how many divisions have you?" '[1] The Soviet analysis of Western behaviour, meanwhile, was based on the view that 'capitalist' states were still dangerous and aggressive, the more so because they were trying to uphold a system which Stalin, and later Brezhnev, believed to be in a 'general crisis'. Hence, Stalin maintained, 'the perils of capitalist encirclement' had not disappeared 'with Hitlerite Germany'.[8] In turn, Western observers pointed to the inherent instability of an ideology and political system which could become so obsessed by outside 'threats' and internal disintegration. Some claimed that this feeling of insecurity dominated the Kremlin's whole outlook and made it dangerously unpredictable.

Four examples can be used to show the interplay of Western and Soviet fears: the original flashpoints of the Cold War – Poland and Germany, the wider strategic area which includes the Western hemisphere and the Soviet frontiers, and the Third World countries of Asia and Africa.

Poland was the first area of real contention between the Soviet Union and the Western Allies. There were, during the course of 1944 and 1945, disputes over the proposed boundaries and government of the reconstituted Polish state. These soon assumed wider strategic implications. Stalin was determined to create, down the entire length of Eastern Europe, a broad band of Soviet-dominated territory which would act as a buffer against any future invasion of Russia from the West. He considered that control over Poland was the most urgent priority, not least because Poland had been strongly anti-Soviet between the wars – in her own right between 1919 and 1934, and as a German satellite between 1934 and 1939. Molotov summed up in September 1939 the uncertainties generated by Russia's western neighbour: 'Poland has become a convenient ground for all sorts of fortuitous and unexpected eventualities that might create a threat to the USSR.'[9] The West, meanwhile, became increasingly hostile to Soviet ambitions over Poland. While they were prepared to acknowledge the Soviet claim to Polish territory east of the Curzon Line, Roosevelt and Churchill were profoundly unhappy about the possibility of permanent Soviet control over

The Cold War to 1980

Polish institutions. Churchill had always regarded Poland as an outpost of Western influence in Eastern Europe, and as a vital barrier against the spread of Communism. Although he and Truman eventually had to accept as a *fait accompli* Soviet control over Poland, they were fully alerted to the scope of Soviet intentions and were determined to make a stand elsewhere.

Germany, meanwhile, had become the greatest single source of conflict between East and West. Details of zoning bedevilled relations at Potsdam in 1945, while the subsequent Berlin crises of 1948 and 1961 had far-reaching significance. What did Germany actually mean to the two sides? Its importance to Western countries was that it acted as a buffer between themselves and the Soviet *bloc*. The first Berlin crisis patterned the whole Western response to the Soviet threat. It resulted, for one thing, in the creation of the German Federal Republic, designed to fill the power vacuum which had existed in Central Europe since 1945. For another, it led to the formation of the North Atlantic Treaty Organization which, by the early 1950s, consisted of the United States, France, Britain, Belgium, the Netherlands, Luxembourg, Denmark, Norway, Iceland, Italy, Portugal, Greece, Turkey and Canada. Its avowed purpose was entirely defensive; by Article 5 of the NATO Charter the signatory powers undertook 'that an armed attack against one or more of them in Europe or North America shall be considered an attack against them all'.[10] The decision to arm West Germany and admit her to NATO in 1955 seemed to provide further security and appeared to be justified by the renewed Soviet pressure on Berlin between 1958 and 1961.

The Soviet view was conditioned by a profound distrust of Germany. Russia, after all, suffered devastating losses at the hands of the Nazis in the Second World War. These were itemized by Molotov in 1947 as 1710 towns and 70,000 villages, 31,850 industrial enterprises and 98,000 collective farms. Above all, between twenty and twenty-five million people were killed, the largest casualty figure sustained by any country in human history. The creation of the German Federal Republic was interpreted as the rebirth of fascist militarism, while her admission to NATO was considered the last straw. Bulganin saw the rearming of Germany as providing the 'means for new aggression' to 'yesterday's aggressors'.[11] The immediate Soviet response was the formation of the Warsaw Pact, which comprised obligations for mutual defence

287

between the USSR, Poland, Hungary, Czechoslovakia, Romania, Bulgaria and Albania. Still concerned about the German problem in the late 1950s, Krushchev sponsored the Rapacki Plan to demilitarize West Berlin. Then, to prevent what he regarded as attempts by the West to bring about economic collapse in East Germany, he sealed the border and ordered the construction of the Berlin Wall (1961). The Soviet leadership subsequently regarded the survival of Ulbricht's régime and the emergence of East Germany as one of the major industrial powers of Europe as a direct result of this policy.

Apprehension also existed over a wider area. American presidents stressed the need to contain Communism behind its frontiers in Asia and, therefore, sponsored military alliances like CENTO and SEATO. They also took the precaution of establishing, at various stages, military bases in Turkey, Iran, Pakistan, Taiwan and Okinawa. Above all, the Monroe Doctrine (which, in 1823, declared that the United States would not countenance any European interference in the American continent) was revived and given new force in two ways. The first was institutional; the Organization of American States was designed as yet another military alliance and as a device for minimizing Soviet influence in Latin America. The second was the precautionary action taken by President Kennedy in 1962 to prevent the Soviet Union from maintaining nuclear weapons in Castro's Cuba. In a public broadcast he announced that Khrushchev had defied 'American hemispheric policy'.[12] In order to exert maximum pressure on Moscow he decided to quarantine Cuba, preparing, as a last resort, the possibility of a surgical air strike on the new missile bases. At the same time, Adlai Stevenson delivered a strong attack in the Security Council on the long sequence of aggressive Soviet actions which had culminated in the Cuba Crisis. Khrushchev, for his part, had complained for some time of the virtual encirclement of the Soviet Union by American air bases. He pointed out, in a letter to Kennedy at the height of the crisis, that Turkey, which contained American missiles, was actually closer to the Soviet Union than was Cuba to the United States. 'Do you consider, then, that you have the right to demand security for your own country and the removal of those weapons which you call offensive and do not acknowledge the same right for us?'[12] As far as Khrushchev was concerned, nuclear war was prevented only by the restraint of the Kremlin.

The Third World entered the calculations of the superpowers

The Cold War to 1980

during the late 1940s and early 1950s. United States policy was based, until the late 1960s, on the 'domino theory'. An extension of the argument of containment, this maintained that each state which fell to Communism would trigger the process in a neighbour. The result was American support for régimes in Latin America and South Korea, and also involvement in Vietnam, the longest and most expensive war in United States history. The official justification was always that military aid was defensive and that it was accompanied by other forms of co-operation, especially economic. Soviet leaders, by contrast, referred to the 'expansionist' tendencies of the United States. Brezhnev, for example, spoke of the 'aggressive war waged by US imperialism in Vietnam'. Soviet relations with Third World countries, it was stated, were not intended to be subversive but assistance to combat the return of colonialism could well be part of a wider aid programme. Each side clearly disbelieved the statements of the other, attributing to all types of aid a great deal of strategy and very little altruism.

*

These strategic rivalries were given a particularly sharp edge by ideological differences as profound as any in history. Adlai Stevenson spoke in the United Nations Security Council in 1962 of 'the conflict between the absolutist and pluralist conception of the destiny of mankind'.[12] Both sides claimed to uphold democracy; both justified their diplomacy in the name of freedom and in the interest of peoples. Soviet Communism stressed the need to eliminate economic and class 'exploitation' by means of irreversible political and social changes. To the West, this implied dictatorship and a denial of the fundamental right of a people to change the system through free elections. There was also a basic difference in their respective views on political parties and constitutions. Marxism-Leninism operated in a one-party state, the purpose of the constitution being to transmit reforms and changes to the people in the most efficient way possible; in practice, if not in official theory, the constitution merely lubricated the Party. The Western democratic tradition, on the other hand, was that the Constitution circumscribed the powers of the various political parties which competed for power within it. This would have been regarded by the Soviet Union as an extension to politics of the interplay of capitalist forces, the emphasis being on the rules of procedure rather than on social reform. In return, Western liberal and social democrats saw in the removal of such rules by the Soviet régime a permanent danger of tyranny which would probably destroy any reforming impulses.

Western views on the future of democracy in Europe were carefully formulated in the Atlantic Charter, prepared by Churchill and Roosevelt in August 1941. 'They desire to see no territorial changes that do not accord with the freely expressed wishes of the peoples concerned.' Furthermore; 'They respect the right of all peoples to choose the form of government under which they will live.'[13] It seemed, at first, that this formula was acceptable to Stalin, who signed the Declaration on Liberated Europe, along with Churchill and Roosevelt, at Yalta in 1945. Under this the three powers promised to help the liberated peoples 'to create democratic institutions of their own choice'. Before long, however, Churchill was attacking Stalin for converting popular front governments into Soviet satellite régimes in Poland, Hungary, Romania and Bulgaria. In his 'Iron Curtain' speech, delivered in Fulton in March 1946, Churchill warned: 'police governments are prevailing in nearly every case' and that 'there is no true democracy'.[14] In the following year Truman told Congress: 'I believe it must be the policy of the United States to support free peoples who are resisting attempted subjugation by armed minorities or by outside pressures.'[1] Western leaders reacted with horror and disgust when Soviet troops invaded Hungary in 1956, and Czechoslovakia in 1968. In the latter case, President Johnson represented the feelings of the Western world when he accused the Soviet Union of having invaded a 'defenceless country to stamp out a resurgence of ordinary human freedom'.[15]

The Soviet perspective was inevitably different. It was argued that Russia never undertook to introduce a Western-style of democracy into Eastern Europe, and that her subsequent actions were designed not to subvert the freedom of smaller countries, but to preserve their socialism from corrupting or destructive influences. Replying to a resolution in the United Nations condemning the invasion of Hungary, Sobolev argued that Hungary had been threatened by 'counter-revolutionary elements', which had succeeded in 'deluding the workers by mendacious propaganda'.[16] A similar theme was used by Brezhnev in 1968 to justify the occupation of Czechoslovakia. He was forced, he said, to take an 'extraordinary step dictated by necessity'. Such necessity arises when 'internal and external forces that are hostile to Socialism try to turn the development of some Socialist country towards the restoration of a capitalist régime'.[17] The common assumption of all Soviet leaders, therefore, was that Western powers, especially the United States, were trying to destabilize Eastern *bloc* countries by exploiting any signs of socialist weakness. Furthermore, it was argued, the United States established a vast economic network, attempting to dominate Europe through the Marshall Plan. The unification of the Western zones of Germany was an example of the collusion of Western capitalism, since, according to Molotov, 'it facilitates the penetration of American and British monopolists into German industry and opens to them wide opportunities for subordinating the German economy to their influence '[18] The American response to this accusation was that the zones were being united and economic assistance granted to prevent Germany from being permanently crippled and impoverished. Besides, it was often pointed out, the Western Allies did not strip their zones of all their industrial assets, unlike Stalin, who insisted on 10,000 million dollars from an already exhausted and impoverished people, thereby adding economic slavery to political subjugation.

*

Two distinct developments are discernible in the period between 1962 and 1980: the movement towards co-operation and détente and the revival of tension which had always been so characteristic of the Cold War.

One reason for the growing desire for coexistence during the 1960s was the grave perils of nuclear warfare and mass destruction, made dramatically clear by the 1962 Cuba Crisis. In a less tense atmosphere, several major agreements were drawn up, including the 'Hot Line Agreement' (1963), the Partial Test Ban Treaty (1963) and the Nuclear Non-Proliferation Treaty (1968). Another impetus was the *rapprochement* between the Soviet Union and the countries of Western Europe. This was initiated by de Gaulle's search for a special relationship between France and Russia in the early 1960s and was enhanced by Brandt's policy of *'Ostpolitik'* at the end of the decade. The result was the 1970 Treaty between the German Federal Republic and the Soviet Union, to be followed by the Four Power Agreement on Berlin (1971), the Treaty with the German Democratic Republic (1972) and the Treaty with Czechoslovakia (1973).

Aspects of European History 1789–1980

The diplomacy of détente focused, in the 1970s, on two major issues. One was the relationship between the superpowers. Clearly the greatest need was for agreement on the control of nuclear weapons, and the Helsinki negotiations eventually produced the Strategic Arms Limitation Treaty (SALT I) signed at the 1972 Moscow Summit by Nixon and Brezhnev. Further talks, between Ford and Brezhnev, resulted in the Vladivostock Accords (1974) which, in turn, were intended to form the basis of SALT II. Meanwhile, the improvement in US-Soviet relations was reflected by agreements on commerce and the transfer of high technology (see Chapter 29). The other major issue concerned Europe. Ever since the 1950s Soviet leaders had aimed at ratifying the status quo in Eastern and Central Europe by means of an all-European conference. In 1973 Helsinki was the scene of an assembly of representatives of all the European states except Albania, together with delegations from the United States and Canada. This 'Conference on Security and Co-operation in Europe' (CSCE) has been described as the closest Europe would ever come to producing an official end to the Second World War by broad-based multilateral agreement. The Final Act, or Helsinki Declaration (1975), contained a wide range of 'baskets', one of which was a set of guarantees of human rights.

Throughout the 1970s, however, détente clearly had its limitations. President Nixon pointed out that it was 'not the same as lasting peace' and that 'the world will hold perils for as far ahead as we can see'.[19] Crises continued to occur, if at less frequent intervals, one example being the military alert called by Nixon at the height of the 1973 Arab-Israeli War. From 1974 onwards a series of factors conspired to undermine détente and, eventually, to wreck the SALT II agreements. One was the disillusionment of the Carter administration with the Soviet record on human rights; another was the fear aroused in Washington by the sudden increase of Soviet activity in the Third World, especially in Angola (1975–6) and Ethiopia (from 1976). The final blow was the Soviet invasion of Afghanistan in 1979. This undermined détente and, during the first half of the 1980s, resulted in the return of the Cold War. After 1985, however, détente was fully restored as a result of the internal reforms and diplomatic initiatives of Gorbachev. By 1989 the Soviet Union had even relinquished its control over Eastern Europe and by 1990 the need for the Warsaw Pact itself had been called into question.

32

Economic and Political Integration in Western Europe 1945–80

The idea of European unity is not new. As far back as the eighteenth century several people, including the Abbé de Saint-Pierre and Jeremy Bentham devised schemes for a European legislature. The term 'United States of Europe', coined in the nineteenth century, was frequently used in the early twentieth century by the Austrian statesman, Coudenhove-Kalergi, and the French politician, Briand. Any hope that Europe was evolving towards a federation was, however, destroyed by the emergence during the 1930s of the most extreme form of nationalism ever known which, in turn, brought militarism and dictatorship to over two-thirds of the Continent's states, as well as the most destructive conflict in history.

The Second World War generated profound disillusionment with Europe's unpleasant habit of producing a major conflict every generation. It is not surprising that the anti-Nazi resistance movements should have led the field in denouncing the destructive forces of nationalism, and in advocating political and economic integration. Their Manifesto, drawn up at Ventotene in 1940 by Ernesto Rossi and Altiero Spinelli, defined the main objective for the future as 'the definitive abolition of the division of Europe into national sovereign states'.[1] This was followed by the formation of the European Federalist Movement (1943) and by a series of conferences which gave practical expression to the belief of the French writer Camus that 'the European resistance will remake Europe'.[1] This 'grass roots' federalism, in turn, influenced post-war politicians and economists who were equally anxious to learn from the experience of

Aspects of European History 1789–1980

Nazi tyranny – men like Adenauer, de Gasperi, Spaak, Monnet and Schuman. The idealism and enthusiasm of the Resistance leaders therefore influenced the new governments, so that, for the first time ever, European integration became, in several states, official policy.

How far did this policy progress between 1945 and 1950? On the whole, practice fell far short of theory, with alliance or inter-governmental co-operation being emphasized at the expense of supranationalism and political unity. This can be seen in the development of the period's three major sets of institutions. The first was the Organization of European Economic Co-operation (OEEC) set up in 1948 to co-ordinate the distribution of American aid in the Marshall Plan. This might have developed into a customs union but any such scheme was strongly opposed by the British government. Secondly, fears for future security brought about the Brussels Treaty (1948) between Britain, France, the Netherlands, Belgium and Luxembourg. But when this was expanded into the North Atlantic Treaty Organization in 1949, and incorporated Canada and the United States, it lost its exclusively European base and adopted a more traditional framework of collective security. The third trend seemed, at first, to be more promising. Numerous conferences were held for the specific purpose of preparing for political unity and the most important of these, at the Hague, resolved 'to transfer certain sovereign rights to the nations in order to express them in common'.[2] The direct result was the Council of Europe, set up in 1949 and consisting of a consultative Assembly. This Council, however, had very few powers and was clearly a much diluted version of the original plan.

The basic reason for the limited success of these ventures was a clash between two different approaches to integration. Some governments favoured a federal model on the lines of the United States, while others preferred a confederal scheme which would resemble the looser structure of the United Nations.

Federalism was ardently supported by the Benelux countries, which had so frequently been caught up in the destructive cross-currents of Franco-German conflict. The French government, still trying to recover from the humiliation of 1940, saw a federation as the most effective way of containing Germany in the future, while the Germans sought a vehicle for reconstruction and reconciliation. Confederalism was the choice of the peripheral states of Western Europe, especially Britain and Scandinavia. Britain had a long

Economic and Political Integration in Europe

tradition of separation from Europe, except over considerations of the 'balance of power'. Hence, Churchill had remarked before the war, 'We are with Europe, but not part of it'.[3] In any case, Britain had maritime and imperial interests, together with a 'special relationship' with the United States. In a conversation with de Gaulle in 1944, Churchill had made Britain's priorities quite clear: 'Whenever we have to choose between Europe and the open sea, we shall always choose the open sea. Whenever I have to choose between you and Roosevelt, I shall always choose Roosevelt.'[4] Above all, Britain was the one country in Europe which was not disillusioned with the appeal to patriotism: Churchill's wartime oratory combined with the experience of victory to reaffirm Britain's complete faith in her own institutions.

Hence there was, by 1950, a clear division between those countries who wanted European unity and those who did not. The latter remained suspicious of all schemes for integration and attempted, where possible, to weaken them. The former, meanwhile, had still to work out between themselves a clear goal and a realistic means of attaining it.

*

The answer was provided by Jean Monnet, director of the French reconstruction programme and a longstanding advocate of European unity. In a memorandum to the French Foreign Minister, Schuman on 4 May 1950, he argued that all the means previously adopted had led to an *impasse* and that this could be broken only by initial concentration on *economic* integration. In time, this would develop an irreversible momentum towards political integration; the Schuman Declaration, issued on 9 May, reflected this view. He stated, as an article of faith, that 'The European federation is indispensable to the maintenance of peace'. On the other hand, 'Europe will not be made all at once, as a single whole: it will be built by concrete achievements which will first create *de facto* solidarity'.[5]

The practical expression of this aim was the European Coal and Steel Community (ECSC). Formed by the Treaty of Paris (1951), this consisted of France, West Germany, Italy, Belgium, the Netherlands and Luxembourg. In the High Authority it possessed Europe's first genuinely supranational institution and one which was intended to have 'legal personality'. In 1957 the leaders of the six members agreed, by the Treaty of Rome, to enlarge the scope of the ECSC by establishing the European Economic Community (EEC) and Euratom. The main institutions of the EEC comprised the Commission, which had powers to instigate and exercise joint economic programmes, the Council of Ministers, in which the key decisions were taken by representatives of each of the member governments; the Parliament, whose deputies were nominated by the national legislatures; and the Court of Justice. A transition period of twelve years was allowed by Article 8 for the establishment of a customs and economic union, which would involve the removal of all internal duties and the adoption of a common external tariff. Common policies would also be adopted for industry, agriculture, transport, capital and services. Ultimately, it was envisaged, progress could be made towards establishing much closer political ties between the member states.

Both the ECSC and the EEC were formed without the membership of the Scandinavian countries or Britain. The former preferred their own arrangements, like the Nordic Council (1952). Britain, anxious to avoid any binding commitments, declined two invitations, issued in 1951 and 1956. The first decision was taken by a Labour government which had no desire to place the recently nationalized coal and steel industries under the control of an external body; a Labour Party NEC document argued that: 'No socialist party could ever accept a system by which important fields of national policy were surrendered to a European representative authority.'[6] The second decision was that of a Conservative government which feared the possible influence on Britain of a continental type of economic planning. Both parties, however, saw the advantage of a free trade area without strings attached. Britain therefore took the initiative in establishing, in 1959, the European Free Trade Association (EFTA), with Austria, Denmark, Norway, Sweden, Portugal and Switzerland. Non-Communist Europe had, in effect, divided into two economic zones; the 'inner Six' and the 'outer Seven'.

Meanwhile, another attempt had been made to establish a political and military system in Europe. In 1950 the French prime minister, Pleven, proposed the formation of a European Defence Community (EDC). His main motive was to allow Germany to rearm, but within a European context; German contingents would be fully integrated into a European defence force under a Minister of Defence, a Council of Ministers and an Assembly. This would have the triple advantage of using German power as a means of replacing

Economic and Political Integration in Europe

United States influence in Europe, preventing the re-emergence of aggressive German nationalism, and providing much needed resources to counter the growing threat from the Soviet *bloc*. The French regarded British support as essential for the success of the scheme, as only a combination of Britain and France could guarantee effective control over German rearmament. The British government, however, was unimpressed by the idea of the EDC, preferring the Atlantic connections offered by NATO. Ernest Bevin declared in the House of Commons that the proposal for a European Army was 'too limited in scope . . . European unity is no longer possible within Europe alone but only within the broader Atlantic community.'[7] Meanwhile, the French Parliament, long divided over the project, finally rejected the EDC, which therefore collapsed in 1954. Eden's government tried subsequently to establish a more loosely structured alternative by enlarging the 1948 Brussels Treaty, through the inclusion of Italy and West Germany, into the Western European Union.

By 1960 it was clear that the only real chance of integration, either political or economic, lay with the EEC. It now remained to be seen whether the aims of the 1950s could be achieved during the 1960s.

*

In one respect the EEC was remarkably successful. De Gaulle described as an 'economic miracle'[8] the rapid enrichment of all six member states and the creation of the world's largest single trading *bloc*. Between 1958 and 1967 the exports of the EEC as a whole trebled, while the volume of world exports only doubled. The indices of the gross national product showed a similar improvement; taking the 1953 index as 100, the GNP of the EEC had increased to 188 by 1965, in comparison with 154 for EFTA and 149 for the United States. Progress was also made in implementing the economic targets of the Treaty of Rome. By July 1968 all internal barriers had been eliminated on industrial goods, iron, steel, coal and agricultural produce; a common agricultural policy and uniform tax system (based on VAT) had been introduced, a common external tariff was in operation, and the member states had adopted a concerted policy on tariff negotiations with countries outside the EEC.

By contrast, any movement towards political unity had slowed down. Economic success had certainly helped remove tension

297

between the nations of Western Europe but had not given a positive boost for federalism. It has been argued[9] that a federation can be established only if a political factor, external or internal, reacts with a background of economic integration. Hence the economic unity of the Thirteen Colonies was transformed into the tighter political structure of the United States as a direct result of the conflict with the British Crown, while the German *Zollverein* was converted into the Second Reich by the statecraft of Bismarck. No such political catalyst had yet appeared within the EEC. If anything, France and Germany pursued, during the 1960s, foreign policies which placed national considerations far above the ideal of political federalism.

On becoming prime minister and then president of the Fifth Republic de Gaulle made it his business to revive France's influence in Europe and to reassert a powerful French identity. Never a convinced federalist, he preferred to focus on *'une certaine idée de la France'* and openly declared as his principle: *'Les nations, ça existe.'*[10] Three distinctively Gaullist policies followed. First, in his determination to reduce French connections with the United States, he withdrew France from the military arm of NATO, committing her to becoming a nuclear power in her own right, and seeking détente with the Soviet *bloc*. Second, he sought a traditional bilateral agreement with Germany in contrast with the Fourth Republic's policy of Franco-German reconciliation within a European context. Third, and most important, he was determined to uphold to the limit French interests within the EEC itself. In 1965, a major crisis developed as de Gaulle insisted on a French veto on certain agricultural policies, even though these were acceptable to the other five members. It took nearly a year before the deadlock was overcome and the result was a severe setback to those federalists who wanted to reactivate the movement towards political unity. The Luxemburg Agreement (1966) provided a compromise which, in effect, acknowledged the right of one member to insist on 'unanimous agreement'. This enhanced the powers of the Council of Ministers, which represented the national governments, at the expense of the more genuinely supranational commission.

By the end of the 1960s and the beginning of the 1970s Germany had also begun to follow a distinctive foreign policy. The Christian Democrats, in power since 1948, had by 1969 been superseded by the SPD, who had always been less enthusiastic about the prospects of European unity. Indeed, the new Social Democratic Chancellor,

	OEEC (Organization for European Economic Co-operation)	OECD (Organization for Economic Co-operation and Development)	European Community	EFTA (European Free Trade Association)	Comecon (Council for Mutual Economic Assistance)	WEU (Western European Union)	Council of Europe	NATO (North Atlantic Treaty Organization)	Warsaw Pact
United Kingdom	●	●	●			●	●	●	
France	●	●	●			●	●	●	
Belgium	●	●	●			●	●	●	
Netherlands	●	●	●			●	●	●	
Luxembourg	●	●	●			●	●	●	
Italy	●	●	●			●	●	●	
West Germany	●	●	●			●	●	●	
Denmark	●	●	●				●	●	
Norway	●	●		●			●	●	
Sweden	●	●		●			●		
Switzerland	●	●		●					
Austria	●	●		●			●		
Eire	●	●	●				●		
Spain	●	●							
Portugal	●	●		●				●	
Iceland	●	●		●			●	●	
Finland		●		●					
Greece		●						●	
Turkey	●	●					●	●	
Malta							●		
Cyprus							●		
USSR					●				●
Poland					●				●
East Germany					●				●
Czechoslovakia					●				●
Romania					●				●
Hungary					●				●
Bulgaria					●				●
Yugoslavia		●							
Albania									

Fig. 1   European integration: membership of various organizations by 1973. Diagram after *The Bartholomew/Warne Atlas of Europe: A profile of Western Europe* pp. 22–23 (Edinburgh and London, 1974)

Brandt, said in 1969: 'In the more purely political field I think we will have to depend upon intergovernmental operations [rather than upon] supranational methods.' This seemed to echo de Gaulle's policy, as did Brandt's search for a bilateral understanding with the Communist régimes in Eastern Europe; in August 1970, for example, the Russo-German Treaty was drawn up, followed shortly afterwards by an agreement with Poland. *Ostpolitik* was criticized by the CDU and CSU on the grounds that accommodation with Eastern Europe could be accomplished only at the expense of further integration in Western Europe.

There was *one* example of progress made during the 1960s. In July 1967 the executive bodies and Councils of Ministers of each of the ECSC, EEC and Euratom were combined into a single Commission and a single Council, within the more generally designated 'European Community'. Yet, by 1969, it was still clear that the spectacular economic progress made by the Six had not yet been accompanied by any real political change. Since the transition period of twelve years, allowed by the Treaty of Rome, had now elapsed, a decision would have to be made about the future of the Community. Yet this decision involved a dilemma. How, on the one hand, could the momentum of evolution be maintained so that premature stratification could be avoided? How, on the other, could further progress be made towards political integration without compromising the national interests considered so important by the Community's two most powerful members?

*

While the continental governments were experiencing these problems, successive British leaders were re-examining their whole attitude to the EEC. The Liberal Party had always been in favour of membership, but the first prime minister to be converted was the Conservative Macmillan. In a broadcast to the nation on 20 September 1962, he said 'all through our history . . . we have still been very much involved in Europe's affairs. We can't escape it. Sometimes we've tried to – but we can't. It's no good pretending.'[11] The Labour Party held out longer, partly because Gaitskell, leader until 1963, was a convinced anti-Marketeer. In 1966, however, Wilson committed his Labour government to seeking entry for Britain, and was determined that he would 'not take no for an answer'.

Economic and Political Integration in Europe

How did the negotiations fare? Five of the EEC members welcomed the British application, but entry was delayed for over ten years because of the vetos imposed in 1962 and 1968 by France. De Gaulle felt that Britain was profoundly 'insular' and 'maritime', and that 'the nature, the structure, the very situation that are England's differ profoundly from those of the continentals'.[12] He feared that Britain would use the EEC merely as a crutch for her own economic recovery; that she would upset the 'special relationship' recently worked out between France and Germany; and that she would act as a 'Trojan horse' within Europe for American political and financial influence. These views were not, however, universally held in France for, on de Gaulle's retirement in 1969, the new president, Pompidou, removed the veto. Negotiations were opened by the Heath government and the Treaty of Accession was signed in 1972, leading to membership in 1973. Subsequent renegotiations and the 1975 referendum, confirmed Britain's place within the Community.

These developments represented a profound reappraisal of Britain's role in the world which, in turn, came from a growing awareness of her economic and political vulnerability.

Britain's economic performance since 1945 had been far more sluggish than that of the EEC countries. For example, her exports grew between 1953 and 1963 by under 40 per cent, in contrast to the Community's average growth of over 140 per cent. Three reasons can be advanced for this: the first was the cost of victory. During the Second World War Britain accumulated enormous external debts and, at the same time, sold many overseas investments and cut back on services. These investments and services had, for over half a century, played a vital part in converting a balance of trade deficit into an overall balance of payments surplus. At first, the true extent of Britain's losses was disguised by American loans and by the post-war weakness of the defeated Axis powers – Germany, Italy and Japan. During the 1950s, however, Germany rapidly reconstructed her shattered industries and, in the process, replaced the type of obsolete plant which was still widely used in Britain. Gradually, the grim truth emerged that Germany's bomb damage was less difficult to repair than the contraction of Britain's investments. Indeed, it could be argued that the smaller degree of physical destruction in Britain actually discouraged systematic modernization in industry. Secondly, Britain continued to pursue an active political role as a major power which was quite out of step with her smaller economic

301

Aspects of European History 1789–1980

base. One example of this was the determination of all post-war governments in Britain to defend the integrity of the sterling area; this was clearly a direct consequence of the commitment which Britain had, in the past, fulfilled as the focal point of a huge empire and as the world's largest trading nation. One historian, in fact, sees a direct conflict between Britain's post-war trading needs and the interests of the City of London.[13] Thirdly, British governments had adopted a more piecemeal approach to reconstruction than had Germany, France and the Benelux countries. Conservative policies fought shy of central control, but even the Labour Party's socialism lacked the consistency of the Continent's 'planned economies'.

By the 1960s British leaders considered that only association with Europe could bring about economic revival. Trade figures seemed to confirm that the future lay with the EEC. During this decade British trade with the Commonwealth increased by 29 per cent (from £1240 million to £1601 million), compared with a massive jump of 230 per cent (£463 million to £1530 million) with the Community. What was now needed was a greatly expanded market which would give British products the same advantage as their rivals. As Macmillan said, referring to Britain's existing limitations: 'How are we going to sell them if the base, the home market, is only a quarter of theirs?'

British decline had also been political. The Suez catastrophe of 1956 showed that Britain was no longer a world power, even though this lesson was not learned for several more years. It also loosened the 'special relationship' with the United States, as the latter had supported several resolutions in the United Nations Security Council condemning Anglo-French action. In the past, Britain might have withdrawn into 'splendid isolation', content to maintain close relations with the Empire. By the early 1960s, however, British colonies were receiving their independence and, in the words of US Secretary of State, Dean Acheson, Britain had 'lost an Empire and not yet found a role'.[14] The solution of the Conservatives was to look to Europe, while the Labour Party at first sought to foster and lead a democratic and multi-racial Commonwealth. Then two events in the mid-1960s, the Indo-Pakistan War and Rhodesia's unilateral declaration of independence, threatened the very existence of the Commonwealth and showed that Britain's leadership was extremely precarious. Membership of a European *bloc* became more and more attractive, especially since exclusion from that *bloc* could mean future isolation and insignificance.

Economic and Political Integration in Europe

Even the longstanding British reservations about the loss of national identity, through unwanted political integration, had been allayed. (The policies of de Gaulle and Brandt showed that federalism was no longer the major target of Western European leaders.) Heath had been able to say in 1961: 'That situation is fully safeguarded and we should not frighten ourselves by false apprehensions about these matters.' By 1970 the situation was still the same. According to Sir Geoffrey Ripon: 'There is no question of the imposition of theoretical solutions from above; no threat of instant federation.'[15]

*

Britain's movement towards the EEC therefore coincided with the latter's considerations about its future. It also provided a stimulus for change. The Community could seek to rediscover its dynamism and to undo the negative effects of earlier internal wrangling by implementing an ambitious and long-term programme of enlargement. This, in turn, would necessitate the overhaul of the Community's economic policies and political institutions. Perhaps, federalists now argued, gradualism and a broad base would also provide the best prospects of political unity.

The Community's enlargement has been carried out by two processes: membership and association. New members have been Britain, Ireland and Denmark (admitted by the Treaty of Accession in 1972) and Greece, Spain and Portugal which entered the Community in the 1980s. Two areas have been granted close association with the Community. The larger is the Third World: at first the connection was confined by the Yaoundé Convention of 1963 to ex-French and ex-Belgian colonies, but the scope was subsequently extended, in the Lomé Conventions of 1975 and 1979, to most of Africa, the Caribbean and the Pacific. Meanwhile, Mediterranean countries were also being given associate status, and a free trade area was established in Southern Europe for industrial, though not agricultural, products.

Economic reform was designed to achieve 'positive integration', or common financial institutions, after the successful 'negative integration', or removal of tariffs, of the 1960s. One example was the formation of the European Monetary System in March, 1979. Efforts were also made to reform the process of budgetary contributions and disbursements, largely on the initiatives of Britain and Italy, against whom the Community budget had tended to discriminate. A major achievement was the adoption of a more distinctively social policy after the 1972 Summit's resolution to give the Community a 'more human face'; this led to the European Development Fund (EDF) in 1975, from which both Italy and Britain benefited.

Political reforms kept the future in mind but were far from spectacular. 1979 saw the realization of one of the long-term projects of the Treaty of Rome – direct elections to the European Parliament. The Community's executive, however, was not substantially altered. It is true that several new institutions were developed, like the European Council and the Conference of Ministers Political Committee. But by 1980 these had not yet merged with the existing Commission and the Council of Ministers. The emphasis seemed, as much as ever, to be on intergovernmental economic co-operation rather than on genuine supranationalism.

To summarize the argument of this chapter, European federalism was an age-old ideal, but became a real proposition only in the powerful reaction against nationalism after the Second World War. It originated as a grass-roots movement, and was then taken over as official policy by several governments. Early initiatives, however, were impeded by the lack of enthusiasm from Britain and other peripheral states. Decisions were therefore made by the Six to concentrate, during the 1950s, on economic integration in the form of the ECSC and the EEC, Britain choosing to remain outside both. The EEC produced spectacular economic success but no further political progress so that Britain, affected by economic and political decline, was able to revise her whole attitude to Europe by the early 1960s. Meanwhile, the EEC went for enlargement and further internal changes in preference to more immediate political unity between existing members. Then, during the latter half of the 1980s, political integration was discussed more regularly and it seemed to some members that an enlarged community could be fully accommodated within a federal structure. Whether such unity can actually be achieved in the long term will, however, depend on the agreement of all members. By 1990 Britain, in particular, remained unconvinced.

33

Nationalism

Among the numerous characteristics of nationalism three are worth particular mention. The first is an awareness, among members of the community, of a natural homogeneity in language, culture (especially literature and music) and social customs. The second is a mass acceptance of the authority of a central government, in the defence of specified frontiers against external enemies. The government sometimes seeks to convert this loyalty into veneration by promoting selected attitudes and transmitting certain values through education and the mass media. The third, the people's awareness of its own unique identity, can be used as a source of energy: either to extend a nation's frontiers at the expense of its neighbours or, conversely, to drive out intruders, whether foreign dynasties or imperial powers.

The nation state has roots which extend far back into the middle ages[1]; both France and England, for example, were incipient nations by the twelfth and thirteenth centuries. Then, during the early modern period, European monarchs gave these states complex bureaucracies so that they could transmit their will more effectively to their subjects. The nation state had, by the seventeenth and eighteenth centuries, become synonymous with centralized government and with the extension of this government's power to all the frontiers.

Nationalism, however, developed rather more slowly. Commitment and loyalty to the nation state certainly existed among the Spaniards, English and Dutch of the sixteenth century, and the

French of the seventeenth. Yet at this stage something was missing. Nationalism is fundamentally the expression of mass commitment above all other loyalties. During the period before the French Revolution, the inhabitants of most countries had other bonds which were still very powerful. One was the *local* connection which comprised a variety of feudal obligations and loyalties which were left over from the middle ages. Another was a profound attachment to *universal* values which, as in the case of religion, entirely transcended the individual state. Thus the commitments of the people were like two separate beams of light, one stopping well short of the national frontier and the other overshooting it. Before a nation state could be fully established the two beams would have to be made to converge *on* the frontier.

English nationalism was given a powerful boost by the puritan revolution, and later by the writings of Locke (1632–1704) and Burke (1727–97). The puritan spirit of English nationalism also spread, with the early settlers and pioneers, to North America. But the absolute monarchs of some of the continental countries were somewhat less likely to speed up the growth of nationalism as an ideology affecting their peoples. Their attention was divided between specific problems (like dynastic consolidation) and universal issues (like religious conflict). Besides, these rulers had no need, or desire, to mobilize mass support. The state, after all, was still considered the personal property of the ruler and the slogan '*l'état, c'est moi*' was hardly likely to promote nationalist fervour. Thus, before nationalism could make any further headway, there would have to be a redefinition of the relationship between the people and the state. This, in turn, would require a political and social upheaval.

*

Such an upheaval was caused between 1789 and 1815 by the French Revolution and the expansion of the Napoleonic empire. During this period nationalism took France by storm and was then transmitted to other parts of Europe, especially to the fragmented states of Italy and Germany.

Although the French Revolution started cautiously, it soon altered radically the individual's relationship with the state by uprooting a host of traditional local interests and sweeping away the remnants of feudalism. As France entered a more ideological phase

Nationalism

from 1793, she came more and more obviously under the influence of the ideas of Rousseau (1712–78). (E. H. Carr describes Rousseau as the 'founder of modern nationalism' in that he 'rejected the embodiment of the nation in the personal sovereign or the ruling class' and 'boldly identified "nation" and "people"'.[2]) Rousseau made two significant contributions to the growth of nationalism. First, he attacked the cosmopolitan outlook of the eighteenth-century Enlightenment and stressed, instead, the people's community base: 'chaque nation a son caractere propre et spécifique.'[3] Second, he redefined the relations between ruler and ruled. In emphasizing the importance of the 'general will', he gave the individual a place within the community as a whole, in turn, the community had the right to expect his total allegiance. Thus 'La patrie est dans les relations de l'Etat a ses membres'.[3] Jacobin leaders like Robespierre, Carnot and Danton used these ideas to develop a common national purpose. According to Danton, 'France must be an indivisible whole'. Mass conscription was introduced to mobilize citizen armies and, with this new weapon, French nationalism overspilled France's frontiers, becoming at the same time more and more messianic. Under Napoleon, nationalism lost some of its association with radical democracy but retained its connection with militarism.

France had a more profound impact on the rest of Europe than had any other power since the days of the Roman Empire. Napoleon, in particular, contributed in two ways to the growth of nationalism beyond the borders of France. First, he dismantled the old institutions and remnants of the feudal system and, in Italy and Germany, consolidated the scattered territories into larger states; he tried, in his own words, to 'simplify their monstrous complication'.[4] The second contribution was more negative, but no less important. His conquests and insensitive diplomacy aroused a series of national responses, ranging from Russia and Spain, to Italy and Germany. This resistance eventually caused the defeat of the French armies in the Peninsular War, the Russian Campaign and the War of Liberation.

During the early years of the nineteenth century Germany underwent a particularly profound upheaval, the catalysts for which were French ideological influence and conquest. German writers like Goethe (1749–1832) had been part of the mainstream of the eighteenth-century Enlightenment and had shared its cosmopolitan base. Gradually, however, German culture acquired a more regional

Aspects of European History 1789–1980

identity as, under the influence of Rousseau, the German Romantics rejected the universalism of the eighteenth century.

German Romanticism began with a linguistic emphasis, as writers like Arndt (1769–1860) stressed the importance of language in national identity: 'The Germans have not been bastardized. They have retained their original purity and have been able to develop slowly but surely according to the everlasting laws of time.'⁵ This was built by Herder (1744–1803) and Jahn (1778–1852) into a broader conception of the German race or *Volk*. Jahn confirmed the movement away from the cosmopolitan outlook of Goethe: 'We seek the same goal, but in Germany instead of humanity.'⁵ Herder introduced the concept of collective creativity in the form of the *Volksgeist*: the cultural achievements of individual writers and painters were outlets for the genius of a whole people. Unfortunately, this people was not yet a nation and Fichte (1762–1814) concentrated his efforts on promoting a political revival and contributing to the defeat of Napoleon. Hegel (1770–1831) went further and emphasized that political regeneration could be accomplished only by greatly extending the power of the state. 'It must be that all the worth which the human being possesses . . . he possesses only through the state.' He added: 'The state is the Divine Idea as it exists on Earth.'⁶

Clearly these expressions added up to a profound change in the concept of the individual's relationship with the community and provided the theoretical ingredients for a powerful national consciousness. But Central Europe was still fragmented politically, a situation confirmed by the Congress of Vienna in 1815. The question which now arose was: how could the national sentiment acquire a political structure? As Jahn said, 'A state without a *Volk* is nothing, a soulless artifice'; but equally, 'a *Volk* without a state is nothing, a bodiless phantom'.⁵

One of the major characteristics of nationalism is that it is ideologically amorphous. It can change shape and adapt to virtually any other ideology, only to switch, if necessary, to something else which is totally different. The creation of nation states in Central Europe shows this quite clearly. During the first half of the nineteenth century German and Italian nationalism identified openly with

liberal and social forces, usually in opposition to the existing establishment. After 1851, however, nationalism in this area increasingly underpinned the establishment and allied with authoritarian
governments.

Italy had been deeply affected by the French Revolution, both
ideologically and structurally. The Italian national movement was
still influenced by France after the end of the Napoleonic Wars; the
Carbonari, for example, was inspired by French ideas in its struggle
against the Austrians. The most important of the Italian nationalist
theorists, Mazzini, allied openly with liberal thought and rejected
the more ruthless Italian tradition of power politics associated with
Machiavelli. Indeed, he considered Machiavelli's era to have been
one of 'corruption and degradation' which it was necessary to 'bury
with the past'.[7] The 1848 Revolutions, however, showed that
spontaneous nationalism, which aimed at establishing an Italian
republic, stood little chance against the power of Austria. It therefore fell to the more conservative Cavour to direct the course of
Italian unification with the aid of a somewhat unscrupulous
approach to diplomacy. Mazzini, disgusted with this turn of events
and with the apparent capitulation of his former disciple, Garibaldi,
complained that Machiavelli had triumphed after all.

German nationalism also co-operated initially with liberalism as
the middle-class search for political power and the desire for
national unity coincided. Again, however, the 1848 Revolutions
showed the need for a different approach to unification and, after
1851, the initiative passed to the authoritarian government of
Prussia. There has always been some controversy as to whether this
was mere capitulation, or whether it was a voluntary change of
direction. Certainly the failure of the Frankfurt Parliament in 1849
closed the door on the liberal pattern of unification, but it could also
be argued that the authoritarian approach was not entirely alien to
German Romanticism, especially to the ideas of Hegel. Also,
economic theorists like List (1789–1846) had constantly urged the
need for economic and industrial progress. Prussia, as it turned out,
provided the model for both state power and industrial might, and
German liberalism resigned itself to what appeared the inevitable.
Baumgarten, the liberal historian, epitomized the attitude to
Bismarck in the 1860s. 'We thought that by our agitation we could
transform Germany,' he said, conceding that the whole liberal
approach had proved erroneous. But then, with Prussia redirecting

Germany's efforts, 'we experienced a miracle almost without parallel'.[8]

This 'miracle' was fully exploited, during the next fifty years, by a series of musicians, poets, philosophers and historians. Wagner, for example, intensified the mystical element of the German *Volk* in his operas, while Treitschke, Ranke, Droysen and Sybel all projected the Second Reich of Bismarck and the Kaiser as the logical, indeed, foreordained outcome of all previous German history. The fusion between the German Romantic spirit and Prussian militarism seemed complete. The way was open for a more assertive display of German power. German nationalism now showed unprecedented self-confidence; Treitschke, for example, boasted: 'From now on German policy can hardly commit any serious mistakes.'

*

We have seen that nationalism can change and adapt readily to different conditions. The period 1871–1914 also proved that it can exist at different levels. These eventually collapsed into each other, to bring about the First World War.

The main level consisted of the nation states which, after 1871, included Germany, France, Britain, Italy and Russia. Between these states rivalries became more and more intense, particularly those between Germany and France, and Germany and Russia. Before 1870 there had existed in France considerable admiration for German Romanticism, especially from Michelet and Quinet, while Victor Hugo had gone so far as to say: *'La France et l'Allemagne sont l'Europe. L'Allemagne le coeur, la France la tête.'*[9] This friendship, however, had never been returned by German writers, except, possibly, by Heine. Then came the shock of defeat in the Franco-Prussian War, which evoked from the French a bitterly anti-German response, which was to be further whipped up by the writings of Maurras (1868–1952) and Barrès (1862–1923). Indeed, Franco-German hostility was the key factor behind the emergence of the alliance systems of the last three decades of the century. Meanwhile, German nationalism had developed a feeling of deep contempt for the Slavs of Eastern Europe, while there evolved in Russia a powerful reaction against German influences; the expression of this took different forms, ranging from the novels of Dostoevsky to the official views of Pobedonostsev. A strong undercurrent of militarism pervaded Russia as well as Germany, intensified by Russian success in the Turkish War of 1877. Dostoevsky, for example, declared that: 'War rejuvenates men. It raises the spirit of the people and the recognition of their worth.' The corresponding German war fever was best expressed by Nietzsche (1844–1900): 'You should have eyes that always seek an enemy – *your* enemy . . . Your enemy you shall seek, your war you shall wage'.[10]

Below the level of powerful and aggressive nations was the level of incipient nationalism. This existed mainly in Central and Eastern Europe in the multi-national empires of the Turks and Habsburgs. Because these two 'prisons' of nation states were of vital strategic importance to the other major powers, the Slavs remained locked up for the whole period in Central Europe, and until 1913 in the Balkans. Germany, for example, bolstered up Austria-Hungary, while Turkey was used by Britain as a bulwark against Russian expansion in the eastern Mediterranean. Power politics on this scale meant, in the long term, a dangerous accumulation of resentment among the Slav peoples. At the turn of the century this was not likely to concern the four governments which dominated Europe, and Joseph Chamberlain in any case believed that 'The day of the smaller nations has long since passed away'.

He also added 'The day of Empires has come.' Between 1870 and 1914 the nationalism of the great powers had overspilled normal frontiers. The resulting 'super' nationalism formed another level and consisted of two distinct varieties. The first was imperialism. Britain, France and Italy all competed for territories overseas, while Germany pursued a systematic policy of colonial acquisition and naval expansion which came under the general term *Weltpolitik*. The second form of expansionist nationalism was the type normally prefixed by the term 'pan'. The Russian variety, pan-Slavism, sought to liberate Bulgarians, southern Slavs, Czechs, Slovaks and Poles from Turkish and Austrian rule and, of course, to extend Russian influence to the heart of Europe. Pan-Germanism was based on two unquestioned assumptions: one was that Germany's frontiers should be extended to include all the German-speaking peoples of Europe; the other, that the German peoples were entitled to *Lebensraum* in the East at the expense of the Slavs. Herder had justified this concept far back in the nineteenth century with the statement that 'The Slavic peoples occupy a larger space on earth than they do in history'.[11]

Imperialism and pan-movements were both potentially lethal,

giving national rivalries a new edge. Although continental considerations had been the main determinants of the system of alliances
which developed after 1871, it was the spread of supernationalism
which promoted the armaments race, especially between Germany
and Britain, and Germany and Russia. By 1914 there was unprecedented tension throughout Europe, ideal conditions for the spread
of war. The *casus belli* occurred, in the area of incipient nationalism,
with the assassination of the Archduke Franz Ferdinand at
Sarajevo.

Nationalism has always had a tendency to schizophrenia. Between
1919 and 1945 it showed greater extremes than at any other time
before or since. On the one hand, there were high hopes of permanent
peace and harmony now that national self-determination had been
accepted as the guiding principle in redrawing Europe's frontiers.
On the other hand, military defeat and economic disaster provided
ideal conditions for the emergence of a new type of nationalism
which was revolutionary, militarist and destructive.

The victorious Allies drew up the peace settlement of 1919 on the
assumption that the Great War had been caused by the aggressive
nationalism of Germany and by the deprivation of the rights of
Germany's minority peoples, especially the Slavs. The answer,
therefore, was to follow the principle of national self-determination
and create a series of new nation states which would also possess a
balanced constitution – so that their nationalism could be demo-
cratized from the very start. Peace in the future could also be
guaranteed by the pursuit of internationalism in the form of the
League of Nations which, according to President Wilson's Fourteen
Points, would afford 'mutual guarantees of political independence
and territorial integrity to great and small powers alike'.[12]
Nationalism would be, at one and the same time, liberated and
controlled; the experience of 1914–18 would therefore come to be
seen as 'the war to end wars'.

At the other extreme, the inter-war period saw the emergence of
what has been called 'inflamed nationalism' in the form of Italian
Fascism, German National Socialism, and Eastern European adapt-
ations of the two. Fascism and Nazism had in common the rejection
of the traditional structure of authority and a contempt for class
barriers. They sought to redefine the relationship between the

individual and the state by stressing the people's corporate identity; according to Mussolini, 'In the Fascist state the individual is not suppressed, but rather multiplied'.[13] The main purpose of the renewed power of the state was to promote external expansion and victory at the expense of weaker neighbours. Hitler, for example, insisted that 'struggle is the father of all things' and that war was man's 'primal condition'.

There is a tendency to consider Nazism as a variety of fascism; but there are, in fact, some differences.[14] Italian Fascism was essentially the vehicle for Mussolini's opportunism and was always subordinated to the *Duce*'s cult of personality. Nazism had stronger and deeper ideological roots which combined the *Volk* of the early Romantics with the theory of racial dominance generated by Gobineau's *Essay on the Inequality of the Human Races*. The result was the transformation of the German *Volk* into the Aryan master-race, in the name of which Hitler oppressed the Slavs, endeavoured to exterminate the Jews, and eventually led Germany to destruction

During the period of German occupation, European resistance leaders came to see the nation state as dangerous and obsolete.[15] Yet once again nationalism displayed a remarkable resilience and capacity for survival. Despite being discredited by the excesses of the 1930s and the Second World War, it became, after 1945, more widespread than ever before.

In the first place, it managed to sustain itself in Europe, although without the extremes of the period 1871–1945. There were those who hoped that Western Europe would abandon the nation state and seek political integration. But progress in this direction was very limited. Since governments invariably insisted on retaining full jurisdiction over domestic and foreign affairs, the nation state was perpetuated rather than undermined. Eastern European countries, too, lost none of their national consciousness. The spread of an international ideology like communism was counterbalanced by national responses to the heavy hand of the Soviet Union. Since 1945, another form of nationalism has gained ground in Europe, profiting from the removal of national tensions between the major powers. Several Western European states have experienced regional nationalism. The Kilbrandon Commission (1969–73) acknowledged the importance of Scottish and Welsh nationalism within the United Kingdom, while the French government is having to come to terms with separatism in Brittany and Provence; the Italian government with claims from Sicily and Sardinia; and the post-Franco régime in Spain with the Basques and Catalans. Whether or not this regional nationalism can be adapted to the existing state and inter-state structures of Western Europe is likely to be a major issue for the rest of the century.

Nationalism began as a European phenomenon and was also an important factor in the spread of European imperialism. Yet, since 1945, it has also been used as a means of pushing back European rule in the Third World. Nationalism in Asia has developed as a series of Western influences implanted onto an historic and indigenous base; this applies particularly to India, Cambodia, Thailand, Vietnam, Burma, Iran and Indonesia, where modernization and the traditions of the strongest ethnic group merged to set in motion powerful liberation campaigns. At first sight, nationalism seemed less appropriate to African conditions, for imperial boundaries had incorporated many different tribes; Nigeria, for example, consisted of over 250 ethnic groups. Yet African leaders like Nkrumah and Nyerere aimed at creating a new allegiance which cut across tribal affiliations and which kept intact the boundaries drawn by the imperial powers. It is true that there were disastrous civil wars in the Congo and Nigeria, and that the numerous border conflicts have given Africa the world's largest refugee population. Yet the alternatives to the nation state, particularly small pre-imperial kingdoms or large political conglomerations, seemed far less likely to succeed. It has been pointed out that Africa contains the largest number of states of any continent on earth and that most of these are relatively stable. Besides, these African nations are no more unreal than those of the Belgians or the Yugoslavs, which have also been created 'from among the ruins of earlier empires'.[16]

*

Nationalism today affects a larger area of the world than at any other time in history and shows little sign of succumbing to other 'isms'. Even a universalist ideology like Marxism, which believes that 'the working man has no country', has settled into national forms; indeed, A. D. Smith refers to 'a proliferation of Marxist nationalisms and highly nationalist Marxisms'.[17] Nationalism retains its dual character and still provides the means for either liberation or oppression. According to K. R. Minogue, therefore, "There is room for both the Sleeping Beauty and the Frankenstein's monster view of nationalism'.[18]

34

Marxism and its Manifestations to 1980

The purpose of this chapter is to provide a brief survey and explanation of the different forms of Communism which emanated from the ideas of Karl Marx. It will outline the basic elements of Marxist thought and show how individual reformulations of this thought reacted with changing material circumstances to produce, by 1980, a series of distinctively regional versions.

*

Despite the quantity and complexity of their writings, it is possible to identify three main constituents in the thought of Marx and Engels.[1]

The first was a determinist conception of society and of the relationship between economic circumstances and political power. The *foundation*, or base, of society was always the state of economic development reached by the ruling class. By the mid-nineteenth century this consisted of either bourgeois capitalism in the more advanced areas of Europe, or decaying feudalism elsewhere. The *superstructure* consisted of the political, juridical and religious institutions by which the ruling class maintained its grip. Alteration of these institutions could be achieved only be removing the economic base from which they sprang.

The second component was the theory of value and profit. The proletariat, Marx believed, was created and used by the bourgeoisie as wage labourers but were always paid far less than the real value of what they produced. The balance of the value therefore con-

Marxism and its Manifestations to 1980

stituted profit, which was used as capital to exploit more wage labour. In this self-perpetuating process it was essential to find new outlets for investment and fresh supplies of labour. When home markets became saturated because of 'epidemics of over-production', capital spread to other parts of the world in the form of imperialism. At the same time, 'unbridled competitive struggle'[2] resulted in the elimination of smaller scale capitalism and the emergence of monopolies. Eventually, capitalism of all types would reach a crisis. This would coincide with the growing strength of the proletariat, which 'becomes concentrated in greater masses' and would seek to overcome its 'misery, oppression, slavery, degradation, exploitation'.[3]

The way in which this change was expected to occur was the third main element of Marxist thought. In their *Communist Manifesto* (1848), Marx and Engels argued: 'The history of all human society, past and present, has been the history of class struggles.'[4] This has not been fortuitous, but had followed a definite course in accordance with certain laws of history which, it has been claimed, Marx uncovered in much the same way as Darwin revealed the process of evolution. The basic pattern was dialectical, and derived from the intellectual methodology of Hegel: that each thesis developed, an antithesis and the resulting interaction produced a synthesis which, as a new thesis, generated a further antithesis and hence revived conflict. Marx developed this at two levels, 'of the external world and of human thought'.[3] Internally, the dialectic has been used ever since by Marxists, and by others, as a method of criticism, examination and analysis. Historically, it was made to show the way in which class conflict developed. Each economic system and class had created its own antithesis, which would inevitably interact with the thesis to form a new system. According to Engels, 'from its origin the bourgeoisie has been saddled with its antithesis: that capitalists cannot exist without wage workers'.[2] Thus, as the *Communist Manifesto* asserted, 'the bourgeoisie produces its own gravediggers. Its downfall and the victory of the proletariat are equally inevitable'.[4] In order to effect this change it might well be necessary to resort to violence, since 'Force is the midwife of every old society pregnant with a new one'.[5] The alternative to bourgeois rule would initially be the 'dictatorship of the proletariat', which would dismantle the capitalist superstructure and extend the powers of the state to cover credit, communication, education, land and the instruments of production. Eventually society and the economy would become fully collective and co-operative in the spirit of communism. This would mean that the coercive elements of the state could disappear, followed by political institutions themselves. Engels believed that 'The interference of the state power in social relations becomes superfluous in one sphere after another, and then dies away of itself . . . The state is not "abolished", it withers away'.[3] What would be left is the Marxist ideal – the 'classless society'.

The actual method of bringing about the 'dictatorship of the proletariat' in the mid-nineteenth century was never clearly stated. Although, in the words of the *Communist Manifesto*, a 'spectre' did indeed 'haunt Europe', it was still mainly a theoretical one. Marx and Engels assumed that the dialectical process, by which capitalism would be destroyed, would operate more rapidly in those countries which had already reached an advanced stage of capitalism than in those which were predominantly feudal. After all, the most developed countries would possess the largest and most discontented proletariats, who would be able to seize the initiative as the economic system entered its period of crisis. On balance, Central and Western Europe seemed the most vulnerable areas; Marx affirmed in 1848: 'The Communists turn their attention chiefly to Germany.'

*

Between 1850 and 1914 the influence of Marx was widespread, but uneven. Two International Working Men's Associations were established, the first in London (1864) and the second in Paris (1869). French socialism, although inclined mainly towards traditional utopianism, developed an influential Marxist wing, while British labour movements combined a few Marxist sympathies with their predominant commitment to trade unionism. As Marx had predicted, however, the new ideology was strongest in Germany.

What had not been foreseen was that there would be a major dispute over the interpretation of Marxist principles. Although this occurred throughout Europe, the most important example was in Germany, which possessed the largest socialist party in the world. Formed by Bebel and Liebknecht, the SPD (*Sozialdemokratische Partei Deutschlands*) sharply criticized the political and social structure of the Second Reich, particularly during the chancellorship of Bismarck (1871–90). The Party's main Marxist theorist, Kautsky, was entirely orthodox, and revolution was an essential

Marxism and its Manifestations to 1980

feature of his policy. This, however, had to be understood in a social and not necessarily violent sense. Co-operation with parliamentary regimes would bring few gains but 'The elections are a means to count ourselves and the enemy and they grant thereby a clear view of the relative strength of the classes and parties, their advance and their retreat. They prevent premature outbreaks and they guard against defeats.'[6] On the other hand, democracy 'is not capable of preventing this revolution. Democracy is to the proletariat what light and air are to the organism; without them it cannot develop its powers'.[6] In contrast to this approach, the case for Revisionism was presented in the 1890s by Bernstein. Marxism should be rescued from its obsession with revolution and allowed to accommodate itself to parliamentary institutions. Once the SPD had attained a majority in the *Reichstag* it could deal with Germany's social iniquities by legislation. Indeed, legislation 'is best adapted to positive social-political work' because it acts as 'a systematic force'. Revolution, on the other hand, was unpredictable and destructive, since it was primarily 'an elemental force'[7]

In addition to the orthodox and revisionist wings of German social democracy there also developed a more radical version of Marxism, led by Rosa Luxemburg and Karl Liebknecht. Before 1914 there was, therefore, a three-way split, and the ideological emphasis of the SPD still had to be settled.

Then came the First World War and with it a much more uniform policy. Far from everywhere destroying capitalism, as Lenin hoped, the war contributed to the breaking of the first wave of militant Marxism in Western and Central Europe. The real victor here was Revisionism. The socialist parties placed nationalism first in every country except Serbia and Russia, and supported their governments. In Germany, Bernstein was now joined by Kautsky (whom Lenin branded as 'renegade'); Kautsky believed that the dialectical process had not yet reached the stage where the overthrow of capitalism was imminent. Adherents to revolutionary Marxism now found themselves the exception rather than the rule and protested in their own way. During the war two offshoots from the SPD formed themselves into new parties. These were the Independent Socialists and the Spartacus League (soon to become the Communist Party, led by Liebknecht and Rosa Luxemburg). Ironically, these found themselves after the war in conflict with an established order which was dominated by the SPD. In January 1919 the government of the

Weimar Republic, of which the SPD provided both president and chancellor, suppressed a Communist rising in Berlin, in which both Luxemburg and Liebknecht were killed. A few months later it destroyed the Soviet Republic of Bavaria, which had been created by the Independent Socialists at the end of 1918.

The pattern was similar elsewhere in Europe. Many Marxists had emerged from the war as Revisionists, accepting the permanence of parliamentary institutions. A smaller number still favoured the revolutionary approach, but now looked to Russia, the new centre of Communism, for leadership and inspiration.

*

While it was becoming apparent that Western and Central Europe would not, after all, be the centre of radical Marxism, a revolutionary impetus was growing in Russia. This was in the form of a new movement, Marxism-Leninism, or Bolshevism. Lenin broke away in 1903 from the more moderate Mensheviks, having already attacked Legal Marxism and Revisionism. He moved in the opposite direction to Bernstein, adapting Marxism to revolutionary conditions rather than to parliamentary institutions. Substantial modifications were necessary, and he once observed: 'We do not regard Marx's theory as something completed and inviolable.'[8] As with other Marxist leaders, in fact, many of Lenin's changes to this theory arose from the force of reappraised circumstances.

Lenin's main theoretical contribution to Marxism was his belief that the first revolution could occur in a more backward country like Russia: that capitalism was most immediately vulnerable at the weakest link in its chain, rather than where it was most highly developed. The war, he maintained, revealed capitalism in decline everywhere, but the process of overthrowing old régimes would actually begin in Russia. Other, more developed countries would then benefit from Russia's revolutionary experience, in return for which Russia would be influenced by socialist developments in the West during the period of the 'dictatorship of the proletariat'.

In his preparation for revolution in Russia, Lenin combined deference to the dialectic with a strong element of pragmatism. He acknowledged that some parliamentary experience was desirable for the development of working-class consciousness and organization. It was even necessary to collaborate with the 'revolutionary

Marxism and its Manifestations to 1980

bourgeoisie' to overthrow the Tsarist régime, since this would bring Russia nearer, dialectically, to the phase of proletarian revolution. At this point, however, Lenin disagreed profoundly with the Mensheviks. The latter, under Martov, argued for a substantial period of parliamentary rule which, in the long term, could be expected to evolve into a socialist system. Lenin, by contrast, considered that the dialectic must be accelerated, and he made this clear in his *April Theses* (1917). After the overthrow of the Tsar by the March Revolution, a Provisional Government was established, based to some extent on Western constitutional principles. Lenin now argued: 'The peculiarity of the current moment in Russia consists in the transition from the first stage of the revolution, which gave power to the bourgeoisie as a result of the insufficient consciousness and organization of the proletariat, to the second stage, which should give the power into the hands of the proletariat.'[9]

Forcing the pace like this obviously eliminated any possibility of a spontaneous revolution, and made a carefully formulated strategy essential. Lenin's solution was the development of a tightly organized Party Central Committee, which consisted of dedicated professional revolutionaries. After all, 'in its struggle for power the proletariat has no other weapon but organization'.[10] The Party adopted conspiratorial methods and the October Revolution, which overthrew the Provisional Government, was a vindication of Lenin's concentration of 'a great superiority of forces at the decisive point, at the decisive moment'. (See Chapter 19.)

The aftermath of the Revolution saw the establishment of Lenin's own version of the 'dictatorship of the proletariat' and the adoption of his interpretation of socialism as the first step towards the ultimate ideal of communism. Considerable coercion was used to accomplish this, although the roles were now reversed: the 'majority' now suppressed the 'minority'. But the possession of power also brought a divergence of views as to the future priorities of Marxism-Leninism. A profound ideological and tactical split developed between Trotsky and Stalin, resulting in the eventual expulsion and assassination of Trotsky.

Trotsky's main contribution was the theory of 'permanent revolution' (or 'uninterrupted revolution'), although this had already been partially incorporated into Marxism-Leninism during Lenin's lifetime. Revolution, Trotsky argued, would not end with the overthrow of bourgeois rule by the proletariat. It must continue, as 'permanent revolution', on both a national and worldwide scale. Nationally, it could end only 'in the complete liquidation of all class society'.[11] Internationally it could attain completion only in 'the final victory of the new society on our entire planet'.[11] Although this fitted in logically with the theory of the dialectic, in practice the worldwide emphasis seemed inappropriate in the 1920s because of a growing disillusionment with the prospect of Western revolutions. The Bolsheviks had been confronted by extensive Western intervention on the side of counter-revolution during the civil war (1918–20) and the spontaneous revolutions in Germany and Hungary in 1919 had been crushed. A sharp reaction therefore occurred; the priority was now to develop 'Socialism in One Country', to make Russia self-sufficient and invulnerable in a hostile ideological environment. This was the principal aim of Stalin, who used the power which he had accumulated by 1927 to restructure Marxist-Leninism in two ways.

First, he elevated the role of leadership to a new pinnacle by redefining, somewhat conveniently, the Marxist concepts of 'base' and 'superstructure'. 'The base gives rise to the superstructure, but this does not at all mean that it merely reflects the basis, that it is passive, neutral, is indifferent to the fate of its basis, to the fates of classes, to the character of the system. On the contrary . . . it becomes the greatest active force, actively assists its basis to take shape and acquire strength, and makes every effort to help the new order to finish off and liquidate the old basis and the old classes.'[12] This directly justified the use of coercion and the development of repressive organs like OGPU and the NKVD, to say nothing of the interference of the leadership in all political decisions. The Party had now become, in effect, 'the instrument of the dictatorship of the proletariat'.[13] The logical conclusion was the systematic elimination of all opposition, since what was needed was 'absolute and complete unity of action on the part of all members of the Party'.[13] (This was actually in contrast to the earlier dialectical controversy which Lenin had encouraged within the Party.)

Second, Stalin greatly accelerated the construction of the Soviet state, concentrating on enlarging its workforce and industrial production. The main reason for this was his obsession with the threat of outside intervention, as he had no faith in the Trotskyist vision of assistance being rendered to Russia by worldwide revolution. To Stalin there was a stark choice. 'We are fifty or a hundred years behind the advanced countries. We must make good this distance in ten years. Either we do it, or they will crush us.'[14] His methods attained a new peak of ruthlessness. The superstructure redesigned the base in a series of Five Year Plans which forcibly collectivized agriculture and converted the Soviet Union into an industrial and military power. (See Chapter 29.)

In the last ten years of his rule, Stalin became the first agent for spreading communism, although not in the way envisaged by Marx, Lenin or Trotsky. Communism did not take over in Western Europe by a series of locally-planned revolutions inspired by the Russian example; instead, it spread over Eastern Europe in the wake of military conquest at the end of the Second World War. The satellite states which emerged were therefore very different from the more advanced societies Lenin had hoped would be a source of inspiration to Russia.

By 1953 Stalin had completely personalized the superstructure in the form of dictatorship. His successors, however, finding the hero cult and extremes of coercion equally unacceptable, proceeded to redress the balance. A destalinization campaign was initiated by Khrushchev, who affirmed in 1956: 'Stalin abandoned the Leninist method of convincing and educating for one of administrative violence, mass repression and terror.'[15] Hence it was necessary 'to eradicate the cult of the individual as alien to marxism-leninism'.[15] But Khrushchev's brand of revisionism did not entirely eradicate Stalinist influences. After Khrushchev was removed from power in 1964, the superstructure was once again strengthened, although Brezhnev stopped short of Stalin's excesses and made no attempt to restore the personality cult. Soviet leaders after 1953 did manage to remove some of the obsessions of Stalinism; they even found a way of using coercion without some of the horror which had once accompanied it. But the revised form of Soviet Communism became, in its turn, rigid and introverted. It was also no longer the only major influence on Communist movements elsewhere.

Stalin had always aimed to keep world Communism as a monolithic organization subservient to Moscow. By the late 1940s this concept was already being challenged by President Tito, who was determined to apply his own brand of Communism in Yugoslavia and who was subsequently expelled from Stalin's Cominform (Communist Information Bureau) for his pains. Worse was to follow as the Chinese Communist leadership emerged as a major rival to

Soviet hegemony in 1949. But it was Khrushchev's policy of destalinization which set the seal on the monolithic image of world Communism and promoted, directly and indirectly, what has been called 'polycentrism', or more pronounced regional variants. This occurred for two main reasons. First, the attack on personality cult undermined the focal point of unity and, because it also attacked one of the ingredients of Maoism, was bitterly resented by China. Peking therefore emerged as a centre to rival Moscow and, in an intensive propaganda war, denounced Khrushchev's line as 'revisionist'. Second, destalinization had a profoundly unsettling effect upon Eastern Europe. Already shaky Stalinist régimes were gravely embarrassed by Khrushchev's revelations of administrative terror and were faced with a series of disturbances which culminated in the Hungarian uprising of November 1956. Khrushchev's reactions to these disturbances shocked the rest of the world and seemed to show that the Soviet Union was more concerned with maintaining control over its satellite states than with preserving or reviving its moral claims for leadership of world Communism. It is ironical that, while the Soviet Union had finally emerged as a superpower with a régime less repressive than of its predecessors, it now inspired less commitment from other Communists than it had during the harsh era of Stalin.

*

An alternative form of revolutionary Marxism had, meanwhile, been developed in China by Mao Tse Tung, both before and after his overthrow of Chiang Kai-Shek's régime in 1949. Chinese Communism was partly a derivation of Russian Marxism-Leninism and partly an adaptation of Marxism to Chinese conditions.

Mao acknowledged his debt to Lenin and the 'salvoes of the October Revolution'[16] which brought Marxism to China. He also learned from the Bolsheviks the importance of organization and conspiracy, which undoubtedly influenced his view that 'A revolution is . . . an act of violence by which one class overthrows another'.[17] Moreover, 'The seizure of power by armed force . . . is the central task and highest form of revolution.'[18]

In some respects, however, Mao reinterpreted Marx and Lenin, adapting their ideas to Chinese thought and conditions. At a philosophical level, he imposed the dialectic on the traditional Chinese concept of *yin* and *yang*, opposites which exist harmoniously within every form or being. He substituted contradiction for harmony, but

324

retained the notion of opposites. Thus 'A thing moves and develops because of such contradictions within itself'.[19] He emphasized, however, that there were two types of contradictions, which he labelled antagonistic and non-antagonistic. The latter contradictions, he maintained, would often have to reconcile themselves in order to deal with the former contradiction. Or, put in political terms, lesser differences should be resolved so that the major enemy could be disposed of.

This approach immediately opened the way for a flexible and pragmatic course of action in bringing about a revolution, and made Chinese Communism highly distinctive. There was to be less emphasis on the internal conflict between classes and more on a united front to overthrow feudalism and imperialism; the implementation of socialism could then follow. Hence he was able to recast some of the fundamental ideas of Marxism and Marxism–Leninism. To replace the regime toppled by revolution, he could conceive 'a joint revolutionary-democratic dictatorship of several revolutionary classes'.[20] He could thus adopt a more flexible and pragmatic approach to the situation in China. He emphasized: 'We are not utopians and cannot divorce ourselves from the actual conditions confronting us.'[21] Since the overwhelming majority of the Chinese were peasants, they had to become the revolutionary force and not remain, in Leninist and Stalinist terms, 'the reserve and ally of the working class'. This creation of a *rural* revolutionary vanguard was Mao's most important legacy, since it could be related to the concept of the 'people's war' and to guerrilla tactics designed for the countryside rather than the cities.

After 1949 trends in China puzzled the rest of the world and there was some controversy as to their real significance. One possible explanation is this. During the 1950s Mao encouraged widespread debate, thus putting into practice his views on contradiction. 'Let a hundred flowers blossom; and let a hundred schools of thought contend.'[22] By the end of the decade, however, Mao had become dissatisfied with the rate of industrial and agricultural growth in China and was concerned that debate was turning rapidly into criticism. Furthermore, he suspected that the Chinese Communist superstructure was becoming as rigid as its Soviet counterpart. He therefore unleashed the 'Great Proletarian Cultural Revolution' in an attempt to rediscover the Chinese revolutionary spirit, thereby 'preventing capitalist restoration and building socialism'. He also brought to a peak his own personality cult and eradicated all internal dissent and external Soviet influences. By 1969, however, the Cultural Revolution had burned itself out and Chinese Communism resumed a more pragmatic course during the 1970s. The most remarkable example of this was the accommodation between China and the West which followed Mao's death. In placing China's immediate strategic interests and intense hostility towards Russia above any ideological conflict with the West, Mao's successors seemed to be acting on the chairman's pre-Cultural Revolution dictum: 'In China and in the present circumstances.'[23]

*

In 1966 Lin Piao said: 'Taking the entire globe, if North America and Western Europe can be called the "cities of the world" then Asia, Africa and Latin America constitute "rural areas of the world".'[24] He added that, since 1945, the impetus of revolution has been 'held back' in the former areas but has accelerated in the latter. Events of the 1960s and 1970s seemed to support this analysis. The revolutionary initiative was captured by Third World Communism while, in Europe, the more moderate Eurocommunism adopted an evolutionary approach.

Third World Communism derived from Marxism, Marxism-Leninism and Maoism. Marx claimed that the bourgeoisie had created 'a world after its own image'. Lenin believed that this had led to the oppression of subject peoples by imperialism, 'the monopoly stage of capitalism'. Furthermore, 'wars waged by colonies and semi-colonies in the imperialist era are not only possible but inevitable'. Mao Tse Tung explained how the overthrow of imperialism could be accomplished, and also how a Communist régime could be established which was related to the needs of the more backward areas of the world; the former by guerrilla warfare, the latter by gearing Marxist-Leninist ideology to the peasantry rather than to the proletariat. He enumerated his tactics of guerrilla warfare in considerable detail, basing everything on the maxim: 'Fight, fail, fight again, fail again, fight again ... till ... victory; that is the logic of the people.'[25] Time and persistence were the vital factors, since imperialism was considered totally vulnerable to popular movements. Western powers were, in his view, no more than 'paper tigers'.

Lu Ting-yi (a member of the Chinese Communist Party Central

Marxism and its Manifestations to 1980

Committee) therefore had good reason for saying, in 1951, that 'the classic type of revolution in colonial and semi-colonial countries is the Chinese Revolution'.[26] But Third World revolutionaries were also swayed by conditions and circumstances within their own areas. Two particularly successful leaders, Ho Chi Minh of Vietnam and Castro of Cuba, were more pragmatic in their outlook even than Mao Tse Tung. Castro, on his own admission, became a Communist late in his career. Undoubtedly, this attention to circumstance has also affected the relations between Third World Communist régimes and the major Communist powers. Although they had a closer resemblance to China, both Cuba and Vietnam chose to maintain close links with the Soviet Union, largely for economic and strategic reasons. The same applied to Angola and Mozambique, the new Marxist states in Africa.

Marxism in Western Europe was characterized by its disillusionment, during the 1950s, 1960s and 1970s, with the Soviet Union. This was in complete contrast to the 1930s and 1940s, when the USSR, despite the excesses of Stalinism, had appealed to intellectuals of the 'far Left' as the 'fatherland of the international proletariat', and had managed to recruit numerous agents like Philby and Burgess in Britain. One reason for this disillusionment was the emergence of the Soviet Union as one of the world's two military superpowers; Western Marxists began to feel that it was now concentrating entirely on national and strategic interests and had lost sight of its ideological role in the world. Another was the alarm felt at the subjection of Eastern Europe. The Soviet invasion of Hungary (1956) and Czechoslovakia (1968) came as a profound shock to Western Communist parties, who vied with each other in condemning Khrushchev and Brezhnev. Yet Western capitalism was still considered unacceptable, whether as free enterprise or in the form of the planned economies now favoured by Western Europe's socialist parties. What, then, was the answer?

During the 1970s, many of the Communist parties in European countries outside the Soviet *bloc* revised their strategies and re-examined their ideologies in a broadly similar way. They were referred to increasingly as 'Eurocommunists', although this label did not imply the loss of national identity by each party or the growth of any international body. Gradually, Communist leaders and spokesmen in Italy, Spain and France built up a new strategy. Radical change was still regarded as essential, in

327

Aspects of European History 1789–1980

Napolitano's phrase, to end 'the anarchy of capitalist development'.[27] The process of change should, however, be accomplished
by constitutional means and the Soviet system should be avoided.
Indeed, Azcárate referred to this type of Communism as a
'parody of Marxism',[28] while Ellenstein declared: 'For us the
Soviet system is neither an example nor a model.'[29] Eurocommunism therefore took the radical step of removing Leninism as a
basic source of inspiration. Its approach to revolution was also
anti-Leninist. Eurocommunists would not seek to disrupt a functioning constitution but, as Carrillo warned: 'In no way do we put
aside the possibility of reaching power by revolutionary means, if
the dominating classes close the democratic paths.'[29] In other
words, revolution was seen as a defensive tactic to uphold democracy rather than as an offensive weapon with which to destroy it.
It is hardly surprising that by 1980 those groups in Western
Europe who regarded themselves as truly revolutionary condemned the Euro-communist parties for being part of the establishment and for turning their back on internationalism.

The constant reformulation of Marxism led, by the 1970s, to its
control of one-third of the world's population; at the same time,
however, it revealed several general problems. One of the original
hopes of Marx and Engels was that an ideology based entirely on
materialism would be best able to guarantee a high standard of
living and a permanent material wellbeing. In practice, the results
of Communist rule were somewhat mixed. The cost of any increase in production was enormous; Soviet and Chinese collectivization produced many millions of human casualties and caused
severe fluctuations in the standard of living. A major dilemma
confronting every Marxist government was how to achieve a
balance between a planned collective economy and a quality of
life for its people which could compete with non-Communist Western societies. The latter, indeed, compounded the problem; far
from falling into headlong decline, as Marx had predicted, they
set a furious pace in economic and consumer growth, especially
after the Second World War, with which even the Soviet Union
had difficulty in competing. Hence most Marxist régimes were
driven to modify some of their policies, and tended to oscillate
between all-out pursuit of industrial and agricultural targets and
periodic concessions to consumer demand. There was, of course,

Marxism and its Manifestations to 1980

no ideological formula for this, each régime being influenced very much by its own problems and circumstances. During the early 1980s the disparity between the Communist world and the West became more marked than ever, necessitating in the Soviet Union a series of reforms under Andropov and Gorbachev.

By the beginning of the 1990s Marxism appeared to have retreated from its high-water mark of the previous decade. Soviet Communism had been radically redefined by Gorbachev to take account of alternative political viewpoints and of market principles in the economy; hardline Communist regimes had collapsed in the former Soviet satellite states in Eastern Europe; the third world Marxist regimes in Africa had been obliged to abandon their dogmatic course; and a number of western European Communist parties had given up their previous titles altogether. Clearly, Marxism was in crisis. But it remains to be seen whether such major changes represent the complete bankruptcy of Marxist idealogy or a particularly active period of adjustment to try to update this ideology's more anachronistic components. It is also possible that the remaining Marxist states which had introduced extensive reform might in the future revert to a more traditional form of Marxism.

35

Imperialism

Between 1815 and 1880 there was a comparative lull in the imperial and maritime conflicts which complicated international relations in the eighteenth and late nineteenth centuries. Three of the five colonial powers had suffered heavy losses and could do no more than safeguard what was left. Spain, for example, had lost Central and South America to independence movements and had to content herself with Cuba, Rio de Oro and the Philippines. Portugal was confined, after being deprived of Brazil, to the African coastal enclaves of Guinea, Mozambique and Angola, while the Dutch were left with only the East Indies and Surinam, after ceding the Cape and Ceylon to Britain in 1815. The other two colonial powers continued to be active. France, deprived by 1815 of one empire, began the task of building another, conquering Algeria during the 1830s and 1840s, extending her influence to Senegal in the 1850s and acquiring direct control over Tahiti, the Marquesas and part of Indochina. Britain, who found her maritime strength enhanced by her gains in 1815, steadily spread her power over Australia and New Zealand, as well as appropriating Singapore (1819), part of Burma (1852), and Lagos (1861). Yet such expansion was relatively peaceful. British and French spheres of influence did not overlap as they had in the eighteenth century, and there was, in any case, an official understanding that the British Empire was replete. The Duke of Wellington, for example, said in 1829: 'I am anxious to avoid exciting the attention and jealousy of other powers by extending our possessions.'[1] In some quarters there was actually opposition to imperial commitments. Cobden, for example, put the fashionable Manchester School view that empire was irrelevant to trade, adding that it would be 'a happy day when England has not an acre of territory in continental Asia'.[1]

Then, during the last two decades of the nineteenth century and the immediate pre-war period, imperial rivalries were renewed, reaching a greater intensity than ever before. The Monroe Doctrine (1823) discouraged European states from turning their attention to the American continent, but Africa, the Far East and the Pacific all experienced partition. British acquisitions during the 1880s and 1890s included Egypt, Nigeria, East Africa, Uganda, Bechuanaland, the Rhodesias, Nyasaland, Sierra Leone, the Sudan, Swaziland, Burma, Malaya, New Guinea and Borneo. The French extended their dominion over the whole of Laos, Annam and Tong King in Indochina, and over the whole of the West African interior. Germany carved out the enclaves of South-West Africa, Togoland, the Cameroons and German East Africa, together with the Pacific possessions of Eastern New Guinea, the Bismarck Archipelago and the Caroline Islands. Italy annexed Eritrea, Somaliland and, in 1912, Libya. Finally, Russia extended her Asiatic interests into the Liaotung Peninsula region of China. By 1914, therefore, most of the globe was under the rule of European countries or peopled by Europeans who had asserted their independence from the original metropolitan power. The only states which had managed to retain their autonomy were Japan (which had Europeanized itself), China (which had to put up with foreign enclaves and unfavourable trade agreements), Siam, Afghanistan, Ethiopia and Liberia.

This second wave of imperialism and, in particular, the 'scramble for Africa', has been the subject of considerable historical controversy, with emphasis accorded to economic, diplomatic, humanitarian and irrational factors. Such a variety of explanations is the inevitable result of the complexity of imperialism; the outward expansion of a country and, even more, of a continent, is caused by a variety of internal pressures, assisted by peripheral conditions as well. The next section of this chapter will, therefore, outline some of the main arguments that imperialism was the result of pressures within and between the European powers. The final section will deal with another approach: that European governments were not always keen on imperial ventures but were, on occasion, drawn reluctantly into colonization.

*

One of the first writers to analyse the pressure exerted by economic factors was the radical J. A. Hobson, whose *Imperialism* (1902) carried the argument that the European states had built up, through industrialization and financial development, a gross inequality of wealth. The concentration of wealth in the hands of the few created a crisis, for this 'surplus capital' could not 'find investments within the country' and had to seek outlets overseas. Thus Britain, Germany and France were forced 'to place larger and larger portions of their economic resources outside the area of their present political domain, and then stimulate a policy of political expansion so as to take in the new areas'.[2] The argument was subsequently elaborated by Lenin, although the latter rejected Hobson's belief that capitalism was redeemable provided that surplus wealth could be redirected to internal 'social investment' at home. Most historians have since pointed out that the Hobson-Lenin thesis does not fit the facts of imperial expansion. There was certainly a huge outflow of investment from Europe, but most of this went to areas which were not subsequently annexed, like Canada, the United States, Latin America and Russia. Hence the accumulation of surplus capital cannot be regarded as a general stimulus to imperial expansion. But this is not to say that economic factors had no influence at all. During the 1880s and 1890s successive British governments showed increased concern about the adoption of protective tariffs by Germany, the United States and other commercial competitors. The British prime minister, Lord Salisbury, for example, complained in 1895: 'Everywhere we see the advance of commerce checked by the enormous growth which the doctrines of protection are obtaining.'[1] Strong political pressure groups emerged, preparing official and public opinion for the transition from purely private enterprise to a more deliberate government policy towards imperialism. Joseph Chamberlain, in particular, sought to revive Britain's commercial supremacy by acquiring new sources of raw materials and outlets for finished goods. The German government, meanwhile, had been strongly influenced by the commercial interests of Bremen, Hamburg and Lübeck in the type of administration it had set up in South-West Africa and the Pacific Islands. Bismarck, on one

332

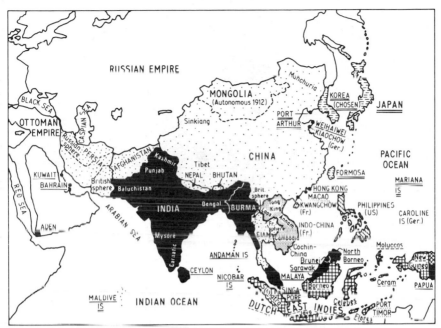

(a) The colonization of Asia by 1914

Colonization

occasion, referred to these protectorates as a 'business proposition', arguing that 'the flag follows trade'.[3] Furthermore, the new *Kolonialrat*, set up in 1890, was always attentive to the representations of the chambers of commerce of Hamburg, Bremen and Cologne.

Pressure groups of this type were not, however, the only force behind official imperialism in Britain and Germany, while in France, it has been argued, 'economic factors . . . were hardly ever responsible for the initiation of . . . colonial policy'.[4] W. L. Langer and A. J. P. Taylor accounted for the spread of imperialism in diplomatic rather than in economic terms,[5] an approach endorsed by D. K. Fieldhouse who believed that 'imperialism may be seen as the extension into the periphery of the political struggle of Europe'.[6] D. Thomson used a similar analogy: 'The naked power politics of the new colonialism were the projection, on to an overseas screen, of the inter-state frictions and rivalries of Europe.'[7]

Aspects of European History 1789–1980

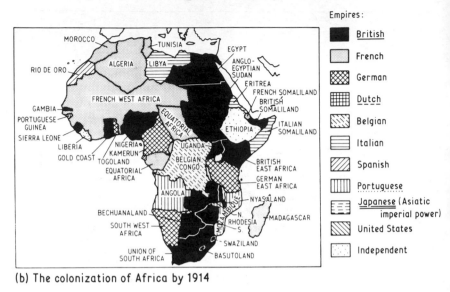

Empires:

- ■ British
- ☐ French
- ▨ German
- ▥ Dutch
- ▨ Belgian
- ≡ Italian
- ▨ Spanish
- ⦀ Portuguese
- ⊟ Japanese (Asiatic imperial power)
- ▧ United States
- ⬚ Independent

(b) The colonization of Africa by 1914

Colonization

It could be argued that Bismarck was partly responsible for this. Concerned that France might try to build an alliance against the newly formed German Reich to avenge the humiliation of 1870, Bismarck sought to isolate the Third Republic and, if possible, to induce a certain degree of dependence on German goodwill. The most effective means of achieving these aims was by creating and exploiting rifts between France and her potential allies. Europe was too volatile for such a design, but collisions in Africa carried little danger of a major war. This reasoning was supported by the Chancellor's celebrated statement that 'my map of Africa lies in Europe'. He was assisted by a revival of French enthusiasm for empire as a means of recovering lost prestige. As Gambetta said, 'In Africa France will make the first faltering steps of the convalescent'.[8] Hence he secretly encouraged France to annex Tunisia in 1881. The result was that Italy, who had plans for the area herself, went through an intense wave of francophobia, eventually joining Germany and Austria-Hungary in the Triple Alliance of 1882. Bismarck also endeavoured to prevent any entente between France and Britain while, at the same time, encouraging the French government to forget the loss of Alsace-Lorraine by

334

seeking compensation in Africa. (He told the French ambassador in 1885: 'Renounce the question of the Rhine; I will help you in securing all the satisfaction you require on all other points.'[9]) As evidence of his good faith to France, Bismarck had been pursuing a policy likely to challenge Britain's position in Africa and the Pacific. He laid claim, for example, to territory adjoining British spheres of influence, and proceeded to annex South-West Africa, Togoland, the Cameroons, Tanganyika and East New Guinea. There was also a domestic reason for seeking confrontation 'at a distance'. After 1884 Bismarck feared that the Kaiser's failing health would soon mean the accession of the Crown Prince Frederick. The latter, openly anglophile and liberal, would almost certainly dispense with Bismarck's services and construct a 'Gladstone cabinet'. On the other hand, his position would definitely be undermined if Britain were seen as a national threat. Herbert Bismarck later admitted, in 1890, that in order to weaken Frederick's power 'we had to launch a colonial policy, which is popular and can produce conflicts with England at any moment.'

How did Britain and France react to these machinations? Under the leadershop of Ferry, the Third Republic took full advantage of the favourable diplomatic situation by extending French influence well beyond the frontiers of Algeria and Senegal. By the time of the Berlin Conference (1885) it was clear that Britain had been out-manoeuvred and that her own interests might well be threatened unless more positive action were taken. From the mid-1890s, there-fore, the 'scramble for Africa' accelerated, assuming a momentum of its own. The alternative to direct annexation was no longer inde pendence but the certain intervention of a European rival. Hence French expansion eastwards towards the Nile, and German activities on the shore of Lake Victoria, threatened British interests in East Africa and Egypt, leaving her with little option but to annex Uganda. Similarly, the German presence in South-West Africa upset the delicate stability of the sub-continent and certainly hastened the colonization of Bechuanaland and the Rhodesias.

Less tangible than diplomatic factors were three other forces, which might be called curiosity, concern and national fulfilment. Curiosity prompted, and was, in turn, kept alive by, the work of explorers like Nachtigal, Barth, Flatters, Brazza, Speke, Burton, Livingstone and Stanley. The controversy over the source of the Nile was followed with passionate interest all over Britain and did much to prepare public opinion to accept a new imperial initiative in 'Darkest Africa'. Similar enthusiasm prevailed in France over discoveries in West and Equatorial Africa. For a while, in President Macmahon's words, 'Geography [had] become the philosophy of the world'.[10] Concern assumed a variety of forms. Missionaries like Moffat and Redman sought to convert whole tribes to Christianity and to promote their material well-being by encouraging contacts with traders. Sometimes the missionary societies put pressure on governments to take a more active role in suppressing evils like the East African slave trade or threats to Christianity. Sometimes the government intervened anyway; the German annexation of Kiaochow in 1897 was a direct result of the killing of two Jesuits in China. Another manifestation of concern was the unquestioned assumption that the indigenous peoples must, for their own benefit, be put into contact with a superior European culture. It was also the duty of the white man to civilize the black. Lord Curzon affirmed in 1907: 'In the Empire we have found not merely the key to glory and wealth but the call to duty and the means of service to mankind.'[1] Other statesmen and theorists emphasized the importance of imperialism as a means of national fulfilment. This was particularly the case in Germany, where Kaiser Wilhelm II openly pursued a policy of *Weltpolitik*, and the historian Treitschke felt impelled to write: 'Every virile people has established colonial power . . . All great nations in the fullness of their strength have desired to set their mark upon barbarian lands.' He added: 'The colonizing impulse has become a vital question for every nation.'[6] The Italian Prime Minister, Crispi, went so far as to claim that colonies were 'a necessity of modern life'.[11]

*

It would be a mistake to consider the parts of the world which came under colonial rule as entirely inert. On the contrary, certain parts of Africa exercised considerable 'pull', particularly on British imperialism; this is an argument stressed by less Eurocentric historians. (According to R. Robinson and J. Gallagher, for example, Britain was drawn into Africa by 'the persistent crisis in Egypt',[12] and the threat posed to British interests by the Boer Republics in South Africa.)

The major concern of the British government was to protect British routes to India, the most valuable part of the Empire, through the Suez Canal and round the Cape of Good Hope. Unfortunately, local problems made the northern and southern tips of Africa very unstable. The Egyptian Khedive was threatened, in 1881, by a major revolt led by Arabi Pasha, who aimed at freeing Egypt from all European influence. The British occupation of 1882 was not the end of the matter, for the great Islamic revolt in the Sudan against Anglo-Egyptian rule necessitated military action by Kitchener, culminating in the Battle of Omdurman in 1898. British rule was dragged further up the Nile and into East Africa by the need to outflank the Islamic threat, and to counter the moves of France and Germany. Meanwhile, the Boer Republics of the Transvaal and the Orange Free State were threatening the long-term British scheme for a loose federation of South African states which would also incorporate the Cape and Natal. The alternative could well be a United States of South Africa, dominated by a republican Transvaal and bitterly hostile to any British influence. Again, therefore, the British Government was receptive to pressure to acquire territory as a means of outflanking or isolating the challenge, in this case promoting the colonization of Bechuanaland on the western border of the Transvaal, and the Rhodesias to the north. The overall result of the two separate processes of expansion was a stretch of British territory from the Cape to the Mediterranean broken only by the German colony of Tanganyika.

It is significant that British imperialism was most actively sponsored by men, like Rhodes, McKinnon and Goldie who operated from inside Africa. Rhodes, who had made fortunes from the diamond mines at Kimberley and the gold reef at Johannesburg, turned his attention to territorial expansion north of the Limpopo, his ultimate intention being to build a rail-route from Cape Town to Cairo. The British government, by granting a Royal Charter to Rhodes' British South Africa Company in 1889, directly sanctioned his activities in Matabeleland and Mashonaland as a relatively inexpensive means of outflanking the threat from the Boers. In extending the range of British influence beyond the Zambezi, Rhodes greatly exceeded the original expectations of the Colonial Office.

Similarly, McKinnon's British East Africa Company, which was given a Charter in 1888 to safeguard British interests against German and indigenous threats, eventually pulled the British Crown into the unexpectedly large areas of Kenya and Uganda.

Even West Africa, predominantly French, had the substantial British enclave of Nigeria, a direct result of the energy and ambition of another local empire builder, Goldie, operating through the Royal Niger Company.

The great powers were drawn into some areas, paradoxically, by resistance of indigenous cultures and leaders to growing European influence. In these circumstances outright conquest took the place of commercial agreements and treaties of protection. The one major indigenous success was the victory of the Ethiopian leader, Menelik, over the Italians at Adowa in 1896, but even this served only to strengthen Italy's commitment to Empire and, ultimately, to shape Mussolini's African policy in the 1930s. Elsewhere, Islamic states which tried through the *jihad* (holy war) to purge themselves of the infidel, succeeded only in laying themselves open to invasion. The British, for example, destroyed the Mahdist state in the Sudan, while the French intensified their efforts in West Africa because of the resistance of leaders like Samori, and peoples like the Ahmadu. Numerous Negro and Bantu states and confederacies were also laid low, examples being the Ashanti, Dahomey, Bunyoro and the Matabele. But, although the indigenous response proved counter-productive in the face of an assertive and aggressive continent, it did establish a precedent for the distant future. Fifty years later, Europe's comparative decline would render it less capable of dealing with colonial rebellions and nationalist independence movements.

36

Decolonization

The peak of Europe's dominance over other parts of the world was reached in the decade before 1914 and immediately after the First World War. Thereafter the process of imperial expansion was gradually transformed into one of withdrawal. This change, at first imperceptible and then gradual, became, during the 1950s and 1960s, an unscrambling of colonies which was even more rapid than the original 'scramble' itself.

This 'decolonization' can be explained in two ways. On the one hand, strong opposition developed within the colonies against the rule of the metropolitan power while, on the other, the power's resistance was lessened by a revised attitude to imperialism which eventually made pulling out seem inevitable. The time-scale of this change was compressed by war; the impact of the Second World War on Europe's Asiatic colonies was quite as devastating as had been the Napoleonic Wars on Spanish and Portuguese America at the beginning of the nineteenth century.

*

The reaction against the imperial powers was threefold: indigenous nationalism in Asia and Africa, worldwide anti-colonialism which was given a forum in international institutions like the United Nations, and, finally, the pressure for decolonization applied peripherally by the two superpowers – the United States and the Soviet Union.

The spread of imperial rule in the late nineteenth century had, in some areas, encountered considerable resistance; this, in itself, was evidence of the deep roots of indigenous nationalism. Nevertheless, this defiance had been too weak in the face of European persistence, mainly because it had been expressed within the traditional context of the tribal war or of the Islamic *jihad*. During the twentieth century, however, anti-colonial movements became much more effective. For one thing, they assimilated European concepts of liberty, equality and self-determination, often combining these with a Marxist attitude to class struggle, and grafting the result to historic pride and cultural rediscovery. Hence political parties campaigned, in the best European tradition, for electoral reform and the control of colonial executives by more widely representative legislatures. At the same time, trade unions and other pressure groups sought to eliminate the economic and social manifestations of racialism. These new tactics were made possible by a social transformation; two colonial legacies which helped destroy colonialism were an educated indigenous élite conscious of its liberating role, and an ever-increasing mass following in the form of a more heavily concentrated urban proletariat.

The impact of the First World War on nationalism was widespread but uneven. It was, perhaps, most profound in the Arab areas of the Middle East. Egypt had a restive middle class, stirred by wartime inflation and ready to back Zaghlul's demands for extensive reforms and for self-government. Milner considered the situation so serious that autonomy was granted in 1922. Pressure also built up in the other Arab states, which had been liberated from Ottoman rule during the First World War only to be mandated to Britain and France. Imperial rule in the Asian sub-continent was also more precarious; the Amritsar Massacre of 1919 showed the depth of Indian opposition and discredited the imperial authorities, even while causing Gandhi to postpone his campaigns of civil disobedience. The British government eventually replied, in 1935, by introducing the Government of India Act which extended the powers of the provincial rulers. It was also generally accepted the sub-continent could, within the foreseeable future, be given dominion status along the lines of Canada and Australia.

Yet, with the major exception of Egypt, no European colonies were carried to full independence on the crest of the First World War. The draft, forced-labour and economic disruption had sharpened indigenous resentment but imperial rule remained, for the moment, intact. The real collapse came with the Second World War. The Japanese conquered most of South-East Asia and Indonesia, and proceeded systematically to dismantle French and Dutch rule. European vulnerability was further demonstrated by the fall of British Malaya, Singapore and Hong Kong. The Japanese occupation of these areas stirred nationalism in two ways. The first was intentional; an intensive anti-European propaganda campaign was combined with the promotion of local officials to replace the newly interned French and Dutch administrators. The second, however, was an unintended by-product of ruthless subjugation: the emergence of patriotic leaders like Ho Chi Minh who were determined, through the use of guerrilla tactics, to eject all forms of foreign dominance, whether European or Asiatic. When, therefore, the French and Dutch attempted to return to South-East Asia in the baggage van of the American armies, they encountered stiff resistance from the Viet Minh and the Indonesian movement led by Sukarno and Mohammed Hatta. The result was the proclamation of the Indonesian Republic and, following the French defeat at Dien Bien Phu in 1954, complete French withdrawal from Vietnam. Meanwhile, in 1947, India had received the independence promised to her during the war; Attlee and Cripps, at least, were realistic enough to see that the clock could not be turned back to the era before the Japanese offensive.

The Second World War also affected the development of nationalism in Africa, although less directly and over a longer period. Extensive economic changes stimulated the growth of trade unionism, particularly in British West Africa. This, in turn, brought organization and militancy to the expression of both political and economic grievances. Nigeria, for example, experienced a general strike in 1945, and the Gold Coast one in 1950. Meanwhile, African nationalism was learning much from the example of liberation movements in South-East Asia and Indonesia. In this respect, as the *Listener* observed in 1954, there was now behind each colonial movement 'the heave of the great shoulder of Asia'.[1] Gradually, the leaders of Tropical Africa – Nkrumah, Azikiwe, Nyerere, Banda, Sekou Touré and Awolowo – manoeuvred themselves into the position which had been reached by Gandhi and Nehru in the previous decade. They hastened the departure of colonial powers who had lost the will to rule but who, nevertheless, considered their presence necessary for the time being. The breakthrough came with the independence of Ghana in 1957, and a veritable host of French and British colonies followed in 1960 and 1961.

There is no doubt that the mobilizing of international opinion played a considerable part in pushing back colonial rule. The United Nations Organization persistently applied pressure on imperial powers and evolved a new understanding of human rights and freedoms. Its role, both political and ideological, became more militant in direct proportion to the number of new Nation States joining the Afro-Asian *bloc*. In 1960, the United Nations issued its *Declaration on the Granting of Independence to Colonial Countries and Peoples.* This was uncompromising in its message to the colonial powers: 'The subjection of peoples to alien subjugation, domination and exploitation constitutes a denial of fundamental human rights, is contrary to the Charter of the United Nations, and is an impediment to the promotion of world peace and co-operation.'² A UN Resolution in 1965 went even further; by this time, colonial rule had become 'a crime against humanity'.³ Similar expressions of hostility to European control had already been expressed by Asian leaders at the Bandung Conference in 1955, and by the Organization of African Unity after 1963. A contrast indeed to Lord Curzon's celebrated statement in 1907 that Empire was 'the means of service to mankind'!⁴ Confronted by such profound hostility in the General Assembly and discovering a new meaning of the 'white man's burden', smaller colonial powers like Belgium followed Britain and France in dumping the possessions which had once given them a pretension to greatness. The single exception was Portugal who became the focal point of the wrath of the Afro-Asian *bloc* until domestic revolution forced her to decolonize in 1975.

Finally, powerful pressure was also applied by the two leading world powers, the United States and the Soviet Union. The former came into being as a result of the revolution of 1775 and incorporated into its constitution the world's first explicitly anti-colonial ideology. American influence has been exerted in two ways. First, official presidential policy has been to put pressure on European states to weaken and cut their imperial connections. In 1918, for example, President Wilson tried, unsuccessfully, to persuade his fellow victors to extend the principle of national self-determination to Africa and Asia as well as to Europe. In 1940, Roosevelt and Churchill differed over their interpretation of the Third Principle of the Atlantic Charter – the 'right of all peoples to choose the form of

Decolonization

government under which they will live'. Roosevelt was looking far beyond the problem of Eastern Europe to the emancipation of British India and the sub-Saharan colonies. Since 1950, a second influence has been exerted by the United States, this time by the American Negro, and the main beneficiary has been West Africa. While the American Negro sought his racial and cultural roots, his African counterpart gained an insight into the organization and methods of civil rights campaigns. Meanwhile, ever since the 1920s, the Soviet Union had kept up a sustained and virulent attack on colonialism, equating it with political and economic exploitation on a massive scale, and offering an ideological pattern of liberation based on class struggle and revolution. There have been moments of co-operation between the superpowers over colonial issues, but these have not prevented them from competing with each other for influence over newly emergent nations and, in the process, accusing each other of 'neo-colonialism'.

*

Imperialism had been immensely popular in the late nineteenth century. Nevertheless, there had from the outset been forces attempting to pull it back. Marx predictably attacked the British initiative in India. 'The aristocracy wanted to conquer it, the moneyocracy to plunder it and the millocracy to undersell it.' Criticism also came from radicals within the Liberal Party, especially Labouchère, Morley and Scott. J. A. Hobson assembled, in 1902, the most complete, organised and logical denunciation of imperialism to date, while Lenin subsequently incorporated some of Hobson's arguments into his own tract *Imperialism. the Highest Stage of Capitalism*. Meanwhile, the British Labour movement had committed itself *en bloc* to Lansbury's 1896 resolution demanding the 'right of all nations to complete sovereignty'.[5] Similarly, the French Socialists and the German Social Democrats attacked government policy over Africa and the Far East. After the First World War opposition to imperialism became at once more specialized and more international. In 1929, for example, the League against Imperialism was established as a result of a conference held in Brussels. By 1939, most of the European Left had come to the conclusion that the continued possession of colonies would perpetuate two major evils. First, colonial administrations were, with varying degrees of justification, open to the charge of racialism and economic exploitation. Second, the diversion of domestic resources into colonial investment was delaying social reform at home and, with it, the emergence of the welfare state.

The conversion of the Right to decolonization came very much later. During the Second World War Churchill affirmed: 'I have not become the King's First Minister in order to preside over the liquidation of the British Empire.'[6] Yet, within ten years, fellow Conservative Oliver Lyttelton was able to say: 'Certain broad lines of policy are accepted by all sections of the House as being above party politics . . . First of all we aim at helping the colonial territories to attain self-government.'[7] By the late 1950s a Conservative prime minister, Harold Macmillan, was referring to 'winds of change' sweeping through Africa, while the colonial secretary, Iain Macleod, spoke of 'a deliberate speeding up of the movement towards independence' in the belief that 'any other policy would have led to terrible bloodshed in Africa'.[8] Two factors had made possible this consensus across the whole political spectrum. Labour's election victory in 1945 started a train of events within the Empire that even the Churchillian wing of the Conservative Party could not reverse after Labour's defeat in 1951. Besides, British withdrawal was made to seem less catastrophic because of the framework of dominion status into which the older colonies had already fitted; this had been confirmed by the Statute of Westminster (1931) as a permanent and regular constitutional device for delegating the powers of the British Crown. Hence decolonization could be made acceptable to the mother country on the grounds that the old Empire was, in effect, being replaced by a new Commonwealth. The French government was less fortunate in its experience. Although it tried to modify its rigid pre-war policy of assimilation, it ran into trouble over its scheme for a French Union; eventually its plans for decolonization took on the appearance of a retreat from the South-East Asian disaster of 1954. A significant change of heart followed Dien Bien Phu as the new prime minister, Pierre Mendès-France, told a shocked nation that France would have to give up parts of North Africa, a commitment honoured by de Gaulle after the formation of the Fifth Republic.

Meanwhile, imperialism was being criticized by a new generation of economists who challenged the whole concept of interlinked commercial and financial benefits which Joseph Chamberlain had once attributed to imperialism. After 1945, empires were seen

Decolonization

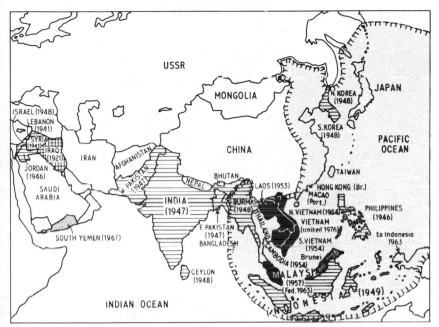

(a) The decolonization of Asia (with dates of independence)

Decolonization

increasingly as a strain on the expenditure of the mother country. After all, West Germany, free of all colonial obligations, was experiencing an economic boom long before it affected the rest of Western Europe. When the other states shed their empires their economies in many cases actually picked up. Fears that the Dutch loss of the East Indies would ruin the Dutch economy proved completely unfounded as firms which had previously operated in Indonesia now redirected their capital and their management skills to the home market, contributing greatly to the Netherlands boom of the mid-1950s.[9] The upheaval caused in Europe by the Second World War also had a tremendous impact on the whole area of policy and was bound to lead to a re-examination of basic priorities. The destruction of Nazi Germany and the Fascist régime in Italy had removed the edge from European nationalism; this meant that it was possible to plan schemes for Western economic integration and political co-operation and, at the same time, made Europe more

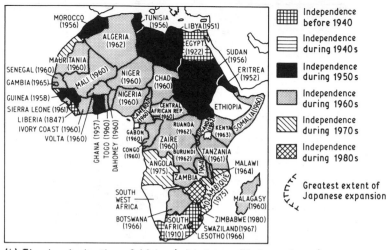

Legend:
- Independence before 1940
- Independence during 1940s
- Independence during 1950s
- Independence during 1960s
- Independence during 1970s
- Independence during 1980s
- Greatest extent of Japanese expansion

(b) The decolonization of Africa (with dates of independence)

Decolonization

introspective and less expansionist. This co-operation was also based on the need for organized defence against the other legacy of the war – an enormously strengthened Soviet war machine. Simultaneous commitments to the EEC, EFTA or NATO necessitated a complete re-examination of the whole meaning of overseas commitments. Naturally, there would have to be a permanent flow of raw materials, including oil, from the Third World to the industrial countries. But, whereas supplies had previously been guaranteed by political domination, it now seemed to make more sense to rely on the self-interest of liberated peoples. Was it not better to promote stable autonomy, rather than to try to maintain unstable dependence?

Post-war Europe, in brief, was in desperate need of reconstruction; but any real recovery would have to be based on an acceptance that she had shrunk in terms of power and influence.

Notes

CHAPTER 1

1 A. DE TOCQUEVILLE: *The Ancien Régime*.
2 J. C. DAVIES: 'Toward a Theory of Revolution', in J. C. DAVIES (ed.), *When Men Revolt and Why*.
3 J. LOUGH: *An Introduction to Eighteenth Century France*, Ch. III.
4 E. N. WILLIAMS. *The Ancien Regime in Europe*, Ch. 8.
5 P. GOUBERT: *The Ancien Régime*, Ch. I, Part 2.
6 K. KUMAR: *Revolution*, Introduction, Part 6.

CHAPTER 2

1 R. R. PALMER. *The World of the French Revolution*, Ch. 2.
2 J. M. ROBERTS: *The French Revolution*, Ch. 2.
3 P. H. BEIK (ed.): *The French Revolution: Selected Documents*, Document 24.
4 D. I. WRIGHT (ed.): *The French Revolution: Introductory Documents*, Document 17.
5 Ibid., Document 18.
6 Ibid., Ch. 5.
7 T. A. DI PADOVA: 'The Girondins and the Question of Revolutionary Government', in *French Historical Studies* (1975–6).
8 A. COBBAN: 'The Political Ideas of Robespierre during the Period of the Convention', in *English Historical Review* (1946).
9 J. J. ROUSSEAU: *The Social Contract*, Book I, Ch. VII.
10 D. I. WRIGHT: *Revolution and Terror in France 1789–1795*, Ch. 6.
11 See C. BRINTON: *A Decade of Revolution, 1789–1799* for a survey of the controversy.
12 G. LEFEBVRE: *Remarks on Robespierre*, trans. in B. HYSLOP: *French Historical Studies* (1958).
13 Quoted in D. I. WRIGHT: op. cit.

14 C. CHURCH: 'In Search of the Directory', in J. F. BOSHER (ed.): *French Government and Society, 1500–1850: Essays in memory of A. Cobban.*

15 M. LYONS: '9 Thermidor: Motives and effects', in *European Studies Review* (1975). Also, *France Under the Directory*, 1975.

16 L. HUNT, D. LANSKY and P. HANSON: 'The failure of the Liberal Republic', in *Journal of Modern History* (1979).

CHAPTER 3

1 R. B. HOLTMAN: *The Napoleonic Revolution*, Ch. X.
2 H. A. L. FISHER: *Bonapartism*, Ch. I.
3 F. MARKHAM: *Napoleon*, Ch. 17.
4 G. BRUUN: *Europe and the French Imperium, 1799–1814*, Ch. 4.
5 R. B. HOLTMAN: op. cit., Ch. VI.
6 Ibid., Ch. V.
7 A. SOBOUL: *The French Revolution 1787–1799*, trans. by A. FORREST and C. JONES: Conclusion.
8 R. B. HOLTMAN: op. cit., Ch. IV.
9 J. GODECHOT, B. HYSLOP and D. DOWD: *The Napoleonic Era in Europe*, Ch. 2.
10 *New Cambridge Modern History*, Vol. IX, Chapter XI: 'The Napoleonic Adventure'.
11 M. LATEY: *Tyranny. A Study in the Abuse of Power*, Ch. 7.

CHAPTER 4

1 F. MARKHAM: *Napoleon*, Ch. 9.
2 G. BRUUN: *Europe and the French Imperium*, 1799–1814, Ch. IX.
3 F. MARKHAM: op. cit., Ch. 14.
4 R. BEN JONES: *Napoleon; Man and Myth*, Part V.
5 J. M. THOMPSON: *Napoleon Bonaparte: His Rise and Fall*, Ch. XII.
6 Ibid., Ch. XI.
7 J. GODECHOT, B. HYSLOP and D. DOWD: *The Napoleonic Era in Europe*, Ch. 6.
8 J. H. ROSE: *The Life of Napoleon I*, Ch. XXX.
9 E. TARLÉ: *Napoleon's Invasion of Russia, 1812*, Ch. 1.
10 F. MARKHAM: op. cit., Ch. 7.
11 J. M. THOMPSON: op. cit., Ch. XIV.
12 E. TARLÉ: op. cit., Ch. 1.
13 J. M. THOMPSON: op. cit., Ch. IX.
14 G. LEFEBVRE: *Napoleon*, Ch. IX.
15 J. GODECHOT: op. cit., Ch. IX.
16 A. BRIGGS: *The Age of Improvement*, Ch. 3.
17 J. F. C. FULLER: *The Conduct of War 1789–1961*, Ch. III.
18 L. W. COWIE: *Hanoverian England 1714–1837*, Ch. XX.
19 J. H. ROSE: op. cit., Ch. XXIX.
20 *New Cambridge Modern History*, Vol. IX, Ch. III.
21 J. H. ROSE: op. cit., Ch. XXXII.
22 Ibid., Ch. XXII.

Notes

23 E. TARLÉ: op. cit., Ch. 6.
24 J. ROPP: *War in the Modern World*, Ch. 4.
25 J. H. ROSE: op. cit., Ch. XXI.
26 E. TARLÉ: op. cit., Ch. 2.

CHAPTER 5

1 W. A. PHILIPS: *The Confederation of Europe*, Ch. III.
2 J. DROZ: *Europe between Revolutions 1815–1848*, Ch. I.
3 M. S. ANDERSON: *The Ascendancy of Europe 1815–1914*, Ch. 1.
4 C. W. CRAWLEY: 'International Relations 1815–1830', in *New Cambridge Modern History*, Vol. IX.
5 W. A. PHILIPS: op. cit., Ch. V.
6 Ibid., Castlereagh's Memorandum.
7 E. L. WOODWARD: *The Age of Reform 1815–1870*; Book II, Ch. I.
8 W. A. PHILIPS: op. cit., Ch. VI.
9 A MILNE: *Metternich*, Ch. III.
10 A PALMER: *Metternich*, Ch. 10.
11 E. L. WOODWARD: op. cit., Book II, Ch. II.
12 G. VERNADSKY: *A History of Russia*, Ch. 9.

CHAPTER 6

1 H. F. SCHWARZ (ed.): *Problems in European Civilisation: Metternich, the 'Coachman of Europe'*, from extract by A SOREL.
2 J. DROZ: *Europe between Revolutions 1815–1848*, Ch. I.
3 H. F. SCHWARZ: op. cit., from extract by H KISSINGER.
4 E. L. WOODWARD: *Studies in European Conservatism*, Part I: Metternich.
5 A. MILNE: *Metternich*, Part I.
6 Ibid., Part IV.
7 A. PALMER: *Metternich*, Ch. 18.
8 C. A. MACARTNEY: *The Habsburg Empire 1700–1918*, Ch. 6.
9 A. PALMER: op. cit., Ch. 17.
10 Ibid., Ch. 15.
11 E. BURKE: *Reflections on the Revolution in France* (1790).

CHAPTER 7

1 P. N. STEARNS: *The Revolutions of 1848*, p. 50.
2 G. A. KERTESZ (ed.): *Documents in the Political History of the European Continent 1815–1939*, Document 44a.
3 D. WARD: *1848: The Fall of Metternich and the Year of Revolution*, Ch. IX.
4 M. KRANZBERG (ed.): *1848 – A Turning Point?*, extract by L. B. NAMIER.
5 E. EYCK (ed.): *The Revolutions of 1848–9*, Document II.6.A.
6 G. A. KERTESZ: op. cit., Document 88b.
7 Ibid., Document 84 (Mazzini's Instructions for Members of Young Italy, 1831).

8   E. J. HOBSBAWM: *The Age of Capital 1848–1875*, Ch. 1.
9   P. N. STEARNS: op. cit., p. 163.
10 F. FEJTÖ (ed.): *The Opening of an Era: 1848 – An Historical Symposium*, Conclusion.
11 P. N. STEARNS: op. cit., p. 91.
12 J. P. T. BURY: *France 1814–1940*, Ch. VI.
13 A. PALMER: *The Lands Between*, Ch. 3.
14 D. WARD: op. cit., Ch. XIII.
15 E. K. BRAMSTED: *Germany*, Ch. 6.

CHAPTER 8

1   See A. J. P. TAYLOR: *The Struggle for Mastery in Europe 1848–1918*, Ch. IV.
2   R. C. BINKLEY: *Realism and Nationalism 1851–1871*, Ch. 8.
3   J. A. S. GRENVILLE: *Europe Reshaped 1848–1878*, Ch. XI.

CHAPTER 9

1   D. MACK SMITH (ed.): *Great Lives Observed; Garibaldi*, Part 3.
2   A. J. GRANT and H. TEMPERLEY: *Europe in the Nineteenth and Twentieth Centuries*, Ch. XVI.
3   *New Cambridge Modern History*, Vol. X, Ch. XXI.
4   D. BEALES: *The Risorgimento and the Unification of Italy*, Document 8.
5   D. MACK SMITH (ed.): *Italy*, Ch. 4.
6   G. M. TREVELYAN: *Garibaldi and the Thousand*.
7   D. MACK SMITH (ed.): *The Making of Italy 1760–1870*, Part 18.
8   D. MACK SMITH (ed.): *Great Lives Observed; Garibaldi*, Part 14.
9   Ibid., Part 1.
10 D. MACK SMITH (ed.): *The Making of Italy 1760–1870*, Part 9.
11 Ibid., 'Cavour to Comtesse de Circourt', 29 December 1860.
12 D. MACK SMITH (ed.): *Victor Emmanuel, Cavour, and the Risorgimento*, Ch. 10.
13 J. RIDLEY: *Garibaldi*, Ch. 27.
14 D. MACK SMITH (ed.): *The Making of Italy 1760–1870*, Part 12.
15 J. RIDLEY: op. cit., Ch. 30.
16 D. MACK SMITH (ed.): *Great Lives Observed; Garibaldi*, Part 11.
17 A. J. P. TAYLOR: *The Struggle for Mastery in Europe 1848–1918*, Ch. VI.
18 D. MACK SMITH (ed.): *Great Lives Observed; Garibaldi*, Part 4.

CHAPTER 10

1   H. BÖHME (ed.): *The Foundations of the German Empire. Select Documents*, trans. by A. RAMM, Document 69.
2   J. M. KEYNES: *The Economic Consequences of the Peace* (1919), p. 75.
3   See W. CONZE: *The Shaping of the German Nation. A Historical Analysis*, Ch. IV.
4   E. K. BRAMSTED: *Germany*, Ch. 5.
5   W. CARR: *Germany 1815–1945*, Ch. 3.
6   F. B. M. HOLLYDAY (ed.): *Bismarck*, Part 1.

Notes

7 W. CARR: op. cit., Ch. 4.
8 A. J. P. TAYLOR: *Bismarck: The Man and the Statesman*, Ch. IV.
9 O. PFLANZE: *'Bismarck's Realpolitik'*, in J. SHEEHAN (ed.): *Imperial Germany*.
10 H. BÖHME (ed.): op. cit., Document 147.
11 Ibid., Document 151.
12 A. J. P. TAYLOR: op. cit., Ch. IV.

CHAPTER 11

1 D. FIELD: *The End of Serfdom. Nobility and Bureaucracy in Russia 1855–1861*.
2 A. J. RIEBER: *Alexander II: A Revisionist View'*, in *Journal of Modern History* (1971).
3 B. H. SUMNER: *Survey of Russian History*, Ch. III.
4 M. T. FLORINSKY: *Russia: A History and an Interpretation*, Vol. II, Ch. XXXIII.
5 W. E. MOSSE: *Alexander II and the Modernization of Russia*, Ch. 5.
6 G. VERNADSKY: *A History of Russia*, Ch. 10.
7 M. S. ANDERSON: *The Ascendancy of Europe 1815–1914*, Ch. 2.
8 H. SETON-WATSON: *The Decline of Imperial Russia 1855–1914*, Ch. II.
9 H. SETON-WATSON: *The Russian Empire 1801–1917*, Ch. XI.

CHAPTER 12

1 M. HOWARD: *The Franco-Prussian War*, Ch. II.
2 T. ZELDIN: *Emile Ollivier and the Liberal Empire of Napoleon III*, Ch. 12.
3 T. ARONSON: *The Fall of the Third Napoleon*, Ch. 4.
4 M. HOWARD: op. cit., Ch. I.
5 N. RICH: *The Age of Nationalism and Reform*, Ch. 2.
6 W. H. C. SMITH: *Napoleon III*, Ch. 12.
7 A. HORNE: *The Fall of Paris*, Ch. 2.
8 W. H. C. SMITH: op. cit., Ch. 13.
9 Ibid., Ch. 7.
10 J. A. S. GRENVILLE: *Europe Reshaped 1848–1878*, Ch. VI.
11 G. P. GOOCH: *The Second Empire*, Ch. I.
12 T. ZELDIN: *France 1848–1945*, Vol. I, Ch. 4.
13 T. ZELDIN: *Emile Ollivier*, Ch. 5.
14 Ibid., Ch. 6.
15 T. ARONSON: op. cit., Ch. 2.

CHAPTER 13

1 G. A. CRAIG: *Germany 1866–1945*, Ch. V.
2 E. EYCK: *Bismarck and the German Empire*, Ch. IV. 3.
3 W. M. SIMON: *Germany in the Age of Bismarck*, Document 38.
4 Ibid., Document 39.
5 T. S. HAMEROW (ed.): *Problems in European Civilisation. Otto von Bismarck: A Historical Assessment*, extract by J. ZIEKURSCH.

Aspects of European History 1789–1980

6   W. CARR: *A History of Germany 1815–1945*, Ch. 5. (The words are those of K. LIEBKNECHT.)

CHAPTER 14

1   A. COBBAN: *A History of Modern France*, Vol. 3, Ch. 1.
2   D. W. BROGAN: *The Development of Modern France 1870–1939*; Book II, Ch. II.
3   M. CURTIS: *Three Against the Third Republic*, Ch. II.
4   W. SHIRER: *Fall of the Third Republic*, Ch. 6.

CHAPTER 15

1   I. GEISS: *German Foreign Policy 1871–1914*; Ch. 1.
2   W. N. MEDLICOTT and D. K. COVENEY (eds): *Bismarck and Europe*, Introduction.
3   A. J. P. TAYLOR: *Bismarck: The Man and the Statesman*.
4   F. B. M. HOLLYDAY (ed.): *Bismarck*; Document: Secret Dispatch from Bismarck to Count von Hatzfeldt, 8 August 1887.
5   H. HOLBORN: *A History of Modern Germany 1840–1945*, Ch. 6.
6   O. PFLANZE: 'Bismarck's Realpolitik', in J. J. SHEEHAN (ed.): *Imperial Germany*.
7   E. EYCK: *Bismarck and the German Empire*, Ch. IV.
8   K. S. PINSON: *Modern Germany*, Ch. XII.
9   G. A. CRAIG: *Germany 1866–1945*, Ch. VII.
10 V. R. BERGHAHN: *Germany and the Approach of War in 1914*, Ch. 2.
11 H. HOLBORN: op. cit., Ch. 7.

CHAPTER 16

1   Report presented to the Preliminary Peace Conference 1919, in D. E. LEE (ed.): *The Outbreak of the First World War*.
2   See I. GEISS: 'The outbreak of the first world war and German war aims', in *Journal of Contemporary History* (1966) I.3.
3   See J. RÖHL (ed.): *1914: Delusion or Design?* (1973).
4   See H. E. BARNES: *The Genesis of the World War* (1926).
5   See S. B. FAY: *Origins of the World War* (1930).
6   See G. P. GOOCH: *Before the War, II. The Coming of the War (1938)*.
7   See A. J. P. TAYLOR: *The Struggle for Mastery in Europe* (1954).
8   See F. FISCHER: *Germany's Aims in the First World War* (1967).
9   For an appraisal of Ritter's views see K. EPSTEIN: 'Gerhard Ritter and the First World War', in *Journal of Contemporary History*, 1966; I.3.
10 See L. C. F. TURNER: *Origins of the First World War* (1970).
11 See I. GEISS: op. cit. Also *German Foreign Policy 1871–1914* (1976).
12 See J. RÖHL: op. cit. Also *From Bismarck to Hitler* (1970).
13 See V. R. BERGHAHN: *Germany and the Approach of War in 1914* (1973).
14 G. A. CRAIG: *Germany 1866–1945*, Ch. IX.

Notes

15 L. C. F. TURNER: op. cit., Ch. 4.
16 J. RÖHL: op. cit., quotation by RIEZLER.
17 V. R. BERGHAHN: op. cit., Ch. 19.
18 W. CARR: *A History of Germany 1815–1945*, Ch. 8.
19 G. A. CRAIG: op. cit., Ch. IV.
20 J. RÖHL: op. cit.
21 L. C. F. TURNER: op. cit., Ch. 6.
22 I. V. BESTUZHEV: 'Russian foreign policy February–June 1914', in *Journal of Contemporary History* (1966), I.3.
23 L. C. F. TURNER: op. cit., Ch. 2.
24 For a full examination of Grey's policy in 1914 see L. C. B. SEAMAN: *From Vienna to Versailles*, Ch. XIV.
25 V. R. BERGHAHN: op. cit., Ch. 6.

CHAPTER 17

1 I. J. LEDERER (ed.): *The Versailles Settlement*, extract by T. MASARYK.
2 E. EYCH: *A History of the Weimar Republic*, Vol. I, Ch. IV.
3 A. J. P. TAYLOR: *The Habsburg Monarchy*, Epilogue.
4 S. MARKS: *The Illusion of Peace*, Ch. 1.

CHAPTER 18

1 B. DMYTRYSHYN (ed.): *Imperial Russia. A Source Book 1700–1917*, Document 42.
2 A. E. ADAMS: 'Pobedonostsev and the Rule of Firmness', in the *Slavonic and East European Review*, XXXII.
3 T. RIHA: 'Constitutional Development in Russia', in T. G. STAVROU (ed.): *Russia under the Last Tsar*.
4 J. WALKIN: *The Rise of Democracy in Pre-Revolutionary Russia*, Ch. 7.
5 H. SETON-WATSON: *The Russian Empire 1801–1917*, Ch. XVII.
6 A. MENDEL: 'On Interpreting the Fate of Imperial Russia', in T. G. STAVROU: op. cit.
7 M. T. FLORINSKY: *The End of the Russian Empire*, Ch. 9.

CHAPTER 19

1 L. TROTSKY: *The History of the Russian Revolution*, trans. by M. EASTMAN, Vol. I.
2 A. KERENSKY: 'The Policy of the Provisional Government of 1917', in *The Slavonic and East European Review* (1932).
3 N. BERDYAEV: *The Origin of Russian Communism*.
4 Quoted in E. H. CARR: *The Bolshevik Revolution*, Vol. 1, Ch. 4.
5 V. I. LENIN: *What is to be Done?*
6 L. TROTSKY: op. cit., Vol. III.
7 A. E. ADAMS (ed.): *The Russian Revolution and Bolshevik Victory*, extract by M. FAINSOD.

8   S. N. SILVERMAN (ed.): *Lenin*, Ch. 3.
9   Ibid., Ch. 2.
10 J. SWETTENHAM: *Allied Intervention in Russia 1918–1919*, Ch. V.
11 S. N. SILVERMAN: op. cit., Ch. 2.
12 C. H. LEGGETT: 'Lenin, Terror, and the Political Police', in *Survey*, (1975).
13 V. I. LENIN: 'The Proletarian Revolution and the Renegade Kautsky', in S. SILVERMAN: op. cit.
14 E. H. CARR: op. cit., Ch. 7.
15 K. KUMAR: *Revolution*, 5.16.

CHAPTER 20

1   See H. NICOLSON: *Peacemaking 1919* (New York, 1939).
2   See J. M. KEYNES: 'Economic Consequences of the Peace (1919) and the Peace of Versailles', in *Everybody's Magazine* XLIII (September 1920).
3   See W. H. DAWSON: *Germany under the Treaty* (London, 1933).
4   See H. VOGT: *The Burden of Guilt: A Short History of Germany 1914–1945*, trans. by H. STRAUSS (1964).
5   W. H. DAWSON: op. cit., Ch. XIII.
6   H. NICOLSON: op. cit.
7   H. VOGT: op. cit., Ch. II.
8   J. M. KEYNES: 'The Peace of Versailles', op. cit.
9   A. TARDIEU: *The Truth About the Treaty* (1921).
10 E. MANTOUX: *The Carthaginian Peace or the Economic Consequences of Mr Keynes*, written during the Second World War and published posthumously (trans. 1952).
11 P. BIRDSALL: *Versailles Twenty Years After* (1941).
12 J. NÉRE: *The Foreign Policy of France from 1914 to 1945*, trans. (1975).
13 W. CARR: *A History of Germany 1815–1945* (1969).
14 A. J. NICHOLLS: *Weimar and the Rise of Hitler* (1968).
15 S. MARKS: *The Illusion of Peace* (1976).
16 G. SCHULZ: *Revolutions and Peace Treaties 1917–1920* (1967).
17 M. TRACHTENBERG: 'Reparation at the Paris Peace Conference', (in *Journal of Modern History* (1979). Also: *Reparation in World Politics* (1980).
18 W. A. McDOUGALL: 'Political Economy vs National Sovereignty: French Structures for German Economic Integration after Versailles', (in *Journal of Modern History* (1979).

CHAPTER 21

1   A. J. P. TAYLOR: *The Origins of the Second World War*, Ch. 3.
2   M. GALLO: *Mussolini's Italy*, Ch. 1.
3   SIR I. KIRKPATRICK: *Mussolini, Study of a Demagogue*, Ch. 4.

Notes

4   M. GALLO: op. cit., Ch. 2.
5   Ibid., Ch. 5.
6   Ibid., Ch. 3.
7   SIR I. KIRKPATRICK: op. cit., Ch. 6.
8   M. GALLO: op. cit., Ch. 7.
7   SIR I. KIRKPATRICK: op. cit., Ch. 5.
10 E. WEBER: *Varieties of Fascism*, Document 1C.
11 M. GALLO: op. cit., Ch. 9.
12 A. LYTTELTON: 'Italian Fascism', in W. LAQUEUR (ed.): *Fascism: A Reader's Guide*.
13 M. GALLO: op. cit., Ch. 10.
14 P. MELOGRANI: 'The Cult of the Duce in Mussolini's Italy', in G. L. MOSSE (ed.): *International Fascism: New Thoughts and New Approaches*.
15 C. LEEDS: *Italy under Mussolini*, Ch. 5.
16 M. GALLO: op. cit., Ch. 15.

CHAPTER 22

1   P. FEARON: *The Origins and Nature of the Great Slump 1929–1932*, Ch. 1.

CHAPTER 23

1   A. BULLOCK: *Hitler, a Study in Tyranny*, Ch. 2.
2   J. C. FEST: *Hitler*, Book 2, Ch. 4.
3   A. J. NICHOLLS: *Weimar and the Rise of Hitler*, Ch. 10.
4   A. BULLOCK: op. cit., Ch. 3.
5   J. P. STERN: *Hitler: The Führer and the People*, Ch. 12.
6   Election figures in this chapter, given as a percentage of the popular vote, are taken from E. R. WHEATON: *Prelude to Calamity*, Table, Parties in the Reichstag 1919–1933.
7   Election figures in this chapter, given as seats in the *Reichstag*, are taken from S. DELMER: *Weimar Germany:* Table in Ch. 9.
8   J. C. FEST: op. cit., Book 4, Ch. 3.
9   See R. KNAUERHASE: *An Introduction to National Socialism, 1920–1939*, Ch. 2.
10 K. SONTHEIMER: 'The Weimar Republic and the Prospects of German Democracy', in E. J. FEUCHTWANGER (ed.): *Upheaval and Continuity*.
11 H. BOLDT: 'Article 48 of the Weimar Constitution, its historical and political implications', in A. NICHOLLS and E. MATTHIAS: *German Democracy and the Triumph of Hitler – Essays in Recent German History*.
12 L. L. SNYDER: *The Weimar Republic*, Document 18: The Weimar Constitution.
13 J. C. FEST: op. cit., Book 4, Ch. 2.
14 J. REMAK (ed.): *The Nazi Years: A Documentary History*, Ch. 4.
15 Ibid., 'Law Concerning the Hitler Youth'.
16 J. C. FEST: op. cit., Book 5, Ch. 1.
17 See K. D. BRACHER: *The German Dictatorship*.

Aspects of European History 1789–1980

CHAPTER 24

1   J. C. G. ROHL: *From Bismarck to Hitler,*|Ch. V, Document 1.
2   Ibid., Ch. V, Document 7.
3   Ibid., Ch. V, Document 6.
4   Quotations from *Hitler's Secret Book (Hitlers zweites Buch)*, written in 1928 but not published until 1961, prepared for publication by G. L. WEINBERG and H. ROTHFELS.
5   H. HOLBORN: *A History of Modern Germany*, Vol. 3, 1840–1945, Ch. 12.
6   G. A. CRAIG: *Germany 1866–1945*, Ch. XIX.
7   J. FEST: *Hitler*, Book 6, Ch. 3.
8   J. L. SNELL (ed.): *The Outbreak of the Second World War*, extract from the Nuremberg Judgement.
9   R. J. SONTAG: 'The Last Months of Peace, 1939', in *Foreign Affairs*, Vol. XXXV (1957).
10   Quotations from A. J. P. TAYLOR: *The Origins of the Second World War.*
11   H. TREVOR-ROPER: 'A. J. P. Taylor, Hitler and the War', in *Encounter*, Vol. XVII (1961).
12   J. FEST: op. cit., 'Interpolation Three'.

CHAPTER 25

1   G. F. KENNAN: *Soviet Foreign Policy 1917–41*, Document 2.
2   A. FONTAINE: *A History of the Cold War from the October Revolution to the Korean War 1917–1950*, trans. by D. D. PAIGE, Ch. 1.
3   G. F. KENNAN: op. cit., Document 1.
4   X. J. EUDIN and H. H. FISHER: *Soviet Russia and the West 1920–1927*, speech by L. B. KAMENEV, 15 March 1921.
5   I. DEUTSCHER: *Stalin: a Political Biography*; Ch. 10.
6   J. DEGRAS (ed.): *Soviet Documents on Foreign Policy Vol. I*; pp. 298–301. Chicherin's opening speech at the Genoa Conference, 10 April 1922.
7   G. F. KENNAN: op. cit., Document 25.
8   W. LAQUEUR: *Russia and Germany: A Century of Conflict*, Ch. 11.
9   *A Short History of the Communist Party of the Soviet Union*, prepared by a panel of Soviet historians, p. 247.
10   See W. LAQUERE: op. cit., Ch. 12.
11   T. H. RIGBY (ed.): *Stalin, Great Lives Observed* series.
12   A. FONTAINE: op. cit., Ch. 7.

CHAPTER 26

1   J. A. S. GRENVILLE (ed.): *The Major International Treaties 1914–1973*, p. 108.
2   P. RAFFO: 'The League of Nations', *Historical Association Pamphlet* (1974).
3   J. A. S. GRENVILLE (ed.): op. cit., pp. 60–1.
4   S. MARKS: *The Illusion of Peace*, Ch. 1.
5   R. HENIG (ed.): *The League of Nations*, II. 3A.
6   C. M. KIMMICH: *Germany and the League of Nations*, Ch. 1.

Notes

7 Ibid., Ch. 10.
8 I. DEUTSCHER: *Stalin: A Political Biography*, Ch. 11.

CHAPTER 27

1 E. H. CARR: *International Relations between the Two World Wars*, Ch. 13.
2 G. JACKSON (ed.): *Problems in European Civilisation: The Spanish Civil War*, extract by F. J. TAYLOR.
3 D. A. PUZZO: *The Spanish Civil War*, Ch. 2.
4 W. L. SHIRER: *The Rise and Fall of the Third Reich*, Ch. 9.
5 D. A. PUZZO: op. cit., Document 20 (Azaña's speech of 18 July 1937).

CHAPTER 28

1 A. ADAMTHWAITE: *France and the Coming of the Second World War*, Ch. 1.
2 M. SCHLESINGER: 'The Development of the Radical Party in the Third Republic: The New Radical Movement 1926–32', in *Journal of Modern History* (1974). The quotation is by MARCEL DÉAT, doctrinist within the Radical Party.
3 D. JOHNSON: 'Leon Blum and the Popular Front', in *History* (1970).
4 D. THOMSON: *Democracy in France since 1870*, Ch. III.
5 S. M. OSGOOD (ed.): *The Fall of France 1940*, extract by P. REYNAUD, trans. by editor.
6 W. SHIRER: *The Collapse of the Third Republic*, Ch. 12.
7 Trans. in D. THOMSON: op. cit., Ch. V.

CHAPTER 29

1 A. G. MAZOUR: *Soviet Economic Development: Operation Outstrip, 1921–1965*, Reading No. 8.
2 R. D. LAIRD and B. A. LAIRD: *Soviet Communism and the Agrarian Revolution*, Ch. 3.
3 A. G. MAZOUR: op. cit., Ch. 1.
4 A. ERLICH: *The Soviet Industrialisation Debate, 1924–1928*, Ch. I.
5 A. G. MAZOUR: op. cit., Ch. 2.
6 A. NOVE: *Stalinism and After*, Ch. I.
7 A. ERLICH: op. cit., Ch. I.
8 Ibid., Ch. II.
9 See M. LEWIN: 'The Immediate Background to Soviet Collectivization', in *Soviet Studies* (1965–6).
10 O. A. NARKIEWICZ: 'Stalin, War Communism and Collectivisation', in *Soviet Studies* (1966–7).
11 See L. PIETROMARCHI: *The Soviet World*, Ch. VII.
12 See R. AMMAN: 'Soviet Technological Performance', in *Survey* (1977–8).
13 W. KLATT: 'Fifty Years of Soviet Agriculture', in *Survey* (1967).
14 K. BUSH: 'Soviet Growth: Past, Present and Projected', in *Survey* (1977–8).

Aspects of European History 1789–1980

15 See J. BRADA and A. E. KING: 'The Soviet American Trade Agreements: Prospects for the Soviet Economy', in *Russian Review* (1973).
16 See A. WOLYNSKI: 'Western Economic Aid to the U.S.S.R.' in *Conflict Studies* No. 72, (June 1976); and V. SOBESLAVSKY: 'East-West détente and technology transfer', in *The World Today* (October 1980).

CHAPTER 30

1 K. HILDEBRAND: *The Foreign Policy of the Third Reich*, Ch. 5.
2 G. A. CRAIG: *Germany 1866–1945*, Ch. XX.
3 W. L. SHIRER: *The Rise and Fall of the Third Reich*, Ch. 19.
4 T. L. JARMAN: *The Rise and Fall of Nazi Germany*, Ch. XV.
5 P. E. SCHRAMM: *Hitler: The Man and the Military Leader*, Appendix II (Memorandum by General Jodl, 1946).
6 J. P. STERN: *Hitler: The Führer and the People*, Ch. 22.
7 W. L. SHIRER: op. cit., Ch. 19.
8 A. BULLOCK: *Hitler: A Study in Tyranny*, Ch. 12.
9 T. L. JARMAN: op. cit., Ch. XVII.
10 G. S. KRAVCHENKO: 'Stalin's War Machine', in *Purnell's History of the Second World War*, p. 1060.

CHAPTER 31

1 C. SETON-WATSON: 'The Cold War – its origins' in J. L. HENDERSON (ed.): *Since 1945 – Aspects of Contemporary World History*.
2 A. FONTAINE: *History of the Cold War from the October Revolution to the Korean War, 1917–1950* trans. by D. D. PAIGE, Ch. 1.
3 Ibid., Ch. 3.
4 Ibid., Ch. 5.
5 G. F. KENNAN: *Soviet Foreign Policy 1917–1941*, Document 29.
6 A. FONTAINE: op. cit., Ch. 8.
7 G. F. KENNAN: 'The Sources of Soviet Conduct', in *Foreign Affairs XXV* (July 1947).
8 D. S. MCLELLAN: *The Cold War in Transition*, Ch. 1.
9 N. V. SIVACHEV and N. N. YAKOVLEV: *Russia and the United States*, Ch. 5
10 *Keesings Contemporary Archives*: 9869A.
11 Ibid., 14249A.
12 Ibid., 19057A.
13 Ibid., 4739A.
14 Ibid., 7770A.
15 Ibid., 22993A.
16 Ibid., 15221A.
17 Ibid., 23025A.
18 Ibid., 8579A.
19 C. BOWN and P. MOONEY: *Cold War to Détente*, Ch. 18.

Notes

CHAPTER 32

1   A. SPINELLI: 'European Union and the Resistance', in *Government and Opposition* (1967).
2   D. DE ROUGEMENT: 'The Campaign of the European Congresses', in *Government and Opposition* (1967)
3   A. WATSON: *Europe at Risk*, Ch. 6.
4   G. LICHTHEIM: *Europe in the Twentieth Century*, Ch. 14.
5   F. VON KROSIG: 'A Reconsideration of Federalism in the Scope of the Present Discussion on European Integration', in *Journal of Common Market Studies* (1970).
6   M. A. WHEATON: 'The Labour Party and Europe 1950–71', in *Government and Opposition* (1971).
7   R. VAUGHAN: *Post-War Integration in Europe*, Document 15.
8   *Keesings Contemporary Archives*, 22246A.
9   F. VON KROSIG: op. cit.
10 D. JOHNSON: 'The Political Principles of General de Gaulle', in *International Affairs* (1965).
11 *Keesings Contemporary Archives*, 19015.
12 Ibid., 19197A.
13 See G. LICHTHEIM: op. cit.
14 U. KITZINGER: 'Britain's Crisis of Identity', in *JCMS*, Vol. 6.
15 S. HOLT: 'British Attitudes to Membership', in G. IONESCU (ed.): *The New Politics of European Integration*.

CHAPTER 33

1   See A. COBBAN: *The Nation State and National Self-Determination*, Ch. 11.
2   E. H. CARR: *Nationalism and After*, Ch. I.
3   A. COBBAN: *Rousseau and the Modern State*, Ch. IV.
4   H. KOHN: *Nationalism*, Reading No. 9.
5   H. KOHN: *The Mind of Germany*, Ch. 4.
6   H. KOHN: *Nationalism*, Reading No. 4.
7   H. KOHN: *Prophets and Peoples. Studies in Nineteenth Century Nationalism*, Ch. 3.
8   H. KOHN: *The Mind of Germany*, Ch. 7.
9   H. KOHN: *Prophets and Peoples*, Ch. 2.
10 'Thus Spoke Zarathustra', First Part, in W. KAUFMANN (ed. and trans.): *The Portable Nietzsche*.
11 H. KOHN: *Nationalism*, Reading No. 3.
12 'President Wilson's Fourteen Points, 8 January 1918', in J. A. S. GRENVILLE (ed.): *The Major International Treaties 1914–1973*, p. 59.
13 H. KOHN: *Political Ideologies of the Twentieth Century*, Ch. XI.
14 See J. DULFFER: 'Bonapartism, Fascism and National Socialism', in *Journal of Contemporary History* (1976).
15 See Ch. 32.

Aspects of European History 1789–1980

16 A. HUGHES: 'The Nation State in Black Africa', in L. J. TIVEY (ed.): *The Nation State.*

17 A. D. SMITH: *Nationalism in the 20th Century*, p. 115.

18 K. R. MINOGUE: *Nationalism*, Conclusion.

CHAPTER 34

1 See also V. I. LENIN: *The Three Sources and Three Component Parts of Marxism* (1913).

2 F. ENGELS: *Anti-Dühring*, extract in C. WRIGHT MILLS: *The Marxists.*

3 V. I. LENIN: *Karl Marx* (written in 1914).

4 K. MARX and F. ENGELS: *Manifesto of the Communist Party* (1848), I.

5 Quoted by LIN PIAO: 'The International Significance of Comrade Mao Tse Tung's Theory of People's War, 1965', in F. SCHURMANN and O. SCHELL, (eds): *Communist China*, p. 343.

6 K. KAUTSKY: *The Social Revolution* (1902), extracts in C. WRIGHT MILLS: op. cit.

7 E. BERNSTEIN: *Evolutionary Socialism* (1911), extract in C. WRIGHT MILLS: op. cit.

8 V. I. LENIN: A Short Biography (Moscow 1959), p. 34.

9 E. H. CARR: *The Bolshevik Revolution*, Vol. 1, Ch. 4.

10 V. I. LENIN: *A Short Biography*, p. 51.

11 L. TROTSKY: *The Permanent Revolution*, extract in C. WRIGHT MILLS: op. cit.

12 Some extracts from Stalin's 1950 writings on language, in T. H. RIGBY (ed.): *Stalin.*

13 J. V. STALIN: *Leninism*, extract in C. WRIGHT MILLS: op. cit.

14 J. V. STALIN: *The Tasks of Building Executives*, extract in T. H. RIGBY: op. cit.

15 N. KHRUSHCHEV: *Speech to the Twentieth Congress*, 25 February 1956, extract in C. WRIGHT MILLS: op. cit.

16 S. SCHRAM: *Mao Tse Tung*, Ch. 3.

17 *Quotations From Chairman Mao Tse Tung* (Peking 1966), p. 11.

18 Ibid., p. 18.

19 MAO TSE TUNG: *On Contradiction*, extract in F. SCHURMANN and O. SCHELL (eds): *Communist China*, Part 1.

20 S. SCHRAM: op. cit., p. 216.

21 MAO TSE TUNG: *On New Democracy* (1940), extract in V. SIMONE (ed.): *China in Revolution*, Part 4.

22 I. DEUTSCHER: *Russia, China, and the West 1953–1966*, Ch. 7.

23 C. P. FITZGERALD: *The Birth of Communist China*, Ch. 6.

24 LIN PIAO: op. cit.

25 *Quotations From Chairman Mao Tse Tung*, p. 68.

26 C. P. FITZGERALD: op. cit., Ch. 7.

27 'Eurocommunism. The long, long march away from Stalin', in *The Economist* (5 November 1977).

28 M. AZCÁRATE: 'What is Eurocommunism?', in G. R. URBAN (ed.): *Eurocommunism, its roots and future in Italy and elsewhere.*

Notes

29 J. ELLENSTEIN: 'The Skein of History Unrolled Backwards', in G. R. URBAN (ed.): op. cit.

CHAPTER 35

1 M. S. ANDERSON: *The Ascendancy of Europe 1815–1914*, Ch. 4.
2 J. A. HOBSON: *Imperialism; A Study.*
3 See M. E. TOWNSEND: 'Commercial and Colonial Policies of Imperial Germany', in G. H. NADEL and P. CURTIS (eds): *Imperialism and Colonialism.*
4 T. E. POWER: *Jules Ferry and the Renaissance of French Imperialism*; Ch. 8.
5 See W. L. LANGER: *The Diplomacy of Imperialism* and *European Alliances and Alignments 1871–1890*; also A. J. P. TAYLOR: *The Struggle for Mastery in Europe*, especially Ch. XIII.
6 D. K. FIELDHOUSE: 'Imperialism; an Historiographical Revision', *Economic History Review*, xiv.
7 D. THOMSON: *Europe Since Napoleon*, Ch. 20.
8 A. J. P. TAYLOR: op. cit., Ch. XIII.
9 W. L. LANGER: *European Alliances and Alignments*, Ch. IX.
10 H. BRUNSCHWIG: 'The Origins of the new French Empire', in G. H. NADEL and P. CURTIS (eds): op. cit.
11 J. JOLL: *Europe since 1870; An International History*, Ch. 4.
12 R. ROBINSON and J. GALLAGHER: *Africa and the Victorians*, Ch. XV.

CHAPTER 36

1 *The Listener* (10 December 1954).
2 K. J. TWITCHETT: 'The Colonial Powers and the United Nations', in *Journal of Contemporary History*, IV, 1, (1969).
3 R. EMERSON: 'Colonialism', in *Journal of Contemporary History*, IV, 1, (1909).
4 See Ch. 35.
5 F. BROCKWAY. *The Colonial Revolution*, Ch. 9.
6 C. E. CARRINGTON: *The Liquidation of the British Empire*, Ch. I.
7 Ibid., Ch. II.
8 D. AUSTIN: 'The Transfer of Power: Why and How', in W. H. MORRIS-JONES and D. AUSTIN: *Decolonisation and After.*
9 See H. BAUDET: 'The Netherlands After the Loss of Empire', in *Journal of Contemporary History*, IV. 1, (1969).

Bibliography

JOURNALS

English Historical Review
European Studies Review
The Historical Journal
History
History Today
Journal of Modern History
Past and Present
French Historical Studies
The Russian Review
Soviet Studies
Survey
Journal of Contemporary History
The World Today
World Politics
Foreign Affairs
International Affairs
Journal of International Affairs
The Economic History Review
Journal of Economic History
Journal of European Economic History
Journal of Common Market Studies

GENERAL

New Cambridge Modern History (Cambridge):
    VIII *The American and French Revolutions 1763–93* (1965)
    IX *War and Peace in an Age of Upheaval 1793–1830* (1965)
    X *The Zenith of European Power 1830–70* (1960)
    XI *Material Progress and World Wide Problems* (1962)

Bibliography

XII *The Shifting Balance of World Forces 1898–1945* (1968)
XIII *Companion Volume* (1979)
XIV *Atlas* (1970).

Problems in European Civilization (Lexington, Mass.):

R. W. GREENLAW (ed.): *The Economic Origins of the French Revolution*
D. H. PINKNEY (ed.): *Napoleon*
H. F. SCHWARTZ (ed.): *Metternich, the 'Coachman of Europe'*
M. KRANZBERG (ed.): *1848 – A Turning Point?*
S. M. OSGOOD (ed.): *Napoleon III*
T. S. HAMEROW (ed.): *Otto von Bismarck*
A. E. ADAMS (ed.): *Imperial Russia after 1861*
H. M. WRIGHT (ed.): *The 'New Imperialism'*
R. F. BETTS (ed.): *The 'Scramble for Africa'*
L. DERFLER (ed.): *The Dreyfus Affair*
D. E. LEE (ed.): *The Outbreak of the First World War*
A. E. ADAMS (ed.): *The Russian Revolution and Bolshevik Victory*
S. W. PAGE (ed.): *Lenin*
I. J. LEDERER (ed.): *The Versailles Settlement*
R. N. HUNT (ed.): *The Creation of the Weimar Republic*
R. V. DANIELS (ed.): *The Stalin Revolution*
G. JACKSON (ed.): *The Spanish Civil War*
L. F. SCHAEFER (ed.): *The Ethiopian Crisis*
J. L. SNELL (ed.): *The Nazi Revolution*
J. L. SNELL (ed.): *The Outbreak of the Second World War*
D. E. LEE (ed.): *Munich*
S. M. OSGOOD (ed.): *The Fall of France, 1940*
N. A. GRAEBNER (ed.): *The Cold War.*

E. H. HOBSBAWM: *The Age of Revolution: Europe 1789–1848* (London, 1962).
R. F. LESLIE: *The Age of Transformation* (London, 1964).
K. R. PERRY: *The Bourgeois Century. A History of Europe 1780–1870* (London, 1972).
F. L. FORD: *Europe 1780–1830* (London, 1971).
J. ROBERTS: *Revolution and Improvement. The Western World 1775–1847* (London, 1976).
C. BRINTON: *A Decade of Revolution 1789–1799* (New York, 1943).
G. BRUUN: *Europe and the French Imperium 1799–1814* (New York, 1938).
N. HAMPSON: *The First European Revolution* (London, 1969).
R. R. PALMER: *The World of the French Revolution* (London, 1971).
G. RUDÉ: *Revolutionary Europe 1783–1815* (London, 1964).
J. GODECHOT, B. HYSLOP and D. DOWD: *The Napoleonic Era in Europe* (New York, 1971).
D. THOMSON: *Europe Since Napoleon* (London, 1957).
R. ALBRECHT-CARRIÉ (ed.): *The Concert of Europe* (London, 1968).
H. G. SCHENK: *The Aftermath of the Napoleonic Wars* (London, 1947).
F. B. ARTZ: *Reaction and Revolution 1814–1832* (New York, 1932).
J. DROZ: *Europe Between Revolutions 1815–1848* (London, 1967).
M. S. ANDERSON: *The Ascendancy of Europe 1815–1914* (London, 1972).
M. WALKER (ed.): *Metternich's Europe* (London, 1968).

Aspects of European History 1789–1980

W. N. MEDLICOTT: *From Metternich to Hitler* (London, 1963).

L. C. B. SEAMAN: *Vienna to Versailles* (London, 1955).

E. H. CARR: *From Napoleon to Stalin and Other Essays* (London, 1980).

J. WEISS: *Conservatism in Europe 1770–1945* (London, 1977).

E. L. WOODWARD: *Three Studies in European Conservatism* (London, 1963).

R. ALBRECHT-CARRIÉ: *A Diplomatic History of Europe Since the Congress of Vienna* (London, 1958).

J. L. TALMON: *Romanticism and Revolt. Europe 1815–1848* (London, 1967).

W. L. LANGER: *Political and Social Upheaval 1832–1852* (New York, 1969).

F. FEJTÖ (ed.): *The Opening of an Era: 1848* (New York, 1966).

D. WARD: *1848. The Fall of Metternich and the Year of Revolution* (London, 1970).

J. SIGMAN: *1848. The Romantic and Democratic Revolutions in Europe*, trans. (London, 1973).

P. N. STEARNS: *The Revolutions of 1848* (London, 1974).

F. EYCK (ed.): *The Revolutions of 1848–49* (Edinburgh, 1972).

E. J. HOBSBAWM: *The Age of Capital 1848–1875* (London, 1975).

L. L. SNYDER (ed.): *Fifty Major Documents of the Nineteenth Century* (Princeton, N.J., 1955).

G. A. KERTESZ (ed.): *Documents in the Political History of the European Continent 1815–1939* (Oxford, 1968).

N. RICH: *The Age of Nationalism and Reform 1850–1890* (London, 1971).

H. GOLLWITZER: *Europe in the Age of Imperialism 1880–1914* (London, 1969).

A. J. P. TAYLOR: *The Struggle for Mastery in Europe 1848–1918* (Oxford, 1954).

M. S. ANDERSON: *The Eastern Question 1774–1923* (London, 1966).

W. N. MEDLICOTT: *The Congress of Berlin and After* (London, 1963).

W. L. LANGER: *European Alliances and Alignments 1871–1890* (New York, 1931).

W. L. LANGER: *The Diplomacy of Imperialism* (New York and London, 1935).

D. K. DERRY and T. L. JARMAN: *The European World 1870–1945* (London, 1951).

C. J. H. HAYES: *A Generation of Materialism 1871–1900* (New York, 1941).

J. JOLL: *Europe Since 1870* (London, 1973).

J. M. ROBERTS: *Europe 1880–1945* (London, 1967).

J. R. WESTERN: *The End of European Primacy* (London, 1965).

G. LICHTHEIM: *Europe in the Twentieth Century* (London, 1972).

R. O. PAXTON: *Europe in the Twentieth Century* (New York, 1975).

H. W. KOCH (ed.): *The Origins of the First World War* (London, 1972).

J. RÖHL: *1914: Delusion or Design?* (London, 1973).

P. KENNEDY (ed.): *The War Plans of the Great Powers 1880–1914* (London, 1979).

F. FISCHER: *Germany's Aims in the First World War*, trans. (London, 1967).

F. FISCHER: *World Power or Decline. The Controversy over Germany's Aims in the First World War*, trans. (London, 1974).

J. C. KING (ed.): *The First World War* (London, 1972).

D. F. FLEMING: *The Origins and Legacies of World War I* (London, 1969).

M. FERRO: *The Great War 1914–1918*, trans. (London, 1973).

Bibliography

A. J. P. TAYLOR: *War by Timetable* (London, 1969).

A. J. P. TAYLOR: *The First World War* (London, 1963).

M. GILBERT: *The European Powers 1900–45* (London, 1965).

S. MARKS: *The Illusion of Peace, International Relations in Europe 1918–1933* (London, 1976).

M. TRACHTENBERG: *Reparation in World Politics* (London, 1980).

H. W. GATZKE: *European Diplomacy Between Two Wars, 1919–1939* (Chicago, 1972).

E. H. CARR: *The Twenty Years' Crisis 1919–1939* (London, 1939).

A. ADAMTHWAITE (ed.): *The Lost Peace* (London, 1980).

M. GILBERT and R. SCOTT: *The Appeasers* (London, 1963).

E. WISKEMANN: *Europe of the Dictators* (London, 1966).

F. P. WALTERS: *A History of the League of Nations* (London and New York, 1960).

E. LUARD (ed.): *The Evolution of International Institutions* (London and New York, 1966).

G. SCOTT: *The Rise and Fall of the League of Nations* (London, 1973).

R. HENIG (ed.): *The League of Nations* (Edinburgh, 1973).

C. M. KIMMICH: *Germany and the League of Nations* (Chicago, 1976).

M. BEAUMONT: *The Origins of the Second World War* (London, 1961).

A. J. P. TAYLOR: *The Origins of the Second World War* (London, 1961).

E. M. ROBERTSON (ed.): *The Origins of the Second World War* (London, 1971).

P. CALVOCORESSI and G. WINT: *Total War* (London, 1972).

B. H. LIDDELL HART: *History of the Second World War* (London, 1970).

W. LAQUEUR: *Europe Since Hitler* (London, 1970).

P. CALVOCORESSI: *World Politics Since 1945* (London, 1968).

S. C. EASTON: *A World History Since 1945* (San Francisco, 1968).

J. WATSON: *Success in Twentieth Century World Affairs* (London, 1974).

A. FONTAINE: *History of the Cold War*, trans. (London, 1969–70).

E. LUARD (ed.): *The Cold War: A Re-appraisal* (London, 1964).

L. J. HALLE: *The Cold War as History* (London, 1967).

D. HOROWITZ: *From Yalta to Vietnam* (rev. London, 1967).

C. BOWN and P. MOONEY: *Cold War to Détente* (London, 1976).

F. S. NORTHEDGE (ed.): *The Foreign Policies of the Powers* (London, 1968).

H. G. NICHOLAS: *The United Nations as a Political Institution* (London and New York, 1975).

M. HILL: *The United Nations System* (Cambridge, 1978).

The Fontana Economic History of Europe (London):

    3 *The Industrial Revolution*

    4 *The Emergence of Industrial Societies*, 2 vols

    5 *The Twentieth Century*, 2 vols

    6 *Contemporary Economics*, 2 vols.

D. H. ALDCROFT: *The European Economy 1914–1980* (London, 1978).

S. B. CLOUGH, T. MOODIE and C. MOODIE (eds): *Economic History of Europe: Twentieth Century* (London, 1969).

S. POLLARD: *European Economic Integration 1815–1970* (London, 1974).

A. WATSON: *Europe at Risk* (London, 1977).

H. ARBUTHNOTT and G. EDWARDS (eds.): *A Common Man's Guide to the*

Common Market (London, 1979).

P. COFFEY: *Economic Policies of the Common Market* (London, 1979).

G. IONESCU: *The New Politics of European Integration* (London, 1972).

J. M. VAN BRABANT: *Socialist Economic Integration* (Cambridge, 1980).

M. B. BROWN: *The Economics of Imperialism* (Harmondsworth, Middx, 1974).

G. LICHTHEIM: *Imperialism* (Harmondsworth, Middx, 1971).

D. K. FIELDHOUSE: *The Colonial Empires. A Comparative Survey* (London, 1966).

D. K. FIELDHOUSE: *Colonialism 1870–1945* (London, 1981).

P. D. CURTIN (ed.): *Imperialism* (London, 1971).

W. J. MOMMSEN: *Theories of Imperialism* (London, 1980).

R. ROBINSON and J. GALLAGHER: *Africa and the Victorians* (London, 1961).

F. BROCKWAY: *The Colonial Revolution* (Hart-Davis, St Albans, Herts., 1973).

A. D. SMITH (ed.): *Nationalist Movements* (London, 1976).

R. EMERSON: *From Empire to Nation* (Cambridge, Mass., 1960).

H. KOHN and W. SOKOLSKY (eds): *African Nationalism in the Twentieth Century* (Princeton, N.J., 1965).

E. H. CARR: *Nationalism and After* (1945).

H. KOHN: *Prophets and Peoples. Studies in Nineteenth Century Nationalism* (1946).

H. SETON-WATSON: *Nations and States* (London, 1977).

K. W. DEUTSCH: *Nationalism and its Alternatives* (New York, 1969).

H. LUBASZ: *Fascism: Three Major Regimes* (New York and Toronto, 1973).

G. L. MOSSE (ed.): *International Fascism* (London and Beverly Hills, 1979).

E. NOLTE: *Three Faces of Fascism* (New York, 1963).

M. KITCHEN: *Fascism* (London, 1976).

F. CARSTEN: *The Rise of Fascism* (London, 1967).

M. VAJDA: *Fascism as a Mass Movement* (London and New York, 1976).

S. J. WOOLF (ed.): *The Nature of Fascism* (London, 1968).

P. HAYES: *Fascism* (London, 1973).

R. N. CAREW HUNT: *Theory and Practice of Communism* (Harmondsworth, Middx, 1963).

C. WRIGHT MILLS: *The Marxists* (Harmondsworth, Middx, 1963).

I. DEUTSCHER: *Marxism in Outline* (London, 1972).

D. MCLELLAN: *Marx* (London, 1975).

D. MCLELLAN: *Engels* (London, 1975).

N. MCINNES: *The Western Marxists* (London, 1972).

G. R. URBAN (ed.): *Eurocommunism, its Roots and Future in Italy and Elsewhere* (London, 1978).

FRANCE

J. P. T. BURY: *France 1815–1940* (London, 1949).

D. W. BROGAN: *The French Nation from Napoleon to Pétain 1814–1940* (London, 1957).

A. COBBAN: *France Since the Revolution* (London, 1970).

Bibliography

A. COBBAN: *A History of Modern France*, 3 Vols (Harmondsworth, Middx, 1969–70).

T. ZELDIN: *France 1848–1945*, 2 Vols (Oxford, 1973).

D. JOHNSON (ed.): *French Society and the Revolution* (Cambridge, 1976).

W. DOYLE: *Origins of the French Revolution* (Oxford, 1980).

J. GODECHOT: *France and the Atlantic Revolution of the Eighteenth Century, 1770–1799* (New York, 1965).

J. KAPLOW (ed.): *France on the Eve of Revolution* (New York, 1965).

P. H. BEIK (ed.): *The French Revolution* (London, 1970).

A. COBBAN: *The Social Interpretation of the French Revolution* (Cambridge, 1964).

A. COBBAN: *Aspects of the French Revolution* (London, 1968).

A. COBBAN: *The Debate on the French Revolution* (London, 1950).

O. CONNELLY: *French Revolution/Napoleonic Era* (New York, 1979).

N. HAMPSON: *A Social History of the French Revolution* (London and Toronto, 1963).

L. MADELIN: *The French Revolution*, trans. (London, 1916).

G. LEFEBVRE: *The French Revolution from 1793 to 1799*, trans. (London and New York, 1964).

J. M. ROBERTS: *The French Revolution* (Oxford, 1978).

A. SOBOUL: *The French Revolution 1787–1799*, 2 Vols, trans. (London, 1974).

M. J. SYDENHAM: *The French Revolution* (London, 1965).

M. J. SYDENHAM: *The First French Republic 1792–1804* (London, 1974).

J. M. THOMPSON: *The French Revolution* (Oxford, 1943).

A. GOODWIN: *The French Revolution* (London, 1953).

R. BEN JONES: *The French Revolution* (London, 1967).

J. M. THOMPSON: *Leaders of the French Revolution* (London, 1929).

M. J. SYDENHAM: *The Girondins* (London, 1961)

G. RUDE: *The Crowd in the French Revolution* (Oxford, 1959).

D. I WRIGHT (ed.): *The French Revolution. Introductory Documents* (Queensland, 1975).

D. I. WRIGHT: *Revolution and Terror in France 1789–1795* (London, 1974).

C. HIBBERT: *The French Revolution* (London, 1980).

N. HAMPSON: *Danton* (London, 1978).

J. L. CARR: *Robespierre* (London, 1972).

N. HAMPSON: *The Life and Opinions of Maximilien Robespierre* (London, 1974).

G. RUDE: *Robespierre* (London, 1975).

J. M. THOMPSON: *Robespierre and the French Revolution* (London, 1952).

M. LYONS: *France Under the Directory* (Cambridge, 1975).

R. B. HOLTMAN: *The Napoleonic Revolution* (Philadelphia, PA., 1967).

J. BOWLE: *Napoleon* (London, 1973).

V. CRONIN: *Napoleon* (London, 1971).

P. GEYL: *Napoleon, For and Against* (London, 1949).

M. HUTT (ed.): *Napoleon* (Englewood Cliffs, N.J., 1972).

R. BEN JONES: *Napoleon: Man and Myth* (London, 1977).

F. MARKHAM: *Napoleon* (London, 1963).

J. M. THOMPSON: *Napoleon Bonaparte: His Rise and Fall* (Oxford, 1953).

Aspects of European History 1789–1980

E. TARLÉ: *Napoleon's Invasion of Russia* (London, 1942).

H. A. L. FISHER: *Bonapartism.*

J. GODECHOT, B. HYSLOP and D. DOWD: *The Napoleonic Era in Europe* (New York, 1971).

I. COLLINS (ed.): *Government and Society in France, 1814–1848* (London, 1970).

J. and M. LOUGH: *An Introduction to Nineteenth-Century France* (London, 1978).

J. M. MERRIMAN (ed.): *1830 in France* (New York and London, 1975).

P. H. BEIK: *Louis Philippe and the July Monarchy* (Princeton, N.J., 1965).

T. E. B. HOWARTH: *Citizen King* (London, 1961).

R. PRICE (ed.): *1848 in France* (London, 1975).

R. PRICE (ed.): *Revolution and Reaction. 1848 and the Second Republic* (London and New York, 1975).

P. GUEDALLA: *The Second Empire* (London, 1946).

J. M. THOMPSON: *Louis Napoleon and the Second Empire* (Oxford, 1954).

T. ZELDIN: *Émile Ollivier and the Liberal Empire of Napoleon III.*

T. ARONSON: *The Fall of the Third Napoleon.*

W. H. C. SMITH: *Napoleon III.*

G. P. GOOCH: *The Second Empire* (London, 1960).

M. HOWARD: *The Franco-Prussian War* (London, 1961).

A. HORNE: *The Fall of Paris* (London, 1965).

R. L. WILLIAMS: *The French Revolution of 1870–1871* (London, 1969).

J. P. T. BURY: *Gambetta and the Making of the Third Republic* (London, 1973).

R. D. ANDERSON: *France 1870–1914* (London, 1977).

D. W. BROGAN: *The Development of Modern France (1870–1939)* (London, 1940).

D. THOMSON: *Democracy in France since 1870* (Oxford, 1946).

M. CURTIS: *Three Against the Republic* (Princeton, N.J., 1959).

J. HAMPDEN JACKSON: *Clemenceau and the Third Republic* (London, 1946).

D. R. ROBSON: *Georges Clemenceau. A Political Biography* (London, 1974).

R. KEDWARD: *The Dreyfus Affair* (London, 1965).

D. JOHNSON: *France and the Dreyfus Affair* (London, 1966).

H. TINT: *France since 1918* (London, 1970).

P. OUSTON: *France in the Twentieth Century* (London, 1972).

J. NÉRÉ: *The Foreign Policy of France from 1914 to 1945*, trans. (London, 1975).

W. L. SHIRER: *The Collapse of the Third Republic* (London, 1970).

J. P. T. BURY: *France: The Insecure Peace* (London, 1972).

A. ADAMTHWAITE: *France and the Coming of the Second World War* (London, 1977).

W. KNAPP: *France: Partial Eclipse* (London, 1972).

S. HOFFMAN: *Decline or Renewal? France since the 1930s* (New York, 1960).

H. TINT: *French Foreign Policy Since the Second World War* (London, 1972).

S. SERFATY: *France, De Gaulle, and Europe* (Baltimore, 1968).

P. M. WILLIAMS and M. HARRISON: *Politics and Society in De Gaulle's Republic* (London, 1971).

P. AVRIL: *Politics in France* (London, 1969).

Bibliography

D. L. HANLEY, A. P. KERR, N. H. WAITES: *Contemporary France, Politics and Society since 1945* (London and Boston, 1979).

GERMANY

A. RAMM: *Germany 1789–1919* (London, 1967).

H. W. KOCH: *A History of Prussia* (London, 1978).

E. J. FEUCHTWANGER: *Prussia: Myth and Reality* (London, 1970).

A. J. P TAYLOR: *The Course of German History* (London, 1945).

E. J. PASSANT: *A Short History of Germany 1815–1945* (Cambridge, 1959).

W. CARR: *A History of Germany 1815–1945* (London, 1969).

H. HOLBORN: *A History of Modern Germany*, Vol. 3, 1840–1945 (London, 1969).

G. A. CRAIG: *Germany 1866–1945* (Oxford, 1978).

G. L. MOSSE: *The Crisis of German Ideology* (London, 1964).

W. M. SIMON (ed.): *Germany in the Age of Bismarck* (London, 1968).

T. ARONSON: *The Kaisers* (London, 1971).

A. PALMER: *Bismarck* (London, 1976).

F. B. M. HOLLYDAY (ed.): *Bismarck* (Engelwood Cliffs, N.J., 1970).

A. J. P. TAYLOR: *Bismarck: The Man and the Statesman* (London, 1955).

O. PFLANZE: *Bismarck and the Development of Germany* (Princeton, N.J., 1963).

W. N. MEDLICOTT: *Bismarck and Modern Germany* (London, 1965).

W. N. MEDLICOTT and D. K. COVENEY: *Bismarck and Europe* (London, 1971).

D. CALLEO: *The German Problem Reconsidered* (Cambridge, 1978).

E. EYCK: *Bismarck and the German Empire* (London, 1950).

H. BÖHME (ed.): *The Foundation of the German Empire. Select Documents* (Oxford, 1971).

K. S. PINSON: *Modern Germany* (New York, 1954).

J. J. SHEEHAN (ed.): *Imperial Germany* (New York and London, 1976).

H. KURTZ: *The Second Reich* (London, 1970).

M. BALFOUR: *The Kaiser and His Times* (London, 1964).

A. PALMER: *The Kaiser* (London, 1978).

K. H. JARAUSCH: *The Enigmatic Chancellor. Bethmann Hollweg and the Hubris of Imperial Germany* (New Haven, Conn. and London, 1973).

J. RÖHL: *From Bismarck to Hitler* (Harlow, Essex, 1970).

V. R. BERGHAHN: *Germany and the Approach of War in 1914* (London, 1973).

H. C. MEYER (ed.): *Germany from Empire to Ruin 1913–1945* (London, 1973).

E. FEUCHTWANGER (ed.): *Upheaval and Continuity. A Century of German History* (London, 1977).

A. J. RYDER: *Twentieth-Century Germany: from Bismarck to Brandt* (London, 1973).

V. R. BERGHAHN and M. KITCHEN (eds): *Germany in the Age of Total War* (London and New Jersey, 1981).

E. EYCK: *A History of the Weimar Republic*, 2 Vols (London and Cambridge, Mass., 1962).

Aspects of European History 1789–1980

A. NICHOLLS and E. MATTHIAS (eds): *German Democracy and the Triumph of Hitler* (London, 1971).

J. HIDEN: *Germany and Europe 1919–1939* (London, 1977).

J. R. P. MCKENZIE: *Weimar Germany 1918–1933* (London, 1971).

A. J. NICHOLLS: *Weimar and the Rise of Hitler* (London, 1968).

M. GILBERT: *Britain and Germany between the Wars* (London, 1964).

S. DELMER: *Weimar Germany* (London, 1972).

A. ASHKENASI: *Modern German Nationalism* (Cambridge, Mass., 1976).

R. KNAUERHASE: *An Introduction to National Socialism 1920–1939* (Columbus, OH., 1972).

J. NOAKES (ed.): *Government Party and People in Nazi Germany* (Exeter, 1980).

K. D. BRACHER: *The German Dictatorship*, trans. (London, 1970).

A. BULLOCK: *Hitler: a Study in Tyranny* (London, 1952).

W. CARR: *Hitler: A Study in Personality and Politics* (London, 1978).

J. C. FEST: *Hitler*, trans. (London, 1974).

N. STONE: *Hitler* (London, 1980).

W. L. SHIRER: *The Rise and Fall of the Third Reich* (London, 1960).

E. B. WHEATON: *Prelude to Calamity: The Nazi Revolution 1933–35* (London, 1968).

P. D. STACHURA (ed.): *The Shaping of the Nazi State* (London, 1978).

K. D. BRACHER: op. cit.

D. ORLOW: *The History of the Nazi Party*, 2 Vols (Pittsburgh, 1969, 1973).

H. GLASER: *The Cultural Roots of National Socialism* (London, 1978).

J. C. FEST: *The Face of the Third Reich*, trans. (London, 1970).

K. HILDEBRAND: *The Foreign Policy of the Third Reich*, trans. (London, 1973).

E. M. ROBERTSON: *Hilter's Pre-War Policy* (London, 1963).

J. P. STERN: *Hitler. The Führer and the People* (London, 1975).

R. GRUNBERGER: *A Social History of the Third Reich* (London, 1971).

K. SONTHEIMER: *The Government and Politics of West Germany*, trans. (London, 1972).

M. BALFOUR: *West Germany* (London, 1968).

T. PRITTIE: *Konrad Adenauer 1876–1967* (London, 1972).

T. PRITTIE: *Willy Brandt. Portrait of a Statesman* (London, 1974).

G. SMITH: *Democracy in Western Germany* (London, 1979).

IMPERIAL RUSSIA/USSR

B. PARES: *A History of Russia* (London, 1926).

B. H. SUMNER: *Survey of Russian History* (London, 1944).

G. VERNADSKY: *A History of Russia* (New Haven, Conn., 1929).

L. KOCHAN: *The Making of Modern Russia* (London, 1962).

B. DMYTRYSHYN (ed.): *Imperial Russia. A Source Book*, 1700–1917 (Hinsdale, Ill., 1974).

M. T. FLORINSKY: *Russia: A History and Interpretation*, 2 Vols (London, 1953).

H. SETON-WATSON: *The Russian Empire 1801–1917* (London, 1967).

Bibliography

J. N. WESTWOOD: *Endurance and Endeavour. Russian History 1812–1971* (Oxford, 1973).

M. RAEFF: *Plans for Political Reform in Imperial Russia 1730–1905* (Englewood Cliffs, N.J., 1966).

W. LAQUEUR: *Russia and Germany. A Century of Conflict* (London, 1965).

A. PALMER: *Alexander I* (London, 1974).

W. BRUCE LINCOLN: *Nicholas I* (London, 1978).

W. E. MOSSE: *Alexander II and the Modernization of Russia* (London, 1958).

D. FIELD: *The End of Serfdom. Nobility and Bureaucracy in Russia 1855–1861* (Cambridge, Mass. and London, 1976).

R. F. BYRNES: *Pobedonostsev. His Life and Thought* (Bloomington, Indiana, 1968).

H. SETON-WATSON: *The Decline of Imperial Russia 1855–1914* (London, 1952).

T. G. STAVROU (ed.): *Russia under the Last Tsar* (University of Minnesota Press, Minneapolis, 1969).

D. PARES: *The Fall of the Russian Monarchy* (London, 1939).

M. T. FLORINSKY: *The End of the Russian Empire* (New York, 1931).

R. CHARQUES: *The Twilight of Imperial Russia* (London, 1965).

D. FLOYD: *Russia in Revolt* (London, 1969).

G. KATKOV: *Russia 1917. The February Revolution* (London, 1967).

E. WILSON: *To the Finland Station* (London, 1940).

A. ULAM: *Lenin and the Bolsheviks* (London, 1966).

L. KOCHAN: *Russia in Revolution 1890–1918* (London, 1967).

H. SHUKMAN: *Lenin and the Russian Revolution* (London, 1966).

G. KATKOV and H. SHUKMAN: *Lenin's Path to Power* (London, 1971).

M. C. MORGAN: *Lenin* (London, 1971).

P. DUKES: *October and the World* (London, 1979).

L. FISCHER: *The Life of Lenin* (London, 1965).

L. SCHAPIRO and P. REDDAWAY (eds): *Lenin. The Man, The Theorist, The Leader* (London, 1969).

A. RABINOWITCH: *The Bolsheviks Come to Power* (New York, 1976).

R. MEDVEDEV: *The October Revolution* (London, 1979).

J. L. H. KEEP: *The Russian Revolution. A Study of Mass Mobilization* (London, 1976).

E. H. CARR: *The Russian Revolution from Lenin to Stalin, 1917–1929* (London, 1979).

E. H. CARR: *The Bolshevik Revolution 1917–1923*, 3 Vols (London, 1950).

E. H. CARR: *The Interregnum 1923–1924* (London, 1954).

E. H. CARR: *Socialism in One Country 1924–1926*, 3 Vols (London, 1958).

E. H. CARR and R. W. DAVIES: *Foundations of a Planned Economy 1926–1929*, 3 Vols (London, 1969).

I. DEUTSCHER: *The Prophet Armed; Trotsky: 1879–1921* (Oxford, 1954).

I. DEUTSCHER: *The Prophet Unarmed; Trotsky: 1921–1929* (Oxford, 1959).

I. DEUTSCHER: *The Prophet Outcast; Trotsky: 1929–1940* (Oxford, 1963).

W. LAQUEUR: *The Fate of the Revolution. Interpretations of Soviet History* (London, 1967).

R. PIPES: *The Formation of the Soviet Union* (Cambridge, Mass., 1954).

Aspects of European History 1789–1980

J. BRADLEY: *Allied Intervention in Russia* (London, 1968).

J. NETTL: *The Soviet Achievement* (London, 1967).

I. DEUTSCHER: *The Unfinished Revolution 1917–1967* (Oxford, 1967).

A. ULAM: *A History of Soviet Russia* (New York, 1976).

G. F. KENNAN: *Soviet Foreign Policy 1917–1941* (Princeton, N.J., 1960).

G. F. KENNAN: *Russia and the West Under Lenin and Stalin* (New York, 1960).

T. H. RIGBY (ed.): *Stalin* (Englewood Cliffs, N.J., 1966).

I. DEUTSCHER: *Stalin. A Political Biography* (Oxford, 1949).

I. GREY: *Stalin. Man of History* (London, 1979).

R. HINGLEY: *Joseph Stalin: Man and Legend* (London, 1974).

R. PAYNE: *The Rise and Fall of Stalin* (London, 1966).

A. B. ULAM: *Stalin. The Man and his Era* (London, 1973).

R. V. DANIELS: *The Stalin Revolution. Fulfilment or Betrayal of Leninism?* (Lexington, Mass., 1965).

A. SEATON: *Stalin as Warlord* (London, 1976).

A. NOVE: *Stalinism and After* (London, 1975).

R. CONQUEST: *The Great Terror* (London, 1968).

E. CRANKSHAW: *Khrushchev* (London, 1966).

A. BRUMBERG (ed.): *Russia Under Kruschev* (London, 1962).

A. BROWN and M. KASER (eds): *The Soviet Union Since the Fall of Khrushchev* (New York, 1975).

A. DALLIN and T. B. LARSON (eds): *Soviet Politics Since Khrushchev* (Englewood Cliffs, N.J., 1968).

D. R. KELLY: *Soviet Politics in the Brezhnev Era* (New York, 1980).

L. PIETROMARCHI: *The Soviet World*, trans. (London, 1965).

G. M. CARTER: *The Government of the Soviet Union* (New York, 1949).

R. W. DAVIES: *The Soviet Union* (London, 1978).

A. Z. RUBINSTEIN: *Soviet Foreign Policy Since World War II* (Cambridge, Mass., 1981).

N. V. SIVACHEV and N. N. YAKOVLEV: *Russia and the United States* (Chicago, 1979).

A. G. MAZOUR (ed.): *Soviet Economic Development. Operation Outstrip 1921–1965.* (Princeton, N.J., 1967).

M. DOBB: *Soviet Economic Development since 1917* (London, 1966).

R. J. HILL and P. FRANK: *The Soviet Communist Party* (London, 1981).

THE HABSBURG EMPIRE, AUSTRIA, CZECHOSLOVAKIA, HUNGARY

A. KANN: *A History of the Habsburg Empire 1526–1918* (Los Angeles and London, 1974).

A. J. P. TAYLOR: *The Habsburg Monarchy 1809–1918* (London, 1948).

C. A. MACARTNEY: *The Habsburg Empire 1790–1918* (London, 1969).

C. A. MACARTNEY: *The House of Austria. The Later Phase 1790–1918* (Edinburgh, 1978).

A. PALMER: *Metternich* (London, 1972).

A. MILNE: *Metternich* (London, 1975).

E. F. KRAEHE (ed.): *The Metternich Controversy* (New York, 1971).

Bibliography

R. J. RATH: *The Viennese Revolution of 1848* (New York, 1957).

F. R. BRIDGE: *From Sadowa to Sarajevo* (London, 1972).

A. J. MAY: *The Passing of the Habsburg Monarchy 1914–1918*, 2 Vols (Philadelphia, PA, 1966).

Z. A. B. ZEMAN: *The Break-up of the Habsburg Empire 1914–1918* (London, 1961).

Z. A. B. ZEMAN: *Twilight of the Habsburgs* (London, 1971).

E. CRANKSHAW: *The Fall of the House of Habsburg* (London, 1963).

K. R. STADLER: *Austria* (London, 1971).

L. VALIANI: *The End of Austria-Hungary*, trans. (London, 1973).

E. BARBER: *Austria 1918–1972* (London, 1973).

M. KITCHEN: *The Coming of Austrian Fascism* (London, 1980).

J. W. BRUEGEL: *Czechoslovakia Before Munich* (Cambridge, 1973).

E. STEINER: *The Slovak Dilemma* (Cambridge, 1973).

S. H. THOMSON: *Czechoslovakia in European History* (Princeton, N.J., 1943).

R. W. SETON-WATSON: *A History of the Czechs and Slovaks* (London, 1943).

J. KORBEL: *Twentieth-Century Czechoslovakia* (New York, 1977).

W. V. WALLACE: *Czechoslovakia* (London, 1976).

C. A. MACARTNEY: *Hungary. A Short History* (Edinburgh, 1962).

D. SINOR: *A History of Hungary* (New York, 1959).

ITALY

D. MACK SMITH: *Italy. A Modern History* (Ann Arbor, Michigan, 1959).

D. MACK SMITH (ed.): *The Making of Italy 1796 1870* (London, 1968).

S. J. WOOLF: *The Italian Risorgimento* (London, 1969).

D. MACK SMITH: *Cavour and Garibaldi 1860* (Cambridge, 1954).

M. SALVADORI (ed.): *Cavour and the Unification of Italy* (Princeton, N.J., 1961).

D. BEALES (ed.): *The Risorgimento and the Unification of Italy* (London, 1971).

D. MACK SMITH (ed.): *Garibaldi* (Englewood Cliffs, N.J., 1969).

C. HIBBERT: *Garibaldi and his Enemies* (New York, 1965).

J. RIDLEY: *Garibaldi* (London, 1974)

SIR I. KIRKPATRICK: *Mussolini. Study of a Demagogue* (London, 1964).

M. GALLO: *Mussolini's Italy*, trans. (New York, 1973).

R. COLLIER: *Duce! The Rise and Fall of Mussolini* (London, 1971).

E. M. ROBERTSON: *Mussolini as Empire-Builder* (New York, 1977).

M. GALLO: *Mussolini and Italy*, trans. (London, 1973).

C. C. BAYNE-JARDINE: *Mussolini and Italy* (London, 1966).

C. HIBBERT: *Mussolini* (Harmondsworth, Middx, 1975).

D. MACK SMITH: *Mussolini's Roman Empire* (London, 1976).

J. WOOLF (ed.): *The Rebirth of Italy 1943–1950* (London, 1972).

SPAIN

S. G. PAYNE: *A History of Spain and Portugal*, 2 Vols (University of Wisconsin Press, Wisconsin, 1973).

Aspects of European History 1789–1980

W. C. ATKINSON: *A History of Spain and Portugal* (Harmondsworth, Middx, 1960).

H. LIVERMORE: *A History of Spain* (London, 1958).

R. M. SMITH: *Spain. A Modern History* (Michigan, 1965).

R. CARR: *Spain 1808–1939* (Oxford, 1966).

R. CARR: *Modern Spain 1875–1980* (Oxford, 1980).

R. CARR: *The Spanish Tragedy* (London, 1977).

R. FRASER: *Blood of Spain* (London, 1979).

G. HILLS: *Franco* (London, 1967).

D. A. PUZZO (ed.): *The Spanish Civil War* (New York, 1969).

R. PAYNE: *The Civil War in Spain 1936–1939* (London, 1962).

S. G. PAYNE: *The Spanish Revolution* (London, 1970).

R. A. H. ROBINSON: *The Origins of Franco's Spain* (London, 1970).

H. THOMAS: *The Spanish Civil War* (London, 1961).

R. CARR and J..P. F. AIZPURUA: *Spain: Dictatorship to Democracy* (London, 1979).

M. GALLO: *Spain Under Franco*, trans. (London, 1973).

OTHER STATES

O. HALECKI: *A History of Poland* (London, 1978).

R. F. LESLIE (ed.): *The History of Poland Since 1863* (Cambridge, 1980).

M. B. PETROVICH: *A History of Modern Serbia*, 2 Vols (New York and London, 1976).

S. K. PAVLOWITCH: *Yugoslavia* (London, 1971).

S. CLISSOLD (ed.): *A Short History of Yugoslavia* (Cambridge, 1966).

S. G. EVANS: *A Short History of Bulgaria* (London, 1960).

G. J. BOBANGO: *The Emergence of the Romanian National State* (New York, 1979).

E. H. CROSSMAN: *The Low Countries 1780–1940 (Oxford, 1978)*.

T. K. DERRY: *A History of Scandinavia* (London, 1970).

J. CAMPBELL and P. SHERRARD: *Modern Greece* (London, 1968).

S. J. SHAW and E. K. SHAW: *A History of the Ottoman Empire and Modern Turkey.* Vol. II: *Reform, Revolution, and Republic: The Rise of Modern Turkey, 1808–1975* (Cambridge, 1977).